'Against the background of the raw mill society in Yorkshire during the 1830s the absorbing story of a woman, a mill heiress, emerging in this long but rewarding saga of the Barforths and their North Country connections. . . . Jagger's rich novel is especially memorable for its characterizations of women.' *Publishers' Weekly*

'A stirring novel, compelling to read, hard to put down.' *Shipley Express*

'A well-spun yarn with hard wearing qualities.' *Western Evening Herald*

'(A) rich and powerful novel.' *Peterborough Evening Telegraph*

'A major new novel.' *Yorkshire Evening Post*

'Women of every age will find this book appealing.' *Library Journal*

Brenda Jagger, married with three daughters, is a Yorkshirewoman who now lives near Bradford. She has worked in Paris and Dundee, and then in the north of England as a probation officer. Her work with 'wayward girls', and her own family, have increased her interest in the female situation, and led to a consideration of what it must have been like in the past. THE CLOUDED HILLS is an exploration of the world through the eyes of a girl in the first half of the nineteenth century, and will be followed by the story of the succeeding generation of women in the Barforth family.

Brenda Jagger

The Clouded Hills

Futura

A Futura BOOK

First published in Great Britain in 1980 by
Macdonald Futura Publishers

First Futura edition 1981
Reprinted 1981, 1982, 1983 (twice), 1984
Copyright © Brenda Jagger 1980

ISBN 0 7088 1827 7

Filmset, printed and bound in Great Britain by
Hazell Watson & Viney Limited,
Member of the BPCC Group,
Aylesbury, Bucks

Futura Publications
A Division of
Macdonald & Co (Publishers) Ltd
Maxwell House
74 Worship Street
London EC2A 2EN
A BPCC plc Company

1

My grandfather, Samson Barforth, built himself a house on the hill above Lawcroft Fold so that on summer evenings, in the company of the woman who was not my grandmother and not entirely the housekeeper she claimed to be, he could look down on the valley he had made his own. And although a more patriotic Englishman never breathed, he was ready enough to admit that he had made a pretty penny out of Napoleon.

He had lit a bonfire of thanksgiving, true enough, to celebrate the Duke of Wellington's victory at Waterloo, but the long French wars, with the constant need for men and for uniforms of good Yorkshire cloth in which to clothe them, had brought prosperity to Barforth looms; and even as he had raised a glass of his best claret to drink the Duke's health, he would not have been sorry, perhaps, to see hostilities start up again, somewhere else. And when the great Duke had entered Parliament and shown himself opposed to Free Trade my grandfather had put his claret away and said hard things about national heroes who, when the battle was over, could think of nothing to do but uphold laws which would keep the price of bread high.

'They've got no place in peacetime, these generals,' I'd heard him grumble to the woman who was not my grandmother, this shocking Mrs Stevens, half his age and far too pretty for anyone's good. 'No place at all. Why should a man suppose that because he knows how to win a battle he knows how to do anything else? Can you tell me that? No, no, of course you can't. But I can tell you, Mrs Stevens, that if the price of bread goes up again there'll be hunger in the cities. And I've noticed, time and again, that when hunger comes, trouble is never far behind.'

And because, as everyone at Lawcroft Fold knew, my grandfather was always right, there was hunger – other people's hunger – through those guarded years of my childhood, men clamouring in our mill yard for higher wages as the price of a loaf continued to rise, and the landlords – encouraged, my father insisted, by the Duke of Wellington and his aristocratic cronies – refusing absolutely to let in the cheap foreign corn that would make everything right.

'Perhaps he doesn't eat much bread, the great Duke,' my grandfather snorted, too angry sometimes to be consoled even by the fluid, feline Mrs Stevens. 'But he grows corn now, I reckon, since we've given him a two-hundred-sixty-three-thousand-pound estate to thank him for saving us from the French. So maybe we shouldn't blame him for feathering his own nest. And what about those gallant redcoats of his, those veterans of Waterloo that he's pensioned off, coming here with their two pounds in prize money in their pockets, looking for work and grumbling when they can't get it or aren't fit for it? What about them, filling my weavers' heads with their fancy notions of liberty and equality that they learned in France?'

But as I played quietly in my grandfather's garden through my warm childhood summers, my sparkling, fur-cloaked winters, not even the prospect of those hard-eyed veterans hungrily prowling our hills had the power to disturb me, for what could a handful of soldiers do – how could the Duke of Wellington himself hope to prevail against Samson Barforth?

My grandfather had been a merchant in his young days, travelling to Lincolnshire with a string of packhorses for the sheep shearing, choosing his wool with care to suit the requirements of the worsted trade, driving a hard bargain, and then coming home again through the deserted Pennine ranges to distribute his stock. First he would go to the combers, who would draw out the long fibres into the creamy coils necessary for worsted yarn; then to the

8

spinners and weavers, working, each man at his own loom, each woman at her own spinning wheel, in their cottages. And, since he was a man who could always see where money was to be made, I suppose it struck him early on that instead of merely carrying the wool and taking his commission, it would be more profitable to retain ownership of it himself, through all its processes, and employ the less enterprising cottagers to weave it for wages.

A hard life, certainly, with much of it spent in the saddle, since it took four spinners in those days to keep one weaver occupied with yarn, and the villages were not grouped companionably together but scattered in hostile, desolate places, stony tracks breaking off suddenly before outcroppings of rock, identical stretches of moorland and steep, faceless hillsides, where a man could wander, lost, for days on end and an injured man might never be found at all. A solitary life, too, both for him and for my grandmother, who could not accompany him on his rough journeyings, and since she knew quite well that many of the village girls were bold and bonny, and that travelling men were not famous for their ability to resist temptation, it may have been partly for her sake that he paused one day at the place called Lawcroft Fold to consider the old corn mill and the fast-flowing stream that refreshed the valley bottom.

He had noted the dampness of the grey moorland air, the grey-peaked hills that tore the rain clouds apart – a guarantee that no waterwheel, in this barren land, need ever be still – and laying down his packs and calling his horses to a final halt, he had purchased the entire property: the mill and the millhouse, the land and the water rights that went with it; he had swept out the dust of the miller's last lean years and transformed himself into that new species of employer, a man who demanded that his workpeople should come to him – not he to them – at a given hour and should remain until they had his permission to leave.

9

The hills around Lawcroft Fold – bare, brown uplands, waterlogged in winter, wind-raked at all seasons – were still alive in those years with a close-fisted, independent breed of men who lived hard and perhaps not too long but who lived as they pleased and had no mind to make changes. They had their handlooms and their spinning wheels, a weekly piece of cloth to be woven as and when it suited them and carted away every Friday to the Piece Hall in Cullingford and offered for sale. They had an acre or so of land apiece, on which to keep a pig and a cow and to grow such crops as could survive the raw northern air and the poor soil. To men like these, who took orders and wages from no one, my grandfather as an employer was not welcome. But perhaps, being as thrifty of emotion as of everything else, they only began to hate him when he introduced into the valley, with great secrecy and some danger, a number of the new machines which, by spinning an eventual eighty threads at a time instead of one, were destined to be the assassin of the spinning wheel.

My grandfather had brought in soldiers to preside at the installation of his machines, while men with hammers in their hands had prowled outside his gates, determined to smash the fiendish inventions that would deprive their women – the spinsters – of work. There were many among them who saw the new spinning frames as a threat not only to earnings but to family life, since a woman who is anchored all day to her wheel, in her own house place, surrounded by her children, has neither the time nor the opportunity for mischief. But let her be idle or send her to a man like Samson Barforth who would put money into her hands, then neither husband nor child could ever know real peace of mind again.

Everyone had heard about the gangs of women employed in the coal mines, strapping, brawling creatures beyond any man's control, crawling half naked down the tunnels with a candle in their mouths and a chain between their legs, dragging a coal cart behind them, in the company of men who were not their husbands: the Law Valley was unwilling to expose its own women to such misery and such temptation.

Samson Barforth was stoned one night as he rode across Cullingford Moor. His windows were broken. He was shunned by the local gentry, who resented his use of the river water to drive his mill wheel to the detriment of their own ornamental fountains; he was shunned, too, by the inhabitants of Cullingford, the nearby market town, who from self-interest and snobbishness followed wherever the gentry led. But my grandfather, being a Barforth, knew that right was on his side, and he experienced no difficulty whatsoever in overlooking abuse and even assault when there was a profit to be made.

'They'll soon see reason,' I could imagine him saying to my grandmother, in the days before Mrs Stevens. 'They can't beat progress, and they can't beat me.' And so it was, for the weavers, momentarily encouraged by the abundance of mill-spun yarn which kept their own looms occupied, were slow to notice the expansion of my grandfather's business, his use of the surplus yarn to weave pieces of his own, so that quite soon he was able to describe himself not only as a spinner but as a full-scale manufacturer of worsted cloth. By the time it was realized that his pieces, being as good as anyone else's but more plentiful and in more regular supply, had attracted the best customers, and that he had no yarn to spare, it was too late.

The old corn mill grew and gave birth to other, sounder structures. A solid, stone house was built for my grandmother – an uncompromising, square-cut pile with a door firmly in the middle, two windows on either side of it, two windows above, and a stone-flagged kitchen, where my grandmother baked her own bread, trussed her own chickens, made soap and candles, and bullied her maids, and where my grandfather added up his accounts and learned to call himself a rich man.

Labour, of course, was always scarce, for no Law Valley man would willingly submit himself to the prison of factory life, and so my grandfather, looking further afield, began to construct rows of cottages around the mill yard: identical two-roomed boxes soon filled by the mass of agricultural labourers who, driven off the southern farmlands by the loss of their free pasture, were drifting rootlessly North, and by the perpetually starving Irish, who would take any man's wages. And when all else failed, it was always possible to strike a bargain with some parish priest or other who, only too glad to empty his poorhouse, would send pauper children by the cartload from as much as two hundred miles away – little abandoned mites too young, some of them, to remember their parents or their proper names, bound as apprentices for a term of fourteen years, boys and girls alike, at the end of which time my grandfather would give them a decent suit of clothes or a good gown and, if they had done well, employment as a free operative in his thriving enterprise.

A long, low dwelling was built to accommodate them, right in the mill yard itself, and when Parliament, at the instigation of Robert Peel, himself the son of a calico printer, decreed that such apprentices should be taught their letters and numbers and a little religion, and that boys and girls should sleep separately and no more than two to a bed, my grandfather obeyed the law, as many others did not, by dividing his apprentice house in two, building a school and hiring a schoolmaster, whose duty it was – my grandfather being of the Methodist persuasion when he could be persuaded at all – to walk the children the weekly five miles to the Church of England the law had specified.

My grandmother, a giantess of my childhood, her stern, well-creased face always surrounded by oddly contrasting butterfly caps of lace and satin ribbon, did her duty strictly by these parish children – valuing, no doubt, their contribution to her ever-increasing comfort – and saw to it that

12

they had an abundance of hot oatmeal twice every day to sustain them through the boom times, when their labour was often required from five o'clock in the morning until eight o'clock at night. And, her favourite colour being blue, she dressed them identically for church on Sundays: dark blue gowns for the girls, dark blue jackets and cord trousers for the boys – even the schoolmaster, in a good blue coat – all of which must be removed on their return from divine worship, since Sunday was often a convenient day for the cleaning of machines.

There were masters, of course, who were less gentle. There had always been tales in the valley of beating and strappings, of infants savagely mauled by the machines or by an overseer's spite, of men who, when their businesses failed, drove their apprentices to the middle of some lonely moor and turned them loose like a litter of unwanted pups to fend for themselves. But my grandmother had always been indignant of such goings-on, my grandfather scornful.

'Bad business,' I'd heard him say. 'Any fool can see that. Treat them right and they'll work. Treat them wrong and they'll run away, and then you'll have to spend time and money catching them or fetching a fresh lot to take their place. And these parish priests drive a hard bargain. Bad business.'

Even when my grandmother died – furious because she had let it be known she wasn't ready and hated to be defied – there had been the sloe-eyed Mrs Stevens to call a doctor to a sick or injured child and to make sure that the 'brats' overseer' was a man of Christian principle and not too rough. But the day of the parish apprentice was over now, for, since the steam engine had been tamed to take the place of the waterwheel and the mills were no longer tied to the banks of rivers, and since fresh famine in Ireland had brought yet another flood of hungry, hardy workers to our shore, the once pleasant town of Cullingford had spread like a giant weed garden, new streets of low, already grimy houses rushing outward to meet the fast-growing ring of factory gates, the black-belching stacks of prosperous factory chimneys; and there were free children in plenty to fill our sheds, kept in order and kept awake by their own hardhanded mothers. The ministrations of the Barforth ladies were no longer required, and although this new breed of factory children seemed smaller and paler than the ones we had fed and housed ourselves – living, as they did, in those mean streets where no Act of Parliament could compel their mothers to put them no more than two to a bed or to teach them to be Christians – there were, at least, more of them, and the work was done just the same.

Mrs Stevens gave her mind now to her pickles and preserves, my mother to her embroidery, and by the time I was sixteen, with Waterloo already far behind us, I was too secure, too convinced of Barforth right and might to be greatly concerned that once again there were soldiers in our mill yard, doing little, it seemed, but lounging and laughing and ogling the maids, but ready, at my grandfather's command, to defend the installation of yet more machines, the new power looms that would force the last hand weaver from the freedom of his cottage workshop or would starve him to death.

The introduction of these power looms, of course, to men like my grandfather, was entirely logical. Since we had spinning machines, it followed as naturally as night follows day that we must have a weaving machine of some sort to keep pace with the vast quantities of yarn we could now produce. But the hand weavers, already losing their struggle to compete with the factories, seeing their earnings cut and their standards falling, seeing their precious freedom eaten away, could not be expected to take so reasonable a view. And since the landowners had once again increased the price of bread and it was rumoured that the younger weavers had taken to drilling with firearms on the moor on warm nights – instructed, one supposed, by those reckless, penniless veterans of Waterloo

– trouble was expected and, being looked for, might well be found.

My father, I knew, would have delayed the coming of the new looms, for, never having known poverty as my grandfather had, he was often inclined to take an easy way and was less urgent, less fixed of purpose. But although the mills were now supposedly in his charge, my grandfather's vision was still acute, his ambition still thirsty, and when he had stumped down from the Top House and ordered, 'Get the looms in, and get the military,' my father had not chosen to disobey.

They were alike in many ways, big men in youth who turned heavy in middle life, vigorous and full-blooded, hearty of appetite, except that my father, being a copy of the original mould, was somehow a little less, his needs more easily satisfied; and perhaps we all knew that it was my brother Edwin – taller, at twenty-four, than either of them – who held first place in my grandfather's heart.

'The Boy,' he called him, in an entirely different tone from the one in which he referred to me as 'the Girl,' and it was Edwin who had gone to fetch the soldiers and the engineers and who had spent long hours in the sheds deciding, with my grandfather, where the new looms were to be placed.

'The Boy knows what he's about,' my grandfather told Mrs Stevens, who, in her turn, made sure we all heard it, and when my brother concluded that nothing would suffice but the building of an entirely new factory, a stone temple of progress and profit, my grandfather chortled his delight.

'We'd best knock this old heap down,' Edwin announced, 'before the new looms do it for us. No shoring up and making do. If we're to do the job at all, then we'll do it right.' And as his vision began to extend to four storeys, six storeys capable of housing not merely the dozen looms on order but five hundred more, I saw my grandfather take on colour, my father fade, and I remembered that, somehow, it was always my father – never my brother

– who would find his horse surrounded by muttering hand weavers, always my father who bore the brunt of some woman's hysteria, who was jostled and threatened and asked if he would be satisfied when the hills were full of walking skeletons.

'Ignore them,' my grandfather said.

'Ride them down,' my brother advised.

But my father could do neither, and there were times when I would have offered him sympathy, had I dared.

'One can see their point of view,' I had heard him tell my mother, speaking low in case my grandfather, from the Top House, should hear him; but unlike Mrs Stevens, who drank in my grandfather's every word, my mother rarely listened to anyone and hardly ever to her husband.

'Isabella,' he said quite harshly, 'does nothing trouble you?'

Smiling vaguely, she murmured, 'Why yes, dear,' and went back to her embroidery.

My mother was a beautiful woman, but beyond the facts of her dark, glossy hair, perfectly oval face, and startling grey velvet eyes, I knew little about her and had never found the way to ask. She was the scent of lavender through my childhood, by no means aloof, since aloofness is a cold thing, a positive thing, and she was far too elusive for that; a woman who gave no orders and made no demands, who always answered, 'Why yes, dear. Of course, dear,' but who was, just the same, as private and separate and elegant as a cat.

My father had caused her portrait to be painted soon after their marriage, showing her in the narrow, Grecian-styled gown of those days, a silver ribbon casually holding her tumbled curls, a dark shawl draping her bare shoulders, her eyes half closed, languorous, her smile making promises it had evidently not been in her nature to fulfil. And standing before it as a child, I had thought her the most exquisite creature in the world and had been amazed that my father did not seem to love her as much as he could have done and that my grandfather did not love her at all.

It is not given to many children to understand the reasons for their parents' marriage, but I knew – because, being a girl and generally ignored, I overheard a great deal and assumed far more – that it was, perhaps, the sole occasion on which my father had gone against my grandfather's wishes. Not that my mother had been in any way ineligible, for, as Miss Isabella Baxter, a master cutler's daughter from Sheffield, she had had a little money and some gentility, and there had been others besides my father who had wanted her. It was simply that the Barforth wives had always been plainspoken, sensible women, useful rather than beautiful, the kind who knew and kept their place, dull perhaps but safe, their feet firmly planted on the ground, and my grandfather had given loud and quite ferocious warning that Miss Isabella Baxter could make no man feel secure. He, too, it seemed, had noticed the languorous smile, the gracefully leaning figure that could entice a man from his duty, encourage him to squander time and energy that should be given to business – the true purpose of a young man's life – and not to pleasure, which should be left for later. But my father, properly enticed, had persisted, and even my mother, for perhaps the first and last time in her life, had made a stand, declaring that she would have no other, and had eventually gone to church to marry him in a cloud of silk gauze and lace that had shocked the Law Valley.

But somehow they had not been happy. Perhaps my father's romantic impulse had not endured. Perhaps my mother's expectations had been too high. Perhaps he had believed she would be changed, on her wedding night, by some mysterious alchemy into the uncomplicated, four-square wife a Barforth really required, while still retaining her exceedingly complex charm; and his disappointment may have caused her to retreat from him, to become even less a Barforth as he, in time, became more. And although my father never spoke a word against her, growing merely a little more morose every year, my grandfather would tell anyone who cared to listen – and when had Mrs Stevens been unwilling? – that he found her lovely face and her skill at fine needlework poor compensation for her feckless, aimless ways and her sad inability to raise her children.

My brother Edwin, it is true, had come roaring into the world like an infant Hercules, and I, despite my inferior sex, was no weakling, but between us and after us a half dozen little Barforths had lived a few sickly months apiece: and since such weakness could not possibly have come from him, my grandfather believed most fervently that it came from her.

I went, often enough, to put flowers on that little row of Barforth graves: brothers Samson and William, sisters Isabella and Emma, Sophia, and a shadow called Lucy I could just remember and who had caused my grandfather to curse and grumble when he was told that her birth would be the last.

'So it's over now, is it?' he'd said. 'That's the best she can do? Two out of eight and no more to follow. Small return, son William, I call it, for what she's cost you. Well, one learns to make the best of what there is to hand, that's the great thing, and at least there's the Boy. Yes, I've got my stake in the future. I've got the Boy. And I reckon the Girl can be made to stir herself, when she's an age for it, and bring us a good man into the house, somebody to stand by Edwin when we're gone. And who knows, William lad, if your Isabella should really prove as delicate as they say – well, I reckon you'll take a solid woman next time, one of our own kind who'd strengthen the stock, because there's the mills to think of and we need every hand we can get.'

There was no open quarrel between them, for my mother quarrelled with no one, while my grandfather was so habitually sharp-spoken that he often seemed angry with the world in general rather than with her in particular.

But her sweet, absentminded smile caused the knotted veins at his temples to swell; her way of talking – very soft, very low, and saying nothing – brought the fierce, mottled colour to his cheeks, and it irked him greatly that my father would not join him and hate her too.

'Aye, lad, it's a bad business,' he would say sometimes, heavy with sympathy, sly with complicity. 'You'd best let the Girl come up to Mrs Stevens and see the proper way to go on, for she's too quiet by half, your Verity. The Boy, now, he's an open book, but it strikes me your girl could turn whimsical and deep. You'd do well to watch her, lad, for we can risk no more of it.'

'She's well enough,' my father said, not altogether defending me, not absolutely denying his wish for a more comfortable wife, and I understood that, as my mother's daughter, I was suspect too and that if I wished to be acknowledged as a Barforth, I would be obliged – unlike my brother – to prove my worth.

They gave me gold earrings the day I reached sixteen, a fan on ivory sticks, white kid gloves, a puppy from my brother's yellow crossbred bitch, a strand of coral, a tortoiseshell comb, to put up my hair; and that evening, in the midst of admiring my presents and instructing me on how the puppy should be fed, my brother casually, defiantly, told us it was time he took a wife.

'Yes, dear,' my mother said. 'Naturally.'

Edwin, who was more inclined to share my grandfather's point of view than I, flushed angrily, stung by her roundabout but effective way of reminding him what a menace he had been, these past few years, to maids and mill hands, and to the farm girl over at Farncliffe Craggs who, last winter, had borne his child.

'You have the young lady in mind then?' my father said quickly, flushing, too, for Edwin had spent the day at the Top House, talking of power looms and weddings, it seemed, with his grandfather, not his father, missing a generation as he was far too apt to do. And as he saw his authority thus whittled away, my father's bitterness escaped its fetters and found its tongue.

'It's a matter not to be taken lightly, and as I know your nature, lad, you'll need a sensible, thrifty woman with her feet on the ground – a woman who wants what you want and understands why you want it – one of your own kind, Edwin. Romance is all very well but it's not hard-wearing, and honeymoons are soon over.'

But my mother, who was thought to hear nothing, notice nothing, and who certainly did not appear to think herself insulted, although I thought it and suffered for her, lifted her elegant head from her needlework and said lightly, 'But he's to marry his cousin, Hannah Barforth, surely? Isn't that what he arranged with his grandfather – or his grandfather with him – long ago?'

'Shall you dislike it very much, Mamma?' my brother asked her, cooler, harder than my father, caring little for the whims of any woman, his cousin Hannah among them. And, my new comb holding my hair in the smooth chignon of womanhood, I was irritated suddenly, quite unbearably, by his smug assumption that Hannah not only would take him but would be very glad to do it.

'Well,' I said, stiff-necked with the unaccustomed weight of upswept hair and tortoiseshell, 'before we like it or not, we'd best know if you've asked her yet. She may not like it overmuch herself.'

And I have never forgotten him, standing brown-skinned, brown-eyed in the sunshine, convinced beyond all question of his ability to take the future by the throat and force from it anything it should be foolish enough to deny him.

'She'll like it very well,' he said, laughing me to scorn. 'There's no doubt about that, or I'd not ask her at all. I'd give no woman in the world the chance to say she'd turned me down. I'll ask her tomorrow, when the new looms come in, and you can dance at my wedding, Verity Barforth, if you can learn to keep your hair from falling down – and maybe you'll catch yourself a husband while you're about it.'

And because I knew he was as irresistible and indestructible as my grandfather, and because I was at an age when weddings were very much on my mind, I believed him and laughed too.

2

They brought the looms in the night, a line of quiet, sluggish carts escorted by soldiers, my brother Edwin at the head of them, leading his army as bravely as any Iron Duke. And although there was a sullen crowd in the mill yard the next morning, they parted, muttering but cowed, to let my grandfather through when he rode down from the Top House to make sure his overlookers and that strange new breed of men called engineers were setting all to rights.

'They'll be in production by the end of next month,' he announced bluntly as he strode back to his horse, glaring at anyone who seemed inclined to argue; hoping, perhaps, that somebody would. And that afternoon my cousin Hannah came to call, knowing, no doubt, that Edwin planned to speak to her and having her answer ready.

She was very tall, my cousin Hannah, and very determined, a Barforth to her fingertips, clever, self-assured, and exceedingly handsome; and if she was still single at twenty-three it was only because she had made up her mind long ago to marry my brother, who, in fact, had always been willing, although my grandfather had not.

No doubt my grandfather had dreamed of someone truly exceptional for Edwin, a girl who combined the practical good sense he had valued in his own wife with Mrs Stevens's persuasive charms; a girl with money, too, and expectations – a millmaster's only child, perhaps, who would inherit her father's business and give it to Edwin. And while Hannah could not be faulted in looks or behaviour, she was something of a poor relation with a family history not unblemished, whose dowry, if there was a dowry, would only be small. Yet Edwin could be stubborn, and my grandfather was eager to see the start of a new generation, to which Hannah might well make a cheerful, sensible, healthy mother; and as she walked into the house that flowery May morning, rather more stately than she should have been in her dull, green gown with its narrow flounces, I had no doubt that she was soon to be my sister.

She was not, strictly speaking, so nearly related to me as she seemed, being the daughter of my father's cousin – another broad, brown-eyed Barforth who had once been in a reasonable way of business at Low Cross Mill not far away. But my uncle, Tom Barforth, who could have lived comfortably on the profits of his weaving sheds, had attempted to live grandly and had kept a mistress in Leeds, spending time with her when he should have been at his mill; quite naturally, he had not prospered. His wife, Aunt Hattie, had been a pretty woman and may even have been good-natured in her younger days, but the constant cheese-paring economy that had been necessary to support his extravagance, her having to wear her own petticoats to shreds while he continued to patronize an expensive Leeds tailor, had soured her disposition and lowered her spirits. With ruin staring them in the face, I had heard, neither she nor my uncle had fought too hard against the fever which had carried them off three years ago, leaving Hannah and her brother and sister to manage as best they could.

'Poor souls,' Mrs Stevens had said mistily on her way back from Aunt Hattie's funeral. 'Poor lambs. Whatever will become of them?'

And, indeed, the situation had seemed so hopeless that Hannah's brother, my cousin Joel, had been expected to sell out, salvage what he could, and take employment. My father, I believe, had even made a tentative offer to take him on at Lawcroft, although my grandfather, who disliked Joel, had declared gruffly – and very likely in Joel's hearing – that Australia would be near enough. But my cousin Joel – who undoubtedly, in face and manner, was much like his father – was cast more truly in the Barforth mould and, taking off his own well-cut jacket, rolling up the sleeves of his fine cambric shirt, had set himself to prove the Law Valley wrong. Although Low Cross Mill as yet was far from prosperous, debts had been paid and men no longer avoided Joel in the street in case he should ask for credit, while Hannah, a far more efficient housekeeper, it seemed, than her mother, kept a good fire in their hearth and plain but wholesome food on their table, and saw to it that Elinor, the youngest member of the family, was as well turned out and well behaved as any girl should be.

'Remarkable young people,' Mrs Stevens often declared, thinking no doubt of Joel, who knew how to charm when it suited him. 'They should be an example to you, Verity.'

Yet, in spite of their admirable courage and tenacity, there was often a harshness about them both, a resentment of their own poverty, a certain contempt for those of us – myself and Edwin included – who had never known hard times, that made me ill at ease.

My mother, had it occurred to her, could have sent her carriage for Hannah that morning, knowing that she and Joel would wish to see the new machines and that Edwin certainly wished to see Hannah, but my mother's arrangements were as insubstantial as her smile – her feelings for Hannah perhaps more definite than she cared to show – and when she saw the sisters, Hannah and Elinor, coming through the gate from the mill yard and up to our door, she looked, for a moment, quite puzzled, as if she could not quite remember their names, except that it was Barforth.

'Oh – yes, dear,' she said. 'How nice – really – how pleasant.' And her voice, without in any way losing its

23

sweetness, reduced Hannah – flushed with her expectation of being the future mistress of this house – to the level of a chance acquaintance who should really not have come in unannounced.

But almost at once my brother Edwin, who had been on fire all day about the looms and had been longing for Hannah to come and tell him how brave and farsighted he was, strode into the parlour, the warm tones of his nature dispelling my mother's coolness; and as he clasped Hannah's hand eagerly in both his own and told her, 'The looms have come,' we all knew he was actually saying, 'Now, at last, will you be my wife?'

'Yes,' she replied, 'they've come. And you had no trouble. I knew you would have no trouble, once you were determined and let them know it. Oh, Edwin, well done, Edwin. Joel has looked in at the mill to see how the engineers are progressing, and I wondered – could I, do you think, go and take a look, too?'

'I came up on purpose to fetch you,' he said, beaming broadly, immensely gratified by her interest and her praise. 'We'll go now, straight off, because I want to talk to you on the way. And then, Mother, if you're agreeable, we're all to meet at the Top House by three o'clock, to take a glass of something, and a bite of something, too, if I know anything about Mrs Stevens. If you're agreeable, that is, Mother, and you've nothing planned for dinnertime – nothing that can spoil?'

'Oh no, dear,' she said, as if the thought of dinner, which we took regularly at four o'clock, had not so much as entered her mind. 'What could I have to spoil?'

But Edwin, determined not to upset his great day, took Hannah's arm in a firm, possessive hold – glad, perhaps, to feel her so solid, so real – and with a nod and a half smile in my mother's direction led her away.

I walked up to the Top House some time later with my cousin Elinor, a girl of my own age, who, unlike the serious-minded Hannah, had few interests in life just then beyond ribbons and ringlets and the contemplation of her own delicate, china-doll prettiness, which did not come from the Barforth side of the family at all.

Hannah and Joel, Edwin and my father all had something of my grandfather about them: 'black Barforths,' with his hooked nose and uncompromising jaw, and even I, although my oval face and smaller features came from my mother, had the dark Barforth eyes, the heavy, chocolate-coloured Barforth hair. But Elinor was pink as a new rose and as fragrant, very much as my Aunt Hattie must have been as a girl; extraordinarily dainty, impossibly vain, with hair of a pale, silvery fairness and eyes a cloudy tint somewhere between blue and green, her slender figure, even at fifteen, elegant in her meagre finery.

My cousin Hannah had one good gown for summer, another for winter, and a sensible bonnet which she wore day in, day out, needing no other decoration than her grand Barforth self-esteem, but Elinor, by ingenuity and skill with her needle and a little unashamed begging from her richer relations, contrived always to appear fresh from the hands of some fashionable city dressmaker. New muslin flounces would appear on the hem of some old dress of mine; a satin bonnet I had long discarded would acquire an ostrich plume taken from a cap of my mother's; a dashing straw hat, freshly crowned with spring flowers and the sauciest knots of ribbon, would be revealed, in whispers, as something for which Mrs Stevens had seen no further use. She would cut herself a wicked little spencer jacket from an evening cloak looted from my grandfather's attic, a sash and matching reticule from the lining, while her pursuit of fans and gloves and costly little bits and pieces was so shameless, so very much like the terrier who gnaws and worries and refuses to let go, that she rarely came away empty-handed.

But today, although her pink muslin dress was worthy of comment, her appearance seemed momentarily to have slipped her mind, and even my enthusiasm for the roses in her chignon and on her sash and the little posy of rosebuds and ribbons dangling from her arm failed to distract her fully.

'I had them from the minister's garden,' she said absently.

'Had them? You mean you took them?'

'Oh – yes, so I did. And why not? Hannah sent me to call – and I had no wish to go – and as I was coming away through the garden, there they were, the first of the season, just the thing for this gown. And I knew he'd never notice. Even if he had, I'd have picked them by then, and he'd hardly have expected me to put them back.'

'But what did you say to Hannah?'

'About the roses? That the minister is a Christian gentleman, which is true, surely? And that he gave them to me, which should be true if he's really a Christian. And if I'd asked him, I daresay he wouldn't have known how to refuse, so I've saved him the trouble, which you could almost say was very good of me.'

But even this example of her own cunning, her skill in playing the featherbrain to outwit her scrupulously honest sister, was not enough to lighten her mood, and as we picked our way up the stony little path to the Top House, she suddenly caught my hand and said urgently, 'Verity, let's hurry.'

'But why? We're not late.'

'No – at least, I suppose not, since I never know what time it is. I leave it to Hannah to tell me. But, Verity, just the same, even if we're not late, let's hurry.'

And glancing nervously over her shoulder at the mill and the millhouse, black in the valley below us, she whispered, 'There were men, you see, on the road as we came down to the mill, and I thought they meant to block our way, and Hannah thought so too although she kept saying, "Nonsense, Elinor, nonsense. Walk straight on." And so I did, for I meant to keep close to Joel. And it was no nonsense either, because they shuffled around us quite horribly, and even Hannah looked scared, which of course she wasn't, because she told me so. Anyway, Joel told them to move aside, and so they did, although some of them were quicker about it than others. But it was the muttering, Verity, and the scowling, and they were all so miserable – all of them, and all those others too, because I looked back, even though Joel told me not to – and they were all over the hillside, little groups of five or six everywhere, just staring down at the mill as if they hated it – staring like trees seem to stare sometimes, although Hannah said I was being fanciful, because trees have no eyes. But that's just the point: they haven't, and yet sometimes they still seem to see – and you'll know, Verity, how baleful they can be. Yes, that's what they put into my mind, fanciful or not – blind trees watching us. It must be the looms they hate, I suppose, and Joel said they were madmen to think they could stand in the way of progress. Although I don't know much about progress – well – if it means they're to lose their livelihood and their homes and live on the parish, then I daresay they don't think too well of it. But I could see what he meant about them being mad. Oh, Verity, do ask your mother to send us home in the carriage, because she won't think of it, and Hannah won't beg – and do please ask her in good time before dark – Verity?'

'Well, of course I'll ask her,' I promised easily, by no means alarmed, since Elinor would say almost anything to beg a ride in a carriage and her fears were usually no more than a means of making herself noticed. 'And if the horses have gone off somewhere or if she doesn't want them to go out again, then you can stay the night with me.'

But to spend the night at Lawcroft Fold, when she had seen it under siege, menaced by that dark human ring of trees, was not at all to her liking, and, as she caught my arm, her eager little hand touched its fear into my skin, sharpening my tongue.

'Oh, Elinor, such a fuss. And what a goose you always are. Trees, indeed. Weavers, that's all, having a grumble about the looms, and what more can they do but that? There's Edwin and Joel, and the soldiers down at the mill, and there's my grandfather. Do you think my grandfather – of all people – would let anyone harm us?'

He was waiting in the garden of the Top House, a gnarled old tree himself, sitting on a bench from which he could see the whole vast, stone-clad outer garment of his enterprises; his mill, his chimney stack, his school, his chapel, the grey tentacles of Cullingford that were creeping ever nearer, the millhouse he had built for his wife, the Top House, built for himself and his final indulgences, the grey smoke of prosperity, rising from the town, blowing eastward today, so that above his head there was even a patch of blue sky, a hopefully glimmering sun.

'So you've come to see me, Verity Barforth, have you?' he said. 'Good. And where's your mother?'

And looking behind him, I saw that my father's eyes were asking me the same question.

Edwin was there already, and my cousin Joel; and although they were superficially much alike, I judged my brother to be the pleasanter, easier man and knew somehow that Joel, for all his show of friendship, did not really like Edwin at all, considered him, in fact, to be a pompous fool and intended to get as much out of him as he could when they became brothers-in-law.

Joel Barforth was twenty-eight that year, somewhat leaner and considerably darker than Edwin, a man who had been wild in his youth – much addicted to cards and bare-knuckle prizefighting, to fancy wines and spirits instead of plain, honest ale – and although, on his father's death, he had shouldered his responsibilities in true Barforth fashion, Law Valley men still treated him with suspicion. In an area where a man's worth could often be measured by the engine grease and dirt ingrained beneath his fingernails, my cousin Joel's hands were always scrupulously manicured; and if, as a child, he had been notoriously threadbare, having been obliged, like his

28

mother, to pay for his father's extravagance, his garments now were always well chosen, well pressed, his boots highly polished, his cravat so elaborately arranged that the Law Valley often wondered how he could find the time. He was, I suspected, shrewd, hard, keen, cunning, one of the truest Barforths of them all – more like my grandfather, even, than Edwin – but my grandfather did not like him, had refused assistance at the height of Joel's troubles which he could easily have afforded to give, and even now when Joel had proved his ability to survive, was inclined to treat him scornfully, giving him no opportunity – when Edwin was there – to shine.

Certainly no one could accuse my brother of wasting time on dress, for it was very clear that even on his betrothal day, with a dozen coats to choose from, he had taken the first one that came to hand: peacock blue, as it turned out, with a yellow waistcoat and checked game-keeper's cravat, a poor showing indeed beside Joel's plum-coloured coat and dove-grey trousers, his white, artfully tucked and pleated shirt, the snowfall of his cravat that proclaimed the sartorial gulf between them. And although I could like him no better for it, I understood well enough why Joel so disliked my brother.

Edwin, with no effort whatsoever on his part, would inherit Lawcroft Fold, while Joel, at considerable personal sacrifice, would be lucky to hold on to his few leaking, broken-down sheds at Low Cross. Edwin had only to express the desire and instantly his grandfather had ordered power looms, soldiers to guard them, a new mill to put them in, leaving Joel to endure his scorching, unsatisfied ambitions. Edwin, at twenty-four, was to marry the girl of his choice, while Joel, four years older, could see no end to his courtship of a certain Miss Rosamund Boulton, who had agreed to wait but could not be expected to wait forever.

He had no greeting for me beyond a slight, formal nod, for I had no part in his schemes for the future. It was very

much in his interests, I knew, to marry his sister Hannah
to my brother, and his sister Elinor to any man with a few
hundred a year who would have her, thus relieving himself
of expense and responsibility and bringing him a step
nearer to marrying his own handsome Miss Boulton. But
I could be of no use to him in that, and, giving Elinor a
look which clearly told her to behave herself, he turned
back to his conversation with my grandfather. And I was
aware that behind his deference he was as bitter and
seething as a bad November, acknowledging my grandfather's malice and returning like for like.

Sitting gracefully on its shelf of landscaped greenery cut
from the otherwise bare hillside, fragrant among its beds
of lavender and carnations and feathery foreign greenery,
the Top House was not a place I greatly cared for. No one
could fault its elegance or its comfort, or feel anything less
than admiration for its airy, high-ceilinged rooms, moulded
in blue and white and gold, and furnished in a lightweight,
light-coloured style Mrs Stevens believed to be French and
which I had always thought too insubstantial for my
grandfather. But Mrs Stevens, who knew all the arts of
pleasing men and practised them lovingly, had scant
regard for the opinions of women and none at all for those
of young girls; and although my brother – and even my
father – often came here to be cosseted and flattered and
to sample her excellent mulled wine, she had a way of
making me feel unnecessary so that I was never sorry to
leave.

But Hannah, the chosen bride, who would be mistress
of Lawcroft, when her time came, in a far more positive
way than my mother, was not to be neglected – certainly
not by Mrs Stevens, who knew my grandfather was not
immortal and that she would have her living to earn when
he was gone – and it was no surprise to me to see her and
Hannah whispering together, Hannah straight and tall
and just a little ill at ease, Mrs Stevens a soft breeze
fluttering around her, murmuring of stolen kisses and

wedding bells and the recipe for her special syllabub, a secret she would entrust to no one else.

She was a slender, boneless woman, Mrs Stevens, moving in a constant aura of rose water and gentle, obliging laughter, a superb housekeeper whose larder shelves were a temptation of savoury pies and pickles, custards and cheesecakes, her kitchen ceiling festooned with glazed, exotically flavoured hams, garlanded with spicy sausages, and, in season, festering with illegal game from Lawcroft Moor. Her seedcakes and spice cakes were famous, her apple jellies miraculous, her bowls of potpourri quite unique, her smile extremely caressing, yet I did not like her, my mother did not like her, and I was relieved to see my cousin Hannah draw back a little, as if she found the older woman's perfume too cloying, her manner altogether too winsome for her age and her station.

But Mrs Stevens was too experienced a campaigner to be unduly dismayed and, quite certain that Hannah would need an ally in time when she came to share a home with my mother, she gave my cousin's arm a final, loving squeeze and came floating towards me with an air of such deliberate secrecy that everybody turned to listen.

'Verity, dear,' she whispered, knowing how well whispers carry, 'it is well past three o'clock. Does your mamma mean to honour us, or has it slipped her mind?'

'I was just wondering the same myself,' Edwin muttered, heavy with his great news. 'She'll be in the garden, I shouldn't wonder, talking to the flowers or watching the grass grow. Well, I've got something to say and I've a mind to say it now—'

'You'll wait,' my father told him, 'until your mother comes.'

But Edwin looked through my father to my grandfather, and seeing the pain in my father's face, I said quickly, 'She'll be here presently. She told me so.'

'Aye, she told you so and promptly forgot all about it, or else she never meant to come at all, which is more likely.

She knows well what I have to say, and why she can't bring herself to like it I'll never know. No – and she'll never explain herself either. She'll smile and say, "How very nice," and I tell you, there are times when it's too much – when it won't serve—'

'Edwin,' my father said dangerously, 'I told you to wait and you'll have the manners to do it, and keep a civil tongue in your head while you're about it.'

'Oh, dear,' Hannah murmured, moving swiftly between them, angry in her turn with my mother for keeping Edwin waiting, angry with my father for taking his wife's part against his son, yet intending her role to be that of peacemaker. But her intervention was not needed, for at the same moment, my grandfather rose lumberingly yet quite majestically to his feet.

'Say your piece, lad,' he ordered bluntly, as if my father were not there at all. 'It's past three o'clock and there's meat on Mrs Stevens's table too good to spoil. Let's hear you.'

I saw, like fragments of stained glass, my father's jealous hurt, my brother's satisfaction at getting his way and his certainty of getting it again, their mutual hostility, and the cold, sardonic gleam in my cousin Joel's eyes as he watched the Barforth ranks so sadly split asunder.

'Well, it's no secret, I reckon,' Edwin said, his strong brown fingers reaching out for Hannah and claiming her with an enthusiasm that touched us all and may have given her actual pain. 'It's time I was wed – high time – and there's no other lass I'd want for a wife but Hannah. They told me to choose a sound woman, one who'd look me in the eye and see things my way, and there's no woman anywhere more straightforward. She'd never keep me waiting and keep me guessing – no, I know where I am with Hannah. And that's what I have to say. We've known a long time how things were likely to turn out between us, and today I told her it was time we got it settled, and so we did. She's to be my wife as soon as she likes – the sooner, the better – and if anybody don't care for it, then it's all the same to me.'

'Oh, Edwin,' Mrs Stevens sighed, 'how beautiful. Oh, Edwin – and Hannah, too – how very moving. We all of us wish you well – all of us, I'm sure.'

As if at her signal, there was a surge of congratulations, of back slapping and kissing, Edwin preening himself like a gigantic, slightly embarrassed peacock, Hannah mindful of her dignity yet conveying to him with every glance, every movement of her square, capable hands that she would be everything he wished, hard-working mistress of his house, enduring companion of his bed, mother of his dozen sturdy sons, with nothing elusive about her, nothing to intrigue him, nothing to plague him or to remind him in any way of his mother. And when the kissing was done we went into Mrs Stevens's high-vaulted, deep-windowed dining parlour to gorge ourselves on her chicken pie, her hot new-baked bread, her almond creams, and my grandfather's wine.

My grandfather sat heavily at the head of his festive board, eating little, gazing with a certain sentimental satisfaction at Mrs Stevens as she performed her intricate little domestic ballet around the table, coaxing the men to partake of this and that, to try just a little more of the other, leaving the women to fend for themselves, not really caring whether they were served or not. The engaged couple remained side by side, stiff with self-conscious happiness, Hannah's smile deliberately cool, her eyes excited and hot, her hand, I thought, still in Edwin's, concealed by a fold of Mrs Stevens's lace cloth. But my father, after some brief discussion with Joel, hovered restlessly a moment or two before retreating to the window seat to stare moodily out of the window which would give him the best view of the path my mother would be bound to take; and when Mrs Stevens offered him a wedge of her chicken pie and a murmur of sympathy I missed neither his irritable gesture of dismissal nor my grandfather's frown.

'We'll drink to the future,' my grandfather said very loud, his glance flickering over my father, leaving him and settling on Edwin. 'Yes – Edwin and Hannah – the future. Let's have the champagne, Mrs Stevens, and while we're about it I'll give you something else to drink to. Now that we're all assembled – all of us, that is, who choose to assemble – I have this to tell you. The new looms will be in production by the end of next month, with more of them on the way and more on order, and it's only fitting that there should be a new mill to house them. Yes, Edwin, I saw my builders yesterday and when it's done, lad, when it's six storeys high, we'll pack it full of every newfangled device those engineers can offer us, so long as there's a profit to be made. That's it, lad, eh? Power and profit, progress, if that's what you like to call it. And it's all to be yours, lad, one day, yours and Hannah's.'

'By God,' Edwin said, his eyes on fire, his knuckles showing white as his fingers crushed themselves around Hannah's wrist, heedless of the pain he must be causing her and which she, gritting her teeth behind her smile, bore like some unflinching shield-maiden of old.

'Oh yes, to the future,' sighed Mrs Stevens, her eyes resting for an instant on my cousin Joel, speculatively, appreciatively, remembering the tales she'd heard of his wild days, imagining for a self-indulgent moment how things could be if she were younger, Joel richer, while he, who could afford to neglect no opportunity, raised his glass to her very slightly, his eyes quite caressing but the brain behind them, I thought, working out exactly what he'd do in Edwin's place and concluding, no doubt, that he'd do it better.

'The future?' my father said, asking a question, his voice toneless, tired. And I would have gone to his side had not Elinor, by no means pleased that it was Hannah's future they were all discussing and not her own, suddenly

34

whispered in my ear, 'Well, if that's the best your brother can do I don't envy Hannah. What a proposal. I shall expect something more romantic than that, especially the first time.'

'And who's going to marry you?'

'Somebody – somebody special. And lots more will want to and be dreadfully upset when they can't.'

'Oh yes, to be sure – hundreds,' I told her lightly, knowing her portion would be even smaller than Hannah's; so small, in fact, that it may not get her married at all. But Elinor, who knew as well as I did that marriages were composed of settlements and vested interests, acreage and who one's father happened to be on good terms with at the time, had enough faith in her own undeniable charms to be able to set these matters aside.

'Oh, I'll get married soon enough,' she announced airily, 'and I know exactly how it will be. I'll have strawberries and champagne for breakfast on my wedding morning, to start off with, and after that I'll sit with my toes on the fender whenever I feel like it. I'm going to have a perfectly lovely time, Verity. I've quite made up my mind to it. Let's both have a lovely time – let's go and ask Mrs Stevens for some more champagne.'

But my father suddenly caught my eye, frowned as if I had somehow displeased him and, instead of following Elinor, I crossed to the window and looked out, hoping to see my mother and knowing I wouldn't.

'Now then, miss,' my father hissed straight into my ear. 'Why didn't she come with you? Didn't I tell you to walk up here, by three o'clock, with your mother?' But he well knew the injustice of expecting me to compel her when he had never found a way to do it himself; and frowning again, he patted my arm – sorry, in his heart, that because of her, and because I had her face, he could not altogether love me.

'She'll come,' I told him. And seeing that I had annoyed him further with my sympathy, I said quickly, 'Father,

Elinor wishes to go home in the carriage. May I tell her yes?'

'Why not?' he said, not caring. 'Just as you please.'

But Hannah, whose ears were in every way as sharp as her eyes and her tongue, was suddenly upon us, flushed with indignation that anyone should be asked to get their horses out on her behalf. 'There is absolutely no need,' she said, rude almost in her wounded pride. 'My sister pampers herself; I'm always telling her so. If her feet hurt, then I'm sorry, but the exercise will do her good.'

But Elinor could be braver, sometimes, than one supposed, was always far shrewder than most people gave her credit for, and her doll's face crumpling with a most becoming distress, her cloudy eyes turning in helpless, tearful entreaty – unerringly – to my grandfather, she whispered, 'But it's not that, Hannah. You know – quite well – that I'm afraid.'

'Afraid.' Immediately the Barforth men stood tall on their earthbound, well-shod feet. 'Afraid? How's this?' And as the tale came spilling from Elinor's lips, protest was loud and, for a moment or two, quite ugly.

'If anyone's harmed you—' Edwin threatened, while Joel, just as threateningly, answered him, 'There was no harm done. I can look after my sisters, I reckon.'

'Oh dear, dear me,' Mrs Stevens murmured, floating between them. 'The poor, poor lambs. And yet there is absolutely nothing to fear. Mr Barforth has said so, and I am sure you can believe him. Mr Barforth has lived through times like these before, and, my dears, he knows. You may all be easy.'

'I'll be easier in a month from now, when the looms are running – if they ever are,' my father said suddenly, astonishingly. 'It's true, what the lass says. There are men on the hillside. I've seen them myself, spoken to them myself, and by God – and I don't care who hears me say it – they have my sympathy. A sheep allows itself to be slaughtered, but a man – well, perhaps I'd fight before I'd see my children starve or put them out to work for a man like me. Yes, so I would, and there's no one here who wouldn't do the same.'

'My goodness,' Mrs Stevens exclaimed, outwardly thunderstruck but inwardly very well pleased to see my father's final fall from grace, for he was handsomer, easier than my grandfather, a man of her own age, and it was my belief that she'd once offered herself to him and been refused. But if she had expected my grandfather to show his anger she was disappointed, for he knew a deadlier trick than that; lifting himself heavily to his feet, he put one hand on Edwin's shoulder, the other on Joel's, his gnarled, old man's fingers gripping them with the tenacity of thirsty tree roots that will not be denied.

'We'll walk a little, lads,' he said. 'Take the air. Maybe we'll go and have a look at these men who choose to set foot on my land. Maybe we'll remind them that my permission's required – you and me, lads. And if you've no stomach for it, son William, then I expect you'll be going home to your wife – if you can find her.'

And it was then that my mother, suddenly, was among us, leaning gracefully in the doorway with hardly more substance than a shadow but with something in her that reduced Samson Barforth's magnificence to meanness, Mrs Stevens's caressing charm to the antics of a bawdy house, my brother and Joel and my cousin Hannah to callow, grasping youngsters who had not altogether remembered their manners.

'Isabella,' my father said sharply, and although I think he meant to say, 'Where have you been?' the words came out, 'Are you all right?'

'Why yes, dear,' she told him. 'Should I be otherwise? Mrs Stevens, do allow me to congratulate you on your table. Is that your famous syllabub and your excellent lemon cheesecake? Delicious – everyone says so – but no, I eat so little – just a sip of wine and a whisper of a macaroon – so kind. Yes, I was sewing, and the time simply slipped away – you'll understand how that can happen, being such a busy woman yourself – and then there was the man – Oh, did I forget about the man? I do believe so. A man came into the garden as I was about to leave and called me back – quite a rough person, I must confess. Ira Agbrigg, he said his name was, and I have no reason to disbelieve him, for he kept on saying it over and over, "Ira Agbrigg, ma'am, that's my name," so I am drawn to conclude he is working for a reward. Ah yes – he bade me tell you that the men are no longer on the hillside and in the woods – not that I ever imagined they were – but that they are all gone to Lawcroft Green. Three hundred of them, he said – a meeting of protest, he called it – and that I was to tell you they are in deadly earnest, that the talk is of desperate measures. Oh dear, three hundred, which perhaps means two hundred, since he was clearly much alarmed and may not have counted right. But even so, there are no more than a dozen soldiers. Ah well, one must hope that it will rain.'

'Rain, Isabella?' my father said, bewildered.

'Rain,' my grandfather echoed, his jaw thrust pugnaciously forward, his face so swollen and mottled with rage that Hannah, mindful of her new duties, planted herself directly in front of my mother and said loudly, 'Rain, Aunt Isabella? Why rain?'

'To put out the torches, dear,' she said reasonably, sweetly. 'For if they have torches, as Mr Ira Agbrigg said they did, then one can only suppose they are coming to burn the mill – which is quite shocking, of course, and most unwise, but quite easy to do, one supposes, since raw wool is greasy, I believe, and easily set ablaze. Dear Mrs Stevens, you have turned quite pale; and Hannah, too. But surely, didn't I hear you just now telling each other that there is nothing to fear – so little, in fact, that my husband may just as well come home to his wife, if he could find her – which, of course, he couldn't, since I am here.'

Like everyone else, I had no idea whether she spoke in

great malice or great innocence; whether she wished to hurt my father or defend him. But one thing I did know, and perhaps it was to alter the whole course of my life: I had thought of my mother as a weak woman, helpless in the face of Barforth disapproval, and I had thought of strength in terms of loud Barforth voices, a hard male fist, a dark Barforth eye. Yet now I had witnessed a new kind of strength, as quietly, airily, almost dreamily my mother dismayed and defeated them all.

3

My grandfather, needless to say, was the first to recover.

'So it's damned Luddites again,' he announced quite cheerfully, a gleam in his eye that may have been satisfaction, since he was a man who not only enjoyed a fight but always expected to win. 'Aye, Luddites. I thought we'd got rid of that particular breed of vermin way back. When was it? Must have been 1812, I reckon – when you were just a baby, Verity lass – when we all got letters signed "General Ludd," saying how they'd murder us unless we rid ourselves of our vile machinery. It was the shearing frames they didn't like in those days, and, damn me, if they didn't mean business. Aye, those Luddite hammermen thought they were heroes all right, smashing down honest men's doors to get at the frames, their pikemen and hatchetmen coming behind; and what they couldn't break they'd burn. Damned heroes – forty thousand men they said they'd got, ready to crush us and crush the King with us unless he toed their line – and set up King Ludd in his place, I reckon. And that was enough – after a fire or two – to scare the smaller manufacturers into giving way. But then they went up against William Cartwright at Rawfolds, over in the Spen Valley, and he was ready – he'd brought in the soldiers and posted lookouts; he'd even set spiked rollers on his stairs and a tub of oil of vitriol on his landing in case they broke in. Not that they did. A round or two of musket fire, that's all – killed a couple of them and wounded a few more, and off they went – scattered them and made them think again. Most of them had had enough by then, I reckon, which is why the ringleaders turned sour and murdered William Horsfall not long after. Aye, I remember Will Horsfall well – a plainspoken man with a decent business over Huddersfield way – and he was ready for them, too. Even had a cannon in his mill yard, as I recall; not that it did him much good, since they waited for him one night when he was riding home over Crosland Moor and shot him out of his saddle.

'Damned Luddites, with their oaths and ceremonies, and their hammers – swore eternal brotherhood, they did, and how they'd suffer hell's torment before they'd turn traitor. And all it took to break them, in the end, was money.

'I'm ready to admit there must have been hundreds – thousands – hereabouts who knew their names and faces, gave them shelter and money and never would have turned them in. But we only needed one greedy man – just one – and when we offered two thousand pounds for the names of Horsfall's murderers, we found him. And that was the end of it, son William, grandson Edwin. We rounded them up, sent them to York to be hanged, and the rest soon went skulking off home. And if the Law Valley remembers them at all, it remembers how hard it was for their women and children to manage without them; it remembers that the machines came in just the same – that it wasn't worth dying for. And these men today aren't real Luddites, I'll be bound. They'll have sworn no oaths nor bound themselves blood brothers. They're just common rioters, without leadership or discipline, and they'll turn tail soon enough. Come, then; we'll all go down to the millhouse and see what's to do.'

But Mrs Stevens, for once, was not of the same mind.

'I must put that child to bed, really I must,' she suddenly cried out, making a dash at the considerably startled Elinor. 'Can't you see she's about to swoon?'

Although Elinor had no intention of swooning and began to say so, Mrs Stevens would have none of it.

'The child can barely keep her feet,' she insisted feverishly, 'which is hardly to be wondered at. But don't concern yourselves. Go and do what must be done, and I will take care of her. A child of her years – and her sensitive disposition – must not be exposed to scenes of violence. It could do her lasting harm – I only pray that the mere thought of it has not harmed her already. But don't let it distract you from your purpose. You may all safely leave her with me.'

And making it abundantly clear that with a sick girl on her hands no one should count on her for very much else, she shepherded the unwilling Elinor away.

We left then in a tight procession that gradually lengthened and separated, my mother gliding effortlessly ahead with no apparent thought of danger, my father stumping behind, heavier of foot, heavier of spirit, unable as always to catch her. Behind them came Hannah, straight-backed, calm, refusing to hurry, walking with a deliberately measured tread since one never knew who might be watching, preparing herself for her new role as my brother's support and inspiration in time of trouble.

But Edwin was not so self-possessed. His immediate instinct had been to stride on ahead, to bar the gate – his gate, his mill, his looms – with his own body if required, but my grandfather could not easily walk alone and, peevishly brushing aside my father's offer of help – 'Look to your wife, son William, ere you lose her again' – he held out an imperious arm to Edwin, the other to my cousin Joel.

'These lads will see me right,' he said, leaning heavily, I thought, on Joel; taking pleasure, perhaps, in crushing his sleeve since he had always mistrusted a dandy and knew that if this coat should be damaged Joel would not find it easy to get another.

'You'll have your work cut out to watch that pretty jacket of yours today, Joel my boy,' he said gleefully, his old man's malice rising into a chuckle. 'There'll be a stain or two on it by nightfall, I shouldn't wonder – and grime under your fingernails, for once, millmaster, if they get to burn the sheds. And what are you doing there, Verity Barforth – mooning about, taking all in and saying nothing, like your mother. Why don't you come and give me your arm and set your brother free? It won't have crossed your mind, girl, that he's eager to get to the fray – that he takes after me.'

And, panting, wheezing, working himself up into a mighty rage – hating me for my youth and my inferior sex, hating Joel for his keen wits that must always be a threat to Edwin, hating my father for obeying him and hurrying after his wife, hating his own body for its weakness when his spirit was eager to take a hundred rioters by the throat – he sank his gnarled old fingers into my arm and came stamping home.

For I believe the millhouse, in his heart, was his home, built when he had been a solid workingman, for a workingwoman without pretensions, who had been content to sit in her stone-flagged kitchen, within sound and scent of his machinery, and had required nothing more for her comfort than the one square parlour, cheerfully allowing him to use the other downstairs room as a countinghouse and, sometimes, a storage space for raw wool. They had stacked wool upstairs, too, in my grandmother's day; in the back spare bedrooms, in the attics, anywhere a corner could be found, and although she was long dead and he had been glad enough to move on to the graces of the Top House and Mrs Stevens, whenever he came here he instinctively looked for her and was not pleased to find my mother in her stead.

'Well then – well then,' he said threateningly, shouldering his way through the door. 'And where's this Ira Agbrigg of yours, Isabella? Spirited him away, have you?'

But Ira Agbrigg was waiting, cap in hand, a thin, pasty-faced, weak-eyed man somewhere around thirty, shabby and shamefaced, a strange blending of terror and determination washing over him as my grandfather and my brother closed in, eager for anything he could tell them and perhaps willing to pay for it but not much liking a traitor, just the same.

'Let's have it all again, lad,' my grandfather ordered. Out it all came: the mutterings and the resentments, the panic, the gnawing, hopeless fears of the cottagers, which, without leadership, might have remained impotent.

'So there's a ringleader, then?' my grandfather said excitedly.

And so, it seemed, there was: Jabez Gott, a young Law Valley man who had been 'away' – in prison, one supposed, for some contravention of the 'gag acts' prohibiting political assembly; a man whose father had been transported to Australia for disobedience, whose brother had been slaughtered by a British sabre on the Manchester battlefield of Peterloo, whence he had gone to demand the right to vote; a man who had lived some time in Lancashire, where the machines had taken a firmer hold, and who had seen starvation for himself. A wizened old man of twenty-two, Jabez Gott, whose eighteen-year-old wife had died in pregnancy, from lack of nourishment, and who openly avowed that he had nothing more to lose. And he it was who, assembling a group of like-minded men around him, had convinced the steadier minds of the Law Valley that soon they would have nothing to lose either, and had gathered up their fear and moulded it, like iron, into a weapon.

'Jabez Gott,' my grandfather said. 'Never heard of him – but I'll keep the name in mind. It's always as well to have a name.' And taking Edwin and my father and Ira Agbrigg with him, he went off to the kitchen to find the

43

only chair remaining from my grandmother's day and to make his plans.

I sat down in my accustomed place by the hearth, knowing that nothing would be required of me. Hannah sat very stiff and straight at my side, puzzled and rather hurt that nothing had yet been required of her. Joel, all too obviously excluded from the war party, stood by the hearth, tapping his foot against the fender. My mother calmly took up her embroidery, and for a long time there seemed nothing to do but listen to the rasping of my grandfather's voice in the next room, the excited rise and fall of Edwin's, the low restrained muttering of my father, as they extracted more names from Ira Agbrigg, whose voice could not be heard at all.

'Poor Mr Agbrigg,' my mother said, looking up from her stitching. 'He is betraying his friends, you know, and is very much ashamed, although I am sure he has his reasons. He may have told himself it will prevent bloodshed and he may believe it – and, for his sake, we must hope your grandfather will remember him. Oh dear, I forgot the name of the man who delivered William Horsfall's murderers to justice – do you remember, just now, your grandfather was telling us they had offered a two-thousand-pound reward? I remember the occasion, too, and it is quite certain that the man, whoever he was, did not receive his money. He died in extreme poverty, I believe, and had been made very miserable a long while before, since no one would speak a word either to him or to his family. They cut him off completely – exiled him – which, of course, he must have expected; he would, no doubt, have moved away, if he had received his money. But, as I said, he did not.

'Joel dear, since one can never be certain what the day may bring, if you should care to change your coat, I feel sure Edwin will have something more suited to the occasion. In fact, I am sure of it, since my son is not very

44

particular. If it eases your mind, dear, do take it off and let me find you another.'

But Hannah, always suspicious of my mother, always resentful at any reference to her poverty, cried out, 'Aunt Isabella, really – how can you suppose – how can you? – that Joel would consider his dress at such a time?'

Sensing, perhaps, the angry tears burning behind her eyes, knowing how mortified she would be if they came to be shed, her brother turned from his contemplation of the hearth and gave my mother a smile that was superficially charming, totally false.

'I really don't know why I shouldn't,' he said calmly, very coldly. 'Most kind of you, Aunt Isabella, but I believe I'll decline. Somebody will have to go and fetch a magistrate, you see – I reckon Edwin's grandfather will be out in a minute or two to tell us so – and if I'm to ride into Cullingford, or out of it, or up to Patterswick to bring the squire, then I'd feel – easier – in my own clothes, Edwin's taste not being the same as mine.'

'Just as you please, dear,' my mother said, amusement hovering at the corners of her mouth.

Although my grandfather was never a comfort to me, I was relieved – as I saw Hannah start to bristle – when the door burst open and the room filled up again with his towering, demanding presence.

'That's it, then,' he snorted. 'Just like last time. Three hundred, this fellow says, assembled on the green, with at least half of them ready to come here and take issue with me. Now then, lads, here's what we'll do. Son William may stay here to guard the women, and as for you boys, one of you can come with me to the mill yard to make sure those redcoats know how to earn their sixpence a day and the other can fetch a magistrate. Edwin, which is it to be?'

'I'll stay. It's my place,' Edwin said, and then he frowned suddenly, for there was glory to be had, too, in riding hard and alone across the troubled hillsides, in going out to meet danger unaided instead of waiting for it, tamely, behind a line of redcoats, at home. And his inability to be in two places at once caused him evident frustration.

'Shall I stay?' he asked himself out loud.

My cousin Joel, still lounging by the fireplace, answered for him. 'Oh, I expect so. You stay and review your troops, Edwin – much the best thing – and leave the rest to me.'

'And what do you mean by that, exactly?'

'Anything you like to make of it.'

'Something low and dirty, I'll be bound,' Edwin snarled. Then, as Hannah made a sharp, horrified sound and half rose to her feet, he turned towards her – remembering, after all, that it was her betrothal day, that Joel was her brother – and said, not altogether apologetically, 'Well, I'm sorry for that, Hannah, because the last thing I want to do is upset you, and I know life hasn't been easy. But it's not my fault I've had the advantages. There's no cause for me to be ashamed because I'm rich and likely to get richer – never been ashamed of anything in my life. And if I was as poor as a church mouse I'd be damned before I'd go about envying other people. And if I was envious I'd make damned sure I didn't show it.'

'Envious?' Joel said, his long, lounging body as taut now as Hannah's, the white-lipped anger in him reaching out for Edwin, who was very ready to meet it. 'Envious? Just tell me that again, cousin Edwin.'

'Yes, gladly, cousin Joel. Can you look me in the eye and say you don't wish those machines down there were yours?'

'Well now, cousin Edwin, I might look you in the eye and say they'd do better if they were.'

And as the two of them moved together, perfectly prepared to thrash each other in my mother's parlour, my grandfather's arm shot between them like a bar of iron.

'You'd say that, would you, Joel Barforth?' he said very quietly. 'Well – for the moment I reckon I didn't hear you. But if you've got yourself into an evil frame of mind, so much the better. You'll get the chance to work it off, I shouldn't wonder, before the day's through. Now go and tell them to saddle you a horse. And you, Edwin lad, come with me.'

The day had clouded over, easing itself now towards evening, and as my mother immersed herself once more in her sewing and Hannah continued to stare down at her tightly clasped hands, her loyalties badly torn, I settled myself on the window seat, my eyes drawn to the mill. The soldiers were still there, taking their ease, but otherwise the yard wore its everyday face: the comings and goings of carts piled high with bales that, from loose corners, shed scraps of wool like dandelion puffs on the night air; other carts heavy-laden with finished pieces, setting off on the rutted, bone-shaking road to Leeds or to the canal which, sluggishly, slowly, carried our goods to Liverpool and the sea.

The sheds would soon be emptying, bringing the yard briefly alive with the busy sound of wooden clogs on stone, the patient outline of female heads covered in the fold of a shawl, the jauntiness of cloth caps set at an angle on wiry, north country curls, leaving behind the engineers and loom tuners, who had an interest in defending the machines, and the soldiers. And who knew how many of our own operatives would go quietly home and how many would find their way to Cullingford Green, to join brothers and fathers and cousins, torch in hand. Could we really be sure that the soldiers, who must have friends – sweethearts even – among the weavers, would risk too much on our account? As the shadows lengthened and deepened, I felt obliged to ask myself if I was brave, and found no answer.

My life, until today, had been as outwardly bland as the long coils of wool combed ready for spinning, perfectly smooth, cloud-textured, cream-textured, and if, inside me, I had encountered a few tangles, if now and again I resented my grandfather's supreme authority, if I could not always believe my brother to be totally in the right, if I wanted my father to love me and my mother to love my

47

father, none of that had been terrible. If I had sometimes felt out of tune with myself, sitting in my mother's cool shadow, realizing I had not inherited her skill with a needle, at least the chair had been comfortable, the fireside warm. I had been safe. Yet now, through the spring twilight, a harsher world beckoned to me – a world where Jabez Gott's wife, a girl not much past my own age, had died of pregnancy and starvation, where Jabez Gott's brother had been massacred at the place called Peterloo near Manchester when soldiers like the ones now lounging in our yard had ridden with drawn swords into a peaceful crowd who had assembled merely to demand a small measure of parliamentary reform, and left more than a hundred men, women, and children bleeding on the ground.

How would I feel tonight if Jabez Gott's brother should die all over again, outside my window, leaving his blood on the cobbles of Lawcroft Fold? How *should* I feel?

My grandfather, I knew, would be triumphant, considering it no more than every Jabez Gott deserved. My mother would make some cool, pointed remark and drift back to her embroidery. Hannah would say, 'Well done, Edwin.' Mrs Stevens would comfort us all with cakes and wine. And I, being a good girl, would eat those cakes, speak when spoken to, give them the answers they expected to hear, not because I feared them but because to be different, in the house of Samson Barforth, was to be alone. But I could not rid myself of the impression of a pair of eyes, flickering somewhere behind my own: huge lack-lustre eyes in a hollow face which may have belonged to the wife of Jabez Gott or to a dozen girls I had seen tramping the hills, a child straddling their hips, going nowhere, wanted nowhere. And forcing myself into their wasted shapes, putting stones beneath my own bare feet and the tugging stranglehold of a child's arms around my neck – a child myself, as they were, bearing other children – I shivered.

'Are you afraid?' my father said, appearing suddenly beside me.

When I nodded he touched my arm briefly, timidly almost, since he had shown me little affection in the past and found it awkward now.

'There's no need. They'll not seek to harm you. They're not savages, just men who see their world coming to an end and who very likely know there's not much they can do about it. Nothing except make a stand, that is – a protest – and when that's all a man has left, who can blame him? Jabez Gott may believe he can set the world to rights by burning Lawcroft Fold, but the men behind him – or most of them – know it can't be as easy as that. They know we'd build again – for somebody will always build, somebody must build – and if they follow Jabez Gott at all it's only to make their voices heard – as men should be heard – because they're too proud to go under without a cry. They know it's over. Before the factories cornered the markets, Verity, there wasn't a cottager of my acquaintance who made less than thirty shillings a week, and now some of them are living on as little as four shillings – or not living, exactly, but keeping body and soul together, taking the outwork it pleases us to give them for as much as we're pleased to pay. They had meat, Verity, when I was a lad, and white bread, and the occasional bottle of rum, but now it's oatmeal and potatoes, and when there's none of that they'll stew nettle broth, aye, and tell you it's tasty and wholesome if you happen to enquire. Poor devils, it's their tragedy to be caught in the wrong place at the wrong time; to have been born when their traditional way of life is ending, when events are moving too fast to do anything but sweep them away. Your brother and your cousin Joel tell me there won't be a handloom in the Law Valley five years from now. Well, they're young men, and hasty, and I'd say longer, a fair bit longer, but it has to come just the same. They'll hang on, for they're a tough breed and stubborn, and not all the millmasters will turn against them. Old Ben Hobhouse, over at Nethercoats, don't care for power looms, but old Ben won't live forever, and his son is likely to be as hasty as mine when the time comes for him to take over. No, they'll be squeezed out – starved out – and even the most pigheaded among them is going to end up using his handloom for firewood one of these bad winters.'

'But if we expand, Father, like Edwin said, they can work for us, can't they – in the mill?'

'Can they?' he said, staring past me to the mill and the bare hillside beyond it. 'I'm not so sure. When your brother builds the new factory he's dreaming of, he'll put a high stone wall around it and a big iron gate, and if you'd been a free, stubborn man all your life, you may not care to hear the clang of those factory gates shutting behind you every morning. If you were a countryman, of course, you'd find it easier, because you'd be accustomed to pulling your forelock to the parson and the squire. But a lad born in those cottages grows up to be his own master, and he'd find it hard having to doff his cap every time he met your grandfather, or Edwin – or me – crossing the mill yard. In fact, he'd find it so hard that I doubt he'd do it at all. He'd more likely turn sour and disobedient and hard to handle. No, they'll keep on doing outwork as long as we'll allow it, but I don't think they'll work for us in the mill – not this generation. And I'm not sure we'd take them.'

'But what then, Father? What else can they do?'

'I don't know, and it troubles me. I think a whole generation may just pass away. Some of them will die, a few will move on, but most of them will strive and struggle for pennies – they'll eat nettles when they have to, and grow old and bitter, I shouldn't wonder, until their children are old enough to be earning. Because the new generation will come to us. And even then, I don't know – I don't know. This afternoon, at the mill, your cousin Joel got his hands on the new looms, and he wondered if a man's strength would be needed for their operation. It seemed to him that a woman would suffice, and women, you know, don't swing Luddite hammers, and they'll accept what's offered them in the way of wages far more readily than a man, especially when they've got children to be fed. So we may prefer to fill our sheds with women. And have you considered the Irish? They've been pouring into Cullingford by the cartload these last few years, since the potato crop started to fail – big, strapping wenches who could make two of most of ours. And everybody knows the Irish will work for less.'

'Are the weavers right, then, Father?' I asked timidly, badly wanting to know, and he made an angry movement, a regretful movement.

'No, of course they are not. One cannot – one should not – stand in the way of progress. In that, at least, I am in agreement with my father and my son. The weavers have no more right to forbid us our machines than we are entitled to deprive them of their means of existence. We should lean towards each other – realize we are of the same species, not alien beings snarling at each other like packs of rival hounds. We are laying up bitterness, Verity, for the future – a cesspit of bitterness – Jabez Gott and your grandfather both – for at the extremity of their views they are both equally wrong.'

But here, it seemed, he had said too much and, giving me a puzzled look, wondering why on earth he was unburdening himself to his daughter, he patted me once again, rather clumsily, on the arm and went away.

My grandfather spent a long time in the mill yard, pacing up and down in front of the soldiers, telling their officer how to handle his men in exactly the same fashion as he often told the parson how to manage his church, the banker his bank; and even if his presence caused the men to straighten their shoulders and button their tunics, they were still an unkempt, ill-favoured assembly and numbered no more than a dozen.

'One hesitates to expect too much of them,' my mother said, nodding pleasantly to the officer, who had caught her eye through the window. 'Perhaps one should consider why they enlist in the first place – meagre pay and meagre rations, and a public flogging every time they misbehave. I doubt if anyone really picks them up when they fall in battle – not all of them, at any rate.'

And, watching the blend of scorn and embarrassment on Hannah's face, I wondered how they would contrive to live together, how I would contrive to live between them, and the arrival of Joel and the magistrate was welcome.

He was Squire Dalby of Patterswick, a man of aristocratic temper and broad acres, a believer in the perfect authority – so far as his tenants were concerned – of the Established English Church, an ardent supporter of the Corn Laws, which had brought hunger to the cities, a subscriber to the view that since God had fixed every man at birth in the place He wished to see him, it was no less than sinful to try to change it. Although he stood for law and order and would have been as ready to hang a child for stealing a shilling as a grown man for slitting his neighbour's throat, he had no liking for upstart manufacturers who, now that they had made their dirty money, were demanding extravagant privileges like seats on the Bench and voices in the House of Commons, which belonged – by law and by Divine Right – only to landed gentlemen.

'Having a spot of bother, are we, Barforth, dear fellow?' he asked my grandfather, making small distinction, it seemed, between Samson Barforth, who owned the machines, and Jabez Gott, who was out to break them. Yet he accepted a glass of wine and a slice of the seedcake Mrs Stevens had hastily sent down from the Top House – assuming my mother's larder to be bare – while the sight of my mother herself, in her light green gauze, her shawl sliding gracefully around her shoulders, appeared to afford him immense pleasure.

'Have we met, madam – surely?' he murmured, quizzing

52

glass at the ready, taking no more trouble to conceal his appreciation than if she had been a milkmaid. Even when my father and my grandfather intervened, for different reasons, he continued to talk to them and look at her.

'Will you not come into the kitchen a moment, Aunt Isabella?' Hannah asked, altogether shocked by the squire's free and easy manner.

'Why, dear?' my mother replied, her grey velvet eyes quizzical and amused. 'What have I to do there?'

And Hannah had no choice but to leave her alone.

'One would expect her to leave the room for her husband's sake,' I heard her mutter to Joel, but my cousin, who had scoured the hillsides on his way to fetch the magistrate, had weightier things on his mind than a little middle-aged flirtation and, striding forward, hastily gave his opinion that the yeomanry should have been called out, and a few stout special constables, to make a show.

'Have we not done enough then, lad, in your opinion?' my grandfather enquired with deceptive mildness. 'You'd do more, would you, if it all belonged to you?'

Hostility would have flared again between Joel and my brother had not Squire Dalby, with a mighty yawn, indicated his total lack of interest in the squabbles, the values, or the opinions of the lower classes.

'Sheep – that's what the trouble is,' he announced somewhat surprisingly. 'Sheep. They don't really want to break your machines, Barforth. Never would have thought of it if some damned Jacobin hadn't come and put it into their heads. Train them in France, you know, these professional revolutionaries – Roman Catholics and atheists every one of them, and damn me if I know which is the worst. France, that's where they go, these malcontents, and when they've got themselves enough liberty and equality, back here they come to spread the word. Not your machines they're after at all – don't care a fig for your machines. It's the rule of law they're out to smash – King and Constitution, that's what they're after – and it won't do, Barforth. Every man was born to his allotted place – I know mine and I expect you know yours – and there's no getting away from it. Find the ringleaders, that's all you have to do. Find the damned Jacobins and send the sheep home.'

It was perhaps a tribute to my grandfather's strength of will that he accepted this landed gentleman's advice in a silence that was malicious, resentful, but absolute.

We were ready, or so we kept telling each other, but suddenly everything outside was quiet: an ordinary evening, deepening, cooling, so much like yesterday that riot, arson, bloodshed receded, became tinged, if only faintly, with ridicule. The soldiers were still waiting in the yard; the engineers and loom tuners and such of our operatives who had elected to stay – Ira Agbrigg among them – were waiting, too, all of them uneasy, some of them afraid, fortified at regular intervals by mugs of ale sent down by Mrs Stevens, who still declined to come herself.

Then, when we had almost stopped looking for them, when all the tension of the day which had frayed our nerves and made us so peevish began to seem unnecessary, then, at that moment, there they were, not violently and clamorously with the great parade of torches we had expected, nor the raucous shouts of hate, but simply there, a dark wedge of silent men, appearing as if they had been there all the time and had only now become visible. Silent and dark, dream figures, lacking substance, so that I was slow to recognize the sound of glass shattering on the cobbles, the bark of musket fire, and unwilling to believe that they were stoning the mill and that the soldiers had fired their warning shots – one hoped – into the air.

I no longer knew if I was afraid. The day had lasted so long, so wearied me, that I simply wanted it to end. With my mother and Hannah, I followed our menfolk as far as they allowed us, to the limit of our garden gate, and watched, listened, drifted a little way from reality, since it all seemed so strange and I felt so tired.

I heard the bulldog rasping of my grandfather's voice, some muttered reply: a wavering, I thought, of ranks, as those who had perhaps not meant to come so far hung back, while others stood their ground. Sheep, Squire Dalby had called them – these ordinary, decent men who, if given the choice, would always prefer right to wrong, good to evil, and who now, feeling the cold, the peril, would have been glad to go away. But no one could fail to recognize the wolf hunger in the men who stood in front, shoulder to shoulder: the true, sworn brotherhood, their thin, taut faces yellow-pale in the moonlight. I understood dimly that although they numbered no more than nine or ten, their intensity, their total fixity of purpose could be well-nigh impossible to resist. If one of them had come whispering to me of injustice and exploitation – a man who was fierce and frail, pitiful and formidable all at once – perhaps I too, had I been poor and uncertain, would be standing there now, somewhat against my will but fascinated, mesmerized, clutching a shawl around me, with a hatchet or a meat cleaver hidden beneath it. And although I knew they were wrong and foolish, and that if it was justice they sought this was not the way to obtain it, it troubled me deeply that I lacked Hannah's certainty, that unlike her and Edwin and my grandfather – or Jabez Gott – I could not tell myself we were absolutely right.

One man, I saw now, had detached himself from the crowd: a thin, youngish man with narrow shoulders clothed in dark corduroy, a shock of sandy hair, hands that seemed made of veins and knuckles – Jabez Gott, no other – making uncoordinated gestures that spoke, somehow, of nerves frayed beyond endurance, of emotions that were running wild, out of control, like a horse that terrifies its own rider. But his voice failed to reach me as, talking excitedly to the men at his back, pleading with them, I thought, to remember the pledges that had been made, he strove to rally them. I wanted desperately to hear him, not because I hoped to hear anything profound or even sensible

– for I did not – but because his violence, his hot, fierce energy reminded me of my grandfather, as he might have been had Fate kept him poor. They were alike – this thin, ragged young man, that heavy, self-centred old one – alike in their need to set their mark on the world, to displace the air around them, and surely they should be able to understand each other?

But Squire Dalby had not come to listen, required no explanations. Advancing as near as he could, quite fearlessly, he drew himself up to his full height, which was not considerable, and bellowed, 'Silence for the making of this proclamation.'

And because he was the squire – even in the Law Valley men knew what that meant – there was a hush, a shuffling of feet, a doffing, in some cases, of caps.

'Now then,' he said, his eyes on the chimney stack, 'I imagine you all know me and what I'm about to do. I'm not sure just why you're here, and maybe some of you are not too sure about it either, but the law doesn't allow these little get-togethers, I'm afraid. And since I represent the law – yes, be very sure of that – it is my duty, as a properly authorized person, to send you all to your homes so that I may go to mine. I am come to read the Riot Act to you, my good fellows, and you must take heed, for once it is read, unless you obey it to the letter, such of you as are apprehended will be adjudged felons, and the penalty for that, as you well know, is death. And if we don't hang you – and I see no reason why we shouldn't – at the very least you'll face transportation to Australia, which I daresay amounts to the same thing.'

And taking a mighty breath, he pronounced tonelessly, tediously, the words which, by their own weight, had crushed the fighting spirit of mightier crowds than this.

'Our Sovereign Lord the King chargeth and commandeth all persons, being assembled, immediately to disperse themselves, and peaceably to depart to their habitations, or to their lawful business upon the pains contained in the

Act made in the first year of King George, for preventing tumults and riotous assemblies. God Save the King.'

I thought, perhaps we all thought, that it would be enough, for even before the squire had finished speaking men had begun to slip away; not many at first, but enough to unsettle the ones who had wanted to fight it out, who had believed in their own desperation and hate, and although I could not hear their mutterings, I knew they were saying, 'What good can we do if we hang?' and 'Who'll feed our bairns if they send us to Australia?' and 'If we make this sacrifice, make martyrs of ourselves, how long will it be remembered?' For them it was over.

But the sandy-haired man – Jabez Gott, surely? – and the half dozen around him were beyond the fear of hanging. As they tried frantically to rally their mates, my heart tore for all of them: for the ones who turned dully away and the ones who hysterically persisted; for my father, standing ashen-faced and sick-hearted; for my brother, looking puzzled, not having expected to be so moved; and for myself, standing somewhere in the wasteland between them, belonging nowhere.

'Desperate measures,' I heard Jabez Gott shout. 'Desperate measures. Remember what we vowed – what we promised.' And then, 'Cowards!' he shrieked. 'It's always the way – always the way. I'm not the first man to look over my shoulder and find no one behind me. But I'll leave my mark – make sure I'm not forgotten. I've not come this far – made this sacrifice – to go away empty-handed.'

But it was over. No more than a handful of men stood around him now, unwilling to leave him but wanting to take him away with them rather than stay, and we all expected him to go. The soldiers had already relaxed their guard, the engineers had crept gratefully back inside the sheds to sample more of Mrs Stevens's ale, Squire Dalby and the Barforth men were already walking back towards the house, making a summer Sunday stroll of it, congratulating themselves and each other. And perhaps it was the loud, self-satisfied note of Squire Dalby's laughter that entered Jabez Gott's mind and pushed it over the edge of reason.

The strolling group had almost reached the gate.

'Well done, Edwin. Oh, well done,' I heard Hannah say; and I heard Squire Dalby answer her, his eyes on my mother, 'No more than one expected, my dear. Just a little talking-to, that's all it ever takes.'

And then, because they were all looking at each other, admiring each other, perhaps I was the only one who saw Jabez Gott break jerkily away from his mates; the only one who saw his yellow-pale face growing, taking on features and textures as it came nearer; the only one who saw the blank eyes, the tears spilling down his cheeks, the thin mouth twisted with the all-consuming, unreasoning need to destroy.

So appalled was I, so fascinated, that my scream of warning came too late.

'Barforth swine!' he shrieked, scattering them with the force of his madness. 'Swine – slayers of the innocent! I said desperate measures – I said it – and you'll never forget me.'

Screaming now with the hysteria of a sacrificial victim – the role he had cast for himself – he dragged a pistol from under his coat and, mistaking his true enemy, pushed my grandfather aside and fired straight into my father's chest.

4

I saw it happen, not once but over and over again through that first unspeakable night, over and over through the months that came after, through the years, the image fading for a while, almost deserting me, and then, when I

58

thought myself free of it, returning to spread tentacles of horror through every recess of my mind.

I saw my father's chest break open and his life pour out of it. I saw Jabez Gott, making no attempt to flee, tear open his shirt, baring his own scrawny chest to the sacrificial knife. I saw the soldiers advance to the slaughter and Jabez Gott begin to bleed. I saw his mates running like hares in every direction, with the soldiers and my cousin Joel after them, their shouting and clattering and the bark of their muskets growing to a sea-roaring in my ears. I saw my brother Edwin sink his head in his hands and Hannah stretch out a hand towards him, wanting to go to him, I think, and finding that her feet had taken root. I saw Squire Dalby, his elegant coat spattered with blood, move to my mother's side, and heard his startled exclamation as, with a long, sighing whisper, consciousness drained out of her and she folded bonelessly to the ground.

I remember, after that, only fragments of the night: the soldiers carrying my father back to the house, only pretending to be careful since they knew he was dead; my mother telling them to lay him on his bed and then, sitting at his side, drawing the bed curtains around them both, shutting herself away with him until the doctor came to tell us what we all knew and to help her to make him decent.

I remember my grandfather stamping, shouting with a gigantic fury which was partly grief-inspired, since he had lost his only son, partly shame-inspired, since they had quarrelled and it could never now be mended.

'You'll get them all, every one of them,' he kept on saying. 'Round them up and hang them. And anybody who gives them shelter is as guilty as they are – isn't that so, Squire? Twelve men. I saw twelve men with that mad devil, and I'll see twelve men hang. If it's the last thing I do, I'll hang them all.'

I remember Hannah, determined as always to do the right thing but doing it awkwardly, wanting to give comfort but unable to hide her disapproval of those tight-drawn bed curtains, her conviction that my mother's insistence on remaining in such close, solitary confinement with a dead man – albeit her husband – was somehow not quite right.

I remember Edwin, not really knowing what to do with himself, the master of the house now, ready to accept his responsibilities but surprised, I thought, at his own tears.

And then I remember myself, drifting like a shadow from place to place, feeling cold and far away, with that loud sea-roaring still in my head, preventing me from hearing or answering when anyone spoke to me.

'Your father is dead,' I kept on telling myself, but they were just empty words that rattled in my mind, so that even when morning came and I had slept a little, my birthday puppy sharing my bed, I would not have been surprised to see him crossing the yard, returning from the mill for his breakfast and his mug of ale.

Downstairs, in the thin, cool light of early morning, nothing seemed changed. In the kitchen I met the same gleaming copper, the same black-faced, evil-tempered stove as yesterday, the same stout countrywoman, our maid Marth-Ellen, baking the day's bread, red-faced with her exertions. There was the same supercilious black cat, the same lazy tabby, my brother's yellow bitch getting up stiff-legged from the hearthrug, my own gangling, enthusiastic puppy, Marth-Ellen calling to me from her bread-board to 'get that little demon out of here.'

The same. Except that my body was tight with tears I could not seem to shed; except that I was cold and could not warm myself, and there were sea waves still, rolling around my head, washing me away from too close a scrutiny of the truth. And when, suddenly, those sea waves receded, I was, for a moment, most appallingly empty, a hollow shell through which a sharp wind was painfully blowing, bringing me, one by one, a procession of images I did not wish to see.

'Your father is dead,' I told myself once more, and, abruptly, the harsh daylight was an assault on my eyes, unbearably, horribly bright.

He had given me a kitten once, long ago, bringing it up from the mill in his pocket and allowing me to find it there, laughing at my delight, pleased perhaps to have stirred the quietness of me to such excited laughter. And now he gave it to me again, the dainty three-cornered face, the velvet striped body nestling in the palm of his broad Barforth hand, my own face eagerly upturned, wanting him to kiss me, wanting to nestle against him, too, yet unable – afraid of a rebuff – to tell him so. And so, through the years, uncertain of his affection, I had half reached out my hand and, fearing he would refuse to take it, had drawn it back of my own accord.

'May I sit beside you in the carriage, Father,' my mind had asked, my feet wanting to carry me across the yard to him, to tug at his sleeve, to jump on his knee, but I had not spoken and he, impatient with my silences, my pleading, uncomfortable eyes, had driven off without me.

And so we had continued.

'Am I pretty, Father?' I had needed to know on the day of my first ball gown when, back from the dressmaker's, I had come demurely downstairs, white-taffeta'd, blue-sashed, hopeful.

And although he would have answered, 'Aye, the prettiest girl I've ever seen,' whether he meant it or not, it was so important to me, I so badly wanted it to be the truth, that I had not asked.

And now, no longer a child, I knew that in his solitude he had needed my love, anybody's love, and still I could find no way to release the tumult inside me, the bitter, futile grieving. A dome of glass, it seemed, like the ones they place over dried flowers, had descended over me; smooth glass, untroubled to the casual eye, while, against the inner side, my emotions beat frantic hands, unable to show themselves. And, one by one, as the memories and

61

the pains had come to me, they trooped back again to lock themselves away in my heart, growing heavier as they remained unspoken.

'She's well enough,' he had said of me to my grandfather, and so it remained; 'well enough,' no more than that, and even then, feeling at last the relief of tears, I could not support the easy sympathy of Marth-Ellen and Mrs Stevens, both of them so willing to comfort me, and rushed out into the garden to find a secret corner in which to cry.

Yet, outwardly, I must still have seemed calm, earning myself a nod of approval from Edwin when I served him his breakfast, and when Hannah came down from the Top House, where she had spent the remainder of the night, I was able to answer her questions and follow the drift of her advice.

'You should go to your mother,' she told me. 'Indeed, you must go to her, Verity, for it can't be good for her, it can't be right, sitting all this while behind those curtains with— It is most odd and I have asked Edwin to send for the doctor again, except that he has no time to go himself and the stableboys are afraid to meet a felon on the way. Joel shall go presently, but in the meanwhile you must do what you can, Verity. Take her a tray of tea and then persuade her to come down or at least to go to another room. And when she is feeling stronger, there are things which really must be done. I appreciate her loss – indeed, I feel deeply for her, considering my situation with Edwin – but your grandfather and Edwin have suffered, too, and really, it is always best, however tragic the circumstances, to keep oneself gainfully employed. I don't wish to put myself forward, but no matter how painful it may be, one has certain duties that simply cannot be set aside. There is mourning to be got ready, for one thing, and since it is the master of the house who has died, the servants should be put in mourning too. Luckily, Elinor and I have plenty of black crepe left over from our own parents, but in your case – well, the most economical way, of course would be

62

to dye the dresses you already have, but I can't really ask them to get a dye tub ready without your mother's permission. And people will be calling or sending to convey their sympathy, and someone must receive them. Really, I am not at all sure what we should do. You are the daughter of the house, but you have only just gone sixteen and may not be up to it – people may not quite like it. Yet if, on the other hand, I do it myself, it may be thought presumptuous, my engagement to Edwin being so recent and no wedding date being set. Verity, do just run upstairs and tell your mother that if she won't come down she absolutely must let me know how she wants things done.'

But my mother had nothing to say to me, and when my grandfather and Mrs Stevens arrived later in the morning she would not speak to them either.

'She was always half cracked,' my grandfather said, stumping his way downstairs, 'and now she's gone altogether. Well, so much the better, for I never liked her – she was never good enough for my son. And now we'll have a fresh start. Where's Edwin, eh, and Hannah? Send them to me, will you, Mrs Stevens, for I'm weary – bone-weary. I'll sit awhile in my wife's kitchen and take a glass of wine, if such a thing's to be found in this house since my wife died. And send the Boy to me, and his lass, and we'll talk of the future. There's no sense now, is there, Mrs Stevens, in looking back? I did what I could, didn't I? And what is there now but the Boy and the future? A good boy, and if the lass has no money to bring with her at least she's straight and plainspoken – at least when she opens her mouth I understand what comes out. So – the wine, Mrs Stevens, and then my lad.'

No more trouble was expected. The crowd had facelessly gone home now, its fighting spirit crushed by the horror of what had occurred. Jabez Gott was dead, and four of his companions with him, shot down by the soldiers; as the day progressed, the others were accounted for one by one, apprehended – with some more timely assistance from Ira

Agbrigg – and despatched first to York and then, one must suppose, to the gallows or a prison ship. And when only two remained at large, and these not ringleaders but young lads merely, both of them thought to be badly wounded, my grandfather began to be certain of his revenge.

He had, perhaps, loved my father at the level where love has nothing to do with sense or even with liking, but there was no doubt that he loved Edwin more, and although he would continue to grieve for my father he would not, in the everyday sense of the word, miss him.

'Life must go on,' he announced, waking suddenly from his reverie in the kitchen rocking chair. 'Yes, and renew itself, eh, Edwin? So we'll have a wedding as soon as may be – and a christening as soon as decent – and then another. That's what your father would say to you if he could, and I'm doing naught but saying it in his stead. I've gained a great deal in my life, lad, and lost a lot, for I had other sons, besides your father, who died in their cradles, and you have brothers in the churchyard who should have been standing beside you today. But never mind that. It's weakness, lad, to look back – and folly. What's done is done, and all I want now is to live long enough to see your children grow – that's all I ask. Just make sure, lad, that there'll be a Barforth down there, making those looms turn, after I'm gone, and another to follow him. That's all I want. And now I'll go back to my own house, Mrs Stevens, and my own bed, for I'm not easy here. Edwin, your arm, if you please—'

My father was in his coffin now, a stranger encased in white velvet and polished wood, exposed in the back parlour for all to see, and since my mother chose to remain upstairs, strange and silent behind her bed curtains, I went with Hannah to the kitchen, lending my seal of approval, while she informed Marth-Ellen when and what we would eat. But, indeed, she scarcely needed me, for Marth-Ellen, who had no intention of losing a good place, was more than eager to gain the favour of Edwin's bride, and perhaps her curtsies and her 'Yes, ma'ams' and 'No ma'ams' finally caused Hannah to acknowledge the change in her situation.

While my father had lived my mother had been the mistress of this house and might have remained so for the first twenty or thirty years of Hannah's married life, presiding over Hannah's affairs, choosing her servants, interfering with the upbringing of her children. For twenty or thirty years Hannah could have been little more than a guest in my mother's house, but now, since my father's slow, disillusioned life had spurted out of him so violently, left him too fast for protest or consolation, Edwin would be the master, his wife the supreme domestic authority over us all. And although she was too proper, too kindhearted to admit it, even to herself, I knew that secretly she must be relieved, that eventually she would be pleased.

'Edwin, do take a little more,' she said as we ate our belated meal. 'Your grandfather told us that life goes on and so it does. This custard tart is not excellent, for the nutmeg must have been put in with a coal shovel, but it is sustaining, and we shall improve the quality presently.'

'I've no appetite, lass,' he told her, but he had, and the excited, only half-suppressed light in his eye when she talked of what they would do 'presently' gave me a twinge of such discomfort that I excused myself and went outside.

The evening was cool again, freshening towards rain, the mill silent as a mark of respect for the dead, although I remembered how Edwin – and Joel, too – had made some protest when my grandfather had dismissed the soldiers.

'You'd do well to keep them another night,' Joel had advised, Edwin agreeing, but my grandfather, having already quarrelled with the officer, vowing he'd have no more red-coated scum in his yard, had turned peevish even with his grandson.

'It's over,' he'd snarled. 'When I say it's over, it's over. Ten of them dead or under guard, two lads dying of their wounds somewhere, and the rest sick to their stomachs of Jabez Gott and his like. They're crushed and finished, and I want no redcoats littering up my yard to remind me of what they couldn't prevent last night.'

And so Edwin had been obliged to content himself with setting Ira Agbrigg to keep his eyes and ears open and, if any further riotous assembly threatened, to let us know.

Life, indeed, for my grandfather, would go on. He would continue to sit on his hillside, I thought, growing richer and harder to manage. Mrs Stevens would continue to pamper him and smile for wages, while here, in the millhouse, Hannah would improve the quality of Edwin's custard, the whiteness of his linen, and would devote her formidable energies to making herself the perfect wife, the perfect mother of Samson Barforth's great-grandchildren. My mother, I supposed, would take up her embroidery again, here or elsewhere, and lead her own life inside her head, as she'd always done. But in it all I saw no place for me. Could I exist, with any degree of comfort, between Edwin and Hannah? Was there any comfort for me in my mother's dream? And, doubting, I felt a vast longing for my father pour out of me like a wail across the mill yard.

And yet the quality of my grieving, even in these few hours, had altered. This morning, in my hiding place by the garden wall, sheltered by the downward drooping of an ancient pear tree, I had wept privately, bitterly, for my father alone: for his loss of life and opportunity, for the terrible waste of him. But now my own life seemed in the night air to swing loose and lonely, with nothing left to cling to.

There was no one, of course, who wished me ill. Edwin was fond of me; Hannah would do her duty; my grandfather, jealous of all his possessions, would guard me vigilantly. But in that dark, solitary hour, I did not wish to belong to my grandfather; I did not wish, in fact, to cling to anyone but to stand and look the world full in the face

66

with my own quiet but not unperceptive eyes and see its colours and textures for myself.

And although I was quiet, certainly, I was neither awkward nor shy. Hannah had thought me too young to receive my mother's callers, but I knew I could have managed everything well enough without her. Hannah would always be deceived by a sanctimonious turn of phrase, a flattering manner, but I, like my mother, often saw beyond phrase and manner to motives and meanings it was not always comfortable to see. Stubborn, my grandfather had once called me, and, remembering my cousin Elinor's gay chatterings of weddings, I thought I might have need of that stubborn streak ere long when Hannah, once established as my brother's wife, would very likely consider it her duty to find a husband for me.

Marriage, of course, would come, as marriage came to all girls of my station, but, since Hannah's taste would not be mine, I would have to take good care to prevent her from laying her well-meaning hands on my future.

When my cousin Joel came out of the house and stood a moment in the doorway, lighting the cigar Hannah would not permit him to smoke inside, I was taken unawares, with no opportunity to avoid him. Not that I particularly disliked him. He was, undoubtedly, handsome, capable of arousing a giggling excitement in certain friends of mine who would have been badly scared had he decided to look their way, but he was also a realist and, knowing that well-mannered, well-dowered young ladies were not for him, had never taken the slightest notice of them – or of me. Yet tonight, with my tortoiseshell comb holding up my hair, perhaps I looked old enough, womanly enough, to merit an instant's attention, and glancing at me beneath lowered eyelids with a certain insolence, a certain amusement I did not like, he came strolling down the path to my side.

'You'll take cold,' he said. 'In fact, my sister asked me to tell you so, should I happen to meet you. You've been out in the night air too long, in her opinion, and I daresay she knows what she's about.'

'I daresay. But I believe I'll stay out a while longer.'

'You may suit yourself. I'm off to the Top House to fetch Elinor and take her home. There's no call that I can see to spend another night under Edwin's roof.'

That should have been enough, and, indeed, I think he was about to go. But then, peering at me through the twilight, he said, 'You're not looking too bright, cousin. This makes a difference to you, then, all this?'

'Of course it does.'

'Of course. I hadn't considered. God knows, I wasn't over-sorry to lose my own father, but that doesn't mean everybody else must be the same, and I reckon it's different for a girl. But you'll do all right, Verity; your grandfather will see to that. There's plenty of money to marry you with.'

'I suppose so. I've never thought much about it.'

'No,' he said, laughing shortly, sharply, not looking at me any longer. 'That doesn't surprise me. The ones who think most about money are those who haven't got it. In fact, when you have creditors waiting to dun you round every street corner, it's hard to think of anything else. But that need never concern you, cousin. They'll marry you comfortably – splendidly, in fact, if you can put your grandfather in the right frame of mind. There's Bradley Hobhouse over at Nethercoats, or Matthew Oldroyd at Fieldhead: they've both got good businesses to inherit – just like Edwin – and they'd both be glad to take you. They'd treat you so well you'd never notice the difference.'

And because I was old enough to recognize his bitterness and his impertinence, and to know from where it stemmed, yet still too young to know how to put him in his place, I said quickly, just to say something, 'You'll be getting married yourself now, I suppose.'

'Oh, you suppose that, do you? And what do you know about it – except what Elinor tells you?'

'It's not a secret, is it?'

'No, no, there's no secret, although the lady's father doesn't like to hear much about it. Yes, for your information and Elinor's, I was thinking of getting married, for Miss Boulton has been waiting a fair while. But I have a problem now, you see, that I hadn't bargained for. Your brother was all set to marry my sister tomorrow, if she'd have him, and he still would, I reckon, which would suit me down to the ground. But knowing the way Hannah feels about doing the right thing, she won't take him until he's out of mourning, which could be a year, couldn't it, for a father? And if I have Hannah to support for another twelvemonth I can hardly afford Miss Boulton. And even then, if Hannah went right now, it would depend on my half-yearly profits before Isaac Boulton would listen to me. Well, I know how to balance my books to my advantage – a trick I learned from my father – but I'm not sure they'll look good enough. So you see, things have changed rather, for me too.'

'I'm sorry.'

'Oh, don't be,' he said airily, apparently much amused. 'We can't all have Edwin's luck. Not many men can afford to marry at twenty-four, without somebody else to pay the bills. Most of us have to wait until we're well past thirty – well past forty sometimes – before we can hope to support a wife; and I'm only twenty-eight, so I've got time.'

But had Miss Boulton? I wondered, as he went on through the gate and up the path to the Top House, for she had seemed to me, on the two occasions I had met her, a flighty, not altogether good-tempered girl whose wild-rose prettiness would soon show thorns. Yet Joel, I decided, was well able to manage his affairs without help from me, and although I was cold now and would have been glad to go inside, to do so would have looked like obedience to Hannah and so obstinately I remained outdoors. And when she came to the window, not seeing me in my dark dress with the light behind her, and called out, 'Verity –

where are you? Will you come in now?' I got up and, keeping close to the wall, slipped around the side of the house towards the gate leading to the mill yard.

I should not have been there, had no wish to be there, so near the place where my father had died, yet Hannah's voice, still calling behind me, 'Verity, Verity, come in now,' served only to push me farther away. And so it was that I opened the gate, walked a step or two into the yard, and realized, without knowing how or what it signified, that I was not alone.

I had heard no more than a rat rustling, somewhere in the dark ahead of me, a common enough sound, for we had rats in plenty and cats, and stray dogs who got into the sheds in the cold weather, yet this, I knew, was a man; no heavy-footed watchman, no engineer going about his rightful business, but someone nervously running from shadow to shadow, who should not have been there at all.

I should, most certainly, have rushed back through the gate and up the narrow garden, shrieking 'Edwin!' at the top of my lungs, but, in that first instant, I froze, as my mother had frozen at the sight of my dying father; although I tried to move backwards, to Edwin, to safety, my feet refused to take me. Who would come here tonight, I reasoned, but a man with a yellow-pale face and sandy hair, sick with hate and the need for revenge? And although that man was dead, twelve others had stood around him, two of them hiding somewhere in the hills, grieving for their companions and their ruined endeavours. And if I stood in their shoes, would it seem right to me to strike another blow, another gesture of crazy defiance before the gallows or starvation took me? I thought that it would and, remembering my father and the yellow-pale, weeping face of his destroyer, I froze again, fear consuming my mind, clouding my reason entirely. I had only to call out and Edwin would come running to defend his property and his sister, yet an instinct powerful enough to paralyse my tongue bade me keep Edwin away. There had been murder and vengeance already – did I want to see Edwin with blood on his hands?

I would creep back up the path and go indoors as if I had heard nothing – as indeed I would have heard nothing had not Hannah's voice driven me here in the first place – and tomorrow, when it was discovered that a few yards of cloth had been slashed to pieces or a bale of wool broken open and scattered in the wind, we would have no trouble in making up the loss.

But I had reckoned without Hannah's sense of duty towards her lover's fatherless, well-nigh motherless sister, her insistent 'Edwin, that child will take cold. Do please go and fetch her in,' so that he was already outside, making his grumbling way down to the yard, when the far shed began to burn.

It seemed, to me at any rate, just a little thing, no more than a candle flame dancing behind the window, uncertain, unlikely to take hold, and I needed to hear Edwin's bellow of rage as he rushed past me to understand that this was arson, another capital crime for which somebody would have to pay.

'Bloody old fool,' he thundered, meaning, incredibly, my grandfather. 'I told him we'd best keep a guard tonight – and Joel told him – but no, he knows best – he bloody knows best. Go and get Joel, for God's sake – there's nothing in the far shed I'm bothered about, but if it spreads—'

I was about to do his bidding when we both saw the man clearly, bent almost double, running across a treacherous shaft of moonlight.

'Let him go,' I shouted. 'Let's see to the sheds,' but the fire was, indeed, not serious as yet, no blaze of vengeful triumph but a smouldering, smoky thing likely to burn itself out, and he seemed not to hear me.

And once again, I recall no more than fragments – wish to recall no more – just Edwin's strong, eager body bounding forward, rich with confidence in itself and its

71

future, knowing that with his long legs, his powerful shoulders, the well-nourished, well-tended bone and fibre of him, he could easily outrun a felon and hold him fast. And so he did, laughing as he caught him by the scruff of his neck and flung him back against the wall, forcing the narrow head and the yellow-pale face up into the moonlight so that I saw again the hollow eyes, the tears spilling from their corners, a lad who knew his nineteen-year-old life was over.

There was no pistol this time. Perhaps I had thought of a pistol, dreaded it – remembering – so that when the boy broke free and I saw the knife in his hand – a long-bladed kitchen knife, a familiar object – it seemed far less terrible.

'Now just throw that down,' Edwin said reasonably, his mind, I think, already going back to the fire, wondering how far it had spread and why the devil I had not gone yet to fetch Joel, and feeling himself so safe, so totally in control, that when the blow fell the sheer surprise of it may have spared him pain.

There came the sounds of men running – Joel, perhaps, who must have seen the fire by now, bringing the coachman, the stable lads – and, half turning his head, Edwin, still despising his adversary, stumbled, lurched forward into a yellow-pale, scarecrow embrace, a hand with fingers like dry sticks groping behind his neck, pulling him nearer, using Edwin's own weight to force that common kitchen blade through his fancy silk waistcoat and into his stomach.

Edwin. My brother Edwin. Why had I never known before that I loved him? And, knowing it now, I threw myself forward, screaming, clawing blindly, aimlessly, ready to put my teeth into the boy's throat and savage him had I been able to hold him.

'I'm sorry!' I heard him scream, his hands biting into my shoulders, trying to free himself of me. 'I'm sorry.'

Even through my madness I could feel the trembling of his body.

'Get away from me! Oh please, get away—' he shrieked,

bringing me to the ground. When I still clung to him he tried to scramble away on all fours, wheezing and whining – sobbing, it seemed to me, unless I was the one who sobbed – until at last there was Joel, fiercely swooping, lifting him and tossing him against the shed wall like a rag doll, picking him up again and beating his head against the stone until the doll stopped screaming.

In the harrowing silence, I dragged myself across the cobbles to my brother's side and knelt very close to him, touched his cheek with a wondering hand, as I had never touched him before, smoothed the heavy brown hair away from his forehead, traced the outline of his jaw with my fingertips, straightened his cravat and the collar of his coat, made him tidy and decent.

'Edwin, love, do look. Your mill's on fire. Do look, darling. They'll soon put it out, so you don't have to worry, but do look.'

And I laid my cheek against his cheek, my mouth briefly on the corner of his mouth.

'He's dead, isn't he?' Joel said, dropping swiftly down on one knee. 'Isn't he?'

And looking up, meeting the flash of excitement in his face, knowing him for a predator, I leaned across my brother's body, hiding the jagged, oozing rent in his waistcoat, and, savage in the defence of my own kind, snarled at him, 'Not yet. Not yet.'

5

We buried them side by side in the corner of the graveyard where my brothers and sisters and my grandmother lay, with ornate headstones of gold-lettered, highly polished marble above them – a huge old apple tree shedding its blossoms on the newly dug ground – and even Squire Dalby, a High Churchman who equated Methodists with

Jacobins, Roman Catholics, and the devil, attended the memorial service in the squat, square chapel my grandfather had built in his wife's day.

It was a soft pink and blue May morning, with a gentle breeze and new sunshine slanting on fresh green: a day for a young man's pleasures, not an old man's heartbreak; yet broken my grandfather certainly was, and everyone who saw him that day, shivering, shrunken, gave their opinion that he and Edwin would not be long apart.

There had been a great deal of sympathy, a gratifying show of respect, messages of condolence reaching us from manufacturers and gentry alike. The Hobhouses of Nethercoats, our chief competitors in the worsted trade, and the Oldroyds of Fieldhead, spinners of high-quality yarn, had expressed their heartfelt sorrow and their readiness to do anything – within reason – to assist. Mr Rawnsley the banker and Mr Aycliffe the builder had paid us every attention, Mr Aycliffe, who was to have undertaken the building of Edwin's new mill, managing not to ask my grandfather what he intended to do about it now. And we had received floral and verbal tributes from some of Cullingford's oldest residents; the aristocratic Colonel Corey of Blenheim Lane, his cousin, the lawyer Mr Corey-Manning – both of them in some way related to Sir Giles Flood, Cullingford's manorial lord – and an assortment of their female relatives, persons of quality not much given to associating with the manufacturing classes but making an exception in our sad case.

Letters had appeared, not only in the *Cullingford Courier* but in newspapers as far off as Bradford and Leeds, praising my father's achievements, my brother's promise, the noble stand they had both made against anarchy. And, in recognition of that stand and the tragedy our family had suffered in their common cause, the local industrialists had subscribed two thousand pounds towards the repair of our mill. My brother's murderer, much of his body in splints from the damage Joel had inflicted on him, had been sent to York with the others to hang, thus ensuring, it was felt, that mill wrecking, machine breaking was now a lost cause in our area; and although I was glad of that, I found no consolation, as Hannah was later to do, in referring to my father and brother as martyrs.

The road leading to the chapel was lined that day on both sides with black-draped carriages which had disgorged so liberal a helping of top-hatted, black-gloved gentlemen and ladies in black crepe and mourning veils that my grandfather's plain little chapel could not hold them all. And so they waited outside until the service was over, some to see what they could see, some because they thought it advisable to be seen, some touched with genuine regret for my father and brother, others weeping simply at the reminder that they too must come to this. A great crowd, their combined fortunes totalling far more than men not born to riches had ever seen a way to earn before, and, behind them, from the mean streets now surrounding the chapel, shawl-covered heads, a line of Sunday cloth caps – Ira Agbrigg among them – coming also to pay their respects to a man who had been known as a fair master.

I rode in the first carriage with my mother and my grandfather, keeping well away from him, uncomfortable with the enormity of his grief and his blind, blazing fury that God had permitted this dreadful thing to befall him. But he had no time for me – no time for anyone – fixing his eyes on the black plumes dancing on the horses' heads, seeing beyond them, I supposed, to the ruin of everything he had lived for. Edwin had been 'his lad,' 'his pride and joy,' and just as he had monopolized him in life, so he refused to share him in death. No one had loved Edwin as he had, consequently no one else had the right to mourn him so intensely, and when Hannah found herself unable to share his view, he had simply ordered her to take herself off to her own home since she had no purpose to serve in his any longer.

I could not recognize my mother's face beneath the

75

swathes of black veiling on her bonnet, yet even in the anonymity of mourning dress she seemed different from the rest of us; and although she was no tower of strength, no comforting shoulder to lean on, I had leaned on her these last days and she had not entirely let me fall.

She had taken my father's death strangely, but her care of Edwin, during the bitter hour it had taken him to die, had been tender, unexpected. She had not comforted him, since a man of twenty-four with the world at his feet cannot be consoled for the loss of it. She had simply held him in his pain, taken him back to his childhood when she'd had the power to make everything right, and afterwards, when Hannah went into some kind of a fit, choking and shaking, staggering about the room and hurting herself against the walls and the chairs, my mother had calmed her and held her too.

I had required no one to calm me. My cousin Joel had carried me up from the mill yard and put me down in the kitchen rocking chair; and I had remained there, motionless, striving in the most appalling silence of my life to fight my way back to reality through those sea waves which were once again swamping my mind. For a nightmare time I thought myself doomed to spend my life curled up with Edwin's blood still on my hands and in my hair, down the front of my dress. But the sea-roaring ceased, as it had done before; my eyes felt sharpened to an acute, distressing observation of the people around me, an observation totally without pity.

Hannah had wandered by me, ashen, unsteady. I thought coldly, She'll get over it. She should have left well alone.

My grandfather had appeared a moment in the kitchen doorway, gasping, blindly groping, and my thoughts told him, That's right, old man, choke – for it was your pride that killed him, and your spoiling. Don't come to me for pity – don't come to me for anything.

Mrs Stevens and our maid Marth-Ellen had come to

peer at me, red-eyed, both of them; uncertain, it had seemed to me, of their own future, for the men on whom they depended were dying. I had not answered them, and when my cousin Joel came in, having changed his soiled clothes and combed his hair, and told Marth-Ellen, 'You'd best see to that child,' her answer had been the simple lifting of her shoulders in a gesture of defeat.

'She'll not let me near her, nor Mrs Stevens, either. Jumpy as a cat with a basket of sick kittens, she is. I've seen it before. It passes.'

But my cousin Joel, as accustomed as Hannah to getting his own way, would have none of that. 'She can't stay here like that, unwashed. Good God, woman, the state of her. Get a can of hot water upstairs in her room, and make her bed ready. I'll fetch her.'

Yet I had no mind, at that moment, to be fetched, and as Marth-Ellen, seeing no reason to take his orders but taking them just the same, had hurried away, I had fastened my eyes on his face, seeing quite clearly his soured ambitions and his present savage hopes, and had discovered that he no longer intimidated me.

'Get up, Verity.'

'I don't think I will.'

'I think you must. Come, love, you can't sit there forever, in such a mess.'

'Why can't I?'

'Well, if you need a reason, because I say so.'

And, my lips parting quite painfully, I had hissed at him, 'Say what you like, Joel Barforth. There's no call for me to take notice of you. You're not the master here – not yet, at any rate.'

And I could have smiled at his sudden recoil, as if a tiny inoffensive sparrow had somehow raised an eagle's beak and bitten him.

But my cousin Joel was a man of experience in the ways of self-defence; had fought his own battles, hard and dirty, all his life and, recovering instantly, had given a short, altogether mirthful laugh. 'Ah well, whatever that means, we'll not talk of it tonight, Verity. You're tired, and you've got your mind in a tangle, so come to bed, love, it's the best place for you.'

He had lifted me easily, held me too tightly for protest, delivering me like an ill-wrapped parcel to Marth-Ellen, to hot water and clean sheets and an unspeakable, tormented night from which I had risen, the next morning, my usual, apparently calm self.

And now, today, we were laying them to rest.

There was a respectful hush as we arrived at the chapel, the gentlemen, who had been strolling up and down discussing their dealings at the London wool sales, grouping themselves in suitably regretful attitudes, the ladies, who may have been wondering how Hannah Barforth, having lost her bright future, would contrive, at twenty-three, to find herself another, raising wisps of cambric to their enquiring eyes. And, had they allowed it, I would have remained in the carriage, closed my eyes, lost myself in my sea waves, and slept.

My cousin Joel was waiting to hand us down. Although he must have moved very fast to have reached our carriage step – having travelled behind us with his sisters – he looked as if he had been there, sorrowfully, calmly, for a long time. Immaculate as always, correct in every detail of black coat and trousers, and mourning bands, he raised his hat to my mother, put a gentle hand under her elbow to help her down and a protective arm around her shoulders to steady her against the impact of sunlight and curiosity, and then, instead of leaving me to manage my skirts and the carriage step as best I might – the treatment he usually accorded to little girls – he held out a hand to me, too, and lifted me with immense care, his solicitude arousing some sentimental murmuring in the crowd.

'Poor lamb,' I heard a woman's voice say. 'She saw her father shot dead, and then they butchered her brother in her arms. Is it any wonder she can barely keep her feet?'

'Aye,' a deeper voice grunted. 'I'd not like a lass of mine to go through that. The shock could turn her head and she'd be never right again.'

And a deeper voice still, 'She'll be right enough. She's a Barforth.'

But then, as my grandfather's mottled, irate head appeared in the carriage doorway, there was a collective intake of breath, a certain drawing back, for although many of them had come to see him weep – thinking it high time Samson Barforth's luck ran out – he was so terrifying, so awesome in defeat that malice and curiosity took flight and silence fell.

He stood for a moment, feet planted foursquare on the ground as they always were, sharp eyes passing from face to face, taking note of absentees as he used to do every morning in the mill yard, daring them all, it seemed, to wonder what he meant to do now with his mill and his money when there was no one but a scatterbrained woman and a half-grown girl to come after him.

I saw his mouth twist itself into a grimace which could have been the sardonic laying down of a challenge – or a barrier to tears – and then, as he took a step forward, an old, desolate man, unutterably bitter, adamantly alone, my cousin Joel came swiftly to his side.

'Take my arm, sir,' he said and, for a moment, it hung in the balance, my grandfather being much inclined, I thought, to push Joel away peevishly. But then he paused, considering, his expression cunning and vindictive, making no secret of his hatred for this healthy young man who was alive when Edwin was dead.

'Aye,' he said, after a long, baleful moment. 'Happen I will take your arm, lad – happen I will, for as long as it suits me.' And putting his hand on Joel's elegant, well-brushed sleeve, deliberately crushing the fabric as I had seen him do before, he leaned his full weight against him and went into his chapel to pray.

There were refreshments afterwards, some of the mourners having come some distance – one or two even from the other side, the cotton side, of the Pennines – and requiring a plentiful supply of Mrs Stevens's ham and pickles and curd tarts to sustain them on their journey home. As we reached our door, the lady herself was there to receive us, come down from the Top House in her black silk dress and her white lace cap to bully Marth-Ellen in her own kitchen and to bathe us all in warm smiles, some of us receiving rather more in the way of her tender care than others.

Hannah, I noticed, who had moved through these last few days like a statue carved in granite, was no longer a particular favourite, being allowed to sit and stare at the carpet as much as she pleased. My cousin Elinor had never counted for very much in any case, but my own importance, it seemed, to Mrs Stevens as well as to my cousin Joel, had increased enormously.

'The dear child has suffered a grievous shock,' she kept on murmuring to the sober, frock-coated gentlemen who were trying not to enjoy their food too heartily or to admire Mrs Stevens herself too openly in the eagle-eyed presence of their wives. And I found that my teacup was constantly being refilled, my plate piled high with slices of seedcake and gingerbread she declared she had made specially for me.

'Clever Mrs Stevens,' my cousin Elinor said, managing even in a plain black gown that was far from new to look extremely pretty. 'She thinks your grandfather can't last much longer and knows that when he dies there's no one he can leave his money to but you. So when you're rich, Verity, and you turn out your wardrobe, do remember me. You'll not want those tortoiseshell combs when you can afford ivory and pearls, will you, and I mean to put my hair up now. Hannah said I was to wait until her wedding but – well – she can hardly expect me to do that now, can she, when there's absolutely no guarantee ...

Heavens, I could still have my hair hanging down my back when I'm thirty, at that rate.'

Elinor's life, of course, was but little changed by the loss of my father and brother. She had spent the night of the riot snugly ensconced at the Top House with Mrs Stevens and had witnessed nothing; now, despite her good intentions, she was growing bored with the white-lipped, rock-hard grief in Hannah that she could not share.

'She should cry more. It would do her good,' was Elinor's verdict, but Hannah had fought all her life against the passionate side of her nature, the part of her which longed now to make some grand, tragic gesture, some pagan expression of mourning like the cutting and burning of her own hair on the funeral pyre. And caught in the straitjacket of her self-discipline, she held herself aloof, with no suspicion, I supposed, that had she left well alone – had she not fussed and fretted about the hour of my bedtime and sent Edwin to look for me – by the time my brother had seen the fire, the felon would no longer have been in the yard to murder him, and she herself would still have been the future mistress of Lawcroft Fold.

Yet such speculation was profitless and unkind, particularly since I was the one destined to take her place. And if that was hard for me to contemplate, my grandfather appeared to find it well-nigh impossible.

'I have no appetite, Mrs Stevens,' he said on his return from the chapel, and turning his back on Cullingford's elite, he retired to a bench in the garden and sat there like some ancient image of weathered stone, his eyes fastened on the mill.

'Oh dear,' Mrs Stevens asked us more than once, 'what am I to do? He should not be out there alone. He will take cold.'

But no one cared to tell him so and, gradually, his friends and neighbours, his keen-eyed competitors, his suppliers and his customers, his minister and his doctor came, one by one, to press my mother's hand and take their leave. And Mr Oldroyd the spinner, Mr Aycliffe the builder, Mr Hobhouse the worsted manufacturer, who all had sons of a similar age, paused a while and made themselves pleasant to me.

'Leave him be,' Joel said, glancing out of the window, hard-faced again, his suave sympathy all gone. 'He has things to ponder, I reckon. Leave him to get on with it. We'll be off ourselves now, Aunt Isabella, but you know where to find me at need. Don't hesitate to apply.'

Even when Joel's hired carriage had rolled away, my grandfather continued to sit and stare at his mill, at his school and his chapel and the long grey rows of his workers' cottages, at the seeds of an empire he had believed would grow and prosper and carry his name into the future – his immortality which would now have to be put up for auction, sold for the profit of a young, unwanted lass.

'Mrs Barforth, can you not speak to him?' Mrs Stevens pleaded, not wishing to hasten his end until she had had the time to negotiate for herself a new beginning, but even as my mother was shaking her head, taking up her embroidery, there he was, glaring at us from the doorway, continuing out loud the conversation he had been having with himself all day.

'So that's it, then,' he announced. 'Yes, that's it – and I'm not broken yet – no. They can think what they like but I'm not finished. I've been down before – never so low as this, but I've been down. And I've always got up again. Life goes on – yes, that's what I said, and I stand by it. Life goes on. And there's one thing we can do now – the sooner, the better. We'll be getting you married now, Verity Barforth. What do you say to that?' And, beckoning imperiously to Mrs Stevens, he stamped away.

I woke late the next morning, and somnolently, unable somehow to bring my ideas together, content simply to lie down on the rag rug by the kitchen fire, my brother's bewildered yellow bitch pressing close beside me, not understanding where Edwin was, I suppose, and sensing something of him in me. And I remained there for a long time, listening to the bitch breathe, thinking of nothing.

Marth-Ellen came and went, leaning over me to tend her oven, never thinking of telling me I was in her way. And as the room began to fill with the basic fragrance of new bread, the slow simmering of broth in the iron pot above the fire, I drifted very far, to a place where no effort was ever required, where nothing ever changed, where – like the dog – it was enough to feel the fire on my skin, to exist at the level of food and shelter and air to breathe: enough, I think, to be alive. Although I knew I would eventually be forced to wake, I chose to delay it, chose not to ask myself why my mother had been summoned to the Top House so early and was so long in coming home.

I dozed a little, rising only to the bare surface of wakefulness when she tapped my shoulder – her eyes rimmed, I noticed, with dark shadows, her own sorrow showing clear in this unguarded moment – and even then, knowing she had something important to say to me, I could only lean drowsily against the dog, ready to drift away again from all complexity, to hide myself in a warm nest of sleep.

But Mother could be sharp when she wished, and quick to make her point for all her apparent vagueness, and sitting down in the fireside chair, the old, creaking rocker with its knitted cushions where Marth-Ellen sat – and my grandmother used to sit – to do her mending, she sent Marth-Ellen away and said, 'Well, since you are so lazy I won't move you. What I have to say will sound as well here as in the parlour. And I must confess it has come a little sooner than I expected and caught me unprepared. Listen carefully, Verity. Someone has asked – this morning – to marry you.'

'Someone?' I said, still drowsy, intent somehow or other on the shading of the dog's coat, the rich gold of her back fading to cream on her legs and belly.

'Verity, are you listening to me?'

'Yes, I'm listening.'

But it neither surprised nor alarmed me that someone had asked to marry me. Amazingly, I did not much care. I wanted merely to be left alone with the dog and the firelight, and I have often wondered if they understood the state of shock I was in and used it for their purposes.

'Well then,' she said, 'since you are listening – I think you must have been long aware that the question of a husband would soon arise, and that even had your father lived, your grandfather would have done the choosing. Tell me, dear – there is no one, is there, no young man who seems more agreeable to you than the others?'

'No.'

'Good. I thought not. I told your grandfather so, and I am glad to be right. Does it surprise you that it is your cousin Joel who has asked for you? At your grandfather's suggestion, I imagine, although I feel sure he would have asked in any case.'

'Why should he do that, Mother?'

'Oh, Verity – my dear,' she said, her hands making a fluttering movement, as if they were looking for her embroidery. 'I think you must know – for I believe you know a great deal behind your quiet eyes – that there would never have been the slightest difficulty in getting you creditably married. Your dowry is far from inconsiderable, and your family connections alone are of great value in the Law Valley. But now, dearest, with Edwin gone, there is far more to you than a mere dowry. Have you not thought of that?'

'Oh yes,' I told her, still not greatly caring, still, incredibly, much inclined for sleep. 'I understand all that. But Joel was to marry Miss Boulton, surely, of Cullingford?'

'Ah yes,' my mother said, smiling. 'Yes, indeed. Certainly there is a Miss Boulton. But their understanding seems to have been only between themselves. Her father had not given his consent, not been properly applied to, so

84

there is no actual commitment – the lady has no cause to sue for breach of promise. He assures us of that. And I think you know, Verity, as well as I do, that your cousin Joel would give a hundred Miss Boultons for the one remaining Miss Barforth.'

'Yes,' I told her, feeling the firelight on my face again, knowing that somehow I would have to rouse myself, have to admit that this was urgent, that it mattered, that it was real. 'Yes, I know about Joel. I know what Joel wants. Why does my grandfather want it?'

'Because he is a dynast. Do you understand what that means? He wants to live forever through his descendants, to be constantly reborn in a line of young Barforth men exactly like himself. Well – we all have our dreams – and it rather looked as if he was going to be cheated of his. Life or Fate or God, perhaps, seemed to have dealt him a blow from which he could not recover – from which many people frankly hoped he would never recover – and now he has found a way to remedy it. That is the heart of the matter. You are all he has left. You cannot run the mill, like Edwin, but, hopefully, you may bear children who can – not Edwin's children, of course, but with something of Edwin in them, the nearest he can get to Edwin. Not just exactly what he had dreamed of, I admit, but his own flesh and blood nevertheless. And although your cousin Joel would be completely out of the question for a Miss Barforth of Lawcroft who had a brother still living – would have been branded a fortune hunter had he ever dared approach you – in these altered circumstances he has much to recommend him. He is a good businessman – possibly better than Edwin and certainly more ambitious than Edwin – and a Barforth, too, which means the name would be carried on. And since his own affairs are in a sorry state, through no fault of his own, he would owe everything to your grandfather – an excellent arrangement from your grandfather's point of view. Far better than marrying you to a Hobhouse or an Oldroyd, who would put his own family's interests first and would not allow him a free hand with your children.'

'And what must I do, Mother?'

She sighed, eased her position slightly, showing no surprise in finding me so docile.

'You must answer for yourself. Certainly no one will drag you to the altar by the hair, but, Verity, my poor Verity, your grandfather has set his mind on this, and I wonder if you have the strength to openly defy him? I must confess to you that I have not. I have never stood my ground and told him what I would and would not do. And on the few occasions when I have tried – well – I have had no success. The only time your father and I held to our purpose was when your grandfather opposed our marriage, and in that I am forced to admit he was right. Affection always existed between us – a kind of affection, at any rate – but we were not suited. And so, you see, a marriage of convenience may succeed as well as any other kind; better, perhaps. Your cousin is handsome and not without experience, and he is only your senior by some twelve years – not a great deal, Verity, for you must know that your grandfather would have no hesitation in giving you to a man of forty or more should it seem good to him.'

'Then you think I must take him?'

'I think you must take somebody.'

'And if I dislike him and refuse him – will you stand by me?'

'I would like to,' she said, her grey velvet eyes holding mine. 'Truly I would like to, as I would have liked to stand by your father – oh, so many times. But it did not seem to be in my nature. You may imagine how much I regret it. But at least I have the self-knowledge to warn you – should the need arise – that I am not to be relied on. And I must tell you, too, that it is not my plan to remain in this house. My service, you see, is over, Verity dear. The Barforths have no more need of me, and I am free. I shall find myself a little nest, not too far away, which you

86

are very welcome to share – naturally – should you find yourself at liberty. I think we could do very well together, you and I, if we were left to our own devices, and certainly I shall be left alone now. But not you, dear. You are of great importance to your grandfather at present, and I can think of nothing which would make him release you. Well, I suppose it is my duty to be more precise and so I will say this to you. Unless your cousin Joel is positively hateful in your eyes – and I know of no reason why he should be – then I think you should listen to him. He will be waiting in the parlour already, I imagine, for he was to follow me down from the Top House in half an hour, and I told him to walk straight in. Verity – your grandfather is thinking of his own interests, not yours – we both know that. But in this case I think your interests may be one and the same. And now that he has found a way out of the snare Fate set for him he will not allow himself to be thwarted by you. He would make your life unbearable, child, for he is a vindictive man, and I don't know who would protect you, since I cannot.'

I got up slowly, feeling light and easy as if I had floated somewhere just a little away from my own body: a spectator, listening as my mother persuaded some other daughter – not me at all – into marriage with a cousin and a stranger.

'Did you really love my father?' I asked, surprising myself. And not expecting an answer, I was even more surprised when she said quietly, 'I told you, there was always affection between us – love, if you like – but in our case it was not enough. We loved without liking, without really approving of each other – or it may be that because we were in love we expected too much of marriage. Yes, you would be astonished, Verity, if you knew how madly I loved your father once, when I was young – an experience I would certainly never wish to endure again. Verity dear, I am not at all sure that love is even a good thing. Friendship – light, warm friendship – yes, that, I think, must be delightful between a man and a woman. But to love with passion can be most painful, and it may not suit your nature any more than it suited mine. Dearest – will you go now and talk to your cousin?'

And knowing that neither she nor my grandfather, nor Joel himself, had for one moment expected me to refuse, I nodded my head.

'Thank you,' she said, and when I looked up in amazement, she smiled.

'Yes, Verity, thank you – for being reasonable, for doing what your grandfather and I both believe, for different reasons, to be the right thing. Thank you for making it easy for us, I suppose. Well then, go quickly, for your grandfather is impatient to have things settled, and I see no point in delay. Joel is precisely aware of your position and his own, so there will be no awkwardness – but, just the same, darling, extract a proper proposal from him. Make sure he asks you very nicely, for, considering all you are bringing him, I feel you are entitled to that.'

He was waiting in the parlour – Joel, a man I had known all my life but did not know at all because he had never noticed me – and now, through the sea mist in my brain, I was curious to discover how he would master the situation, how he could possibly speak of marriage to me without appearing pompous or ridiculous or quite simply greedy.

But as my mother had said, he was not without experience, and coming towards me, he said quickly, 'Your mother has spoken to you, then?'

'Yes.'

'She has explained – everything – fully?'

'She has.'

'And what have you to say to me?'

'I thought you had something to say to me?'

'Ah yes,' he said, his mouth lifting at the corners with a wry amusement, a consciousness of his own false position that I perfectly understood. 'You're going to put me through it, are you?' that smile said. 'Going to get your money's worth? Well, and why not? I don't blame you. In your place I'd very likely do the same.'

For a moment, I was tempted to follow my mother's advice, to be coy and capricious, as any girl, surely, at such a moment has a right to be; tempted to force him to some explanation of his motives and to ask him how it was that he could so easily give up Miss Rosamund Boulton. I wanted to see, I think, just how far he would go; if, at the fear of a refusal, he would spin me some wild yarn of an affection for me he had felt obliged to conceal, or if, letting his reckless, insolent grin flash out, he would confess himself eager merely for my inheritance and dare me to complain.

But finally, the idea of making him play the lover seemed too grotesque, too dangerous, since it would surely annoy him, and later, when he was my husband and in total control of my life, he would not remember it kindly. And so, setting the pattern of our future lives together, choosing the way not of submission but of common sense – having long known the peril of asking for more than could be easily given – I offered him my polite smile of everyday and said, 'Shall we walk up to see my grandfather, since he is expecting us?'

'Is that your answer to me?'

'Why, yes – at least . . . Yes, that's my answer.'

'Good,' he said, his eyes narrowing, the brain behind them busy with his shrewd calculations. 'Excellent.'

Then, almost boyish with relief, more nervous, it seemed, than I, occupied with my own nerves, had supposed, he added quickly, chuckling through the words, 'You don't want me to go down on my knees, then, hand on heart?'

'No, I surely don't.'

'Thank you,' he said, laughing no longer. 'Really, Verity, thank you, for being so reasonable. Your grandfather said you'd be a good girl, but then, old men don't understand these things. And I wasn't sure. You'll be all right with me, you know. I reckon you could have just about anybody, the way things have turned out, but I can look after your affairs better than Bradley Hobhouse, and although Matthew Oldroyd knows what he's doing, he's a shade too careful of his coppers and it's not what you've been used to.'

As I smiled again, polite and friendly – a reasonable girl who understood how these things were done – he put in, perhaps without meaning to say it, 'And, Verity, you are – pretty, you know, really very nice.'

My grandfather was waiting, not for an answer, since there had been no question in his mind, and seeing him in his doorway, tenacious and eternal as a thirsty old tree, his roots deep in the hillside, I knew how impossible it would have been to disobey. Not even my father had been able to do that, not even Edwin, and as I submitted to his sharp-cornered, dusty embrace, I knew that at least he was offering me an established place in the only world I knew. And the night following my father's death, when I had determined to stand on my own feet, seemed very far away.

'Capital,' my grandfather said, twisting my ear with the rough affection best bestowed on a dog. 'You'll make a good little wife if you put your mind to it, and Mrs Stevens will tell you how to go on if your mother can't explain aright. Capital. They thought I was beaten – I could see them yesterday, wondering how much I'd take for the mill, telling themselves they'd bide their time until the business was run down and I was desperate. Aye, let them wait. Let them wait forever.'

Later, when Joel had gone away – having explanations to make, I supposed, to his sisters and to Miss Boulton – my grandfather, full of claret and self-satisfaction, winked his shrewd, sharp eye at me and said, 'Don't worry, lass. I've taken his measure, and he'll treat you right. He knows which side his bread's buttered, yon lad. And he's a hungry man. I never liked him, I admit it. While Edwin lived I kept my eye on him, to make sure he never got in Edwin's way. But that's all changed now. I've told him, if he frames himself, if he shows me he can handle the business, then it's his – or yours, which amounts to the same thing. And if he can't, then I'll sell it over his head. That's what I told him, and it won't harm him to believe it. But it won't come to that because he wants it too bad, he's too hungry for it, and by God, I'll make him earn it before he's through.'

And chuckling, wheezing slightly with his wicked glee, he clasped me in another acrid, uncomfortable embrace and sent me back down the hill a bride.

6

In matters of religion my cousin Hannah's interests tended towards the organization of parish affairs rather than anything of a mystical or emotional nature. She was, of course, a Dissenter, as we all were, since no Law Valley manufacturer worth his salt would join the common herd on the hard back benches of the Established Church while the squire and his lady sat in well-upholstered state in front. No Hobhouse, no Oldroyd – certainly no Barforth – would listen meekly to the parson whose job it was to preach obedience to the squire, contentment with one's humble lot, and to warn against the mortal sin of nurturing ideas above one's station. Such things would do well enough for farm labourers, tied to their cottages and to the squire's whim, but some of these energetic West Riding clothiers had, in their youth, heard the Wesley brothers preaching at the pithead, in the foundry yard, on the edge of a ploughed field, anywhere a congregation could be brought together, and had taken more comfort there than among the squire's aristocratic splendours. Although the first plain chapels such men had built were becoming more elaborate now that money was in good supply and there was an undoubted tendency for the manufacturers themselves to sit in front, their operatives crowding behind, at least the sermon was about industry and thrift, the virtue of not being late for work in the morning – the virtue, in fact, of work for its own sake – and the Hobhouses and the Barforths were well pleased.

Hannah, too, believed in all these things, was always industrious, had no choice but to be thrifty, and, preferring good deeds to good intentions, had deeply involved herself in the Sunday School movement, the movement for the abolition of the slave trade in our colonies, missionary societies and Bible societies, the tedious visiting of deaf old ladies and the sick. She was also far too convinced a Christian to grudge her brother the good fortune which should have been hers and, whatever her private torment, had congratulated me on my engagement with immense composure – had ventured, even, to express her pleasure that we would, after all, be sisters. But on one point she was adamant. Due to my recent loss the wedding must be delayed at least a twelvemonth, and from this view she would not budge.

The rules of conduct, she argued – the rules of decency – were perfectly clear. One remained in mourning and, as far as possible, in seclusion, three months for a brother or sister, six months for a mother or father, a full year for a husband or wife. And since I had lost a father and a brother, in such shocking circumstances, she felt the customary six months should be doubled to twelve, and that no bridal arrangements could be made until then.

'Certainly I mean to observe the full twelvemonth,' she informed me tartly, considering herself, in her heart, I think, to be a widow.

But my grandfather, a man of an older, bawdier generation, held firmly that once one had put a man under the earth with the best headstone one could afford above him, the rest was nonsense. No amount of black armbands and crepe veiling would bring Edwin back, and, ignoring Hannah – disliking her now quite openly and unjustly because she reminded him too sharply of his loss – he stipulated that I should be married as soon as my mother could have me ready.

'Three months at the most,' he said, calculating that at that rate he could have his great-grandson in the spring of the new year.

And so, as May and June dissolved in the blue sun-flecked air of high summer, I spent my days walking the moorland paths above Lawcroft Fold with my brother's old yellow bitch and my own gangling puppy, careless of Hannah's newfangled notion that it was improper for a young lady to walk out alone. And when it rained, I sat on the hearthrug, dreaming into the empty grate or watching as my mother's pale, narrow hands transformed lengths of batiste and muslin and cambric into the intricately tucked and pleated nightgowns, the frilled and embroidered petticoats I would need for my marriage.

There were trips to Cullingford, too, where feathers and fringing and lace could be obtained, packages to be collected at the Old Swan yard, where the coaches from Leeds and Manchester swept in and out several exciting times a day. Every afternoon, there was a sewing woman, come all the way from Cullingford Green, to stitch me into the crepe de chines and gauzes, the taffetas and the brocades that would equip me to be a wife. There were vast discussions about the width of a skirt, the number of flounces to be added to its hem, intense consultations over the merits of cashmere and silk crepe shawls, the right shade of blue for a hooded velvet evening cloak, the amount of ribbon and lace that would make a bonnet dashing without being ostentatious, whether gigot sleeves were still in or had gone, sadly, out, so that the marriage seemed to be far more concerned with fabric and design than with Joel.

Indeed, I saw little of him, for it was more to his advantage to woo my grandfather, who had the power to call the wedding off, than the young bride, who had not, and his visits to me, made either on his way to the Top

House or back from there, were brief, his mind too full of warp and weft, profits and percentages, for romance.

'Only think of it – getting married to old Joel,' Elinor said with sisterly irreverence. 'Only think of that.'

But thinking of it was precisely what I could not do, and it seemed best to take each day as it came, allowing myself to be manipulated this way and that by the sewing woman, allowing Elinor to root through my cupboards and submitting to her judgement when she told me, 'You can't possibly want this yellow muslin now, Verity; it's not at all the thing for a married lady, so I'd best take it off your hands. Oh – and you have the slippers to match, don't you, and the little bonnet with the pansies on the brim. I'd best take them, too.'

We could not, of course, be married in my grandfather's chapel, the Dissenting clergy not then being empowered to conduct the ceremony of marriage, and so we went to the ancient, smoke-grey parish church, erected by some distant four-hundred-year-old ancestor of Sir Giles Flood, lord of the manor of Cullingford. It stood at the top of the steep cobbled street called Kirkgate, dominating the town, its steeple – which once, in Oliver Cromwell's day, had been hung with wool packs to protect it from Royalist cannon – standing graceful and beautiful against the skyline, a swan among a duck pond of factory chimney stacks. And I was driven there on a hot August morning, in an open carriage, wrapped in my bridal veils, my grandfather sitting in grim self-satisfaction at my side.

My mother had kissed me that morning, a cool butterfly's wing against my cheek, one of the ingredients of that kiss certainly being goodbye.

'You will be glad to know that my own plans are very nearly complete,' she had told me almost a week before, as she sat at her sewing. 'Squire Dalby has offered me a cottage on his estate at a most moderate rent. A charming little house with a walled garden, just one room and a dining parlour with two bedrooms over and two attic rooms over that – ample for me to manage with a man and a maid. No horses, of course, and no accommodation for them, but it is very near the village and people are very kind. I expect you would lend me yours, at need, and Squire Dalby has kindly promised his gig, although naturally one does not wish to presume or to create too much obligation. Yes, dear, I think it will suit me very well – and it will suit your husband too, I make no doubt, for no man can really relish the idea of setting up house with his wife's mother.'

And so I understood that when I returned to the mill-house as Joel's wife, I would be alone.

I wore a white dress with a high, ruffled collar, a bell-shaped skirt ending in twelve rows of deep, lace-edged frills, swansdown and orange blossom and white satin roses to hold my veils, high-heeled slippers that raised me to the middle of Joel's ear – and the middle of my grandfather's ear too, which surprised me since I had always thought him such a giant of a man.

'You look well, lass – very well,' he said as we paused in the church porch; grudgingly, I thought, since I may have looked too much like my mother. And then, with his hard hand firmly on mine, he marched me down the aisle, darting glances of triumphant venom at the Aycliffes and the Oldroyds and the Hobhouses there assembled, their heads uncovered, their backs stiff with disapproval since there was not an Anglican among them, and, in any case, this wedding was all too sudden, would have given rise to some unkind speculation and a discreet scrutiny of my figure had not my grandfather's intentions been so well known.

Not even my grandfather had expected Hannah to walk behind me with flowers in her hands and a smile painted on her aching lips, but Elinor was part of my bridal procession, startlingly fair in pale blue gauze, as unlike her brother in appearance as it was possible to be, although they were like enough in vanity and self-seeking.

I suppose I was pretty too that day, as all brides seem to be, for there was a hush as I entered the church, and then a murmur: a tribute, perhaps, to the frailty of young girls who are brought to the altar by hoary old men and handed over to strangers.

And then there was Joel, waiting at the altar, as beautiful in his way as Elinor, with a white rose on the lapel of his dove-grey jacket, a white brocade waistcoat, a drift of white sea foam for a cravat, his black hair vigorously curling, one brown hand taking mine instantly as my grandfather released it, his grip smoother, perhaps, but just as firm.

I had not often heard the wedding service before, being the first of my generation to marry, but as with so many of life's rituals, I had not really pondered its meaning, and, in my case, many of the words did not apply. I could obey Joel, certainly; in fact, I would be well advised to do so, but I wasn't sure just what was meant by honouring him, and as for love, perhaps it was not essential; he had not asked me for it in any case. Yet I made my vows easily enough and, as I did so – as I became his wife – my property and my expectations passed from me into his charge, so that when his turn came to make the promise 'With all my worldly goods I thee endow,' he was already in possession of the wherewithal to keep it.

I had entered the church door an heiress who, had I been of full age, would have been able to dispose of my fortune at will, to sign contracts, to enter into agreements, but from the moment our vows were spoken, everything I had or earned or came to inherit belonged automatically to him; and he was not even called upon to guarantee that he would be kind.

He could leave me, if he chose, without in any way forfeiting the use of my money. But I, unless I gained his consent, could never live apart from him. He could take my goods and chattels and sell them without my consent; he could clothe his mistress – if he had one – in my silks

96

and satins, give her my jewels. He could remove my children from my care whenever it suited him; in fact, he could do anything he pleased with my property and my person, since now, as a married woman, I had no legal identity of my own. And if, occasionally, there were a duchess or some other powerful lady who sought a divorce, a special Act of Parliament was first required, and I could not imagine His Majesty's government concerning itself with the wrongs of a Mrs Joel Barforth of Lawcroft Fold.

My marriage, like every other marriage I had ever heard of, would be for life, and if the law now chose to ignore me, at least I knew my grandfather would not. And I smiled very pleasantly as I walked back up the aisle, particularly at Emma-Jane Rawnsley, the banker's daughter, and Lucy Hobhouse of Nethercoats Mill, both of whom had sworn to be married not only before me but before one another as well.

Due to our recent tragedy there was no elaborate reception, no need to hire the Market Hall in Cullingford as we would have done in happier times – just a wedding breakfast prettily served by Mrs Stevens, with a lace-covered table festooned with flowers, cake and champagne and colourful, frothy confections that left no memory on my tongue. There was my mother, her mourning dress set aside for the day, wearing pale lilac, her mind apparently elsewhere as Mrs Hobhouse of Nethercoats and Mrs Oldroyd of Fieldhead tried hard to discover on what terms she really stood with her new landlord, the squire. There was my grandfather, planted foursquare at the head of the table, his eyes gloating, gleaming, as they rested on Mr Aycliffe the builder, who was still wondering about the contract for the new mill, or on Mr Hobhouse, his chief rival, who had hoped, no doubt, to get me for his son Bradley and to see Barforth looms making money for Nethercoats.

There was Bradley Hobhouse himself, a young man I had known all my life, making eyes at my cousin Elinor, ignoring his mother's determined efforts to push him towards Emma-Jane, the banker's daughter, plumper than Elinor but considerably richer. And there was Hannah, with a mourning brooch made of my brother's hair set in gold at the neck of her dress, her face pinched as if by cold, smiling as if her mouth hurt her; Hannah speaking sharply to Elinor for flirting with the Hobhouse boy, and then disappearing altogether, to be discovered by Mrs Stevens, as I heard later, on the attic landing crying her bitter tears.

Finally, after a bee swarm of good wishes and some heavy-handed teasing, when my stomach was a little queasy from Mrs Stevens's subtleties and too much champagne, it was evening and I was left alone to contemplate the harsh reality of getting into bed with my cousin Joel.

Since the mill had a prior claim on his time, there was to be no wedding journey. We were to have the Top House for a day or two while my grandfather and Mrs Stevens paid a visit to Leeds; and my grandfather's ornate bed, with its ocean of pillows and bolsters, its heavy fringed canopy, and the gross, unbidden whispering in my head of what he and Mrs Stevens did there, were enough to unnerve me.

'Don't think about it, dear,' my mother had murmured on leaving, having taken an unusual amount of champagne herself. 'It's not as if there was anything you had to do – any skill that you might lack. Not a bit of it. He will know what he's about, and at the very most you have only to follow his lead. And these tales one hears – you know, of brides who go mad with shock or have their hair turned white – well, darling, one never actually meets anyone to whom that happened, so I rather think we may discount it altogether. Naturally you may show surprise, because it is all rather surprising at first, I must confess – but not terrible, not fatal. I speak lightly, Verity my dear, because I find it the best way. My own mother told it to me quite differently, for she had a finely developed sense of the dramatic, and I found it no help at all. Take things lightly,

Verity, as I try to do. I think you will find that whatever happens – however badly one is made to feel – the very best defence is to seem not to care.'

Although I understood her meaning, for there was enough of her in me for that, the long wait my husband imposed upon me, leaving me sitting bolt upright in that giant, alien bed while he smoked a cigar and then another, surely, in the room below, added nothing to my composure. The suspense, I thought, would be far more likely to drive me mad than the other – a matter I understood mainly from a few farmyard observations and which I thus expected to last no more than a moment – and when at last I heard Joel's step on the stair and he came into the room, alien himself in his richly patterned dressing gown, his face very dark in the candle flame, I felt more relief than alarm – pleasure, even, at the thought that soon now I would be allowed to go to sleep.

I expected, I think, an immediate assault in the dark, but, leaving the candles burning, he sat down on the edge of the bed, ready, it seemed, at this unlikely moment, for conversation.

'Well then,' he said, a smile just lifting the corners of his mouth, 'so it's done—'

And because he was my wicked, grown-up cousin, experienced in the ways of the world, it did not occur to me that, sitting there in my best embroidered nightgown with my hair hanging loose again in little-girl fashion as he used to see it, I seemed so familiar to him, so very nearly a sister, that he was nervous, too.

'Yes,' he said, his smile flashing out suddenly, its wry humour directed, I suppose, at us both. 'So here we are – and you must be quite terrified, I suppose.'

'No, I'm not.'

'Oh, my word – are you not? Or do you simply mean to be brave, grit your teeth and endure all the amazing things I shall do to you – for I suppose they will amaze you. You can't have the slightest notion—'

'Yes I do,' I answered stoutly, stung by his condescension; unaware, in my total ignorance of physical desire, that the prospect of doing those things with me – his little, sad-eyed cousin – was proving far more difficult than he had bargained for.

'Oh no you don't, I'd put money on it, for your mother will have told you nothing – not dear Aunt Isabella. One wonders if she even knows herself.'

And although I couldn't vouch for that, not really being too certain of what he meant, I insisted tartly, 'I'm not such a goose. I'm not blind either, and Edwin said things sometimes – to the stableboys when he forgot I was by.'

'Ah well, in that case, if Edwin said things, what can I possibly tell you?'

And, remembering against my will his eyes watching Edwin die and knowing I must not, at any cost, remember it – never – that it was absolutely essential for me to obliterate it totally, at once, I said quickly, to cover the forbidden images with words, 'I know Edwin had a child, two or three years ago, from a farm girl, and I know how much my father had to pay.'

But my sole example of worldliness did not impress him.

'Oh, so you know that, do you,' he said coolly. 'Well, I reckon my sister Hannah knows it too, although she'd die before admitting it. Just think, Verity, if that child had been a boy instead of a sickly girl, you might not be here tonight. Your grandfather might well have decided to adopt Edwin's child – whether his farm-girl mother had liked it or not – and then you'd have been left in peace. Only think of that. I wonder if it's what they mean by destiny?'

'Oh – I don't know anything about that. And anyway, what does it matter? I am here, aren't I?'

'Now I'm not denying that,' he said. 'Not for one moment.' And getting up, he walked to the window, looked out, came back to my bedside, and, putting the tips of his fingers experimentally on my shoulder, ran them down my arm and back again to my neck, tracing the outline of my ear, concentrating perhaps so hard on his own reaction that he missed the rigidity of my body, the flush of embarrassment staining every part of me.

'You really are very pretty, you know,' he said musingly. 'Listen – I won't pretend I've looked at you too closely in the past, because – well, you were always forbidden fruit where I was concerned. If I'd come near you before, they'd have chased me off mighty quick and that would have ruined Hannah's chances. So I didn't look, and you're not a flirt to put yourself in a man's way; just a quiet smile, a "Good evening, cousin Joel" – a deep one, like your mother, I've heard tell, and that doesn't displease me. Your grandfather may not think much of your mother, but she's got style, Verity, a fine, high-stepping style – Dalby's noticed it all right – and I can see you'll be the same. Never flustered, never at a loss for words, but always soft-spoken. You'll make an elegant woman, Verity; the kind other men will look at and say, "By God, he must be doing well to afford her." And I like that.'

And his voice trailing away, his hand clenched itself in a movement of impatience and then went quite roughly into my hair.

'I should wait,' he said. 'I should be patient and give you time. I know it, and I know I won't do it. Verity, I can't tell how innocent you are, or how sly – because my sister Elinor has never been so dainty as she looks – but one thing you can't know about and that's need. How could you? It's not a feminine thing, need. It's a man's demon and it's been biting me too long now. Listen, Verity, they'll have told you certain things about me, or you'll have heard them talking – I've had my wild times, I admit it, but they ended – because my father was wild too – and I've been obliged to deny myself pleasures to which I'd grown accustomed. I'm not making a confession, because I'm not ashamed – oh, damnation take it, how am

I to make myself clear without putting you to fright. Have you any idea at all of what I mean?'

'Oh yes – yes,' I told him, anxious now to have it over and done with.

But he shook his head, knowing quite well, I suppose, that Verity Barforth, at sixteen, whose experience of the world stopped short at the limits of the Law Valley, had small chance of understanding the split in his nature between the part of him that found it well-nigh incestuous to desire her and the part of him that was ready, most ardently, to desire any woman.

'I don't believe you,' he said. 'But let's see – let's just see what progress we can make from here.'

To begin with, as my mother had said, although his stroking hands on my arms and shoulders were strange to me and his tongue, parting my lips, took me by surprise since I hadn't realized a kiss was quite like that, it was not pleasant perhaps but not terrible. Something, I thought, to which I could grow accustomed, as every other married woman I knew had grown accustomed. Not really alarming at all, until I realized he had shrugged himself out of his dressing gown and was naked. And the shock of being clasped in that nude embrace released a flood of images in my mind – of my grandfather's weathered, old man's body in this very bed with Mrs Stevens, panting and grunting as Joel was beginning to do – images that flicked my already uneasy stomach to nausea.

'Take off that nightgown,' he muttered.

When I began to protest and ask him how he dared, he almost snarled, 'Take it off. It makes you look like a child, or a damn nun waiting to be crucified. Take it off.'

'Then put out the candles.'

'Not I. I'm no peasant to make love in the dark.'

'Good heavens – you mean to look at me?'

'Aye. And if you want to spare yourself the sight of me you'd best close your eyes.'

And so, my eyes tight shut, I pulled my mother's finely

stitched cambric over my head and delivered myself up like a sacrifice, my head swimming again with the obscene posturing of my grandfather, revolted beyond any appreciation of Joel's skill or the realization that, while not for one moment forgetting his own pleasure, he made a decent effort not to hurt me.

But he would have done better perhaps, that first time, had he been less skilful, had he simply taken me without expertise, merely with a little kindness, instead of giving way to his rich enjoyment of the female body, his determination that every one of his senses should be satisfied, that every part of him should be replete – not only hands, mouth, and loins but eyes and nostrils, and the mischievous curiosity that led his tongue to explore the whole surface of my skin, the curves and crevices at which I rarely looked myself.

And so the act I had believed would be so quickly over prolonged itself, rising in intensity as his teeth possessed themselves of the lobes of my ears, the point of my shoulders, and my breasts, not painfully but compellingly, so that I knew I was being devoured, that he was taking me slowly, inch by inch, inside himself, and that I would never be whole again. And because no one had ever spoken to me of pleasure, because I had learned that this whole process was designed to give men satisfaction and to make women pregnant – and my grandfather certainly required me to be pregnant – I grew more bewildered with every caress.

I had been ready for discomfort and embarrassment. Nothing had prepared me for Joel's lingering enjoyment. In my total ignorance of sensuality, I became so desperate for a conclusion that the final pain of penetration was not unwelcome, since that much at least I understood, and even Joel's body nailed shuddering to mine, his long, inexplicable groaning, were not so much a shock as a promise of release.

'Don't fret,' he told me when it was over, turning away

from me and breathing hard. 'Women aren't supposed to like it – ladies, that is, at any rate. And if a woman don't care for it with her husband she's not likely to look elsewhere when he goes off to Norfolk for the wool clip. So don't fret, Verity.'

Yet even I, through the fear and ignorance that had been the breeding ground of my disgust, even I could tell that although his agile brain had accepted the shortcomings of our situation, his restless, experienced body had not been satisfied.

7

Those first months of marriage were awkward but polite, dominated completely by my grandfather, who, sitting on the hillside above us – baleful, all-powerful – had every intention of making Joel earn his keep.

He was in the mill yard every morning at five o'clock, watch in hand, eyes peeled for latecomers – as my father, but not always Edwin, had done – since time is money, and no one should be allowed to waste anything that belonged to a Barforth. He spent his days in the sheds, constantly answering my grandfather's summonses to the Top House to explain himself, and his evenings, more often than not, in the countinghouse, checking through old accounts, poring over old ledgers, building up a meticulous picture of Samson Barforth's commercial past and what he, Joel Barforth, could make of the future. And from the very first their ideas on that future were in conflict.

My grandfather, in fact, did not require ideas from Joel. He wanted, quite simply, a caretaker for the next generation, someone to hand over the business intact to a new Edwin, as he had planned to give it to the old; he had no desire, now, for change. And, indeed, since the attack on our mill interest in power looms had declined generally in the Law Valley, not from intimidation but from what was seen as sound common sense.

'I see no reason for it,' Mr Hobhouse of Nethercoats had announced. 'The most I ever pay a hand weaver these days is seven shillings and seven pence a week, and when I can get my job done as cheap as that, what do I gain with expensive new machines – paying these fancy engineering fellows to look after them when they break down, and having to reinforce my sheds to take the weight and the vibration – that's all I'll get – that and the risk of getting shot at one night on my way home. There'd have to be money in it, lads, a deal of money, afore I'd risk that.'

And although my grandfather could see the possibilities of power weaving as clearly as Joel – or as clearly as Mr Oldroyd of Fieldhead, whose spinning machines could produce more yarn than the handlooms could accommodate – he was determined now, it seemed, that everything at Lawcroft should remain as it was, a monument to Edwin Barforth's memory rather than a steppingstone to Joel Barforth's greater glory.

On his return from Leeds, after our wedding, he had immediately required Mr Aycliffe the builder to attend him at the Top House and, without Joel's knowledge, had cancelled all arrangements for the construction of a new mill.

'No use for a new mill when there's nothing to put in it,' he'd said to Joel, 'for I've cancelled the new looms, while I was at it. I reckon you've got enough to be going on with, my lad. More than you ever dreamed you'd get your hands on, I'll be bound. So let's see how you tackle it – let's see you keep it turning over, nice and steady – the way my son William used to do.'

But if my father had been content with the position of workhorse, scapegoat, Joel was not. As the near-bankrupt owner of Low Cross he had been obliged to struggle from one day to the next, delighted merely if he could meet his commitments; but now that he was acutely aware of the changes in the world outside the Law Valley, of so many new inventions and hitherto unheard-of opportunities, my grandfather's tight curb rein choked him, drove him sometimes to the limits of endurance. But because my grandfather held the purse strings and had the power, at any time, to sell the mill or simply close it down, those limits could not be passed, and Joel, with a venomous fury lurking behind his eyes, was obliged to smile, to persuade – to beg, even – when it would have suited him far better to fly at my grandfather's throat.

Our area was famous for the manufacture of calamancoes and shalloons, heavy worsted cloth that, with care, could last a lifetime.

'A Barforth calamanco,' my grandfather was fond of saying, 'can last a woman all her married life and still have enough wear in it to serve her daughter when she's gone.'

And when Joel remarked that although this may have been all very well in the old days, perhaps the younger generation of women would not wish to wear the same garment so long, my grandfather was not merely scornful but very much annoyed.

'You'd cut the quality then, would you, lad,' he snorted, 'to make a quick penny? Aye, and that's your father coming out in you, fast and flashy – turn anything off his looms, your father would, if he thought he could sell it. But I notice his customers never came back twice.'

'There's no question of that, sir,' Joel said, keeping his temper, although I felt the snap of it. 'It's a question of supplying what's needed, and in these days, when there's more cash in hand for luxuries, when people get about more and new fashions are coming over all the time from France, it strikes me that women aren't looking for something they can keep a generation. And where's the sense in producing plain, hard-wearing cloth you can't sell? Lightweights are going to pay better, sir, in the future; I'm convinced of it. Fancy lightweights – power-woven.'

'Aye,' my grandfather snarled. 'Fancy lightweights for fancy ladies. You'd know all about that, I reckon – millmaster – like your father before you.'

And I knew – Joel knew – that had Edwin put forward this idea it would have been hailed as a flash of brilliance: 'Damn me, but the Boy knows what he's about,' instead of 'Keep your fancy ideas to yourself, millmaster, or bear in mind what they did to your father.'

Yet Joel, quietly, with the assistance of Ira Agbrigg, the weaver who had brought us news of the riot, began experimenting with lightweight worsteds at his own mill, Low Cross, a matter which, when it came to my grandfather's attention, provoked the most serious argument they had yet had.

In the first place the employment of Ira Agbrigg did not please him.

'Damn the Judas,' he had said, having spotted him in the crowd at Edwin's funeral. 'Give the fellow a guinea and send him on his way.'

And the fact that Joel had not obeyed but had made use of him – and illicit use at that – would have been enough to raise a storm.

But Low Cross itself was really the heart of the matter, for my grandfather could tolerate no division of loyalties and grudged every second of Joel's time that was not spent at Lawcroft Fold.

'You'll get rid of it,' my grandfather ordered. 'Get rid of it. I told you before you were married that I'd carry no deadwood. Sell it if you can, knock it down if you can't, and I'll have no more tales about buyers who don't come up to scratch. I've never seen any of those buyers of yours – don't believe in these buyers. Well, you can save yourself the trouble of inventing another, for I'll find a buyer myself.'

'I must ask you not to do that, sir.'

'What!' my grandfather yelled, stung by the quiet insolence of Joel's manner. 'Ask me? Tell me, more like, and I'll take no orders from you. I'll have that muckheap sold up, lock, stock, and barrel, this time next month, if it's the last thing—'

'Hardly without my consent, sir.'

And seeing the veins swell on my grandfather's forehead, seeing his purple mottled colour, I cringed, looked away, and held my breath.

'So that's it,' he whispered. 'Your consent. And what have *you* to say to anything? You'll consent whenever it suits me, you young scoundrel, and be glad to do it – and if you don't it's not only Low Cross I'll put under the hammer.'

But even the ultimate – the everyday threat – could not deter Joel on this occasion.

'Low Cross is my sisters' home, sir. And the sale of it, as it is now, will hardly provide them with another.'

'Aye, your sisters – and what do you care about your sisters? It's your looms and your damned fancy worsteds you're thinking of, my lad; sneaking there and wasting time with that Judas – time that belongs to me, time I bought and paid for, like I bought and paid for you—'

'Very likely, sir – but, nevertheless, my sisters do live in the millhouse.'

'Then get them married,' my grandfather snarled, altogether beside himself, knowing, I suppose, that he could not really deprive Edwin's intended bride of a home and he had no intention of offering her any alternative. 'Get them established – get rid of them – tell them to look lively and take themselves off to the marriage market. And when they've gone, Low Cross goes with them.'

And so Low Cross was given its reprieve, and Ira Agbrigg with it, my grandfather having forgotten him, it seemed, in his rage against Joel, but there were to be no power looms, no fancy lightweight worsteds, no changes.

'Your time belongs to me, lad,' my grandfather reminded him grimly, frequently, and even on Sundays, when the mills were quiet, he watched Joel carefully, chuckling, I think, when he saw him go down to the empty sheds rearranging them in his mind, taking possession, making complex calculations to suit the day when his time would be his own again.

I existed between them, hardly noticeable in the glare of their mutual hostility, sole mistress now – since my mother's departure for Squire Dalby's hamlet of Patterswick – of Lawcroft millhouse, the place where I had been born, expected, suddenly, to answer Marth-Ellen's questions about the pickling and the preserving, the contents of larders and closets, expected to know what my cousin Joel might wish to find on his plate at dinnertime.

To begin with, there were often dramas, for, unlike my father and brother, who required food simply to be hot and plentiful, Joel had a complicated appetite, a carry-over from his wild days, when he had tasted – in Manchester, I suppose – the new style of cooking from France, brought over by the refugees from Napoleon's wars. And although Hannah had certainly never provided such delicacies – believing that the sense of taste, along with all the other senses, was better suppressed than encouraged – his new responsibilities had increased his expectations, and he openly found Marth-Ellen's plain roast meats and batter puddings dull.

There were dramas, too, about the polishing of his boots and the laundering of his linen, for Marth-Ellen had a heavy hand with a goffering iron, and his shirt frills were rarely to his liking.

'Hannah did them for him when he was at home,' Elinor confided. 'For mercy's sake, don't let her know I told you, for it was always a great secret, but our poor old Bertha could never do anything right for him, and we couldn't afford anyone else, so Hannah did all the goffering and the dainty work. Poor Hannah, standing for hours in the kitchen, all hot and flushed and her hair coming down – no wonder she was ashamed of it. So come on, then, Verity, I know you're a married lady now and I'm just a silly chit from the schoolroom, but you are going to tell me things, aren't you? I'm absolutely relying on you, for Hannah won't say a word – although now I come to think of it she may not be too sure about it, either. So do tell, Verity – there's really no one else. And – while we're on the subject – whatever happened to Rosamund Boulton?'

I had, of course, nothing to say on the subject of Miss Boulton, since no one – least of all Joel – had thought fit to inform me of her reaction to his marriage. If she had loved him, then no doubt she had cried; if not, then by now she was probably already in careful pursuit of another lover – in either case, there was nothing I could reasonably do about it.

But Joel's domestic grievances were another matter, and although I was still awkward and uncertain in his nightly embraces, I found no difficulty in slipping into Marth-Ellen's kitchen to whip him up a syllabub liberally laced with brandy, according to Mrs Stevens's famous recipe, nor hardship in taking a leaf from Hannah's book and using my own agile wrist and patient disposition to manipulate the goffering iron. And gradually I began to discover not only how to cope but even, sometimes, to get my way.

I was surrounded by natures far more aggressive and urgent than mine, gigantic tempers which flared and fumed and threatened, against which my own protests could not be heard. And so, when my grandfather bellowed, 'Get rid of that damn dog of Edwin's, it ain't healthy and it's got fleas,' or when Hannah, grimacing over a slice of Marth-Ellen's gingerbread, informed me, 'Do you not think, Verity, that this house is getting too much for a woman of Marth-Ellen's age? In your place I would send her to Patterswick, to your mother, and hire myself a pair of clean young girls,' I made no attempt to defend either my dog or my maid.

'Why, yes,' I said smiling, allowing no opportunity for argument. 'Yes, I'll do that – presently.' And I did nothing.

I found, too, that such things as badly polished boots could easily be remedied – that housekeeping, in fact, was not the mystery Mrs Stevens chose to make it – and since I became almost immediately and most obligingly pregnant, no one, so far as I knew, had any cause to complain.

I did not ask myself if I wanted a child, since that had been the sole purpose of my marriage, nor did I expect any great show of delight from Joel, who wanted Lawcroft for himself and not for a son who, in this early life at least, would be monopolized – and spoiled – by my grandfather. But the Top House greeted the news with predictable joy, Mrs Stevens floating down the hill at once to make my grandfather's requirements known. I must sit with my feet on a stool, must take large, nourishing meals to build his great-grandson's bone and fibre, must walk no farther than the garden gate. And here, once again, I scored a small triumph.

'Do you know, Mrs Stevens, I think you had best go back and tell him that it would not be wise to coop me up like that for the next six months or so. Tell him I am the type to go into a decline unless I have my day's supply of fresh air, and what would happen to his great-grandson then? Tell him you can read all the signs, and he will believe you.'

'Why, Mrs Barforth,' she said, 'how sly—'

But my grandfather had been out of sorts lately, and, always anxious for her own future when his began to seem uncertain, she did my bidding, ensuring that I was allowed to take my carriage exercise with my cousin Elinor, the only other person I knew with time to spare.

Elinor, of course, was waiting, too; she had been waiting six out of her sixteen years for the man who would become her husband, and although her early dreams of some young landed gentleman had been modified to close consideration of the Hobhouses and the Oldroyds, she was determined, at all costs, not to be left on the shelf.

Certainly, her situation, in the upheaval that had swept

over us all, had not changed for the better. If Hannah had married my brother, Elinor's position, alone with Joel and possibly Miss Boulton, would have been difficult but only temporary, for Hannah would have moved heaven and earth, and my brother Edwin with it, until a suitable match for her sister had been found. Edwin, with his liberal allowance, could have added something to Elinor's portion; enough, at any rate, to make her interesting – not, perhaps, to a Hobhouse, but to some small tradesman who would know the value of the Barforth name. But my grandfather, deeply suspicious of Joel, put very little ready money his way, while Hannah had not only lost her taste for weddings but, whether she realized it or not, was in no hurry now to part with her sister and face life alone.

Not that anyone had asked her to do so. At my wedding Elinor had experienced no difficulty in attracting the notice of the square-cut, bull-necked Hobhouse boy, nor in having her thigh surreptitiously stroked by the portly, pious Mr Oldroyd, whose ailing wife had not yet obliged him by falling sick enough to die. But when that lady finally did succumb to one of her many maladies, her husband would remarry carefully, to his profit. And when it was time for the Hobhouse boy to take a wife, it would be Emma-Jane Rawnsley, the banker's daughter, or plain Amelia Oldroyd of Fieldhead his mother invited to tea, not Elinor.

'There has to be somebody,' she told me. 'Somebody will see me, somewhere, and realize he absolutely can't live – yes, yes, I've been reading novels again, which Hannah doesn't approve, but it must happen like that now and again, surely, or how would they know to put it in all the stories?'

And so, since to be admired she had first to be seen, I went over to Low Cross two or three times a week in the good weather, although plumper and more breathless as time went by, and took her for a drive.

The millhouse at Low Cross was one of the pokiest and dingiest I had ever seen: a dark, square box, not set apart like ours behind its high stone wall but tacked on to the mill itself, so that no more than the thickness of a single wall separated my cousins from the clatter of looms and the coarse conversations of their operatives. The ceiling was low and oppressive, the windows, in an effort to keep out dust and grime and the shouted obscenities of wagon drivers, tiny and always tight-shut, while the door opened directly onto the yard, exposing the Low Cross young ladies to stares and sniggers, which they had long learned to ignore. Not a house in which I would have cared to live; no fit place, indeed, for Hannah, should she ever find herself alone, and often enough, when Elinor, hearing the sound of my carriage, came tripping across those soiled cobbles as if they were a summer meadow, I felt certain that her prettiness and her determination would have their reward. And when I thought of Hannah, my heart sank.

We went, of course, invariably to Cullingford, which was not, in that first year of my marriage, the grim city it later became, having still something of the country town about it: a market square with an old grey-white cross, and two old coaching inns at either side of it – the Old Swan, where one could take the coach for Manchester or Liverpool any morning of the week, and the thriving, bustling Wool Pack, where coaches were coming and going all day to Wakefield, York, Halifax, Bradford, and Leeds. There was the old Market Building on the Wool Pack side of the square, the upper floor of which could be hired for dances, concerts, or weddings, while the ground floor was devoted to the sale of vegetables and cheeses and the unsightliness of the meat and poultry trade. On the other side, the Old Swan side, the Piece Hall stood in all its ancient glory, its gates still opening promptly at eight o'clock every Thursday morning to admit those who had woollen goods for sale and those who wished to buy.

From Market Square one could still see patches of green on the hills that encircled the town; one could still wander pleasantly up the steep, cobbled slope of Millergate to buy a bonnet or a fan, stroll to the top of Kirkgate, even steeper and stonier, to inspect the fine stone tracery of the parish church, or spend an exciting half hour at the bottom of Sheepgate, where crumbling old warehouses stood with their feet in the canal and one could find low, sinister-fronted shops where carved ivory and intricately tooled leather were offered for sale. There were mean streets too, an unsavoury crisscrossing of alleyways behind the main thoroughfares where once-decent houses, now in decay, had been divided up to accommodate a faceless multitude. But they kept themselves aloof, it seemed, and although the streets were alive, on market days, with top-hatted commercial gentlemen come to do business at the Piece Hall or at the Old Swan, where additional piece rooms were provided, it was not difficult to remember that Cullingford had once been little more than a convenient place to cross the stream, a village lost in the isolation of bare, impenetrable moorland, where no stranger ever came.

My grandfather and others like him – the Hobhouses and the Oldroyds, the Aycliffes – had brought prosperity to Cullingford: I was well aware of that. It was, without doubt, because of them that the coaches came and went, that the inns were flourishing and the name of Cullingford was known outside the Law Valley, and yet they did not altogether belong here, nor really anywhere else.

The old divisions of society had been easy to understand. There had been the king and, under him, his dukes and earls and other noble lords; and, beneath them, a multitude of country squires – all drawn together by common interest and inclination into a ruling class, supported by the parsons, who, more often than not, were younger sons of the noble houses. In the countryside there had been the peasants, tied to the farmers, who, in their various ways, were tied to the squires; in the towns, small shopkeepers and tradesmen plying their crafts with an apprentice or two, minding their own business; and, in the cities, a mob, having no rights, much given to unlawful assemblies which, occasionally, had to be put down.

But now this sudden machine age had produced a new breed of men: men without either pedigree or prestige, who had discovered other roads to wealth besides the possession of broad ancestral lands or the wielding of a sword, and who were fast becoming too rich and too clamorous for the gentry to ignore.

Yet they still continued to ignore us. Some twenty years ago, I knew, an Act of Parliament had been obtained 'for the lighting, paving, watching and improving the town of Cullingford,' a measure which required the appointment of a Board of Commissioners, all to be leading citizens, men of substance and good character. Yet, although the increase in trade, brought about by the manufacturers, had made the Act necessary and most of them were men of substance and exemplary behaviour, not one place on the board was made available to them. The appointments had gone to Sir Giles Flood, lord of the manor of Cullingford, although few of us had ever seen him, to his son and his son-in-law, to his cousin Colonel Corey of Blenheim Lane, to Colonel Corey's cousin, the lawyer Mr Corey-Manning, and to others who had property in the town but were not well known here.

And it may not have been any great consolation to men like my grandfather that so far all the commissioners had achieved was the lighting of the better streets, the removal of a number of hog styes and muckheaps, and the employment of a few quite elderly watchmen who, patrolling the town with their lanterns and rattles – when the weather was not too inclement – added little to our security.

The landed gentry, with their protective agricultural policies, their belief in the natural harmony of castle, altar, and throne, had no intention of allowing power to fall into the hands of a pack of greedy, upstart manufacturers who would allow cheap foreign corn into the country to feed their operatives and would foul the countryside with their chimney stacks and their chapels. And although one could sympathize with their determination to hang on to their privileges – just as one could sympathize with the workers who, by smashing the machines, were trying to hang on to theirs – one could not expect men like my grandfather, wedged uneasily between, to be content.

Yet, on my afternoon drives with Elinor that spring, there were no outward signs of conflict, unless it was that I, not yet seventeen, was too preoccupied with my approaching motherhood to notice it, and that Elinor had no time to spare for any miseries but her own.

'I'll be an old maid' was the burden of her song that lilting April, as she sat beside me in a cast-off dress she had transformed beyond recognition, my old tortoiseshell combs in her fine, fair hair. 'Yes, I can see it coming. I'll be an old maid and I won't be good at it. Hannah, now, she won't take it too badly, because she had Edwin and she can say her heart is in his grave – and, really, that sounds very fine. I wish I could say the same. But by the time your grandfather dies and Joel can afford to give me a portion, then I'll be too old to care. Or Hannah won't let me go.'

'Nonsense,' I told her, feeling her shiver and seeing, through her eyes, the image of Elinor Barforth, beautiful, enchanting, made for life and love, withering to waste. But she would not be consoled.

'No,' she insisted, her chin unusually resolute, her cloudy blue-green eyes swimming with her easy tears. 'I'll turn sour – if I let it happen to me, and there are times when I think I'd do anything to get away. Yes, Verity – think of it – sitting with Hannah in that dark hole, day after day, pretending not to do the ironing – hating it – getting plain, getting old – while Emma-Jane Rawnsley squeezes herself into a wedding dress, for she's as fat as a sow, and Lucy Hobhouse calls in her carriage to bring me a piece of her bride cake. No, I won't have it, Verity. I'll do something – get away somehow – I'll fall in love with somebody unsuitable and run off with him, and even if they bring me back in disgrace, or he abandons me and I have to crawl back, at least I'll have had something – I'll be a fallen woman, and that's better than being an old maid. And if I can't do that, then I'll marry beneath me, even if it means living in a cottage and doing the washing and not having a nursemaid. Even that – why not? – it's what Rosamund Boulton means to do. Oh well, I daresay I shouldn't talk of her to you, and I daresay you won't be interested to know, but she's always thought well of herself, and when Joel cried off she thought there'd be plenty of others. And so there were, Master Matthew Oldroyd among them, but when it came to marriage her dowry's not much better than mine and it wouldn't do. So now she's angling for a farmer out in Wensleydale, just an acre or two and a cow and no society. Dreadful – but before I'll sit at Low Cross waiting to die with Hannah, I'll do the same. You don't understand, Verity. You've got Joel. You may not like him – in fact, I don't always like him very much myself – but he's a husband.'

But by the time I took her back to Low Cross that day, her tears had dried, her china-doll face was composed again, and her manner was that of a carefree young lady entering her baronial hall. It was only as I waved her goodbye that I began to wonder why, for the last hour, I had felt so unwell.

The sun was warm, certainly, for an April day, the road stony and the carriage badly sprung, but I was not one for vapours and it came as a surprise to me when, walking from the stables to the house – for we had no carriage drive – earth and sky rushed suddenly together, crushing me between them to a momentary blackness. And when the day returned, I was again surprised that the face peering anxiously into mine was not one I knew but one which I had seen before – thin, yellow-pale, and so sickeningly reminiscent of Jabez Gott that I almost fainted again.

'Who are you?' I gasped, but he did not feel his identity to be of much concern.

'Agbrigg, ma'am,' he said without explanation. 'See, there's your Marth-Ellen coming running. Here, lass, help your missus into the house and I'll go fetch the master.'

'No,' I said desperately, assuming he meant my grandfather, the last person in the world I wanted by me now. 'You'll do no such thing.'

But he was off, hurrying stoop-shouldered towards the mill, and I was relieved when, some time later, Joel appeared.

'What ails you?'

'What should ail me? I'm starting the baby, I suppose.'

'Is it time?'

'It could be. I'm not sure. Who was that man, the one who came to fetch you? He called you the master.'

'Yes,' Joel said, smiling. 'He would. That's Ira Agbrigg – a good lad. Your grandfather calls him Judas.'

'And he calls you the master?'

'So he does. A forward-thinking lad, Ira Agbrigg. Believes in the machine age, like I do, and he knows your grandfather don't much like him. But he's not after affection. He wants to rise in the world, and he'll cling to my coattails so long as I'm going in the right direction – upwards. Verity, are you in pain?'

'No,' I said fiercely, refusing to be in pain, realizing now, when it was too late, that I did not want a baby after all, that I was too young, that I would not know what to do with a baby, that I was afraid of dying. 'No, no, I'm not in pain. And if I am, then it's not what you think, not what I said. I've eaten something, that's all.'

'I reckon I'll send for the doctor, to be on the safe side, and your mother.'

'If you want to give them the trouble of coming all this way for nothing, then you can suit yourself.'

And as he turned to go and issue the necessary commands, I shrieked his name. 'Joel!'

'Yes. I'm here.'

And he reached me, it seemed, in one stride, just as the pain which had been tiger-prowling somewhere at the small of my back struck out again in a knife thrust that almost forced me to my knees.

'By God,' he said, much alarmed, as strong men often are by these female processes. 'Sit down. Here, let me help you to the rocking chair, and then wait, just wait, while I get somebody on the road to fetch the doctor.'

But, clinging to him, tugging him back towards me, half laughing because I could see he feared I would give birth then and there and that for once in his life he would be helpless, and half crying because there was now no doubt that I would give birth sooner or later and was still unwilling, I said quickly, my tongue breaking loose from all restraint, 'No, no, there's no hurry. It goes on for hours – days. It goes on forever. Listen, do listen for once, my grandfather made me have this baby, and if it kills me don't let it go to the Top House. Promise me. If I die take the baby to my mother, keep it away from him.'

'You'll not die,' he said, the pugnacious set of his jaw warning me he would be furious – with me, with death itself – if I did. But having made up my mind to it, I was not easily dissuaded.

'How do you know? Unless you think you're God, like he does! Promise me.'

'All right. You'll not die because you're a Barforth and you've got too much to live for, but I promise. Trust me.'

'I don't know that I do.'

And putting his hand under my chin, not pinching it now in that smug, cousinly way of his but holding it steady, holding me steady, so that I could look at him, he answered, 'Now just you listen to me, Verity Barforth. He may be your grandfather and he may think he owns you – and that he owns me, too – but he's an old man and I reckon we can

119

let him keep his delusions. You're my wife, Verity, and no one – understand me, no one – harms my wife, nor my child, nor anything else that belongs to me. Not so long as I'm alive, they don't, and I'm good for a long while yet. Now, do you trust me?'

And in this one case, if in no other, I did.

'So it's a bargain then,' he said, holding me now very close with a firmness that reassured, a gentleness that surprised and calmed me. 'Now will you let me fetch the doctor?'

But, my hands wildly twisting together around his neck, I could not let him go, and picking me up, he carried me into the hallway and up the stairs, calling out instructions as he went; and he lay me down, once again with that gentle firmness, on my bed.

'Joel, don't leave me. Don't leave the house, especially when my grandfather comes. Don't let him send you to the mill.'

'He'll send me nowhere, and if you don't want him here he won't come, I'll see to it.'

And smiling at my shocked expression – for how could anyone, even Joel, refuse entry to my grandfather – he slid an arm beneath my shoulders, supporting me against his chest, and my labouring body took comfort in his lean, hard strength, my panic subsided. But when, after a brief respite, the pain struck again and I sank my face, gasping, into his shoulder, his arm tightened and his own face, when I could open my eyes to see, had turned pale. And when I said weakly, 'Oh, Joel, I fear I am crumpling your jacket,' both his arms came around me and he replied, 'You may tear it to pieces if you will, if it eases you.'

'I think I shall not do that.'

'No, but, Verity, sweetheart, I didn't know you felt like this about your grandfather. I thought you were . . .'

'What? On his side, against you?'

'Aye, that's one way of putting it. It's not so? You've no love for him, have you?'

'Heavens, I've never thought of loving or not loving. I'm just afraid of him, that's all.'

'There's no need for it. Verity, look at me. I can take care of you. And I don't promise what I can't perform. Only a fool does that and I'm nobody's fool.'

And taking me once more in his arms – his compassion astonishing me as greatly as his sensuality had done on our wedding night – he held me, rocked me, stroked my hair to give me comfort, and stroked the small of my back to ease my pain, guarding me from my fears and from my grandfather, until the doctor came.

8

My son was born the following day, arriving, when he finally made up his mind to it, without too much fuss, and, lying back among my pillows, luxuriating in my body's release from bondage, I thought, I shall have peace now, and was, very soon, disappointed.

'I imagine you will call him Edwin,' Hannah said, stiff-lipped, her colour very high. 'It would seem most appropriate – and I feel sure everyone expects it.'

'Oh, my little Samson,' cooed Mrs Stevens an hour later, bending over the cradle. 'My darling little Samson – his great-grandfather's pride and joy. I suppose he is to be Samson – surely?'

'There'll be no Edwin and no Samson,' Joel told me, ominously quiet, not looking too closely into the cradle but claiming what was in it as his own, just the same. 'You may name him as you please, since you had the trouble of bearing him – except that he'll not be an Edwin, nor a Samson either.'

And he strode away, leaving all explanations and recriminations to me.

'My goodness,' my mother murmured, 'such a fuss. I

would suggest William, for your father, except that with so many high tempers and high expectations to contend with, perhaps it wouldn't be wise. Maybe one should look outside the family. What do you say to Augustus, or Alexander, since he is certainly destined for greatness? Or why not name him for St Blaize, the patron saint of wool combers. That may satisfy them all.'

And so he became Blaize Barforth, a tiny, angry scrap in the family cradle, his tight little face bright red, his hair a true Barforth black; an amazing creature – a baby – and, as I had foreseen, I did not know what to do with him and was appalled at his crying, horrified by his helplessness. Puppies I understood, and older children who could tell me what ailed them, but this newborn human, who could not hold up his head, defeated me, filled my whole mind with the worst anxiety I had ever known, so that I lay awake that first night – and for many nights after – my ears straining through the dark, listening, agonizing, in case he should cease to breathe.

'My dear,' my mother told me, 'he is perfectly well. He cries from hunger, which indicates a healthy appetite.'

But my mother had lost six of her eight babies and, quite feverishly, I did not trust her. Nor did I trust the nurse she had found for me in Patterswick; a strong, solid, clean-looking girl, I was forced to admit, but her eyes were small and crafty, pig's eyes, and how could I be sure she would not drug my baby with laudanum to make him sleep or let the kitchen cat get into his cradle and smother him?

I could not have said, at that stage, that I loved him, for he was still a stranger, oddly unconnected with the heaving burden I had carried inside me for so long. I was, quite simply, afraid for him and, had I been permitted, would have taken him into my bed, into my arms, like a mother cat in her basket, and put my claws into anyone who tried to touch him.

But I was not, of course, permitted to do that, for

touching him appeared to be the prerogative of all comers: my grandfather, snatching him from the cradle at every visit, whether he was sleeping or not, and holding him up to the light; Mrs Stevens, appearing whenever she had an hour to spare to wake him and then rock him back to sleep; Mrs Hobhouse and Mrs Oldroyd, when they came to call, claiming the right to pick him up an examine him a moment or two, comparing him with their own children, and scraping my nerves to shreds.

But eventually a morning came when I was no longer altogether astonished to find him still alive; when the nursemaid suddenly had a kind smile to compensate for her pig's eyes and a firm but gentle hand as she put my noisy, healthy son into my arms; a morning when I was concerned, once again, with my own face in the mirror and delighted with the new lightness of my body; when I rediscovered my appetite for hot chocolate and new bread and remembered that, in a day or two, I would be seventeen.

My grandfather went to Lincolnshire soon after to visit old friends of his wool-buying days, and, taking advantage of the fine weather, I made myself free of the Top House garden, installing myself there, under the flowering cherry trees and the budding lilac, my son on one side of me, my dogs on the other, while Mrs Stevens, who had never had a child – nor a real husband either, for that matter – advised me on the care and upbringing of mine.

'Bear with her,' my mother advised me one sparkling afternoon when, after a veritable lecture on infant feeding, she had gone inside to prepare our tea. 'She is only safeguarding her position, after all, for your grandfather suffered a severe chill through the winter and has not entirely recovered his strength. Do you know, it struck me only the other day that, really, he is quite a small man, when I used to think him so large. And since, of course, I know perfectly well he stands over six feet high, it can only mean that he has lost a great deal of flesh. And no one can blame poor Emmeline Stevens for wondering what she will do when he is gone.'

'Will he not provide for her?' I said lazily, not really caring, watching my son's miniature fists flailing in the sunlight, his miniature rage at his failure to reach the pink and white blossoms dancing overhead, barely listening until something in her manner warned me she was using Mrs Stevens as a bridge for something else.

'Oh, I hardly think so, not adequately at any rate. I often wonder, you know, about women like Emmeline Stevens. They think themselves so clever and fine, but really their position is most precarious. They can inherit neither a man's money nor his prestige when he dies, and during his lifetime have little more of him than the side of his nature his wife is perhaps glad enough to be without. Not a pleasant existence, and bear in mind that, with no marriage contract to protect them, they can be cast off the very moment they fail to please, without a shred of reputation left – which is very much the same as dismissing a maid without a testimonial. And, of course, they invariably are cast off, for men may desire them but they are never respected, and desire is so fleeting, you know – only respect endures. But Mrs Stevens, I imagine, will survive, for she is no novice and knows the pitfalls of her profession. She was in service once, at a great house somewhere in Derbyshire – a very pretty little parlourmaid she must have been – and I often think she would have done far better had she listened to the young gardener who could have married her instead of setting her cap for her master, who, of course, felt obliged to dismiss her once his passion had cooled. And that has been the way of it ever since. She is quite accustomed to being discarded, our Mrs Stevens – except that, each time it happens, she has grown a little older. And what can it cost you, dear, to be patient?'

'Was I sharp with her? I didn't mean to be.'

'Not very sharp – I merely wondered if her way of life was so distasteful to you that you could not bear her. There have been others before her, of course, for your grandfather has always been an exceptionally lusty man. I believe all the Barforths are so. Certainly your Uncle Thomas – Joel's father – and I must honestly confess to you that your own father made very many visits to Leeds about which I chose not to enquire. I took the view that they did not really concern me – that such things are in a man's nature – a view I know your grandmother shared. For even your grandfather was most discreet during her lifetime. He has many faults, but he took great care never to embarrass his wife. She knew, you see, that he valued her, as his wife, above everything else, and she felt herself in no way threatened – in no way insecure. Men do not discard their wives as they do their mistresses – and I have every reason to believe your grandmother was an exceedingly happy woman.'

Silence for a moment, then the sounds of the dogs panting in the sun, the child stirring in the warm, safely padded world of his cradle, birdsong somewhere among the cherry trees. A holding in of breath, a reluctance to move myself towards understanding, a reluctance to feel.

And then I said carefully, 'Mother, is there something you want to tell me about Joel?'

'No, no,' she said. 'Absolutely nothing, for I know nothing about him. I merely took the opportunity to express an opinion, for we had so little time for conversation before your marriage. I sent you into the world all unprepared, my dear, and here you are, a mother already, so there is nothing I can tell you on that score. And as for the other – your husband may become a model of fidelity, but if he should not – if he should conform to the family pattern – Oh dear, how hard this is to express without appearing insensitive – but these fiercely energetic men, these competitive men with their hunting instincts so finely developed, these greedy men, if you like, who cannot bear to have anything pass them by – And when they are so often away from home . . . My dear, if it happens it will probably mean very little to him and should not unduly distress you. It is necessary to treat these matters with sense rather than feeling – believe me – and after all, you did not marry through a sudden fit of emotion. If now, dear, you can become friends, use friendship as a foundation on which to build; then I think you will be well served. I set great store by friendship, Verity; I believe I once told you so. If I could choose I would always prefer a friend to a lover.'

'And can you choose?'

'At my age I think I can. Squire Dalby and I are friends.'

'Do you mean to marry him?'

'Oh, my dear, hardly that,' she said, the trill of her laughter easing the load between us, 'even if he would have me, which seems unlikely. His wife has been twenty years in her grave, and he has a son and a grandson waiting to inherit – I can't think he would embarrass them with a worsted manufacturer's widow, at this late stage. No, no – friendship, that is my aim. Warm but peaceful friendship – no demands, no jealousies – free, open friendship. You would not believe how delightful it can be.'

Mrs Stevens served tea in the garden, and afterwards when my mother had returned to her friend the squire, I continued to sit awhile under the blossom trees, wondering if Joel would be unfaithful and concluding that he would; concluding, since my mother would not have mentioned it otherwise, that he already had. And what did I really feel about it? Would it, indeed be pointless to have any feelings at all, since I had no power to prevent it? Certainly I could throw hysterical fits as his mother had often done; I could whine and complain to my friends, as she had; I could even go to my grandfather, who, although he might privately consider male adultery to be a far more trifling offence than being late at the mill, would defend me. He would even use it as an additional rod with which to scourge Joel.

'So there's more of your father coming out in you, lad,

is there? And there's a short answer to it. If you can afford a harlot's bills, then I'm paying you too well, and since it's my money and my time you're spending, I'll have to cut you down to size.'

And that would result in something far removed from friendship between me and Joel.

The truth was that events had moved far too quickly for me. Only a year ago, this very month, I had sat in this same garden with my cousin Elinor, two little girls beneath anyone's notice, while Hannah had dreamed of her wedding, Edwin of his power looms, and Joel had brooded over how he was to settle his father's creditors. And now, a year later, Edwin and my father were gone, I was Joel's wife and the mother of his son – and I had only just stopped being sixteen.

Joel had given me a bracelet for my birthday, a thin twist of gold; he had even fastened it around my wrist and kissed my hand with a casual gallantry I found decidedly pleasant, until he had spoiled it all by pinching my chin and ruffling my hair in his old cousinly fashion. He had kept his promise and remained beside me through my long hours of labour, leaving only a moment or two before our son was born when the midwife, shocked and somewhat unnerved by his presence, had shooed him away. And afterwards, when I had been weak and tearful with relief, he had filled my room with flowers and kept his temper – certainly for my sake – when my grandfather, declaring them unhealthy, had demanded that they should all be taken away.

'Flowers,' my grandfather had snorted. 'Damn things belong in a garden – or a whorehouse. They'll take up the air and choke the bairn. Flowers – I reckon that's another of the damn fool notions you've picked up from your father.'

But Joel, quietly and with, for him, immense patience, had replied, 'My wife was glad to receive them, sir. She's tired, you see, which is hardly to be wondered at, and I've no mind to upset her. In fact, I don't see my way to denying her anything right now that could give her pleasure.'

And although my grandfather had grunted and grumbled and stamped his feet all the way downstairs, I had kept my flowers.

Nor had he been impatient to reclaim his conjugal rights. A month, the midwife had told me, was as much as most men allowed their wives before they came pestering again, but Joel had shown no such unmannerly haste.

'Don't fret,' he had told me, that firm hand gentle once more beneath my chin. 'A brute I may be on occasion, but not the kind to risk putting you through this agony again in a hurry. Take your time, get your strength back, and when you're ready just let me know.'

When, touched by his consideration, I had shown myself ready sooner than I might otherwise have done, he had treated my newly healed body almost with respect and, for a while thereafter, had taken such care as he could not to impregnate me again. And remembering the midwife's harrowing tales of women forced to go on producing one child nine months after the other, I had been intensely grateful.

In exchange for that and for his support and protection, his casual, tolerant affection, could I acknowledge his physical appetites to be greater than mine; his physical curiosity, as a man, in need of more variety than mine, as a woman, and accept it as natural for him to supplement the deficiency elsewhere? Presumably both my mother and my grandmother had done exactly that and retained their dignity, while Joel's mother, who had not accepted it, had become a shrew, a hysteric, and a nuisance. Did I, in fact, see such acceptance as a basis for the friendship my mother had talked of? I thought I did not. Was there no way for us to approach each other – for I was willing to admit I had much to learn, if he would be prepared to teach, and to admit that I, too, had skills and knowledge that he lacked

– and surely the fact that we shared a roof, an inheritance, a child, must mean more to him than any chance encounter? And if, sometimes, I still saw his face looking down at Edwin, his ambition leaping towards the mill, the looms, the heiress, before the breath was out of my brother's body, I would try to forget. And if I could lock that memory away, surely he could bring himself to look at me and realize that my hair was no longer in pigtails, my eyes no longer so quiet as they used to be. But my thoughts were sketchy and could not have been put into words, and how could I, barely seventeen, make Joel sit down and listen while I outlined my scheme for a better future?

How did I visualize that future? What did I really feel for the man I was still sometimes surprised to call my husband? He was, without doubt, hard and calculating, but these were traits of which my Law Valley heart could not wholly disapprove, and I had admired him, often enough, for his sharp, sardonic wit, the fierce energy that took him, after a day of gruelling labour, to Low Cross, where, in flagrant disobedience of my grandfather's wishes, he would work long into the night, repairing, adjusting, operating with his own hands the looms that wove his experimental fancy worsteds. I had seen him ride home at dawn, dirty and drained, with no more than an hour to spare before Lawcroft demanded his presence again, and had seen the narrow, glittering anger in his eyes, instantly suppressed, when my grandfather, noting his fatigue, had made some scathing hint of an evening spent in wine and cards.

'Watch him, lass,' he would tell me at such times. 'I can see his father in him, plain as day.'

But it was not my uncle Thomas Barforth but Samson Barforth himself I could see in Joel, and my grandfather's iron qualities in this younger, handsome man were not displeasing. And he was handsome. There was nothing now in his long, hard body that I found offensive, nothing to shock me when he strode naked across my bedroom floor with a branch of candles in his hand, the flame turning his skin to amber and darkening his eyes and his vigorously curling hair, adding brilliance to the sudden flash of his teeth as he gave me his bold pirate's grin.

Yet the fact remained that we had not chosen each other. We had been brought together to fulfil my grandfather's desires rather than our own and, being very much aware that Joel had desired other women and had sacrificed a woman he may even have loved whereas I had desired no one, sacrificed nothing, I was afraid to expect too much. Had he spoken to me of love on our wedding night I would have been offended, and yet now the possibility of love between us stirred, tantalized the fringes of my mind, and then I paused and grew cautious as I remembered his casual fingers pinching my chin, his teasing voice calling me 'little cousin,' 'sweet cousin' sometimes, but 'cousin' just the same. And on the occasions when a more intense feeling had arisen or had started to arise – when I had become 'sweetheart,' 'little love,' occasionally 'darling' – I could not forget how he always turned it away with a laugh and called me 'cousin' all the more.

I was woman enough now to know what troubled him. He had seen me growing up alongside his sister Elinor, a little girl at a time when he, twelve years my senior, had already started to think of women. It was surely not to his discredit that the mental barrier which prevents men from desiring their sisters had made it difficult for him, in the early days, to desire me.

But could that barrier now be crossed? Certainly I had never regarded him in any way as a brother. Throughout my entire childhood I had seen him as a man full-grown, a potent, predatory male, and had listened with rapt attention whenever his mother, my Aunt Hattie, had come whispering his misdeeds to my own mother.

There had been a married lady in Harrogate, of good family, older than Joel, who had ruined her reputation for his sake; an irate husband who could not be expected, Aunt Hattie feared, to take the matter lightly. There had been an actress in Leeds, a singer of bawdy music-hall songs, with no reputation to lose but every intention, according to his mother, of ruining Joel's health. There had been another actress, who had cost him money he could not afford, a mysterious woman whose source of income was never named, who had made him scandalous gifts of clothing and encouraged his taste for fine wines. There had been a frenzied episode in Manchester with a young widow, whose letters, when my Aunt Hattie had finally managed to read them, had made her blush. And there had been Rosamund Boulton.

He was a sensualist then, my cousin, my husband, but no despoiler of virgins. A man with a taste for women of character: mature, forceful beauties beside whom I must appear tame indeed. Although I had a fair enough opinion of my own character, privately considering myself to be as honest as anyone else and a shade more intelligent than some, and although my face and figure did not altogether displease me, I knew I lacked the flamboyance, the variety, the experience to which Joel had grown accustomed.

Not that I believed he ever deliberately hurt me. I had not forgotten his compassion in the hours before Blaize was born. I knew he was fond of me and pleased with me more often than not; and I knew, dimly, that I should perhaps be grateful he had not attempted to use his skill and charm to turn my seventeen-year-old head and make me fall in love with him. He had not amused himself with my untried, uncertain emotions as some men could well have done. He had done nothing, in fact, by Law Valley standards, about which I could reasonably complain. And, at the end of the day, I could do no more than admit the wisdom of my mother's words. If Joel took a mistress, if he already had a mistress, it would mean very little to him. Whatever it meant to me – if it made me angry, or if I were stung by the injustice of it; if it gave me a sense of failure or futility, or even if it hurt me – my best defence would be to pretend that I did not care.

Elinor deserted me somewhat that fragrant May, being little inclined to sit and marvel at the infant Blaize when Emma-Jane Rawnsley was fast reaching an understanding with Bradley Hobhouse's mother, if not with Bradley himself. And so she took her carriage drives with Emma-Jane, keeping her eyes peeled, to the great annoyance of Mrs Rawnsley, who knew quite well what Elinor was up to, even if Emma-Jane did not. But Hannah paid me regular visits, growing more stately than ever in her plain brown taffeta, her mauve silk, the mourning brooch of Edwin's hair always on her collar, and although she was not fond of babies in the physical sense and appeared most ill at ease on the few occasions Blaize was allowed on her knee, she was his godmother and took her responsibilities seriously.

Indeed, an afternoon with Hannah was always a serious business, for she was more engrossed than ever in the Sunday School movement, spending a full eight hours every Sunday at Ramsden Street Chapel, near Low Cross, where poor children were taught first to read and then to read the Bible, and spending considerably longer than that in explaining to the minister how best to organize his congregation. Ramsden Street Chapel, it seemed, depended very largely on Hannah's support; it would, I feared, be very likely to crumble and fall down should she ever desert it. So accustomed was I to her feuds with various old ladies who dared to question her advice and, on one or two occasions, had gone so far as to accuse her of bullying the minister, that when, one afternoon, she broke off in mid-sentence and said, 'Verity, I believe you are acquainted with Mr Morgan Aycliffe,' I assumed he was chapel business too.

Only her silence, the tension vibrating inside her as it sometimes did in Joel, made me look at her and realize that, whatever it was, it was personal, vital, enormous.

'Am I? Mr Aycliffe the builder? Oh – just barely acquainted with him, Hannah, although I think my father knew him well. I understand he is in a very large way of business, and he was to have built Edwin's mill—'

'Yes,' she said, her cheeks, always highly coloured, flooding with crimson. 'He has told me so.'

'You are acquainted with him yourself, then?'

'Yes,' she said harshly, angry suddenly, as if it were none of my business; furious, I think, at her own tongue-tied, girlish confusion. 'You may recall, some eight or twelve weeks ago, that a Dr Blackstone came to Ramsden Street to speak to us about the abolition of the slave trade? Certainly you recall it, for I remember telling you how pleased we were at the attendance. Mr Aycliffe was there. No, he is not a member of our congregation, but we had extended our welcome to everyone, and he was there with Mr and Mrs Rawnsley, who presented him to me and asked me to take tea with them afterwards, which I thought most kind. Mr Aycliffe was impressed by the speaker and remarked how well the meeting had been organized, which caused me some embarrassment when Mrs Rawnsley failed to restrain herself from telling him I had been the organizer. In short, we had some conversation about abolition, and about Sunday Schools – which he considers a good thing – and since then we have met several times, under the supervision of Mrs Rawnsley – and once in the street, by chance, when I saw no harm in pausing a moment, since Elinor was with me. There was no harm, surely?'

'Surely not.'

'His wife died a year ago,' she said, flinging the words at me as if they were stones. 'Naturally he has observed the full mourning period, as I have. In fact, he came out of black armbands only ten days ago—'

And, understanding that she was drowning in embarrassment, pleading to be rescued and too proud to cry for help, I said quickly, 'And has he spoken to you?'

She looked, for a moment, quite horrified, very much on the brink of tears, but instead of weeping she straightened her back and said resolutely, 'I think you know what your brother and I meant to each other. I will not dwell on it. And I daresay you are very much shocked to hear me mention Mr Aycliffe – or anyone – when it has been little more than a year. And I would like you to understand that it is in no way the same – that my feelings, as such, are not involved – merely that we appear to have a great deal in common, a certain similarity of thought—'

'But has he spoken to you – of marriage?'

'No,' she said, her chin very firm. 'But unless he had that intention – taking into account his strict code of conduct – I do not think he would have approached me at all. And he has singled me out most particularly. Mrs Rawnsley herself has remarked on it – she is always remarking on it, which is really why I felt obliged to tell you.'

'And if he does speak to you? Will you take him?'

'Oh – as to that— The correct procedure would be for him to speak to Joel, and I am undecided as yet. I can only say he is a good man who champions a great many charitable causes, and I could be of use to him in that. And he has had much suffering, with which I am well able to sympathize. His wife died of some lingering malady of the nerves which greatly distressed him, and he has a most unsatisfactory child. Perhaps I could help him there too.'

'Hannah,' I told her, 'the Aycliffe boy is hardly a child; he must be well turned twenty – easily twenty-two.'

But the idea of a stepson very nearly her own age did not seem to deter her, and at the end of an hour I was in no doubt that however thoroughly she had convinced herself that this marriage could be no more than a Christian duty, in reality she was as eager to escape the mill yard of Low Cross as Elinor. While the prospect of allying herself to the rich, highly regarded Mr Aycliffe, of being a married lady able to dispense charity instead of receiving it, filled her with a wild delight.

'I'll tell Joel,' I promised, and, when I did, his answer was immediate, triumphant.

'By God, Verity, if she can land Morgan Aycliffe she'll do well for herself – and for me. How far can we rely on it?'

'Far enough, I think. He must have made his intentions fairly clear if Ramsden Street Chapel is taking notice.'

'But he could still cry off. Is there a way to fix him?'

'Hardly,' I said, remembering that not even Rosamund Boulton had found a way to fix her man; and, just possibly catching the drift of my thought, Joel gave a short laugh.

'No, I suppose not. No way Hannah would be prepared to take, at any rate. So – what's to be done? How does an old stick like that go about his courting?'

'I don't see what we can do. But if he's serious, then I suppose he'll do something himself. He could call on me, I suppose. He must know she comes here a great deal, and if he calls to see me, then he has a chance of seeing her – and you.'

'That's it,' he said. 'He'll call. And when he does, take care your grandfather knows nothing of it. I don't know what Morgan Aycliffe's worth but being his brother-in-law would do me no harm if I ever had to go cap in hand again to Rawnsley's bank. And if he's even considering marrying her – knowing there's nothing much to come with her and I've not much to add to it – then he must have confidence in me. And that wouldn't please your grandfather. Is that Marth-Ellen of yours fit to serve him tea, if he comes?'

'I'll see to it.'

'Yes,' he said, 'I believe you will.' And, in a high good humour, he reached out his hard hand and, with a cousinly gesture of affection, pinched my chin.

The millhouse had been designed for the convenience of a millmaster who wished to keep an eye on his operatives, not for the entertaining of guests, and so, in anticipation of Mr Aycliffe's call, I had them clear the front parlour of the paraphernalia of housekeeping, got out my wedding china and washed it myself, supervised the preparation, every teatime, of wafer-thin bread and butter, the polishing of silver spoons, dressed myself carefully, daintily, brought flowers into the house, created as best I could an atmosphere of tranquillity and grace that would, surely, induce romance. But I could have spared myself the pains, for romance seemed to be neither in Morgan Aycliffe's mind nor in his nature.

I had seen him a hundred times before, but, because his life had had no bearing on mine – and because he was of another generation – I had never noticed him, and, when he finally rode up to my door and got stiffly, almost huffily down from his tall roan, it was as if I were seeing his thin, grey face and his long, grey body for the first time. He was somewhere between forty-five and fifty, with a back so stiff that I wondered, with a seventeen-year-old's inclination to giggle, how he would ever manage to sit down, and then watched, with the respect he easily inspired, as he folded himself neatly into a chair, with his long, rather bony hands placed precisely, one on each knee.

'Dear Mrs Barforth,' he said, his voice somehow dry and bony, too, 'I feel this visit to be sadly overdue. Indeed, I have long meant to call with my congratulations on the birth of your son. My word, what exquisite roses, the very first of the season – such a tasteful blending of colour—'

Watching him closely, only half listening to the easy, oily flow of his voice, I had the same impression of suppressed energy that Joel gave me, except that in Morgan Aycliffe's case, the suppressing was by his own hand, as if his own virility made him uneasy. And it occurred to me that he may not be so straitlaced as he seemed.

His clothes, it was true, were of a clerical sobriety, sombre in the extreme, but the fabric was expensive and the cut excellent; the watch chain across his dark, unpatterned waistcoat was solid gold, and the black onyx ring on his finger elaborate and costly, his fingers themselves many years away from any actual contact with bricks and mortar. And, in those first few moments, I did not find him a comfortable man.

But, like most men of business, he knew how to make himself pleasant, and, having paid my bread and butter the compliment of eating it and allowing me to send for more, he crossed one leg with meticulous neatness over the other, pressed the tips of his skinny fingers together, and commenced the true purpose of his visit, the delicate business of presenting his credentials as a prospective bridegroom without in any way committing himself should his intentions change or the lady herself prove unworthy.

A cautious man, Mr Aycliffe, and a lonely one, he told me; the more so since he and his late wife had enjoyed a rare harmony, which had made his bereavement doubly hard to bear. He had kept his wife's room exactly as it had been in her lifetime, her toilet articles remaining just as she had left them, her pincushion and embroidery frame in their accustomed places. He had not really expected, he told me, to recover from so tragic a blow, but, needless to say, there had been his business to consider, contracts to fulfil, workmen to be kept in employment, and, recognizing his responsibilities, he had not shirked.

'Life must go on,' he said, and I had the impression, most discreetly conveyed, that for Morgan Aycliffe life was going very well indeed.

He did not, of course, mention the soundness of his financial position, although his references to his good relations with Mr Rawnsley the banker were enough to convince me of that. But, knowing Hannah's connection with Ramsden Street, he confessed to me, with a rueful smile, that his own religious views were somewhat unusual. He was, in fact, a little of one thing, a little of the other; a Dissenter, I concluded, when he was among Dissenters, yet a man who, aware of the privileges conveyed by the Anglican Church, saw no reason to shun them. Not that he, personally, wished to attend the universities of Oxford and Cambridge – open only to Anglicans – yet his instinct was always to be on the winning side, to keep his options open. A subtle man, then; a clever man who, although he would not say so, and no doubt for vastly different reasons, was as eager for marriage as my cousin.

'My wife was a most unworldly person,' he told me, 'one who preferred the security of her own home and was never plagued by curiosity as to the hurly-burly of life outside. Her anxieties were all of the kitchen and the store cupboard, and it was my pleasure and my pride to be able to shield her from other cares. She has been sorely missed.'

'I daresay your son has been a comfort to you,' I said, and, his lips parting in the smile of an indulgent father, he replied, 'Yes, indeed. We stand very close together, Crispin and I, although sons, my dear Mrs Barforth, as you will soon discover, have minds and wills of their own. An excellent boy, Crispin – something of a dreamer, and with his mother's delicate disposition, but a fine son. I had him trained an architect, you know, at some inconvenience and expense, but he has no head for the building trade – he dreams of building castles instead of houses for honest working folk to live in. But that's his mother in him, for she was often fanciful, and he'll learn. She indulged him, I fear, almost to excess, for he was her pride and joy, and although the effects of her pampering on his character have not all been for the best, I could deny her nothing in her later years. And so my son has been somewhat spoiled, I confess. Yes – spoiled – but we are, little be little, setting ourselves to rights. I hope you may come to know him, Mrs Barforth.'

'I hope so too.'

'Most kind,' he said, beaming his approval, taking my hand on leaving with a fulsome warmth that was clerical in feeling and left me in no doubt that he would come again.

And, while I was mulling him over, my door opened and

Elinor came into the room, complaining bitterly because the Rawnsleys and the Hobhouses had set her down in the top road, above my grandfather's house, so that she had been obliged to walk and had mud on the hem of her dress.

'The old cat,' she said, referring to the highly suspicious Mrs Rawnsley. 'She could have set me down at the door. She could see that roan horse as plain as I could – obviously a gentleman's horse – and she wasn't even curious. All she wanted was to send me walking down the hill; putting me in my place, I expect she calls it. And it's not my fault if people look at me instead of her fat Emma-Jane. Three gentlemen raised their hats to me today in Market Square – complete strangers – and I didn't smile at them first, whatever Mrs Rawnsley says. Well, so he's been to declare himself, has he? Aycliffe, I mean. What do you think to him?'

'I'm not sure.'

'Well, I'm sure,' she said, and, swinging her reticule in one hand and her frilled parasol in the other, she spun round slowly in a dancing movement, her skirts billowing like the wings of a yellow butterfly, showing off her beauty and grace, her lightness of heart, until she stopped moving and I saw the tense, resentful anger in her face.

'I'll tell you what I think, Verity. It's disgusting, sermonizing and sighing and making eyes, and his wife not cold in her grave—'

'Well, not too warm either, darling, since he wore black for a twelvemonth—'

But my attempt at lightness did her no good, and, stamping her small foot, her cheeks scarlet with her doll's anger, she almost shouted, 'I'll tell you about him. He's old and stale and his wife hated him. Lingering malady of the nerves, he calls it, but the truth is, he frightened her to death. And his son hates him, too. They say his son wouldn't speak to him at the funeral and not for a long time after. He's rich and he's mean and he's old and what I want to know is, if Hannah marries him, what is going to happen to me? You haven't thought of that, have you? No. No one has. Let's get Hannah married, that's the great thing – let's get Hannah settled. But there's me, Verity. What's going to happen to me?'

9

Joel had expressed his ignorance of Morgan Aycliffe's exact worth, but, in the days that followed, he hastened to inform himself and was well pleased with the answers. About Mr Aycliffe's building enterprises we already knew, since he was responsible for the newer part of Cullingford, somewhat larger than the old, but Joel, after a few visits to the Piece Hall and the Old Swan and other hostelries where businessmen were wont to congregate, was able to track down hints of Aycliffe involvement in canals, turnpikes, and coal mines, of inherited money and money still to inherit, which filled him with a pure and lasting delight. And, Law Valley men being notoriously close-mouthed, much inclined to 'hear all and say nowt,' we knew such hints were to be relied on. Admittedly the existence of a son, the spoiled, fanciful Crispin, was something of a drawback, since, when the time came to carve up his father's estate, he would be bound to take the lion's share.

'He could live somewhere between ten and twenty years,' Joel calculated happily. 'Call it fifteen – which would bring Crispin well into his thirties, with Hannah's children, if she has any, still too young to have got their hooks into the business. Well, I'd like it better if there was a chance of Hannah's getting the lot, but there's plenty for all, I reckon, and I'll have it in writing from him, once we get started, that she's to be well provided for.'

And so, on the whole, it was decided that no better brother-in-law could possibly be found.

'He's old,' Elinor declared, wrinkling her nose. 'Never

mind, Hannah, you'll be a widow that much sooner. So, if you think it's what you want – if you think it's worth it – then I'm happy for you.'

But Hannah, too nervous, I think, to bother with Elinor, took refuge in dignity and refused to quarrel.

'You are all making a great fuss,' she said, 'and I hope you will not be too disappointed if it comes to nothing – for I have by no means made up my mind.'

But she had, and because I knew how intensely, how dreadfully, she was longing not for the man himself but for the smooth, gold ring that would liberate her from the restrictions Cullingford imposed on its spinster ladies, I gave Mr Aycliffe the most encouraging of welcomes when he called, and, since he could not call at Low Cross, where there was no adequate chaperone, I invited Hannah and Elinor to stay with me. And although, as May entered into a warm June, he had not yet proposed, each visit committed him a little further, each slice of seedcake made it more difficult for him to withdraw, and the irrepressible Elinor was soon talking of bridesmaids' dresses and giggling at the thought of calling Morgan Aycliffe brother.

'I'm determined she shall have a decent wedding,' Elinor told me. 'No poky little affair in dove grey with a new feather in her bonnet. I shall persuade her into white satin if it's my last day's work – because she'll never wear it afterwards and I can easily cut it up and make it over again to fit me. And I think I shall wear white, too; not satin, because I'll have the satin in any case – something gauzy and lacy, with frills caught up with blue ribbon. And my hair in a great big Apollo knot with a white rose in the middle. And Bradley Hobhouse will see me floating down the aisle and he'll look at Emma-Jane Rawnsley's buck teeth and he'll know he can't live without me, no matter what anyone has to say to it. Yes – and when they threaten to cut him off with a shilling I shall plead with him to give me up, of course, knowing quite well he won't. And then I think they'd better forgive us and let him make an honest woman of me, because I would like a proper wedding in the parish church with all the bells ringing. Yes, that I would.'

She laughed, dancing around the room again, enraptured by her own imaginings, and then, her dainty feet returning abruptly to earth, she sighed. 'Ah, well . . . I just wish Hannah and her old gentleman would hurry themselves up. They just sit there, in the parlour, and talk about the condition of the poor and how to go about freeing the slaves in the West Indies. And if it's left to her they'll go on like that forever. All he needs is a little push – I told her so last night and I thought she meant to slap me, she was so put out. But it's true. In her place I could get him to propose in ten minutes, and so could you, I reckon. She thinks these feminine wiles, as she calls them, are beneath her, but I don't think it's wily: I call it common sense. And what about this famous son of his that he keeps promising to bring with him and never does? It strikes me that Master Crispin Aycliffe may not altogether like the idea of a new mamma and a parcel of little brothers, all wanting a share of the Aycliffe estate. And I can't say I blame him. I wouldn't like a new mamma of my own age. Just think of it – if you can bear to. It's perfectly disgusting.'

'Hannah doesn't think so. And, after all, Crispin Aycliffe is a man with his own life to lead. He may not even live in the house with them. He may get married, or go out to the West Indies and begin freeing the slaves. Perhaps you should smile at him, instead of Bradley Hobhouse, when you get your white gauze . . .'

'Yes,' she said, suddenly extremely serious, concentrating so hard on this new possibility that all else was forgotten. 'Yes, of course. I could marry Crispin Aycliffe, couldn't I? Is it legal, Verity, do you suppose, for a girl to marry her brother-in-law's son? It doesn't sound legal and, with my luck, he'll adore me and it won't be. Do you think our minister would know? Oh, I do wish Hannah would stir herself. All she needs to do is be a little more approachable – she needs to give him the eye, in fact, and she'd have a fit if she heard me say so, although it's perfectly true. I could show her how to do it in a trice – I was born knowing how to do it.'

And as Morgan Aycliffe appeared just then at the parlour door, with Hannah behind him, Elinor caught her sister's eye, her own eyes sparkling with a look that said, 'Come on, Hannah, this is how it's done. Just you watch me,' and, stepping forward into a shaft of sunlight, she gave the sober gentleman a smile of such studied enchantment, such innocent, fascinating mischief, that he took a step backwards, most hurriedly, towards the safety of Hannah, startled and, it appeared, considerably displeased.

But at least our wish to meet the elusive Crispin was soon gratified, for, a few days later, Mr Aycliffe invited us to dine, not at the comfortable hour of the late afternoon we were used to, but at the fashionable city dinnertime of six o'clock, a notable departure from tradition in the Law Valley.

I wore, for the first time, the long velvet evening cloak my mother had given me before my marriage and, under it, a gown of cream-coloured crepe de chine, cut with a simplicity that had pleased Joel, while Hannah's brown silk, equally simple, had seemed to him too plain. But there was no doubt at all that Elinor was looking her best in a gown the colour of sharp, fresh lemons, a confection of gauze over silk which she had persuaded me to buy against my better judgement, feeling it to be too pretty for my nature, but which, after a change of ownership, having been shortened and tightened and further embellished with knots of satin ribbon, was perfect for hers.

'I've quite decided about the son,' she whispered to me as we were setting out, intensely serious beneath her teasing, scatterbrained manner. 'I've quite stopped thinking of Bradley Hobhouse. I called on Emma-Jane the other day, and he was there, and really, I could see he's just the

143

kind to do as his mamma tells him. So if he did run away with me he'd only run back again. Now I've been making enquiries about Mr Crispin Aycliffe, and they say at Ramsden Street Chapel that he will do anything if he thinks his father may not like it. And if I got myself married to Crispin before the old gentleman had a chance to marry Hannah, I suppose he wouldn't like that at all.'

'But have you even seen him, Elinor?'

'No. Have you?'

And it seemed suddenly strange, very strange indeed, that in a town like Cullingford, I had not.

'They say in Ramsden Street,' Elinor murmured, lowering her voice to a thrilling whisper, 'that his mamma would never let him play with the other boys in case he took cold or skinned his knees. And they also say, my dear – and do listen carefully to this because it is really quite special information, and Hannah would have the vapours if she knew I knew – they also say that since his mamma died, he drinks.'

And she put her head on one side like a graceful little monkey which, having just performed a trick, is waiting for a reward.

The Aycliffes lived in the select area of Cullingford known as Blenheim Lane, a narrow, leafy thoroughfare beginning with the ancient, venerable home of Colonel Corey, cousin to Sir Giles Flood, our ground landlord, and ending with the new, elaborately stone-fronted houses and the self-conscious gardens of men for whom the need to live in their factory yards no longer applied. Mr Thomas Rawnsley the banker lived here, with his plump daughter, Emma-Jane, Mr Corey-Manning the lawyer, and his sister, Mrs Roundwood, her husband being the owner of our newspaper, the *Cullingford Courier and Review*. There were some smaller houses, too, all in a row, belonging to a Corey widow and a pair of Corey-Manning spinsters; their upstairs windows, surely, giving them a view of the Fleece Inn, where, in the absence of an adequate courthouse, Colonel Corey sat, in his capacity as magistrate, whenever there was a poacher or a debtor to be put away, or the father of a bastard child to be forcibly reminded of his obligations. And in a discreet position in the middle of the lane stood the Aycliffe dwelling, as tall and grey as the man himself, set well back behind its ornamental iron gate, in a pool of tree shadow.

The hall was dimly lit, cool and hushed as a chapel, except that the panelling, fragrant with beeswax and almost black in colour, was of a quality unknown in Ramsden Street, while the staircase, growing from the centre of the hall and branching to left and right, had bannisters like ribbons of ebony, carved here and there with fruit and flowers.

Mr Aycliffe was there to greet us, narrower than ever in his black evening clothes, offering us a thin, faraway hand, and it was immediately apparent to us all that his money was older than ours, that he had progressed from the stage of accumulation to that of display.

The house, I supposed, was not comfortable in the chintzy flowery way of Mrs Stevens, but its subdued elegance spoke to my nature, its uncluttered drawing room, furnished with the gleam of silver against dark walls, the graceful swan-curving back of a fragile sofa, a fragile chair – so different from the millhouse, where chairs were designed to take the weight of a heavy, tired man – delighted my eye. And it took me a breathless moment or two to realize that its perfection was also oppressive, a setting for the jewel of a man's success rather than a home.

I could not imagine a woman leaving her embroidery on that sofa, nor a boy growing up here, surrounded by so much silence, so many frail and lovely porcelain figurines, so many pieces of fine enamelled glass displayed in black lacquer cabinets or set out on small tables of dark, polished wood. And, indeed, among the first awkward spurts of conversation and the even more awkward pauses, we were all aware that the boy, the wayward son, was nowhere to be seen.

Hannah, her emotions gathered into a spot of colour beneath each cheekbone, sat in silence. Elinor frankly stared, admired, coveted, while Joel – who also had it in his nature to spend money on objects that could neither weave nor spin nor reproduce their kind – hid his own covetousness by a slight air of nonchalance, as if he were used to seeing such treasures every day of his life.

But I was not, and, my eye alighting with pleasure on the two black basalt urns, one on either end of the marble mantelshelf, I said, 'How lovely. They are – Wedgwood – are they not?'

'Yes,' he replied, his thin mouth sketching a smile, rather as if it grudged the effort. 'My urns – very true – you will not have seen their like in these valleys.'

And after his contemplating them for a moment with a gloating that was in no way austere, an expression of intense annoyance suddenly pinched his face.

'Good heavens, they are not straight,' he muttered, so absolutely furious that, thinking he had detected some major fault in their construction, I half expected to see them shatter to ruin and was relieved when, crossing to the fireplace with a rapid step, he moved the urn on the left a fraction to one side so that it exactly matched the position of the one on the right.

'I cannot bear it,' he told us, 'when things are set awry. It should be a simple matter for the girl, when she dusts, to put my things back as she found them. I am not asking her to devise artistic arrangements of her own, not asking her to think— Yet I have never had the good fortune to employ a servant who could understand how painful it is to me when I see my possessions in disorder. The beauty of a pair of vases is that they should be a pair, standing in harmony with each other. If they are disarranged but a half inch it irritates me, offends me, like a false chord in

146

music – a matter which even my wife was quite unable to comprehend.'

It was at this mention of his mother's name that Crispin Aycliffe walked into the room.

He was, as we had supposed, perhaps twenty-two, with a narrow, finely moulded face which could, one day, grow lean, and hair, shading from pale brown to honey fair, cut in feathery layers across a high forehead; his light bone structure gave no great impression of strength, although there was nothing in that first glance to indicate the invalid, the recluse, or the drunkard. He looked, in fact, very much the carefully brought-up young gentleman who, his family fortunes having been made a generation or two ago, had escaped the toil of the factory yard, and he would have been handsome enough, in his pale, insubstantial fashion, to please anyone had his expression not been so peevish, so frankly bored.

'Good evening,' he said, bowing with false dancing-school courtesy to me and Hannah and Elinor but not looking at us.

'Good evening,' he said to Joel, offering him a disinterested hand.

'Good evening,' we replied, Hannah stiff with nerves, Joel with a certain grim amusement, not caring a fig for being disliked if there were a profit to be made. But Elinor, seeing nothing beyond his cool civility, caught her breath and blinked in delighted surprise – for what was the bullnecked Bradley Hobhouse to her now? – and, as Crispin Aycliffe turned away, she gave to his father, somewhat by mistake, a smile that held all the sparkle of crystal in candlelight. And once again, Morgan Aycliffe's thin mouth pinched its disapproval, his eyes, for an instant, looked hunted, as if this display of girlish charm was every bit as abhorrent to him as a pair of ill-matched urns.

We went into dinner then, Mr Aycliffe giving me his arm, Hannah walking stiffly with Crispin, Elinor with Joel, her feet barely touching the ground and her mind, I thought, on a fast coach for Gretna Green, the only one of us to be unimpressed by the pale green damask of the dining-room walls, the mahogany sideboard inlaid with satinwood, the long table, its surface polished to the sheen of glass, the epergne and candelabra of embossed silver, the cost, the value.

There was a portrait, well lit by a branch of candles, of the lady who had died, according to Hannah, of some lingering malady of the nerves, and, according to Elinor, of fright occasioned by her severe spouse. But her painted face looked calm enough, as if she bore him no grudge, and, noting the pearls painted around her throat, I knew that Joel – and possibly Hannah, too – would be quick to assess their worth and wonder what had been done with them now.

'I have no daughter,' Mr Aycliffe said, startling me, since I thought he had read my mind and was about to tell me the whereabouts of his wife's jewels. Although he simply meant to apologize for the lack of a hostess, the point was clear to us all. He had no daughter and consequently his wife's pearls would be available, surely, to her successor, unless, of course, his son should, in the meantime, marry a lady capable of making her claim.

A manservant attended us, an ageing, anonymous black shape, but a manservant, not a girl. And, having expected the food to be anonymous too – in keeping with our host's deliberately clerical manner – I was surprised by the collops of veal in a buttery, peppery sauce that lingered on the tongue and by the wine that was not clerical at all. Mr Aycliffe did, indeed, apologize for the variety and abundance of the wine, suggesting that it was done for our sake since he knew my grandfather kept a good cellar, but, although he drank less than Joel and considerably less than his son, his dry fingers curved themselves with a collector's appreciation around the long, ornamented stem of his glass and his tongue savoured the bouquet with a lingering pleasure that – whether he liked it or not, and whether Hannah liked it or not – could only be called sensual.

But perhaps Hannah was less shocked by this new aspect of her lover than she might have been. Certainly all this caressing of his possessions – the possessions themselves – had, at first, seemed strange to her, and being strange had seemed wrong, but she had no deep-rooted objection to comfort, having preached the merits of the frugal life from necessity rather than conviction, and the image of herself presiding at this luxurious board did not displease her.

And certainly Mr Aycliffe's conversation was altogether beyond reproach.

'Yes,' he said, raising his glass to admire the effect of candle flame on the dark red liquid, 'as you know, I am much concerned with the Sunday School movement, although there has been criticism – ah yes, a great many people have explained to me the dangers of educating the labouring classes. I have been warned that it can serve no purpose but to make them discontented with their lot, and, naturally, I would be the last man alive to ignore the folly of educating anyone beyond his station. But that, you see, is where my critics are in error, for how much better to educate these young men ourselves, carefully choosing the information that can be of use to them, than to have some radical hothead come along and unsettle them with nonsense – and dangerous nonsense too. We teach them to read the Bible, to be industrious, right-minded, and grateful, and I think no one can refuse to acknowledge the valuable service we perform.'

And, as he had clearly paused for some sign of appreciation, we gave it to him, murmuring, 'Most valuable,' 'So very right,' all of us except the son of the house himself, who continued to stare at the wall, his fine face unutterably bored – drinking, I thought, more than he should and eating little – the fingers of one long, well-tended hand tapping irritably on the table.

149

'I suppose you must agree with your father?' Elinor asked indiscreetly, saying the first thing that came into her head to attract his notice.

And, his eyes going through her again, past all the primrose fairness she was so willing to offer, he said, 'Oh indeed I must,' and returned, quite rudely, to his wine.

But Elinor – who had conquered Bradley Hobhouse and knew of no reason why she should not conquer the world – was not to be put off, and, believing the best way to impress one man was to show herself off to another, she turned to Morgan Aycliffe, not because she wished to flirt with him but because he was the only other man in the room besides Joel, and even Elinor could not flirt with her brother. But her effect on Mr Aycliffe was once again unfortunate, bringing back that pinched expression to his eyes, that thinly quivering distaste to his nostrils, so that I felt bound to intervene with some dull little remark about Charity Schools – charity in general – which won me a flash of blue-green anger from Elinor's eyes and Mr Aycliffe's gratitude.

We left the gentlemen alone soon after, knowing our manners, and returned to the drawing room, where, presently, the faceless manservant brought us tea and coffee in cups of a terrifying fragility, and little cakes coated with almonds.

Feeling the tight agony of Hannah's nerves, I said, 'It has all gone very well.'

'Oh, I do hope so.'

'Of course it has,' Elinor trilled, and, getting to her feet, began a dancing, twirling promenade around the room, her skirts flying so close to the objets d'art so perfectly displayed on their low tables that I painfully held my breath. 'Of course it has – of course – it's as good as done. He just wanted to see if you matched his statues and his vases, and how best to place you – an inch to the left, an inch to the right. Well, let's give him something to think about.' And as she came to a halt by the mantelpiece, her wicked hand shot out and set the black basalt urns quite roughly askew.

'Stop her,' Hannah said desperately, too horrified to move, and, jumping up, knowing how destructive her mischief could be, I slapped Elinor hard across the arm and sent her back giggling to her place.

'Put them back,' Hannah said. 'Put them straight. Please.'

But somehow I couldn't get it right.

'Is that it?'

'No.'

'Oh – I can't do it. Is that it?'

'No.'

'Oh – heaven help us, there's somebody coming.'

And the door opened, bringing Crispin Aycliffe to my side.

'Allow me,' he said. 'Oh no, don't be alarmed – my father is not directly behind me. He is still at the table with your husband pretending he don't care for the port, so we have ample time. Now then, I have often heard him say four inches from the edge of the mantel shelf, four inches from the Meissen bowls – so, how does that seem? Is that it?'

'I think so. I think it will do.'

'Yes – although I cannot suppose it will do for him. But don't be concerned for that. It is fairly safe to assume that when a man rearranges his vases as much as my father does, he enjoys it, so you have actually afforded him a pleasure. Will you take a little more coffee or tea? I was told to entertain you, and you must really give me the chance to be obedient.'

'No, nothing more, thank you,' Hannah said, her stomach too cramped with anxiety, I thought, to cope even with tea.

But Elinor, still mischievous and giddy, accepted as eagerly as if he had promised her a pearl in the bottom of her cup and, stirring in her sugar, said, once again indiscreetly, 'Was that your mother in the dining-room – the portrait, I mean? She must have been a very lovely lady.'

'Oh, I wouldn't say she was lovely,' he answered, his face completely without expression. 'Not a bit of it. That likeness was taken long ago, before this malady of the nerves you will have heard about. She became very wasted, very spoiled – not lovely at all the last time I saw her.'

His light, sardonic eyes moved slowly from Elinor's face to Hannah's and remained there.

'How terrible,' Hannah said, her voice barely under control, knowing how pointedly she had been reminded that, in his view, his father had not waited overlong to find a replacement.

And without meaning to speak at all, I heard my voice say, 'I am so sorry for you.'

'Are you?' he said, the fine arch of his eyebrows raising in surprise, taken aback, as I was, yet ready enough, I think, to say more, to ask me why, had not Joel and Mr Aycliffe come back just then. At the sight of his father, he gave me a slight inclination of his head and withdrew not just his body to a far corner of the room but his personality with it, the kind of escape I had often seen my mother make.

A difficult young man, certainly, who would be a sharp thorn in Hannah's side; a dangerous, complex enemy to her peace of mind, who would have no reason to listen if I tried to explain that Hannah meant no harm, that she was a good, sensible woman who should be allowed her chance in life. A young man who was unlike anyone I had ever met, who aroused my curiosity and my compassion. Yet, driving home that night, more than half asleep, I had room in my head for only two things, the pinched face of Morgan Aycliffe, entering the room after dinner, noticing at once that his urns had been tampered with again, and the realization that throughout the entire evening he had not addressed one word directly to his son.

We did not see Mr Aycliffe for some days after that. His half hour alone in the dining room with Joel had provided him with an ideal opportunity to speak his mind, but he had not done so, and when his absence extended to three days, five days, we began to be puzzled and alarmed.

'He's decided you don't match his furniture,' Elinor said with wicked glee. 'You're too tall to fit on the mantelpiece and you're the wrong colour for the hall table.'

But at the end of the week, on the eighth day, a note was delivered announcing Mr Aycliffe's intention of calling that afternoon, if Joel could spare an hour of his time. Hannah and Elinor, as it chanced, had driven over to Patterswick to visit my mother, and I made sure I was in the kitchen when Mr Aycliffe arrived, coming out at the end of an hour only to peer from the window to take note, from his manner and Joel's, that all had gone well. And so, going back into the kitchen to supervise Marth-Ellen's cakes, I was unprepared for Joel's voice yelling. 'Verity – come quick,' and downright alarmed when I found him in the front parlour shaking with laughter.

'Joel – what is it? Whatever is it? Didn't he propose?'

'Oh yes,' he said, wiping his eyes and then succumbing again to those undignified whoops of delight. 'He proposed all right. By God, Verity, he proposed. The damn fool has asked me for Elinor. Yes, you may well stare, for I did the same. I thought he had mistaken the name and told him so, which didn't please him. But no, it's Elinor he wants. Elinor. Damn me, I always knew he was the kind to have one hand on a prayer book and his other up a housemaid's skirt, but I never thought he'd lose his head this way. The fool – I ask you – with all his urns and his vases and his Napoleon brandy – has there ever been such a fool?'

10

It was, of course, perfectly disgraceful – scandalous, even – and, beneath my immediate pity for Hannah, I too could feel laughter stirring, for I did not like Morgan Aycliffe and would not be sorry to see him discomfited. But then, as Joel began to whoop again with his unkind mirth, suspicion bit into me and I said, experimentally, hopefully, 'So that's the last we shall see of Mr Aycliffe.'

'Oh – hardly that.'

Altogether aghast, I sat down, shuddering slightly as the ludicrous image of Morgan Aycliffe in a nightshirt suddenly burst into my mind, sickening me.

'Joel – you can't possibly . . . Oh, Joel, you can't consent.'

'Why can't I?'

'Because Hannah—'

'Hannah has nothing to do with it anymore,' he said, laughter draining out of him, leaving him hard and hurtful in the face of my opposition. 'If he can't have Elinor he won't come back for Hannah, you can be sure of that. He didn't find it easy – believe me – standing here, asking me for my seventeen-year-old sister. He knew exactly what I was thinking, and what everybody else is going to think – and say, behind his back – and he didn't like it at all. But he did it. That's how mad he is for her, and if he don't get her he'll bolt – so Hannah's lost her chance either way.'

'So you consented.'

'I did.'

'And Elinor? You mean to force her, then?'

'Force her? What the devil makes you think I'd have to force her?'

And, as that grotesque image of the grey-faced widower in his night attire once again danced into my mind, I cried out, 'Because she won't take him willingly – you know she won't.'

'I know no such thing,' he said, and as he looked at me keenly, recognizing the disgust in my face, I saw his temper snap and felt it reach out for me with a crouching snarl, designed to hurt.

'You don't understand us at all, do you, Verity – me and Hannah and Elinor? Won't take him? She'd give her eye-teeth for him – yes, yes, yes, indeed she would – for him and for the dress allowance he can give her and for the pearls he can put round her neck, and for her own carriage so she can stop begging rides in yours and Emma-Jane's. That's what's been biting her these last few weeks, because she thought Hannah was going to get all that, and she'd be left on the shelf. And if he's not pretty, then neither is Bradley Hobhouse, who's just younger, and that don't last. But how could you understand, Verity, when there's always been your grandfather to put his hand in his pocket every time you had a whim or a fancy? So don't judge what you can't comprehend. Elinor would do anything to get out of the hole her father left her in – as Hannah would.'

'As you would?'

'I reckon so,' he said, the sting of his anger so venomous now that I turned and walked away from him, finding, to my own surprise, that by the time I had reached the refuge of my bedroom and bolted the door, I was in tears.

It was his affair, then; his and Elinor's and Hannah's, the three of them together. Deciding to take no part in it, I called my dogs and, walking up the path past the Top House, followed the track beyond my grandfather's garden that led to the open moor. And when the dogs had had their run and my shoes were full of stones, I sat with Mrs Stevens, drinking tea and watching, from my grandfather's hillside perch, as the carriage returned from Patterswick and stopped at the millhouse, and Hannah and Elinor went inside.

'I'll take some more tea, Mrs Stevens, if you please,' I said, and sipped it slowly, allowing the time to pass – an hour at least – before I saw Joel come out of the house and walk across the yard to the mill. And then, after having another slice of gingerbread and calculating that the coast would be reasonably clear, I took my leave, entering the millhouse cautiously by the kitchen door and hurrying up the back stairs to find Liza, the nursemaid, and give Blaize his supper.

I put my son to bed, sat for a moment enjoying his total contentment, and then went back to my own room, hoping for solitude, but it was not long before there was a discreet knock and Elinor's fair head appeared enquiringly around the door.

'I expect you are very angry with me,' she said, walking flat-footed like a little girl across the floor and sitting, hands neatly folded, in front of me, waiting for her scolding.

'You mean to take him, then?'

'Oh yes, indeed I do.'

And when I began to ask her how she could, she made a decisive movement with one hand that reminded me very strongly of Joel.

'How could I not? And I didn't steal him from Hannah, no matter what anyone has to say. I never even thought of him, for he seemed positively to dislike me, except that I suppose he did that on purpose, to stop himself showing that he liked me too much. Or so Joel says, anyway.'

'And what of the things you said? That he was old and stale and that he frightened his wife to death?'

'Oh that,' she said, half sighing, half laughing. 'Well, I talk a great deal, don't I, and mean less than the half of it, you know that, Verity. But I am not so stupid – really. Sometimes it's better to appear stupid and go prattling on because otherwise who would ever notice me? Emma-Jane can afford to have buck teeth and never say a word, because half the men in Cullingford owe money at her father's bank. But I'm a poor relation, and all I'm entitled to say is "Please" and "Thank you kindly." And, you see, if I did that, then I'd be treated like a poor relation, which is even worse than being one, and I made up my mind long ago not to let that happen. Joel and I, you know, we're both the same; we'd do anything for money. I sometimes wonder what we'll ever find to strive for once we have it. So I'm not stupid. I know Bradley Hobhouse would never run off with me, Verity – and, far worse than that, I don't think I'd have the courage to go in any case. And that's quite terrible, you know, when you think how just dreaming about it has kept me going. So I have to do the best I can. And Mr Aycliffe must love me enormously, wouldn't you think, to risk the gossip, because they won't take kindly to it at Ramsden Street, I can tell you.'

'Elinor,' I said very slowly, 'if I catch you flaunting yourself, just once, in front of Hannah, then I shall slap your face until it swells, even if it should be on your wedding morning.'

'Oh, Verity,' she said, laughing, rubbing her cheek with a hand not entirely steady, 'how fierce you can be in your quiet way. But Hannah can defend herself, you know, and you may save yourself the trouble of slapping me, for she has done it already. She flew at me like a spitting cat and boxed my ears soundly, I can tell you, with Joel not lifting a finger to stop her. But listen, Verity, Hannah doesn't love him, you know, and now it makes no difference to her whether I take him or not – except that if I don't take him there'll be two old maids at Low Cross instead of one. And I'm not cut out to be an old maid, I've told you that often enough. I can't go on prattling and dreaming forever, and what else can I do? I don't care for the chapel and good works like Hannah. I don't want to teach Sunday School, and I can't manage, somehow, to feel sorry for the slaves when I'm not free myself. And those sugar plantations and cotton plantations are so far away. I can't even begin to imagine them. But I can imagine myself, Verity, in a few years, if I stay at Low Cross. And there won't be another Mr Aycliffe.'

'But he's so much older than you, Elinor, and so stern.'

'And so rich. And I'll be good at being rich. He likes beautiful things. Didn't you see him, the other night, with his statues and his fine wines. I won't help him with his Sunday Schools, like Hannah, but I can look pretty – that's what Joel told me to do: to look pretty and keep my mouth shut. And that must be what he wants. There must be two sides to his nature, I suppose: the serious side that wanted Hannah and the fancy side that wanted me – and my side won. Oh, Verity, don't be too cross. I'm going to have such a lovely time. Strawberries and champagne for breakfast, just like I always told you, except that I'd stopped believing it and now it's coming true. Hannah will get over it, and you don't want to spoil it for me, do you?'

'No, I don't. But, Elinor, do you really understand about marriage – I mean?'

'Oh,' she said airily, 'about kissing and being in the same bed? Well, it's not such a mystery.'

But Elinor's mother had been dead a long time, and because I could not imagine Hannah explaining in any great detail, or even fully understanding the details herself – and because Morgan Aycliffe was repulsive to me and I assumed he must repel her, too – I said rather primly, 'There's a great deal more to marriage than kissing.'

'Oh yes,' she said, 'a great deal more, and I won't be the first to live through it. We kept dogs, Elinor, like you, and pigs, and I've heard my mother say many a time that men were just the same.'

I did not expect Hannah to appear at breakfast the next morning, but it was Elinor who shirked, Hannah sitting straight-backed at the table while serving buttered toast and honey to Joel, when he came up from the mill, as if nothing of any importance had occurred. And I was aware of the bond between the three of them: a shared determination, bred of their shared poverty, that no personal

158

sacrifice was too great if the interests of their family would be served; a bond which prevented Hannah from blaming either of the other two, although I knew she was mortified, horrified, sick at heart.

She had wanted that marriage herself, desperately, but now, having boxed her sister's ears and called her a thieving minx, after a night of self-torture and humiliation, she was almost awe-inspiring in her calm.

'I have a great deal of plain sewing to do,' she told me when Joel had gone back to the mill. 'I will take it upstairs and sit in the window. The light is better there.'

'Yes, of course.'

And then, visibly drawing herself together, she said, 'Naturally you will have heard that my sister is to be married?'

'Yes, indeed.'

'Yes – and I daresay you may have been surprised, although you must admit that there has been nothing in any way improper. When a gentleman becomes a regular visitor at a house where young ladies are to be found, he must eventually declare himself – we all know that to be the rule – and since Mr Aycliffe has declared himself, I can see no occasion for talk – gossip – you will know what I mean. Certain acquaintances of ours – Mrs Rawnsley, for one, and Mrs Hobhouse, I daresay, since they are always together – have expressed the view that Mr Aycliffe's interest was in my direction. But that was no more than supposition – I always said so, you have heard me say it – and I should not like it if they were to – to—'

'They will not,' I told her, knowing she meant 'to commiserate.' And, watching the proud, painful squaring of her shoulders as she picked up her work basket and walked away, I made up my mind to see Mrs Rawnsley and Mrs Hobhouse as soon as I could, and to suggest to them, without exactly telling a lie, that Mr Aycliffe may well have proposed to Hannah first and been refused.

My grandfather, as expected, was not pleased at this

piece of good fortune which had come Joel's way. He had ordered him to get his sisters married and out of Low Cross, certainly, but he had had a shopkeeper or a schoolmaster in mind, not another financial giant like himself who could encourage Joel's habits of independence and disobedience. Although he might well have given Elinor the wherewithal to settle herself nicely into a dairy or a schoolhouse, he now elected to give her nothing. But Mrs Stevens, for whom weddings were occasions of great heart-searching, came down from the Top House whenever she could, to help with the trousseau, and, once again, it seemed that marriage was a purely feminine matter, a choice between lilac gauze and sky-blue satin, with which the bridegroom – once he had been securely attached – had nothing to do.

My mother came quite often too, adding her fine stitching to the growing pile, and, while Hannah undertook the plain sewing of the household, my mother, Mrs Stevens, Elinor, and I sat in the stone-flagged kitchen – Blaize gurgling in his cradle beside us – concealing ourselves behind the companionable hum of our voices and the plying of our needles, with fashion books strewn all about us and a pot of tea constantly brewing by the fire.

It was, of course, to be the best trousseau ever seen in the Law Valley, for Joel would not have his sister go out a beggar, and even though Morgan Aycliffe was willing to take her on promises alone, he would at least give her the means to cut a dash. And since cutting a dash was a matter well understood by both Joel and his younger sister, we were busy indeed.

'Oh, do stay just a little longer, Mrs Stevens,' she would plead. 'Just fit me into this yellow silk again, for I've a dreadful feeling I measured wrong last time and it needs another inch off the hem. And if I don't know for sure it will nag me and nag me, and I'll never sleep tonight. And you will come tomorrow, dear, dear Mrs Stevens, won't you, because you are so good and clever—'

And Mrs Stevens, whose burden was growing every day heavier as my grandfather's temper grew shorter, his constitution weaker, would smile through her fatigue – for a Mrs Morgan Aycliffe was a different matter entirely from a Miss Elinor Barforth – and promise to come if she could. Indeed, she rarely failed, for, as my mother had once told me, she had her future to consider, and her attentions both to Elinor and to me were most marked.

'Dear Mrs Barforth, dear Miss Elinor,' tripped from her tongue like summer rain, and, whenever there was a dispute between us, which happened not infrequently, her tact was altogether a work of art.

'I think Mrs Barforth is right, Miss Elinor, my dear, because this pattern is certainly gay – excessively so, Mrs Barforth, as you say. But then, glancing at it again, although it wouldn't do for Mrs Barforth at all, since she likes simple, elegant designs which suit her so well – perhaps on Miss Elinor, who is in quite another style— So pretty. What do you think?'

And, holding up a length of sprig muslin, having called me elegant and Elinor pretty, she would leave the decision to Fate, or to my mother, on whose taste we could all rely.

Yet there were times when Elinor's bubbling excitement and Hannah's rigid control were hard to bear, and times when Joel's odd blending of self-satisfaction and ill temper distressed me. Could it be that, after all, he had his doubts about giving his sister to this dry, difficult man? Was his conscience indeed stirring, while ambition and self-interest forced him to ignore it? Yet we were the same age, Elinor and I, and capable of making the same judgements, and although I was often overwhelmingly anxious on her behalf, I could detect nothing in her own manner but unsullied delight.

Even when she heard the news of Emma-Jane Rawnsley's engagement to Bradley Hobhouse, she merely chuckled and said, 'Poor Emma-Jane. She will have his mamma to contend with, and I hope she may find a way to deal with her, for I am sure I never could. If she thinks she is to be mistress of Nethercoats she will have a rude awakening, for Mrs Hobhouse is quite the most managing woman I ever met, and I should not like her putting her long nose into my cupboards. Well – thank goodness there is no mamma-in-law in Blenheim Lane to bother me.'

But did she ever give a thought to other things in Blenheim Lane that could bother her: to the silence, to those perfectly spaced basalt urns, to Mr Aycliffe himself. And had she considered how Crispin Aycliffe, who had been hostile to a stately woman like Hannah, must feel now that his mother's place was to be taken by a girl of seventeen? Had she considered that his presence could prove far more disturbing than any mother-in-law?

We dined once again at the Aycliffe house – Joel, Elinor, and I – this time with Mr and Mrs Rawnsley as fellow guests, neither Hannah, who had not been expected, nor Crispin Aycliffe, who most certainly had been, choosing to appear. The next morning, unable to stand Hannah's extreme politeness, her absolute refusal to ask how the evening had gone although she was longing to know, I called my dogs – in whose company I was never ill at ease – and took my familiar walk past the Top House and out to the moor.

It was high summer then, the sky behind me yellow with the slow penetration of sunlight through the pall of factory smoke, but I turned my back on the town, striding quickly away from it to a point where the tufted upland grass was sharp-scented and even the sky shredded, first to a cleaner grey and then to blue.

Hannah, I knew, did not approve of my lonely ramblings; she had even spoken to Joel about my breach of convention, the necessity for a suitable companion, but he had made nothing of it, and, that morning, leaning against the wind, letting the dogs run free – the puppy now as big as her mother and not always ready to obey either of us – my mind was so full of the bare, brown curve of the land, the nearby music of moorland water, the tangy freshness of space and solitude, that I failed to recognize Crispin Aycliffe until he spoke my name.

I had seen him approach in the distance, a man walking a horse, a dark-green-coated figure that could have been anyone, and I had thought only to call up my young dog, who would be very likely to snap at the horse's legs. But it was the old bitch who came obligingly to heel, the young one pausing for an instant, flighty and nervous, dancing away, and then pausing again, taunting me to give chase.

'They are very large dogs, Mrs Barforth,' a man's voice said, 'for a lady.'

The wind striking me a capricious blow, whipping the ribbons of my sunbonnet into flight and my hair into disarray, I looked up and saw him, hat in hand, smiling, his mouth no longer sulky, his face almost boyish without its studied boredom.

'Should you be walking here, Mrs Barforth, quite alone?' he asked, and, knowing that his father shared many of Hannah's narrow views, I shook my head.

'No, I daresay I should not, for I always go home with stones in my shoes, but someone must walk the dogs.'

'Your dogs?'

'Yes – at least the young one is mine, and the old one belonged to my brother, so I may say she is mine now too.'

'Your brother Edwin?'

'Did you know him?'

'Oh – barely. We shared a term or two at the grammar school, but I cannot say we were friends. You are not in the least like him.'

'I suppose not. But do you often take this road, Mr Aycliffe? It seems a little out of your way.'

'Indeed it is,' he told me, his eyebrow making its fine, quizzical arch, 'since it leads only from Cullingford to Lawcroft Fold, and then on to nowhere. I was coming to pay you a visit, to apologize to you and to Miss Barforth for my absence at dinner last night. At least, I intended to come, but somehow my horse rode on, until your house was behind me – so I dismounted and I am walking back.'

'Why? In case you should ride past us again?'

And for an odd, uncomfortable moment, I saw him in that sombre, beautiful house, hiding his bruised feelings behind that quizzical, insolent lifting of the eyebrow, that sardonic curving of his mouth, while his father ordered him to saddle up and ride over to Lawcroft without fail to pay the visit that common courtesy demanded, that filial duty absolutely required.

'The girl is to be my wife, and you will go to her, as you should have done a month ago, and you will say everything that is proper, everything that is due to her as my intended, everything that is due to me as your father. I am not answerable to you, boy, but you are answerable to me, and you would do well not to forget it.'

And because he was indeed answerable, because his father held the purse strings and would not hesitate to draw them tight, he had ridden over to Lawcroft, looked down at it from the moorland road – sick, I thought, with anger and disgust – and ridden on, needing a moment more of clean air and space to equip himself for the ordeal of taking Miss Elinor Barforth's tiny hand and declaring himself ready to love her as a son.

'It would seem,' he said quietly, 'that I gave serious offence by my failure to dine——?'

'Not to me, certainly.'

'Possibly not. But to your husband and to – your cousin?'

'Oh, as to them, they are both quick to take offence and quick to recover.'

'But you will nevertheless accept my apology?'

'Of course.' And, feeling again the abhorrence in him that prevented him from even speaking Elinor's name, I quickly added, 'And I will convey it to my cousin. She is not at home today, but she will gladly forgive you. You may tell your father so.'

'Oh,' he said, 'thank you,' his hand adjusting something

at the horse's head, his attention apparently elsewhere, until my young bitch, planting herself at a safe distance from flying hooves, set up a howling that caused the fine bay animal to shiver. It was not until my flighty young dog had gone dancing off into the wind and his horse stood, sullen and offended but peaceful again, that he looked at me very carefully and said, 'Is Miss Elinor Barforth really not at home?'

'Well . . . yes, as it happens, she is at home, but she is very much occupied with my mother and our housekeeper, and I know they don't wish for a visit from anyone today.'

'And is it so very obvious that I don't wish to pay one?'

'Yes,' I said, my eyes drawn directly to his face. 'And there is no reason in the world why you should apologize for that. I perfectly understand why.'

'Do you?' he said, his eyes half closing with a weary gesture I had observed in him before. But he was not ready yet to accept my sympathy, and when his eyes opened there was no weariness in them any longer, but keen, cool sarcasm, tinged unmistakably with spite.

'And why is that, Mrs Barforth? Do you imagine I object to my father's choice of a second wife?'

'I think it can scarcely please you.'

'Oh, but it does. It pleases me enormously.'

And when I shook my head he laughed, not pleasantly, a snap of malice once again in his face.

'You are quite wrong, Mrs Barforth – so very wrong, believe me. I am delighted – totally enchanted – with Miss Elinor. And if there is something undignified or question-able in the spectacle of a man of my father's years cavorting with a child – and I imagine she is very much a child – then, well, that delights me even more. I am not, as you may have noticed, particularly attached to my father, but even I – Mrs Barforth – in my worst moments – could never have devised so complete a punishment for him as this. They have the very greatest chance of unhappiness I

165

think I have ever observed, and if you knew me better you would understand that I could hardly object to that.'

But it was too much, too personal; I was too aware of the hurt in him, smarting beneath his cruelty, too ready to sympathize, and I said stiffly, 'Mr Aycliffe, we do not really know each other, and you should not speak to me like that.'

'No,' he said, instantly the courteous young gentleman minding his manners, his smile rueful and charming, expecting to be forgiven. 'Of course, I should not. I know that very well, and yet I allowed myself the liberty – indulged myself – because, well, you feel so very sorry for me, don't you, and so I knew you would forgive me. I have taken advantage of your kind heart, you see, just as I used to do with my mother, for it is quite true that I have been very much indulged. Have I really offended you?'

'No. But I must be getting back now.'

'Then I have offended you.'

'No, not in the least.'

'Then why must you hurry back to Miss Elinor – who is not at home? But, of course, if you must, then I am sorry for it, especially since we may not have the chance to talk again.'

'Why is that? Are you going away?'

'Yes,' he said, smiling. 'Indeed I am, and you may tell me how glad you are of it, if you wish, for your cousin's sake. I am going to France and, hopefully, to Italy, in pursuit of architectural knowledge – not forever, alas, but for long enough to prevent my sour face casting a gloom over the start of your cousin's marriage. Naturally I shall attend the wedding, for it would be thought odd in Ramsden Street otherwise, but I shall leave straight after. I am at pains, you see, to spare my new mother the slightest degree of awkwardness.'

'No, you are not,' I said sharply, speaking to him very much as I would have spoken to my brother Edwin, and, throwing back his narrow head, he burst into a peal of real, uncomplicated laughter.

'You think I am merely feeling sorry for myself, then?'

'I don't know about that, and perhaps you have good reasons. But this is not of my cousin's making, you know. She is young and her life has not been easy, and really, when it comes down to it, she can only do as she is bid.'

'Yes, indeed,' he said, suddenly very serious, gentle almost. 'You are right, of course. How terrible to be a woman. I have often thought so. God knows, I am not so free as I could wish, but a woman has no freedom at all. And, worse than that, she knows she never can be free. I think that would drive me mad. There is always someone pursuing you, isn't there – father, brother, husband, children, eating your time and energy and believing they have a right to it, allowing you no rights at all. I find it terrible, and yet I have done it myself, for I laid all my burdens on my mother's shoulders, no matter how weary she was. And if I take a wife I shall doubtless do the same. But you are quite right, Mrs Barforth; your cousin is not to blame, and you clearly would not wish to see her made miserable.'

'Indeed I would not.'

'And I have worried you on her account. Please forgive me. The fact that my father and I cannot live in peace together does not exclude the possibility of his being at peace with someone else. I have a bitter nature, I think, and often I make too much of things. Your little cousin may be exactly what my father needs, and, in that case, she will do well enough.'

I turned and walked forward, towards Lawcroft, my back now to the thin blue sky, my face to the smoke, and he fell into step beside me, his horse following with supercilious grace while my old yellow bitch pressed close to heel, the puppy continuing her frenzied ballet on the borders of the track. It was late afternoon, the earth heavy with the accumulated heat of the day, the town a charcoal sketch in the distance, the roof of the Top House just visible now, beckoning me home to a world where the uncomfortable truth was rarely spoken. And, looking up at Crispin Aycliffe, accepting his presence lightly and naturally, as if I had known him as long as Edwin, I said, 'Was your mother very unhappy?'

'My dear Mrs Barforth, whyever should you think of such a thing?' he said, his brows raising again in that defensive arch of sarcasm. 'My mother was surely the happiest creature alive, for she had everything any right-minded woman could desire; I have heard my father tell her so a hundred times. A house in Blenheim Lane, her carriage, pearls . . . My word – happy? I should say so.'

And I could only hope that if these grand possessions had not sufficed for the first Mrs Aycliffe, they would surely content the second.

We strolled the rest of the way to the Top House in silence, and, as he bent over my hand, I told him, 'I shall envy you when you go to France. I have been to Leeds and twice to Sheffield to visit my mother's family, and if I get to London before I die I shall consider myself well-travelled. So I shall think of you, when you are looking at your palaces and your churches.'

'Yes,' he said, 'do think of me. Who knows, I may even find a beautiful princess looking down at me from one of those palace windows and come home with a royal bride to dazzle Ramsden Street.'

And so there was laughter at our parting, a surface gaiety, draining abruptly out of me and causing me to speak sharply to the dogs as he rode away. He would go to France and Italy; Joel, to London or anywhere else he chose; Elinor would go to Blenheim Lane, which in her eyes was as exciting as Samarkand, and Hannah, surely, would grapple with her disappointments and wrest something out of life, while I would stay here, neither happy nor unhappy but smiling, maintaining order, keeping the peace, and being quiet, reasonable, and serene. And for one brief moment of fierce intensity – a moment I did not relish at all – I wondered when life was going to begin.

11

They were married on a cool September morning that spoke of summer's end, Elinor in a cloud of white gauze over satin, looking like some frail creature of air and moonlight as she entered the church on Joel's arm, followed by two little girls, cousins from her mother's side of the family, whose presence spared Hannah and me the embarrassment of being bridesmaids. And I suppose, when one accustomed oneself to the stark contrast of dainty, fairytale bride and long, grey, withered groom, that it all went very well.

Hannah was there, of course, smiling through her ordeal, clothed in brown silk and the grand mantle of her Barforth dignity – the brooch of Edwin's hair on her collar again – and a fine gathering of Hobhouses and Oldroyds and Rawnsleys attended, brimming with good wishes and curiosity. The professional classes, too, were represented: Mr Corey-Manning the lawyer, bringing his spinster sister, and Mr and Mrs Roundwood of the *Cullingford Courier and Review*, arriving, a bare second before the bride, with a cousin of theirs, Dr Overdale, who, having recently moved to Blenheim Lane, was fast establishing himself as Cullingford's most expensive physician.

My grandfather had agreed to come, declaring himself eager to see Aycliffe go to his doom, but somehow he had not found the energy, was not up to it, although Mrs Stevens was there, and my mother, on Squire Dalby's arm, their appearance causing considerable excitement among the 'manufacturing' ladies, who, having no good opinion of Isabella Barforth, would, nevertheless, have given a great deal to make the squire's acquaintance. And occu-

169

pying a pew near the back of the church were Mr and Mrs Isaac Boulton with their younger, married daughter Catherine and their elder, still single daughter Rosamund, who had been abandoned by Joel for my sake.

'You will not mind my asking the Boultons,' Elinor had said. 'It would seem odd to leave them out, for we have known them forever. I have stayed at their house often enough, and Rosamund, who is so clever with her needle, has always helped me with my dresses.'

Although I had agreed that it would seem most odd if they were not included and that I knew of no reason why I should mind, I found myself looking closely at this girl, a woman now of twenty-five or twenty-six, who, by waiting for Joel, trusting him, had landed herself, it seemed, firmly on the shelf. She was tall and well proportioned, with bright, almost bold dark eyes and high colour in her cheeks, her dark hair fashionably arranged beneath a dashing military bonnet, her hands hiding themselves in a feathered muff dyed to the exact blue of her gown. She looked smart, self-possessed, capable, the kind of girl who could dance all night and be first downstairs, fresh as a daisy, the next morning. Quick-tempered, perhaps, and flirtatious; disappointed, certainly, although she did not show it, and I would have been less than human had I not wondered what she thought of Joel now, what he thought of her. And, pondering her situation, I saw Crispin Aycliffe nodding to me from the other side of the aisle.

'Good morning, Mrs Barforth,' he said quietly.

'Good morning, Mr Aycliffe,' I replied.

And I found I had clenched my hands tightly, gripped by an uncanny, unnerving sensation that of all the people here assembled this pale young man was the only one who knew me; the only one, besides myself, who was entirely real.

There was champagne later, Elinor still in her blissful dream, her husband, and his son, too, looking as if they felt the cold, and it was not long before he whisked her away on the honeymoon I could scarcely contemplate, escorted to the coach by Messrs Hobhouse, Oldroyd, and Rawnsley, who, for one night at least, would gladly have been in his place, while Hannah, free at last from the obligation to smile, broke a plate, kicked my old bitch, and reduced Marth-Ellen to tears.

I had given a great deal of thought to a wedding gift, settling finally on a dessert service, complete with sauce tureen and ice pail, decorated with painted roses in more shades of pink than I had believed possible. And driving to Blenheim Lane to present it, after their return, I think I expected to find Elinor sunk in shock and despair and bitter regret.

'Is Mrs Aycliffe at home?' I enquired of the manservant, nervously preparing myself for a denial, but instead the door of the room we had been brought up to call a parlour but which was now a drawing room burst open and Elinor herself, ringlets and ribbons dancing, came tripping out to greet me.

'Oh, darling, how marvellous,' she said, without really looking at the china dishes, which had been purchased, in any case, to impress her husband. 'Wilkinson will put them somewhere, and then Mr Aycliffe will put them somewhere else when he comes home. Wilkinson, do see to it, and then tea, please, in the drawing room, with lots of cakes.'

And I concluded, from the faceless Wilkinson's almost imperceptible shudder, that the first Mrs Aycliffe had never presumed to take tea with friends in the drawing room, among all the precious glass and porcelain – or, indeed, had perhaps never invited friends at all.

'Are you well?' I asked her, puzzled, because although she looked well, it hardly seemed likely. But Elinor had a certain toughness, a certain coarseness, in her nature that not only enabled her to find her husband's marital endeavours amusing but made her quick to appreciate the power his desire gave her.

'My dear, he'll do anything for me,' she said, letting me see the new ring on her hand and the wide gold bracelet around her arm. 'Anything – I have only to ask – and all because he just wants to look and look at me. My dear, you can't imagine – I thought I'd be quite frightened, but he's so careful. I suppose it comes from handling all this porcelain. And do you know, that's exactly how he makes me feel – precious porcelain. I'm not even to worry myself about the housekeeping. We have Wilkinson and Mrs Naylor for that, and a host of girls. . . . I'm just to sit here, looking pretty, and whatever I want I just have to ring for it. When he comes home, he'll just gaze at me all evening – I don't even have to think of clever things to say. And he gave me champagne on my first morning too – oh my, I'll never forget it – although I do wish strawberries had been in season.' And she broke off, giggling not in the least coyly.

'You find it all quite – quite pleasant, then?'

'You mean . . .? Oh well, naturally, one has to make a fuss at first, because it's expected, but, as they say, one doesn't die from it, and I think I may well endure ten minutes of puffing and panting for all this. In fact, I believe one could actually get to like it if – well – I do, that's all.'

With a younger man, I thought, a handsomer man. And, not realizing he was in my mind, I asked, 'And what of Mr Crispin Aycliffe?'

'What of him? He's gone. Didn't you see his sour face at the wedding? Looking down his nose at everything as if there was a bad smell? Well, he's gone to France, where there probably is a bad smell, and if he never comes back I shan't be sorry. Although he will come, of course, because my husband needs him to look after the business and our other financial affairs. Oh my – did I really say that? Our financial affairs – how absolutely splendid that sounds. Anyway, that's why we need Mr Crispin.'

A princess, I thought, looking down from a palace window, pink towers and spires, rose-tinted sky and water;

and it suited him. A rich and royal bride coming back to Cullingford to put Elinor's nose out of joint. And because that suited him, too, I found myself smiling; I was glad that he, at least, if only for a little while, was free to find his own way.

'Perhaps he won't come back,' I told her. 'Perhaps he'll make a rich, exciting life for himself somewhere and have a new adventure every day . . .'

'Or they'll hang him,' she said, quite viciously, ringing her bell for more tea and then, when it arrived, leaving it to go cold as she took me upstairs to see her silver-backed brushes, her scent bottles her trinket boxes, but not as yet, I noticed, that marvellous double strand of her predecessor's pearls.

Yet she was well and I was glad of it, as one must be glad for anyone who sees a dream come true, and if I was uneasy, perhaps it was only because I disliked the idea of describing it all to Hannah when I got home. But the necessity, as it happened, never arose, for, as I descended from the carriage, Ira Agbrigg, that bringer of evil tidings, was standing there, cap in hand, his odd, lashless eyes respectfully lowered as he handed me a message from Mrs Stevens that my grandfather was ailing.

I had known, I suppose, that he would die eventually, sooner rather than later – as Mrs Stevens had known it – but knowing is not believing and we were both of us unprepared and terrified, she at the loss of her livelihood and I at the loss of this supreme authority who, by standing between me and the lesser authorities of father and husband, had offered me the possibility of appeal. 'Father says you may not,' they had told us as children, and both Edwin and I had always answered, 'But Grandfather says we may.' And it had always sufficed.

But now the doctor – the smart new Dr Overdale from Blenheim Lane – decreed that it would be a matter of days, a week at the most, and felt obliged to defend himself by repeating the warnings he had given on his previous visits about the effect of the wine and the food and – although he did not exactly say so – of Mrs Stevens on the overweight, overage bulk that was still, although only barely, Samson Barforth.

'He has had these attacks before,' Mrs Stevens told me desperately. 'Five or six these last two years, and he has always recovered. Dear Mrs Barforth, surely, there is hope?'

But I did not think so and she did not think so; and, as she moved sadly away, I was aware for the first time of age in her face, the tiny lines around her eyes, the slackening of her jaw now that her mouth was not smiling, the sheer fatigue of a woman who has turned forty and dares not admit it.

My mother was sent for, Hannah and Joel came, but my grandfather, waking from his drugged sleep to the realization of his end, was not reconciled. Death was just another enemy to be grappled with, and when he understood that he could not defeat it, that it had mottled his cheeks and clogged his chest for the final time and that soon it would be at his throat, he lay back in the ornate bed where I had spent my wedding night and consoled himself by hating us all.

'You were the ruin of my son, Isabella Baxter,' he growled at my mother. 'You took him from spite and broke him, and now you lead a harlot's life – playing the whore for Dalby like Emmeline here plays the whore for me – except that she's a silly whore and I'll wager you're a sour one.'

And when Mrs Stevens, tears streaming down her face, leaned forward to adjust his pillows, he struck her quite hard, making himself cough again, and told her to take her fool's face out of his sight.

'What good are you to me now?' he shouted. 'And I'll not have your weeping and wailing – that's not what I paid you for and I don't want it. You'd cry as much for a sick cat, woman – damnable, stupid woman. Get out. Get out, now. I don't want you, haven't wanted you for a long time. Get away. I want my wife.'

And that, after ten years of her devotion, was his goodbye to her.

Nor would he allow Joel in the room with him.

'Tell him to wait downstairs,' he snarled, 'like the lackey he is. He knows where to find the will afterwards – that's all that bothers him – and so he can wait. Maybe he reckons I'm taking too long and he'd like to slip up here and hold a pillow to my face – aye, he'd like that right enough. I should never have let him have the Girl. I should have given her to Morgan Aycliffe's lad, as I intended. Aye, you didn't know that, did you, Verity? Aycliffe spoke to me and I was agreeable, but then Edwin died and I didn't want Aycliffe's bony hands on my mill. No – but I tell you this – if I'd strength left I'd go down now and fire it myself, just to spite yon lad downstairs. That I would – just to spite him.'

And then, for a long, aching time, he was quiet.

I thought he would not wake again, for his breathing became shallow as the night wore on, and his face chalk white where the purple mottling had not touched it, but death was neither so simple nor so clean, and towards morning he awoke, his eyes shooting fiercely open but his body limp and feeble and needing care. Even then there was another long day, with the September sunlight slanting in through the drawn curtains, hardly sweetening the foul air, Mrs Stevens somewhere outside, pathetically hovering, and Joel waiting for his inheritance, while my mother and I sat one on either side of the great bed, hypnotized by the shallow breathing that seemed sometimes to stop and then, by the sheer effort of will, started painfully up again.

The doctor came, shook his head, made his murmurings, and then went downstairs to wait with Joel, who, after all, would be the one to settle his fee, and even then, as the night fell again, my grandfather did not die, his body and soul welded together, it seemed, by his determination to keep Joel waiting a while longer.

'Would you like to rest?' my mother offered, and, when I refused, she fell asleep gracefully, her head resting on the chair back, her hands folded.

Perhaps I dozed, too, for suddenly I was wide awake, aware that the candles had burned low, that something was wrong and I was to blame.

And then he whispered, 'Verity.'

'Yes, Grandfather.'

I had to come close to hear him, for his voice was dying before him, the touch of his hand as it grasped mine like crinkled old paper that would flake and shrivel in the fire.

'I don't like him,' he said. 'Yon Joel – he's like me, I know it, but I don't like him. But I've left him the mill for your sake. I could have cut him off, sent him to the devil – but you're his wife and you'd have had a poor time of it then. So I've left you everything, Verity, which is the same as leaving it to him since you can't touch it while he lives – and he'll live. By God, he'll live. I should have given you to Aycliffe's lad – cut my losses and married you as I'd intended – but I wouldn't be cheated, you see. I thought I could have Edwin again. Thought I could – but no – and it doesn't matter now – damn it – doesn't matter.'

And slowly, the room became empty, terrifyingly, totally still.

'I think,' my mother said, quite coolly, 'that he has gone.' And, reaching forward, she unclasped his hand from mine and then smoothed my hand with both of hers, washing his dead touch away.

'Poor man,' she said with no expression whatsoever in her face. 'He admitted defeat at the end, and I shall try not to be glad of it. He absorbed so many people's lives – your father's certainly – and there is no doubt that he was a selfish man. I used to hate him so dreadfully. Yes, Verity, really hate him. I used to long for his death. Yet here it is, and, as he said, it doesn't matter now. Go quickly, dearest, and tell your husband and our poor Emmeline. She at least will shed an honest tear.'

And, bending over him, with a steady, almost impersonal flick of her wrist, she closed his eyes.

Hannah and Mrs Stevens were in the darkened hall, Hannah maintaining the solemn face she believed to be death's due and Mrs Stevens sobbing quietly for those ten years of devotion that were ended now and for the next ten years which might well prove lean indeed. But before I could speak, the parlour door flew open and Joel, pushing them both aside, took me by the shoulders, his fingers gripping hard, as if he felt the need to shake the news out of me.

'He's dead, isn't he?' he said, the same words he had used on another occasion, the same excited glitter in his eyes, and when I nodded, although his lips didn't move, I heard his mind say, 'Thank God for that. I thought we'd have the old devil to shoot.'

Mrs Stevens sat down, just that, with no apparent intention of ever getting up again, and although my mother was to pass the night at the Top House, Hannah, considering them both somewhat featherbrained, decided to stay too. But Joel dismissed my offer to remain with them and I soon found myself walking down the stony pathway beside him.

It was a crisp night, the sky twinkling with cold stars, the air coming down from the moor spicy with autumn, and, as I let it wash over me, I was aware of my own aching weariness and a certain silence within me that should have been grief. But there was no silence in Joel and once we were out of earshot – the black bulk of the mill just discernible below us in the night – his hand closed around my arm with the effect of an iron claw.

'Did he say anything about his will? Has he left it to you – as we agreed?'

'Yes – everything.'

And, as he came to an abrupt halt, his tension and his

triumph poured out of him with the effect of a long, shuddering sigh, telling me that until this moment he had not been certain.

'Right,' he said. 'That's it, then. The first thing I do tomorrow is talk to my brother-in-law Aycliffe about building. And as soon as we get the old devil underground I'm away to Lancashire for the best power looms I can find, and a man who can adapt them to suit my purpose.'

But the mention of power looms chilled me, and I whispered, 'Won't there be trouble?'

'Machine breaking? I reckon not. Ira Agbrigg keeps me well informed and there's no Jabez Gott now to stir them up. I doubt they even need reminding what he looked like, swinging in the Castle Yard at York, but if they do Ira Agbrigg can take care of it. There'll be no trouble.'

'Will we move to the Top House?'

'Yes – not that I relish it, with your grandfather's mark all over it – not when I've a mark of my own and the wits and the guts to make it. But the mills and the machines come first, and the Top House will serve until I've cash to spare. And I need the millhouse at Low Cross for Ira Agbrigg, since I've a mind to make him manager there, and he has a wife and a parcel of brats to come with him. So there's Hannah to fit in at the Top House, too.'

Although the prospect of accommodating Hannah made my heart sink, the face of another woman – even more in need of a home – swam into my mind.

'What will happen to Mrs Stevens?'

'Mrs Stevens? What should happen to her?'

'Well, something – surely?'

'Oh, as to that,' he said, shrugging his total indifference to her fate in a manner I found displeasing, 'women of that sort should know what they are about. I believe your grandfather may have left her five hundred pounds, and I daresay she feathered her nest, these past ten years, at his expense. More fool her, if she didn't.'

And, remembering my mother's light voice telling me,

'She is quite accustomed to being discarded, our Mrs Stevens,' I was suddenly very angry. I had disliked her because I had seen her as part of my grandfather, had laughed at her honeyed wooing of every man she met, her cloying, transparent self-seeking, but the reality of her – her no longer being young; knowing that when her beauty finally faded and her five hundred pounds was done, she could well be faced with the stark choice of the brothel, the workhouse, or the street – that reality touched me very deeply. Emmeline Stevens, the woman who no longer mattered to the men who had used her once her usefulness was done – men like my grandfather and Joel, for they were alike, who took women for a variety of purposes, to satisfy a range of appetites, as they would take any other commodity. And her plight convinced me of two things: that no woman could really grow accustomed to being discarded and that it was no particular virtue on my part but merely an accident of birth which prevented me from standing in her shoes. And I made up my mind that when we moved to the Top House I would ask her to stay.

I went home then, feeling the cold, leaving Joel to contemplate his new possessions a while longer, but I was still at my toilet table, brushing the tangles from my hair, when he came into the room, carrying a tray with a bottle and glasses, and a branch of triumphant candles.

'Champagne,' he said, vibrant, victorious, and totally joyful.

'Champagne?'

'Yes – champagne for a funeral. Shocking – but then I'm not always a hypocrite, you see, Verity, and I'm a free man tonight. He was a bad old devil, your grandfather – I know that, you know that – and maybe I'll be the same at his age – so, if you outlive me, you have my permission to celebrate my passing with champagne, and good luck to you – you and my son together. But this is my time now – just starting – and I'll do the celebrating.'

And lifting his glass to the light a moment, he smiled at

it, saluted it almost, and drank greedily, his whole body rich with enjoyment.

'You'll drink with me?'

'Yes.'

'Good. But then I knew you wouldn't refuse. You always give me what I want, when I want it – don't you, Verity? Always so good and polite – except that I'm not a polite man, girl, and tonight I'll need more than that. Tonight your politeness won't be enough.'

'Whatever do you mean?' I said, withdrawing from him.

And, laughing at my obvious perplexity, he refilled his glass and swallowed the wine once again with powerful, full-throated pleasure.

'I'll tell you, Verity. I thought he'd never die, that old man. I thought he'd live to plague me until I was old myself and soured by the burden of him – too old and dry to care. But he's gone and I'm in my prime, and, by God, I like it. I need to revel in it, Verity; I need to burn the pleasure of it out of me tonight, so I can show a decent, sober face tomorrow, when I stand by his coffin. And I need you to revel with me.'

'I don't – I don't know – I don't think––'

'No, you don't know, and you don't think, and maybe you can't – maybe it's not in you. But it's a challenge, if nothing else, and that's always been my style. I like to fight and I like to win, and what I win I value – so let's see, shall we, what we can do with you, to stop you saying, "Yes, Joel," like your mother used to say, "Yes, William," and for the same damn reasons – because it's easier to say yes and get it over with. Come here.'

But my body had turned completely cold, as awkward and tense as on our wedding night, and, stung by his mockery – and perhaps to give myself a little time – I cried out, 'Well – you may talk about challenges, but you didn't put yourself out to win me before we were married. You let my mother do your proposing for you, and you were grateful enough to me for not making a fuss.'

'Ah yes,' he said. 'That hurts, does it? That makes you cross? Good. Your grandfather was the challenge that day, sweetheart, not you. And now it's your turn – now that I've got time to spare. Yes, yes, I was an unfeeling brute. Get angry with me – very angry – lose your temper, Verity.'

'No, I will not.'

'Oh yes you will – just think about my making you take Hannah to live with you, and what she thinks should be done with your dogs.'

'What about my dogs?'

'Didn't I tell you . . .?'

'Joel—'

'Ah well – it's not the moment – but Hannah says it's not right for a lady to have dogs that size. And I have to admit – gun dogs – something odd about gun dogs, I'm bound to agree. So get yourself a pair of spaniels, if you like, and as to the others, perhaps Hannah's right. Perhaps I'll tell you to get rid of them.'

And whether it was true or merely some part of the strange game he was playing, it was an exercise in power – between me and Hannah? between me and Joel? – and I knew I'd have to fight; I knew, incredibly, that I wanted to.

'I won't do that, Joel.'

'Won't you, by God.'

'No, by God.'

And I could not miss the snap of excitement in his eyes, the heat in his fingers as they closed around my wrist and pulled me towards him.

'You'll defy me, then?'

'I'll defy you.'

'And if I take the brutes out now and shoot them? What then? You know I could, and would.'

'I know.'

'And . . . ?'

'Don't, that's all.'

181

'My word,' he said, his eyes flickering over my bare shoulders. 'Defiance, and disobedience. Rebellion, then?'

'If you like.'

'Oh, I do, I do.'

'Leave me be,' I shouted, struggling in his arms, realizing he was hurting me, although I could feel no pain, and suddenly, as his mouth came down on mine, a great, uncomplicated, wholehearted fury welled up inside me, liberating me utterly from the restraints of common sense. Sinking my teeth into his lower lip, I twisted both my hands into his hair and tried hard to get my knee into his groin, to hurt him any way I could, so that, overbalancing, we fell together onto the bed, Joel freeing himself, laughing, catching my wrist and pulling me against him.

'That's it, darling,' he said. 'Come on, stay angry a while longer.'

Howling now with the birth of most uncharacteristic temper, I began to strike out, hitting him anywhere, not hurting him at all, I suppose, since he went on laughing, but needing to strike, welcoming the fierce release of energy that quickened my breath and the glorious loss of dignity.

'Damn you,' I threw at him, seizing a pillow and vainly battering him with it. 'You think you're so marvellous . . .'

'I do,' he said. 'Come, I'll show you.'

Taking hold of the pillow, he tugged it sharply forward and then, as I fell on top of him, turned swiftly over so that I was beneath him, our mouths snapping and biting at each other a moment longer, before my body, of its own accord, acknowledged its need and made no effort to escape when he eased his weight away and, casting his eyes over the entire length of me, put his mouth delicately against my stomach and let it travel upwards, inch by lingering inch, to my own mouth, which, for the first time, and most astonishingly, was waiting.

'It's called pleasure, Verity,' he said, his breath teasing my ear and the base of my throat. 'Why leave it all to me? In your place I'd make damn sure I got my share. When

I touch you like this I'm telling you you're beautiful – it's the best way I know. Since I reckon I'm not ugly, you can tell me that, too, can't you, in the same fashion?'

Pleasure, alien to my nature, yet there it was, in his skin, in the intricacy of his bone and muscle beneath my fingers, in the earth-scent of him, in the flaunting challenge of him. Pleasure in my own skin, too, rising up in breathless expectation from every pore, so that my body expanded in the glow of it, languorously stretching, languorously sighing itself towards him until, quite suddenly, something stirred hesitantly, almost secretly, a tiny thread waking, growing, its tendrils coiling, delicately spreading. And as I intently bent my whole mind on that tiny thread of joy, determined not to lose it, not to frighten it so that it would shrivel away to its birthplace at my body's core, he said, 'Shall I stop now?'

'What . . .?'

'Shall I stop? Let you go to sleep?'

'No! Don't – please, Joel.'

And afterwards, when the threads had joined together into my body's first sensual rejoicing, when I had clung to him and cried aloud with ecstatic amazement, he lay smugly on his back and told me, 'You'll know now what I mean by need. Ah yes, I've got you now, Verity. You'll miss me, girl, next time I'm away. You'll be sending to the Old Swan to see what time my coach gets in, and getting yourself ready. And I'll bring you perfumes, the next time I'm in London – the kind my sister Hannah doesn't approve of – and you'll wear them for me.'

But for all that he had shown me of the nature of need and pleasure, for all he had spoken of challenges and triumphs and the gifts he would bring me, he had made no mention at all of love.

12

We took possession of the Top House as soon as my grandfather had been decently carried out of it, and there, almost exactly nine months later, my second son, Nicholas, was born. My daughter, Caroline, followed fourteen months after that, her birth proving so difficult, so unlike the other two, that Mrs Stevens – who could be relied on to know such things – warned me that, for a while at least, there would probably be no more.

My recovery from that third confinement was slower, too, and I spent the summer of my daughter's birth sitting in the garden of the Top House, as my grandfather used to do, looking down on the recently completed six-storey mill Morgan Aycliffe had built for Joel from a design supplied by his son Crispin, large enough to accommodate upwards of eight hundred power looms, and which had cost £80,000 of my grandfather's money.

'Yon lad's overspending himself,' declared Mr Oldroyd of Fieldhead, who had the reputation of being ready to cut a currant in half.

'I reckon old Samson Barforth would turn in his grave if he knew,' muttered Mr Hobhouse of Nethercoats, who still maintained, with some violence of language, that power looms had no place in the future.

But neither Mr Aycliffe the builder nor Mr Rawnsley the banker appeared to share that view, and within two years of my grandfather's death, Joel's commercial standing in Cullingford was high. And when the new looms began to come in, slowly but very surely replacing the old, there was a grumbling and a growling but little more, for Cullingford was by then in a state of explosion, surging out from its centre to swallow every available stretch of green separating it from the surrounding villages, and then swallowing the villages themselves, so that one could no longer tell where Cullingford ended and Fieldhead, Thornwick, or Lawcroft Fold began.

At the start of the century there had been only two mills of any size in the region of Cullingford, ours and the Hobhouses', but now, less than thirty years later, as other men besides Joel saw the advantages of this new machine age, there were already fifty, with the prospect, it seemed, of fifty more, the monstrous belching of their chimneys fast discolouring the rows of back-to-back cottages with which Morgan and Crispin Aycliffe had covered the fresh grass, had driven away the memory of birdsong.

And the town in which I had grown up, comfortable little Cullingford with its 13,000 souls, was now a sprawling, black-faced, uneasy giant, where some 43,000 people earned – or did not earn – their bread.

In the streets around Joel's other mill, Low Cross – Simon Street and Saint Street, Gower Street – the tall houses designed for the original, quiet inhabitants of a sleepy market town had been reduced to anthills where the Irish – in perpetual flight from famine – crowded five and six and ten to a room; a wild, foreign people, alien in speech and religion, not understood and so mistrusted. And every day saw the arrival of the landless agricultural poor – on foot, most of them, their possessions and their children on their backs – coming North in seach of work.

Although there was work, not all were fit for it, not all would take it, and there was always resentment brewing beneath the grime, always the possibility of another Jabez Gott somewhere in the tenements of Simon Street or those rows and rows of dingy, identical cottages thrown up by the Aycliffes.

It had happened, I suppose, as my father had foreseen: for the hand weavers in general, even when hunger began to bite, would not take work in the factories, and those who did could neither settle nor give satisfaction. Accustomed to working very much as they pleased, to staying up all night Monday and Tuesday to finish the week's work by Wednesday, making Thursday and Friday into a holiday if it suited them, they – like the farm workers, with their habit of following the seasons – could not adapt to the steady flow of work required day in, day out, by a machine. When the sun shone and they had enough cash in hand to meet immediate requirements, many of them quite simply would not appear; others would come in the afternoon when they had finished digging their allotments or tidying their hen runs – and when the millmasters retaliated by keeping wages low to ensure regular attendance and by imposing fines on latecomers, it was not understood. But, as Joel had seen from the start, a woman – a very young woman – had strength enough to operate a power loom, and, although women and children had always worked in the mills, increasingly now men were required only for the skilled work of loom tuning or the heavy work of loading and lifting. And since hand weavers were usually small men with no spectacular endowment of muscle, the hard labour – at Lawcroft and on Mr Aycliff's building sites – was reserved for men of farming stock and the Irish.

'Bloody thieving Barforth bastard' was scrawled one morning on the garden wall of the Top House, but Joel, who drove a smart, high-perch phaeton down to the mill these days, with a glossy grey mare between the shafts, did no more than smile, remarking that perhaps Hannah's Sunday Schools were not such a good idea after all if this was what came of teaching the poor to write.

But Hannah's Sunday School was more than ever her pride and joy, her control of Ramsden Street Chapel as absolute as Joel's control of Lawcroft, and although she was not popular with the entire congregation, as he was not liked by all his operatives, there were few who cared to disobey either of them. Hannah, of course, had not welcomed her move to the Top House – certainly not in the dreadful capacity of spinster sister-in-law, and certainly not with Mrs Stevens remaining as housekeeper – and she had made her feelings immediately clear.

'You are surely not thinking of keeping that woman on,' she had told me the day of my grandfather's funeral, when Mrs Stevens, only an hour earlier, had wept with gratitude in my arms. 'For it would be thought most odd – the whole of Cullingford being aware of the terms on which she stood with your grandfather. I must ask you, Verity, to consider my own position in this, for I really cannot be expected to associate so closely with her.'

But, from necessity, they got along well enough, tolerating each other as they tolerated my dogs and my children, and there could be no doubt that, as a housekeeper, Mrs Stevens had no equal in the Law Valley.

The Top House, enormous for my grandfather alone, was less spacious now, but there was an adequate drawing room and dining room for the entertaining of guests, a back parlour for my day-to-day living, and a small oak-panelled room behind it where Joel could retire with his newspapers and his accounts and the cigars his sister found so offensive. There were my grandfather's lofty bedchamber, new-furnished and new-painted, two cosy rooms for Hannah and Mrs Stevens, and two cosy rooms to spare; the attic floor was pleasantly converted to nurseries, with space for the nursemaid Liza, my old Marth-Ellen, and the girls already in Mrs Stevens's employ. We had the garden, the carriage drive, the stables with rooms above them for the coachman and his lads, and although it was not enough for Joel, it had, at least, the bones of the gracious living he required – a step, no more, in the direction he wished to take.

He had been, to begin with, a hungry fighter, goaded by pride and poverty, ferocious in his energy and his desires, and now, with Lawcroft at his feet, his appetite had not abated. He had his phaeton now, sure enough, to take him down to the mill, but he was there, in the mill yard, every morning at five o'clock as he had always been, to see the engines come on; there, at the mill gates, to see the first of his operatives arrive; there to see the last of them leave, letting them know that if their hours were long, his were longer. He was there in the sheds, too, throughout the day, appearing without warning, unerringly locating the source of trouble or idleness, making it abundantly clear to all of them, from managers and overlookers to weavers, spinners, and even the young 'pieceners' and 'scavengers' who twisted together the broken threads and retrieved the waste, that there was no job at the whole of Lawcroft that he had not done himself at one time or another, no job he was not prepared to do again, if the need arose. And it was well known in the Law Valley that men who had worked for Bradley Hobhouse and even for Matthew Oldroyd, neither of whom were fond of soiling their own hands, had a rough ride when they came to work for Joel.

Yet his wages, to men who understood his requirements, were good and his treatment of those wise enough to know he could be neither fooled nor flattered was fair.

'Don't tell me why you *can't* do it,' he would demand of a loom tuner faced with the apparent wreckage of a machine or a shed manager with an impossible delivery date to meet. 'I can think of a hundred reasons why not. What I want from you are the reasons why.'

And, more often than not, the machine was mended, the goods went out on time, a bonus was paid, the successful man's name entered into the credit side of Joel's memory.

'I don't ask the impossible,' he told them. 'If I can do it, so can you.'

For the ones who could not there was no alternative but to go, cap in hand, to the likes of Hobhouse or Oldroyd.

'You don't suit me' was all Joel ever told them, winning himself no popularity in the town, nor in the Piece Hall either, where other manufacturers grumbled that he had enticed their best men away with money and sent them his dregs.

He had supervised, or so it seemed to me, the laying of

188

every brick during the building of the new mill, accepting no delays, refusing to deviate an inch from his original plan.

'It won't suit me,' he said bluntly to Morgan Aycliffe whenever that wily gentleman suggested some little time-saving alteration. 'It might suit you, since I daresay you'll charge me the same whichever way we do it, but it won't suit me. I ordered what I need, and I reckon that's what I'll have, if you please, Mr Aycliffe.'

Nor did he expect those around him to be idle, and I was quick to learn which tasks he considered appropriate to a wife. He did not require me to be skilled in the making of soap and candles as my grandmother had been, nor, particularly, in the art of fine needlework or the correct arrangement of garden flowers, but he demanded far more than Morgan Aycliffe, who could content himself with a pretty face, and more than Bradley Hobhouse, whose placid Emma-Jane talked of nothing but her children and her squabbles with her mother-in-law. Joel wanted, expected, a wife who could grow with him; who could provide a setting for the things his money could buy; who could cope efficiently, without assistance from him, with the administration of a large household, improving the quality of life's surroundings with a skill and taste as new to Cullingford as the power looms themselves. And so, having Mrs Stevens to do my cooking, Liza to take the donkey work out of minding my children, I set to work on my social graces and my mind until, quite soon, when Morgan Aycliffe spoke of Sèvres and Meissen, I could answer him with Minton and Derby, and when Crispin Aycliffe spoke of Wordsworth and Coleridge, I knew they were poets and not cotton spinners from across the Pennines. And, by reading Joel's newspapers, I knew about the Corn Laws and the vexing question of parliamentary reform.

And I had my own, quite separate pleasures, my long, moorland ramblings through grey-veiled, cool spring mornings, saffron-yellow summers, biting, steel-tinted winters, with a dog sniffing close at either side, a sudden, soot-coloured bird rising up startled in my path, an awareness of small creatures, busily nest-building, life-building in the damp, roughly springing grasses, the interlacing of old trees. And, as those seasons blended and re-blended, first one toddling child, then another, emerging from the cocoon of babyhood to explore the wide, amazing world of the Top House garden.

I was not, it seemed, a woman who could take much joy in pregnancy, unlike my friend Emma-Jane, who had become pregnant on her wedding night, or thereabouts, and who viewed her body's basic biology with great pride, making it the constant subject of her conversation. Pregnancy to me had been a loss of freedom, a small invasion, but motherhood I found to be quite otherwise, and although I did not constantly wish to increase the quantity of my offspring, I was well pleased with those I had.

I had thought babies to be all alike, until the unique miracle that was Blaize. For a while, I pitied other women with their quite ordinary children. Then in the months before Nicholas came, I had worried in case this second child should be no more than a pale copy of the first. And it had taken me a day or so to accustom myself to adoring this new variation of the Barforth face, to understand that I could love them both, differently yet equally.

There was little more than a year between them, with their identical dark Barforth curls, their insistent Barforth voices making their requirements known from the start, and then the wonder of two Barforth natures growing together yet quite separately. Blaize was the winning one, the artful one, his hair fading from black to a deep brown, his eyes the same smoky grey as my mother's. He would always get his way by a sweet, guileful smile, would always bide his time, while Nicholas, the true 'black Barforth,' ebony-curled and amber-skinned, the handsome one, was ever resolute and impetuous.

Blaize from their earliest nursery days would say, 'I don't think I'll do that'; Nicholas, scowlingly, standing his ground, would declare, 'I will not do it.' And far more often than not, it would be Blaize, bowing gracefully with the wind, transferring adult tempers to his belligerent brother, who would obtain the favour, the forgiveness, who would avoid whatever task he had not wished to do, while Nicholas would end in angry, pent-up tears, taking his own punishment furiously, proudly, and even his brother's if I were not there to intervene.

'You can't deceive me, Master Blaize,' I would tell him, my heart bleeding for my younger son, understanding very well the pride that made him hide his weeping face in a corner, that made him pull away from my consoling hands. 'I know what you're up to, Blaize Barforth, getting your own way with Liza, blaming everything on your brother. You'll not get your way so easily with me.'

But Blaize would smile his pointed smile, so like my mother's, his clear grey eyes as innocent as hers, something behind their untroubled surface telling me that for all my scolding it was his unquestioned belief that I loved him best. 'Oh yes,' those eyes told me, 'I know you have to defend him, but he's only Nicholas and I'm Blaize.'

The enormity of his self-esteem, his complete certainty that the world properly belonged between the palms of his brown, Barforth hands, seldom failed to move me to laughter.

And then there was Caroline, my daughter, the female born of my own female body, without whom I would not have been complete. My daughter – beautiful from her moment of entry into the world, with black silk hair and eyes the colour of a midnight sky, an enchantment who, on the battleground of the nursery floor, knew of no reason why she, a girl, should not be the conqueror.

'She's very strong, and very noisy,' the nursemaid Liza told me, with less than wholehearted approval. 'She'll take some quietening down, ma'am, I'm telling you, when the time comes.'

But the time had not yet come when it would be necessary to explain to her that a young lady must be meek, with the appetite of a bird and motionless as a lily, and so when she put her fist into Blaize's mocking eye, stole Nicholas's pudding, and raced them both, shrieking, around the garden, I refused to listen when Liza clicked her tongue, when Hannah said, 'That child, Verity, really she gives me the headache,' refused to wonder when Joel, who rarely noticed his children, announced, 'That one should have been a boy.'

We no longer took our dinner in the middle of the afternoon. We had luncheon now, at midday, which, by pushing our dinner hour into the realm of moonlight and candlelight, enabled us more easily to entertain and wear our evening clothes, as the landed gentry had ever done. And if Mrs Hobhouse and Mrs Oldroyd, who believed the gentry had no morals, did not quite like it, family pressures soon obliged them to follow suit. While Mrs Aycliffe – my cousin Elinor – liked it very well, and although her husband did not permit her to give large parties, fearing possible damage to his porcelain, she could be counted on to sparkle at any gathering of mine.

I gave a dinner one warm evening for no better reason than to show off the new pale blue watered silk on the drawing-room walls, and the new pale blue chairs to match, which toned well, I thought, with the deep red velvet sofas we had purchased the year before. And, as usual, Elinor was the first to arrive, coming early – before her husband – to chat and chirrup and arrange herself advantageously in the light, so that the next person who entered my drawing-room door would see her perfect pose and might lose the desire to look at anything else.

Strawberries and champagne, perhaps, were no longer served for breakfast in Blenheim Lane, the honeymoon and the first intensity of her husband's enraptured gazing being long over, but the glow of his possessions still warmed her and the pleasure of curling up, kittenlike, with her vast saucer of Aycliffe cream still appeared to suffice. And even the arrival, one after the other, of two little girls and a series of miscarriages to follow had barely disturbed her blissful dream.

The children, who could clearly never be admitted to the hushed Aycliffe drawing room, had been from birth so absolutely confined to the nursery, to the back stairs, to a world apart, that Elinor, when they were brought down to her for ten minutes at teatime, treated them carefully, with a faint air of surprise. Children, certainly. But her children? Incredible. And it was always with relief that she gave them back to Nurse.

But tonight she was clearly agitated, and since painful emotion in Elinor was usually associated with her stepson, I settled myself to listen, and was not sure I would be able to sympathize.

Crispin Aycliffe had indeed spent some time in France but had soon been called home again. His designs had been required for Joel's new mill at Lawcroft, for an extension the Oldroyds were building at Fieldhead, for those rows of uncouth cottages, and although he went away again whenever he could, his father – especially now that the other children were beginning to arrive – had no intention of dispensing with his services. Morgan Aycliffe, perhaps, had never looked too closely at his infant daughters – had certainly never wanted them – but they were a responsibility and a burdensome one at his age. They had to be provided for, as Elinor had to be provided for, and having lost his own inclination for the building trade – preferring to pass his days in financial manipulations of a more subtle nature and his evenings gazing at his porcelain and his wife – he began to rely more and more heavily on his son. Crispin was needed at home, and at home he must stay. But he remained unwillingly, fretfully, and in everything but his professional capacity as an architect he was a most unsatisfactory son. Or so Elinor had told me, and so she was about to tell me again.

'I am come early on purpose to say they will be late,' she said. 'And if they come at all I shall be astonished, for they have had such a set-to. He has not slept at home for three nights, so where he has been sleeping you may well imagine, and you know my husband cannot abide such a thing. And when he came in this evening – looking exactly as one would suppose – he laughed and said he would gladly go away again if his appearance gave offence, and that it would suit him well enough to take rooms somewhere and spare us the sight of him altogether. Well, and I wish he would, but my husband will not hear of it – he thinks people would talk and say it was because of me. A young man's place is at home, he says, until his wedding day – which means I shall be burdened with him forever, for he will not look at the girls my husband proposes, and the girls he does look at – well – you will know what I mean. And he will not leave without his father's consent, because of the money. So – there they are, having their set-to in Blenheim Lane, and your dinner spoiling. And what about Hannah? If Crispin does not come we shall be odd numbers at table, and Hannah will very likely refuse to dine.'

But the sound of new arrivals wiped all thoughts of Hannah, and of both Aycliffes, from Elinor's mind and she was altogether composed, dimpling with delight, as the Hobhouses were shown in, the more so when she realized that Bradley's wife, her old rival Emma-Jane Rawnsley the banker's daughter, was dressed, like herself, in yellow.

'Oh, look, Emma-Jane,' she said wickedly, 'look how alike we are.'

Patting her own gauzy, primrose skirts into artful disarray, she went skipping across to Emma-Jane's side so that all of us – especially Emma-Jane's husband – could see that if Elinor were a primrose, Emma-Jane could only be a full-blown, well-fleshed dandelion. But if he still retained a taste for primroses – as he may well have done – he was a Law Valley man, with his priorities in good order, and before he had finished shaking hands with Joel, I knew his acquisitive eyes had tracked down every new item the room contained, and calculated its worth.

Not that Bradley was himself short of money, his father's recent death having made him the master of Nethercoats and the several hundred handlooms it contained. And if Joel had been an easier man, Bradley – notoriously easy himself – would have been ready enough for friendship and praise; he might even have taken his advice about the power looms he was now anxious to buy. But Joel was not easy, and I suppose Bradley knew, as my next guest, young Matthew Oldroyd of Fieldhead, knew, that he had little respect for men like themselves – and my brother Edwin – who had never had to struggle.

And as they stood one on either side of him on the hearthrug, downing their sherry and ready for their dinner, talking yardage and how much one could expect to get for it, I sat with Emma-Jane and Elinor, and Lucy Oldroyd, who had once been a Hobhouse, and waited nervously for the Aycliffes.

Hannah came into the room, in her favourite brown silk, looking very aloof and very handsome, and received a nod and a faint smile from Emma-Jane and Lucy, a good enough greeting for a spinster lady of no particular fortune and autocratic temper.

'Is your husband not well?' she asked Elinor, rather as if she were about to add, 'And is it any wonder?' But just then, as I was about to slip away and warn Mrs Stevens that we might be less than ten at table, we heard the doorbell again and the Aycliffes, father and son, were among us.

'Oh, there you are,' Elinor said, obviously startled. 'And not a minute too soon.'

But, ignoring her, they took my hand in turn, the father first and then the son; their lips spoke courteous words without meaning, their mouths smiled, and no one would notice – except Elinor and me – that throughout the entire evening, and tomorrow evening, and very likely the one after, they would not address a single word to each other.

'Oh dear,' she whispered, pressing her hands together. 'I can see it was very bad. They have been talking about her – his mother – and my husband will not forgive him for days and days. Oh dear – the dreadful boy, if only he would get married and go away. There must be someone, Verity – someone respectable – that he could take a fancy to. And if not, then I hope he runs off with a married woman and disgraces himself entirely, so that I may be rid of him.'

We had dinner then, Mrs Stevens's favourite soup rich with its liaison of eggs and cream, turbot and ducklings and spicy fruit tarts, wine from my grandfather's cellar, by no means exhausted yet; and the table decorated with garlands of rosebuds at every corner, with a vast arrangement of ferns and fruit and flowers in the centre.

'My word, this is very nice,' Morgan Aycliffe said accusingly, raising his glass to the light, admiring the crystal as much as the golden, altogether impeccable liquid it contained. 'Very nice indeed, Barforth – mighty well done.'

For the first time that evening Joel glanced at me, from the other end of the table, seeing the woman I had created to fit his requirements, the sensible, quiet little cousin grown up to be a sensible, self-possessed wife, wearing his diamonds in my ears, his silk on my back, a woman other men would look at – as he had told me on our wedding night – and say, 'By God, he must be doing well to afford a woman like that.'

As I took the ladies back to the drawing room after dinner, leaving the gentlemen alone, I wondered as I passed Crispin's chair how he would amuse himself: if he would merely drink his port and stare at the wall or if, quite casually, he would toss some hot, controversial stone into their pool of conversation, making the sluggish, after-dinner waters sizzle. Catching my thought, he looked up and smiled, his eyebrows making their fine arch, and, as clearly as if it were happening inside me, I knew that his head ached, that those three nights of low company had soured his stomach and his spirits, that if there had been pleasure he could no longer remember it.

'Verity?' Hannah enquired from the doorway, puzzled, thinking I had found something amiss with the table.

Shaking my head, I hurried away.

'I hope they will not be too long,' Emma-Jane said, taking up the whole of a red velvet sofa with her wide skirts, not really caring how long they were since men were of little interest to her now that she had one of her own. But Elinor, who cared a great deal, sighed and shook her head.

'Then you will be disappointed, for I expect they will be hours – discussing their dirty politics – how long it is going to take the poor old King to die and when he does will the new one agree to extend the franchise – and if he does, who is to get the vote and who is not. And for my part I'm weary of it – absolutely – so that I don't care if they give the vote to the sheep and pigs, or shoot the Duke of Wellington, as Mr Aycliffe seems to think they should, or ask the Pope to come and sit in the House of Commons.'

'Lords,' I said, well used to Elinor's vagaries. 'I expect he'd feel easier in the Lords.'

But Hannah, always ill-tempered at dinner parties, especially when the gentleman invited to partner her was the neglectful, moody Crispin Aycliffe, said tartly, 'The franchise is of great importance, Elinor. Think a little before you speak, and then perhaps you'll understand that Cullingford – with upwards of 40,000 people – must have its own Member of Parliament. It is really quite vital.'

'Oh, stuff,' Elinor told her. 'And if we get him, he'll end up in Sir Giles Flood's pocket – or in my brother Joel's – and even if he doesn't, what exactly can he do for me? Will he build us a suite of assembly rooms like they have in

Bradford and Leeds, so we can give real balls occasionally instead of having to make do with the market buildings and all those foul smells from the shops underneath? Oh no, he'll just try to get the Corn Laws done away with, if he's Joel's man, so they can bring the price of bread down and Joel can pay lower wages. And if he's Sir Giles Flood's man he'll try to keep the Corn Laws in so the farmers can charge what they like. And, whatever they do, I don't care, because I'm in the family way again and I don't expect to survive it.'

'Oh, darling,' I said, laughing, 'how nice – and you'll survive.'

But this news, which should have been of interest to both Lucy and Emma-Jane, met with a sudden, stiff silence, a blank staring into space that was caused by the presence of Hannah, a single woman, before whom it was improper to speak of anything remotely connected with the marriage bed. And their quite spiteful determination that Hannah – who was far more intelligent than either one of them – must be excluded from any kind of adult conversation, must be kept totally in the dark, was somewhat amusing but considerably unkind.

Yet there was nothing very much wrong with either Emma-Jane Hobhouse or Lucy Oldroyd. They were neither malicious nor angelic, neither brilliant nor stupid, just ordinary women who enjoyed the good things of life and wanted more of them but were not uncharitable, Emma-Jane being mainly concerned with her pregnancies, Lucy with her apparent inability to become pregnant at all. They were, I supposed, happy, yet, thinking of Bradley Hobhouse and the penny-pinching Matthew Oldroyd, I could not imagine why. Clearly then, marriage to them was not about personalities but about position, security; nor was it about surprises, since neither Lucy nor Emma-Jane would ever wish to be surprised. It was enough for them that the days should follow one after the other, comfortable, cushioned, peppered with identical joys and sorrows, their calm broken by nothing more serious than a tiff with their mother-in-law or a chipped plate; enough that nothing should be asked of them that they did not immediately understand; enough for them to say, 'I am Mrs Bradley Hobhouse or Mrs Matthew Oldroyd. And this is my house, my son, my new blue chairs.'

I am Mrs Joel Barforth, I thought, with no identity apart from his. Mrs Joel Barforth. Not Verity any longer, but a serene, cool-eyed woman – Mrs Joel Barforth – who could discuss porcelain and poetry and politics, who knew the names of dozens of French sauces and how they should be served and which wines should accompany them, who understood pleasure and need, now that her body had matured – and was sophisticated enough, even, to understand that sometimes her husband took his pleasures elsewhere. And since I had accepted the limits of our relationship, there was no reason – surely? – why I should not be happy, too.

'It is because of my condition they are so cross,' Elinor whispered to me, and, seeing my blank expression as I emerged from my reverie, she hastened to make herself clear. 'My husband hates me to be pregnant, you know that. The alteration to my shape offends his eye, and he finds it indelicate in other ways. He will not come near me for months before, and months after, for which I am not at all sorry, although it makes him very nervous and prickly as a porcupine. And then, people tease, you see, and congratulate him as if it was a miracle at his age – which only serves to remind him that I am young and he is not, for which I am not at all to blame. And Crispin, of course, is thinking of himself, for if I should have a boy his own position is threatened. My poor Prudence and Faith can cost him no more than a dowry apiece, but a little brother would put his long nose out of joint. And so you see, there I am, between the two of them. And when my husband dies I have no idea what will become of me, for that odious Crispin will turn me out with nothing but my petticoats if he can find the way. Oh dear, how hard it is. I think I am going to cry.'

But, as her lower lip began to tremble, the double doors opened, bringing the gentlemen back to us again, and instead of weeping, she gave them all a brilliant, welcoming smile.

'I expect you will have noticed,' she murmured to me a while later, 'that Bradley Hobhouse has not spoken a word to me all evening, which, in Emma-Jane's place, I would find most suspicious, considering the way he has been looking – and looking – oh my. I can only hope my husband is still too furious with his son to notice, or I shall have to answer for it. And it is not my fault, after all.'

But, blessedly – for I was tired now of false smiles, false conversations – it was almost over, and quite soon Mr Aycliffe had Elinor in her cloak, allowing her just a moment to display the swansdown lining before he bade her, quite sourly, to stir herself since tomorrow would be a busy day.

'Aye, busy enough,' Bradley Hobhouse yawned, stretching his luxurious, weighty frame, with no intention, I thought, of making that grim five o'clock trek to the mill yard now that his father could be none the wiser. But Matthew Oldroyd, whose father was still hale and hearty enough to kick him out of bed if need be, made a sign to his Lucy that she understood, and all three carriages were brought round to the door.

'Goodbye, and thank you, Mrs Barforth,' Crispin Aycliffe said as I accompanied them into the hall, his hand very cool – a boy's hand almost, narrow and lightly boned; a scholar's hand, perhaps, although I knew nothing of scholars.

'Goodbye, Mr Aycliffe. I think your father is already in his carriage – waiting.'

'Oh, then he should wait no longer, for I believe I may walk.'

'Oh – do you think so?'

'Yes,' he said, smiling, understanding my concern and not offended by it, enjoying it even. 'I think so.'

And taking his hat, he went outside, still smiling, and walked, quite slowly, past the Aycliffe carriage.

'Good night, sir,' he called out, tipping his hat at a jaunty angle, making no reply when, from the dark interior his father hissed rather than spoke the one word 'Crispin,' making the name itself into a threat, a dire warning. 'You try me too far, boy,' that furious whisper said, and the insolent tilt of Crispin's hat replied, 'Not far enough, sir – not yet.'

Hannah went quietly to bed and, when we were alone together, Joel said, 'Well – envy. I like it. They'd be content with what I have, here and now, Bradley and Matthew. They'll call it success if they can hold on to what their fathers leave them. And so I make them uneasy when they see I'm not satisfied. They get to wondering where they'd be without Nethercoats and Fieldhead behind them, and the answer is right back on the muckheap. I feel good tonight, Verity—'

And, sensing his mood of jubilation, of revelry, I expected his arms around me and waited, half smiling, ready to match his excitement with a quiet one of my own; needing, I think, to be repossessed, to have my own troublesome identity burned away, blended once more with his. But, instead of touching me, he crossed to the window, looked out, and paced a few quick steps across the floor, his fiercely crackling energy a discomfort on the air, his need for revelry apparent, but not, it seemed, with me.

'I'll – er – go out for an hour,' he said. 'It strikes me I'd best drive over to Low Cross and see what the night shift are doing. There's a piece I'm waiting to have a look at, and I reckon it should be off the loom by now.'

And because he had taken the trouble to explain himself instead of simply telling me, 'I'm off,' and going, I knew he was lying.

'I'll go up to bed, then,' I said.

Nodding agreement, he reached out a casual, cousinly hand – yet again – and pinched my chin. 'Yes, love, go to bed. It's a long way to Low Cross in the dark – there and back again.'

'So I may expect you when I see you?'

'I reckon so.'

'Yes – good night, then.'

'Good night, Verity.'

And when they brought his phaeton to the door, I refused to lift a corner of the heavy velvet curtains or the shrouding, confining lace to see in which direction he drove away. I refused to listen to hoofbeat or heartbeat, or anything but the calm shell of myself which assured me that – like my mother and my grandmother before me – I understood, I accepted, I was not threatened. 'If it happens,' my mother had said, 'it will mean very little to him.' And I had no intention of asking myself – not tonight, not ever – what it meant to me.

13

That same year – my twenty-second – saw the death of the King, our fourth Hanoverian George, an event not much regretted except, perhaps, by his Prime Minister, the Duke of Wellington, who was left with the hushing up of a royal scandal or two and the certainty of a general election.

He had been a man of appetite, King George, accustomed to breakfasting on pigeon pie and champagne, with brandy, hock, and laudanum to follow; and a great lover of other men's wives, although he had locked his own out of the Abbey on his coronation day. His only child, Princess Charlotte, having died in childbed, he was to be succeeded by his brother, the Duke of Clarence, a fussy, well-meaning old gentleman who, it was thought, in his eagerness to please might listen not only to the Duke of Wellington but to the clamorous voice of Reform.

And Reform, of course, was the only answer, for although some of us were very rich that year and some of us very poor, we all had our grievances. We were not content.

In the countryside, men turned into landless labourers by the enclosure of common pasture and driven to despair by a series of harsh winters had taken to burning hayricks and breaking the threshing machines that were rendering their muscles obsolete. In Ireland, there was unrest: a growing Catholic demand for freedom from Protestant England, trouble in the streets, and the Lord Lieutenant – the Duke of Wellington's brother – attacked in his box at the theatre. Here in the newly industrial North, the hand weavers were tightening their belts, withdrawing into the bitter, resentful brooding of men who want to work and cannot, supported in many cases entirely by what their wives and children could earn in the mills. And since the millmasters, in their determination to keep their sheds full all day, every day, adhered to their policy of low wages, those earnings were rarely sufficient.

In France, there was revolution again, a bloodless, businesslike affair this time, exchanging one king for another, not to suit the convenience of a haughty aristocracy or the demands of a radical people but due entirely, we were led to believe, to the calculations of cool-eyed men of business. And whenever there was revolution in France its unsettling effects were felt here, too, not only among the London mob and the northern political unions – notoriously easy to unsettle in any case – but among businessmen of our own, who, now that the accumulation of money was less difficult, less of a challenge than it had been, were beginning to appreciate the attractions of a new challenge – political power.

In that troubled year of 1830, there was no one, it seemed, who wished matters to continue just as they were – no one, that is, except the Duke of Wellington and his following of country squires, our own Squire Dalby among them – for even the aristocratic Whigs, that party of impeccably born grandees, were ready for change, if it could help them to oust the Iron Duke from power.

Reform, then, of Parliament, was the only answer, for, in a country where a mere fraction of the population had the right to vote, no effective change could otherwise be brought about. Parliament existed, we had been told, to serve the interests of property, not of individual people, but the trouble was that since the original boroughs had been created, 'property' had shifted somewhat – had moved North, for the most part – so that towns which had once been flourishing were now almost deserted, while others had transformed themselves from hamlets at a river crossing to thriving centres of human endeavour. And although these dwindling old boroughs had lost their importance and their population, they still retained the right to send a representative to Parliament – ready to support the agricultural interest – while the new industrial towns were not represented at all.

The county of Yorkshire as a whole, the largest in England, sent only two members to Westminster. The ancient city of York had a member of its own, and the city of Hull, along with a dozen other antique boroughs, many of them remote country places by now and in the pocket of some great landlord who would bestow them on promising young men of his own choosing who would be guaranteed to handle matters his way. But Leeds, Bradford, Sheffield, Wakefield, Halifax, Huddersfield, Cullingford were not enfranchised; they had no one in Westminster to speak for them, and now that trade was expanding, now that Yorkshire cloth was becoming a new wonder of the world and Yorkshiremen were anxious to secure that world very much as their oyster, the matter was growing urgent.

The issue of Reform became so sensitive, so vital, that in November of that year, the Duke of Wellington's government was defeated, three months after an election victory, an event for which the great Duke was himself entirely to blame, having risen to his feet and informed the nation that the extension of the franchise was so abhorrent to him that he would not countenance it at any price.

Not only would he refuse to bring forward any such measures himself, he told a shocked House, but he would consider it his duty to oppose them when proposed by others. In the Duke's opinion our electoral system was perfect, the distribution of votes just as it should be, since he and all his friends had one and, apart from the soldiers in his army, he had probably never met anyone who did not. But, as with many old men, however distinguished, the ducal eyes were focussed on the past, and his apparent conviction that votes should be reserved for gentlemen was his undoing. A fortnight later his resignation was in the hands of our new, uncertain King William, who was perhaps not too sure about Reform himself, while the manufacturers of the Law Valley – who were very sure – began meeting quietly to discuss what a Member of Parliament of their own would be worth to them, and how best to use him.

'Sir Giles Flood will be sure to have his man ready,' Morgan Aycliffe lectured us one evening when we had gone to dine with him and Elinor, who was looking unwell. 'Yes, Sir Giles still thinks of Cullingford as an extension of his own stable yard, and as soon as the Reform Bill goes through he'll have his man ready – his son-in-law, or one of the Dalbys, or some bright spark from London who won't even trouble to make a speech at the hustings. So we must prepare, Barforth; we must make absolutely certain that the first member for Cullingford will speak for us – will be one of us . . .'

And seeing the scornful tilt of Crispin Aycliffe's smile and the not altogether kindly amusement in Joel, I understood that Mr Aycliffe was ready now – with a son who could be trusted with the mundane details of the building trade, if not its profits – to pass on to higher things. He was not only willing to stand for election himself, he most ardently desired it; he longed, in fact, for the pomp and circumstance of it and would be mortally offended should his candidature be set aside, and yet, unprepared to expose his emotions, he wanted not merely to be invited but to be coaxed, wooed even, and was relying on Joel to do him this service.

But Joel, in matters of emotion – as I could have told him – was not to be relied on, and, taking a lazy sip of wine, his nostrils quivering with what may have been appreciation of its bouquet but was more likely suppressed mirth, he answered, 'Aye, he'd best be one of us, but I don't know who'd care to tackle it. I certainly wouldn't, so anyone who is thinking of asking me would do well to think again. Not much in Bradley Hobhouse's line either, although I daresay Emma-Jane may fancy a trip or two to London.'

And here, Elinor, whose pregnancy was not going just as it should and who had not really been listening, caught the words 'trip to London' and said eagerly, 'I can't think why you don't go yourself, Mr Aycliffe, for it would suit you – and it would suit me. Yes, Morgan, you must be our first member. I've absolutely set my mind on it, and you've talked of it so much that I can tell you want to – don't you?'

And as her voice thinned to astonishment and faded away, perhaps only Morgan Aycliffe's son was not surprised at the effect of her indiscretion. I had seen Mr Aycliffe's disapproval before, had seen him pinch his face and set his entire body into rigid lines of outraged dignity, but I had not seen his temper, which, suppressed like all his other feelings, was a twisted, fearsome thing when it broke free.

'Mrs Aycliffe,' he said in no more than a whisper, 'do not, if you please, address me by my first name in public.'

That was all he said, but that whisper chilled me, speaking as it somehow did of punishment – not by violence but by a long, cold, suffocating silence in the days to follow when he would not address a single word to her.

'Oh dear,' she muttered. 'If I've said something amiss, then I really don't know—'

'You've said no more than we were all thinking,' Crispin Aycliffe cut in swiftly, getting up from the chair where he had been lounging, apparently half asleep, and coming to stand face to face with his father. 'Naturally you must sit for Cullingford, sir – if the Bill goes through. That's my opinion, and I feel sure Mr Barforth will endorse it.'

And as he raised his glass, with his eyes, very cool, very steady, on his father, Joel got up, too, glass in hand, and said, 'We'll drink to it, then. You can have my vote, Aycliffe – if the Bill goes through.'

'Oh, don't worry about the Bill,' Crispin told him, his eyes still holding his father's. 'There'll be a Bill all right. The country wants reform, and so our leaders – because they want to stay our leaders – will give it to us. But what kind of reform it will be I couldn't say. Just enough, I imagine, to satisfy those with the power to make a fuss – should they not be satisfied. You'll get your member for Cullingford, you can be sure of it, but they'll fix the property qualification so high that not more than a thousand of you, out of the 43,000 in this town, will have the right to elect him.'

'And what,' Morgan Aycliffe said, speaking again in that chill whisper, 'is amiss with that?'

'Nothing, sir, if you happen to be among the thousand.'

'As I will be – as *you* will be.'

'Quite so.'

And all the time their eyes were locked together, the ferocity of whatever was between them drinking up the air so that I could hardly breathe.

'You must excuse my son,' Morgan Aycliffe said, his thin lips sketching themselves in a completely mirthless smile. 'It is well known that young men who travel abroad, at their father's expense, often pick up disease, and my son has succumbed to the germ of revolution. He subscribes to the dangerous, the comic notion that every man should have the vote, without property qualification – without any qualification at all. Yes, you will be shocked, Barforth, for so was I when I first became aware of it, and I only mention it now since your wife – and certainly my wife – can hardly comprehend the extent of his folly, the implications and the threat to their own persons. Yes, he sympathizes with the penniless, you see, since he is penniless himself, more often than not, by the fifteenth of every month. You should beware of him, Barforth. He would give the vote to the operatives in your factories, and I cannot think you would take kindly to that.'

But Joel, whose only creed was to buy in the cheapest market and sell in the dearest, had small interest in political speculations of so wild a nature and no interest at all in Aycliffe's tantrums with his son. When he opened his mouth to reply, I think that he almost yawned.

'Well, as to that, he may do so any time he has a mind, for, if they got the vote, they'd have sense to know they'd have to use it my way. So, since I can count my operatives just as surely as Squire Dalby and Sir Giles Flood can count their tenant farmers, you'd be putting upwards of a thousand votes in my pocket, thank you very kindly.'

'And if they voted against you they'd lose their jobs, just as Dalby's tenants would lose their smallholdings?'

'Well, I reckon that's what they'd expect, and I reckon they'd not be disappointed.'

'And the fact that there would be a certain similarity of conduct between yourself and the squire, to whom you are politically opposed, does not concern you?'

'Concern me?' Joel smiled, automatically reaching out for the cigar he could not smoke here, in the Aycliffe drawing room, although it was permitted in mine. And he seemed so large, suddenly, so dark, and Crispin so light, so easily broken, that my mind urgently whispered, 'Don't hurt him.'

'If you mean,' Joel went on, 'that we both know how to take care of our best interests, me and the squire, then I don't see anything to concern me in that. I don't blame Dalby or Flood or the Duke of Wellington himself for keeping a hold on their privileges – because nobody will take mine away from me, you can rest easy on that score.'

'Yes, I feel sure I might. And yet you would deal harshly with the privileges of others, if they happened not to accord with your own?'

'Wouldn't you?' Joel asked him, easily, tolerantly, more inclined for amusement than anger. 'Surely – if it came to it – wouldn't anybody? Take the Corn Law, for instance. The Duke of Wellington and his associates, the Dalbys and the Floods and the rest of them, are farmers – corn growers – and who am I to blame them for wanting to keep the foreign corn out and their own profits high? I'd do the same if I stood in their shoes. But from where I stand, I want the foreign corn in, so that my operatives can afford to eat without pestering me for higher wages. So I have to support Lord Grey. He's likely to give me what I want not because he cares about my wages bill but because he wants the Duke of Wellington's job. That's what it comes down to – not so much conviction as common sense. They may cut each other's throats at Westminster any day they please, but what I do believe in – most sincerely – is that I shall take good care they don't cut mine.'

'Ah yes,' Crispin said, smiling too. 'I think we may all rest assured as to the continued good health of your throat. And I admire your honesty, at least, Mr Barforth. You don't pretend to hold any deep political conviction, or any kind of conviction at all – as some do.'

But this was too much for Morgan Aycliffe, who, suspecting his own convictions – or supposed lack of them – to be under attack, suddenly inserted himself into the conversation like a knife blade, too angry now for good manners, driven most painfully against his will to break his lifelong commandment that Aycliffe linen, dirty or otherwise, should only be washed in the strictest privacy.

'There will be no universal suffrage,' he hissed, as if it were an entirely personal matter, a misdemeanour of Crispin's he was determined to put a stop to. 'It is an indecency – a madman's dream.'

And the locking of eyes, the clash of wills began again.

'I believe you are wrong, sir.'

'I believe I am right.'

'That is your privilege.'

'What right has a man to say how a country should be governed unless he has property in it?'

'Because he is a man, sir. And because government should be concerned with people, not exclusively with possessions. Because we are Christians, sir, or profess to be, and have learned about brotherhood.'

'Easy to say, my lad, when you possess nothing and never show yourself in chapel.'

'As you say, sir.'

And as Crispin walked across to the decanter to refill his glass, Morgan Aycliffe threw at him, in that hideous whisper, 'And you drink, boy – you drink.'

'Yes, sir,' Crispin said coolly. 'So I do.' And raising his glass to his outraged parent, he saluted him, smiled, and drank it down.

'I am not well,' Elinor said, scrambling to her feet. 'Mr Aycliffe, I am not at all – as I should be. Oh dear, oh dear – Verity, will you come upstairs with me? I am not well.'

Although her interruption was timely and she did indeed appear very much out of sorts, her husband did no more than give her his permission to withdraw, showing no disposition at all to comfort her.

I did not expect to see Crispin Aycliffe again so very soon, for it was not his habit to pay polite calls or take tea with ladies, but the following afternoon brought him to my drawing room, a rueful smile on his lips and his air that of a naughty schoolboy who can usually wheedle his way back into anyone's good graces.

'I am come to make my apologies, Mrs Barforth.'

'I wish you would not. There is no need.'

'I think there must be. Can you deny that I behaved badly?'

'Oh – quite badly – very badly, if you like. But if you had good reasons – if it helped – then it doesn't matter.'

And when he began to say something, hesitated, and then seemed unwilling to continue, I said quickly, 'I was not offended. I am not going to pretend otherwise. And that is the end of it. May I give you some tea?'

'No – no, thank you – no tea. But if I may sit with you a while – for the polite interval . . .?'

And already I knew that if he never took another step towards me but remained on the edge of the blue satin chair, a yard away, he was still too close.

'Is my cousin Elinor quite recovered?'

'I have not seen her today. She must have remained upstairs.'

But we were not talking about Elinor at all; we were simply talking, using words because only true friends – true lovers – can really be silent together, and we could be neither. Yet words do not always obey the tongue. It was certainly unwise of me, instead of making some remark about the inclement weather, to ask him, 'Do you truly dislike your father?'

And it was unfair of him, perhaps, to lean forward so eagerly and give me an honest answer. 'In my better moments I do. It's far easier, you see, to dislike him – as he dislikes me – than to feel sorry for him.'

'Will you tell me why?'

'I would tell you anything, Mrs Barforth. My father dislikes me for many reasons, some of them very simple. Because I am young and he is not. Because my uncle – my mother's brother – has recently made me a small allowance – not a great deal but enough to permit me to be mildly disobedient. Because I am sinful, as he calls it, and not ashamed by it, while he is not sinful at all – since it is not sin in marriage, surely? – and is frequently alarmed by his own desires. Those are the simple reasons, but mainly, I suppose, it is because I remind him of my mother.'

'And she was – she was unhappy, I suppose?'

'Oh yes, quite dreadfully. I think the very foundation of my childhood was her unhappiness, for I was always aware of it. I used to hurry home from school when I was quite a little boy, convinced that something terrible had happened to her – and often enough I would find her weeping or could see that she had heard me coming and had tried to calm herself. I felt quite unable to stay away from the house for too long, in case she needed me – in case she was in danger . . .'

'And was she in danger?'

'Physical danger? No, of course not. My father is not a violent man – not with women and fine china, at any rate – and he would never have lifted a finger against her in anger. It was his disapproval she feared, and unfortunately she could do nothing right for him. In his opinion she was a most unsatisfactory woman – as I am a most unsatisfactory son – and eventually she began to believe him. She lost faith in herself, since he had none in her, and when that happened, she began to fade.'

'But what did she do to displease him?'

'Oh, a hundred little things that his eyes magnified out of all proportion – the incorrect arrangement of his vases, a glove left on a chair, a careless word, so that eventually she would hardly open her mouth in his presence. She was, I think, naturally high-spirited, even a little scatter-brained, rather like your cousin Elinor, except that she lacked Elinor's resilience, Elinor's tough Barforth fibre. She was warmhearted and sensitive and perhaps not too brave. Her spirit bruised easily, you see, and my father found her unhappiness insulting. He could not admit that it stemmed from him. There had to be another reason, and so he decided she was not well, an invalid prone to odd fancies. He isolated her from old friends and from the possibility of making new ones; he isolated her most luxuriously, but it was a prison just the same – and so, in a way, he suffocated her. He gave her everything he believed she ought to have, except light and air, and so she withered. And he was angry with her, so angry that she withered even more. He was angry the day she died, and so was I. I still am. There's no more to it than that, except that I, too, find it hard to breathe in his atmosphere.'

'And what will you do? Will you go away again?'

'Oh, I hardly think so,' he said with a forced nonchalance, his familiar, sardonically arched brow. 'How could I possibly be spared now that my father is acquiring a taste for the political life, which has never been cheap. He will need me to keep a sharp eye on his interests – and even on his wife – while he is away at Westminster. No, no, my father needs me, and I am very good, you know, at my profession. I believe I know how to squeeze together more human souls per acre than any other man in the Law Valley, which may not have been the purpose of my architectural studies abroad but is certainly most financially rewarding. My cottages may fall down in a year or two, I admit, and I have never pretended, even to the poor devils who have to live in them, that I could not do better. But they are cheap, you see – unsanitary, ugly, but cheap. And our profit margin is very high.'

'I'm sorry.'

'Why? Because I'm ashamed of my work? Yes, I am ashamed of it – it's the same feeling my father has, I suppose, every time he feels the urge to get into bed with his wife, which is perhaps one of the reasons I pity him.'

'Mr Aycliffe, I don't think you should—'

'No, of course I should not speak to you like that – not to a lady – a lovely lady – but you understand me, Mrs Barforth. Don't you?'

And because I did, because I could feel my heart

pounding, the air entering and leaving my lungs, because I could hear the stirrings of that uncomfortable identity inside me which claimed the right to hope and feel – to comfort this man if I wanted to comfort him, to say, 'Yes, I understand. Go on. Share your pain with me. Let it create a bond between us. And then, when it doesn't hurt any longer, who knows?' – because of that, I knew it was time to send him away. All my choices had been made for me, long ago, by others. I had no rights, no personal hopes. I was the wife of my husband, the mother of my children; I could have no identity beyond that, and I must tell him so.

But, after all, it seemed he did not need to be reminded, for he got up, clearly preparing to take his leave, and I got up, too, nervously extending a hand.

'Once again you will have to forgive me,' he said. 'Perhaps I am too sensitive to climate – I see a great deal of misery around me, in those fine new slums I have created, and I tend to absorb too much of it. Mrs Barforth, did you know that my father once spoke to yours, or perhaps to your grandfather, about a marriage settlement between you and me?'

'Yes – yes, I knew—'

'And that I – because it was my father who had proposed it – turned sulky and would not agree to meet you . . . No, you couldn't know that, nor how bitterly I regret—'

'Mr Aycliffe.'

'Yes, Mrs Barforth.'

I could not, for a moment, remember the words which meant 'I think you had better go' and, remembering, found my tongue heavy and awkward when I forced it to speak.

'Yes,' he said, 'I think you are right. I will leave at once – naturally—'

And when he had gone I sat down, folded my hands, closed my eyes, and sought for silence with immense determination.

14

I did not wish to see Crispin Aycliffe again, of that I was very certain, but to avoid him would not only have appeared odd, it would have meant avoiding Elinor, too. And since her pregnancy was not going as it should, I continued to call at Blenheim Lane and so continued to meet him there, and elsewhere, and to show him the neutral civility of caution, the preservation of oneself from unnecessary pain.

'Good morning, Mrs Barforth,' he would say to me. 'Are you well?' And I would answer, just as coolly, 'Very well, thank you. And you?' And that was all.

But Elinor, sickly and depressed – fanciful, as her husband had begun to call her – aware, perhaps, that he no longer gazed at her quite as he used to, was inclined to blame Crispin for all her ills and would greet me every day with some fresh example of his spite.

I would find her, more often than not, in her bedroom, curled up on a sofa surrounded by the lotions and potions of sickness, the odds and ends of idleness with which her husband had forbidden her to clutter his drawing room. Her hair would be hanging girlishly down her back, her thickening body hidden, as best she could, in a swathe of lace and frills, and before I had taken off my bonnet, her tale of woe would begin.

'Well, and I am glad to see you, for no one has even glanced at me the whole morning. They brought me my tea and toast at nine o'clock and since then I could have died and would have been quite cold by now. Yes, and I am obliged to sit up here because he fears my medicine glass may spill over on his carpet or that I shall put it down on his satinwood table and it will leave a ring . . . And if I am not well enough to go downstairs tonight, will he come and sit with me? Yes, when he's eaten his dinner and read his paper and quarrelled with his son – yes, and when he does come in he'll straighten all the bottles on my table and tidy up my books and my needlework before he even asks me how I am. And then he'll sit like a cat on hot bricks, without a word to say about anything but that abominable young man. It's Crispin's fault. It's Crispin who makes him so nervous, and if I lose this child and myself with it, then I shall know who to blame. Oh, there was such a set-to the other night, Verity, and right outside my bedroom door, in the corridor where everyone could hear them. He had come home very late – indeed I think it was almost morning, for it was quite light – and since he has to pass this door to reach his own, my husband heard him and, oh my goodness, Verity, the things they said to each other. I suppose he was not quite sober – for my brother Joel was never sober when he came home so late, except that my father was never there to see – and my husband called him spendthrift and feckless, and then they began about the allowance he has from his uncle, and how my husband had tried to put a stop to it. And then my husband told him he was not fit to have it, since all he did was squander it on revolutionary newspapers and women of bad character. So there they were, going at it hammer and tongs, until my head ached, and I could hardly look Mrs Naylor in the eye the next morning when she brought my tea, because she must have heard them, too. He wants me to lose this child, I'm sure he does. He doesn't want a half brother with a half share in the business. That's why he's always provoking me, and provoking my husband – or else he wants my husband to throw him out so he can say it was because of me, and ruin my reputation. Yes, I do believe he does, for I have heard my husband say to him a hundred times that he will not let him go. "You will stay here, boy, and do your duty until I decide your duty is done." That's what he tells him. Oh dear, what an odious creature he is. And to think that when I was younger and didn't understand things so well, I wondered if he might marry Hannah. I used to think any husband was better than none, but I'd have her stay single all her life before I'd see her take him.'

But Hannah had made some slight arrangements of her own, Ramsden Street Chapel having acquired a new minister that year, a square, plain-looking man of thirty-five, red-haired and most distressingly freckled but more than ready to appreciate Hannah's administrative talents. At about the same time, on a visit to my mother, she had made the acquaintance of the new incumbent of Patterswick Church, a pale, rather beautiful young man who, experiencing some difficulty in communicating with his parishioners – his accent being vastly different from theirs – had been most grateful for Hannah's advice. And so, between the two of them – the forceful Methodist Mr Brand and the beautiful, timid Anglican Mr Ashley – her days, somewhat to my relief, were full.

'She won't marry them,' Elinor told me. 'It's Ashley she likes best and Brand she thinks she ought to like best, and so she'll hover between the two and miss them both. And really, one wonders, isn't that the best part – the courting, when you're always nice to each other and you've got your own bed to go home to? Ah well, if I die having this baby she can marry Morgan Aycliffe after all – if it's legal.'

But, towards the end of November and the sparkling, frosty beginning of December, there were times when she decided she might well live a little longer and, since her husband did not like her to appear in public once her pregnancy began to show, my services were often required.

'You may go to your brother's house and nowhere else,' Mr Aycliffe told her, requesting me privately to invite no other company when she was there – for Bradley Hobhouse had sniggered the last time he had seen her in that condition and would certainly do so again – but Elinor, like Joel, would always take a yard for every inch one gave her and saw no reason to deny herself the excitement of our winter lectures on the slave trade.

217

We were, of course, dedicated opponents of this pernicious traffic, both in the sugar plantations of our own dominions and the cotton plantations of America, and, to renew our enthusiasm, we would be visited from time to time by some reverend gentleman or other lately returned from the West Indies, who would regale us with all the horrors of human degradation. Sometimes there would be exhibits, bullwhips, thumbscrews, leg irons – now and again with blood still on them – and there would be tears from most of us and indignation from us all, and Lucy Oldroyd, more often than not, would be carried outside in a dead swoon. And for a few days afterwards we would feel chastened and would count our blessings and be kind to one another, until the West Indies and America began to seem very far away and we very small, and we slipped back into our everyday selves again.

Speakers, of course, varied. Some of them were pompous, some tedious, some downright embarrassing in their emotion or their enjoyment of the sin and shame of it all. Some were forthright and sincere; a few dwelt rather too lovingly on the fine female bodies put up naked for auction. A few, like Mr Richard Oastler of Huddersfield, that great champion of Abolition, were magnificent, never to be forgotten. But whatever the quality of the oration, the experience, in the dull, grey wasteland of our northern winter, did us good, and as we arrived at Ramsden Street schoolhouse that December evening, although we had heard it all before and knew, in fact, that the battle for Abolition was almost won, excitement was not lacking.

And perhaps Elinor was doubly content because, at the last moment, she had almost been prevented from coming at all for lack of the male escort her husband considered essential. Mr Aycliffe, who was himself a leader of the Abolitionist cause in Cullingford and who had been expected to take his accustomed place on the speaker's platform, had been obliged, quite deliberately I thought, to cancel; while Joel, in response to Elinor's frantic note, had merely shrugged his shoulders and gone off to his Oyster Club, a group which met supposedly for political discussion but mainly for the sampling of oysters and cold punch in the best room at the Old Swan. And having resigned myself to an evening in Blenheim Lane, making soothing murmurs to Elinor's well-nigh continuous complainings, I had been surprised to find her dressed and smiling, standing in the hall on tiptoe with eagerness.

'Don't take off your cloak,' she said, 'for Crispin is to escort us, which is very kind of him, except that I believe he is doing it mainly to annoy his father, who doesn't wish me to go.'

'Then perhaps you should not go.'

'Nonsense,' she said. 'Nonsense. He didn't expressly forbid it. He just said it was impossible since I had no one to take me. And now that Crispin has actually offered, I don't see how I can be blamed.'

And Crispin, handing us into the carriage, his face once again a mask of weariness and boredom – a stranger – said coldly, 'Oh, you may rest easy on that score, Mrs Aycliffe. I shall take the blame entirely – I think we shall both make very sure of that.'

It was not far to Ramsden Street, a bare quarter of an hour of close confinement with a man who should not have cared for me enough to be unkind, whose presence or absence should have meant nothing to me. Yet I was aware of every breath he took, aware of the fresh scent of lavender on the surface of his skin and the odours of a living body beneath it, of blood flow and pulsebeat, of the texture of nerve and muscle, the texture of the heart; while, entirely divorced from logic or common sense or the natural desire to preserve myself from shame or hurt, my fingertips desired to touch him, my skin desired to be touched by him – glowed, expanded, basked almost in that desire. And I was terribly afraid.

There were a great many carriages already in Ramsden Street: the Hobhouses', bringing Emma-Jane and her mother-in-law; the Oldroyds', bringing Lucy; a single vehicle carrying a collection of the Corey and Corey-Manning widows and spinsters – Anglicans, every one of them, but willing to stretch a point on this occasion. And as we entered the schoolhouse there were other people, sitting on the back row of chairs: small shopkeepers and tradesmen and clerks in their best corduroy jackets and Sunday boots, and Ira Agbrigg, the mill hand who had come to warn us the night my father died and who, having attached himself to Joel's shadow, was now the manager of the small but thriving Low Cross Mill, Joel's old home.

But prosperity, I noticed, had not touched him outwardly, for, sitting self-consciously in the middle of the room – in a kind of neutral ground well behind the millmasters' families but in front of the clerks and grocers, the old-clothes dealer and the pawnbroker, who doubtless remembered him of old – he was still a thin man, bones and angles and anxieties taking refuge beneath a good winter coat. And because I understood the gnawing unease from which he suffered – for he was no longer a mill hand, would never be a master, was mistrusted by his old associates and despised by the new – I paused and spoke to him.

'How do you do, Mr Agbrigg, and where is Mrs Agbrigg this evening? Is she not well again?'

He had married a woman even thinner and paler than himself, a sad-eyed, lashless little mouse who, almost annually it seemed, brought forth another child, a whimper of humanity that sometimes lived and just as often did not.

And, as I passed on, leaving him flushed and grateful, Crispin Aycliffe whispered, 'That was most generous of you, Mrs Barforth; most condescending. You have made the poor fellow very happy.'

The platform party was already assembled, the Reverend Mr Brand looking extremely plain, extremely serviceable; the visiting speaker too bearded and bewhiskered and buttoned up in his dark clothes to have any identity other than 'the speaker'; and Hannah, having organized the meeting, having booked the speaker and paid his expenses, supervised the placing of the chairs, the proper arrangement of books and pamphlets, cups and saucers, and the collection plate, feeling justified tonight in putting herself forward.

This was, after all, her Sunday School. Hers was the voice which decided every issue; hers the voice which settled every crisis, from the number of pupils to be taught and the nature of that teaching to the quality of tea to be served at evening meetings and the exact purpose of those meetings themselves. Hannah it was who dispensed charity and patronage, who sorted out the 'good poor' who could be helped from the 'bad poor' who deserved their poverty and should be allowed to get on with it. And although there were still a few old ladies who resented her authority, who attempted to stage a revolution from time to time and occasionally deserted altogether to the Baptists or the Congregationalists, I could think of no occasion on which she had failed to get her way.

'See how she enjoys it,' Elinor whispered, settling herself in the centre of the front row. 'The new minister is quite in her shadow, just as if this was her own drawing room and he the husband with nothing to do but pay the bills. And, only think, she doesn't even have to order his dinner, you know, or worry about his ill humour, for he will never be ill-humoured with a woman who is free to go or stay as she pleases. No, no, he'll be sweet as pie, for he'll not risk losing Hannah to the Baptists, you may depend upon it.'

The Reverend Mr Brand rose to his feet and, asking for silence, introduced the speaker by name and reputation, managing to make some reference to Hannah's skill and devotion to her Christian duty as he did so; and, my mind registering no more than Hannah's careful lack of expression and Emma-Jane Hobhouse's quick, peevish frown – for she, too, was a Christian lady, pregnant and overburdened, doing her duty in quite another way – I found myself unable to attend, unable to care.

There had been slaves hereabout, I knew, in my grandfather's day: young African women brought to a lonely farmhouse in the Dales by men who had been answerable to no one and obliged to make no explanations when the women had disappeared. They had been murdered, Emma-Jane Hobhouse declared, raped and most horribly murdered, for one could still hear their ghosts on winter nights wailing for freedom. And suddenly I heard the echo of that cry in my own heart, for was I not bound, in my way, more tightly than any cotton picker, any harvester of sugarcane, since they, at least, had the hope of freedom? And I was aware of Crispin Aycliffe again, lounging in the chair beside me, his legs stretched out with an ease that was quite insolent, his eyes half closed.

'I have seen little children torn from their mothers' arms,' the speaker was saying. 'Infants torn from their mothers' breasts, human souls shackled in cold iron, beaten and abused so that you may take sugar with your tea – sugar, my friends, a luxury unable to sustain life itself but for which lives are sacrificed . . .'

And although it was true and terrible and must be stopped, I had no easy tears like Emma-Jane and Lucy and Elinor, no flush of indignation like Hannah, nothing but a vague, aching sadness and, behind it, the cool voice of reason, telling me there was more to slavery than sugar, bidding me to remember the cotton mills just a few miles away across the Pennines, kept alive by slave-picked cotton from America. And I knew, had Joel and I been born those few miles farther west, that our prosperity – and Hannah's – would have been based on slavery, too.

Yet there was nothing to do but endure until the bearded speaker had recounted his full catalogue of horrors, leaving us hushed and shocked and weeping, and Mr Brand took the floor again to suggest that, in the absence of Mr

Morgan Aycliffe, his son, Mr Crispin Aycliffe, might wish to say a word or two in the speaker's praise.

'Why, yes,' Crispin said, without surprise, hardly shifting himself from his position of insolent ease. And then, as the congregation turned towards him with courteous attention – since, after all, his father had contributed most generously to the cause – he got up, smiled, stretched himself a little, and smiled again.

'Dear sir,' he said with perfect, dangerous politeness, 'I have found you a most accomplished speaker, and a most tactful one, for in the midst of all your emotions you never once fell into the trap of reminding us that were it not for the cotton mills next door to us, in Lancashire, the plantations of the American South could serve no purpose and thousands of miserable African slaves could be set free. And since we all of us have friends and relatives who spin cotton for a living – and a mighty good living it is, too – we are grateful to you for not troubling our consciences with that.'

And as he gazed coolly around the room, where the women were busy dabbing their eyes and gathering together their shawls and gloves and the men were wondering how much or how little they should drop into the collection plate, and if they could now evade Miss Hannah Barforth's eagle eye and slip outside to smoke, perhaps only the speaker, the minister, Hannah, and I were aware of what he had really said.

Don't, I thought urgently, willing him to hear me. Don't do this, Crispin, for if you shame your father like this he will manage to hurt you for it. And, for an instant, as he began again, I was reassured, and then almost instantly appalled.

'I had the honour recently,' he went on, 'to spend an evening in the company of Mr Richard Oastler, a name you will all know and must certainly respect, since he has done more perhaps than anyone else in our area towards the abolition of colonial slavery. I found him to be – as I

223

had expected – a most honourable, most pleasing gentleman, and perhaps I can do no better, on this occasion, than quote some of his own words.'

'Yes, yes,' Mr Brand said, inexpressibly relieved at this mention of Richard Oastler, that eloquent champion of the oppressed. 'Please do so, Mr Aycliffe. They could be none other than well received.'

But, as Crispin reached into his pocket and brought out a neatly folded sheet of newsprint, I saw the alarm in the speaker's face and his hand hastily clamping itself on Mr Brand's arm, warning him of danger. And I saw that it was too late.

'I have in my hands,' Crispin said, still speaking coolly, lightly, 'the copy of a letter written by Mr Oastler to the editor of the *Leeds Mercury* some few weeks ago, and which may interest you – alarm you. I will not bore you with the whole, nor will you be likely to ask for more. Very well, he begins – and I must stress again that these words are Mr Richard Oastler's, not mine. "It is the pride of Britain that a slave cannot exist on her soil." '

And here, as Crispin paused, there was an obedient murmur of agreement, for this was exactly what Mr Oastler could have been expected to say.

But Crispin's voice went on, light, impersonal, and gradually silence fell, a hushed, uneasy, unwilling attention. ' "The pious and able champions of Negro slavery should have gone further than they did, or, perhaps, to speak more correctly, before they travelled so far as the West Indies, should at least for a few moments have directed their attention to scenes of misery, acts of oppression, and victims of slavery even on the threshold of our homes. Let the truth speak out. Thousands of our fellow creatures and fellow subjects, both male and female, the miserable inhabitants of a Yorkshire town, are at this moment existing in a state of slavery more horrid than are the victims of that hellish system, colonial slavery." '

'Mr Aycliffe,' Hannah said, very angry, on her feet now, her body tense.

And, giving her a slight bow, still smiling, he said, 'Miss Barforth,' and carried on: ' "The very streets" – and I quote Mr Oastler again – "are wet with the tears of innocent victims at the accursed shrine of avarice, who are compelled not by the whip of the slave driver but by the equally appalling thong or strap of the overlooker, to hasten half dressed to those magazines of British infantile slavery – the worsted mills in the town and neighbourhood of Bradford." Yes, yes, I do agree, as I am sure you have all noticed, that Mr Oastler is talking of Bradford, all of ten miles away, but we have worsted mills in Cullingford, too, and so it is reasonable to assume that we have a slave trade of our own. May I continue?'

'You had better not,' Hannah said, her fists tightly clenched, but there was, after all, only so much that a spinster lady, in these circumstances, could do, and, pausing a moment to allow the frozen silence to bite, he smiled at her once again.

'I cannot agree, Miss Barforth, really I cannot, for I have heard you on many occasions – you and my father – express the depth of your admiration for Mr Richard Oastler. I have even heard you call him an inspiration to this your favourite cause, and I feel that in your heart you will be glad to give him a hearing. Listen then. "Thousands of little children," he tells us, "both male and female but principally female, from seven to fourteen years of age, are daily compelled to labour from six o'clock in the morning till seven in the evening, with only thirty minutes for eating and recreation. Oh, listen," he bids us, "to the sorrowing accents of these poor Yorkshire little ones." And he continues, "If I have succeeded in calling the attention of your readers to the horrid and abominable system on which the worsted mills in and near Bradford are conducted" – and I think that we here in this room are near enough to Bradford to feel ourselves included – "then I have done some good." There is just a sentence more. "Christians should act and feel for those whom Christ so eminently loved and declared that of such is the Kingdom of Heaven. I remain, yours, etc., Richard Oastler, Fixby Hall, near Huddersfield, September 29, 1830."

'And since Mr Oastler's information derives from his friend Mr Wood of Horton Hall, himself a manufacturer of some substance, we may assume it to be correct.'

Silence again – of shock, almost of disbelief – a general averting of eyes, of pretending it had not happened at all or, if it had, one had not noticed it oneself – rather as if he had performed some act of gross physical obscenity. And then Hannah, too furious now for dignity, looking more like Joel than I had ever seen her, leaned forward across the speaker's table – Mr Brand and the speaker seeming almost to cower behind her – and hissed, 'You would not dare say these things if my brother or some other man of standing were here to oppose you.'

'But I have said nothing, Miss Barforth,' he told her, still elaborately polite. 'These are Mr Oastler's words, not mine, and if there are those in this hall – and I believe there are – who have laboured in the mills themselves as children, perhaps you will allow them to judge.'

And, bowing again – to Hannah, to Elinor, to the speaker, to Emma-Jane Hobhouse, but not to me – he walked quite slowly down the aisle between the rows of seats and went outside.

He was waiting for us, of course, in the carriage, for he would not abandon his father's wife, in her condition, to be taken home by strangers, and he had been obliged to wait some time, since the meeting had not been easy to disperse and Hannah, who was to come back to Blenheim Lane with us, had at first refused to ride with him. Even now, although Elinor allowed herself to be handed into the carriage with something like a giggle, Hannah refused to be touched, and seated herself.

The night was very cold, a threat of snow hovering

226

beyond the dark, the ground iron-hard, and, as the horses strained to take us up one hill and down another, the panting of their overburdened chests and the creaking of harness were the only sounds. We sat in sharp-edged silence, Hannah's anger cooling now, like molten iron, to a point where she could fashion it into a weapon, and, suddenly, without condescending to look at him, she said loudly, 'Mr Aycliffe, I have to tell you that you have behaved abominably.'

'Yes, of course you do.'

'And I must also advise you of my intention to inform your father of what has occurred.'

'Yes, of course you must.'

And not another word was spoken.

Mr Aycliffe had not yet returned when we reached Blenheim Lane, and as we were shown into the hushed splendour of his drawing room, the walls seemed to close around me like a tomb, the richly furnished burial place of a king, perhaps, but a tomb nevertheless, a place of concealment for the dead, and taking a nervous step or two, I spun round to Hannah, already seated, and asked her, 'Is this necessary? Is it even wise? Should you not consider Elinor and her condition – and the effect further quarrelling could have on her?'

'I hope I know my duty to my sister.'

'I wonder if you could be mistaking it.'

'Indeed. I am not quite certain what you mean by that, Verity. And I must tell you I find your own attitude surprising. I expected to see some indignation in you, for my brother's sake, since he was clearly among those singled out for attack.'

'Well – that may be so, but I think your brother is quite capable – like Mr Aycliffe – of handling his affairs without my assistance.'

'Are you accusing me,' she said, getting to her feet, 'of interference – of meddling? Are you suggesting that I am acting from spite?'

And the honest blaze of her indignation defeated me, convincing me that Hannah, in the pursuit of what she sincerely believed to be right, could not be diverted.

'No, Hannah, you are not spiteful, but I still wonder if, for Elinor's sake, we should try to keep the peace – to make the incident seem less rather than more?'

'Oh, don't worry about me,' Elinor cut in, installing herself by the fire, more animated than I had seen her in a long time. 'I feel quite well – almost new again – and Crispin must want his father to hear about it, otherwise he'd hardly have done it in Ramsden Street – would you, Crispin? – and I'm sure he'd rather hear it from Hannah than from Emma-Jane.'

My stomach twisting with anxiety, I walked out into the hallway, thinking I heard a carriage, and, turning, found Crispin behind me in the half dark.

'There is nothing you can do,' he said quietly. 'Don't try to defend me, Verity – Verity. No one else will, and you can't stand against them all.'

And, stupidly, the sound of his voice speaking my name – saying 'Verity' instead of 'Mrs Barforth' – pierced some unwanted source of emotion inside me and brought me close to tears.

'Are you really so unafraid as you seem – so careless of what your father will say to you?'

'Oh no,' he said. 'No one is quite so careless as that. I care rather more, I think, than he will ever believe. I am bound very tight, you see, and so I must cut deep to be free.'

'Free? To do what?'

'More than I have yet done. More than talk – and dream. More than build ratholes for men to live in. More than that. You would do the same, I think, Verity, if you could.'

And I have always thought he meant to touch me, and that I would not have resisted, had not Hannah appeared

228

in one doorway and his father, almost simultaneously, in another.

'I heard the carriage,' she said, feeling even now the need to explain her presence in the hall when, as a guest, she should have kept to the drawing room, but the pallor of Morgan Ayrcliffe's face, the inexpressible disgust written clear across his thin features, reduced her to silence. And as he came slowly through the door, walking as if his limbs hurt, Crispin said, 'I fear you are too late, Miss Barforth. My father, it seems, has met someone on the way who has performed your task for you.'

Mr Ayrcliffe paused, carefully divested himself of cloak, hat, and gloves, handing them without haste to his manservant, and then, going past us into the drawing room without so much as a glance at Crispin, said tonelessly to Elinor, 'I will bid you good night, Mrs Ayrcliffe.'

'Oh, but I am not in the least tired. I wish to—'

'I will bid you good night.'

'Oh why, sir?' Crispin said. 'She merely wishes to witness my downfall. Surely you can indulge her in that.'

And, as they at last faced each other, it was clear that the older man was straining himself to his limits to keep his self-control while the younger, by any means at his disposal, was determined to break it.

'I will deal with you presently, boy – privately. When my wife is safely abed, and these other ladies removed from your insolence.'

'Oh – as to that – I am not sure I have a mind to be dealt with, sir. In fact, I think I may walk into town and take the air.'

'You will do,' Morgan Ayrcliffe said dangerously, 'exactly as I bid you.'

'I wonder.'

'And I do not wonder. You will come when I call you and go where I send you, because you can afford to do no other. You owe me obedience. It is your debt to me and I shall demand payment in full.'

'And if I refuse the debt, I wonder how you will set about collecting it.'

And pressing back against the wall, I saw that even Hannah was afraid, and understood that we were witnessing a kind of murder, a deliberate amputation of the last shred of affection that bound them together.

'Go to your room, boy. Go now. Stay there until I call you. And remember you have no mother now to throw herself between us—'

'No, sir, I have no mother, and I will not go to my room just now. Not until I have told you that you and I must part, sir – sadly but finally.'

'No,' Morgan Aycliffe said. 'Never. I am not a fool, boy. I know you do these things to provoke me and drive me to the point of dismissing you, but you have not succeeded. You will stay here, in my house. I am your father. I am entitled to your support – your gratitude – and your labour.'

'Why, sir? To provide dowries for your daughters and an easy life for your widow when you are gone? No – no – I think not. And do not threaten me, sir, with changes in your will, for you mean to disinherit me in any case when my usefulness is done. I know that very well. And so do you, Father, so do you, even though you may not yet have called your lawyers, even though you may not even have admitted it to yourself. Admit it now. Acknowledge the pleasure it would give you on your deathbed, knowing you had worn me out in your service, when all the time you had left your fortune away from me. And perhaps I have no mind, Father, to let you die so happy. Nor have I a mind to stay and watch you drain the life out of that silly child over there, as I saw you drain it from my mother—'

And, at last, it was enough. I saw Morgan Aycliffe's face dissolve and then re-form itself again into a living snarl, as far beyond his control as the arm that, raising itself, struck his son hard across the mouth.

'Oh dear,' Crispin said. 'I wish you had not done that. You have not hurt me, Father, do not think it. I merely regret it for your sake. You have struck me often enough before and I realize it pains you far more than it pains me, as you have always told me – yet you have always recovered. No doubt your little wife will know how to console you.'

It was Hannah who put herself between them, who said, 'This is too much,' and who led the suddenly helpless Mr Aycliffe away.

I took Elinor upstairs, without gentleness, without sympathy, and bundled her into her bed, refusing to answer when she gurgled, 'That looks like the end of it, then. He's going. And I hope you don't blame me for being glad, for you can see what a brute he is, and that he would never have treated me fairly. Silly child, indeed. Well, I may be silly, but I'm here, in my warm bed, and who knows where he'll sleep tonight. Do stay, Verity. Talk to me a little, for I'm too excited to rest.'

But, barely staying to bid her good night, I hurried to the top of the stairs and waited, hiding myself away like a child at a party spying on her mother's guests. Hannah came across the hall, a glass in her hand, opened the drawing-room door and went inside, shutting herself in most decidedly with the man who had not, in the end, chosen her as his wife. The old manservant appeared, a heavy bag in his hand, placed it by the hall table, and went away again. And then, 'Crispin,' I whispered through the gloom, using his name at last, and went running downstairs to him.

'Where will you go?'

'Oh, somewhere – not far – don't worry. I shall be quite safe.'

But, in the dreadful turmoil of my nerves, his safety seemed in doubt, his father's malice a thin winding sheet to bind him and choke him, and I said urgently, 'Did you have to make him so angry? Could you not simply have packed your bags and gone?'

'Yes,' he said gently. 'So I could. I have done it before. And he could give out that I was travelling abroad for my health or on his business, as he has done before. And sooner or later someone would come to tell me that he is getting older, his strength is failing – he is in need – and I would have come back. As I have done before. And so, this time, I have been monstrously rude to him before witnesses, two of whom will not keep silent. I have given him the opportunity to present himself to his little section of the world as a wronged father, and I think the role will suit him. Certainly no one will blame him for what has happened tonight, and that is what matters to him, you see. He is as susceptible to guilt as some people are to the measles, and now that he no longer needs to feel guilty on my account – for Miss Hannah Barforth will soon convince him I am not worth it – he can let me go. There will be no reprisals, Verity, but I am so very glad to see that you care.'

'Oh – as to that—'

'Yes – as to that—'

And carefully, very carefully, he touched my cheek with the very tips of his fingers.

'I am not in love with you, Verity – at least, I have tried not to be. But I think I could love you – very much, very much – if you would allow it. And you would not allow it, would you?'

'I cannot allow it.'

'No – quite rightly.'

And, seeing the strain in his face, the immense fatigue, I knew that none of this had been done lightly, with a shrug and a quizzical lift of the eyebrow, as he had pretended.

'I really will be safe, you know. I have a small allowance from my uncle – the famous fifty pounds a year my father swears has led me into mischief – and so I shall not starve. Verity, will you tell me to leave. I am finding it very hard to say goodbye.'

'Yes, you had better go. Much better. Goodbye.'

And as he walked away, into a bitter night, a harsh December that had already begun to murder the poor, the homeless, the weak, I knew poverty myself, for the first time – poverty of the heart – and weakness, and the terrible conviction that I too had lost my rightful home.

15

The Duke of Wellington, his government defeated, was gone now to sulk in the House of Lords and to make gloomy predictions that any extension of the vote would open the floodgates of revolution. But the spirit of disobedience was abroad again, and it was not only the industrialists who cried out for Reform.

'Cullingford must have the right to elect its own member to Westminster,' Mr Aycliffe thundered whenever anyone was near enough to hear him, and although he merely meant that a small section of Cullingford, comprising Joel and Bradley Hobhouse and a few trustworthy managers and shopkeepers and tradesmen should have the right to elect Morgan Aycliffe, support was now coming to him from lower sections of society, from curly-headed Law Valley men with cloth caps and callused hands who said, 'Aye, let the millmasters take on the squires so that when our turn comes we'll find it that much easier to take on the masters.'

Reform, then, had become a matter of time, of degree. Wellington and his government had been ousted for denying it, and his chief opponents, Lord Grey and Lord Russell, who during their long time in opposition had been regularly promising it, had no option now but to perform;

and so, in March of that year, 1831, Lord John Russell entered the House of Commons, where one third of the constituencies represented were controlled outright by one hundred aristocratic landlords – nine of them by the Duke of Newcastle, whose members called themselves his ninepins – and lay before it his scheme for improvement. Boroughs with less than 2,000 inhabitants were to be disfranchised completely; those with less than 4,000 were to elect one member only, instead of two, thus creating plenty of spare seats for allocation to the northern towns. There would be rather fewer members than before, and, the vote being extended to all men in the boroughs who occupied, as owner or tenant, property worth ten pounds a year, there would be half a million new, somewhat well-to-do voters to elect them.

Naturally, under this system, some would fare better than others. In London, and even in Manchester, where rents were higher, a ten-pound property qualification did not imply any great social standing, but in Leeds and Bradford, in Halifax and Huddersfield, in Cullingford, where rents – and wages – were very low, enfranchisement was mainly a middle-class, purely masculine affair; for although there were extremists like Crispin Aycliffe who demanded one man one vote, no one, in my hearing, had suggested offering the vote to a woman. And had anyone done so, the result would have been laughter.

Not exactly revolution, one might have thought – in fact, I did think so, although no one asked for my views – but there were many who saw it very differently. The industrialist Joel Barforth could hardly challenge the authority of a Lord Grey or a Lord Russell, both sprung from the ancient nobility, secure in the accumulated wealth and privilege of generations, but he could challenge a smaller country squire like Eustace Dalby – even a bigger one like Sir Giles Flood – and, fearing a transfer of power from themselves to this new, cunning, aggressive race of millmasters, the squirearchy was quick to take alarm. Forces were mustered. The Duke of Wellington, speaking from his wife's deathbed, reaffirmed his view that responsible government could not be carried out to suit the whim of public opinion, that this Bill was simply a prelude to further Bills which would eventually sweep away the House of Lords, the Church of England, the monarchy, the last vestiges of decent society. But the Whigs were in no position to retreat, and, when the Bill passed its second reading in the Commons by only one vote and seemed certain to be thrown out by the Lords, the Whig Prime Minister, Lord Grey, demanded that Parliament be dissolved and a new general election fought solely on the issue of Reform.

'The Bill, the whole Bill, and nothing but the Bill" was the battle cry of the election that April. In London, the Duke of Wellington's city residence, Apsley House, was attacked by a Reform mob, his windows smashed and his railings torn up, while his duchess lay dead inside. In the southern counties, where distressed agricultural labourers were still burning hayricks and getting themselves hanged for it, it was felt that some change, any change, would be welcome. The Reform Bill would not cure all ills, but it would be a step forward, which, at the very least, was better than standing still. Many people, if questioned, would not, perhaps, have known exactly what they expected from it, but in the industrial towns of the North, this second generation of manufacturers were in no doubt at all. They needed a voice – a great many voices – in Westminster, to smash the abominable Corn Laws and advocate free trade, to make laws to suit the North for a change, instead of the agricultural South. And so clamorous were they for Reform that their operatives, seeing perhaps that at this stage there was little in it for them or merely finding the habit of opposing the employers too strong to break, turned their backs and gave their attention to men like Mr Richard Oastler, who, in that election month of April, ignored the burning issue of Reform altogether, requiring instead that all candidates should support the introduction of a ten-hour working day.

But the Reforming Lords Grey and Russell received the mandate they had requested, sweeping back to Westminster with a majority that made the proposal of a second Reform Bill inevitable. And while Squire Dalby prepared to sell his estates while he still could in order to go abroad – before someone suggested the setting up of a guillotine in Cullingford Marketplace – and my husband, and the husband of every woman I knew, went down to the Old Swan to toast the new era – their era – in champagne, I sat with my cousin Elinor in the darkened room considered appropriate for such occasions and watched the birth of her third child.

Nothing, from the start, had gone entirely right with this pregnancy. It had made her very sick and very stout, had puffed up her ankles and her face, had hidden her pretty, pointed chin and her dainty features, had taken the lustre from her hair and depressed her spirits, so that for the last few weeks, from a combination of self-disgust and the certain knowledge that her husband no longer found any pleasure at all in gazing at her, she had taken to her bed and cowered there like a sick animal.

'There is a concoction of chamomile flowers and mullein leaves I know of,' Mrs Stevens had offered, 'which will put the shine back into your hair.' But so low had Elinor sunk that even this could not cheer her.

'What does my hair matter,' she said, 'when I am going to die, in any case. Everybody knows the third child is the dangerous one – the killer – and I only hope it is a boy so that my husband may be spared the ordeal of marrying again and inflicting this nastiness on someone else. Now, is that not noble of me, Verity – to think of others at such a time?'

But her attempt at humour – and nobility – merely reduced her to fresh tears and when, in the fearsome dark – with her husband not yet returned from the Swan – she gave birth to another tiny girl and did not die, she simply turned her face into the pillow, weeping now from sheer weakness, and refused even to look.

'Give it to its nurse,' she said when the midwife tried to press the fragile bundle upon her.

And seeing the woman's shocked expression and not wishing to hurt her feelings – nor to give her an opportunity to gossip – I took the child myself – not a pretty child but just a red, angry scrap of wails and creases – and, because it had not asked to be born, rocked it and held it tight.

'You have another daughter,' I told Morgan Aycliffe much later, while Elinor slept, and although his disappointment must surely have been great, his face registered no more than a kind of thin disdain.

'Tell me, Mrs Barforth,' he said, carefully removing his gloves, 'is it – in your opinion – a strong child?' And when I said that it was not, he refrained, quite visibly, from exclaiming, 'Good. Good,' letting me know, wordlessly, that although a son might have served him as a replacement for Crispin, a daughter – a third daughter – could not be welcome. 'Perhaps she may not survive,' his pinched, thoroughly weary expression told me. 'Perhaps it would be as well if she did not.'

But the little girl, although she lay suspiciously still for a day or two, managed to cling to life – as is often the way with females – and was soon installed in the nursery at the top of the house with her sisters, to be cared for by Nurse and suckled by a placid, heavy-breasted farm girl, who, between them, spared Elinor the necessity of seeing her at all.

And Elinor, in fact, still had no desire to see her, and not much inclination, even when the first month was over, to leave her bed.

'Oh yes,' she told me, 'they keep bringing her down to me and thrusting her under my nose – and I make the right noises because it is easier to pretend than to have them nagging me and whispering to each other that I am unfeeling. But, to tell the truth, she looks exactly like the other two, and I can see nothing to go into raptures about. And what does my opinion matter, in any case? It is my husband who will decide what is to be done with them. I shall have nothing to say to it. They are calling her Cecilia, by the way – Hannah suggested it, although I can't think why, since I know of no one of that name in our family. Prudence, Faith, and Cecilia – well, good luck to them. No, Verity, I do not wish to get up today. Hannah has been bothering me about it all morning, but if I know nothing else at least I know when I am comfortable.'

Even Hannah, who still reigned supreme at Ramsden Street Chapel and whose opinions did not pass unheard at Patterswick Church, who could bend both the Dissenting Mr Brand and the Anglican Mr Ashley to her will, met defeat at the hands of this passive little sister who, when asked to get up, simply closed her eyes and went to sleep, or, when forced to her feet, declared herself to be dizzy and fell back into bed again.

'She must be made to accept her responsibilities,' Hannah declared, but there was a growing feeling in Blenheim Lane that not much could be expected in the way of responsibility from the second Mrs Aycliffe. And when tiny Cecilia began to vomit and whine and grow tinier than ever, it was Hannah who lay in wait for the wet nurse and caught her ruining her milk by swigging gin; Hannah who spared Morgan Aycliffe the unpleasantness of dismissing the woman – who was drunk and abusive – by doing it herself; Hannah who found a healthy replacement and had her safely in the Aycliffe nursery before the next feeding time.

'What an entertainment we have had this afternoon,' Elinor told her husband on his return, 'for the wet nurse was drunk, and there was such a set-to – such a deal of huffing and puffing that I had to get up and watch the fun.'

But his reply was no more than a gradual tightening of

his features, that look of thin disdain so habitual with him, and, as her voice began to ebb away and her gaiety with it, he merely said, 'I am appalled.' And I couldn't tell if his contempt were directed solely at the nurse, at Elinor, or at himself.

The days of his enraptured gazing – the days of strawberries and champagne – were so totally at an end that even their memory, I think, distressed and amazed him. And if he could not forgive himself for the sensual impulse that had led him to propose to the pretty young sister instead of the sensible older one, he could not forgive Elinor – it seemed – for inspiring it. The difference in their ages alone did not disturb him too much, for Hannah was herself very much his junior and, in a world where women were apt to die young anyway, in childbed or from the strain of raising large families, a man could be forgiven for taking one who could be expected to last. It was simply that, his passion having cooled, Elinor had nothing else to offer him but a vivacity he found unseemly and a fertility that filled him with dread. He had fallen victim to lust, he had been tempted and had succumbed, and now, saddled forever with this prattling child, he felt he had been cheated. Lust, it seemed, was not splendid, as he had hoped, but untidy. It was a clutter of knitting needles and medicine bottles in his drawing room; a drunken country girl, her breasts swollen with sour milk, stumbling across his threshold; it was a nursery full of little girls who, one day, would surely escape their place of confinement and lay sticky fingers on his porcelain, who would defile his Wedgwood and his Coalport, his dignity and his purse. And because Elinor was lust, who had played him this foul trick, had lost him his son and failed to provide him with another, he chose to turn his thoughts in other directions, to the parliamentary career which would enable him, more than ever, to avoid her.

'You may inform Mrs Aycliffe I will not be dining at home this evening,' he would tell his housekeeper as she presided over his solitary breakfast, and Elinor, much relieved, would plan her day around her own whims and fancies, her callers and her growing number of aches and pains.

'I am not quite well this morning. No, no, I really don't know what ails me – a little dizziness, a slight pain behind the eyes. I could get up, but it hardly seems worth it since I shall only go back to bed again. And, I ask you, what is there to get up for? They can all manage splendidly without me. When I make the effort and go downstairs in the evenings I can do nothing right, for my husband has been so morose since Crispin left. And was that my fault? I suppose it was. Just as I am to blame for having girls instead of boys.'

Crispin. Although at the command of good sense I decided not to think of him, only the surface of my mind obeyed. I continued, as I had always done, walking my dogs every morning on the moorland road above the mill, taking tea with Emma-Jane and Lucy, submerging myself in the life of my household, the lives of my children, inviting my husband's friends to dine. I engaged a nursery govern-ess on Hannah's recommendation: a well-starched Mrs Paget to supplement the services of my nursemaid, Liza. I taught my six-year-old son Blaize to read, and was astonished – and made much of it to Emma-Jane and Lucy – when I discovered my five-year-old Nicholas had some-how taught himself. I brushed my daughter's hair at bedtime, enchanted by its fragrant, sable coils, and told her the stories my old Marth-Ellen had once told me, rejecting the new books of moral fables given to me by Hannah.

I promised Caroline a kitten for her birthday that year – a gift my father had once made to me – and took her, hand in hand, down a country lane in search of the old woman who kept white cats and usually had a litter to dispose of. Although all through the bumpy drive, jumping up and down beside me in the carriage, she had talked of a white, fluffy kitten – 'Snowy,' she'd said, calling out to the passersby. 'We're going to fetch Snowy' – when we finally located the low stone cottage and found a basket alive with all the colours of a casual feline mating, she had been so enchanted by deep tiger stripings, a little black-and-white patchwork body, a pair of transparent eyes saucily winking from a head the texture of grey velvet, that I, enchanted with her, had understood the impossibility of making a final selection and had allowed myself to be convinced that if she had a kitten, then Blaize and Nicholas should have one too. And giving way to her pleas of 'It's only fair, Mamma,' and her very plausible fears that if we left them behind their wizened owner would be more than likely to drown them, I had come away with the striped tabby for Caroline, the grey for Nicholas, the black-and-white for Blaize, arriving home to a frozen welcome from Hannah, to a sharp reminder that Mrs Paget, the governess, was averse to animals in her nursery; to Nicholas, who demanded the black-and-white cat because Blaize had it; to Blaize, who, privately not caring much for cats at all, hung on to it because Nicholas wanted it; while Caroline, cutting through their dispute with an imperious hand, declared that since they did not know how to behave, she would have all three.

'They'll be mine,' I told them, 'every one, before the month's out, unless you learn to care for them properly.'

'Oh, I'll look after mine all right,' Blaize said.

'And so will I,' Caroline told me. 'Better than him.'

Yet by the end of that first month, after a great deal of boasting from Blaize that his cat would soon be big enough to eat the other two, after a great deal of petting and ribbon tying from Caroline, who considered hers the prettiest, I found only Nicholas beside me when I put out the daily saucers of milk, the fish scraps and meat scraps; only Nicholas to concern himself and go hunting with me whenever one of the mischievous trio could not be found. And, as so often before, my heart bled for him when, having accepted their food from his steady hand, the fickle creatures stalked away to jump, purring and flirtatious, on the lap of my other son, the careless and charming Blaize.

I found peace in the smooth unwinding of my days. I drove to Patterswick to visit my mother, sorted linen, made potpourri with Mrs Stevens, ordered new clothes, and experienced pleasure, sometimes, when my husband made love to me – sometimes not – and irritation whenever he reached out that cousinly hand to pinch my chin. And when, from time to time, it seemed that my last meeting with Crispin Aycliffe had been the only real thing that had ever happened to me, I closed my eyes to it, closed my mind to it, and hurriedly went about my daily tasks.

It would have been easier, of course, had he gone away altogether, but Mr Richard Oastler's letter to the *Leeds Mercury* had created a mighty stir in our community, and by so publicly associating himself with it, Crispin had become involved. He had gone from his father's house to spend a few days at Fixby Hall, where Richard Oastler was employed as steward by its owner, Squire Thornhill, and where, Mr Oastler having diverted his considerable energies from the slave trade to the cause of oppression nearer at home, Crispin was introduced to the Huddersfield Short Time Committee, headed by Mr Oastler and dedicated to the shortening of the industrial working day.

And instead of going on from Fixby Hall to London or to his uncle, on whose favour he must now depend, he had come back to Cullingford, where a Short Time Committee of our own was forming, and had taken lodgings at the Red Gin, a public house of ill repute somewhere in Simon Street. He was often to be seen in the company of Mark Corey, an illegitimate son, rumour had it, of our gallant Colonel Corey of Blenheim Lane, who, unlike his supposed father, was a revolutionary, a ne'er-do-well, and owner of a scurrilous weekly newssheet, the *Cullingford Star*.

'The Bill,' then, 'the whole Bill, and nothing but the Bill.' But to Richard Oastler and Mark Corey and Crispin

Aycliffe, and to a multitude of workingmen – and a multitude of other men who had no work – it was not the Reform Bill but the Ten Hours Bill that mattered. Since the masters would not reduce the working day voluntarily, they must be forced to do it. The factory children – and the women, too – must have legal protection. And although there had been Factory Acts before, which had made very little difference to anyone, at the mere hint of further legislation the manufacturers reacted very much as the Duke of Newcastle had done when, criticized for evicting tenants from one or other of his nine constituencies because they had not voted his way, he had replied, 'Have I not the right to do what I like with mine own?'

It was not that all millmasters were the savage demons it suited the *Cullingford Star* to have us suppose, for, like any other breed, they varied from the very good to the very bad, with a great many in between who were sometimes one thing, sometimes another. There were men like Bradley Hobhouse, who, from indolence rather than any definite streak of cruelty, set a target of production for every day and allowed his overlookers to achieve it in any way they pleased. And since the time-honoured Law Valley method for keeping factory children awake was to strap them or duck their heads in a cistern of cold water – and since the accident rate at Nethercoats, from exhausted children falling into the machines and having their clothes, their hair, and sometimes their limbs torn off, was unusually high – Emma-Jane wore a very long face when the town, suddenly, became flooded with copies of Richard Oastler's letter, one of which found its way into her carriage and one, wrapped around a stone, through her parlour window.

At the other end of the scale, there was Mr John Wood, the worsted manufacturer from Bradford, who had contributed £40,000 to Richard Oastler's campaign and who, in his own mill, provided baths, and seats for his operatives to rest on, and allowed them half an hour for breakfast and

243

a lordly forty minutes for dinner. And somewhere among them was Joel Barforth, expanding faster than anyone, still building larger premises that would need more hands, more women, more children, more overlookers greedy for their bonus if production was kept up and certain of their dismissal if it was not. And if these overlookers, who needed the money, worked little girls of eight and nine for seventeen hours a day to earn it, and strapped them to keep them on their feet, I knew that Joel, unlike Bradley Hobhouse – who preferred not to look – would be well aware of it.

'I ask them to do nothing,' he announced, when pressed, 'that I have not done myself. I worked at Low Cross with my father from seven years of age, and when my mother set her mind on sending me to school I walked there, five miles, summer and winter, and back again, and then worked half the night when we were short-handed. And I'll tolerate no interference in my affairs. I'll allow no spineless government official into my factories, telling me what I can and can't do, any more than I'd allow him into my wife's bed.'

And Emma-Jane Hobhouse, who was dining with us, rushed to agree. 'Really,' she said, 'I believe this Richard Oastler is merely out to make mischief or to get his name in the newspapers again, now that the slave trade campaign seems almost over. Poor man, one could almost pity him, for he is only the steward of Fixby Hall, not the squire, and having been so idolized for his work for Abolition, is quite beyond his station; one can see that he doesn't want to sink back into obscurity. But why should we be made to suffer for it? And I tell you this, if this horrid Ten Hours Bill ever came to pass, we should not be the only ones to grumble at it. Ten hours of work sounds very fine, but has he stopped to wonder how people are to manage on ten hours' wages? If we stopped our engine at the end of ten hours and sent everybody home, most of them would stand outside the gates and beg to be let in again. And if parents were unwilling to send their children to work, what on earth could we do to force them? They couldn't manage without their children's wages, that's the truth of it – my word, we've all seen women dragging their children to work by the ear or chasing them into the yard with a possing stick. Really, Mr Oastler should confine himself to what he knows, like managing Squire Thornhill's estate, for if he has all this time to spare for our affairs, one can only assume he neglects his own.'

But Emma-Jane was troubled in her conscience, and every morning, as I walked out with my dogs, I found myself pausing on the path above the Top House and looking down at the mill, enclosed by its high stone wall set with black iron spikes and a massive iron gate. I was never awake these days to hear those gates clang shut at half past five precisely, separating the early risers, who deserved their day's pay, from the latecomers, who did not. But I would be on the path sometimes by half past eight, breakfast time, when the gates opened again for a quarter of an hour and the latecomers would be let in, reprimanded, fined, while others, who had already been at work a full three hours, would come out into the yard for a breath of soot-flecked air, a slice of bread and dripping, and to make water before the engine came on again, when they would need permission to leave their looms.

There would always be a line of children outside the gate, tiny girls five or six years old with bundles in their arms which could have been rag dolls but which were babies, coming to the mill to be fed. And, gradually, a woman would detach herself from the crowd, suckle her baby, hand it back to its five-year-old nursemaid, and go hurrying away, with two or three of her older children about her, to her labour. And although I wanted to deceive myself, my eyes refused to lie and I saw how small these children were, how crooked, how pale, how many threw one leg inwards as they walked, how many had one shoulder higher than the other or were bent at both knees from straining bones that were still soft.

Children had always worked in the mills, and I had never questioned it. My grandfather and my father both had employed them, and before that they had worked for their own parents, in the cottages, where the whole family had laboured hard to produce their weekly piece. Country children went gleaning at harvesttime and fed pigs and chickens on bitter winter mornings; city children cleaned crossings, made lace, swept chimneys, and were expected to fend for themselves as soon as they were able and were expected to leave home, in many cases, and go into service at twelve or younger to make room at the family table for new little ones. No one had ever told me that childhood was a time of idleness, for even I, as a little girl, had been required to mend linen, to help with pickles and preserves in season, to make myself generally of use. And at least, as Emma-Jane put it, the factory children were spared the burden of having to learn to read and write. But that troupe of pale dwarves filing listlessly into the mill – twisted bodies that, if they grew at all, could only become twisted men, scarred women – got into my dreams, lodged themselves somewhere behind my eyelids, so that they were never altogether out of view.

'Naturally,' Hannah said, 'although Mr Oastler is guilty of gross exaggeration, there is abuse. The Hobhouse mill leaves a great deal to be desired. And Bradley Hobhouse should be made aware that if he allows young persons of both sexes to mingle together so freely, without adequate supervision, then promiscuity can be the only result. It has been brought to my notice that some of his overlookers are men of most unsavoury repute and since factory girls mature so rapidly – due to the heat in the sheds, one supposes – Well, I have heard of two cases of girls from respectable families in Ramsden Street who have been most vilely led astray by their employment at Nethercoats.

Someone should speak to Emma-Jane before the *Cullingford Star* gets to hear of it and we are all made to suffer.'

But the flaunting factory queens of Hannah's imaginings never crossed my path, while the sad-eyed, crook-shouldered boys and girls I did encounter showed no signs of the energy required for seduction. They were, quite simply, too weary, and it seemed to me that the scorching heat of the sheds instead of maturing them would be far more likely to wither their vital impulses away.

Yet how could I, the wife of Joel Barforth, protest? How could I do more than keep silent when, in that glorious Reform year of 1831, Mr Michael Sadler, the member for Newark and formerly an importer of Irish linens in Leeds, lay before the House his bill for the protection of young persons in factories and for the regulation of the working day? If the bill became law it would be illegal to employ anyone under the age of nine, although in the absence of any official registration of births, this would be difficult to enforce and the old Law Valley attitude – 'if they're big enough, they're old enough' – would still apply. Young persons between nine and eighteen would be permitted to work no more than ten hours a day from Monday to Friday and a mere eight hours on Saturdays.

And, in the general protest, I kept a determined silence. When the proposals of Sadler's bill were issued in pamphlet form by Crispin Aycliffe – firmly established now at the *Cullingford Star* – and distributed throughout the mills, my silence deepened and extended itself, so far as possible, to my mind.

'Don't think for one moment that Crispin Aycliffe cares about the factory children,' Hannah said hotly. 'That young man has joined Oastler's campaign merely to annoy his father. He knows perfectly well that when Cullingford is enfranchised Mr Morgan Aycliffe will stand for election, and his aim now is to embarrass him. That young man is not an idealist. He is simply malicious.'

And when, one afternoon, we met Crispin Aycliffe face

to face as we were crossing Market Square and he was coming perhaps from the Red Gin, Hannah refused to acknowledge his bow, stared through him, and seemed ready to walk through him had he not stepped aside, her hand gripping my elbow like a vice, so that I was bound to follow. And that night, plagued by the memory of his smile that had said, 'Don't worry. I know you have to pretend to hate me,' I looked closely, cruelly, in my mind's eye, and admitted that every morning when I set out with my dogs I longed to see him coming towards me through the mist. And, terrified by the intensity of that longing, I decided I would walk my dogs on the moorland path – in the place where he knew he could find me – no more.

I was Joel's wife. That was my reality, and all else was illusion. And although I had been too young and too dazed on our wedding day to understand the vows I made, I knew they could not be broken. In my heart, perhaps, I could neither love nor honour him, but my only hope of living in peace was to pretend that I did.

As so often before, it was Elinor who tested my resolve.

The possibility of her husband's election as Cullingford's first Member of Parliament had at first meant little to Elinor. But once the implications had been pointed out to her – prolonged visits to London, even a house there – she had taken on a new lease of life.

'I must have something fit to wear,' she announced, finding no difficulty at all in jumping out of bed now that she had something to get up for, and when I called again it was to find her upstairs, certainly, but surrounded by lengths of satin and silk brocade, lace and beads and feathers, and by a tall, dark woman I almost recognized.

'No, no,' Elinor called out. 'No need to ask me how I am, for I am very well. Tell me, how do you find this blue brocade? That is more to the point, for Rosamund here swears it matches my eyes, and I am afraid it turns them green. Oh, Verity, you are acquainted with Miss Boulton, are you not?'

And although our acquaintance could not be a happy one since she, being still single, could not be expected to forget that Joel had deserted her to marry me, we bowed and smiled and talked at some length about fabric and design and the pleasure she took in creating gowns for others to wear.

I calculated that she must be around thirty now, a slender woman who would, in ten years, be gaunt and elegant rather than beautiful, with a great deal of charm but little softness in her dark face; a woman who had tried to marry several times since Joel and who now, her family's affairs not having prospered, was obliged to supplement her income with her needle.

'I make a great many wedding gowns,' she told me. 'When Estella Corey, Colonel Corey's daughter, married last spring, she wore one of my creations and ordered her entire outfit from me for her London season. Oh yes, I am kept very busy in Blenheim Lane.'

And, knowing what was expected of me, I murmured, 'You must make something for me, when you have the time to spare.'

'With great pleasure, Mrs Barforth – and for your little girl too, should you ever require it. And dare I ask you to visit me in my new premises? Yes, I am about to embark on a new venture: a shop for the sale of ready-made children's clothes of the very highest quality. The latest London designs and a few ideas of my own to make them really exclusive. The very first shop of its kind in the area; and, depending on its success, I mean to add ladies' wear, bonnets and shawls, slippers, fans, perfumes, all the little luxuries I am sure you are accustomed to sending to London for. Why go to so much trouble and have such a long wait and then find they have sent the wrong colour or that it was not really what one had in mind when it can all be obtained here, from me, in Millergate. Oh, I am so excited, Mrs Barforth, so full of plans—'

And noting down Elinor's instructions, making a quick

sketch of something she declared could be safely left to her judgement, she picked up her fashion books, her pin-cushions, the tools of her trade, and hurried briskly away.

'Well, and I don't know why she should be so abomin-ably pleased with herself,' Elinor muttered, suddenly very cross. 'Always running here, running there, in and out of everybody's houses, tittle-tattling as she goes. Well, she may think herself very clever, but she wearies me, that's all – just wearies me.' And her small, smooth fingers flexing themselves as if they needed something to break, she gave way to a sudden, spiteful impulse, her mouth turning hard and crafty as she said, 'And perhaps she is clever at that, for her new shop is really very smart – all powder-blue velvet and little gold chairs – and knowing the price of property in Millergate and the kind of stock she intends to carry, I'd dearly like to know where the money is coming from. A partner, she says, smug as a cat in a cream pot, but who? Yes – what I would give to know that.'

Silence for a moment, a brittle thing, easily passed over. But I was in no mood suddenly for social conventions, and instead of replying, 'Who indeed?' and talking of something else, I said slowly, quite pleasantly, 'I doubt you would give a great deal, Elinor, since you must know already.'

'Oh,' she said, startled. 'And what do you mean by that?'

'I mean that if someone has invested money in Miss Boulton's shop, then it is probably Joel, and if you didn't think so – or know so – you would not have mentioned it to me in the first place.'

'Verity,' she said, her cheeks flooding with pink, her eyes with tears, for she was fond of me and wished me no harm. 'Verity, I'm so sorry. I don't know why I said that. I felt so miserable suddenly – seeing that woman so full of energy when I have none at all, and seeing you so serene – and now I feel so wicked and so – so – dreadful—'

And, for a moment, it was dreadful, for this was a name

I knew, a face I knew, no anonymous expensive woman in London or Manchester. This was different – frightening.

'It doesn't matter,' I said.

'Oh, but, Verity, it does matter.' And, fearful now, knowing that her brother Joel would not take kindly to this gossip, remembering what a clever, vindictive enemy he could be, she whispered, 'What are you going to do? You won't ask him, will you? Tell him?'

'Oh – what should I do? I imagine I'll order a dress from her, and one for Caroline, for if the franchise comes, there'll be parties and dinners, and we must look our best. And I have to agree that it will be most convenient not having to send to London every time one wants a decent cashmere shawl.'

'Don't you care at all?' she asked, still speaking in that sad little whisper, her face, emptied of its vivacity, seeming quite plain.

'Oh – as to that – what good would it do me to care? And since it would be foolish, I fully intend not to put myself in the trouble.'

'You can order your emotions – just like that?'

'Well – so it seems. Or perhaps I simply behave as if I can.'

'How like your mother you are, Verity.'

'Yes. I believe so.'

'But I am not,' she said, her hands clenched into those futile fists again. 'I am not. I thought I was so clever once, Verity – being a woman, getting all this without having to work for it, curling up on a cushion like that girl in the nursery rhyme and eating strawberries and cream all day. But I didn't know how long the days are – I just didn't know . . . He doesn't want me now, Verity; he just thinks about politics and makes me feel I'm in his way – makes me feel a nuisance, a failure. And he wants that election so badly it's making him peevish, making him ill. Don't you think he looks ill?'

Her next question hovered unspoken between us, for

how could she say such a thing, how could I listen to it? Yet her mind spoke, and mine heeded.

'Do you think he'll die soon, Verity? Do you think he'll die and set me free?'

16

September brought the coronation of our new King William, a less than wholehearted event, perhaps, since he was elderly and ailing and arrangements had already been made for a Regency in case he should die before his niece, twelve-year-old Princess Victoria, had reached eighteen. But we gave a dinner, nevertheless, loyally toasting him in champagne, and, the Reform Bill being almost won, it was suggested that evening, around my dinner table, that a committee be formed to erect a hall in some suitable part of Cullingford, where the nation's great events could be celebrated in style.

'It will not be easy to find a site,' Morgan Aycliffe said dryly, as if it mattered little to him in any case. 'However, on reflection, there may be one possibility. Not cheap, of course, but central – most convenient – and the committee, I feel sure, would not wish to pinch pennies.'

Nor, it seemed, should we wish to economize on the question of architecture.

'You will be wanting a room large enough for dancing, I imagine,' Morgan Aycliffe said wearily, finding it all a great nuisance. 'And a reading room and lecture hall too, one would suppose, and if one is to follow the fashion of Leeds and Bradford and add a billiard room – well – the cost, of course, must escalate accordingly. The Bradford Public Rooms, too, I fear, are sadly ornate, a deal of fancy stonework and ironwork, which can never be cheap and may be thought unnecessary – unless, of course, it would grieve the ladies should we seem to lag behind. Yes –

ballroom, lecture hall, reading room, billiard room, adequate facilities for the convenience of patrons and the preparation of refreshments, a reception hall with a staircase – for I fear the ladies will expect a staircase of decent proportions where guests can be received – and a retiring room. Hmmm, yes, I doubt it could be done for less than ten thousand pounds, although, of course, I cannot commit myself to an estimate made off the cuff.'

And although everyone knew that Mr Aycliffe had certainly worked out his figure most carefully in advance and would lose nothing by it, no Law Valley man would blame him for that.

The money was to be raised in thirty-pound shares, each share conveying a vote on its owner and ladies being permitted to vote by proxy. And since Joel, by speedy purchase of shares, had placed himself, perhaps from force of habit, in a position of command, the Assembly Rooms became yet another outlet for Hannah's fierce energies.

'If we are to do it at all,' she announced, quoting an old Barforth maxim, 'then we must do it right,' and, taking Mrs Stevens with her as chaperone – at some inconvenience to me – she set off on a visit to inspect the public buildings of Bradford and Leeds, returning with copious notes, drawings, and measurements, and a few warnings.

'Naturally I do not wish to put myself forward,' she told the more important members of the committee, assembled once again informally in my drawing room. 'And, given my religious commitments, I do not think anyone can accuse me of encouraging frivolity. The Reverend Mr Brand, I must admit, does not approve of dancing, but I am inclined to feel, like the Reverend Mr Ashley, that in moderation it can do no harm. And the practice of giving charity balls, as they do in Bradford, is a most practical and pleasant method of doing good. I must point out, however, that should we hold such functions the price of the tickets must never be lower than one guinea apiece, and that the tickets themselves should only be purchased

253

at the invitation of a committee member. Naturally not even this system is foolproof, and undesirable elements will, from time to time, slip through the net, but if it is strictly adhered to one may at least have the satisfaction of feeling one had done one's best. It is also the custom in Bradford to admit visiting businessmen on a yearly subscription basis, and I must tell you that this custom, although exceedingly popular with the young ladies, is not entirely without risk. In the main these men are of good standing and place too high a value on their business connections in the town to seriously misbehave. But very little is known about some of them, and, in any event, one would in no way wish to be accused of organizing a marriage market. However, that must be left for others to decide. Now, as to the question of design . . .'

And, with a few well-chosen phrases, Hannah, excessively demure yet somehow totally dominating in her eternal brown silk dress with the mourning brooch of my brother's hair still on its collar, demolished Morgan Aycliffe's dreams of a highly ornate, highly priced Gothic palace quite beyond recall.

'I believe we should think along simple, classical lines,' she announced. 'Doric columns, elegance rather than ostentation. I happen to have with me a drawing . . .'

And, anticipating no more difficulty with this group of hardheaded businessmen than her two devoted, obedient parsons gave her, she produced a neat sketch almost from thin air.

'Here it is,' she said. 'Most competently done, and, besides its artistic merits, perhaps Mr Aycliffe could tell us if it is feasible, if – should we have cause to celebrate enfranchisement this year – it could be ready in time. And then, of course, there is the matter of decoration, curtains and floor coverings and furnishings – and colour. White walls, I fear, are unwise, for they soil so quickly and give off so much glare. I think one must have a little more imagination than white. I may go to Bradford again for a second glance.'

But soon there was less cause to hurry for, on October 8, after passing successfully through the Commons, the Second Reform Bill was thrown out by the Lords, resulting in riots in most of our major centres of population, a new bitterness in the conflict between industrialists and squires. In Cullingford the windows of the Coreys and the Corey-Mannings, our most prominent representatives of the gentry, were broken, an event not entirely lacking in prestige since the Duke of Wellington's London house shared the same fate. There was a great deal of arson, too; the Duke of Newcastle's Nottingham home and a large proportion of the city of Bristol went up in flames, while the traditional November 5 bonfires were livened up that year by effigies of unpopular bishops – twenty-one of whom had voted against the Bill – burning away beside Guy Fawkes and the Pope.

Troops were called out and a great many people died – some of them for their convictions, some of them by mistake, not a few because they were too drunk to get out of the way. Yet they could all have saved themselves the trouble, for the government was in no mood to give way, and, in December, a Third Reform Bill was placed before the Commons, not much different from the first, while our Whig Prime Minister, Lord Grey, made it clear that if the Lords persisted in refusing it yet again, he would ask the King to create enough new Reform-minded peers to push it through.

The main problem, of course, was the Duke of Wellington, who, when the Bill showed its monstrous head for the third time in the Lords, rose to his feet – too deaf to hear criticism or protest, too proud to care even if he had – and duly talked it out, bringing us closer to revolution than we had ever been.

The government resigned, leaving the King with no one but the Duke of Wellington with courage enough to try to form another. There was an immediate run on the Bank of England, as industrialists like my husband withdrew their funds in obedience to the Radical slogan 'To beat the Duke go for gold' and, in addition, declared that they would pay no taxes until they had their way. In the northern cities, men of a more violent nature – who saw middle-class freedom as a steppingstone to their own and who fully shared the Duke of Wellington's view that once Reform had begun there would be no stopping it – began to barricade the streets. Suddenly the country was on a war footing, class against class, and once again, as in the year my father died, there were tales of armed gangs drilling in the woods and of soldiers sharpening swords that would not all be used – if matters came to that – against the mob.

I did not expect myself to be attacked, for I could see no profit to anyone in that, but so ugly was the mood of the streets, so haphazard the violence brewing beneath the very cobbles, ready to slay as indiscriminately as the typhoid, that I stayed close to home, confining my children and my dogs to the garden. Yet when I did walk out, drawn once again to the pathway above the mill, I could still see that faceless bee swarm of women in the mill yard, waiting with the patience of weariness and need for the gates to open, totally submissive, as men know women must always be submissive when there are children to be fed. And I wondered just what the Reform Bill meant to them.

I had accompanied Hannah often enough, these past months, on her missions of mercy in Patterswick for her Reverend Ashley, and in the grey-faced, mean-spirited alleys behind Ramsden Street, where the gutters ran foul with sewage water and the occasional rotting carcase that had once been dog or cat. And although I could do no less than admire her zeal, I returned always unsatisfied, for Hannah visited only the 'good poor,' carefully selected by her two reverends, who could be trusted to behave decently before a lady and who, if they failed to act upon her advice, at least knew how to thank her for it. And, indeed, Hannah's advice was, in most cases, perfectly sound. She was undoubtedly justified in advising a young mother that her eight or nine small children would do better if they showed clean faces and clean pinafores to the world, although with their living in one of Morgan Aycliffe's two-room cottages, where the sole source of water – a solitary tap in the middle of the grimy street – was only turned on for an hour or two every day, she did not state how this should be achieved.

'I think,' she lectured, gently but firmly, 'that eight children – or is it nine? – are quite enough, for there is no more space, either upstairs or downstairs, for another mattress, and your older boys and girls are getting too big now to sleep together. It is high time you thought about hanging a curtain to separate your bedroom, half for your husband and yourself, half for your daughters, while your boys must use the floor downstairs as best they may. My sister-in-law may have some curtaining fabric to spare – oh good, Verity, I felt sure you would – and if Mrs Stevens could make it up and we could supply some brass rings and a rod – yes? I think we may make all decent, in that case. But really, my dear, there must be an end to it – large families are all very well for those who can afford them, but you must remember that you cannot.'

And although the young woman gave her most fervent agreement, it was not kind of Hannah, in my view – since she had not specified just how further pregnancies could be avoided – to be so cross when, on a subsequent visit, she found the girl with tears in her eyes and a tenth child already showing under her none-too-clean pinny.

'It was him, not me,' she said, gesturing towards the mill, where her husband was employed. 'He had a drink one Friday night and that was it, wasn't it. What could I do?'

'Nothing,' I told her, but Hannah, with whom all men, even my brother Edwin, had been careful, did not believe

257

that any woman could be taken against her will or could give herself, knowing the consequences, merely to avoid a black eye and a few foul phrases.

'I will ask Mr Brand to speak to the husband,' she said as we came out of the dim, acrid little hovel into the wet and littered street. 'But I am beginning to feel we are wasting our time in this case. If they had restrained themselves to begin with and settled for two or three children at the most, then they could have done well enough, but now they seem to have set their feet on a downward path. And if the husband is drinking his wages, I can see nothing but the workhouse at the end of it.'

And so the young family was transferred, with one blink of Hannah's eyelids, from the list locked firmly in her mind marked 'deserving' to a second list marked 'feckless, ungrateful, not worth the trouble.'

Yet there were many others, pensioned-off servants of Squire Dalby's and old weavers of my grandfather's day, all of them existing meagrely in tied cottages, who welcomed Hannah's visits, glad of the soup and cakes, the knitted blankets and shawls and the sound of another human voice she brought them, and were by no means unwilling to doff a cap or sketch a creaky curtsy at her comings and goings.

'What a marvel she is,' the Reverend Mr Ashley often told me. 'Take care of her, Mrs Barforth, I beg you, for I cannot imagine how the parish ever managed without her.'

'A fine, noble lady,' the Reverend Mr Brand thundered at me. 'The very finest it has been my privilege to meet.'

Yet neither the pale, beautiful Mr Ashley nor the plain, vigorous Mr Brand proposed marriage, and when I wondered why – being anxious to get her settled in her own home and away from mine – my mother surprised me by declaring it was because Hannah would not permit it.

'I cannot speak for Mr Brand,' she said, 'since I barely know him, but our Mr Ashley would marry her rather than lose her. Oh yes, yes, I am well aware that he would prefer to remain single, for he is indeed somewhat too frail for the married state, but if Hannah wanted him he would not know how to resist. She would need to do no more than make her wishes known. Yet why should she limit herself to Mr Ashley and his hundred pounds a year when, by marrying neither, she can have the better part of both? Yes, yes, I know how sorry you feel for her, because of Edwin and Mr Aycliffe, but only think, dear, how easy her life must be. She has the devotion of two men without any obligation whatsoever, and as to children, if she feels the lack of them, I imagine she can help herself to her sister's. Elinor would not miss a child or two, or even three, and how convenient for Hannah, to be spared the ordeal of actually bearing them.'

'And you think that would be enough for her?'

'Oh, my dear,' my mother said, laughter trilling out of her like birdsong, 'it would have been quite enough for me.'

But in Hannah's case, as I watched her stooping to pass the doorway of some low cottage, a heavy basket on her arm, or standing straight-backed, straight-souled, before a committee or a Sunday School class, or before Morgan Aycliffe himself when he explained to her – not to Bradley Hobhouse or to Joel – why the Assembly Rooms were not rising fast enough, I was not sure. My mother had learned to be content with life's surface – as I was learning to do – but Hannah, like Joel, needed to be in the battle itself, wielding pike and gun, and even precise control of Mr Ashley and Mr Brand was not enough.

Her nature, like Joel's, craved the stimulus of constant challenge – a craving so intense that she became physically ill, with headache or toothache, when it remained unsatisfied – and, again like Joel, she was constantly, restlessly in search of new worlds to conquer and hampered, at every turn, as he was not, by her sex. Naturally she could not offer herself for election should the franchise come, but she could support the man who did – Mr Aycliffe or another

– and although her feminine modesty would not allow her to utter one word in public on his behalf, she could assist him in the composition of speeches and articles that were stylish ánd tasteful and contained nothing which could be used against him at a later date. She could not herself preside over the meetings of the Assembly Rooms Committee; she could merely preside over the president, her brother, who found it amusing to impose his sister's wishes on Hobhouses and Oldroyds and Corey-Mannings, and on Mr Aycliffe himself. She could not, as my mother had suggested, bear children, but her orders were the only ones to carry weight in Elinor's nursery, and it was Hannah who decided when little Cecilia should be weaned, when a doctor should be called to diagnose Prudence's spots or Faith's cough, and how much fresh air and sunshine should be allowed to all three. And eventually, although her official home was still with me, she had her own room in Morgan Aycliffe's house and her regular place at his table, directly beneath the portrait of his first unhappy wife, with his second unhappy lady welcoming the intrusion since she was thus spared the necessity of conversation.

'I have put some of my thoughts on paper about the free trade issue, Miss Barforth – jottings, merely – and would be glad of your opinion,' Mr Aycliffe would casually murmur. And she, some time later, would reply, 'Most concisely put, Mr Aycliffe – a masterpiece of verbal economy. Should you wish me to make a fair copy I would be most honoured.'

'Ah – the honour would be done to me, Miss Barforth. And should any little irregularities of style present themselves to your notice, by all means feel free. . . .'

'What a good thing he did not marry her,' my mother said after dining one evening in Blenheim Lane, 'for they could never have had so immaculate a relationship had she been his wife. Had he married her he would have been obsessed with his obligation to desire her body – or his lack of it – but, as it is, he is free to value her mind, while poor Elinor must bear the burden of the other side of him. But what about the son – that most interesting young man? I have heard he is associating with anarchists and atheists and the landlady of the Red Gin. Can it all be true?'

And I was bound to say it was. Perhaps I had looked for Crispin this past year as I had walked dutifully beside Hannah, my charity basket on my arm, through those foul courtyards cobwebbing their way behind Ramsden Street; perhaps I had hoped for him, wanted him to appear suddenly through the constant yellow-grey gloom of those back alleys. But he was never there, and I had taught myself that his life, like mine, was full and had no room for strangers.

And I could not doubt that his life was full, for – setting aside the rumours concerning his relations with his land-lady – his work with the Short Time Committee and his contributions to the *Cullingford Star* had made him a great hero to some of us, a great nuisance to others, and his name and face so well known that I was often obliged to hear others discuss him, although I did not discuss him myself.

'He's a grand lad, young Mr Aycliffe,' my maid Marth-Ellen told me, having heard news of him from her sister, who lived in Simon Street. 'Do anything for anybody, he would – give you the shirt off his back if you asked him for it. Fetch a doctor, he will, any time of the day or night – and pay, sometimes, I reckon, since not even old Dr Turner goes to Simon Street these days unless he gets his money in advance. And when there was no money to bury Maria Flaherty – her next door to my sister's granddaughter – and nobody bothered about her because she was sodden with drink and killed herself with it, just like it killed her man last winter – they say it was Mr Aycliffe who put his hand in his pocket for the funeral and kept an eye on the bairns until her sister could be got to take them. Aye – Maria Flaherty – and she was a filthy young slut at the best of times. They think a lot of Mr Aycliffe in Simon Street.'

But Hannah judged differently.

'Don't think for one moment he cares about the factory children,' she continued to insist. 'He has still no other motive than malice towards his father.'

And perhaps, to begin with, her judgement had been partly true, for Crispin had never pretended to be noble and was not above taking his revenge. But he had lived now, for more than a year, in an alleyway somewhere behind the Red Gin, a typical, short, narrow street of identical two-room houses thrown down on a patch of clay and engine ashes, with a dung heap at one end and a swill tub at the other, put there by a pig farmer who would pay a penny or two for the communal slops. For more than a year he had viewed misery not from Hannah's lofty if well-intentioned heights but at the range of his nostrils and the pores of his skin. He had woken in the night to the whimpering of the woman next door, separated from him by a paper-thin wall, as she gave birth to another unwanted child; and he had listened to her bitter complaints and then her wail of anguish because the child, after all, was dying and there was no money for a doctor. He had grown accustomed to the sound of distress and the violence that it breeds; to the men – and the women – coming home from the gin shop and the beerhouse, needing to break something or one another, taking sex as they took combat and strong drink because these, at least, were desires that could be satisfied and one had to do something to feel alive.

He had seen the children too, staggering home like sleepwalkers every night, drowning in grime and dust and fatigue; misshapen old men of nine or ten, some of them, who whined and shivered all night in their sleep from the ache of limbs that would never be straight again. He had heard them in the morning too as they were shaken awake in the cold dark and pushed out into the street to begin again on that treadmill of heat and noise and toil, going round and round like mice on a wheel until some of them fell off and were whirled away forever.

There was a girl that year at the Hobhouse mill who, when her sister became entangled in the machinery, tried to pull her out and had her own arm torn off, both sisters bleeding to death before they reached the infirmary.

'The girl fell asleep at her work,' Emma-Jane told me defensively. 'And although it's tragic and horrific and I'm very sorry, I don't see how Bradley can be blamed for it. The overlooker should have kept her awake, that's what he's there for, after all. I've told Bradley to dismiss him, as a gesture, because, after all, if he lets the girls fall asleep, one can hardly feel any confidence in him.'

But we learned some days later, through the agency of Mark Corey's *Cullingford Star* – from the pen of Crispin Aycliffe – that these girls, being the sole support of an ailing mother and six infant brothers and sisters, had, since the age of eight, been in the habit of getting up at half past three in the morning to walk several stony miles to Nethercoats, where, in temperatures of seventy-six degrees, they endured fourteen hours of hard labour, returning home as they had left it, in the pitch dark, arriving sometimes with cracked and bleeding feet, and frequently much bruised about the shoulders from the overlooker's strap.

'Is it any wonder,' the article concluded, 'that such girls become lethargic? It would seem more a matter for wonder that one of them possessed the courage, or the humanity – in so inhumane a world – to attempt to save the other from destruction, thus destroying herself in the process. And if anyone should ever pause to enquire – which seems unlikely – why the machinery was not turned off at once, one must remember that someone, possibly with a bonus to earn, may not have understood the hurry.'

And beneath Crispin's skilful, dramatic words, the Hobhouses' discharged overlooker was allowed to have his say.

'Yes, I have a strap to beat them with,' he agreed, 'although that's mainly for the boys. I just give the lasses a clout, more often than not, across the ear, and that does the trick. Yes, the mothers complain sometimes, or some of them do, but they've been bairns themselves, like I have, and they've had their share. They know, same as I do, that if the masters want to employ bairns, there's only one way to make them work. If they stay awake they stay alive, and what's best – a clout or two, or a lick with a strap, or happen a right good kicking, or going round the shaft and ending up dead? What do they expect? The masters bring the bairns in, and if they don't attend to their work they hold the rest of us up from doing ours, and then the masters complain. And if there's any other way but the strap, then I'd be glad to know it, because I'm always sorry afterwards – every time, I'm sorry.'

'Despicable man,' Emma-Jane Hobhouse almost sobbed, without making it clear whether she meant their former overlooker or Crispin Aycliffe. 'Making it out that it's all Bradley's fault, as usual, and it's not, because he didn't make those girls get up so early and walk all that way. Their mother brought them to the mill and begged us to give them work. "Ailing mother" indeed; well, maybe she is ailing, and I don't wonder. But what this obscenity of a newspaper forgot to mention is that there's a father too, who hasn't done a stroke of work for years – no, not a stroke; he just stays in bed all day getting his wife pregnant and sending his children into the mill so he can spend their wages on drink. No, they forget about that.'

But, in the next issue, the *Star* remembered and, in a damning article undoubtedly from Crispin's pen, we were made aware that not all working-class parents were noble or unwilling to sell their children into slavery. There were mothers who wept at the mill gates as they saw their children absorbed into the heat and dust, and fathers who grieved and raged and shouldered as much of the burden as they could. But there were also couples who, living in a permanent state of drunken squalor, bred children solely for the money they could eventually earn, beg, or steal.

'And why should you be surprised at this?' the *Star* thundered, shattering our momentary self-righteousness. 'Why should anyone be surprised when one considers that these same parents were themselves brutalized and abused in childhood – "pauper brats," some of them, brought here when five years old from the poorhouses of the South, to work, eat, and sleep in our mill sheds, knowing nothing, from that young age, but the overlooker's strap and the parson's weekly reminder that it is all the will of God.'

And below was an illustration of an overlooker's black leather thong, set into its short, evil-looking handle, and of a Negro slave, well fed and curly, his chubby hands raised in grief for the diminutive, almost skeletal white child who was about to be whipped.

'This should be put a stop to,' Morgan Aycliffe said, holding a copy of the *Star* shaking between his outraged fingers and recognizing his son's authorship, I imagine, even better than I did.

But Joel, who had never suffered much from embarrassment and was a stranger to guilt, merely shrugged and smiled.

'Then we'll put a stop to it. It shouldn't be difficult. Even a rag like this costs money to produce, and these lads who are producing it – whoever they may be – will hardly have much of their own. So they're either begging it or borrowing it, and all that's needful is to locate their source of supply and block it or cut it off altogether. I'll see to it myself when I get the time, but for now I'll put Ira Agbrigg onto it. A good man, Ira, for secrets. He'll ferret it out, and then you may leave the rest to me.'

But even Ira Agbrigg, just then, had little time for secrets or very much else, as the Reform issue rose, once again, to the boil. This third Bill, introduced in December and passed triumphantly by the Commons, had been thrown out by the Lords, yet again, in May. Lord Grey, having requested the King to create enough new peers to push it through, had been refused and then he had resigned. The Duke of Wellington had been sent for, either to form a government or to stage an aristocratic *coup d'état*, depending on one's point of view, but it was soon clear that his efforts, however valiant, could not succeed. He could find no one really willing to stand beside him and, by the middle of the month, the Reforming Lord Grey was back again, informing a possibly nervous monarch that he must either agree to the creation of new peers and get the damnable bill into the Statute Book or suffer the consequences. And since there could be little doubt that those consequences might well include not only the loss of his throne but the loss of his head, he had no alternative but to agree.

The Third Reform Bill became law on June 7 in the year I was twenty-four, the Duke of Wellington and one hundred of his supporters – who could not bring themselves to vote in favour – saving the royal face somewhat by abstaining altogether so that the wholesale distribution of new peerages would not be required. Bradford, Leeds, Halifax, Manchester, Sheffield, Cullingford were all enfranchised. The middle classes, the industrialists, the master tradesmen, the shopkeepers, the better-class householders, those who paid a minimum rent of ten pounds a year – even Ira Agbrigg, former mill hand and now manager of Low Cross – were all free.

But I was a married woman, for whom, like infants and idiots, the law allowed no freedom, and, like the other women of my class, I turned my mind to silks and satins – for the Assembly Rooms and the Reform Bill were completed together, and we were to give a ball.

17

Morgan Aycliffe and Hannah between them had created for us a classical palace of culture and entertainment, faced by fluted Greek columns and long, shallow steps; a swan of a building, preening itself among a collection of lesser barnyard fowls, the old shops and warehouses clustered around it. It had a square hallway, elegantly marbled in black and white, with a staircase rising majestically from it to reach a broad landing where guests could be received and ushered through the double doors to a long, high-ceilinged apartment, the lecture hall and ballroom, lit by the most magnificent chandelier Cullingford had yet seen, a waterfall of crystal donated by my husband in my name, to the mortification of Emma-Jane Hobhouse, who, having already provided the blue velvet curtains – and made a great song and dance out of her generosity – could not, with decency, increase her offer. Nor could she grumble, being pregnant again and not really fit to be seen, when it was decided that Elinor and I should act as hostesses at the great Reform Ball, Lucy Oldroyd, being of a retiring disposition, having declined, while Hannah, who had certainly earned the honour, being single and, consequently, out of the running.

I had no idea how much she minded. The Assembly Rooms had undoubtedly risen as much by her efforts as by the exertions of Morgan Aycliffe's bricklayers. Hers had been the tenacity of purpose, the vision, the determination to thwart even Emma-Jane, who had really wanted green velvet curtains and had been prevented from supplying them only when Hannah had told her that blue would go better with the chairs.

'What chairs?' Emma-Jane had asked, looking blankly around the empty room.

'The chairs Mr Aycliffe has asked me to order on his behalf,' Hannah explained calmly, finally, so that Emma-Jane, instead of demanding that the order be altered or cancelled, said, 'Oh, I see,' and waited, quite meekly, until the straight-backed blue-and-gilt chairs were delivered and she could match her curtains accordingly.

Yet, on that grand gala opening Hannah would have no choice but to stand behind me and her younger sister, behind Emma-Jane, even – unless Nature provided the young Mrs Hobhouse with some other way, that evening, of occupying her time – and although it would be the duty of every man present to pay attention to me, Joel Barforth's wife, very few would trouble to notice his unmarried, undowered sister.

'Perhaps she should marry the Reverend Mr Ashley for the occasion,' Elinor suggested languidly. 'Even his hundred pounds a year would guarantee her a place in the receiving line, if that's what she wants. Although what she'd do with him afterwards, I really couldn't say.'

But Elinor, surprisingly, had lost her own enthusiasm for balls lately, and although there were some mornings when she was ready to take the Assembly Rooms by storm and others when she would arrive, mischievous as a kitten, merely to disagree with anything Emma-Jane Hobhouse proposed, there were other occasions – many occasions – when, quite abruptly, in mid-speech, mid-air, her vivacity would drain away, leaving her blank-eyed, peevish, not knowing where to put herself.

'I'm not well,' she would declare. 'I'm tired.' And, with no more excuse than that, she would walk out of tea party or luncheon party, walk out of church – once in the middle of a Hobhouse christening – or, if she happened to be in her own house, would retire upstairs, leaving her startled guests to their own devices.

'I had a headache,' she would tell me, 'and that's that. Yes, it may have given offence, but I can't be expected to know in advance how I'm going to feel. I'm just not brave, that's all – or stupid. I know Hannah would sit downstairs and smile no matter how much her head ached – and I expect you'd do the same. But why? Why should I put myself through agony for Emma-Jane Hobhouse, or for anybody else for that matter? It's just not worth it. And if they do it for me, then that's their business, and I surely don't appreciate it.'

But whether or not she meant to attend the Assembly Ball – and I found it hard to believe that Elinor, of all people, would be able to stay away – she ordered a sky-blue satin gown from Rosamund Boulton for the occasion and made substantial purchases of fans and silk gloves, ivory combs, and a great many other things she did not need.

I went with her to that new, smart-as-paint little shop in Millergate, with Rosamund Boulton's name in pink above the door, and, since everyone else I knew had commanded their ball gowns from her, I did the same, allowing her to dissuade me from my original choice of white silk to a quite different idea of her own.

'I could see you in this light green, Mrs Barforth – a very cool, elegant shade which would certainly become you, for one should dress to suit the personality as well as the face and figure. And since, with your dark colouring and your height and slenderness, any shade would suit you, I feel we should concentrate on a general impression of poise – serenity. Do try this green, Mrs Barforth.'

And, as she swathed that length of silk crepe around me, smiling, professional, totally self-possessed, I understood how much Joel meant to her, that she would rather strangle me than dress me but would dress me, just the same, if she could, in the one colour she knew Joel disliked.

A small triumph, which I almost allowed her – a woman turned thirty still so achingly in love with the man who had abandoned her at twenty-three – and then could not allow, so that as she threw the fabric across her counter and began to measure, I called out, 'One moment, Miss

Boulton – may I change my mind. I think the white, after all.'

'Oh,' she said, hating me, her scissors hovering. 'Just as you please, Mrs Barforth, of course – although I must say I'm surprised.'

'Yes, but you'll do it for me, Miss Boulton, won't you, as I've asked – and I'm sure it will be beautiful.'

But I could not trust her, and although I attended the fittings and let her mould the dress on me, I went privately to the best needlewoman I knew, my mother, and spent quiet, mellow afternoons in her house at Patterswick, watching her ply her needle as I had done all my life, her tranquillity touching the seeds of my own, so that, in her presence, I was at peace. She made me a dress of cream-coloured gauze over a foundation of embroidered silk, a delicately worked tracery of cream on cream, with billowing, transparent sleeves and a skirt as light as a summer cloud, and when I took it home and hung it beside the white brocade Rosamund Boulton had made too tight across the bodice, I forced myself to think of her with Joel and to assess just what it meant to me. And I had not anticipated how completely I would fail.

She had wanted him once and had been willing to wait for him against her father's advice. He had wanted her, too, but not enough to forgo the Barforth inheritance for her sake. They had met again, perhaps not too long ago, when all her subsequent attempts at matrimony had failed, and if he had put money into her business – and I was sure he had – then she was his mistress by now, had been his mistress before the loan, would continue to be his mistress for as long as it gave him satisfaction. And did I care? Should I care?

He's with her now, I told myself that night when he failed to appear at dinnertime; he's gone to the Old Swan for his oysters and his punch, and then to the shop, to her, just about halfway between the Swan and home. I saw him letting himself in through the back door, enjoying the deception and the knowledge that she had been waiting for him, longing for him, all day as his wife never seemed to do. I imagined him taunting her, talking business, making her wait a while longer, when all the time he could sense the heat in her, the need. I stripped him in my imagination, took off his expensive coat and fine, cambric shirt, which, even in a moment of passion, he would fold carefully on a chair back, remembering the days when such garments had been beyond his means. I looked at the long, hard curve of his back, the breadth of his shoulders, the scattering of dark hairs on his chest and arms, the skin that could look like amber in the candlelight, the arrogance and power and beauty of him. And then I stripped her too; I made her thinner, perhaps, than the truth of her, angular but ardent, wanting pleasure, knowing how to give it. I put her in his arms and found, to my amazement, that I could go no further, not from anguish of the heart but from the sheer physical refusal of my brain to function. At the precise moment of their joining together something inside me that controlled the source of my imagination snuffed out and the coupling did not take place. They still lay there, somewhere in the back room of that smart new shop, but they were unreal – as I was unreal – dolls merely, and when I tried to bring them and myself to life, I encountered nothing but fog and confusion.

And so I had two ball gowns, two pairs of satin slippers, two feathered fans – one white, one cream – yet I almost missed the dance itself, for two weeks before the great event I miscarried a child I had only vaguely begun to suspect, thereby annoying my husband, who, though by no means a fond father, was not pleased to see Bradley Hobhouse with five sons and another on the way when he had but two.

'Oh my,' Elinor said, coming to perch at my bedside, 'if you are going to be ill, then I had better be ill too, for I really cannot stand at the head of that staircase alone.'

But Joel required the presence of his wife at the Assembly

Rooms on that memorable, sultry summer night, and since it did not seem to cross his mind that I could fail, I got up and, in reply to his brusque 'Are you all right?' replied that I was very well.

'You are a little pale, dear, and a little hollow in the cheeks,' my mother told me, 'but it suits you – it makes you look mysterious and just a little sad, which men will always like since it appeals both to their protective instincts and to their curiosity. And if Mrs Stevens can do up your hair very high on the crown of your head, then it will make the hollows deeper, and you will seem sadder and sweeter than ever. Can she do that?'

She could and did, forming a heavy, intricate coil threaded through with cream rosebuds after rinsing my hair in her special lotion of aromatic vinegars and herbs and brushing it to a fine shine.

'Beautiful,' she murmured, cooing over me, patting the folds of my cloudy, gauzy skirt with affection, for I was her pet and her treasure these days, the recipient of all her cosseting as my grandfather had once been. And although I knew that these loving gestures were merely the tools of her exhausting trade – that of making herself pleasant to strangers – at least with me she could allow her own cheek muscles to sag a little, her ankles to swell in the heat; she could take her nap in the afternoons; she could be, in fact, a comfortable, gossipy, middle-aged woman. And she was grateful.

Joel came into the room as she left it, impressive as he always was in evening clothes, and, looking me up and down, he said decisively, 'Yes. I saw it in your cupboard and thought it plain, but you'll make the others look overdressed, and that's good – that's good, Verity. You may like to wear these with it.'

And he took, quite casually, from his pocket a necklace of cream-tinted, velvet-textured pearls and held them out to me.

It was a complicated piece, three strands worn high

around the neck with a fourth hanging halfway to the waist, a diamond droplet at its centre, and, putting it on, I stood for a moment before my mirror, entranced by its sheer loveliness, quite breathless but not precisely grateful. He would not ask for the jewels to be returned to him tonight, when the dance was over, as Morgan Aycliffe did, nor would he keep them hidden away under lock and key and oblige me to beg his permission to wear them, as Elinor had to do. On the contrary, he would be glad to have me wear them as often as I liked since the reason for their purchase was not only to give me pleasure but to show the world that in this glorious Reform year of 1832, when Bradley Hobhouse was known to be losing money through his own mismanagement and Matthew Oldroyd was not making quite so much as his father before him, Joel Barforth was a man who could offer his wife toys such as these.

And so, turning myself this way and that to see the lamplight probing the velvet heart of the pearls, the wild heart of the diamond, I murmured, 'Thank you, Joel,' without really looking at him.

'That's what I like,' he said, laughing. 'I give her a fortune in jewels and she says, "Thank you, Joel" – no more than that.'

'What would you like me to say?'

'Oh, exactly what you did say – it's enough. After all, if you'd been a boy, you'd have had the mill, wouldn't you, and the money, and I'd still have been scratching a living at Low Cross, so there's no need for raptures.'

And he would have been married to Rosamund Boulton, I thought, shivering suddenly, so that I reached for my shawl and told him quite crisply that we must not be late.

I took my place at the head of the stairs without too much apprehension, for although I was to receive guests they would mainly be the people I had known all my life, and such strangers as there were could only be the Leeds and Bradford equivalents of the Hobhouses and Oldroyds, and the party our manorial lord, Sir Giles Flood, had warned us he would bring.

We had not, in fact, expected Sir Giles, since he was rarely seen in Cullingford itself, preferring to transact his business with us from the safe distance of his hunting box in Leicestershire or his town house in Belgravia. But our recent enfranchisement could not have escaped him, and although he could have no hope of winning the newly created constituency of Cullingford – being as dedicated to the landed interest as the Duke of Wellington himself – his presence here tonight indicated that he meant to put a candidate in the field.

'It is merely to annoy us, don't you see?' Elinor whispered as we mounted the staircase together. 'Mr Aycliffe is definitely to stand as representative for the manufacturing interest, and because the squires are so piqued about the Reform Bill getting through, they have decided to take up this business of the ten-hour day. And although Richard Oastler and Michael Sadler seem really to care for the factory children, I am very sure Sir Giles Flood does not. He only wants to get back at the manufacturers for daring to push the franchise, so he will put up his own candidate – someone not to win but just to make a nuisance of himself and force my husband to spend more on his campaign funds than he need have done. Anyway, that is what my husband says, and it sounds very complicated – and very likely – but what I really want to know is where did you get that dress and why are you not wearing the one Rosamund made you? She will think you most unkind and I – well – I think you are sly.'

But her spirits were too high that night to be much affected even by the sight of my pearls – finer than the ones she was allowed to borrow, now and then, from the shrine of the first Mrs Aycliffe – and standing beside me on the landing, taking an occasional little skipping step in her excitement, she seemed her old, irrepressible self again.

Below us, the hall, lit by another Barforth chandelier,

was like a rose garden, with vast arrangements of pink and white blossoms lining the walls, twining themselves around the columns, climbing the staircase, while every long, shallow step was crowned with a bowl or a basket of flowers. In the rooms behind us, my household staff and Elinor's and Emma-Jane's, along with an army of hirelings, were standing, we hoped, at their posts beside the buffet tables, while below us and to our right, in what would be the reading room, a full-scale supper was to be served. The orchestra, selected by Hannah, was in its place, and her blue-and-gold chairs waited to receive the happy, the excited, the disappointed, the footsore and the weary, while I, as the first carriages began to roll by, remembered I had barely touched my dinner and that I would be obliged to stand here a very long time.

'Thank God I am not a duchess,' Elinor muttered as the first self-conscious arrivals began to drift upstairs. 'Imagine having to do this three or four times a week in the Season. One is bound to get a headache after an hour of it – in fact, I can feel mine coming on already.'

But this kind of entertainment, as well as the Assembly Rooms themselves, were new to Cullingford, and after our having talked of little else for weeks, our having spent the day laying out gown and gloves and pelerine, and the afternoon wiring our ringlets into place, the temptation to come early and actually see for ourselves was too great. By ten o'clock Millergate, Market Street, and Kirkgate were blocked with carriages and the rose-garden staircase had become a multicoloured moving tapestry, with a gigantic communal smile, a collective hand reaching for mine, and a voice – my voice – repeating, without any assistance from my brain, 'How nice to see you. How very nice to see you. We are so glad you were able to come.'

The Hobhouses and the Oldroyds arrived in a cluster, strong colours, warm laughter, Emma-Jane feeling herself sufficiently close to me to be frankly jealous of my pearls, Bradley saying, 'Hmmmm, well – they must have cost a

275

pretty penny,' and then bolting away to the refreshment room, as if he thought Emma-Jane might suddenly demand the same. And after them came the stream of lesser people, the newly enfranchised 'ten-pounders' who had reason to celebrate – our own managers among them, some of them shaking my hand with a brash self-confidence, some with a studied charm that reminded me of Joel in his younger days, while Ira Agbrigg's thin, silent wife turned so pale when I spoke to her and her eyes became so terrified that I would not have been surprised to see her turn and run for cover like a cornered vixen.

My mother and Squire Dalby brought Hannah with them, the Reverend Mr Ashley walking a pace or two behind, looking delicate and pale and very well pleased, since the Reverend Mr Brand, who did not approve of dancing, could not be here. Indeed, Mr Brand's objections had been so strong that he had attempted to dissuade Hannah from coming herself, but 'I shall take no harm,' she had told him, and, as she came striding towards me, her mind clearly on the hundred last-minute details she assumed I had forgotten, I did not doubt it. She looked competent, eagle-eyed, regal, a grand personage who deserved a second, respectful glance and something rather better than a hundred-pound-a-year country parson dangling at her skirts.

'Why are you wearing flowers in your hair?' she asked me, plainly considering my cream rosebuds an insufficient headdress for a millmaster's wife, and, answering her, I was unaware of Rosamund Boulton until she was standing before me, holding out her hand, her smile freezing on her lips as she saw my gown.

She had come with her father, her married sister, and her brother-in-law, a respectable family party which would only be noticed for the challenging, almost desperate beauty of Rosamund herself. She was in gleaming, dazzling white satin – chosen to put my white brocade in the shadow – a dress she had moulded to her body to accentuate every

276

long, lithe curve of it; a bold, provocative outfit which would not please many women but would draw the eye of every man. There were red roses at her waist and in her hair, and a long feathered fan swishing nervously, irritably in her hand, belying a restlessness beneath the sophisticated, professional charm that would appeal to these Law Valley men who, like Joel, could rarely resist a challenge.

'Why, Mrs Barforth, how delightful you look . . .'

'Thank you, Miss Boulton, and so do you.'

'But that dress, Mrs Barforth – if I have ever seen anything so exquisite I really can't remember when.'

'How kind,' I said, making no explanation, wondering why I was being so cruel when I did not hate her, when it would be so easy for me to say, 'It was a gift from my mother – totally unexpected,' and relieve her mind of the agony of wondering why I had set aside the dress she had made me herself.

Did I know about her and Joel? And if I did, could I put a stop to it? Would he abandon her all over again to please me? Those questions, I knew, would haunt her throughout the dance, would torment her until she could snatch a few words with him, ask him, warn him, plead with him, annoy him, since he would not take kindly to her fears and jealousy tonight. And, knowing this, understanding the how and the why of it, I kept silent and let her go.

Sir Giles Flood and his party, quite naturally, were not expected until the last, and when a breathless lad came running upstairs to tell us their carriages were in the street, I knew a moment of alarm, quickly suppressed, since Sir Giles Flood was but another arrogant, overbearing, rich old man, and I had known plenty of those. But perhaps I was unprepared for the size of his party, the size of the man himself – a full six feet and a half, or so it seemed, of aristocratic ennui – a manorial lord indeed, his cousin, Colonel Corey, whom I often saw in Blenheim Lane, faded to insignificance beside him. Colonel Corey's daughter, Estella, was there too, now the wife of a dashing Captain

Chase, who had come in full-dress uniform; and, behind them, a half dozen young men and several young ladies, none of whom could possibly be Lady Flood.

'My dear Mrs Barforth,' Colonel Corey said, coming towards me, bringing a rich odour of brandy and cigars, a certain bluff geniality, with him. 'My word, this is all very nice – and very nice of you to have us too – very civil, enemies in the camp, eh? But we won't worry about that tonight. Are you not acquainted with my cousin, Sir Giles? No, I imagine not, for you would have been in the schoolroom the last time he came among us. Giles, dear boy, let me present Mrs Barforth to you. You won't regret it.'

'Mrs Barforth?' the lord said, offering me two limp and languid fingers by way of greeting. 'Now then – let me see – there's a Samson Barforth somewhere, as I recall – pushy kind of a fellow – he'll be your husband, ma'am, I reckon?'

'My grandfather,' I told him, my nerves jangling but my voice quite cool. 'He died some years ago.'

'Did he, by Jove,' he said, and as he glanced down at me, his lordly lips began to twitch slightly at the corners with the birth of a smile.

'Very happy to make your acquaintance, Mrs Barforth,' he said, the two limp fingers becoming a hand, holding mine far too long with lordly privilege, until his cousin, Colonel Corey, who appeared eager to hold my hand too, said, 'Don't frighten the girl, Giles,' and elbowed him aside.

'Good evening, Mrs Chase,' I said, very much amused. 'Captain Chase.' And then, assuming that I knew no one else, I paused, waiting to be introduced, and found myself holding out a hand to Crispin Aycliffe.

'My goodness,' Elinor said, forgetting both her manners and the impression she too was making on our ground landlord. 'Oh my goodness.'

But Sir Giles's arrival had brought the entire Assembly Rooms Committee out onto the landing, Morgan Aycliffe and Joel among them, and, in the shadow of Sir Giles's august presence, there was nothing to do but smile.

'Mrs Barforth,' Crispin said to me, bowing formally over my hand.

'Mr Aycliffe.'

But Elinor gave him the very tips of her fingers, gingerly, as if she thought her husband might snatch them away again, while everyone else – except Lucy Oldroyd, who was too softhearted to snub anybody – managed, in the confusion of that overcrowded landing, not to greet him at all.

'I'm sorry,' Emma-Jane hissed into my ear. 'I don't want to make a scene, but I really can't speak to him. After all those vile things he's written about us I don't know how he can show his face – upsetting me when I'm like this . . .'.

And Bradley, his mouth dangerous, muttered into my other ear, 'Let him talk out of turn just once, Verity, and I'll take him outside and thrash him. By God I will.'

'I feel cold,' Elinor breathed, pressing close beside me, using my body to shut out the sight of her husband making some tight-lipped, grey-faced remark to Mrs Chase, his mouth moving as if every word gave him pain. 'Don't you feel cold, Verity? I feel cold – perhaps I'll just slip away and get my shawl.'

But our manorial lord, having dined exceedingly well, required now to be entertained, and, reaching out a commanding hand, he clasped my elbow and led me into the ballroom, the crowd parting before us with a docility I found astonishing and which he did not notice at all.

'Let's get things going, eh, Mrs Barforth – breathe a little life into the proceedings,' he said, and, taking me to the centre of the room amidst a light flutter of applause, bowed and clicked his heels, knowing, with the supreme self-confidence of those born to greatness, that the orchestra would at once begin to play a waltz.

And because there was nothing but Crispin in my mind,

the fact that I was dancing with Sir Giles Flood, who had every intention of flirting and making love to me if he could – since he was known to be obliging in that direction – bothered me not at all. I could be in no doubt that had Crispin come alone, without the protection of Sir Giles, he would have been asked to leave; he would have been hustled roughly downstairs and booted out into the night as likely as not. And why was he here? What connection had he with the Floods and the Coreys, other than his association with Colonel Corey's bastard son Mark? Had he known them in London, or in France? And would they stand by him if Bradley Hobhouse took too much wine and turned his threat into a promise? And if Bradley made trouble, who would stop him, for although Law Valley men were not barbarians they were not too sophisticated to enjoy a rough and tumble; and, if it came to it, I knew that even Joel would be ready to take off his jacket, provided there was someone to hold it for him, and use his fists. And I did not want Crispin hurt – not by anyone, but most of all not by my husband.

'Creating quite a stir, our young Mr Aycliffe, don't you know,' Sir Giles said, clearly well satisfied, and, sensing my interest as a man experienced with women can always do, he grinned broadly, 'Ah, I see you are wondering about him too – just what he's doing here with me and my cousin and those young sprigs. But he's a bright young man, young Aycliffe; exactly what we need. A champion of the people, no less, and it's the people we're after, you see – the little people who haven't got the vote this time but are bound to get it sooner or later – and when they do it won't be our fault, you know. No, no, it was the present government who lowered the drawbridge, and when that happens everybody is sure to get in sooner or later. And if one can't keep them out – if one can't beat them, m'dear, one joins them. No more than common sense, I should think. Yes, the industrialists will take this constituency in September, make no mistake about that, but we'll put up a fight, make our impression, not on today's voters, but on tomorrow's – all those poor devils who work in your mills, m'dear. How long is it? Fourteen, seventeen hours a day? Can't be allowed, you know; simply not decent – no wonder this Ten Hours Bill appeals to them. Never heard of it myself, I must confess, until young Mr Aycliffe let me know about it, for which I'm entirely grateful, since it sounds like a very good thing to me. And with Mr Aycliffe himself to spell it out for us, I don't see how we can fail. No, the millmasters can win this time, but I'll see a man of my own as member for Cullingford before I'm through, for when all's said and done, m'dear, it is my manor and you can't deny me my entitlement to have my say.'

'You mean Mr Crispin Aycliffe is going to stand for office?'

'Well, in a manner of speaking, I rather think he is. Young Captain Chase, my cousin's son-in-law, is my official candidate, for he needs a job of work to do and I'm inclined to keep these things in the family as much as I can. But he's from the South – Godfrey Chase – don't understand the natives, and they can't make head or tail of him – but with Crispin Aycliffe there, you see, to answer the questions and make the speeches, young Chase has no need to open his mouth at all. And if he does, we can rely on Crispin to tell him what to say. Aycliffe for the industrialists, m'dear, and Aycliffe and Chase for the squires. Well, if that don't confuse them, I'll be surprised, for it confuses me.'

And there it was, the whole story; concise, obvious, quite dreadful. Morgan Aycliffe for the manufacturing interest, to enable him to get away from his wife; Crispin Aycliffe for the gentry, for his nuisance value and to interpret for the real candidate, Captain Chase. And my first thought was: Poor Elinor – poor little girl. They'll crush her between them.

18

I danced next with Colonel Corey, while Sir Giles took
Elinor; then Mr Corey-Manning the solicitor, Mr Lucius
Attwood the brewer, Mr Roundwood, owner of the *Cullingford Courier and Review*, with Dr Overdale, and with a
multitude of other worthy men who wished to dance with
their hostess as good manners required and then to retire
to the refreshment table as quickly as they could. And, on
each occasion, when I had been complimented on my looks
and the appearance of the rooms, I was asked if I had
heard about Crispin Aycliffe.

'Interesting times ahead,' Colonel Corey told me. 'Fine
young man, our Crispin – met him through a relative of
mine – not anyone I expect you'd know, Mrs Barforth –
just a young man of my acquaintance. But yes, he'll be a
great help to my son-in-law. In fact, I doubt if the captain
could manage without him.'

Mr Attwood the brewer, who had a troublesome son of
his own, considered the whole affair to be criminal and
thought that Crispin should be publicly flogged at the cart
tail as they'd known how to do in the old days.

'Used to tie their wrists to the tailboard of some old
wagon,' he said with relish, 'and then we'd drive it slow
from the Old Swan to the Bee Hive at the top of Millergate,
flogging all the way, with a gang of urchins chucking stones
and dung and anything else they had a mind. And when
a lad had been through that he soon found the way to
mend his manners. We had more respect in those days,
and more gratitude. Youngsters knew what they owed
their fathers, and how to pay it. And now look where we've
got to – a lad like Crispin Aycliffe, who looks as if he
couldn't knock the skin off a rice pudding, turning against

his own class and setting out to make a fool of the man who raised him.'

And, spluttering with indignation, Mr Attwood forgot the dance was over and went on holding my hand, muttering furiously, until Matthew Oldroyd came to claim me.

Whirling around that polished floor, dazzled by the play of light from Joel's chandelier, clasped in one set of middle-aged arms after another, I found that I needed no more than a fraction of myself to smile and play the polite game of question and answer, leaving the rest free to observe, to taste the atmosphere around me. And it was not sweet. I saw Elinor raise a hand to her lips to stifle a giggle and then, her husband's eyes on her, back away towards the double doors, seeking escape. I saw the huddled outrage of the Hobhouse and Oldroyd ladies, a closing of ranks, stone-cold stares and hastily drawn-in skirts as Crispin Aycliffe passed by. I saw Rosamund Boulton edging towards Joel, raising an enquiring eyebrow, possibly the only person in the room who was too intent on her own affairs to care, or even to have heard about the Aycliffes. But Joel, although well aware of Morgan Aycliffe's position, had no intention of allowing it to spoil his evening. After all, no one would be heckling Joel Barforth at the hustings. Appearing not to see Miss Boulton – although I imagine he saw her very clearly – he strolled across to the manorial party, standing every inch as tall as Sir Giles Flood, and, having made himself generally pleasant – having nodded with a certain grim amusement to Crispin – he began a lighthearted but prolonged conversation with the real Tory candidate, Colonel Corey's son-in-law, Captain Chase. And Miss Boulton knew as well as I did that Joel's interest in the gallant captain extended no further than his wife.

She was fair and sharp-featured and somewhat distant in her manner, Mrs Chase – Estella Corey, who had ordered her wedding gown from Rosamund Boulton; a girl of twenty, perhaps, who knew her own worth, since her mother had been a Flood, and whose languid airs and graces contained their fair share of Flood arrogance. Not a beautiful girl, not even pretty with her pale, watery eyes and her abundant teeth, but a thoroughbred, a challenge, the kind of girl that Joel, in his Low Cross days, had never dreamed of being able to afford – which would, in itself, be enough. And as he bowed over Estella Chase's limp, well-bred hand and led her into the dance, I saw Miss Boulton's face stripped, just for a moment, of the smile, the wit, the brilliance, the bold sparkle, and become a brittle mask of anguish.

But then there was Morgan Aycliffe, appearing in the doorway, looking very much as he always did, a long, grey, mournful man, no stranger to distress, and Hannah, striding purposefully towards him with the Reverend Mr Ashley trailing far behind. Planting herself before him, shielding him from the public view, she began to talk earnestly, telling him, no doubt, that the shame was Crispin's, not his, and that if any awkward questions should be asked she would be glad to deal with them on his behalf.

Crispin did not approach me. By now, my mother and Squire Dalby had joined the Floods in the charmed circle of chairs they had installed near the refreshment table – where, for the rest of the evening, until they left immediately after supper, they remained, drinking quantities of claret and champagne, talking and dancing exclusively with each other – a party within a party – Estella Chase breaking the rule only to dance again with Joel. Crispin sat with apparent ease among them, with one of Sir Giles's young ladies on either side of him, and gradually, since most people were intent on enjoying themselves and it was a personal matter anyway, everyone but his father and Hannah and the hot-tempered Emma-Jane managed to forget him.

Supper was served downstairs on a long table covered with white damask and a multitude of expensive dishes –

veal, chicken and oyster patties, cold roast turkeys and hams, trifles and creams and mountainous ruby-coloured jellies, a veritable feast – with Emma-Jane Hobhouse installed in an armchair at the head of it, placidly eating one plateful for herself and the next for the baby, kicking quite visibly inside her.

'I cannot help thinking that Mrs Hobhouse would have done better, in her condition, had she remained in the security of her own home,' I heard Morgan Aycliffe say to Hannah and, meeting his cold, fastidious eyes and the protective blaze in Hannah's, I understood that sympathy would not be well received by either. Clearly, for both of them, it was a case of what could not be mended must be ignored and since one could not take one's only son by the throat, call him 'Judas,' and sink a carving knife into his heart – as Mr Aycliffe may well have liked to do – the next-best thing was to pretend that he did not exist at all.

'Elinor has gone upstairs,' Hannah told me, 'to the retiring room, to rest.' Then, as Mr Aycliffe went off to fetch her a glass of lemonade, she lowered her voice and said, quite crossly, 'She says she is unwell, but I have just been to see her, and there she is, curled up on a sofa, chatting away to Emma-Jane Hobhouse's maid and your Mrs Stevens – having her forehead rubbed with rose water and her supper brought up on a tray. And when I told her I thought she should come down she said, "Oh, I'm comfortable here, and I've seen everything I want to see downstairs – it wasn't really so exciting, was it, as one might have thought." Do you know, Verity, it's my belief she's actually bored – bored, when this awful thing has happened to her husband – and I can't tell you how much it grieves me to see my own sister with so little sense of – well – duty, responsibility. She should be here, shouldn't she, at his side – not leaving it to others. Oh dear, Mr Ashley is over there looking quite forlorn, trying to make conversation with Miss Boulton – and why she should be in such a sulk I can't imagine. Do go and rescue him,

Verity, for women of her sort positively intimidate him – and my conscience would not allow me to leave Mr Aycliffe just now.'

But Miss Boulton, her smouldering, snarling temper just barely under control, intimidated me too and, escaping from Hannah, I let the crowd engulf me, carry me into the hallway and up the stairs towards the ballroom, where I concluded – from Miss Boulton's state of mind – that Joel was dancing with Estella Chase again. But before I reached the doorway a couple standing close together in a corner of the landing caught my eye: a girl I didn't know who had clearly just been paid a compliment, her young face looking upwards, beginning to smile, displaying the inviting curve of a young neck and shoulders, and Crispin smiling down at her, aware of the invitation. And my whole body suffered such a pang of sheer physical anguish that I rushed forward, quite blind, heedless of anything but my need to get away, not to look, not to know that he could and did desire someone else.

This, I thought wonderingly, is jealousy. This is the suffering you wanted to feel for Joel and could not. This is what Rosamund Boulton is feeling. And it was as terrible to me as that first clawing agony of childbirth, which, in my panic, I had thought would never end. I had expected to die, then, in the hours before Blaize was born and, for a brief moment, I expected to die now. But one does not die so easily and, biting my lip, breathing for an instant as deeply as I could, I made my eyes see again, forced them to pick out of the haze before me the slender, azure shape that was my mother, the stumpy black and white of Squire Dalby, the brittle, arrow-fine silhouette of Estella Chase, her eyes interested, calculating, her own thoroughbred curiosity aroused, as Joel led her back to her chair.

'My dear,' my mother said, hurrying towards me, 'what is it? You have turned quite pale.' And because she thought my concern was for Joel and Mrs Chase, I smiled and was calm again – so calm that even when Crispin came through

286

the door alone and stared hard at me, questioningly, I did not flinch.

'You will not endear yourself to your friends by dancing with me, Mrs Barforth,' he said, 'but perhaps you will not mind that.'

'Dear Mr Aycliffe,' my mother answered him in her vague, ever accurate way, 'I do not think my daughter is much inclined to play the great political hostess. I think we may safely leave that to the Duchesses of Devonshire and Newcastle, who are not likely to show their faces in our Assembly Rooms.'

And, having reduced it to its proper size – having shown me how to defend myself should anyone criticize – she drifted away.

The ballroom was quite empty, most people not having yet returned from supper, Hannah and Mr Aycliffe safely out of sight, Joel in conversation again with Captain Chase, talking through the husband to the wife, too intent on searching out a response in this difficult, unusual woman to notice me. There were a few couples dancing, young people escaping to each other while their chaperones were eating, and Rosamund Boulton, who had followed me upstairs and was now sitting beside her father, venomous and painful with her jealousy, her eyes clawing Joel's back as he displayed his peacock arrogance, his stallion vitality, to Estella Chase. Ira Agbrigg was there too, sitting stiff and uncomfortable in his new clothes beside his terrified wife, always on hand, one felt, should Joel need him. And, as I began to wonder if they had been too shy to go down to supper and if I, as hostess, should make sure they were fed, the music started up, Crispin touched my arm, and everything but that ceased, entirely, to exist.

'Do you think I was wrong to come here?' he said.

'Yes – if all you meant to do was hurt your father.'

'And you think I am wrong to involve myself in the election – to try and win it for Captain Chase?'

'That depends.'

'On what?'

'Do you really care about the factory children, Crispin?'

And my use of his name, because it came so naturally, made the pressure of his hand on mine seem natural too.

'Oh – as to that – do I care? Not every day. I could consign them all to the devil quite cheerfully, many a time, and take the train and be rid of them. I find caring to be a great encumbrance. A man is well advised to avoid it – except the lucky ones among us, that is, who manage to care only for themselves.'

'You mean – men like my husband?'

'Yes, of course I do.'

'Then you should not say it – not to me.'

'Of course I should not. I should not be dancing with you, either. I have taken an unpardonable liberty, for when the dance is over I shall walk away quite freely and you will be left to explain yourself to your family, who will not be pleased with you. Verity, do you still walk your dogs on the moor in the early morning?'

'No – no, I don't – at least, hardly ever. But never mind that. What do you really mean to do, Crispin – really – with yourself, and your life?'

'Oh,' he said, 'do I want to be a politician, you mean?' And, laughing, he whirled me around for a moment in a silence altogether without strain, since our minds and our bodies were still talking to each other.

'No, I think, on the whole, I would rather not. It is just that – how can I explain it, Verity? You must know my father well enough by now to realize that I was raised in almost total silence. Yes? And because of that, perhaps I need to make a noise in the world. And if I am to make a noise it may as well be a useful one, may as well serve a purpose. Not the best of motives, maybe, but as good as another – and honest, I think, since I have nothing to gain by it. I have no care for my soul, as my father has, since I am not acquainted with such things, and society allows me

288

better ways of working out my frustrations than it does your cousin Hannah. Yes, I have seen her many a time, picking her way through the back alleys, looking as if she had a peg on her nose, and you with her. No, no – how could I have spoken to you? She would have come between us at once to protect you from my contamination – and she would have been right. Verity, will you walk your dogs tomorrow on the top road?'

'No.'

'No, of course not – but if you should be there, around nine o'clock, and you should happen to take the path that forks to the right past Lawcroft—'

'I never go that way.'

'Naturally – it is much too solitary, and I imagine you could not walk so far as the flat stones beyond the ridge, the ones that fan themselves out like a skirt, that the locals call Old Sarah. It is a very rough pathway, almost no pathway at all, and there is always mist on such high ground, before the sun gets up. Where may I leave you – since the music has stopped? Shall I take you back to your husband?'

But I saw now as the music drained out of my mind, as the room became real again – such a petty, tawdry little room, such a sham – that Captain and Mrs Chase were taking their leave, were already out on the landing, with the Hobhouses and Hannah and a wedge of solid, vindictive Law Valley faces glaring at us, blocking Crispin's path to safety. And fear touched me.

'No, no. Go quickly now. The Floods are leaving and you must not stay here without them.'

'But I cannot abandon a lady in the middle of a dance floor. And what can you possibly suppose they would do to me?'

'I don't know – no more than jeer at you, perhaps, or snub you, which breaks no bones—'

'Exactly. And if I am to be a politician I must accustom myself to jeers and snubs, you know.'

'Oh yes, I daresay you must, but not now – please. Oh dear, your father has come in and is standing where you cannot possibly avoid him.'

'Supposing, of course, that I wish to avoid him,' he said, and holding my hand a moment in both of his, he bowed and walked quite slowly through that hostile crowd, as I had seen him do once at Ramsden Street, straight towards his father. But those who were hoping to see blood or tears or both were doomed to disappointment, for there was nothing in the slight inclination of Morgan Aycliffe's head to speak of outrage or humiliation and nothing in Crispin's equally slight acknowledgement of the greeting that spoke of insolence.

'Good evening, sir,' Crispin said.

'Good evening,' his father answered, and, bowing again, the older, greyer man walked forward, smiling his taut smile, into the illuminated room, and the younger went lightly downstairs, both of them faithful, for the moment, to their family creed of silence.

I came home in the lilting, magical light of the summer dawn, a rose-tinted sky warming the smoky town, yet even at that hour there were people in the streets, black, bent outlines, shawl-wrapped for protection, not from the cold of the season but from the cold of fatigue; a sudden crowd of children appearing like a flock of starlings with enough energy left to stare at the carriage, to hurl a random stone. But I had no pity that night, no curiosity, no awareness of anything beyond myself and the strange conviction that my whole life had shrunk from its full twenty-four years to the few hours I had spent with Crispin Aycliffe. The years had been long and smooth, slipping easily one into the other; years of reason and good sense, quiet pleasures, quiet sorrows, effortlessly acquired, easily forgotten. And although I knew I would have to be content with them again – for I was neither wanton nor brave – my life suddenly appalled me.

It would last, I thought, another twenty, another thirty

years or more, and then, at the end of it, what could I find to say of myself should anyone enquire? Would it content me, on my dying day, to know that I had been sensible, logical; that I had never deliberately harmed anyone? Would it be enough to know that I had never suffered because I had never allowed myself to feel?

'Verity, I have something to say to you,' Hannah announced abruptly, leaning towards me from the corner of the carriage. 'And indeed, I am very sorry to have to say it at all. But you should not have danced with Mr Crispin Aycliffe.'

'Should I not, Hannah? And why is that?'

'You must know very well why,' she said, perfectly ready to be angry, since I was, after all, only her little cousin, no matter who had married me, and she assumed Joel, in this case, would be on her side. 'His behaviour during this past year cannot have escaped you – those articles of his accusing better men than himself, your husband among them, of malpractice, which is easy for him to say when he has nothing to do himself but sit about in gin shops and alehouses. And then, to appear tonight, among the very people he has so much maligned, with no other motive than to taunt his father – and you must agree he could have had no other motive than that. Your encouragement of him appeared odd, Verity. It attracted notice, and not very favourable notice at that. Needless to say, Mr Aycliffe himself did not speak a word against you – but others, unfortunately, were less charitable.'

'And I am sure you defended me very ably, Hannah.'

'Naturally – as I would always defend my own family. But, since I had no idea at all as to what possessed you, it was not an easy task.'

'Well, I am sorry for that. I was merely doing my duty as a hostess, or so I thought – and I suppose I remembered about the prodigal son and how he had been welcomed home in the Bible, and imagined I was doing right. And to refuse him would have seemed quite odd, you know, for I had already danced with Sir Giles Flood and with Colonel Corey and Captain Chase, all of them in the same party – of the same persuasion.'

'It is not at all the same,' she said, furious now because I was being frivolous and devious, my mother's daughter, who had done a great deal of dancing, it seemed, while she, who had organized the proceedings, had hardly danced at all. 'It is not Crispin Aycliffe's politics I am complaining about – since he has none, in any case – but his nature. Sir Giles Flood remains loyal to his background. Crispin Aycliffe has betrayed his. He is a snake in the grass, no more and no less, and if you are unable to see the damage he has inflicted, and intends to go on inflicting, on his father, then I must assume you have deliberately closed your eyes.'

'Small chance,' Joel said tersely, his legs stretched out on the seat, 'of closing mine with this racket going on.'

But Hannah, although she depended on Joel for her daily bread, was not afraid of him and had no intention of curbing her tongue for his sake.

'My opinions may count for little,' she said acidly, 'but it is my right and my duty to express them. And in my view, Mr Aycliffe was entitled to the support of his friends this evening – entitled to a certain rallying round in which neither of you chose to participate. And since he is, after all, our brother-in-law, he must have felt it deeply. I am sorry for that, and so, I imagine, is he.'

The carriage having come to a halt outside our door, she got down without assistance and strode inside.

'She is, as it happens, quite right,' Joel said, helping me down, and I nodded, grateful to her now, in fact, since her anger, and my need to defend myself, had cushioned the true cause of my malaise.

'Yes. I do know that. Unfortunately she tends to say the right thing in the wrong way, often at the wrong time, so that instead of seeing the error of my ways I simply lose my temper.'

'Temper?' he said, laughing, throwing a casual arm around my shoulders. 'Temper, Verity? I can't imagine it. I've seen you cool and a shade sarcastic, but honest-to-God temper – no, not you, love. Not that I'm complaining about your way of saying things – far from it, for I've never heard you speak a word that wasn't to the point; I've never seen you put a foot wrong.'

And, drawing a deep breath of pure, uncomplicated satisfaction, he held me against him, pressed my head against his shoulder, and ruffled my hair, not so much as a lover but as a conqueror, a man fully entitled to take liberties with a woman who knew the art of keeping other men at bay.

'You were perfect tonight, Mrs Joel Barforth. If I hadn't seen you growing up here, at the millhouse, I'd have thought you very definitely out of somebody's top drawer, and I might have been curious, wanting to find out a lot more about you. And that's exactly how I want my wife to be. Make them curious, Verity; look expensive and hard to please, keep them guessing . . .'

But once upstairs, when my pearls were locked away in the jewel case he had given me for the purpose – large enough, I noticed, to accommodate his future generosity – and my lovely dress was neatly bestowed in its cupboard, his mood of warm approval altered, quickened to the restless excitement I knew of old, which would end, surely, in a great unleashing of sensual revelry. And, lying back on my pillows, waiting, I was more inclined than I had ever been for his caresses. I wanted him quite suddenly, quite desperately, to make love to me. I wanted to be repossessed; wanted him to burn away the emotion I had felt tonight for another man, in the heat of our legally coupled, eternally coupled bodies; wanted him to drown my newborn heart-searchings in a floor of physical pleasure. I wanted, at the end of an hour or so, to be limp and bruised and exhausted, my body so submissive, so grateful, so satiated, that there could be no thought left in me anywhere of Crispin Aycliffe.

I wanted my body to be enslaved and mesmerized by Joel's body; wanted to be so totally overwhelmed by rapture and the certainty of its renewal that I could forget the hope of love. I wanted, in fact, to be safe.

'Why don't you come to bed?' I asked him. 'Do you mean to pace the floor all night?'

But if there was invitation in my voice he did not hear it and, flinging himself down beside me, his weight disarranging my pillows, he reached out not for me but for a cigar, inhaling the tobacco with unashamed greed.

'Your sister would have something to say to you – and to me – if she knew you smoked in bed.'

'I daresay, but then my sister can be narrow in her ideas, we're both agreed on that. What did you make of the Floods, Verity?'

'Which one of the Floods?'

'Whichever one you fancy.'

But the fancy was his, not mine, and lying so close beside him, I could feel the huntsman's blood stirring in his veins as he remembered Estella Chase's cool eyes and languid hands, the supercilious airs and graces that had intrigued him at the dance. And it seemed to me, noting the wry amusement tilting his mouth, wrinkling the corners of his eyes, that only decency prevented him from saying to me, 'She has an eye for me, our high-toned Mrs Chase. Didn't you see her, making out she wasn't looking and then looking, hard as she dared, under her eyelids?' And, because I had seen it, and because Rosamund Boulton's hungry, despairing eyes seemed only to have added spice to the challenge, I said coolly, 'Sir Giles was very much as I expected, and Mrs Chase, too, although she is quite plain.'

'Aye,' he said, his mouth more amused than ever. 'So she is, although she doesn't know it. And a woman who thinks so well of herself must have her reasons. Plain as a pikestaff and thinks she's an empress – doesn't it make you wonder?'

'Not much.'

But my coolness, like my invitation, escaped him, and, angry now and fearful, with Crispin Aycliffe swimming resolutely back into my thoughts, I knew a moment of fierce refusal, when it was impossible to continue lying here so close to him with the spectre of another woman, another man hovering between us.

'I'm tired, Joel,' I told him, sliding deliberately against him as I pretended to settle down to sleep, inviting him now in a fashion he would not overlook.

'Are you, by God? We'll see about that,' he said, throwing back the bed covers, his hands and his mouth good-humoured before they became urgent. He was fond of me, pleased with me, generous and tolerant, with an easy affection that he never questioned, that gave him no pain, especially now that I had obliged him by growing into the kind of woman he had always intended. Yet when it was over, when my limbs had quivered with joy and continued to throb with the memory of it, the inner core of me was not possessed, not protected, neither satiated nor enslaved but as tumultuous as if he had never touched me at all. And, frozen by the warm air of that summer morning, I lay for a long time awake while the careful fabric of my life, so painstakingly, sensibly constructed, tore itself to shreds around me, warning me that I might never again be truly at peace.

19

I had never experienced difficulty in getting out of the house early in the morning, to go walking with my dogs, yet on the morning after the ball my entire household –

except its master, who had left, as usual, for the mill – seemed to block my way.

'My dear, you cannot get up,' Mrs Stevens told me, determined not to be robbed of the hour of gentle backbiting she had clearly promised herself. 'You were not in bed until the small hours and you must rest – naturally you must – until luncheon at the very least. I doubt if Mrs Aycliffe will get up all day, and Mrs Hobhouse certainly will not, for she was delivered of another boy not three hours ago. I heard it from the laundry maid. Another boy – yes, that makes six – but never mind, dear, you may have a dozen yet, and there's not one of hers so bonny as Master Nicholas nor so artful as Master Blaize.'

And when Mrs Stevens had been disposed of, Master Blaize and Master Nicholas themselves came to me with a demand for justice, with Liza following behind with demands of her own. There had been toothache in the night, Caroline so noisy and demanding in her pain that she had disturbed everyone's rest, and now, peevish from lack of sleep, Blaize had pulled the tail of the grey cat and then Caroline's hair; Nicholas, in defence of the kitten rather than his sister, had slapped Blaize, who, as was only to be expected, had slapped him back. In the resulting affray, a bowl had been overturned, and there was porridge on the nursery floor, murder in Liza's heart, and broken china.

'I can't do nothing right with them,' Liza muttered, peevish herself and bristling when Mrs Paget, the governess, flowed smoothly on the scene, so well starched even at this hour that I wondered if she ever went to bed at all.

'Please don't concern yourself, Mrs Barforth,' she told me, eternally smiling. 'Liza should know better than to bother you with trifles. They do show off so, madam, when you are here. Each one wishes to impress you, which is only natural.'

And although I knew she meant for me to run along until teatime, when she would bring them all brushed and starched for my inspection, I had it in me that day to remind her that they were, after all, my children and sent her away.

I took Caroline on my knee, sitting in the nursery rocker as I used to do in the cosier days before Mrs Paget came and, holding her hot, tousled little head against my cheek, murmured wordlessly to her, letting her delay me, crumple my dress, disarrange me, so that I would set out too late for temptation or would not go at all. And when Nicholas, still furious about his cat, planted himself before me and said accusingly, 'Why are you talking secrets to her?' I pulled him against me and whispered nonsense into his ear, combing his dark curls with my fingers.

The boys were both at school now, and although Blaize, sitting cross-legged and mischievous on the window seat, would have remained there all day in delicious idleness, Nicholas had always been aware of the passing of time, like any true Barforth, and was soon restlessly tossing his head beneath my hand, unwilling to be late.

'The carriage will be waiting,' he said, conscious, it seemed, even in childhood of the cost of carriage horses and aware that it did them no good to stand fretting in the heat any longer than they had to.

'Let it wait,' Blaize answered him. 'It's our carriage.'

And, to Blaize, it was 'our' school too, since it had not taken him long to discover that the grammar school very largely owed its existence – and the headmaster, Mr Blamires, his career – to the donations it pleased Joel and Bradley Hobhouse and Matthew Oldroyd to give. And that being the case, he had no more fear of the redoubtable Mr Blamires than he had of my maid Marth-Ellen.

I had taken them both, three months ago, to present them to Mr Blamires, with Blaize unashamedly holding my hand and Nicholas walking resolutely alone. As Joel's wife, I had been treated with immense courtesy and had listened with equal courtesy to the man who had once given Joel the smattering of Greek and Latin he had never used again, and promised to do the same for his sons, who also would have small use for it. But young gentlemen must, at least once in their lives, translate a sentence or two of Virgil, a line of Plato, and so they now set off every morning, making the journey by carriage that Joel had made on foot, the immediate difference between them being that whereas neither had any aptitude for the classics, Nicholas cared more than he need have done, and Blaize cared not a scrap.

'What's the good of it?' was Blaize's opinion, tossing his books carelessly into a corner. But failure of any kind having a bitter taste to Nicholas, I opened his books myself, struggling one lesson ahead of him, finding sometimes that Blaize, leaning carelessly against my shoulder, would, with a flash of brilliance he never troubled to sustain, breathe life into those dead sounds, laugh with delighted surprise at his own cleverness, and stroll away.

I would have kept them at home that morning after the dance. I would have been glad to notice a rash, to hear a cough; would have been glad of any excuse at all to tuck them up in bed and imprison myself in watching over them. But Nicholas was soon straining at my leash; even Blaize showed a perverse willingness to comb his hair, straighten his collar, race Nicholas for the best place in the carriage. And when they had driven off, and Caroline had curled up and fallen peacefully asleep – no longer needing me, either – I found the dogs waiting, puzzled and hopeful, on the driveway, and was most painfully aware that it was still but a quarter past eight o'clock.

There was, as Crispin had said, a mist on the top pathway. It swallowed the dogs as they ran ahead of me, so that I was constantly obliged to call them back. And I was startled by each sudden appearance of their wet, dark gold shapes, by every shift of air and cloud that could but did not reveal Crispin Aycliffe coming towards me. He would not, of course, be there. I did not expect him; I had embarked on this long, uncomfortable expedition simply to prove the lightness of his intentions. Yet when I reached the ridge, panting a little from the roughness of the ground, and saw him leaning against the pile of rocks known as Old Sarah, the ill temper in his face, his mouth as tight-drawn, almost, as his father's, startled me and made me angry, too.

'Good morning,' I threw at him through the grey cowl of rain-decked air. 'Not that it's good, and not that you seem overjoyed to see me.'

'No,' he said, getting up, his face still set and closed. 'I was hoping you wouldn't come – sure you wouldn't come. It would have been far easier.'

And, as he came towards me, the dogs, catching my temper, converted it to danger, so that the old bitch bristled, baring her teeth, and the young one, not designed for heroics, cowered behind me, stretching her neck, and began to howl.

'You'd best make them behave,' he said, smiling at last, and when it was done and they had gone running ahead to sniff the puddles and taste the morning, he told me, still quite roughly, 'Hoping you wouldn't come has nothing to do with wanting – you do see that, don't you? I've been up here a long time, waiting, long before there was any hope of seeing you, because there seemed no point in being anywhere else. And I think I may have gone on sitting here all day if you hadn't come, cursing you and being grateful at the same time. Can you understand that? I don't even know you very well, Verity, yet I can't see beyond you. You block my way to other things that are well within my reach. And I have to resolve it now, one way or another, since you are here and I don't believe you would have come lightly.'

'No, not lightly, although I don't know just why I came at all. And now I think I had better go away again.'

'Better?' he said. 'Yes – much better, not that you will – not that I'd allow it. These things don't happen so tidily.'

And, catching my wrist, he spoke my name sharply and pulled me into his arms.

'Don't,' I said, just as sharply, awkward now and bitter because this was only what any other man would do, seizing his opportunities, and if this feeling – this hope – should curdle and turn sour it would leave me with nothing I cared to remember. And when he would not obey, the mist got into my mind, coiling itself around my precious common sense, so that I heard myself cry out, 'Stop it. Not this way. Don't take me – that's what Joel does. Can't you let me give something, freely, for a change?'

'Verity,' he said, his voice shaking. 'Oh my darling – absolutely – when?' And the enormity of what we had both said affected my nerves so strangely that I laughed, and, after a startled moment, he laughed too.

'Before you tell me when,' he said, ruefully but easily now, his arm almost companionably around my shoulders, 'perhaps we should consider where, for we can give nothing to each other in this high wind. And I do not suppose you would come to my lodgings, would you?'

'You know that I would not – not now, at any rate. Perhaps never. Crispin, what are we saying to each other? What are you asking me to do? And why am I even listening to it?'

We had come back to the rocks again, instinctively seeking shelter from the wind and, as we leaned together against the stone, he took my hand, kissed it, and then slid both arms around me, holding me gently and lightly as my body knew it had always wanted to be held.

'Verity – my Verity – I am as scared of this as you are. I have all my life wanted one deep, intense relationship, one total commitment – and it shouldn't be with you, my darling – certainly it should not. Yet everything brings me back to you. And it is no easier for me, no simpler, than it is for you. No man in his right mind would choose to love a woman who is not free.'

'If you love me.'

'If? Yes, perhaps you are right to doubt it. And that is what we have to discover, surely – for if all I am to you is an adventure, and all I really feel for you is desire, then we shall soon know it. And don't frown at me and wrinkle your nose when I mention desire, for I am not ashamed of it – no – and you should feel no shame, either. It is not the whole of love, but love wouldn't be entire without it, Verity, and I don't mean to conceal my desire for you.'

'Perhaps we should pray that that is all it is, then – just desire.'

'I daresay. But don't speak of it so contemptuously – just desire; don't underestimate it. And don't worry about it, either. Don't be alarmed, for I am not asking you to desire me – not until you want to, until you can. I won't hurry you. I have harmed you enough by bringing you this far. Believe me, I know very well that I should have gone away months ago, without speaking to you; that even now I should leave you in peace – shouldn't I?'

'Oh yes,' I told him, combing his fine, flyaway hair back from his forehead with my fingers, my body utterly content with him, dangerously at ease. 'Of course you should leave me in peace, just as I should refuse to see you again. We both know what we should do, there is no difficulty about that. And what puzzles me most is why I am no longer terrified.'

'Are you not?'

'No – at least, I think I would be if I could really believe it. It all seems so unreal that it doesn't trouble me – not yet. Crispin, I don't know what time it is. I simply feel it is time for me to go.'

'Yes, of course. Will you kiss me goodbye?'

'Oh no – much better not.'

But, face to face in the shelter of the rock, the mist torn apart now by shreds of sunlight, I put my hand carefully on his cheek and my mouth carefully, carefully, on his, as one would kiss a sleeping child, lingering to retain the odour and texture of him in my mind, to carry his lightness, the cool delicacy of him home with me to cherish, to sustain me, in case I should never see him again.

'Thank you,' he said, very quietly, and as I called my dogs and walked away from him over the roughly springing grass, I was happy – blindly, rapturously happy as children are in the blissful days before they learn of consequences and folly, of guilt and retribution, when it is enough to hold a single, perfect hour in the hand and call it good. I was happy and alive, the blaze of my joy, the sheer richness of its transforming me into the Barforth I had never really been, as powerful as my grandfather – as powerful as Joel – until the shadow of his house fell over me again and drew me in.

'My dear, you are wet through,' Mrs Stevens called from the gate. 'Do hurry, for it is about to rain again – and Mr Hobhouse has called to announce his new son, although we knew it already, and Sir Giles Flood has sent roses, a mass of them, which I have put in the hall with the card well displayed. An excellent card, perfectly plain – a gentleman's card, which Mrs Hobhouse would be delighted to have on her mantelpiece – and Mrs Aycliffe too, I shouldn't wonder. No, he has not sent flowers to either of them, for I enquired most particularly of his coachman. Do hurry, dear, and take off those wet shoes, for there has been such a set-to upstairs. The governess came to ask me for a drop of brandy since Caroline has had toothache again, and Miss Hannah happened to be nearby – and Miss Hannah has strong views against giving spirits to children, as you know, and has never been shy of expressing them. And Mrs Paget is simply not a woman who can be spoken to in quite that way. You had best see her at once, for I am sure she means to pack her bags, and Mrs Hobhouse would take her gladly, you know, now that she has six children to look after, and her Mary-Jane has got so old.'

For a moment, her words flowed through my mind

without meaning; they were addressed to another person, at some other level of understanding, and not to me.

Mrs Paget, who had no intention of leaving, allowed me to persuade her to stay, largely, she implied, because she knew I could never manage my unruly children without her. Hannah, by no means pleased with me and my haphazard domestic arrangements – even though she herself had recommended Mrs Paget to me in the first place – took herself off on Assembly Rooms business, church business, her charity basket on her arm; and when I had admired my roses, and spent an hour consoling my daughter and separating my warring sons, when I had eaten my luncheon, I drove over to Emma-Jane's to pay my compliments and deliver an embroidered shawl and lace cap for her child.

I had not expected to be shown upstairs, but Emma-Jane, six times a mother now and with a peasant resilience she saw no reason to conceal, was not averse to company, and although her nurse, intent on dramatizing the occasion, whispered to me, 'No more than a few moments, ma'am, if you please. I dare allow no more than that,' I found Emma-Jane sitting up in bed surrounded by pillows and plum cake and all the clutter of a hearty teatime.

'Well, and so I have done it again,' she told me, her mouth full of fruit and spice and brown sugar. 'Another boy – nothing but the best for my Bradley. And look at him, not a day old yet and strong as a little bull already. He's the image of my brother, Ben, which won't suit my mother-in-law, although if he was fair and blue-eyed and skinny she'd still insist he looks like Bradley. That was the first thing she said this morning, after he was born. Not "Is he well?" or "Are you well, Emma-Jane?" but "Oh, my word – he's my little Bradley all over again." Well, her little Bradley stands six feet tall and weighs upwards of sixteen stone, so I'm bound to think her cross-eyed. But do have a slice of cake, Verity, or a macaroon – yes, I know I'm not eating for two anymore, but what else is there for me to do, sitting here in bed for the next three weeks, for Nurse won't let me set a foot to the floor until then. I can't help it if I don't feel frail when I ought to. I'll be as fat as a pig when I do get up, but that doesn't matter, does it, after you're married. Nobody expects a mother of six children to have a shape, after all. But he's a bonny baby, isn't he? And, do you know, Verity, lying here with nothing to do but think about it, I really believe I'd like a girl next time.'

Next time, I thought, looking into the cradle at the scowling little face and inhaling the milky, powdery odour of the newborn. And remembering my own miscarriage, only a month ago, I was possessed suddenly by a great surge of panic, a total dread of being pregnant again, a refusal to accept – as Emma-Jane seemed happy to do – that this was my sole purpose, that I had no choice.

'He's beautiful,' I said, knowing I had not said enough, but the cooing and gurgling Emma-Jane thought proper to the occasion – and which she herself had lavished most generously on my own children – was beyond me that day, and it was a blessed relief when Nurse came, full of her own importance, to shoo me away.

Mrs Stevens had accompanied me, having some business to transact with Emma-Jane's housekeeper, and while I waited for her in my open carriage, watching the slant of the August sun on the dark, square house, the dark-leaved shrubbery around it, thick hedges and bushes relieved only sparsely by a dull purple, an uncertain yellow, Bradley himself – who should have been at the mill – came to join me.

'Yes,' he said, answering my congratulations, 'six boys – six workers and not a dowry to find. You'd best watch out, the rest of you, for the town will be alive with Hobhouses ere long, and if they're like me and have six apiece, then it's a dynasty I'm founding.'

But his smug, entirely natural satisfaction in his own virility went no deeper than a layer or two of skin, a roll or two of the fat which his massive frame could still carry with dignity; and as Mrs Stevens came hurrying across the carriage drive – making a great show of not wishing to keep me waiting, although, truth to tell, it did not worry her at all – he leaned towards me and said hurriedly, much too casually, 'I hear Joel has made an offer for Sam Carter's mill at Tarn Edge.'

'Oh – I don't know, Bradley. He may have done.'

'Yes, and a mighty big offer at that, since Sam Carter never gave anything away.'

'I imagine so.'

'And I expect Joel will throw all the handlooms out and put power in – not that I blame him for that, although it means more men out of work and I can't take them. I doubt if Matthew Oldroyd can take them, either. I hear tell Joel wants the Carter place for some new lustre cloth – something to suit the fine ladies who have too much money to spend – and that sounds like Joel, eh? Won't say a word about it himself, but they're saying plenty at the Piece Hall and the Old Swan – they even say he's to start building again.'

'I really don't know, Bradley.'

'My word, I should say not – and if you did you wouldn't tell me, of course you wouldn't. He once blacked my eye, Joel, when we were youngsters, you know. I knocked his coat off a peg when we were at the grammar school, fooling about, as lads do, and kicked it around the floor a bit, never thinking it was the only one he had. And he damn near killed me. Your brother Edwin tried to separate us, and damn me if he didn't go for Edwin as well – took the pair of us on and smashed us both into the ground – not because he was bigger than us, or tougher – it couldn't have been that – so I reckon it was because he was angrier. It wasn't a lark to him, like it was to us; he didn't care how much we hurt him so long as he could hurt us back – and, by God, he hurt us. Headmaster gave him a fair flogging afterwards – reckon he couldn't sit down for a month – but

305

nobody ever touched his coat again, I can tell you. And now I reckon he'll have more coats than any man in the Law Valley, although he's short on sons, Verity – and that won't do, my lass. A man in his position, with all those mills to run, needs sons, so you'd best put your mind to it, girl.'

And planting a kiss on my cheek, managing, as he always did, to disarrange my bonnet, he helped Mrs Stevens up beside me and stood on the carriage drive – a man who had never really been angry, never been hungry – waving, smiling, until we were far away.

I was not inclined to return home, and so we drove, inevitably, to town, down Blenheim Lane, past Colonel Corey's handsome, mellow home, and the Fleece Inn across the way, where he still sat as a magistrate, for lack of more dignified accommodation, to the dread of poachers and debtors and fathers of bastard children for many miles around. There was no need to hurry past the Aycliffe house, since Elinor would still be in bed, but I was glad to see her curtains drawn just the same. I was relieved when the good houses petered out, giving place to the bad, which, in turn, brought us to Kirkgate and Millergate, a smart new shop with Rosamund Boulton's exhausted face in the window, the Piece Hall and the Old Swan, enjoying its last spurt of glory now as a coaching inn, since the railway was coming every year a little nearer, Morgan Aycliffe having already chosen a site and set about evicting the inhabitants to make room for a station and, eventually, a station hotel.

It was a Friday afternoon, and, Thursday being payday, the streets were full of men with money in their pockets who would not go back to work until the cash ran out; men who had been gloriously drunk last night, less gloriously today, who would snarl and prowl tomorrow at the stale tag end of pleasure, until there was nothing else to do but go home to be cursed and clouted by their wives, to push one brood of children out of the door and set about making another.

There were children too in the streets, as there always were; children locked out of their homes while their mothers were at work, children abandoned altogether or just wandering, the infants who had not yet been sent to the mills straighter, chubbier than their wizened seniors but puny just the same, pasty of face and foul of tongue, splashing their feet in the sewage channels and pelting filth at passing carriages.

'One should do something about those wretched creatures,' Mrs Stevens said tartly, clearly having deportation to Australia in mind, but, leaning forward to smile at one ant cluster of tousled heads and receiving giggles and vulgar gestures in reply – for these were not my cousin Hannah's worthy causes who had had their hands and their imaginations washed in Ramsden Street – I thought of Crispin, who had chosen to live among them, and smiled again.

And from Crispin my mind went to his friend and now, apparently, his associate, the Tory member for Newark, Mr Michael Sadler, whose Bill for the introduction of the ten-hour working day had found scant favour in Westminster, resulting in nothing more definite than the appointment of a Select Committee empowered to make further enquiries. But Michael Sadler, addressing the House of Commons in March, when the agitation for parliamentary reform had been at its height, had shocked even that sophisticated body by displaying one of the black leather thongs, a necessary tool, it seemed, of the West Riding overlooker's trade. The House heard of the heat and dust of the sheds, the stench of grease and gas and sweat, the deformities, the degradations, and, when it refused to act – since the manufacturers could always find enough doctors and parsons to swear that such things toughened the body and purified the soul – the Short Time Committees decided to act for them.

There had been a massive Easter pilgrimage organized by Richard Oastler and his friend, the fiery Parson Bull, curate of Bierley; Mr Oastler himself marching out of Huddersfield with brass bands playing, to meet contingents of Short Timers from all over the West Riding, who had gathered in Leeds. I was not sure how many came, for the number varied depending on who was telling the tale and no one could guess how many fell by the wayside, for it was twenty-two miles from their starting point to the Old Castle Yard in York and many of them were ill-shod, undernourished, poorly equipped to handle the rough overnight going and the continually pouring rain. But a great many, certainly, were there the next morning to stand around Mr Oastler in the Castle Yard and to exchange with him that burning promise which had been the main purpose of the ordeal: Our children shall be free.

And although newspapers like the *Cullingford Courier and Review* and the *Leeds Mercury* had made fun of the whole affair, suggesting that Oastler saw himself as a king dispensing justice to a grateful populace, their very malice brought the plight of the factory children and the activities of the Factory King to the attention of many who had been unaware of them before. My maid, Marth-Ellen, told me that when Oastler returned home, after that Easter day, having walked a total of ninety miles, the soles of his feet peeled away as he removed his boots, a small matter, which in no way delayed his journey to London, to give evidence before Mr Sadler's committee.

Parson Bull had gone to London, too – and Crispin Aycliffe – armed with the names and circumstances of hundreds of families whose children were deformed from stooping and straining in the mills. They had taken with them a few terrified examples of oppression: the girl from a Leeds poorhouse who had pulled her six-year-old bones out of place by dragging heavy baskets; the boy who, at the age of eight, had such pain and weakness in his legs that he had to be carried a mile to the mill, every morning, by his brother and sister, all three of them getting a beating if they were late. The committee heard of the ten-year-old child who was tied to an iron pillar and beaten by his overlooker, then gagged and forced to run round and round a loom, past this same overlooker, who would sometimes strike him and sometimes not. They heard about the fourteen daily hours of labour, the appalling accidents, the promiscuity, the tub in the yard which was all some factories had by way of privies, for men and women alike. They heard how impossible it was, in such circumstances, for parents to educate their children; to do little more than put their exhausted, unwashed bodies to bed on Saturday night and wake them in time for work on Monday morning. They heard of fathers who, unable to find employment themselves, were refused Poor Relief unless they agreed to send their children to the mills; of fathers who were heartbroken and bitter at the harm they were forced to do to their own infants; of fathers who would sell their children's souls for a drop of gin.

And all this in a Christian land, the richest, most progressive nation in the world; all this beneath my feet, inside my nostrils, behind my eyelids, sleeping inside me, as I had slept myself until Crispin had opened my heart; and my eyes, of their own accord, had opened too.

He had said nothing to me that morning of his visit to London, his meetings with Michael Sadler; the devout politician, the battling churchman Parson Bull; with Richard Oastler, the land agent, the countryman whose flamboyance and sincerity could so move and uplift city crowds. He had said nothing to me about the pathetic scraps of humanity who had told their harrowing tales to Sadler's committee, nor how he and Oastler and Parson Bull had persuaded them to speak, had soothed their fears of retribution from their employers, had fed them and consoled them on the bewildering journey to London and back again. He had said nothing of all that, but I understood now that he had half hoped I would fail him not merely because of the dangers and distresses inevitable in an affair with a married woman but because he had no real room in his life now for personal affairs at all. Perhaps, as Hannah said, he had joined Oastler's campaign in the beginning to obstruct his father – in fact, I felt fairly sure he had – and I believed, as he had told me at the dance, that there were indeed many times when he wished he could walk away from it all and be free again. But I did not think he would walk away, and I wondered – with sorrow and affection and a whisper of jealousy – if he had already found his total commitment, his intense relationship, in a way he had not bargained for.

Yet I had done nothing from which I could not withdraw. I had not committed adultery and could see no likelihood of ever committing it, since the moment of wild passion necessary for an act so contrary to my education could hardly take place on a stretch of public moorland and I knew that to visit his lodgings in secret, or find some other place of concealment, would be totally beyond me. And so we could not be lovers, from lack of opportunity and from a certain incredulity inside me that made the idea seem almost laughable. Men committed adultery, and women like Rosamund Boulton who had little to lose; women like Estella Chase, perhaps, with enough noble blood to despise the conventions. Our late Queen Caroline had done it, and there were plenty of factory girls who, in times of unemployment, would take to walking the streets. But what had that to do with me? Was it even what I desired?

I tried to see myself in bed with Crispin – tried to find a bed to put us in – tried to see myself dressing hurriedly in some unfamiliar place, rushing home breathless and fearful, lying, covering my tracks, perpetually ill at ease. And I could imagine no love strong enough to survive such furtive, hasty couplings, such shoddiness. Yet, even so, I knew I was no longer prepared to set aside the one real relationship life had offered me. I was entitled to something, surely – entitled to claim a small measure of love and freedom, so that at least, later on, I would have something to remember. And I understood now, even more clearly, why I had almost suffocated at Emma-Jane's bedside and trembled at the sight of the cradle, knowing that I could have a dozen children yet and that my own fertility would prove to be my jailor.

'And was it a pretty baby?' Mrs Stevens asked, catching my thought.

Leaning towards her confidentially, making sure of her attention – knowing full well she was hoping to hear some spicy detail of Bradley Hobhouse's sexual appetite, reputedly prodigious – I said, 'Very pretty – like all babies. But, do you know, Emmeline dear, I've just been thinking it over, and it strikes me that I'm in no hurry to have another child.'

'Ah well, dear, that I can understand,' she said, suddenly very interested in the shop front, the passersby. 'But one takes what God sends.'

'Do you think so?'

'My dear – of course I think so. And we all know what a lottery it is, how some of us bring forth every springtime and think nothing of it, whereas others go for years and years with never a one.'

'Oh, come now, Emmeline,' I said, warning her by my unaccustomed use of her first name that although my tone was light, I was not in jest. 'Can it really be such a lottery as all that? You lived with my grandfather for ten years, and with other men before him, and you don't look to me like a barren woman. Was it really chance, Emmeline?'

'Dearest,' she said, colouring slightly, 'my situation was never, in any way, similar to yours. You should be aware that one of the things a man values in his wife is her fertility, and one of the things he values in his mistress is her lack of it.'

'Then there *is* something – I knew it – something one can do?'

'Verity,' she said, and I could see she was both shocked and alarmed, 'what are you asking?'

'Not a great deal – Emmeline dear. You have brewed me potions to make my hair shine, and perfumes, and tooth powders, and tonics to make me strong. I have conceived four times already – is there no way of ensuring me a little rest?'

'No way that is certain – and, Verity – please, dear – your husband has a right to his children. I think it could be considered criminal in a wife to deny him knowingly – certainly he would think so. Why, Mr Hobhouse was saying just now that you need more sons, and I am sure Mr Barforth would not quarrel with that.'

'But I would quarrel with it, Emmeline,' I said, and, taking her by the wrist, I fixed her with a stare I knew she could not withstand for long. 'It is my body, Emmeline. They call it "labour," and so it is, hard and dangerous; and they call it "confinement," and it is that too. And my body has laboured and been imprisoned four times, and, for a little while, that is enough. We are not all made the same. I cannot lie in bed and stuff myself with cake for three weeks every year like Emma-Jane and talk about my "next one" like she did, with her new baby less than a day old. You had better help me, Emmeline – really – you had better.'

'Oh dear,' she said. 'Oh, Verity – how is it that you have become so hard? You were never hard . . .'

'No – not hard enough. But I am still sensible, Mrs Stevens, and so are you. And you will help me, dear. You know you will. What else can you do?'

'There is more of your grandfather in you than I thought,' she told me. 'Your grandfather and your mother blended together. My word. My goodness – yes, of course I will help you, Verity – naturally dear, anything you say.'

And we completed the rest of our drive in silence, having much, I believe, to consider privately.

20

It would end, I decided, with the fine weather, when the hazy, amber mornings of October choked themselves in November fog and sleet; when the white-cold of December and the nasty, sodden miseries of January and February made it impossible for us to linger on the moor. And by the time spring came again he would be too engrossed with his Ten Hours Committee and I would be pregnant, perhaps, with Joel's child, since Mrs Stevens could only offer me help, not certainty. He would have thought better of it, or forgotten, and I would be in no state to remind him. But, before the snow came, I went out as often as I could to Old Sarah's Rock, allowing him each time to possess a little more of me, wanting him to possess the whole, so that when he told me, 'You'll come to my lodgings, Verity – yes – yes, you'll come soon,' I was beginning to believe him. And although I was often afraid, I felt no shame since, of the three of us, the only one who really enjoyed his life was Joel.

Joel had taken exception, certainly, to the findings of Michael Sadler's committee, but he saw it merely as a nuisance, not as a threat.

'Let them legislate,' he said, 'if they will – if they can – which I doubt, for Parliament, after all, is composed of men of affairs who are more likely to see things my way than Richard Oastler's. And there's always a way round it. If I have a likely lad who wants to work more than the law allows, what's to stop him putting in his ten hours at Lawcroft and another four or five, or as much as he likes – or as much as I like – at Low Cross? And even if our Mr Michael Sadler has thought of that, I doubt he can find a way to stop it. And I don't whip my employees. I don't even whip my horses, or my wife. Do I?'

And, pinching my chin, he went breezily on his way, too busy with the purchase of Carter's mill at Tarn Edge and his pursuit of Estella Chase to wonder about my sudden interest in Reform.

The Ten Hours Bill, if it ever came, was to be set aside, then, at Lawcroft, an obstacle, like all others, that Joel would not long allow to block his way. But one evening towards the end of October he came striding into the house, his face so black with rage that I, who had seen his rages often enough before, stood hastily back from this one, knowing it to be different. And then, because it could concern my meetings with Crispin, I hurried after him, carefully opening the study door he had slammed so violently shut and stood for a moment on tiptoe, wondering if I could weather the storm.

'What is it, Joel? Has something – gone wrong?'

'Wrong? Oh no, no – what could be wrong? In my superbly run enterprises how could anything go amiss? One of the old sheds at Low Cross has burned down, that's all – early this morning.'

And, for a moment, I was infinitely, blessedly, relieved.

'Oh – but it didn't spread? It wasn't a big fire? For we saw nothing—'

'No. It didn't spread, and if you had seen smoke on the horizon, would it have concerned you? There's a deal of smoke hereabouts, and mill fires are common enough. And the shed was due to come down anyway.'

'So it wasn't serious?'

'Did I say so? No, it wasn't serious, or shouldn't have been – except that there were fifteen children inside.'

'Oh, Joel – no, Joel—'

'Oh yes – locked in, I might add, and nobody could find the key—'

As I struggled against nausea his fist came crashing down on the table and he snarled, 'That bloody Agbrigg. He'll make Low Cross pay, he tells me – and so he has – but there's cheap labour and cheap labour, and if he has to bring in Irish brats by the dozen from God knows where – if he has to take in waifs and strays from off the streets and let them doss down in the old sheds – well – I warned him, no trouble, nothing that the *Cullingford* bloody *Star* can get hold of. And so he has to lock them in at night – for their own good, he tells me – to keep them off the streets or stop them from entertaining men on my woolsacks, or some such bloody nonsense. He wants to keep them respectable – playing the parson, doing his own bit of reform – and so he locks them in and goes off to a prayer meeting and lets them burn themselves to death. God knows what the real Reformers are going to make of that.'

I sat down in the deep armchair by the desk, suddenly very cold, as if the ice of an intense winter had entered the room, a living presence, blue-lipped, skeletal, making me shiver.

'They were all girls, then? Young girls?'

'Yes – twelve-year-olds, I reckon – fourteen, some of them, maybe.'

'And some of them younger?'

'Agbrigg says not. And I intend to believe him.'

And he sat down, too, on the other side of the desk, took a cigar from the heavy silver box and inhaled deeply once and then twice, his eyes narrowing against the smoke; he was intensely shaken, I thought, and unwilling to admit it, determined to show nothing but the indifference of a Matthew Oldroyd, the defensive bluster of a Bradley Hobhouse. And I was surprised, puzzled – oddly disturbed – to see that he felt more than that, to realize that, whether he liked it or not – and he did not like it – he could not view this tragedy impersonally, that those fifteen 'operatives' had acquired fifteen quite separate faces – young faces which, because they mattered more than he felt they should, had weakened him.

'Are there no relatives?'

'Not yet, though no doubt they'll appear should I decide to put my hand in my pocket. And maybe I would. I've

315

paid compensation often enough before, looked after the widows and orphans and doctors' bills, which no law in the land obliges me to do and which is more than the Hobhouses have ever done. But then, if I do it now and some clever devil from the *Star* gets to know about it and mentions my name to Richard Oastler – says I'm buying silence, or easing my conscience— No, no, no – if they get their Bill through and try to enforce it they can't inspect every mill in the country. They'll pick out the names they know and come ferreting in what they hope are the right muckheaps. And I won't stand for it.'

'And are they all – all—?'

'Dead? Twelve of them. They took the other three to the infirmary, but they can do nothing—'

'Dear God—'

'Yes. Quite so. An accident, Verity – we all know about accidents. We've grown up with them. And my record's good. I have twice as many employees as the Hobhouses and only a quarter of the accidents – except that now I've had fifteen in the same place at the same time. Where you have machines, you have injuries – it's bound to happen.'

'Yes, I suppose so. Where you have machines – and children—'

'And what is that supposed to mean?' he snarled, his hot temper flowing swiftly around the other things he was feeling and did not wish to feel, obscuring them from his view. 'I don't need a lecture from you on factory children, by God, I don't. And I didn't invent the machines. I haven't got it in me to invent anything. All I know is how to use whatever comes to hand. I can recognize a need and work out how to fill it at a profit – that's all. And if anybody says one word – just one word – about my methods and my motives, then I'll put another corpse in the graveyard. And if you have nothing better to do than sit and stare at me, you can just take yourself off, girl.'

But the quick, defensive flaring of his anger was soon over and, when I made no move to leave, he said quietly,

'You'd best pay a visit to Agbrigg tomorrow, for he's taking it badly – thinks I may use him as a scapegoat, I expect, if it comes to it.'

'And would you?'

'Very likely. But, as it happens, I don't see the need for it. But go and talk to him, just the same, for he'll appreciate it. And take Hannah with you, for he's of an Evangelical turn of mind – an odd sort of a fellow, really. And when he tells you he locked those girls in to keep them straight, you can believe him.'

It was not a duty I wished to perform, and so, to get it over and done with, I set off early the next morning, Hannah, large with her good intentions, beside me. And perhaps it was only in my imagination – since mill fires, truly, and fatal accidents with them were very common – that ordinary passersby, working girls who were usually eager to stare at a lady's carriage, avoided my eye. And although I had made up my mind, long before we reached Low Cross, that I would not look at the gutted shed, it loomed on the edge of my consciousness from the moment of our arrival like the reeking pit of a nightmare into which one is bound to fall.

Low Cross – where Hannah and Elinor and Joel had been born and brought up – had never been a favourite place of mine, sunk in its stagnant little hollow much too near the centre of town, drawing its work force from nearby Simon Street, where, nowadays, in houses that dripped with damp and shook with the passing of every cart, the Irish were packed in six or seven to a bed. It was here that men murdered each other, sometimes, on Friday nights; here that the fevers started in the hot weather, and where not everyone could hope to survive the winter. It was here that one's eyes smarted from the stink of garbage and sewage, from the streams and gases rising out of the canal – strong enough, it was said, to blacken silver, strong enough, certainly, to take the breath away. It was here that the unpaved, rutted alleyways, sodden with cess water, swarmed with mongrel dogs and mongrel brats, snapping and snarling together in raucous harmony. A malodorous, unmannerly place, these days, Simon Street – home of the Irish and Ira Agbrigg and the Red Gin – a place where no lady, not even Hannah with her charity basket, any longer dared to tread. Yet today, as they opened the mill gates for us, the familiar clamour seemed hushed, and once again I felt hostility, a menace of silence telling me I would do better to take myself and my sleek, well-nourished carriage horses and go away again.

The millhouse, too, was as gloomy as I remembered it, its windows tightly sealed against soot and noise, sun and air, its low-ceilinged parlour painted a dingy brown, which Joel – since it had sufficed for his mother and his sisters – had seen no reason to change. Yet, for the Agbriggs, who had raised eight of their eleven children in two rooms at the mean end of Sheepgate, it may have seemed spacious enough. Not that there were eleven children now, the processes of nature having reduced the number to some five or six, all of them straight-limbed enough since their father's rapid promotion in Joel's service had taken the older ones out of the mill before too much harm had been done, the younger ones having escaped it altogether. But they were puny just the same, fleshless and bony as if it took more than one generation of good feeding to make up the loss, their eyes deep-set in faces that had the pallor of an old candle, and quieter, I thought, than healthy children ought to be. And it was as well that their father, seeing the carriage, came hurrying across the yard to greet us, for his wife, sitting in her dim, dark brown parlour, her curtains drawn as a mark of respect for the dead, seemed unable to say a word.

'Ann, we have guests, Ann,' he urged her quite gently, almost with pleading. 'Mrs Barforth is here, and Miss Barforth, the master's sister – Ann. Ann, love.'

But she could manage no more than a wan smile, her eyes no longer terrified as on the night of the dance but completely dull, dark smudges merely in a face so lifeless that it was hard to believe she could really see anything at all. And it was her son, a boy of about twelve, who set chairs for us and asked if we would take tea.

'No, no,' Hannah said, torn between the natural emotion of seeing her old home again in the hands of strangers and her quick response to human distress – her fingers itching, I imagined, to set this poor woman to rights. 'You are not well, Mrs Agbrigg, which is not to be wondered at – in fact, you are not well at all. Mr Agbrigg, your wife is clearly not herself – would she not be better in her bed?'

'I have tried, Miss Barforth,' he said humbly. 'And young Jonas here has tried. And neither of us can move her.'

'Then how long has she been sitting here?'

'Since early morning, ma'am. She was all night at the infirmary with the bairns we sent there, and when she came home she sat down and has not spoken since. What shall I do, ma'am?'

And, rising to her feet, hovering between genuine compassion and a strong desire to investigate the Agbriggs' domestic arrangements, which she did not expect to be satisfactory, Hannah said, 'You may leave her to me, if you will, for this will not do, you know. If she has been up all night she must rest, and even if she cannot rest she must not sit here, in full view of the curious. Come, Mrs Agbrigg, we will go to your room. Your son – Jonas, isn't it? – will come with us to help you climb the stairs, since I have every reason to know they are dark and steep, and then, when you are quite comfortable, we will have some tea. Mrs Agbrigg.'

'Ann,' her husband said, pleading again, 'go with the lady, love. Go with the lady.'

And Ann Agbrigg, hearing them both, I think, at a great distance, rose very slowly to her feet, the habit of obedience – even in shock – being too strong to break, and meekly, with head bowed and hands patiently folded – the posture of a mill girl waiting at the gates – followed Hannah from the room.

'I am truly sorry, Mr Agbrigg,' I said, uncomfortable at being alone with him, for although he was the most respectful of men, there was still, beneath the sober frock coat, the gold watch chain, the careful attire of respectability, something desperate and strange about him, the same hunger I had seen in the men who had killed my father and my brother, that blending of fierceness and frailty I had found so moving and so terrible.

I knew little about him. He was simply Ira Agbrigg, who had attached himself to Joel, a small opportunist clinging to a great one. Mr Agbrigg, he was called now, and in Simon Street men doffed their caps to him; a member of Ramsden Street Chapel, a pillar of the community whose son – this same, sharp-eyed Jonas – attended the grammar school with Blaize. A resourceful, useful man, Joel said, although the roughness of his speech still closed many doors to him and, in Joel's view, his thin, tired wife would hold him down.

'That's what comes of marrying young,' Joel had said. 'He should have waited – found himself a woman who could keep up with him – instead of losing his head over the first mill girl who caught his eye. Strikes me she'd be happier in a back-to-back in Simon Street, which is where she came from, and that's a pity. He can't like it, the way he strives his guts out to improve their standards, when she can't even improve herself.'

And, knowing how Joel would have treated a wife who could not 'keep up,' I had expected to see the same impatience and resentment in Ira Agbrigg too and was surprised by his evident deep concern.

'She takes life hard,' he told me. 'Always has. Worries over silly things – feels uneasy all the time, for no reason. And this has been too much for her. We've lost six children out of eleven, Mrs Barforth, and I'm not complaining about that because I know plenty who've lost more – some

320

who've lost every one they had – but Ann took it bad each time, and now it's all come back to her. She's grieving for the bairns who died here last night, and for her own bairns all over again – and trying not to blame me for it all, I shouldn't wonder, because she won't want to blame me – never wanted to blame me for anything. Am I to blame, Mrs Barforth?'

'Oh, Mr Agbrigg – I really don't think—' I began, not knowing what I thought.

But the tragedy which had clogged my tongue had served to loosen his and, forgetting his awkwardness and his humility, he burst out, 'Can't you understand why I locked those girls in, Mrs Barforth? You can see what it's like in this neighbourhood – Simon Street, Gower Street, Saint Street? You're a lady but you must know what goes on here – they say every other house is a knocking shop and I've no reason to think otherwise. And those girls were no better than any others. An extra shilling was riches to them, and if I hadn't kept my eyes open they'd have gone out to earn it any way they could, and ended up diseased and in the family way – ruined. Mrs Barforth, you should have seen them when they came here – oh, they came in dribs and drabs, not in cartloads like in the old days when the parish priests used to send us up here, in consignments, a hundred at a time. Dribs and drabs, it is now. Some of them were turned out into the street by their own kin, to fend for themselves, because they were taking up too much room or because the mother had a new man in the house and the girl was getting bonny; some of them orphaned and wanting to keep out of the workhouse; some of them in danger from their own fathers when they were drunk. It must be hard for you to understand, Mrs Barforth, just what it's like to be homeless and rootless, how a twelve-year-old girl can be alone in the world, except for the village constable and the poorhouse overseer, and the brothel keepers in Simon Street. But I understand – that I do – and so I let them sleep in the old shed, not as part of their wages – although I expect Mr Barforth thinks I should have deducted something – but just to give them a roof over their heads. And when they started getting out at night and made a disturbance in the yard, I locked them in, not to keep them at their work as people are saying but to keep them off the streets. I wanted to do some good, not that I'll be believed, because even if they don't go so far as to accuse me of murder, they'll make out I had vile intentions of my own – young girls and a man with a sick wife – it's easy to say. I'm not liked here, and I know it. They don't care to see one of their own get on. They don't mind the gentry having money, because that's inherited – got without effort – but when a man like themselves rises above the average it makes them feel bad – makes them wonder why I can do it when they can't, and they don't like that. Not that I am one of their own, if the truth be told.'

And, seeing my surprise, realizing that by his speech I had taken him for a Law Valley man, he shook his head and smiled.

'No, ma'am, I'm not a native of these parts, although just where I did come from I couldn't rightly say. I was brought here, in a consignment, when I was too young to know my right name or age, or where I was coming from. I was a parish apprentice, ma'am, and before that I'd been in a poorhouse somewhere – left on the doorstep, I reckon, by my mother, whoever she may have been, and she may have been no older than some of those bairns who died here yesterday. I grew up in the sheds, Mrs Barforth; we all did, all my consignment – eating, sleeping, working in the same room, boys and girls together, dossing down anywhere on sacks and heaps of waste, bound until they said we were twenty-one. And of the hundred who came up with me I doubt there's more than a dozen alive today – and I may be forty, ma'am, or thereabouts, and they could be no older. Well, I had no name, like I told you, so they called me Agbrigg because that was the village my overlooker came from, and then later, when I thought I'd better have a Christian name like everybody else, I called myself Ira, after one of the Hobhouses, because I thought it might bring me luck. And so it did. I never got crooked in my limbs, ma'am; never bowed at the knees like most of them, and though I've got strap marks across my back, at least my back itself is straight – I don't really know why. And then I met my Ann, which was luck enough for any man, and I made promises. I said we wouldn't starve, that I'd take her out of the weaving shed and put a decent roof over her head and keep it there – and so I have, and more besides.

'I knew I had to do more than just grumble, more than just envy folks that had more than me, if I wanted something of my own, and so I went to Sunday School – got myself washed and tidied up and spent my days off learning to read and write instead of at the cockpit and the pothouse like my mates. And once I could read I was free. I saw what the machines could do, Mrs Barforth; I saw the changes they'd bring, just like your husband did, and that's why I brought your mother that warning. It wasn't treachery. It was common sense, because you can't stand in the way of progress. I know that – and you must know it – but they don't know it down there in the yard, Mrs Barforth, and you can't tell them. All they see in me is a crawler, a greaser, a sneak, doing his master's dirty work – and it's hard for my Ann. I can stand it, but she's got no friends now, you see. Her old mates don't trust her anymore, and she's not one for solitude like me. She doesn't talk much but she likes to feel part of things, and it's hard for her now when her old neighbours pass her in the street – it's hard for the children, too. My Jonas – my eldest – is a clever lad, doing well at school, and Mr Barforth tells me he can find a place for him – a good place – for which I'm grateful. And I can afford to keep the girls at home to help their mother – there's no call for them to go out and earn a penny, I'm proud to say. But they get

323

beyond my Ann sometimes, talk about things she's never had the chance to understand, and they get out of patience when they think she's slow – especially Jonas. And she's mighty fond of Jonas. She takes that hard, too.'

'I'm sorry. If there is anything I can do—'

'Why no, ma'am,' he said, remembering, with visible discomfort, that I was Joel's wife. 'Nothing at all – beyond the honour of this visit, for which we are most grateful. But you have not had tea, Mrs Barforth – you must take something before you go. Yes, yes, indeed you must.'

And, solely to please him, because I knew he would fret about it otherwise, I drank the weak brew he eventually managed to serve me, and kept on repeating, 'How delicious. How very refreshing,' until I felt a perfect fool.

'That young woman must pull herself together,' Hannah told me as we drove away. 'With five children to think of she cannot afford to indulge herself by going into a trance. You won't believe this, but they have no maid, just a woman who comes in to scrub. Can you imagine that? Naturally they can afford it – I have some idea of the wages my brother pays, and they could easily manage a cook and a parlourmaid and a skivvy, and at least a man outside. Mrs Agbrigg never had a word to say, but the boy was quite talkative – a good sensible boy, young Jonas Agbrigg – and from what he says it strikes me that although his mother insists she wants to do the work herself – and may even believe it – the truth is that she doesn't know how to handle servants and is afraid to try. And it won't do, you know. In the first place it looks odd for a man in his position not to have servants, and she'd be far happier in herself once she'd made the effort. She feels she's letting her husband down – which, of course, she is – and the cure for that is to assert herself, convince herself that Mrs Ira Agbrigg is worth something and need stand no nonsense from anyone.'

And although she was – as so often – quite right, I could

324

not help wondering if Hannah's strong medicine would do more harm than good.

I drove next to the infirmary at the top of Sheepgate, somewhat to Hannah's dismay since public hospitals, designed for the accommodation of whores and vagrants, victims of gin-shop brawling and others who could not afford to be decently cared for in their own homes, were not greatly to her taste. But I had made up my mind and, having first sent the coachman inside to enquire, I found it impossible to remain in the street and, jumping down, went through the door and into what could have been the sparsely decorated hallway of an ordinary dwelling house.

Inside there was a sweetish, unpleasant odour and the impersonal shabbiness of a public building no one had thought to beautify, and, having expected a great hustle and bustle, some official instantly on hand to ascertain my business, I was amazed to find myself alone but for two young men lounging against the stair rail, one of them a stranger and the other Crispin Aycliffe, who, with a cool, formal nod of his head, seemed to be warning me to keep my distance.

And I would have gone willingly back into the street, dreading these inevitable chance encounters, the necessity for falsehood, had his companion not made a sudden move towards me, an excited flash of recognition in his face.

'Your conscience troubling you, then, Mrs Barforth, is it?' he said, rougher than Crispin, smaller but fiercer, a fighting cock of a man with the flamboyant good looks one glimpsed sometimes at a fair. A gipsy lad in a good coat and an exceedingly fancy waistcoat, not at all the kind of man I would have expected to speak to me.

'I beg your pardon?'

'Conscience, Mrs Barforth – or your husband's con-science? You've come, with your basket of goodies, have you, ma'am, to ease the last moments of the dying. Very commendable, except that you're too late, I fear. They've all gone – all fifteen of them – so there's nothing left for you

325

to do but buy them a headstone – something really splendid, with a nice inscription, I should think.'

'That's enough, Mark,' Crispin said very quietly. 'We're not campaigning against women.'

But the man – Mark Corey, certainly, of the *Cullingford Star* – his face quite ghastly, having just come downstairs from viewing those nightmare bodies, was devoured by a need to strike out at someone, anyone, and he paid no heed.

'Are we not?' he said, speaking rapidly as if he had so much to say, so much protest inside him, so much outrage that he must rid himself of it or choke. 'Are we not campaigning against them all? She's Joel Barforth's wife, isn't she? And what objection has she ever made to living on his blood money – and living well? Can she be innocent, Crispin – really – or even decent, when she lives with a man who picks twelve-year-old girls up from the streets, locks them in his sheds, and throws the key away? Maybe she's just never thought about it, Crispin, so ask her, tomorrow, in your article – and all the others like her – and see if she can reply—'

'Easy, Mark,' Crispin said, for indeed the man was very close to tears. 'Easy, old friend,' and, as they clasped hands and drew close together, the understanding between them excluded me, their absolute certainty of being right defeated me, a woman who could see fragments of right and fragments of wrong everywhere.

'I'll take you to your carriage,' Crispin said, his hand giving Mark Corey's a final, reassuring squeeze, and turning, walking quickly outside – running away – I could not speak to him, had no idea at all what I could possibly – ever – say to him again.

'Well, I did warn you,' Hannah told me as our carriage clattered smartly up the hill, away from the town and the silent, shawl-clad figures standing around the infirmary door. 'And now I suppose you have got yourself soundly insulted, for you must know who that young man was. No, no, not Mr Crispin Aycliffe, we all know about him. That was Mark Corey, who calls himself the editor of the *Star*, which he calls a newspaper. And, indeed, I hardly think he has the right to call himself Corey for that matter. He may be a natural son of Colonel Corey's – although the colonel himself has never said so – but that would not make him a Corey, would it? However, somebody paid for his education, for he was at the grammar school with Crispin Aycliffe, and then they tried to make a churchman of him, which was clearly doomed to fail. He went to France, of course, as they all do, to get their revolutionary ideas, and since then he has been persecuting us with his dreadful newspaper. I know all this because Mr Morgan Aycliffe has told me.'

'But you know so many things, Hannah.'

'I am not stupid,' she said robustly. 'And one thing I do know, and that is why Crispin Aycliffe and Mark Corey were at the infirmary. They are going to write an article about the fire, not because of Ira Agbrigg – for who has ever heard of Ira Agbrigg? – but because they believe they have found something to use against Joel. And whether it is the truth or a lie will in no way concern them. And so if Mr Corey insulted you just now, you must let Joel know of it so that he can take appropriate action – so that people may understand they are dealing with a bully and a liar, not some kind of avenging angel.'

But when we returned to the Top House to find Joel most unusually at home in the middle of the day and he demanded, 'How did you get on?' for the first time in my life I took refuge in assumed frailty and answered, 'Oh, I am not quite well, Joel. I have been too long in the heat and dust and my head aches. Hannah will tell you about it. I think I must really lie down.'

21

The *Cullingford Star* made its appearance some two or three days later, a shoddy publication printed on coarse paper, as different as could be from Mr Roundwood's *Courier and Review*, which, on the whole, told us things we were glad to know, such as the progress of Mr Morgan Aycliffe's political campaign and the brilliant success of our Assembly Ball.

The *Courier*, predictably, had reported the fire at Low Cross as a tragic accident, finding it unnecessary, in an area where industrial fires were common, to indulge in speculation about keys and what may or may not have been the reason for those locked doors. But the *Star*, which some kind soul pushed under our door in the early hours of the morning, not only speculated, it accused, assassinated, presented, with a pen dipped in venom, a picture of man's brutality to his own species that curdled the blood.

No relatives of the dead girls had yet been found. No proper record existed of their names and ages. And so who were they? And were there others, confined somewhere in a slavery baser than any West Indian plantation? How many young persons from Simon Street and Gower Street and Saint Street were missing from home? And since, as always, there were dozens, hundreds, unaccounted for, had they perhaps been taken into captivity? Was this, then, how profits were made? Had a certain well-known local industrialist found a speedier way to amass his millions? Had it come to him one night around the second magnum of champagne that instead of paying low wages he would do better to pay no wages at all? And so a picture was built up of Ira Agbrigg scouring the Simon Street area in the dead of night like a vampire, looking for vagrants, the little lost children, the straying lambs, to lure them back to Low Cross, lock them up, and work them until they dropped.

One was asked to consider a Roman galley with soldiers patrolling the benches with whips, pausing here and there to unshackle a dead oarsman and toss him overboard while a replacement was fastened in his place. And on the deck of such a galley would be a cold-eyed, cold-hearted gentleman who saw nothing amiss with using the bodies of his fellow creatures to speed his transportation, consuming them as casually as a present-day engine consumed coals. And the readers of the *Star* were asked to pity such a Nero, to understand that such a man, so devoid of humanity, would surely bring about his own destruction. They were asked to bear in mind the tale of King Midas, who, having requested of the gods that everything he touched should turn to gold, found that his food and drink became metal on his tongue, and his wife a golden statue in his arms, and that such a man was doomed to spiritual decay, a vast inward rot, and was certain to putrefy in the midst of his splendours.

'You will take action against them, of course,' Hannah said, handing the paper back to Joel as if it were a dead rat, her nostrils revolted by its imagined odour, and, taking it from her, folding it carefully, he put it in his pocket and smiled.

'I don't know that I shall, not direct action in any event, for if I put them out of business, I'm Nero again, aren't I, and they're martyrs to their cause. And every cause needs its martyrs – my word, yes, the more the merrier – so I doubt I'll oblige them in quite that way.'

'But you won't simply ignore it – let them get away with it?'

'Did I say that? I don't think I did, you know.' And, pushing back his chair, he said to me, 'And how is my wife this morning? Does your head still ache? You'd best not sicken just now, my girl – unless you're breeding again –

for we've a funeral to go to tomorrow, and if you're not there some fool is going to swear I've turned you to gold.'

And, seeing through his eyes, I had a vision of Rosamund Boulton encased in precious metal in her shopwindow, and of Estella Chase hardening in places since she was perhaps not yet entirely possessed; and I understood the content of his smile.

My old bitch was not inclined for exercise that day, preferring the comfort of a hearthrug to the first snap of cold in the autumn air, but the young one did not fail me and went loping ahead, knowing her way by now to Old Sarah's Rock. There was a fine veil of rain in the air, a pale grey sky with a patchy grey mist beneath it, and the ground was so heavy with water that the hem of my dress became unwieldy, my progress unsteady, my spirits as dark as the bare fold of the land before me, cowering at the approach of winter. And when I came upon Crispin, standing in the shelter of the rock, Mark Corey's words were there, like poles in the ground, between us: 'Can she be innocent?' And because nothing, to me, had ever been entirely black, entirely white, I knew there was no answer.

'Well,' he said, 'you are looking at me very strangely, and so you must have read the *Star*. Is he going to sue?'

'No.'

'I thought not. And you are angry with me?'

'Am I?'

'Verity,' he said, throwing back his cloak and opening his arms and his mind towards me in a gesture that always moved me, always drew me irresistibly towards him like a homecoming, a return to the source of my true self. 'Verity, Verity – I am sorry for what happened at the infirmary – sorry for what Mark said to you – but he doesn't know you and you don't know him, which is a pity, for you would like each other.'

'Do you think so? Would he permit himself to like me, when I have gorged myself for so long on blood money?'

And I did not know why I had spoken so sharply when

the last thing I wanted – the one thing I could not bear –
was to quarrel with him.

'Don't,' he said, growing sharp in his turn. 'Don't,
Verity. Mark Corey may not please everyone on first
acquaintance, but he has strong feelings, sincere emotions,
and after the horror we had just seen – after that – he was
not in command of himself and neither was I. And because
of that horror – to ensure that it never happens again – can
you blame me, Verity, for my need to strike out? Yes, yes,
I know my words were inflammatory – a deliberate play
on the emotions – a savage personal attack on a man I
happen to dislike for very private reasons – I admit it
freely. But there was enough truth there to justify every
syllable of it – and if you had seen those girls you would
understand why. Verity, we must settle this between us,
for it is not the end of it. I know how awkwardly you are
placed, but I could not bear it – and I must tell you this
– if you tried to defend him.'

I disengaged myself from his arms and walked a step or
two away from him, knowing how easy it would be to offer
him my wholehearted support, to say, 'Yes, Crispin, tell
them anything – take any atrocity you can and enlarge it,
invent it, anything, because the end justifies the means.'
And so it did, for the children had to be protected; I knew
that now as well as he. A way must be found, somehow,
anyhow, to allow them their childhood, to guarantee them
shelter and time and space in which to grow and, when
childhood was done, an opportunity to live with dignity.
But was it not too easy, too obvious, to fasten one's hatred
on Joel and others like him, to imagine that curbing him
or removing him would solve everything? Did we, in fact,
know how to recognize our oppressors, or were we all
oppressors, all self-seeking, all of us to blame? An accident
of birth had made Mark Corey a radical and Joel Barforth
an industrialist, just as that same accident could so easily
have reversed the roles of my grandfather and Jabez Gott.
And how many, I thought, even down there in the mill

yards, once their own needs were satisfied, would lift a finger to help others? Not many, it seemed to me, not many, and although it made none of it right, it made it difficult, a maze of human good and ill through which I could not find my way. And concluding that our salvation could only come from inside ourselves – from a maturing of our own greedy, childish, grasping, frightened human hearts – and because I saw no possibility of such a universal change, I wondered why I could not tell Crispin an easy lie, settle it as he wanted it settled, and think only of myself and him.

'I am not making excuses,' I told him. 'It is just that I know someone else who saw those girls, someone who went to the infirmary with them and stayed there until they died, and who has barely spoken a dozen words since.'

'Mrs Agbrigg?'

'Yes. I think it unlikely she ever learned to read, but she has a clever son who can read for her. And if he doesn't tell her about your article, then someone else will.'

'Yes,' he said. 'I know. I met her at the infirmary, and however sorry I'm inclined to feel, I can't afford it, Verity. She's a nice woman, but her husband did lock that door, and because that door was locked those children died. Verity, it's as clear-cut as that, isn't it?'

'No, Crispin. Nothing could ever be so clear-cut as that – not to me. I would want to know why he locked that door. He says it was to keep them off the streets, and although I don't say he was right nor that it was right for them to be there – because that certainly wasn't right – what I do believe is that he was trying to do the best he could, as he saw it.'

'Agbrigg? My God, Verity, the man's a positive disease. They detest him at Low Cross.'

'Only because he's close to Joel, and they detest Joel.'

'Exactly.'

And suddenly it was no longer a question of Low Cross

or the *Cullingford Star* but our own personal triangle, its spikes threatening now to impale us.

'I cannot bear to hear you defend him,' he whispered, his face blanched with jealous anger, as perhaps mine had blanched with fear. Yet instead of throwing myself against him and vowing that I detested Joel as heartily as anyone at Low Cross – as Crispin wanted me to do, as I wanted to do – I said, much too calmly, 'I am not defending him. I know what Joel is – after all, he is my cousin. I have known him all my life. And even if I wanted to defend him it would be a waste of time, since he doesn't care what people think of him.'

'No, he doesn't care what men think of him, that I grant you, but where women are concerned— You know he has other women, don't you?'

'Stop it, Crispin.'

'Why? You do know, don't you, about Miss Boulton? And Mrs Chase now too, it seems, according to Mark, who is, after all, her half brother—?'

'Yes, I know. It doesn't seem to matter.'

'It matters to me – because he has you too.'

And, covering his face briefly with his hands, he shuddered, quite violently, a movement of distress that banished all my hesitation and brought my arms around him.

'So that's jealousy, is it?' he said, smiling, nuzzling his head against mine. 'I thought I was above it, you know, but I'm not, and it hurts. What are you going to do for me?'

And when I merely held him tighter he laughed, making a joke of what we both knew to be the most urgent thing in our lives.

'I know what you can do. You can come and live with me, on my fifty pounds a year, in my attic at the Red Gin. How would that suit you?'

'In some ways it would suit me very well.'

'Yes – or I could move away from here and find

333

responsible employment, in London perhaps, for I am, after all, an architect not without talent and there is money to be made. I could earn the wherewithal to keep my own carriage and a cook and a parlourmaid, and all the little niceties we've both been accustomed to. And you could spend your days waiting for me to come home and saying, "Yes, dear. Quite right, dear," every time I expressed an opinion, like my mother used to do. And we could feel very triumphant because Mrs So-and-So had left a card, or very desperate because she hadn't. Would that suit you better?'

'It would hardly suit you at all.'

'I suppose not, and I might not even be very good at it. I have often wondered if I could ever turn sour, like my father, if I began to feel out of place with my life. Perhaps there is enough of him in me for that. So what now, Verity?'

What indeed? The sky, I noticed, had clouded over, and there was a chill wind sighing across the surface of the moor, bending the stiff grasses: a dull, clammy morning, promising more rain, heralding a cold ending of the year. And feeling the numb misery in him, knowing what he was steeling himself to say, I knew it would be an act of love to say it for him.

'Perhaps we should not meet again – not for a while, at any rate.'

'That is not what I want, Verity.'

'Oh – I think, in a way, it is. There are too many things standing between us, and I think you are afraid to find me more of a Barforth than you imagined – or that circumstances may force me to become so. I think you are afraid I may turn you away from the path you have chosen – and I think you may be right.'

He leaned, for a moment, quite heavily against the rock, and my own body, too, was weak; a great weight, it seemed, was pressing against my forehead, a certain bewilderment that I, who was not brave, had found the courage to say these things.

334

'How clear your eyes are,' he whispered, 'and how small you make me seem. I am no more reasonable, you see, than any other man. I knew you would dislike my article, yet I wanted you to lie to me and call it brilliant. I wanted you to be unquestioningly on my side. I need that exclusive devotion, and yet I am not prepared to give it. I have found something to do with my life, and it seems I cannot part from it. I am a poor creature sometimes, Verity, for it is not in me to say goodbye to you.'

And it was a blessing that my dog came suddenly careering back to me and, rearing up, clapped muddy paws on my shoulders, almost overturning me.

'Foolish animal, you are quite wet through – get down, be still. I had better take her home, for she is shivering and the moor must be running with water. Silly girl, you have no sense at all.' And, brushing my hands against my cheeks, I said unnecessarily, 'It is coming on to rain,' knowing that the sudden flurry of raindrops would offer me some concealment if I began to cry. 'Crispin, I had better run, for Mrs Stevens is obsessed with the weather and she is likely to send the carriage for me, as far as it can come.'

'Yes, of course. Of course – Verity—'

'No,' I said, wildly perhaps, for me. 'No' – forbidding him to hold me back, refusing absolutely to listen, and, obsessed with my determination that we must part this way, as loving friends, I turned and fled, unaware until I reached the road again that my dog had not followed me and then leaving her, for the first time, to find her way alone. And that day I truly understood how necessary it is sometimes to fall ill, how the only way to survive is to draw the bed curtains and creep inside the sheets, remaining motionless, untouchable, until one can bear to face the daylight again.

And I had need, in the days that followed, of all my strength, a full measure of my reason.

To begin with there was the funeral: fifteen small, plain

coffins, and a multitude of silent figures lining the way to the churchyard, crowding into the church, so that, walking past them to a front pew, I had a panic sensation of drowning, could feel them surging forward in a great wave to overwhelm me. But they had nothing with which to harm me but their silence, and when the short, awkward service was over, every face I looked at turned away from me, every eye avoided mine.

Hannah was there, and the Agbriggs – Ann Agbrigg invisible beneath her mourning veils – and Mark Corey, standing in a corner of the church porch, giving Joel a look of hatred and contempt to which Joel replied by coolly tipping his hat. But not even Mark Corey could dispute the evidence of the relatives, who, appearing in some miraculous fashion, had no complaints to make, and everything would have gone smoothly had not Mrs Agbrigg suddenly paused on her way to the carriage and fluttered to the ground with no more substance about her than a silk scarf in the wind.

'I feared it would be too much for her,' Hannah told me, pulling off her gloves briskly when we reached home and looking around her for the appearance of the tea tray. 'Mr Agbrigg says she didn't wish him to face the ordeal alone, which is very commendable, but it is a pity, just the same, that she could not keep her feet. It may have given a false impression, which would do her husband more harm than good.'

But, by nightfall, we learned Mrs Agbrigg was suffering not from remorse but from a fever contracted, it was thought, at the infirmary when she had kept watch at those nightmare bedsides.

'They took a vagrant in that night,' Hannah said, managing to be well informed even at this crisis. 'An Irish girl from heaven knows where, quite filthy, complaining of dizziness and pains in the head, and then they let her go or she simply went away leaving her fever behind her. Poor Mrs Agbrigg. I hope she is strong enough to bear it – I do indeed. I have sent Marth-Ellen to enquire if anything is needed in the way of linen or remedies, for the Agbrigg girls are barely old enough to understand the doctor's instructions and they have no other woman in the house. Marth-Ellen has taken soup, too, which I am sure you do not mind, Verity, and I think it would be as well to send her tomorrow – every day, in fact, for I am not at all sure they know how to manage on their own.'

But, by the end of the week, Marth-Ellen, too, had taken to her bed, burning and freezing in turn, her head wrenched apart by an iron claw, she told me, a knife blade somewhere in her chest.

They never gave the fever a name. We had had cholera and typhus, and our seasonal epidemics of diphtheria and smallpox, and we could all recognize the consumption that withered away so many women and the choking coughs that carried off our babies. But some ailments which came to ravage us, nailing us to our beds and then abruptly departing, had no name and were called, simply, fever. And this was one of them. First it came upon the Agbriggs and the teeming dens of Simon Street, where one lived or died according to one's own strength, since a doctor was rarely called there; then Marth-Ellen, bringing the sickness into my house; then Lucy Oldroyd, and a child of Elinor's, and three of Emma-Jane's; then the Reverend Mr Brand, who lay alone in his house for two days until Hannah went to look for him; and then, early one morning, my governess, Mrs Paget, begged me to come and look at Nicholas.

Fretfully tossing his covers, he was lying in bed, red and cross, hurting, he told me, just hurting. But by afternoon he was cooler, demanding food and entertainment and making a great fuss, and it was Blaize who lay flushed and much too quiet, shivering with cold although his skin burned to my touch.

'Don't alarm yourself unduly,' the doctor told me. 'Such a strong child – a little Hercules – his body should make light work of this. It is not so, you understand, with nursing

337

mothers, and new babies, with the old and the weak and such like. But a fine little chap like this should fight his own way through. Moisten his lips a little if you cannot make him drink, keep him warm, say your prayers – there is nothing more, at this stage, one need do but that.' And I understood he was telling me there was no cure, that some lived and others did not, and I would have to wait and see.

I sat down at the bedside, pressing my hands together, striving to be calm, and remained there, sometimes with Hannah, sometimes alone, for the rest of that day and night and the day that followed, obsessed with the need to make him drink, cradling his painful little body against my shoulder, appalled at the fierce, dry heat of him as the fever glazed his eyes, swallowed the roundness of his cheeks and pinched them into the bare bones and hollows of sickness.

'He must sweat,' Hannah said, knowledgeable in the progress of the disease since she had already nursed Marth-Ellen and Mr Brand. 'He must drink – and he must sweat.' And I knew she was hurt when suddenly I pushed her capable, well-intentioned hands away and declared I could manage alone.

'Call me when you need me,' she said, deeply offended, deeply concerned, for this was her brother's house, her brother's child, and she had never had much faith in me. But Joel was away in Manchester, knowing nothing of Blaize's condition, and there was no appeal.

'I will look in every hour,' she told me, 'for you will need to sleep eventually, Verity. And although your devotion is commendable, I have to tell you that it lacks good sense. Make no mistake about it, he is very unwell and your experience of nursing has not been great.'

And although, once again, she was quite right, panic had made me stubborn and I meant to have my way.

But a moment came that second night when, jerking myself awake from a momentary doze, I was heartened by a fine beading of moisture on his brow and then became almost immediately terrified by the sudden drenching of his body, sweat dripping from him like the layers of a candle. Having done all the other things the doctor had required, having dabbed his forehead with cologne and his lips with water, I went down on my knees and tried to pray. But my conversations with God had always been conventional, impersonal, and even through the raw reality of my grieving, I could think of nothing to say.

I knew well enough that few women expected to raise all their children. My own mother had buried six, Joel had lost two elder brothers and a number of sisters, Emma-Jane Hobhouse was the sole survivor of five; I myself had attended the funerals, throughout my childhood, of a dozen of my playmates carried off by measles, by typhoid fever, by a strange, nameless wasting away. 'You're too fond of those bairns, missus,' the old woman from whom I had bought the kittens had told me. 'And in the long run it doesn't pay. Keep your distance, lass, or you'll end by laying up grief for yourself. I had thirteen once and now never a one; half in the graveyard, a pair at sea, the rest God knows where.' Yet now, when it seemed that my turn had come, I was not resigned.

I had loved him for seven years, first as an extension of my own body and spirit and then for himself: Blaize Barforth, unique, unrepeatable. Now, as he lay melting before my eyes in that dreadful sweat, the full horror of his loss struck me a mortal blow from which I knew I would not heal. I had lost my father and my brother, had seen them struck down, bleeding, but the anguish I had felt then was nothing compared to this. I had known, even when that sorrow had been at its height, that I would learn, however painfully, to live with the memory of it. But now, frantic and blind with panic, I would have torn out my own life willingly if somehow I could have injected it into my son.

I could not bear to lose him, could not contemplate a

world without his cool, mischievous smile or his unshakeable belief, even when I so often seemed to favour his brother, that I loved him the best. And in this moment I did love him the best.

I heard my voice, or perhaps only my thoughts, promising, 'Let him live and I will try never to think of Crispin Aycliffe again.' And in case I weaken, I will allow myself to become pregnant again, which will please Joel and punish me enough in itself.

Having made my bargain, I rested my head on my son's counterpane and, for a very long time, wept.

I slept too, as Hannah had said I would. Then, waking with blind eyes in the darkness and certain, in that first conscious moment, that he was gone and I had let him die alone, I experienced the most intense gratitude of my life when I found him not only alive but sleeping more naturally, sweating still but better than before.

I got up clumsily, my body cramped and aching, and, going over to the washstand to rinse my face and hands, I heard the door open. Hannah, I thought, hoping to find me asleep. Without turning round, I whispered irritably, 'He's much improved – and I can manage perfectly well. I'm quite all right.'

'Good,' Joel said. 'I'm delighted to hear it.' So astonished was I to hear his voice that I answered sharply, ungraciously, 'What are you doing here?'

'Well, and where should I be?'

'In Manchester, surely, until Friday?'

'Yes, except that I had a message to say that I was needed at home.'

'Not from me.'

'No,' he said, coming slowing into the room. 'Apparently not from you.' And standing by the bedside, looking down, he murmured, 'He is my son, you know, after all.'

'Yes,' I said, sitting down suddenly, lulled by the miraculous rise and fall of the child's breathing, my son who was also Joel's son. 'Yes, he is, and he even looks like you. I thought not. I thought it was Nicholas who had your face; and Caroline, both your face and your manner. But he's like you. And like me, too, like my mother . . .'

'Well,' he said sharply, although the hand he closed abruptly over mine was surprisingly unsteady, 'isn't that just as it should be? Part of me and part of you. But you say he is better, truly?'

'Yes, yes. I see you have no more faith in me than your sister.'

'Verity, Mrs Stevens met me at the doorway and pleaded with me to make you go to bed. You can trust me, surely, to sit with him until the doctor comes?'

'Oh yes, indeed, but I think I will stay with him myself, just the same.'

And so, obstinately, since I could hardly stand, barely see, I remained guarding my child as I had done on the day he was born, until the doctor came. Only then would I allow Mrs Paget to relieve me and Mrs Stevens to put me to bed.

I slept a long time, the whole of a crisp autumn morning, the amber beginnings of an afternoon, waking to find my room awash with sunshine and Joel, standing at the window, asking me if I could eat breakfast, luncheon, tea?

'Yes, all of them, I think. But first, Blaize . . . ?'

'Yes, he's mending. And the other two are showing signs of nothing but wickedness, which Hannah says is normal.'

'Hannah would.'

'I daresay, but what shall I ask them to bring you, my lady? Will you have a tray and eat in bed?'

And when it came and I had devoured hot muffins and gingerbread, and Joel, sitting at my bedside in his shirt sleeves, had most surprisingly poured my tea, he said, 'Tell me something – do you dislike my sister?'

'No, as it happens.'

'And what does that mean?'

'Oh, there are times when I feel that I want to dislike her, but actually I don't.'

341

'I'm glad,' he said, his hand closing once again over mine, startling me. 'Because if you did dislike her I'm afraid you would have to endure it. No, no, I'm not trying to set her above you or any foolishness of that kind, and I'm well aware that she is high-handed and obstinate and fond of her own way, as I am myself. But when my father died, Verity, with his affairs in such a tangle, Hannah stood by me like a rock, and I have no mind to forget it. You don't know what it means, Verity, to owe money, to watch the lads you were at school with change direction when they see you coming in case you want to borrow – or to go into the Piece Hall and find them all too busy to talk to you. They were all waiting to see me fail, Verity, and, by God, they'd have enjoyed it, because not one of them could have got himself out of the mess I was in – certainly not Bradley Hobhouse, or your brother Edwin, either. And I was doing it. Even without your grandfather's money, I was doing it. Low Cross was beginning to come straight, and I'd have got on all right. I'd have managed – me and Hannah – you do see that?'

'Oh yes,' I told him, passive, yawning, still too full of sleep to care what I said. 'You'd both have done well. She would be married now to my brother, and you to Miss Boulton, and we'd have been obliged to go on sending to London for our shawls and fans.'

'Quite so,' he said, standing up, his face suddenly very keen, very careful, and then, with neither guilt nor swagger nor anything else in his voice, he asked me, 'You know, then, that I financed Miss Boulton's shop?'

'I do.'

'And what conclusion do you draw?'

'Oh – that your financial arrangements are not my concern, unless you choose that they should be.'

'How very reasonable,' he said, again expressionless. 'And how like you. You may take it that my conscience troubled me on her account, for reasons we both know of and have never had any reason to discuss. Do we have any reason to discuss it now?'

'I don't think so.'

'Neither do I.'

And as he leaned towards me, the warm, male scent of him, the odours of wine and tobacco that lived on the surface of his skin, the good, red blood flowing vigorously underneath reminded me of the bargain I had made, that if Blaize lived I would conceive another child. And although the vow itself had lost its urgency – for he was alive and I would soon convince myself he would have lived in any case – the need for a barrier between me and Crispin Aycliffe seemed more than ever vital.

'You know that I've bought Carter's mill at Tarn Edge, don't you?' he said. 'Yes, of course you do, and I've bought a ten-acre site just beyond it, because I reckon we've lived here long enough, Verity, in Samson Barforth's house. I want a decent house of my own before I'm forty, and once I've got the mill altered to suit me, it strikes me we could landscape a few of those acres and build ourselves a palace while we're about it. What do you say?'

'Yes,' I told him, understanding simply that from Tarn Edge I could not walk my dogs on Lawcroft Moor, would be spared the agony every morning of denying myself the chance to look for Crispin; and, drawn together by this new enthusiasm and by our realization last night of what it could mean to lose a son, there was a brief companionship between us.

'Well – the mill first, of course – business before pleasure or there'll soon be no pleasure at all, as Bradley Hobhouse is starting to discover. And then I'll have a house my sons can be proud to live in when they're grown.'

'And your daughter.'

'Naturally, my daughter, and with the dowry I can give her she'll be able to marry wherever she likes. They'll be clamouring for that girl of mine, and not just manufacturers, either – landed gentlemen, titled gentlemen, why

343

not? She could have any one of the Hobhouse boys, but what could they give her except money, and I can give her plenty of that – she'll be used to that – so a title may be the only thing left for me to buy her.'

And as he grinned down at me, making light of it yet meaning it just the same, there was something about his nakedly expressed ambitions that made him seem younger, less sinister, unless it was that I was older and no longer so intimidated by this wicked, handsome cousin, twelve years my senior, who had always looked down his nose at little girls.

'Lady Caroline – good heavens,' I said, sliding lower into my nest of pillows, knowing how easily his sensual curiosity could be aroused, refusing to be troubled by his faithlessness since I myself was faithless, now, in spirit.

'My word, Verity – if I thought you were the kind of woman who'd invite a man into her bed in the middle of the day, I might just take advantage of it.'

'Are there such women?'

'Ah well,' he said, nudged into remembrance of Miss Boulton, his eyes careful again in the strong daylight. 'And if there are, they have nothing to do here, between us, surely? Are you growing up, cousin?'

'That – or growing old. And don't call me cousin.'

'What a shrew,' he said, taking my chin between his hard, pinching fingers. 'What a scold. It's no bad thing we're cousins, Verity – that you've always been a Barforth. If you'd been a Hobhouse you'd have been nagging me by now to do something for Bradley, thinking about Nethercoats instead of Lawcroft. But, in our case, your interests are exactly the same as mine, and that's what binds people together – that's what counts. Other things can be very pleasant – friendship, for instance – but, however warm it is, however interesting, it's here today and gone tomorrow and only a fool puts his faith in it. Friendship has no bones. But property in common, blood in common, children in common – there you have the real bricks and mortar of life. And you're at the very centre of it, Verity. So, sweet cousin, does anything worry you?'

'Nothing,' I told him. 'Nothing at all.' And although he was offering me a reassurance I did not need, since I felt perfectly secure of my place in his life, I was ready once more to accept it.

'I'm sorry,' he said gruffly, having little experience of apologies. 'Sorry you didn't feel the need to send for me when you thought Blaize was dying, that you were so surprised to see me after Hannah sent the message in your place.'

'I'm sorry, too.'

And briefly, as our eyes met, we reached out, hesitating, on the borders of an unknown pathway that could lead us beyond the barriers that had always held us apart, but both of us, I think, nervously aware of the risk, afraid of failure.

'They are my children,' he said. 'I may not appear to notice them, for my father never noticed me, unless it was to call me to help him load a wagon or get him up the stairs when he was drunk. But they are my children. They'll never see me drunk and incapable, and when I make them work it will be to their advantage more than mine. I'm saying – I don't know – they're my children and yours . . . And, by God, if we'd lost that little demon it would have hurt me.'

Although he could not have spoken the words, I understood his half-acknowledged thought and answered it, for in the event of that loss we could have turned neither to Estella Chase nor to Crispin Aycliffe but only to each other in our grieving.

22

I conceived another child and almost immediately miscarried, as I had done earlier that year, but as Blaize continued to thrive, I decided that my bargain with God could now be considered null and void, and I returned to the contraceptive practices that even Mrs Stevens privately thought wicked.

But others were less fortunate than Blaize. Elinor's little girl recovered and the Reverend Mr Brand, dragged from the jaws of death by Hannah's iron will alone, it seemed, but my old Marth-Ellen, in her sixty-eighth year, died almost apologetically, as if she had left behind a pile of ironing to be done. And, following her coffin back to Patterswick, her native place, I could not forget that it was Hannah who had sent her to the Agbriggs, the source of the infection, and I was bitter and unfriendly towards her for days.

The Hobhouse child survived, although he was sickly afterwards, causing Emma-Jane so much anxiety that she, too, miscarried the girl she had set her heart upon and had such trouble conceiving again that she came to our versatile Mrs Stevens for remedies which I begged should not be confused with mine.

Lucy Oldroyd recovered her health, and Rosamund Boulton's married sister, and the housekeeper to the Corey-Mannings – those of us who were well fed and had the means, in that raw November, to warm ourselves. But in Simon Street, where the diet was oatmeal porridge and weak tea, there was a great deal of dying, a terrible blending of sorrow and anger and apathy, of those who wished to burn down the whole world for vengeance and those who were simply too tired to care, of those who went quietly, almost gladly, and those who wished to take Ira Agbrigg – or Joel Barforth – with them.

Ann Agbrigg recovered, too, slowly and quietly as she did everything, but perhaps the fever, after whetting its appetite in Simon Street, had become more virulent, greedier, when it reached her children, for they were among the last to be infected, all five of them at once, presenting a volume of nursing care so completely beyond Ann Agbrigg's strength that Hannah, who had never lacked courage and knew no one else would be likely to help the vampire of Simon Street, went to Low Cross and undertook it herself. And I cannot imagine how she found the words to inform Ann Agbrigg, not yet risen from her own sickbed, that although the eldest boy, Jonas, and a girl, Maria, seemed likely to recover, the other three, in the space of two days, had passed from sleep to death as imperceptibly as the pale guttering of a candle.

The Agbrigg funeral was the most terrible I had yet attended, Ann Agbrigg, dead herself in all but the movement of her limbs, being supported by the two children who were all that were left to her after she had suffered the painful, hopeful agonies of childbirth eleven times. And although they were whispering in Simon Street that this was divine retribution, I doubt if she was aware of it, for her eyes seemed quite blind, her vision very far removed from the things she could not bear to see, her mind turned inwards or backwards or simply refusing to function at all. She shed no tears, made no moan; she was simply there, obediently standing and sitting as she was bid, and it was her husband, fully conscious of his loss, who really needed the support of young Jonas's arm.

He had aged ten years, Ira Agbrigg, in that harrowing week, and had lost flesh I had not thought he possessed to lose, so that now the skin, stretched tight across his yellow-pale face, looked as if it could split, pierced by his cheekbones and the awkward, painful movement of his thin lips. Yet, for all that, he thanked me for my presence at the cemetery and for my graciousness in returning to his home to drink tea and eat a slice of seedcake I assumed Hannah had provided.

'Miss Barforth has been an angel of mercy,' he said. 'It overwhelms me to think of it – such a fine lady concerning herself with us. She sat up all night with Maria, telling me to take my rest since I had my business to attend to on the morrow. And both Jonas and Maria owe their lives to her. My wife could not – cannot – she is not recovered yet. Mrs Barforth, you have seen her – she won't speak to me, or can't, and doesn't seem to hear me – she couldn't believe, could she, what they are saying? – about punishment for those bairns who died in the shed? The doctor says she's numb with shock and it will wear away, but if it should not – ? Everything I've ever done has been for her, Mrs Barforth, and if she can't see it, doesn't want it, what good has it all been?'

Yet we had other things, quite soon, to distract us from our grieving, for December brought us two events of great moment: the first elections ever to be held in Cullingford and the engagement of my cousin Hannah to the Reverend Mr Ashley, Anglican parson to my mother's ever-devoted, High Church, High Tory squire.

I had not expected her to choose Mr Ashley, particularly since her attention to the Reverend Mr Brand during his bout of fever had thrown them into such close contact that certain ladies in Ramsden Street thought their marriage not only imminent but essential; while Joel, sharing my astonishment, was seriously displeased, considering a hundred-pound-a-year parson no fit mate for his favourite sister. But my mother, growing younger, it seemed, with the passing of each tranquil day and utterly content to sit gracefully on life's fence and observe, with gentle irony, those of us who still played life's games, saw little occasion for surprise and none at all for haste.

'Do not,' she told me, 'make plans as yet to give her bedchamber to Caroline, for we cannot expect a speedy conclusion. Mr Brand, I feel sure, would have insisted on marriage within a six-month, and indeed I am amazed that he has managed to stay unwed so long. But Julian Ashley, my dear, is the very man for betrothals and will not mind how long it lasts – forever, if that should be what Hannah has in mind. And, you know, dear, even a betrothal gives some status, at very little cost. She will have no more to do than come over here two or three times a week, which is what she does anyway, put some order into Mr Ashley's affairs, and then rush off to do the same for Mr Morgan Aycliffe and Mr Ira Agbrigg, neither of whom, it seems, can rely on their wives. It may well be, dear, that someone – at Ramsden Street perhaps – has dropped a hint that her interest in those two gentlemen could be sentimental as well as charitable, and in that case, what better way of killing the rumours than to get herself engaged to a third. She will have to sacrifice Mr Brand, I suppose, since he can hardly allow the promised wife of another parson to meddle in his parish affairs. But Mr Brand may have made himself too pressing, you know. He may have seized what he thought were opportunities when she went to nurse him – for parsons are men, after all, like the others – and I think that would have frightened her away. At least she can rely on Mr Ashley, for he will not even recognize his opportunities, much less take advantage of them. Odd, isn't it, how things turn out. When they were both girls I thought Hannah plain and awkward and imagined she would become gaunt in later life, ungainly, while Elinor had the kind of loveliness one knew would never fade. Yet here they are, Hannah, in her thirties now – as Edwin would have been – striding through life like an Amazon queen, and Elinor, so much younger, looking quite extinguished. How sad, she was so vivacious, that little one, so full of herself, so appealing. Her loss of spirits pierces my heart. One must hope to see her bloom again if her husband goes to Westminster, for surely he will take her with him?'

349

And simply by putting the question, my mother acknowledged that she had her doubts, for Morgan Aycliffe's political ambitions had a certain bachelor, even monastic quality about them, and what troubled me most was that Elinor, who should have been on fire to go to London, seemed not to care.

'Oh, he tells me nothing,' she said. 'If I am to go I shall be informed of it, and if I am to stay he will arrange the housekeeping with Mrs Naylor and all the rest with this Mr Adair who has come to manage his business. And it is all the same to me.'

Yet, knowing Elinor, I could hardly believe her.

'You will not want to know us when you have your fine house in Belgravia,' said Emma-Jane Hobhouse, pregnant again and so huge that it surprised no one when she later produced her twins, increasing the total of her sons to eight. And when Elinor turned her head away, too listless to reply, I found myself making excuses on her behalf, explaining that since Mr Aycliffe's parliamentary duties could occupy him no more than half the year, there seemed little point in going to the expense of a second family home, when everyone knew a gentleman alone could manage perfectly well in two rooms with a manservant and an occasional cook.

But the election had first to be won and, through November and December, a new fever mounted, centred on the respective campaign headquarters, situated at the Bee Hive and the Old Swan.

We had won the right to return two members, the industrialists putting Mr Morgan Aycliffe and a somewhat faceless cousin of Mr Lucius Attwood the brewer, a Mr Thirlwell, into the field, our manorial lord, without any hope of winning – for the nuisance value only – offering us Captain Chase assisted by Crispin Aycliffe, whose expenses, it seemed, were being met by Colonel Corey, father of the radical editor Mark Corey and cousin of Sir Giles Flood. And instantly the town was divided between the manufacturers and those who wished to gain their favour, who were solidly behind the party which had given them the franchise, and the gentry and the workers, combining together to support the Duke of Wellington or, as the workers saw it, the party of Richard Oastler, which advocated factory reform.

Mr Aycliffe, immensely dignified in dark grey Cullingford – one hoped Barforth – cloth, made few promises in his speeches, pledging himself simply to support Lord Grey, the Prime Minister, to whom we owed our freedom, and his meetings would have been sober and probably very dull had he not been heckled constantly – not by Crispin, who knew that a father-son conflict would not win general favour, but by the highly excitable Mark Corey himself, who, surrounded by a group of like-minded friends and an outer ring of tough-grained, determined Short Timers, demanded to know Mr Aycliffe's views not only on the Ten Hours Bill, to which he was necessarily opposed, but on any other subject that seemed likely to embarrass him.

The question of allowing Methodists and members of other non-Anglican groups to attend our ancient universities was not touched upon, since Mr Aycliffe – representing a 'millocracy' that was largely non-Anglican – would be bound to support it. Nor was he challenged on the Corn Laws, since their repeal would be to the advantage of both Mr Aycliffe and the average workingman, and to Mark Corey himself for that matter. But, with his hands in his pockets and his tongue in his cheek, Mark Corey, in all the flamboyant splendour of his scarlet waistcoat and his spotted gamekeeper's neckcloth, made his appearance whenever Mr Aycliffe was due to speak, cutting through the candidate's well-chosen words – chosen, in many cases, by Hannah – with the very questions he did not wish to answer.

Would Mr Aycliffe support the abolition of stamp duty on newspapers so that the workingman could afford to read them? Clearly Mr Aycliffe would not, although, surrounded by a mighty gathering of those same working-men, he clearly did not like to say so. Would the honourable gentleman support the abolition of the death penalty for offences other than murder or treason? What, in fact, were the candidate's views on crime and punishment? Would he put a stop to flogging in the Army? Would he work for the emancipation of the Jews – many of whom were settled in Leeds and might well bring their skills and culture to Cullingford – so that they could enjoy the same rights as a Methodist? Did he believe in the secret ballot, so that no man, squire, parson, or manufacturer could influence the vote of another? And when Mr Aycliffe had made his clipped, noncommittal replies, taking great care to offend no one, since there was no telling which way the wind would be blowing next year or even tomorrow, he would stand on the steps of the Piece Hall, or wherever he happened to be – looking so dry, so grey beside Colonel Corey's mischievous, quite beautiful bastard son – and submit himself to questions from the crowd, those toughs from Simon Street, and Gower Street and Saint Street who, although not entitled to vote themselves, felt perfectly free to pelt him with abuse and garbage and to smash the windows of the Old Swan, an occurrence so many times repeated in that election month of December that in the end the landlord made do with wooden shutters and the glazier's bill somehow found its way to us.

Crispin's main task, of course, was to introduce Captain Chase to the mass of workingmen not yet empowered to vote; no easy matter since the captain's cultured accent could neither be understood nor be taken seriously, giving rise to such gales of laughter that eventually he stopped speaking altogether, leaving Crispin free to put forward his own quite revolutionary ideals. Captain Chase imagined he was promising a measure of factory reform. Crispin Aycliffe made it clear that if every man in the mill yard, every man in the country, had his vote, then promises

352

would be unnecessary. With the vote in his pocket the workingman could demand his freedom, not beg for it, and dismissing the ten-pound franchise as an insult, he declared that the only qualification should be a man's status not as a householder but as a Briton.

Yet this doctrine, while appealing to the Simon Street masses who could not hope to own property – and, I confess, to a married woman like myself, who could own nothing, either – did not find favour with everyone. There were men – overlookers' sons, maybe – who, by hard work and sacrifice and with perhaps not too many brothers and sisters to bar their way, had raised themselves a little above the rest, escaped from Simon Street to the new stone terraces of Sheepbridge Lane – men who, one day perhaps, by their own efforts, would be ten-pound householders and who saw no more reason to share their privileges than Sir Giles Flood would have done.

Nor was the vote itself considered such a prize if, after all, they would be obliged to use it to suit the masters rather than themselves. And although Crispin's explanation of the secret ballot was clearly of interest to some of them – shabby, keen-eyed lads with the wit to plan ahead, who wanted more out of life than a jar of ale every Friday and a quick tumble on a pile of waste with any mill girl who was willing – there were others who, accustomed to living from day to day, went about drunkenly and foolishly declaring that if they got the vote they'd be glad to sell it to the highest bidder.

The vote, then, in a town where only approximately a thousand out of a population of 43,000 were entitled to it, was seen at present as a middle-class issue; and although some of these workingmen were ready to demand it and fight for it, while others would not trouble to use it if it was theirs, they were all agreed that there was little one could do about it this December. Radicals like Crispin Aycliffe and Mark Corey might say what they pleased about the rights of man, but neither of those gentlemen had a half

353

dozen children to feed through the winter, and although in general Cullingford men were quite ready to use their fists, when the time was ripe, and firearms if necessary and available, not all of them were.

But Crispin, surrounded by his escort of Short Timers – those rugged, dedicated men who knew exactly what they wanted and were willing to fight for it, sacrifice for it, today, right now, as long and as hard as they had to – stood daily on the Piece Hall steps, with Captain Chase smiling benignly at a safe distance behind him, and spoke about the factory children. And this, at least, unlike the franchise, was immediate, urgent, possible; this concerned them all.

And when Crispin threw at them, 'Do we want a ten-hour day for women and children?' they thundered back, 'Aye, that we do.'

'And who is trying to cheat us of it?'

'The masters – Barforth, the robbing bastard.'

'And who will help us?'

'Oastler – and Sadler – Richard Oastler, the Factory King.'

'And what do we need to help Richard Oastler? What do you need to help our Factory King?'

'The vote,' they screamed, suddenly seeing the sense to it, wanting it now, this minute, not next year or the year after when we could all be dead. And although Colonel Corey, who was paying Crispin's expenses and who had no difficulty at all in understanding the West Riding accent, must have seen this as a serious misuse of his money, Crispin was carried shoulder-high around Simon Street, while the Red Gin was the only hostelry in town to keep its windows intact.

Our own windows, needless to say, were less fortunate; a well-aimed brick landed squarely on my dinner table one evening, accompanied by a scattering of glass that entirely missed the industrialist, Joel Barforth, slightly injuring instead the sympathetic parson, Mr Ashley, Hannah's timid fiancé. But some days later, as Joel drove his phaeton into town at a spanking pace, stones were thrown at his horse's legs, causing the valuable animal to bolt, foaming and dangerous, down Sheepgate, where a street market was being held, overturning fruit stalls and vegetable stalls and a swill tub or two as it went; it was brought under control at last by a Joel Barforth who, forgetting his dignity, had reverted to the wildness of his younger days and, jumping down from his damaged vehicle, smashed his fist into the first grinning face he saw.

'Bloody thieving Barforth bastard' appeared once again on our factory walls, in letters a foot high, put there, one supposed, by persons well known to our dogs and our watchmen, since neither had complained, and although Joel was quick to recover his temper and continued to drive his phaeton to town, I took out my carriage, those last few days, only to deliver my sons to school and to fetch them home again.

Polling day dawned cold but dry and clear, greeted by the ringing of church bells and the clamour of the singing, parading crowds who, since they could not vote, intended at least to enjoy themselves. And when the Old Swan and the Bee Hive had both been pelted with stones and filth by a grubby, cheeky gang of boys whose only political conviction was to do as much damage as they could, and all the bunting, blue and orange alike, had been torn down and made away with, the candidates themselves became fair game.

A bombardment of eggs greeted Mr Morgan Aycliffe at his first appearance of the day, considerably injuring his self-esteem, although the same lads, having raided somebody's hen run, dashed immediately across town to throw the remainder at Crispin and Captain Chase; while the third candidate, the colourless Mr Thirlwell, was, for a long while, prevented from setting out at all by a gang of Simon Street toughs who had invaded his lawn.

But the result was never in doubt, and anyone with the

most rudimentary knowledge of arithmetic could have worked it out.

Mr Aycliffe and Mr Thirwell between them would share the votes of the manufacturing interest – the mill-masters themselves, their managers, the tradesmen and better-class shopkeepers who served their needs; while only the Coreys and the Corey-Mannings and a few shopkeepers situated in the Simon Street area, who wished to avoid trouble, would vote gentry. Dr Overdale, who attended gentry and manufacturers alike, would, of course, be in something of a dilemma, while the town's innkeepers were, in some cases, unreliable, having made promises, with professional geniality, in both directions. But, on the whole, there were no surprises, other than Mr Boulton, Rosamund's father, who, against his own best interests, voted for Captain Chase, in protest perhaps at the party of the manufacturers, one of whom had seduced his daughter, while one or two others, torn between their private convictions and pressures from Simon Street or Lawcroft or Blenheim Lane, found it wiser to fall ill or be called out of town and not vote at all.

And, waiting at home as a woman should, far more concerned for my old dog – Edwin's yellow crossbred bitch – who had died early that day, than for the House of Commons and all who sat therein, I was not surprised – not even very interested – to learn that Morgan Aycliffe had topped the poll, Mr Thirlwell following discreetly behind, and Captain Chase, for all Crispin's efforts, barely visible in the distance.

Joel sent me a message to join him at the Aycliffes', with a case of champagne – and Hannah – and we dined there, very late, very lavishly, but with little real enjoyment, for I was still grieving for my dog, and Mr Aycliffe himself was plainly weary, suffering perhaps from a depression of the nerves that often comes when some great object has been achieved.

'What a triumph,' Hannah told him on arrival. 'And so richly deserved.'

And for Hannah Mr Aycliffe's thin lips did sketch a smile. But to the rest of us he was merely polite, having invited us only because the circumstances required it; because victories must be celebrated with due pomp; because, after all, he was a 'public man' now and knew his responsibilities. Yet, for all his attentions and courtesies, it was all done so joylessly, the performance of an arduous duty rather than a pleasure, that it would have been better had it not been done at all.

'Mrs Barforth, I believe this pâté is to your liking, do take a little more.' But, as always, I was so deeply aware of the staggering value of his china that the scrape of my knife on the exquisite Wedgwood plate seemed sacrilegious and I felt his own watchfulness and the careful hovering of his housekeeper, Mrs Naylor, so unnerving, that I had no appetite.

'I think we may consider the day fairly won,' he told us, leaning back in his carved oak chair, his thin, dry fingers caressing the stem of his glass in a way I found unpleasant, perhaps because I knew how rarely these days he caressed his wife. 'Yes, a triumph for good sense. A victory. And, for me, a new beginning.'

'You will excuse us, I am sure,' Elinor said abruptly, having no mind, it seemed, to sit placidly by while he gloated over a beginning in which she did not play a part. 'You may take as long as you like over your port.'

And while Hannah slipped upstairs to count the children and interrogate their nurse, I went with Elinor to her too elegant drawing room to take coffee, appalled, as I always was, by the fragility of the cup.

'Is Faith quite recovered from the fever?' I asked, merely to start a conversation, and she answered listlessly, as she had been doing all day, half listening, uncaring.

'Yes, I believe so.'

'And you? You seem worn out.'

357

'Yes, so I am. Quite worn out.'

'From what?'

'Oh – from doing – doing nothing, I suppose. And don't you know that it is the hardest thing of all – doing nothing, all day, all night – passing the time. I find it a weary business, at any rate.'

And then, after a short but heavy silence, an uncomfortable thing, she said, 'I am not to go with him to London, you know. It is quite definite.'

'Oh – I'm sorry, Elinor.'

'Yes. I daresay. Mrs Naylor is to look after me and the glass and the china. Nurse is to look after the children. Mr Adair is to look after the business and see to the household bills – to tell me how much I may spend and what I may spend it on.'

And, before I could think of anything which might console her, she hissed suddenly, quite viciously, 'I am to have no money, Verity; no allowance. I am to apply to Mrs Naylor for pin money, who will then apply to Mr Adair, since it is not proper for me to approach him direct. I am to sit here all day and listen to the clock ticking my life away. I am fit for nothing else, you see – not even for breeding. He is leaving me, Verity, don't you see that? Oh, very politely and correctly, as he does everything, and in such a way that no one else will even notice. And, of course, I shall have everything he thinks I require – and I shall certainly have the children, since he can't wish to bother with them himself. But I am to be abandoned, Verity, just the same – cast off. Fat Emma-Jane can keep her husband, and mousy little Lucy Oldroyd, and you – but not me. And I was the pretty one, wasn't I? The prettiest of you all? Isn't that so, Verity – can you deny it?'

'No – you were the pretty one, Elinor. You still are.'

'I hate him – hate him. Do you know that?' she whispered, shuddering with the violence of her emotion, and, jumping to her feet, she picked up a tiny porcelain shepherdess, not unlike herself, and dashed it wildly

358

against the fender. And then, as the delicately painted face and the frilly, lace-edged porcelain body disintegrated, I saw my vivacious, impossible, lovable cousin Elinor crumble with it.

'Oh dear God,' she said. 'Dear God – dear God—' And watching her trembling with fright, cowering away from the consequences of her action – knowing she would not be pardoned – I remembered her as she had been on the night, seven years ago, when she first came here to dine, dancing and swishing her skirts around this same room, not caring a fig for Mr Aycliffe and his porcelain, while Hannah and I had trembled. And I was saddened beyond belief.

I heard their feet crossing the hall – her husband's and mine – and, swiftly gathering up the pieces, I went hurrying to meet them.

'Oh, Mr Aycliffe, I do not know how you will ever forgive me, for I have done a dreadful thing—'

'Surely not, Mrs Barforth.'

'Oh, I do fear so.'

And I held out to him the evidence of Elinor's crime.

'It is not usual for me to be so clumsy, but I caught it with my skirt as I was passing . . . Oh dear, naturally I will replace it—'

'Such generosity,' he said, his voice empty of all expression, 'is quite beyond you, ma'am. It cannot be replaced. Please think no more about it.'

And although that was all he said, I knew that I had been accused of a heinous offence, judged and condemned, and that if he lived to be a hundred he would never find it in his heart to forgive me.

23

There was no doubt that Joel was getting richer, a fact which could not hope to find favour with everyone, and when his purchase of Tarn Edge became common knowledge and speculation arose regarding his plans for the splendid ten-acre slope of Tarn Rise, Emma-Jane Hobhouse chose to settle the matter by calling to enquire.

'I hear you're building a new house, Verity?'

'Yes – so it seems.'

'And what about this one? Is it to be sold?'

'I really couldn't tell you.'

'No? Well, it reached my ears that Joel was thinking of making it over to Hannah as a wedding gift, which I can only put down to foolish gossip since everybody knows a house of this size to be quite beyond Mr Ashley's means. No, no, I said, when I heard it, if Hannah Barforth chooses to marry a parson, then it follows that she wants to live in a parsonage – doesn't it stand to reason?'

But Hannah, as my mother had foreseen, was in no hurry to marry at all and replied to Joel's cutting enquiries as to time and place, and her exact plans for Mr Ashley's hundred pounds a year, with a simple 'When I'm ready, brother.'

Mr Brand had gone out of her life now in a considerable huff, but Mr Morgan Aycliffe, following his departure for London, communicated with her far more frequently than with his wife, and to compensate her for the loss of Ramsden Street she now had the Agbriggs, parents and children, whose affairs required a great deal of attention.

Ann Agbrigg had not recovered her health. She was simply there, a presence in a chair by the window, giving no trouble, eating what was set before her, managing, with some help from her daughter, to keep herself clean and tidy, but no more than that, a shadow who could neither appreciate her husband's success nor understand the sorrow she caused him.

'Poor man,' Hannah said, fairly often, clearly puzzled by his attitude. 'It is quite pathetic to see them together. People think of Mr Agbrigg as such a hard man and yet, before his wife, he reminds me of nothing so much as a hopeful dog with a bone. And when he lays it at her feet and she doesn't even notice I do believe he hides in a corner and cries his eyes out. Poor little woman. I see no possibility of a change, but they are so glad of my visits that I can hardly fail them, and left to themselves they have no idea how to carry on. They are doing their parlour in a lighter shade – did I tell you? My suggestion, of course, since they think of nothing for themselves, and I always did find those dark browns and greens altogether depressing and often wondered what my mother was about to select them in the first place. And Maria is to go to Mrs Turnbull for lessons. Mr Agbrigg had placed her with a most unsuitable woman, some person advertising herself as a teacher of deportment and needlework and French and who had no samples of her own work to show me when I called, and failed to pronounce one word of a foreign language in my hearing. You see how gullible he is? Mr Agbrigg had taken her for a lady and dared not question her word. Well, I questioned it, and now Maria is with Mrs Turnbull, an old acquaintance of mine, who keeps an excellent establishment. Not a brilliant child, of course, Maria; a little mouse, which is what one would expect. The boy, Jonas, however, is really very quick and doing very well at the grammar school. I had a word with Mr Blamires, his headmaster, the other day, and he is really quite impressed with young Jonas – which is rather more than he could say for Blaize, who seems to have divided his time there so far between sulking and fighting.'

'He has only been there a little while, Hannah.'

'Yes, and I imagine Mr Blamires is well aware of it,

although in view of Joel's position in the town, and his generosity, he would not say so. I am very fond of Blaize, as you must know, but he can be very high-handed at times, and I almost wonder if you have been too tender-hearted, and my brother too busy, to check him as you should. And Nicholas, I believe, is just the same. I wondered, too, Verity, now that the boys are at school, should you not give some thought to Caroline? Mrs Paget is all very well when it comes to washing and dressing and doing up her ringlets, but in matters of education – and discipline – I find her a trifle lax. Caroline should now be embarking on some regular course of study, and my friend Mrs Turnbull could help you there. She is constantly receiving applications from suitably skilled ladies, many of whom are willing to enter private employment, and Elinor has taken on a Miss Mayberry, with whom we are all well satisfied. Do think it over, Verity. Caroline may have a great position waiting for her in the future, and you would not forgive yourself if you failed to prepare her for it. Have a look at Miss Mayberry when you are next at Elinor's and hear what Elinor has to say for her.'

But Elinor, when applied to, had little interest in governesses or anything else.

'Miss Mayberry? Oh, she's well enough. She lives upstairs with the children and brings them down, now and then, at teatime to wish me a good afternoon in French. And when I decide to take them for a drive she comes, too, because Mrs Naylor wouldn't trust me alone, I suppose – and occasionally she lets Prudence in here just before dinner and makes the poor child pick out a tune on the piano. It's supposed to be a treat, although I don't quite know who is being treated since it turns the child chalk-white and makes her sick afterwards, and I confess I don't enjoy it. But, naturally, they know best – Miss Mayberry and Nurse and Hannah—'

'If you think it makes Prudence ill, why don't you forbid it?'

'Oh, my dear,' she said, making a languid, rueful gesture. 'Do you know, one evening I quite made up my mind to do just that – I almost did it. But then – well – the fuss and the ill temper and Hannah being sent for next morning to tell me I'm failing in my duty – and convincing me, as she usually does. And then having to apologize to Miss Mayberry and having her running around me for a week or two asking my permission for every little thing, because I'm sure she doesn't want to lose her place. No, no, in the end it seemed best just to look away and think about something else, and then applaud prettily and say, "Well done, Prudence. Well done, Miss Mayberry." Much better – and, of course, there is one consolation, because Mrs Naylor cannot bear to see the children in the drawing room – she hovers, my dear, in absolute agony, even now when there's nothing much left for them to break. What she'd really like it is to put the whole room under dust covers, but since my husband did leave the furniture I assume he meant me to sit on it – and sometimes I think I actually prefer the room this way.'

Although I had been deeply shocked at first to see the drawing room denuded of its treasures, Mr Aycliffe having taken his favourite pieces to London with him and placed the rest in the safe custody of the attic, I had to admit that I was more comfortable now, more inclined to linger. The polished, inlaid tables carried nothing more awe-inspiring these days than dried flowers under glass, a china milkmaid and ploughman, an apple women, rosy, rustic children and an assortment of dogs and lambs and bright yellow chicks, the purchases of Morgan Aycliffe's earlier years, long since outgrown but which Elinor, discovering them packed away in an old tea chest, had arranged to suit her own uncritical eye. And, on her good days, when Emma-Jane Hobhouse came to tea and compared her own, rapidly expanding waist with Elinor's girlish nineteen inches, or Daniel Adair, her husband's manager, remembering her husband's age and how attractive she would be as a widow, almost turned himself inside out to impress her, then Elinor was at ease in her drawing room – mistress, at last, of her surroundings.

But not all her days were good and far too many afternoons I would find her prostrate on her couch, not knowing what ailed her except that she was weary – weary – Weary to death and without care as to when it came.

'The trouble is,' Hannah said, 'that she will not stir herself. She could be busy now with her husband's affairs. Someone must go about the constituency and assess its mood so that he may be informed as to what people are saying and thinking. And since Elinor cannot, or will not, then I feel obliged to undertake the task myself. Oh yes, I know it is not my place and may give rise to gossip, but if Mr Aycliffe should ever lose his seat for lack of information which Elinor could have supplied, it would not go well with her. And while I do not wish to see her in distress, I do feel that a man in public life should be able to rely on the support of his close relations, and that Mr Aycliffe has been most unfortunate in that respect.'

Unfortunate indeed, but Elinor, surviving every one of Hannah's lectures, continued to fluctuate between a lethargy so stifling that she could barely trouble to raise her hand and periods of intense activity when she would have herself driven furiously around town, inviting everyone she met to tea, and spending her husband's money as fast as his manager, Mr Adair, would allow.

'I do not need another evening gown,' she would say to Rosamund Boulton, 'but since I am here, I may as well have a look – and yes, you may make me up that sky-blue satin, and the black one, Rosamund dear, while you are about it, for it will make a perfect foil to my husband's first wife's pearls. No, no, there is no need to take my measurements. My waist is still nineteen inches, which Emma-Jane considers scandalous at my age, for I am almost twenty-five and should rightly look like an old crow by now. Well, one day I shall turn thirty, I suppose – like you, Rosamund

– but in the meantime have you nothing to age me? For when I go to London someone may mistake me for my husband's daughter, and we cannot risk that. But never mind, for we can always send my sister Hannah in my place.'

But such outbursts were often followed by a sick melancholy that I could not dismiss, like Hannah, as mere childishness.

'Leave her to wallow,' Hannah advised, 'which is what I mean to do, for if I stay I shall box her ears.'

But solitary brooding, in my view, was not the medicine she required, and one summer night she kept me talking very late in Blenheim Lane, holding my hand and chatting, not of her present sorrows, but of our shared childhood, so that travelling home in the warm dark I was heavy and sentimental with a past that had always contained Joel.

Yet where was Joel tonight? A mile away, perhaps, or two, but no closer to me than Morgan Aycliffe to Elinor. And was my life, as a woman, less empty than hers? Admittedly, Joel had not physically abandoned me. He was here, in my daily life, in my bed more often than not, and it did not wound me if, when he took me in his arms, he thought of the aristocratic Estella Chase or some other chance-met adventuress, since I invariably thought of Crispin. But, for all my good sense and my desire for peace, for all his talk of our shared interests, could it really suffice? And, knowing that it could not, I prayed suddenly, quite fervently, that I could be like Emma-Jane Hobhouse, engrossed with her own fertility and the tittle-tattle of everyday life, a woman at peace in this man-made world.

Was I, in fact, the freak of nature, Emma-Jane the norm? And if she were the breed of woman society required, should I not try to resemble her, to cover my body and my mind in layers of her complaisant, contented fat so that I too could doze in the afternoons with my mouth open, and argue for weeks about what constituted a perfectly baked apple tart? Or should I admit that, in a world where

Emma-Jane personified success, I was doomed to failure and, having come to terms with that, should I withdraw, like my mother, and watch that unbalanced world pass by? Pondering these questions, I was not immediately aware of the tumult in the streets.

Polling day now was six months past, but Cullingford, having enjoyed its first taste of political upheaval, was not unwilling for more, especially since the December electorate had not favoured the cause of the factory children. Crispin Aycliffe's policies had been soundly defeated in Cullingford; a Mr George Banks, a convinced Ten Hours man, had fared no better in Bradford. Richard Oastler, the Factory King himself, had been rejected by Huddersfield, while Mr Michael Sadler had failed to secure re-election at Leeds, leaving the Ten Hours Movement without a voice at Westminster. And that – or so Bradley Hobhouse and some others declared – was the end of that; or should have been, until battling Parson Bull of Bierley made the journey to London and persuaded the intense, deeply religious Lord Ashley to take up the Ten Hours cause. Lord Ashley had never seen a factory child or been aware, at any conscious level, that such abuse existed, but the Reverend George Stringer Bull had found no difficulty in persuading him to reintroduce Sadler's Bill to the House.

'Damnable interference,' Bradley Hobhouse had muttered. 'And what does this Lord Ashley know about my weaving sheds? Do I go and tell him when to plant his corn, or whatever he does on his estates? Ten hours, indeed. It takes me ten hours to cover my overheads, and I need five more, at least, after that, to show a profit. And if I lose, they all lose.'

But Joel merely shrugged and replied, 'We'll not lose. We've got honourable members and our own, now, haven't we, at Westminster, and what did we elect them for but this? So let Morgan Aycliffe and the rest of them earn their keep or when they pass the begging bowl round again they'll get nothing from me.'

And so it was, for although the Ten Hours Bill was given a first reading, the newly elected industrial members knew what was expected of them and, drawing solidly together, had little difficulty in convincing the House that Sadler's committee, however moving and horrendous, had been too one-sided to justify legislation. Evidence had been heard from mill hands and midwives, parsons and idealistic land agents, from victims and their sympathizers, but the manufacturers themselves had not been allowed to state their case. And once again it was thought better to delay, to gather more facts, to appoint a Royal Commission this time instead of a mere Select Committee like Sadler's, which, instead of shipping cartloads of wrecked humanity to London, would come North, to interview masters and men in their native surroundings and see for itself.

These commissioners, as it turned out, were gentlemen of the very highest integrity, but in that summer of 1833, to the mass of workpeople, who had learned to expect very little from gentlemen – honourable or no – they seemed no more than the tools of a government willing to play the masters' game. And when Richard Oastler, still smarting from his defeat at Huddersfield, thundered out his warning that the commissioners were coming to cheat the people, not aid them, the simmering brew of discontent came once more to the boil.

For months past, ever since it was known that the commissioners would be coming, the air had somehow tightened, and I had grown so conscious of eyes peering at me suddenly from beneath a shawl, shooting me quick glances from the shading angle of a cloth cap, watching, speculating, that for the first time I began to share Emma-Jane's fears of intruders in the night, of shadows that became strangling hands, raping hands, and I dreamed again, often, of that gaping hole in my father's chest and of my brother's dead face.

The Hobhouse mill, I knew, was watched night and day by silent relays of Ten Hours men, determined that Bradley should make no attempt to clean up his sheds or install decent privies before the commissioners came; and Tarn Edge, where building was taking place, had been singled out, not openly like Nethercoats, since Joel was a harder, trickier man than Bradley, yet so thoroughly that I could no longer visit it without that nightmare sensation of eyes in my back, of someone pale and twisted with little to hope for and little to lose watching me just beyond the edge of my sight.

And when the commissioners arrived they were met by bitter crowds who harassed and hustled them, and by Oastler's partisans, the hard-faced Ten Hours men, who followed them from town to town on horseback, a grim escort they found impossible to shake away. There were mass meetings and processions. In Bradford so many threats were made against them that Mr John Wood had felt obliged to refuse them entry to his mill since he could not guarantee their safety. And, returning from Elinor's that summer night, brooding on my personal demons, I had forgotten that the enemy, as they were called, had reached Cullingford and that Joel, even now, was in consultation with them – over dinner, one supposed – at the Old Swan.

Naturally, in this atmosphere of suspicion and hostility, it had been impossible to entertain them at home, to the chagrin of Mrs Stevens, who, like Joel, had great faith in the effects of well-seasoned sauces, well-chosen wines and cigars; and so, in his superbly cut evening clothes, a heavy gold ring on either hand, a pearl in his necktie, a gold-topped ebony cane, and a black silk hat, Joel had gone down to the Old Swan to assure the honourable gentlemen that, unlike Mr Wood, he was able to offer them his protection in Cullingford, no matter where they wished to go. And I cannot imagine they doubted him.

But now, abruptly, I was aware not only of disturbance

368

around me, to which I was no stranger, but of wood smoke pricking my eyelids, reminding me, in my reverie, of bonfires, Guy Fawkes and November, until, with a start, I woke up to an airless, over-warm July.

'What is it, Thomas?' I called out.

Busy with the restless horses, who were no fonder of wood smoke than I, my coachman, who had served my grandfather and still thought of me as a chit of a girl to whom not much respect was due, merely grunted, as if I should have seen for myself. 'Trouble. And there'll be more unless I turn these brutes around.'

But Blenheim Lane was not only very long but very narrow, the trees in full summer leaf joining hands in places overhead, and, having passed the Fleece, whose yard would have given us a turning space, there was nothing to do, in the growing crowd, but continue forward.

I heard Thomas curse as the horses – which he had always thought too high-bred and fancy for a carriage, too much of Joel Barforth and not enough of Samson – became fractious at the scent of fire; and, as I leaned out again, he shouted, as my grandfather would have done, 'Get in with you, lass. You don't want them to recognize your face tonight.' And, whipping, cursing, furious at being saddled with the responsibility of his master's wife when he didn't much care for the master and it was my own fault anyway for gadding about at night instead of staying at home as a decent woman should, he set off again as best he could.

I had no hat, no cloak, just a knot of ribbon in my hair and a light summer shawl, a gauzy complement to a dress which seemed suddenly too bright, a clean fresh lemon that could not hide in a corner, which could identify me: 'That's Joel Barforth's wife. Stop the bitch.' And because I knew it could happen – that they could drag me about the streets by the hair, abuse and defile me – because my father's life had bled away through that hole in his chest and they had impaled my brother on a kitchen knife six inches long, I was afraid.

Kirkgate and Millergate, as we lumbered down their steep, cobbled sides, were a mess of abandoned carriages and broken shop fronts, littered with stray dogs and cats and stray children gorging themselves on the scattered pickings of Mr Wilmot's grocery, Miss Timmins's bakery, the Fearnley sisters' tea and coffee shop, places I knew and could barely recognize now in the tumultuous dark. And, at the bottom of Millergate, where it joined Market Square, we were forced to halt.

They had built a bonfire in the Old Swan yard, a huge, smoking pile beneath the windows of the supper room where the commissioners, and Joel, had gone to dine. As a great tongue of flame leaped suddenly into the air, I heard them shouting Joel's name and saw him appear at the window, open it, and, with the cool arrogance that made him so detested and so feared, lean against the window frame with the nonchalance of a spectator at a show.

I saw the firelight pick out the gold buttons on his waistcoat, the flash of those white teeth against his dark face as he made some remark to the men in the besieged room with him; I saw faces looming out of the crowd, leering, grinning, hating, unreasoning, beyond any appeal I could make to them, functioning now not as men and women who could know pity and good sense – although they would know it again tomorrow when it could be too late for us all – but as part of a crowd that could kill and maim with no more responsibility than a raindrop must feel for the devastation of a storm. In the morning it would not be their fault. In the morning someone else would have thrown the stone, wielded the knife, tossed that burning piece of wood through the Swan door. In the morning some of them would not even remember what it had all been about in the first place, while others, remembering, would be sorry or ashamed; and others still, feeling that not enough had been achieved, would be ready to start again. But now, with the calm that extreme fear sometimes brings, I recognized that I was trapped and that, since I could not rely on Thomas and could not reach Joel, I would have to save myself. And as the crowd parted to let a solid wedge of Ten Hours men come through, I clasped my hands and held my breath, like a child who, by closing his eyes, hopes he will not be seen.

I did not at first recognize what they were carrying on their shoulders, there in the tossing, uncertain torchlight, and when I did the shock alone carried me to the far edge of panic. And although I told myself that the thing they were holding aloft was not Joel – for he was still there at the window – it was so sickeningly real, the cut of the coat, the elaborate shirt frill, the width and height of him, that part of my mind refused to believe it was just a doll. And as they paraded their effigy once, then twice around the inn yard – giving Joel time to recognize himself, should he need it – and then heaved it savagely into the fire, my mind, for one brief, harrowing moment, caught the odour of flesh burning, the agony of a man screaming soundlessly through the flame. And, drenched as I was by that torrent of hate, it seemed to make no difference that Joel's living face was still at the window, looking down.

I tried to look away and could not; I tried to close my eyes and could not do that either, and so, like everyone else, I watched the doll burn, saw the legs disintegrate, the chest open to disgorge heaven knew what garbage as the expensive coat shredded away and the shirt frill, the face, the tall silk hat were devoured, one by one. And because the hate was there, because they truly desired him to suffer this torment, it was real again and terrible. And when it was over, when the doll lay in ashes and symbolic murder had been done, all eyes were raised to that long upper window, where Joel was still leaning, glass in hand, against the sill.

'Bloody thieving Barforth bastard,' they shrieked at him.

And, looking down, smiling – that white flash of perfect

teeth against his amber skin – he raised his glass to them in cool salutation, drank, bowed, and went inside.

And most strangely, in the great howling and screaming that went up around me, the brandishing of torches and shaking of fists, I found that I was smiling too.

But there still remained the matter of my own safety, and in that sea of faces swamping the square, spilling out into the adjoining streets as water does in confined spaces, I could see no help, no hope at all. I doubted if any of these men would offer violence, in the normal way of things, to another man's woman – although they would all indulge occasionally in a rough and tumble with their own – but this was not a night for normality, for remembering how ashamed one would feel afterwards, and when the fire began to burn low and Joel, after all, had not burned with it, I would be a natural target for their frustrations. No one, I thought, had recognized the carriage as yet, so intent were they on the Old Swan and the men inside it – and, indeed, there were many vehicles in the square, cut off as I was from escape – but eventually, quite soon, although some would drift away back to their homes or to the ale-houses, the bitter ones, the hurt ones, the ones perhaps who had nowhere else to go, would stay and, seeing the carriages as a symbol of life's injustice, would vent their hate against them. And I had no mind to sit in a fragile box on wheels while they pelted me with stones and filth and the maddened horses, plunging out of control, jolted me to destruction.

'You'd best get down, missus,' old Thomas grunted, appearing suddenly, his head close to mine. And when I could do no more than stare at him, appalled by the very idea I had had in mind, he said, quite furiously, 'Come on, lass. They don't know your face so well, but they know mine and they'll remember in a minute or two whose horses I drive. And if you're sitting behind me they'll soon work out who you are and I can't be responsible for what they'll do to you. These aren't mules, you know, these fancy high-steppers, and if they lose their heads there's more than you to get hurt.'

And when I went on staring, he picked up the carriage rug and threw it at me.

'Put this round you, lass, and get down – get down. Get into the Swan if you can, and if you can't then get to the back of the crowd and make for the top of Millergate. And if you don't see me there, knock on a door – there's decent houses at the top end of Millergate – and get somebody to take you in, or take you home, or send a message. And look sharp about it.'

No one, for a very long time, had told me to 'look sharp,' certainly not a coachman whose sole concern should have been my safety. But, realizing he did not mean to abandon Joel's mettlesome horses here, where they could trample a dozen other women underfoot – women far closer to him in background and temperament than I – I nodded, swallowed hard, wrapped the rug awkwardly around me, and got down.

Millergate, I thought, Millergate, and, shockingly, having lived here all my life, I had no idea where Millergate was, so little notion of which way to turn that I simply moved blindly away from the carriage, thinking that anywhere, surely, was better than here. No one spoke to me or tried to stop me, no one deliberately blocked my way – for, after all, without my carriage and my fringed parasol, my deep-brimmed satin bonnet, who was I anyway? But I had never been in a crowd before, had never experienced the accidental jostlings and pushings of strangers, had never inhaled the stale breath and sweat of people who were unknown to me, and I found it terrifying.

Millergate, I thought again. Please, Millergate, for indeed there were houses there with little gardens and decent front doors, a maid to give me tea and a man to take a message home. But Millergate swam away from me, came back a moment, and then was not Millergate at all but some narrower place, unlit, malodorous. And when I

373

turned back there were too many people behind me, too many eyes, so that, keeping my head down, I blundered again and was truly lost.

Yet to be lost here, in my native town, was ridiculous and, pressing close to the wall, I paused a moment, forcing myself to reflect. These could only be the alleyways that cut between Millergate and Kirkgate, glimpsed a thousand times as I drove by, and if they were foul and damp, dens of vice and dens of disease, at least they were short. I had only to keep on walking in the same direction and eventually a paved, gaslit thoroughfare – Millergate or Kirkgate, I no longer cared which – would open out before me. I had only to keep on walking – no more; I must, in fact, keep on walking, and, hurrying forward, my useless satin slippers paddling through murky water, I felt my identity shred away from me and knew real terror. I was just a woman alone in the streets at night, fair game for any man, and the fear of being recognized as Joel Barforth's wife no longer seemed important. I was appalled now merely by my own helplessness, by being a woman who could be forced into a corner, abused by unwashed hands and coarse mouths, held down by the scruff of the neck as dogs hold bitches. And with the spectre of so much degradation reaching out to touch me through the hot dark, I rushed off sightlessly again, my breath catching painfully in my chest, meeting nothing but blank walls, a pathetic mouse – scurrying through tunnels that engulfed me, until at last a hand caught my wrist and an unknown voice said, 'Mrs Barforth.'

'No. No I'm not. Let me go.'

'Wherever to, God love you, for you haven't an idea in your head as to your direction. I saw you get down from your carriage and you've been going round in circles ever since.'

Oddly enough, the fact that the stranger was a woman did nothing to console me.

'Just let me go, that's all, whoever you are – out of my way. I don't know you.'

'No. But I know you, sweetheart,' she said, tightening her grip on my wrist. 'You're high-and-mighty Barforth's wife, all right, not a doubt about it. Lost your carriage, did you? No, no, don't try to take a swing at me, Miss Verity, because you're not up to it. I'd have you down in the muck before you knew what had hit you.'

And then, dragging me close against her, her face almost touching mine, she muttered, 'Don't think I want to do this, because I don't. I don't care what happens to you – however bad it is, you'd deserve it – and you'll get it, my lass, soon enough, if you stay here. The lads are still mostly down at the fire, but they'll be back ere long and they'd gobble you up alive, little lady, make no mistake about it. So I've got to take you to Crispin, darling, haven't I, because if I leave you here and he finds out about it, he'll lose his good opinion of me. And I wouldn't want that to happen. So come on, love, come to Crispin. It's what you want, I suppose, same as he does – and if you're even half a Barforth you won't be slow to take your opportunities.'

And fascinated, overpowered, with no more will to resist than Ann Agbrigg, I followed her.

24

I had never seen the Red Gin at close quarters before; I knew of it simply as the haunt of brawlers and malcontents; of godless, rootless men and immoral women – of whores. Now, with my hand firmly in the grip of one of these – a bareheaded, brazen creature swinging her hips, tossing her long black hair – I found myself walking down a passage as narrow and unpleasant as a greasy ribbon and then mounting a rickety, littered back stair to a room I most certainly should not have entered.

'Wait here,' she said. 'I'll fetch him.'

Although I heard her turn the key in the lock and had no guarantee that she had really gone for Crispin, I sat down almost like a well-behaved child at school, with no thought of escape.

There was a lamp burning on a scarred wooden table, bare floorboards, bare walls, a narrow iron bedstead, a kitchen chair, books in tidy piles, writing materials: the bare essentials of existence. A monk's cell, I thought; obsessively neat – where Morgan Aycliffe, not Crispin, could have taken refuge to scourge his soul. And, from the inn below it, the noise of unkempt revelry seeping through the floor, the tight-packed anthill of the street across the way, of the room next door, the intimate functioning of strangers' bodies constantly within range of eye and ear and nostril, no longer separated from me by the thickness of stone walls, an acre of rose garden, a carriage drive. And although it was troublesome, it was in some ways a protection.

He was a long time in coming but when the door finally opened I could see he had been running.

Unprepared for the emotion in him and the emotion in me leaping forward to meet it, I said, quite harshly, the first words that entered my head. 'Who was that woman?'

And because he had not expected me to say that, it steadied him, gave us both a breathing space.

'She is Dinah McCluskey, the landlady here. She told me what happened, and, Verity, your coachman should be whipped. He should never have left you to make your way alone.'

'Oh, he was thinking of the horses, I expect, for they would cost a great deal of money to replace, whereas women come cheap enough. Only think, if the horses had been damaged, Joel would have been obliged to send to Tattersalls in London and pay out a thousand guineas or more. And what could I cost? Just a rather splendid headstone, and he wouldn't even have to go out of

Cullingford to replace me. So Thomas knew what he was about.'

'Verity,' he said, 'are you – quite well?'

'No. I think I am probably hysterical but I expect I shall be able to contain it. And if I did have a fit, would it matter – here? Would anybody trouble to enquire?'

'I am very sure they would not. In fact, you could scream your head off and no one would dream of interfering. It would simply be assumed I was beating you – which all women deserve from time to time and some of them enjoy – and if you opened the window and shrieked, "Murder," they would only suppose you deserved that too.'

'I am in your power, then.'

'No,' he said, his voice losing its forced lightness, his face tightening. 'You are not in my power. You know that very well. I think you must stay here awhile, for there is still an ugly-tempered crowd in the streets, and then I will arrange for you to be taken home. I have nothing to offer you but brandy, I am afraid, and even Dinah may have difficulty in finding tea at this hour.'

'Brandy, then. It won't harm me. It kept my grandfather alive during his last years – or so he said – and he was never wrong.'

The glass he gave me was of fine-cut crystal, incongruous in those meagre surroundings, and the brandy may well have been superb, although, as I crossed the room and stood by the window looking down at the putrid alleyway, it burned, then numbed my tongue. And I knew that whatever happened between us would be of my choosing; he would remain cool and polite, convincing me, perhaps, of his indifference, if the woman, Dinah McCluskey, had not said to me, 'Come to Crispin. It's what you want, I suppose, same as he does.'

'Were you in the square?' he said quietly. 'Did you see the burning?'

'Yes. And I saw Joel salute the crowd afterwards. I don't

377

know what I should have felt about that, but actually I was proud of him.'

'I'm sorry.'

'You shouldn't be. I've told you before – he's my cousin. I understand him. My father would have been shocked and upset, and my brother would have blustered and tried to break a few heads – and got himself killed all over again. But my grandfather would have done exactly as Joel did, and whether you liked my grandfather or not – and I didn't like him at all – you had to admit that he was magnificent. I don't always like Joel too much either, but that has nothing to do with being proud of him, of giving him credit for courage and audacity – or for wishing he was on your side. Because he'd do a lot more for your cause than Mark Corey – if he believed in it, or if he could see a profit in it.'

He smiled, ruefully, unhappily, his face very pale in that uncertain lamplight; thinner, I thought, the fine, fair skin creasing at his eye corners, the eyes themselves a paler blue, as if they had been washed by fatigue. And, knowing beyond question that I loved him, I wondered why I had made my voice so hard, why it seemed so essential to explain that I had an odd, unlikely respect for Joel, too.

'Barforth pride,' he said, trying to make his voice light again. 'Is there no end to it? I have never seen you so fierce.'

'I daresay, and you may well see me fiercer, for I want to know how that woman was aware of a connection between us.'

'Because I told her of it.'

'Crispin, for heaven's sake, how could you do that?'

'Because she is kindhearted and intelligent and can be trusted to listen when the brandy talks and to keep quiet about it afterwards. She is exceedingly common, I grant you, but if she had not followed you from Market Square, I dread to think what might have befallen you. You should be grateful.'

'So I am, grateful indeed. What did you tell her?'

378

'Would there be any purpose in repeating it?'

'There may be.'

'Verity,' he said, his voice no more than a whisper, his eyes closing briefly as if, suddenly, his head ached. 'Don't do this to me again. Don't come close to me and then disappear in my hands like smoke – not again. It may hurt you, too, but it crucifies me, Verity.'

'What must I do, then?'

'Nothing, for nothing has changed. I am no more able to support you than I was before – less able, for the election cost me dear and I am in debt for every penny. And now that my face is well known, and my opinions, people apply to me for assistance and I am rarely able to refuse. If we ran away together we would have a merry procession following us, your husband and my creditors – you may as well know it.'

'Yes – yes. I know it. Now tell me what you have said to Mrs McCluskey.'

He walked a step or two away from me and back again, catlike in his tense, delicate testing of the air around me, making a valiant effort to persuade himself not to touch me, not to attempt my downfall, reminding himself how much I had to lose, vowing he would do nothing to harm me even if I, foolish woman that I was, seemed so strangely willing. And his resolve made me smile, for I knew – in my mood of foolishness and strangeness – that he could not keep it.

I had asked him, long ago, not to take me, to allow me the chance to give, and now, watching his painful hesitations, his longing to commit himself and his fear of commitment struggling inside him for mastery, it struck me that for the first time in my life I was free. No one – except Crispin and Dinah McCluskey – knew at this moment where I was, and if people were searching for me they would not look here. Liberty, brief perhaps, but liberty just the same, and what did brevity matter since life itself was short and uncertain and I could have been killed down there in the street or could have died six months ago of the fever. And suddenly, basking in a newfound strength that had all the warmth and fragrance of sunshine, I saw no shame in acknowledging not only my love but my desire for this frail, beautiful man, not only the matching of our minds but my body's sheer, basic need to possess him, to give itself into his possession.

'I can't ask you to be my mistress,' he said, a schoolmaster lecturing me, lecturing himself. 'Can I? Not again. I asked you once and you gave me no reply – there could be no reply, I understand that, and so we parted.'

And, reaching out my hand and winding an arm around his neck, I told him, 'I'm not so sure. I think it was because you feared I would persuade you into some little villa and make a respectable man of you. But now, since your creditors would not allow that in any case . . .'

'Verity, don't laugh at me. I love you. I don't always know why, and God knows I've tried not to, but I love you.'

'And I love you.'

And in those first moments, our delight had the wondrous, almost innocent quality of children discovering the scents and shades of the world, a slow wandering through enchantment as his hands gently removed, one by one, the pins from my chignon, his mouth smiling and tasting, his nostrils deeply inhaling, as I shook my hair loose against his face. We had waited a long time, yet now there was no hungry falling upon each other, no cause at all for haste. And standing a breath away from him, I understood at last the pleasure of display, no longer submitting my body to a man's eyes but offering it, pausing at the unfastening of each tiny pearl button, raising my arms above my head with a rich, sighing content as my bodice fell away, glad of the lamplight on my bare shoulders and the contours of my breasts, proud suddenly that those breasts were still smooth and firm, that my legs, emerging from the froth of my petticoats, were long and slender at the ankles, loving my own body at that moment, beneath the caress of his gaze, because he loved it.

And even then, when the fine, lightly boned moulding of him, the fragile blond skin with its silk-scattering of fair hair, had moved me to an immense, wondering tenderness, we gazed a while longer until, with the very tips of his fingers, he touched my forehead and my cheeks, my mouth, the outline of my ears and throat, the length of my breastbone and thighbone, while I, stretching my arms above my head again with that same languorous sighing, turned slowly round, my body ready now to dissolve in his, to flow over him and into him like a rich, unhurried stream.

The bed was hard, with a lumpy pillow and a scratchy blanket, and there were still the street noises, still the raucous merriment of whores and drunkards from below, squalid and wicked, if any of it had been real. But it did not concern me, for the real world had become very small and I had nothing to do in it but devote myself to the pleasures of Crispin Aycliffe, pleasure far more complex and delicate and nervous than the forthright explosions of male joy to which I was accustomed. I was, in that hour, his most devoted and willing slave, lost and bemused with adoration, wanting nothing but the rich reward of his skin against my skin, the lightness of his bones beneath my fingers, so drunk with giving that my own pleasure took me by surprise and left me too mindlessly content to remember that I was now an adulteress, who ought to be ashamed and afraid.

'Truly,' I told him, breathless and laughing, wanting him again already in my mind, knowing he needed to be reassured, 'truly that must have been perfect.'

And he smiled. 'Of course. Did you think that I could ever be less than a perfect lover?'

And then, leaning over me, his elbows one on either side of my head, his smile gone, he said quickly, 'I was never more nervous in my life – terrified of offending you or hurting you or not pleasing you enough. Love me, Verity.'

'I do.'

'More than you love anyone else?'

'Easily – but then, who else do I love?'

'Your children,' he said, sitting up. 'You love your children.'

'Yes, I do.'

'I have seen it in your face, sometimes, when you look at them. Your tenderness has moved me.'

'That displeases you?'

'Dear God, no. It delights me, except . . .'

'Yes – except?'

'Except that I am honest enough to care that our love could harm them, and base enough to know that I will not sacrifice it.'

And brushing my hand the length of his tense, anxious back, an indulgent, comforting gesture that was not unmaternal, I told him, laughing at him, loving him, 'Crispin Aycliffe, you have spent years of our lives trying to entice me into your bed, and now that you have me I do believe your complicated nature is looking for reasons to regret it.'

'Ah – then you must hold me in your arms a while longer and smooth my fears away, for I am soon melancholy, particularly when I have been very joyful. I need a great deal of cosseting and spoiling, Verity – I warn you.'

And so, taking him in my arms, his head nuzzling against my shoulder, I turned his fine, fair hair around my fingers, dropped light, quick kisses on his eyes and ears and chin, the hollows and angles of his delicately moulded face, kissing the hurt child in him that was still lost in the dark until the man awoke and he made love to me again quite briefly but with an assurance that enabled him to open his eyes in the moment of pleasure and smile.

It was time, then, to go and, disengaging myself from him with the infinite care one bestows on objects of enormous value, enormous frailty, I got up and stood for a moment, surveying the bare little room – the monk's cell

– smiling at the cheap, ugly furnishings, the damp patches on the walls, the scarred boards underfoot, as if they were priceless treasures.

'I thought this would be the worst part,' I told him. 'Getting up, getting dressed, hurrying out into the street – I thought it would seem sordid – that I wouldn't be able to bear it. Yet here I am, doing it, and the only thing in my mind is that I love you.'

'Thank you,' he said, getting up, the rueful smile back on his lips. 'I believe you said that to put me at ease, because you knew I would be worried about it, too. You will come to me again, Verity?'

'Yes. I don't know where – for I don't know that I could possibly come here alone without discovery – but I'll find somewhere. People think me placid and easy to manage but, in fact, when I am determined, I can generally get my way. Now – you will have to help me with these tapes and these infernal little buttons – and I do not think I can do up my hair alone.'

We dressed without embarrassment, wound my hair into a plain but convincing knot, laughed at the frothy burden of my petticoats and their awkward fastenings, and instead of the shame, the dry-mouthed dread of discovery that I should have felt, my mind refused to be distracted from its rich glow of remembered happiness.

'You have committed adultery,' reason accused me, and my conscious mind replied, 'Next time I will bring a big, deep-brimmed bonnet so that I can simply cram my hair inside it and run.'

'Adultery is a crime,' reason said. 'Before God and before the law. And it is not the same law for a woman as for a man. Society excuses a man, but an adulterous woman is worse than a leper. And Joel, whatever he may do himself, would hurt you if he caught you.'

But my mind, raising an impatient finger to its lips, answered, 'Hush – don't interrupt – don't annoy me –

383

don't distract me from looking at him, from remembering, from planning how I can come to him again.'

And then, standing at the door and seeing Crispin in the good blue coat he had worn at the hustings, growing shabby, I noticed, at the lapels and the elbows – reminding me of the debts he could surely never repay on his fifty pounds a year – I asked him, 'Crispin, how long have I been here?'

'Well, I have never been a man for the exact time, especially since I let my watch go, but it cannot be less than two hours.'

'Dear God—'

'No,' he said, quite sharply. 'Don't ask God to help you. You can rely on me for this. You are not accustomed to deceit, but I served a long apprenticeship. My mother taught me to lie, for my father surrounded us with so many rules that the only way we could breathe was to deceive him. And so I know what I am about. You cannot walk home in those foolish slippers, which saddens me, since I would enjoy a long stroll in the moonlight, and unless we happen to meet your coachman on the way, the only thing for it is to go to the Swan.'

'Will Joel still be there?'

'Oh, I imagine so. He will have cause to celebrate his own triumph, for it is not every man who is elevated to the level of Guy Fawkes. Oh yes, he will still be there – and he will be very much obliged to me, I imagine, for rescuing his wife.'

As a spasm of discomfort, a prickly, unpleasant thing, briefly crossed my mind, he put a hand under my chin, forced my head up, and made me look at him.

'Do you doubt me already? Do you think I have made love to you only to humiliate your husband? Do you think he even entered my head just now? And if you tell me he entered yours you will mortally wound me.'

We walked, hand in hand, down the rickety staircase, the greasy passage, into the alleyway, picking our way through

384

noise and stink and litter, and, with his arm around me, my whole body was still dazzled by his nearness, throbbing with a blissful, butterfly joy that extended no further than every footstep, every single intake of breath. Enchantment and then, too soon, the glimmer of gaslight, the windows of the Swan beckoning in the distance, so that I paused in the shadows, my feet growing heavy and unwilling to tread a paved road again, and the outline of the square, the Market Cross, the Piece Hall that I knew so well striking me as alien, hostile, dangerous.

And in the moment before we entered that illuminated space, tension gripped him suddenly, painfully, and he said, 'Tell me, Verity – tell me—'

'I love you.'

'And then – and then? More than that—'

'I love you best – much more than anyone else.'

'Than anyone?'

'Yes, yes – more than I could ever love anyone.'

'Thank you,' he said, the taut pressure of his nerves sighing out of him. 'So – come then, my darling, I'll take you across the way to the Swan and teach you how to lie.'

The square had emptied now, a light wind tasting of ash and the memory of burning stirring the debris underfoot, reminding me of a ballroom, forlorn with departed gaiety, but the Swan still sat there in its accustomed place, humming and glowing with good cheer, ready to cater all night long to the appetites of those who were prepared to pay. Walking now a polite distance away from me, with no greater familiarity than a solicitous hand beneath my elbow as I negotiated the mess in the inn yard, Crispin saw me safely bestowed in a back parlour, procured the landlady to attend me, and then, with apparent coolness, mounted the stairs to find Joel and inform him of my plight.

'Barforth, dear fellow, if I might have a word – yes, I daresay I am the last man you expected to see here tonight, and no – very civil of you, but I won't take anything just now. The fact is – well, your wife – no harm done as it turns out, although there could have been – by God, there could have been. Caught up in that little spot of bother, it seems, on her way home from your sister's – my step-mother's. Damned coachman couldn't see his way through, took fright and made her get down. Some fool's notion of picking her up at the top of Millergate, if she ever got there, which of course she didn't. Exactly, Barforth – that's the very word I'd have used myself. Found her in Cropper Alley – yes, that's right, Cropper Alley – could have been the great Wall of China for all she knew. Absolutely worn out and a bit shaken, but luckily I got to her before anybody else, and she's downstairs with Mrs Parkin. What you do to your coachman, of course, is your own affair, but I expect you'll be taking Mrs Barforth home.'

And hearing the light, drawling note of his voice as they came downstairs together, my mind turned rogue again and I was very near to laughter.

'By Christ, Verity,' Joel said from the doorway, appalled, I think, by the mud-splattered hem of my dress, my fouled slippers, my bare, quite dirty feet at ease on Mrs Parkin's good stool. And I thought: How big he is – how dark – basic colours, black and red and great bands of gold – compared to Crispin, behind him, turquoise and lilac and misty, muted shades blending his personality together like a spring evening.

But I said, with great composure, 'Yes, I am in a state, which is hardly to be wondered at, and I would like very much to go home.'

He had, of course, been drinking for hours, was as drunk as he ever permitted himself to be, but he was steady on his feet and decisive in his movements as he turned away from me to Crispin, wanting to be rid of him, I thought, since he had no mind to scold me, or whatever he meant to do, before strangers.

'I am very much obliged to you, Aycliffe.'

'Oh, my pleasure – really – absolutely my pleasure, you may believe me.'

As they shook hands and Crispin bowed slightly towards me in leave-taking, I was aware once again of laughter welling up inside me and stifled it instantly, knowing that if Joel heard it and ever discovered the cause he would kill me for it.

And why, I wondered, did I have so little care for that? Why did I refuse, obstinately, to bow myself with shame and terror when my position was both shameful and terrifying?

'You are quite sure,' Joel said, coming towards me, 'that no one harmed you – quite sure?'

'Why, yes. No one spoke to me at all. I was pushed and jostled a little but no more than anyone else, and I hope you do not mean to blame me for it. I stayed late with your sister because she was in her miseries again, and when Thomas told me to get down and walk to Millergate, I could see the sense to it.'

'Sense? There was no sense at all. He should have brought you here or stayed where he was until the crowd dispersed, or forced himself a way through – they'd have stood back soon enough when they saw it was either that or being ridden down. But, in any case, you are not to blame – bedraggled little sparrow that you are – and I will deal with Thomas later. Come now, I'll take you home.'

'There's no need to take me. Just send a message and they'll come to fetch me. Don't leave your guests on my account.'

'My guests will do very well without me for an hour or two. Just throw those shoes into Mrs Parkin's fire, for I'll not have them in my phaeton, and we'll be on our way. Come – if you had less than six inches of mud on your skirt I'd carry you, but – evening clothes costing what they do – you'll have to manage as best you may.'

But he lifted me a step or two, just the same, across the splinters of charred wood, the brim of what had been a silk hat wedged grotesquely among them, warning me all the while to keep my muck away from his trousers, and, as he tossed me up into the phaeton, I was still happy, still blissfully, gloriously lost to reason. I felt intensely alive, rich and beautiful and clever, my senses and appetites sharpened so that colours seemed brighter, sounds clearer, champagne or spring water equally delightful, and I could have rolled myself in the summer grasses, as young animals do, from sheer joy in living. And, my mood extending to Joel, I wondered if he felt this exultation when he had been with a woman he desired; and then, abruptly, I pitied him, for Joel, who wanted to possess the whole world, had surely never possessed this. Joel, I was quite certain, had never been in love in his whole life. How could his restless desires, his conquests and his triumphs compare with the emotion I was feeling now?

Poor, magnificent, all-powerful Joel. And pitying him – still too dazed with joy to understand that I had cause enough to pity myself – I could feel the reserve I had always felt towards him melt away and I could accept him, value him, exactly as he was.

'Thomas goes in the morning,' he said, taking a corner dangerously, setting the dust flying. 'Or he goes tonight, if I catch him.'

'Oh, he'll not mind that. He's old and ready to go to Patterswick to live with his sister – and he's heartily sick of me.'

'Is he, by God.'

'Yes. I was in the square, Joel. I saw the bonfire, and I saw you raise your glass to them afterwards.'

'Did you?' he said, his smile flashing out as it had in the inn yard. 'And what did you think of that, little cousin?'

Smiling too and closer to him in some odd, quite terrible way than I had ever been before, I answered, 'I'll tell you, cousin – I thought I had never liked you so well before in my life.'

388

25

My mother, being desirous of inspecting the site of our new property at Tarn Edge, had arranged to meet me there the following day and to take me back to Patterswick with her for tea, an expedition which should have given me ample opportunity for a private conversation had not Hannah announced at breakfast, 'I think I had better come with you, Verity. In fact, I think Mr Ashley would expect it of me on such a pleasant day.'

While I finished my tea and toast and ran upstairs for my bonnet, our numbers were again increased, first by Elinor driving up at a spanking pace and calling out, 'My miseries are entirely gone. What – are you going to Patterswick? Excellent – I'll join you, for I hear you had an adventure last night and you can tell me on the way,' and then by young Jonas Agbrigg, who, coming to return a book Hannah had lent him, eagerly accepted her offer of a drive.

'You can take Jonas up with you, Verity, and I will ride with Elinor,' Hannah decided. Since the introduction of Jonas Agbrigg filled Blaize, then Nicholas, then Caroline with an overwhelming desire to come too, I set out surrounded by children while my two cousins followed behind, in the Aycliffe carriage, most comfortably alone.

It was a day of great heat, a blue and gold sky, a thirsty land gasping between the intense reds and yellows of summer flowers, the moorland spiky and crackling underfoot although I had not walked there that morning. And still – my crime already a day old, my body having accommodated Joel's waking desire that morning quite automatically, my mind making little of it, my mouth having smiled and lied as I repeated the story of my escapade to Hannah, to Mrs Stevens, to Elinor, as I would go on repeating it to the many who would ask – still I was happy. And if this mindless, girlish bliss – these symptoms of first love – were ridiculous in a woman of twenty-six, three times a mother, then I was content to be ridiculous. And if they were dangerous – as they undoubtedly were – then, when the time came, I would suffer. And, amazed, amused even at my own recklessness, I smiled at every passerby, even at young Jonas Agbrigg beside me in the carriage, and asked him, 'How is your mother, dear?' although I did not like him and knew that, to him at twelve years of age, his ailing mother was an embarrassment, a nuisance.

'She's very well, ma'am,' he answered dourly, although I knew she had taken to wandering lately, suddenly not being there when, just a moment ago, she had been quietly in her accustomed place.

'A tremendous anxiety,' Hannah had told me. 'She was on Cullingford Green two days ago and had to be fetched home on a tatter's cart, and last week Mr Blamires of the grammar school met her on the road above Lawcroft: she had no idea where she was going – was ready, in fact, to go anywhere with anyone, like a stray dog. Fortunately Mr Blamires recognized her and took her back to Low Cross, but eventually she is bound to encounter someone who will be differently disposed and one trembles to think what may happen then. For her own safety she ought to be restrained – no, no, not with chains, you silly goose, although it would come to that, I fear, if her husband could not afford to care for her at home. I mean simply that they should lock her door and bar her window, but Mr Agbrigg will not hear of it. He looked as shocked as you when I suggested it. Yet what else is to be done? Is she to be left to walk under somebody's horses, or into the canal – for I declare she has no more sense of danger than a toddling child – or to fall into the hands of some villain who would take advantage of her? It would give me no pleasure to turn the key in her door, but I assure you that, when I consider the alternatives, I would force myself to do it.'

As I looked at Ann Agbrigg's clever son, scuffling with my own children for what seemed to them the best place in the carriage, I wondered if it had shamed him when Mr Blamires, his headmaster, had brought his mother home, and if he too would be willing to turn that key.

The surviving Agbrigg girl, Maria, was of little interest to Hannah; a quiet little thing who could do nothing more exciting than sew a straight seam. But the boy Jonas, as plain as his sister, as long and angular and yellow-pale as his father, had a sharpness of intellect – altogether above his station – which had quickly claimed her notice.

A graceless boy, Jonas, sullen and secretive, who had fallen foul of his teachers in the early days until Mr Blamires – most discerning of headmasters – had taken Hannah aside and confided in her that Jonas, far from having difficulty in keeping up with his socially superior classmates, had so far surpassed them that, in some cases, even the masters were finding it impossible to keep up with him.

'Mr Blamires was quite taken aback,' she in her turn confided in me. 'Naturally, every master dreams of a brilliant pupil, but considering the thousands of pounds the Hobhouses and Oldroyds – and the Barforths, of course – have given the school, the poor man was very much alarmed at seeing all the prizes go to an Agbrigg. I sympathized, of course – who would not? – but I was quick to make Mr Blamires aware that no suggestion of holding Jonas back could find favour with me. After all, one never knows what a boy like that may do in the future – what heights he may reach – and how would one feel then if one had not encouraged him?'

Since that day, Hannah had set herself the task of encouraging Jonas Agbrigg as much as she could, earning herself a place perhaps in his memoirs should he ever achieve greatness, while he had attached himself to her good graces with a willingness that made me suspect he was neither so unworldly nor so unpolished as he seemed. A calculating child, I thought, unlike my own sons, who lived like greedy butterflies from one sunbeam to the next, unlike my daughter, who thought the world existed for her pleasure, unlike my own children altogether, who were, just then, causing the alien Jonas so much discomfort with their jostling for position that Hannah called out, 'Verity, can you not keep those children in order? They will have Jonas out on the road ere long if they are not checked.'

'It's our carriage,' Blaize said, clear-eyed and innocent, knowing Hannah could not hear him.

'It's our road as well,' Nicholas muttered, compelled to go one better, not caring whether Hannah heard him or not.

'And I don't like him,' Caroline declared. 'He smells.'

And although the odour Jonas exuded was that of good, cheap soap, nothing to be ashamed of, the look in his pale, slightly uptilted eyes would have worried me had she been older or more available to his spite.

My mother was waiting for us at Tarn Edge, in Squire Dalby's open landau, chatting to Daniel Adair, the Aycliffe manager, who may have had business on the site or may simply have made it his business to be there, since he was a man who enjoyed an audience, particularly of women. And as he helped us down and began to tell us where my drawing room would be and to explain the proposed width and magnificence of my hall, it struck me that one did not often see an Irishman, in these parts, in such a perfect state of health.

He was a man of thirty-five, not tall but square-cut, powerful, with a perpetually smiling mouth and a merry eye, quick to spot its own advantage; a man who, having been instructed by Morgan Aycliffe simply to run the business at a profit and no questions asked, could be relied on, one felt, to feather his own nest with a kind of good-humoured rapacity that would make him popular even among those he robbed. And although he very likely believed that young women were fit for nothing but bed and breeding, while old ones should be firmly anchored to washtub and kitchen stove, nothing could have exceeded the gallantry of his escort, the courteous tilt of his head as he listened to Hannah's questions, the clarity of his replies, the twinkle in his eye as he let himself be discovered looking at Elinor and me, and even my mother, in a way that said, 'Naturally I could never presume to touch, for I'm just a common man, but I'd like to – I'd really like to.'

I stood a little apart, for I had been here often enough before and knew the dimensions of the house, the distance from the mill, how a high stone wall and a future circle of trees would screen me from the unpleasantness of factory life; how, in fact, the firm of Morgan Aycliffe, master builders, would assist me to turn my back on the factory altogether by giving my front windows a view of open fields and a stretch of unblemished sky above them. I knew that I was to have a thick hedge of rhododendrons around my wall, sweet-scented shrubs and half an acre of roses to take the factory smells from my air, a paddock for my children to race their ponies with another wall around it, massive gates and a gatekeeper, and more trees to ensure my privacy. I knew it was to be not just a house, or a home, but a palace for an industrious industrial prince, with myself, his gracious, perfectly mannered consort, inside it.

And I knew I would be that consort. I would give him everything he asked of me, as I had always done, because I could see no other way. I would be obedient and sensible and crafty, and what I could not have by right, I would get, like any other bondswoman, by stealth.

'What are you dreaming of?' my mother asked, gliding up to me in her fluid fashion. Then, catching the drift of something in my face with which she did not wish to involve herself, she said quickly, 'I have the feeling Hannah is in no hurry to see the completion of this house. I suppose your removal from Lawcroft must force her to consider her

393

own position. If she intends to marry Mr Ashley she should certainly name the day, for there seems little point in moving up here with you only to remove again to Patterswick. Mr Ashley is entirely at her disposal – would not dare, I imagine, to be otherwise. Will she marry him, do you think? They tell me Mr Brand has entered the lists once again. Is he, after all, likely to succeed?'

Indeed, Mr Brand, fully recovered from the fever by now and fully aware of what Hannah's loss was costing him in time and effort, had taken to calling on me lately, planting himself squarely in my drawing room at teatime, or any other time he could find an excuse to call, and bewailing not Hannah's engagement to Mr Ashley but her conversion to the Church of England which it entailed.

'It is her soul, Mrs Barforth – her bright, pure soul.'

Yet I didn't think that Mr Brand, as he swallowed his tea and his emotion, was really thinking of Hannah's soul. He wanted her in bed with him, I believed, and the mother of half a dozen red-headed, earthbound children just like himself, and if she meant to become a parsonage wife at all – and I had yet to be convinced of it – I thought she would be more comfortable with him than the ethereal Mr Ashley.

But – and I could not have explained this to Mr Brand – it was not really Mr Ashley, at the moment, who stood between them, nor Morgan Aycliffe, either, but the simple matter of Jonas Agbrigg's education.

'Jonas must go to Oxford or Cambridge,' she had decreed. 'His calibre demands it.' And since only members of the established Church of England were eligible for these ancient seats of learning, it followed – in her view – that Jonas must give up his Methodism and be received, by Mr Ashley, into the Anglican fold.

'It seems to me quite pointless,' she said with true Barforth logic, 'to allow these fine points of religion to ruin an entire career. I am convinced our Lord never intended it, for if one fails to help oneself when the opportunity arises I do not think one should expect anyone else to make up the deficiency. I have explained to Mr Agbrigg – who has very simple views on religion and is far more humble with the clergy than he has any need to be nowadays, considering what he is earning – that he has no need to attend the Anglican church himself, simply to allow Jonas to do so. I have offered to take him with me to Patterswick, provided I may continue to use your carriage, which should cause you no inconvenience since you have the use of Joel's on Sundays, and Mr Ashley will, of course, be only too pleased to receive him as soon as I have convinced the father.'

And so, until Jonas's confirmation had taken place, or until another enthusiasm came along, Mr Ashley had little to fear.

'Oh, I fancy she will be moving up here with us,' I told my mother, and she gave me her vague, pointed smile.

'Yes, I fancy you are right – in fact, I imagine we will all stay very much as we are. Only look at Elinor – skipping along beside Mr Adair and allowing him to believe she is laughing at his witticisms although, in fact, she is merely thinking that she is looking her best today and is not listening to him at all. Poor child, her husband will not die so very soon, you know, for these melancholy men who find life such a burden can be relied on to live forever. Only think what an attractive widow she would make – I am certain Mr Adair has thought of it – with her own enchanting face and figure and all Mr Aycliffe's money, since one supposes he has disinherited his son, and Elinor's children are all girls. A temptation for any man, and Mr Adair appears very ready to be tempted. Well – I am sure he can be very rough when he is not being very charming, and once he got his hands on Elinor and the business he would probably cheat her daughters of their dowries and would take no notice at all of Elinor's headaches. But, at least, he would not be melancholy, so perhaps there would be no headaches – perhaps we should see her blossom again as Mrs Adair. How sad – for she will be Mrs Aycliffe, I think, not perhaps until her dying day but until it is too late for blossoming. Poor lamb, perhaps she would do better to concentrate on being Mrs Aycliffe, since it is so clearly her destiny – and stop trying to share it with her sister – since I can see nothing else for her.'

As we got back into our carriages and Mr Adair waved us a hearty goodbye, I wondered, all the way to Patterswick, how much my mother knew – or guessed – for the advice she had thought appropriate for Elinor could just as well have applied to me.

There was very little to distinguish Squire Dalby's village of Patterswick from a dozen like it, a cluster of grey stone cottages housing his dependants, the paler grey of the church, a few farms squatting among the folds of the land, my mother's house with its ivy-covered wall, its garden mossy and overgrown, its low, oak-panelled rooms dim and cool at all seasons, haunted by a scent of hyacinths that had lingered from generation to generation, the squire's own ancient dwelling just a leafy, shady walk away.

And there, in my mother's flowery, chintzy parlour, an apple-cheeked country girl served us tea, with a silver kettle and basin, on rose-patterned china, and chocolate cake and angel cakes and sticky gingerbread, to which Blaize and Nicholas and Caroline helped themselves raucously, the plates emptying before Jonas Agbrigg's lashless eyes until Hannah delivered her sharp protest and my mother sent the girl for more.

But Jonas, it seemed, had no appetite; he was almost embarrassed by the confectionery Hannah heaped on his plate and was sitting so awkwardly that Blaize, quick to spot his opportunities, needed only to jog his elbow slightly to send that plate flying, the chocolate cake landing squarely, creamy side down, on my mother's pale, decidedly costly rug.

'Oh dear,' she said. 'What a pity. Do have another slice.'

But Hannah, who had seen Blaize's wicked elbow as

well as I had, put her own plate down smartly and enquired in a voice not to be ignored, 'Verity, do you intend to let that pass?'

'What, dear?'

'I think you know very well.'

And when, unwilling to make more of the incident than I had to, I continued to look vague and to sip my tea, she turned furiously, very directly, to the culprit himself.

'That was an extremely wicked thing to do, young man. You have damaged your grandmother's carpet and upset a fellow guest.'

'Not me,' Blaize answered innocently, rudely. 'I didn't drop my cake. It was him.'

'Because you pushed him.'

'No, I didn't,' Blaize told her.

'No, he didn't,' Nicholas told her too, his eyes less innocent, the set of his jaw declaring his readiness to do some pushing on his own account.

'He didn't, either,' Caroline said, quite certain that her opinion must settle things once and for all.

And, finding the whole thing ridiculous and futile, taking note of Hannah's mounting fury and Elinor's barely stifled yawn, I got up and shooed my sons outdoors.

'You did push him, didn't you?' I told Blaize, blinking at the impact of the strong sunlight. And, blinking too, he smiled, his eyes very nearly on a level with my own.

'Oh yes, of course I did. I know you saw me, and I knew you wouldn't give me away to Aunt Hannah.'

'Indeed – well, it wasn't kind of you, Blaize. He may not be a likeable boy, but he's had a sad life, and apart from that, as your Aunt Hannah told you, he is a guest.'

'I didn't invite him.'

'That makes no difference. Neither did I.'

'And you don't much like him either, Mamma. I know you don't. And even if you did, you'd still be on my side.'

'Don't be too sure.'

Yet it was true and, as his easy self-assurance inclined

me, as always, to laughter, I felt a chill whisper of warning inside me, repeating Crispin's words, 'I am honest enough to care that our love could harm them.' And sickeningly aware that it was true, I peered keenly at Blaize, his smoky eyes inviting me to share his mischief, and at Nicholas, standing on my other side, darker, deeper, his feeling for me more intense, perhaps, than his brother's, and I knew that no part of my love for them, or for Caroline, had changed. I would love them every day of my life. And I wished them to be free and whole and individual. But would they, even when they no longer needed or desired my day-to-day caring, extend the same understanding to me? Could they ever accept that my love for a man who was not their father removed nothing from my feeling for them?

Blaize perhaps, who would be worldly, I thought, when he was grown, might come the closest. But Nicholas, insecure enough to be jealous, would suffer, would clench his fists and bite back his tears, and I could not be sure what Caroline would make of me.

'I am base enough to know I would not sacrifice it,' Crispin had said, and I could not sacrifice it either.

'Where have you gone, Mamma?' Blaize said, cutting through my reverie.

And smiling, flinging an arm around each of them, I answered, 'Oh, not far.'

We were to visit the squire after tea, and because an invitation to Dalby Hall was such a rarity, even Elinor found the energy for a brisk walk to the lodge gates, with my children, having been reprimanded once again by Hannah, racing around her, while Hannah herself, taking the sullen young Agbrigg with her, went off in search of her fiancé.

'Come, dear,' my mother said, clearly not wishing to be alone with me. 'We should go up to the Hall, too. The squire has company already – his grandson and his daughter-in-law, who always upsets him – and since he has nothing to do in the summer, when there is no hunting and shooting, he spends a great deal of his time drinking and he may not even recognize Elinor so late in the afternoon. I think I may be needed to make things smooth.'

But I had come expressly to talk to her, as she seemed to know very well, and I shook my head.

'Elinor will manage the squire well enough, Mother, and there is something I wish to tell you.'

'Are you quite sure, dear,' she said, looking round for her embroidery in her old, vague manner. 'Quite sure? Things tend to become so real, I find, when one talks about them. Perhaps if you just think about it a little longer – whatever it is – it may become less urgent—'

'I doubt it.'

'Then after tea, dear – when the squire is settled and Elinor can occupy herself flirting with his guests, and the children can play with the puppies, if young Master Agbrigg ever condescends to play – or if he is even a child – Did I tell you about the puppies, ten of them – five black and five yellow? I wondered, in fact, if you would care to choose one to replace your poor old bitch – Edwin's old yellow bitch—?'

'Mother . . .'

'Be very sure, Verity.'

'Yes. I am in love with Crispin Aycliffe, Mother, and he with me.'

'Oh dear,' she said, executing several quick, apparently accurate stitches in the cushion cover she was making. 'Oh dear.'

And then, laying down her work, folding her hands, she gave me her tranquil faraway smile and moved her shoulders in the faintest sketch of a shrug.

'That strikes me as most unfortunate. Yes, I caught a spark of something between you a long time ago, I confess it, and when I heard that he had rescued you last night so romantically, I wondered . . . But, Verity, why have you told me this? Surely, I ought not to have been told?'

'Because I need you, Mother. It did not end last night, and I may need an alibi, a meeting place, and, in the final instance, a refuge. I think you owe me that, Mother.'

'Owe you?'

'Yes, since you persuaded me, when I was very weak, into a marriage which suited your convenience more than mine. If you had allowed me time to recover from my father's death and Edwin's, I might have remembered the kind of man Joel is, and shown more defiance.'

'Oh no,' she said, taking up her work again. 'No, no, Verity. Let us remember things as they actually were. If I had allowed you the time you speak of you might have defied me – which I doubt – but you would not have defied your grandfather for long. You know that perfectly well, child.'

'Yes, of course I do.'

'And have you been so very unhappy with Joel?'

'No. Neither happy nor unhappy – just sensible.'

'Quite so – whereas Crispin Aycliffe has not been sensible at all. Apart from the fact that he threw away his inheritance in a most reckless manner – you may or may not know that he is considerably in debt to Colonel Corey and to others, I believe.'

'Yes, I know that.'

'Then what future does he offer you?'

'None. He has chosen his own way of life, and I know I cannot share it.'

'But do you at least hope for a change – do you feel able to persuade him into more profitable attitudes?'

'No – at least, I hope he will change but I am sure he will not.'

'Then why, darling? Why take this dreadful risk at all?'

'Because I want something, Mother – something in my life before I'm old – something of my own choosing – something I want, not something somebody else thinks I should have. And he's all I've ever wanted. Wanting nothing was pleasant in its way, very safe and warm and rather superior at times, but I can't go back to it now. I've lived on half feelings and lived very well, but it was a kind of emotional virginity, and like the other kind, once it's gone then that's the end of it.'

'I see,' she said, very gravely for her, and, sighing deeply, looked down at her hands.

'Verity, my dear, I suppose you realize that Joel would never – absolutely never – be prepared to allow you the freedom he permits himself.'

'Yes, I realize that.'

'Nor would his own moral shortcomings even incline him to tolerance. Dearest, I believe he would treat you most savagely and vindictively should the occasion arise. And the sad thing is that no one would blame him. The law would allow him to do just what he pleased with you, and all your friends, even the women – especially the women – would declare it no more than you deserved. It is not precisely a stoning to death these days for an adulteress, but something very like it. And his own adulteries, which appear to have been many and various, would win you no sympathy. You would simply be told that it is different for men. Dearest, I believe he is fond of you, in his way, and that would only make him worse.'

'Well – and I believe I am fond of him too.'

'And just as determined, I see, as the rest of them – the Barforths.'

'I fear so. I have grown up, Mother. You cannot manage me any longer by drifting away into your embroidery, for I will follow you and involve you – for, as I have said, you owe me this.'

She got up, still light in her movements but very slow; crossing to her window, sheltered by its tiny, diamond-shaped panes and its widely frilled chintz curtains, she looked out a moment at the sunshine, not to warm herself, I think, but to check her security.

'They are right,' she murmured, 'the ones who say it is different for men, for they designed the world by themselves, for themselves, and although you and I can well imagine what it is like to be a man – an individual who claims the right to work and speak for himself and who does not bear children – I doubt if there is one among them who knows how it feels to be a woman. They make me smile, these radicals like Mark Corey and your Mr Crispin Aycliffe, when they talk of freedom, for what do they know about it when they cannot even imagine a servitude from which there is no escape. A man who is thrown into prison knows his cell has a door, and a man imprisoned by poverty can strive and hope for better days. But we are born slaves to our own fertility, and how does one escape from that, especially since nature has bound us further by equipping us with emotions, so that we generally love the children we bear? I have had eight children, Verity, a task which has eaten away seventeen years of my life, years of great weariness and some pain, when I simply functioned at the level of any other breeding, nursing animal and had no time to ponder on my humanity or my intellect, no time at all for what men call the finer things of life. Wasted years, I might add, since you are the only one left alive. That is the full tale of my life, Verity. I have had eight children, some half dozen miscarriages, and I can do fancy needlework. You may engrave that on my tombstone when the time comes, for there is no more.

'Clever women are not happy women in our society, my dear, you must know that, for although men may greatly desire us, they do not, in general, like us. And if some totally effective means of avoiding pregnancy should ever be found, many men would rise up against it in horror and call it sin, simply from the fear of setting us free. "Keep her pregnant and you'll keep her out of mischief," they say, and what they really mean by mischief is not infidelity but independence, their own unwillingness to lose us as domestic servants and to compete with us in other fields of endeavour. You were always far more intelligent than your brother Edwin. I believe your cousin Hannah could manage Lawcroft Mills every bit as efficiently as Joel. But if you were given the opportunity of real work, real responsibility, would you be willing to devote so much time to the niceties of your husband's dinner or his shirt frill? Would Hannah be so tireless in her arrangement of the altar flowers, or so happy to compose Morgan Aycliffe's speeches and allow him to pass them off as his own? Naturally not. It takes a very clever man, Verity, to accept intelligence in a woman – a very clever man, indeed, to value it. Mediocre men will always feel threatened by it, will need to console themselves by clinging to their man-made myth that woman is no more than a kind of high-grade cow. And, since the majority of men – and women – seem to be quite mediocre, they will keep you down. And, if you deviate from their rules – my dear, they will slaughter you.'

'Yes, Mother. But I have no skill for fine needlework, you see. And I am not totally lost to reason. I will obey the rules. I will be deceitful and cunning, and I will tell lies to my husband very cheerfully, as he tells lies to me. And he will believe me because it suits him to believe me. There is no question of elopement or open scandal, Mother. I am not a romantic girl. I could, perhaps, persuade Crispin to give up his social ideals and come away with me – for Joel would not actually murder me, and although he would be unpleasant, it would in no way break his heart. And if I refused to come back to him and went on refusing long enough I think he would let me go, for his vanity would not allow him to live with an unwilling woman. I would be poor, of course, but reasonably secure, for Crispin would never desert me, even if he wanted to. And when he began to blame me for forcing him into a mould he did not like, we would still be polite to each other – bored, perhaps, and sad, but polite. And I will not do that to him. I know how fragile love is, Mother. It is not likely to last long in this harsh climate. And when it is done I shall not ask you to help me again.'

The afternoon, outside her window, had deepened from dancing noontime gold to a rich, quiet amber, draping itself warmly around her apple trees, wrapping the sleepy, nodding heads of her lupins, the musky, full-blown faces of her roses, in a gentle haze, encircling the whole house and garden with fragrance and serenity. And I knew she would not refuse me.

'Well then, since I cannot dissuade you, and you seem to know your peril, what must be done?'

'I wish simply to know that I may rely on you at need – although you once told me that you were not reliable.'

'Ah yes. But I was weaker then. Your grandfather was still alive, and although I never vanquished him, no one else has seemed so very terrible to me since he has gone. I tremble for you, Verity. You see yourself clearly now, and Crispin, but afterwards he will go on his way – merrily or sadly – but he will go free, and you— You say love is fragile and I hope you may be right, for how could you ever bear it if it should last?'

'Was that the church clock?' I said. 'Striking four? We should really go and rescue the squire from Elinor, and his ancestral hall from Blaize and Nicholas.'

And, knowing there was nothing more to say, she caught up her bonnet and her shawl, gave me mine, and, glancing affectionately around her flowery little room, smiled to herself, glad, I suppose, that among her portion of life's misfortunes, she had never found herself – or, at least, not for a long time – in love.

26

The factory commissioners stayed some days among us, conscientiously compiling and comparing facts, interviewing anyone who would speak to them and ignoring the Ten Hours men – still dogging their footsteps – who would not.

'I have no idea what happens inside my sheds,' Bradley Hobhouse informed them, 'any more than I know what goes on in my wife's kitchen. I do know how much my machines are capable of producing, for it is my business to know that, but the rest is up to my shed managers. If you call a man a manager and pay him a manager's wages, it's only common sense to let him manage, wouldn't you think? That's what I think, at any rate, and so if you require personal details regarding my employees, I must refer you to my managers. Good morning to you, gentlemen.'

'The parents of the children in our employ do not complain,' Matthew Oldroyd, the worsted spinner, offered. 'In fact, we have children thrust upon us – more than we can take – and indeed, since we are primarily engaged in spinning, I fail to see how we could continue without them, for only very small children are able to go under the machines to join the threads when they break. And if the threads are not joined the yarn cannot be spun. I assure you it is not heavy work, and although I do take very small children – smaller than in the weaving sheds – I do not know where they would go otherwise, for their parents would never think of sending them to school. They would be left to roam the streets with nothing to eat and every temptation to steal, and I cannot think they would be better off. Here, at least, they are warm and dry. And if their mothers are employed here too, as is usually the case, they may find each other at dinnertime. Deformities? Yes. Some of our children are crooked but I do not know that they were straight when they came to us. Some of them are not crooked. We have a great many attractive youngsters in our employ. Promiscuity? That is hardly my concern, sir, unless it takes place on my premises, which it does not – or very rarely. I believe some of our girls become pregnant before marriage; others after. And yes, some of their babies die, some do not. I could not say how many, or for what reason. Beatings? Do you reprimand a school-master, sir, for flogging his pupils? I have had many a flogging myself, as a boy, and took no harm from it. Vast numbers of children cannot be allowed to run wild, sir, among machinery. They must be kept in hand and kept awake—'

And every overlooker who was interviewed muttered sullenly, 'We have our own wages to think of. If the bairns don't frame we can't frame neither.'

And every parent said, 'We need the money.'

But Joel personally escorted the commissioners around Lawcroft and Low Cross and Tarn Edge, and he told them simply, 'I am here to make a profit. That is my sole purpose. I did not build these factories with the charitable aim of providing employment for those who could not find it elsewhere. My aim, unashamedly, is to make money for myself and my family, and, assuming that my employees are similarly motivated, I pay good wages and provide better facilities than anyone else in the Law Valley. And, once again, I do this not from charity but from common sense, since any man or woman works better if he, or she, is decently treated. And since my operatives come here for the same reason as myself – money – I imagine they must be well satisfied. There is no process in my mills, gentlemen, from the meanest and dirtiest to the most complex, that I cannot do and have not done myself. And if the profit is mine, then I take the risk to go with it. I could lose everything overnight, as you well know, and there would be no Royal Commission appointed to look into my well-being. I would be considered capable of taking care of myself, and so I am – so is any man worthy of the name. Yes, gentlemen, I do employ children; girls mostly, who, by the time they are twelve or thirteen, are often the main wage earners of their families, capable of supporting their parents in some cases. And since a reduction in their working hours would mean a corresponding cut in wages, I cannot think they would welcome it. Is there promiscuity in my sheds? Not while the engines are running, gentlemen, I do assure you. How would I be personally affected by a ten-hour day? You will have been told, of course, that we take ten hours to cover our overheads and require the remainder for our profits. Well, if you have heard that you have been talking to badly organized men, for I can sometimes make my profits before the rest of them are out of bed. No, the ten-hour day in itself does not alarm me, although you must bear in mind that when you speak of ten hours for women and children, the men are involved too, since it would not pay me to keep the engines running for the men alone. However, that will in no way prevent me from fulfilling my orders and keeping my customers satisfied, for, no matter what conditions prevail, an industrious man can always make his living.'

The commissioners, however, when all had been said and done, found that there was room, indeed, for improvement, and eventually the gist of their report found its way into the *Cullingford Star*. They had evidence enough, they declared, that the children employed in factories worked the same number of hours as the adults, the effects of this labour producing, in many cases, permanent physical damage. They had been made aware that such children, by reason of those long hours, were unable to receive any kind of education and would be too exhausted to profit by it if they did. They had noted too that at the age when these children entered the mills and were exposed to such massive injury, they were not free agents but were sent there by parents or guardians who took full possession of their wages. Consequently, in their opinion, a case was more than fully made out for the interference of the law.

But even that was not enough, for when, after much wrangling in the House, legislation was at last introduced that same year, it was not a Ten Hours Bill, or anything like it. Children between the ages of nine and thirteen were to work no more than forty-eight hours a week and were to be given some elementary education during working hours; young persons of thirteen to eighteen were not to exceed sixty-nine hours, while children under the age of nine were not to be employed at all. And, to give the Act some bite, four factory inspectors were appointed and given the awesome task of enforcing it. But it was by no means the sweeping, cleansing instrument of reform that had been looked for, and men so far apart as Joel Barforth and Richard Oastler himself were quick to spot its inadequacies.

The length of the adult working day was still at the good pleasure of the masters. The mills would be open, engines running and looms turning, twenty-four hours of the day if necessary, so that youngsters who wanted to work, or were being forced to it by needy or greedy parents, could be shunted from mill to mill, to do their eight hours here, another eight hours there. It would be an astute or remarkably lucky inspector who managed to plug such a loophole as that.

And although Mr Oastler talked hotly of strikes and how he would teach the factory children of any master who broke the law to wreck the spindles with their grandmothers' old knitting needles, I knew of no mill-master who paid much heed to him.

'It has been most cleverly done,' Crispin told me, bitter with disappointment. 'The situation was becoming ugly and so, to take the heat out of it, they gave us something. Not enough to satisfy those of us with sense to see into the future, but enough for those who, never having had very much anyway, didn't expect a great deal. And so now, although the Ten Hours men know they've been cheated, the troops have gone home. And not even Oastler will be able to get them out again in a hurry.'

A perfect opportunity, perhaps, for me to say, 'What will you do now, Crispin? Surely – isn't the fight over? Can't you think of yourself now – and me?' But I had learned already that for a man like him there would always be another battle, the interval between being no more than preparation for the fray.

We met, that summer, that beautiful, deep-gold autumn, once again on the moor, only one dog now frisking around us in the fragile early mornings, the hazy evenings. And because I had always walked my dogs that way, and had always been so sensible, so good, so beyond reproach, no one suspected me. But it was never enough. The undulating landscape, the sudden outcroppings of rock, sheltered us, offered us an illusion of safety, but I could not give myself to him on the hard ground and could not – absolutely could not – visit him again at the Red Gin. And so, instead of sin or heartbreak, guilt or fear of retribution, our main preoccupation was where to go to make love.

For a blissful September fortnight there was an empty cottage of Squire Dalby's, just over the rim beyond Patterswick, so that I could leave my carriage at my mother's and go hurrying through the sweet-scented afternoon – a little stroll before teatime – to throw myself laughing and breathless into his arms – and return while the kettle was still boiling. Sometimes there was an apartment belonging to Mark Corey, the back room of a leather-goods shop in Sheepgate, reached casually through the shop door; the merchant was paid to look the other way when I arrived, with my face well hidden beneath bonnet or shawl, my carriage being sent to deliver calling cards and messages with instructions to collect me in Millergate in an hour's time. And finally, there was a hut beyond Old Sarah's Rock, belonging once again to Mark Corey, with a bare, flagged floor, a chair and table, and a bed with a thin mattress that was an agony to my nerves, my dignity, the small of my back.

'Oh, darling – wait a second – is someone there?'

'No, no – only the dog, scratching.'

'Oh, the dog – if anyone sees her, they'll know—'

'Know what? That we're making love, or trying to, at this hour of the morning? No one would ever believe it. Law Valley men make love at night, in the dark, and they think everybody else must do the same, so we're quite safe.'

'Hardly that. And you're a Law Valley man yourself.'

'Sometimes I wonder. Perhaps I'm a changeling, left on

my father's doorstep in a basket. Darling, don't you want me at all?'

'You know very well that I do, or you wouldn't ask.'

And, with great, good-humoured gentleness, he would coax me to that hard, unlikely mattress and ease me beyond awkwardness to a dreamy, hazy state where my body could float effortlessly into love.

'I know you can't be at ease here,' he told me, 'but I need you this way, to reassure myself. I even like to see you shiver and make that little grimace of distaste when you first come in here, because then I know you must love me very much to come here at all. How much, Verity?'

'More than you deserve.'

'Ah, yes – but that won't do, you know. You have to say how much, or I'll go away hungry, and won't manage to sleep or eat, and you'll worry—'

'All right. I love you – entirely – quite dreadfully.'

'And it hurts you – when you don't see me?'

'Oh yes – badly.'

'Good,' he said, rolling over on his back, laughing at himself and yet sighing at the same time, with a content I knew would not last for long.

'What a spoiled child you are, Crispin.'

'Oh yes – I was a spoiled child once. And what an ideal state that was. It suited my nature exactly. I have been trying to get back there ever since.'

'Well then – and don't I spoil you enough?'

'Will you come to my lodgings?'

'No. And why should you want me to? It is scarcely more comfortable there than here.'

'Because it is a barrier, and I want you to cross it. It may help me to cross a few barriers of my own. Will you come?'

'Not yet.'

And on that point alone he could not move me.

But in everything else my only aim was to please him, not in the servile sense of making him pleased with me but in giving him pleasure, in coming to understand the shades and humours of his mind and body, in nurturing and nourishing them and making them grow. My own body could not always find pleasure on that narrow mattress, could never achieve it at all in the furtive little room behind the leather shop, but my ability to filfil his needs and quench his constant thirst for reassurance, to ease the tight tangle of his nerves so that he sighed, and wept sometimes, with physical satisfaction, had an acute, altogether special pleasure of its own. And the difference between my lover and my husband was that whereas Joel needed women, Crispin needed me.

Yet his uneasy nature had other needs beyond my strengths and skills as a woman, and although his concern for flesh-and-blood humanity may have been, to begin with, a reaction against his father, a man whose dust-dry emotions were reserved for glass and china, having found his cause he would not use it merely to strike attitudes, as the flamboyant Mark Corey sometimes did. He would not – as Mark Corey could well do – rise to prominence one day as a radical politician and become almost indistinguishable from the grandees it was his business to oppose. He would not, in fact, be successful in any way that I could understand success. Yet, since all the things I had been taught to desire had always been within his grasp, the choice had been deliberate, and I was bound to accept it.

'If I am to be of any use to these people,' he told me, 'then I have to understand them. I have to know not what I want them to have but what they want themselves. I have to know what it feels like to be them. And I can only do that if I am myself cold when they are cold, if my nostrils are offended by the same smells, if I am exposed to the same dangers – and even then it is not enough, since I am not imprisoned in misery as they are. I am an educated man. I can walk away from it, back to the affluence my education could bring me. And because there is no way for me to actually feel the hopelessness of a man who was born in Simon Street and knows himself condemned to die there, I can simply observe it at close quarters and write about it in Mark's paper. Little enough, but I have started to receive invitations now to lecture up and down the country, to groups who had no idea such harsh conditions existed anywhere in this Christian land of ours – which is little enough too, Verity, but something – a drop in the ocean, but that's what oceans are made of, surely?'

And so he continued to live, precariously, above the Red Gin on his fifty pounds a year, borrowing when his allowance did not suffice and, more often than not, giving the money away.

'Yes,' he said sweetly, 'I know you think me irresponsible. It is simply that I was brought up to believe money grew in my father's pocket, and I cannot rid myself of my lordly attitudes.'

But to the Barforth side of me debt was a far more shameful thing than adultery, and I would never pass an opportunity to scold him.

'Crispin – Crispin – you have lent money to half of Simon Street, from what you tell me – and how many do you think are even grateful?'

'Very few. None, perhaps, since they will never be able to repay me and they must find it a great nuisance, feeling obliged to cross the street to keep out of my way.'

'Then why do you do it?'

'Why not? I am not looking for gratitude.'

'Of course not – but they use you, Crispin. All this rent that cannot be paid and these doctors who will not come without the money in advance. Yes – yes – I know that happens – but does it happen every time? Do they always use your money for that, or does it go in drink?'

'Not all of it. Some of it, of course. But sometimes, Verity, all that is needed to separate life from death is a shilling. Imagine that. One can buy a life for a shilling – a sick life, admittedly; usually a very young one. And if I

412

have a shilling, and I must confess there are occasions when I don't— Verity, don't fret, I am only really in debt to Colonel Corey, who obliges me because of Mark. And Mark is into him for thousands.'

'I daresay. But he is Mark's father, after all – or so one supposes.'

'One supposes correctly.'

'Oh, I don't care about that. He's not your father, at any rate, and how do you mean to repay him? Obviously he expects it. He has made you sign for it, hasn't he?'

'Yes, yes – but he knows quite well I shall have nothing until my uncle dies. It was all arranged on that understanding, and he's not a bad old stick, Verity. He has money to burn and what could he possibly gain by prosecuting me for debt? If he gets me locked up there is no way in the world I can ever repay him, since my uncle would probably disown me, and it would upset Mark no end, which matters to the old boy. He's always been ready to do anything for Mark, except marry his mother, of course, which is only out of consideration for his daughter, Estella Chase, who doesn't mean to share her inheritance with a stepmother. And if you're wondering what would happen if Mark and I fell out, then don't, because we've known each other too long for that. Verity, if I frittered it all away on extravagant living, then I'd allow you to be angry, but I don't.'

'No,' I told him, sharp with anxiety. 'One can see that. Isn't it time you had a new coat? You've worn that one so long I can't remember you without it – and it's getting thin at the elbows.'

'Is it? Yes, I believe you're right. I suppose Joel has dozens and dozens of coats, hasn't he, all spotless and well brushed and not a button missing anywhere? Odd, isn't it, the way things work out sometimes. He only had one coat when we were all at school, and I remember standing in the crowd while he very nearly massacred Bradley Hobhouse for trampling on it. I was quite a little boy then, of

413

course – younger than Joel and Bradley – and every morning my mother dressed me up in something fresh and new, and every night my father inspected me from top to toe to make sure I'd kept myself clean. And the dramas we had about a mud stain, or a loose thread – you can't imagine.'

'Well, that must have been a great nuisance for you, but you can't wear that coat much longer because it will soon fall apart. Crispin – you wouldn't . . .?'

'No,' he said, very decisively for him. 'Darling, the amount of pin money you receive may be magnificent – in fact, I'm sure it is – so magnificent that you simply don't know what to do with it, and I'd be doing you a service if I took some of it off your hands. But no, you must not give me things – really, you must not.'

'What nonsense. If you were rich, you would give me presents, wouldn't you?'

'Certainly. I pass sleepless nights wrapping you in sables and diamonds and cloth of gold – which does nothing to help my insomnia, quite the reverse.'

'And yet you will not allow me to buy you a simple coat?'

'I will not.'

'Is that logical?'

'No. But is it logical for you to refuse to come to my lodgings? Verity, I shall wheedle and cajole, I warn you, and grow angry and shed a few tears, so you had better come now and save us both the trouble.'

And I could not tell him, for perhaps I did not know, that my hesitation was in part due to his bold, black-eyed, exceedingly common landlady, Mrs Dinah McCluskey, who had told me, at our brief meeting, how much she valued his good opinion.

But in all other ways my life flowed on, that summer and autumn, with astonishing serenity. I supervised the affairs of my household; I engaged a governess, a music teacher, and a drawing master for Caroline and found Mrs Paget a place with Emma-Jane, who, with nine sons already and the likelihood of nine more, would need a nurse for many years yet. I spoke, sensibly I thought, to the headmaster, Mr Blamires, about the progress of Blaize – who did not appear to be progressing in any useful direction – and of stubborn, surly Nicholas. I spent lazy, gossiping afternoons with Mrs Stevens, lulled by the beckoning tones of her voice. I discussed pregnancy with Emma-Jane and the lack of it with Lucy Oldroyd, took tea with the Reverend Mr Brand and conveyed his messages to Hannah, leaving her in no doubt that she was sorely missed in Ramsden Street. I took my carriage exercise up and down the town and smiled warmly at Colonel Corey whenever he raised his hat to me. I gave dinners for Joel's colleagues, friends, enemies, anyone he wished to use or make envious or impress. And when Squire Dalby came to tell me that he wished to marry my mother I gave my consent and was instructed by Joel – who could see the advantages of having the squire as a father-in-law – that I should do my utmost to persuade her.

Morgan Aycliffe came home in the autumn, thinner and greyer but wearing his new authority well, a sombre, deep-purple aura about him that, after six months at Westminster, spoke already of state secrets, the crushing burden of high office.

'He should have been a Roman Catholic,' my mother said, 'for he would have made an excellent cardinal. One can imagine him, so sleek and sinister, flitting among secret passages with vital documents concealed in his sleeves and a great ruby ring with poison in it too, I shouldn't wonder. Oh dear, perhaps it is just as well that cardinals are not allowed to have wives.'

And indeed, I could detect no signs of improvement in his relations with Elinor. He had acquired, certainly, something of the professional politician's automatic charm of manner, enough at any rate to supply me and Emma-Jane and Lucy, the wives of his principal supporters, with such details of the London scene he thought would please us. We learned of the animosity between the King and the Duchess of Kent, mother of Princess Victoria, the royal heir, and her determination to act as Regent should he die before Victoria became eighteen. We learned of the savage disposition of the King's brother, the Duke of Cumberland, and how it would suit him if Victoria never reached eighteen, so that the young princess lived in constant fear of kidnap or murder or worse.

We learned, too, that the present government, which had given us the franchise, could see stormy waters ahead – very stormy – yet the exact details of tempest, flood, or act of God were not considered fit for ladies, could only upset us, and were reserved strictly for our husbands – who would be unlikely to tell us – and for Hannah, whose nervous system, while remaining ladylike, was evidently considered by Morgan Aycliffe to be superior.

'He can never marry her, you know,' Elinor said one evening as we sat alone in the drawing room. And as her dainty, pointed face crinkled with smiles, these last few bleak years seemed to have been wiped away from her, and she was her old, irrepressible self again.

'What a thing to say, Elinor, when he is married to you.'

'But that is exactly why he can never marry her. A man cannot marry his wife's sister, even after her death, which seems rather unfair since what difference can it make when one is under ground. But, at least, they have nothing to gain by murdering me, have they?'

And although the trill of her laughter filled the room – adorned again, I noticed, by some of its more valuable objets d'art – I remembered my mother's airy description of secret passages and poisoned rings, and I shivered. Not that I believed Morgan Aycliffe capable of putting down a stray dog with his own hands, much less murdering his wife, but that could make it no easier for Elinor – the pretty one, who had expected so much from life – to know that this old, grey man, having once lost his head on her account, considered her now simply a nuisance and a bore.

Yet, that night, it did not seem to trouble her greatly and, noting that she had the late Mrs Aycliffe's pearls around her neck again and a new sapphire on her hand, a new sky-blue satin gown from Miss Boulton, an air of pert self-assurance, a certain awareness of her own worth that the Barforth side of me recognized and approved, I wondered if she had at last come to terms with her situation and herself and elected to make of it the best she could.

As to my relations with my own husband, I cannot think that he, at least, was aware of any change. He was extremely occupied that year, with his new mill, his new lightweight cloth, the branch line to Cullingford, which was soon, it seemed, to materialize and make him – the possessor of abundant railway shares – an even wealthier man. He was busy with engineers and architects, designers and craftsmen of all kinds, who swarmed thick as August flies at Tarn Edge. And when he was at home, he discussed footage, acreage, mileage, profit, and – since profit was happiness and he was determined to be happy – the necessity of making more.

I saw Rosamund Boulton too, often enough, at her shop, and judging by her forced smile and her strained, tight-lipped courtesies, I suspected that profit was all Joel cared to discuss with her these days too. And profit there certainly was, for Miss Boulton's business was thriving, spilling over into the shop next door, where she had opened special departments for the sale of shoes and shawls and garments of a more discreet nature, direct – or so she said – from France. But affluence did not appear to suit her, for she was often ailing, prone to unexplained backaches and headaches and attacks of ill temper, relying more and more on her fresh-faced young assistants to spare her the necessity of making herself pleasant. And, although Estella Chase had gone to London in the spring and remained there long after her husband came North for the grouse,

Joel was himself in London two or three times that year, in Liverpool and Manchester more than he need have been, I thought, if railway business had been the only attraction, and, glimpsing Miss Boulton's face in an unguarded moment, I concluded she knew rather more about that than I.

'So your husband has gone away again,' Elinor said to me one morning towards the end of the hot weather. 'Well, mine will be off again before long, and I shall not grieve over it, for I find Mr Adair much easier to manage.'

And, patting her skirts and her ringlets, preening herself as she had done as a girl but with an allure now that belongs only to a woman, she put her head close to mine and murmured through a half sigh, half laugh, 'While we are on the subject of Mr Adair – and naturally I would say this to no one else, Verity – I do believe the foolish man has taken it into his head to fall in love with me, which is quite impertinent when one remembers that five or ten years ago he was nothing but a common bricklayer. Yes, only think – my husband left me in Mr Adair's charge because I could not be trusted with the spending of my husband's money, and now all I have to do is flutter my eyelids and sigh when the bills come in – which never succeeded at all with my husband – and Mr Adair has not a word to say. Not to me, at any rate, although certainly explanations must have been made to my husband – and good ones too, since he has not reprimanded me either. And that, you know, is certain proof that Mr Adair is clever and cunning as well as most obliging. I must thank him – if I happen to remember it – when I see him again.'

'Not too warmly, I hope.'

'Good heavens, no, Verity, dear – a bricklayer? Hardly. But enough to put him firmly on my side, for there is something else . . . Oh well, I really shouldn't tell you this, but since I am going to anyway I had better tell you now, at once, and all that can happen to me is that I will have longer to feel guilty about it.'

'Oh dear, Elinor—'

'No, not yet. I have done nothing yet, but Mr Adair is not the only one who has been paying attention to me lately. It is Bradley – Bradley Hobhouse – and there is no need to stare, because you know very well he would far rather have married me in the first place, if his mamma had not made such a fuss about money. Well, he has been looking at me again – exactly as he used to – which is hardly surprising when one looks at Emma-Jane, who reminds me of nothing so much as a cottage loaf.'

'Yes, so she does, but then Bradley is no feather either.'

'I should say not,' she said, chuckling quite greedily. 'But he carries it well, Verity. He eats and drinks and sleeps, he's fat and good-humoured and easy, he's pleasant . . . Oh, don't be alarmed, I'm not thinking of running away with him again. He can barely afford the family he has, much less take on a second, and poverty would suit neither one of us. It's just that, on the days when he has been looking at me, I feel better than on the days when he hasn't – unless Mr Adair has been looking, which, just now and again, rather makes me tingle inside and makes me wonder – oh, quite wicked things. It does me good, and that's enough – really – quite enough. For now, at any rate.'

Take care, I thought, yet I was not the one to speak to her of the sanctity of the marriage bed, to remind her of loyalty and true dealing, when I had seen precious little of either, when I was myself, in fact, entirely true to no one.

Life, it seemed, was movement, transition, and a time would unavoidably come when I would be forced to take a step backwards or forwards, to open a door, to say goodbye to Crispin or not say goodbye to him. And since I could not, at that moment, visualize, much less solve, the problems of our remaining together, I chose not to think of them at all. I would allow myself this season of good weather, this time of youth which, having eluded me at sixteen, had come to me now, ten years too late. And when the days cooled and clouded over, when the moor was wind-racked and rain-scoured with November – when winter deprived us of our hiding place – then would be time enough for contemplation.

27

Ann Agbrigg died that winter, an early casualty of the cold weather and her own careless wanderings, having too little interest in life, perhaps, to cling to it. She died in complete silence, a death merely of the body, the spirit having long since withered. And, standing at her graveside, I understood her husband to be far beyond consolation.

'Naturally, I went to them at once,' Hannah told me, 'and although Mr Agbrigg eventually arranged everything as I suggested, he was quite strange. She had been dead for some hours when I arrived and he was still sitting at her bedside, in the dark, and was quite sharp with me when I covered her face and sent him away. One simply cannot afford to brood, especially when there are children to be considered, and I must admit I was shocked to hear Mr Agbrigg say he would gladly give his children twice over to have his wife back again. Oh, I know people are apt to say wild things at such times, but Mr Agbrigg was quite calm, quite matter-of-fact about it, and, with everything considered, I cannot excuse his behaviour to Jonas. I have always known Mr Agbrigg to be a hard man, but to accuse Jonas of being glad of his mother's death – relieved, he said, because now she could embarrass him no longer in front of Mr Blamires, nor hold him back from his grand ambitions – well, I find that hard to forgive.'

'But it's true, Hannah – surely?' I said, remembering young Jonas Agbrigg's careful, crafty eyes, and she shrugged, making an impatient movement with her hand.

'Well, of course it's true. She would have been an

420

embarrassment and a hindrance to him. I know that and you know it, but Jonas, who has an excellent disposition, could have no such feelings about his own mother, and it was wrong of his father to suggest them to him. She was a hindrance to her husband, too, whether he likes to think so or not, for she had no notion as to the management of her household affairs, and if Joel means to make him manager at Lawcroft, as I believe he does, the poor woman would never have settled here. She would have gone wandering back to Simon Street at every opportunity, and I suppose what is making him so bitter is that he knows quite well he should not have taken her away from there in the first place. He must have been aware of his own capabilities, even as a young man when he first went courting, and he should have chosen a girl who had it in her to grow with him.'

And so Ann Agbrigg was laid to rest by a husband too bitter for tears, and, a month later, Ira Agbrigg, the parish apprentice, who knew neither his real name nor his exact age, was appointed manager at Lawcroft and invited to occupy the millhouse where, long ago, he had come to tell my mother of his workmates' intention to riot.

'We should do the house up for them, don't you think?' I suggested to Hannah, expecting her to take care of it herself, but her own affairs were coming to a head just then and, glancing up at me from her breakfast-time correspondence – a great deal of it to do with Mr Aycliffe – she said absently, 'Yes, for Mr Agbrigg will not dare to change anything – or will not think of it. If you can prevail upon them to get some good chintz covers for their parlour chairs you will do them a service, Verity. And Jonas should have Edwin's old room, I think, for the fireplace there is the only one that does not smoke, and he will need a good fire to study by. And speaking of Jonas – and since I imagine you will be having a good sort-out before you move to Tarn Edge – there is a bookcase in the back spare bedroom doing nothing at all. If you should care to make

Jonas a present of it he would be much obliged. In fact, if you are agreeable, I will arrange for it to be delivered at once, since Tarn Edge is nowhere near completion and Jonas must have somewhere to put his books.'

But, in fact, our move to Tarn Edge could not really be so far distant as Hannah envisaged, for, under Mr Daniel Adair's expert eye, the walls were growing into the recognizable shape of a house, each brick, each pail of mortar advancing the moment when Hannah must name her wedding day. Certainly Mr Ashley expected it, and Mr Brand lived in dread of it; even Joel, whose scathing eye had seen from the start that Mr Ashley would never become a bishop, was reconciled, had already made some grudging financial promises. And when Mr Ashley was offered the living of Redesdale, some fifteen miles away, Patterswick Church being required now for a relative of Squire Dalby's, we knew there could be no more delay. She would have to marry him now and content herself with the affairs of one parish, or she would have to break with him and expose herself once again to the onslaught of Mr Brand and the sheer inconvenience of the single life.

'I thought in the spring,' she told me at Christmastime, having already made an excursion to Redesdale, with my mother as chaperone, to inspect the church and parsonage and to ascertain the disposition of the local squire's lady – a feeble creature, it seemed, too occupied with her dozen or so children to give Hannah much trouble. 'Yes, Easter,' she said, quite decidedly.

And so Mr Ashley ate his Christmas dinner at my table, in peaceful, placid silence, willing to fetch and carry and smile when one asked him to, willing to be married or not to be married, offering no opinion of his own even on the vexing question of Irish church reform, which, Mr Aycliffe declared, could well bring the government down in the new year.

Elinor was there too that Christmas day, and her three little girls, three dolls identically dressed in blue satin

422

frocks and lace pantalettes, three pairs of round blue eyes and three heads of elaborately wired ringlets, shading from light brown – Crispin's colour – to Elinor's pale, silvery gold. Three little mouths too, which never spoke a word since Morgan Aycliffe believed that if children must be seen then they should not be heard, and he was much inconvenienced all day by the noise my own children made, by Caroline's constant bids for attention and the sorry spectacle of Blaize and Nicholas coming to blows for no better reason than an inborn desire for combat.

'He started it,' Nicholas shrieked, probably quite correctly.

'Well, come and finish it then,' Blaize taunted, grinning wickedly, bracing himself to receive the full weight of his brother's irate body which knocked the pair of them to the ground in a pummelling, biting-and-scratching back-alley tumble which was every bit as lethal as it looked. And when Joel, who had not been unacquainted with back alleys in his younger days, took them both by the scruff of their necks and booted them through the door with instructions to go and kill each other somewhere else, Morgan Aycliffe's horror at the prospect of damage – not to young bones, which would heal, but to the hall furniture, which would not – was so great that Hannah took him away to the library for a soothing discussion on church tithes and whether or not we should send troops to Portugal.

'They're just boys,' Caroline explained with infinite condescension to her Aycliffe cousins, who had no experience of the species. And since there were times when I too found boys somewhat trying, I settled the four little girls around me and for half an hour told them the fairy tales of my own childhood, my old Marth-Ellen's legacy to me.

Faith and Cecilia, the two younger Aycliffes, curled up beside me in the big chair, barely listening, lulled simply by my voice and a physical contact to which they, raised entirely and impersonally by nurses, were unaccustomed.

But Caroline, who had heard the stories before, was concerned largely with her dress – the cloud of pink gauze over silk she had found on her bed that morning – her new coral beads, her newly pierced ears, threaded temporarily with silk ribbon, with the doll wearing an exact copy of her own party frock, its dark ringlets tied up, like hers, with pink velvet. And Prudence, the eldest and plainest of my nieces, was clearly unimpressed by the quality of my entertainment; did not, perhaps, set much store by fairyland at all.

'That can't be right, Aunt Verity,' she said suddenly, frowning at her narrow, immaculately shod feet. 'If the princess was so silly as to keep getting herself caught over and over again by that dragon, and then putting everybody to so much trouble to rescue her, I don't see how she could have been a good queen. She should have helped herself more.'

'Oh, darling, yes, but it's just a story.'

'Well,' snorted Caroline, who would, without doubt, have made an excellent queen, 'I'd like to see you set about fighting a dragon.'

'I would,' Prudence said, her chin resolute, 'if I had to.'

'No you wouldn't. You'd run. You'd run screaming for your mamma.'

But the idea of running to Elinor for assistance was so foreign to Prudence that, frowning again, concentrating hard, she was about to justify her claims to courage when Caroline, not altogether enjoying the sight of Faith and Cecilia nestling so cosy on my knee, announced scathingly, 'Well, no silly old dragon would ever catch me.'

'And if he did,' I told her, tugging at a stray ebony ringlet, 'then he'd soon bring you back.'

And Caroline, saucily grinning, believing herself, like Blaize, to be my favourite child, made a sudden leap forward to fling her arms around my neck, roughly dislodging Faith, who bore it stoically, and Cecilia, who started to cry, bringing the Aycliffe nanny, who was never far away, instantly to her side.

'Dear me, Miss Cecilia, you've crumpled your frock, which I can't wonder at, sitting so gracelessly. And Miss Faith. Young ladies keep their backs straight, my dears, and their knees firmly together, and never, never do they allow their own backs to touch the backs of the chairs in which they are sitting.'

And with her pale eye telling me that, with my shoulders comfortably supported by cushions, I was setting something less than a good example, she took her charges away.

'Verity, dear,' Elinor said, slipping her arm through mine, 'shall we have a headache, you and I? We have nurses for the children, and Hannah for my husband. Joel is bored with all of us, and Mr Ashley will not even notice we have left him alone. Come upstairs and let me tell you how Bradley Hobhouse took quite five minutes to help me into my cloak last night at the Assembly Rooms, and how Mr Adair positively swelled up – yes, just like a toad – with jealousy. Oh, I can't tell you how much I liked that, Verity. Do come upstairs, because I want to talk and talk and talk about it, and we'll be quite wicked, shall we, and ask Mrs Stevens to bring us a bottle of wine, or two. This coming year is going to be good to me, Verity. I can feel it.'

We celebrated the new year – Elinor's year, as she kept on insisting – with a charity ball at the Assembly Rooms, a glittering, fancy-dress affair, the proceeds of which, with tickets at two guineas each, would be considerable – to be used for the relief of our ever-increasing poor. And although few of the men, if any, would condescend to fancy dress, believing their evening clothes to be quite fancy enough, competition among the ladies was murderous.

'They will all dress up as queens,' my mother told me when I asked her advice. Depend upon it – and heavy queens too; a dozen Elizabeths, with ruffles and stiff brocades, and as many Mary Stuarts and Good Queen

Philippas, so very well wrapped up in wimples and long sleeves. And they are right, of course, since most of them will not suffer from being wrapped up a little. Now you, Verity, I wonder – since Elinor, in the mood she is in, will certainly do something spectacular – have you thought of what you mean to do yourself?'

'I rather hoped you would do it for me.'

'Yes,' she said, smiling, well content with herself these days, since a proposal of marriage from a High Tory squire, even if she had no mind to accept it, was no mean achievement for a woman of her age and origins. 'That is what I supposed. In fact, I have a small idea . . . Should we, perhaps, give some thought to the Empress Josephine, Napoleon's lady?'

'Should we? And how was the Empress Josephine?'

'Oh, light as thistledown, in transparent muslins and gold sandals, with bare feet with gold lacquer on her toenails – Grecian and wicked. Quite a simple costume to arrange, since I have the very dress you need upstairs in one of my boxes, a dress I brought with me when I married, and of which your father's mother did not approve. Shall I fetch it? I have the gold sandals too.'

'And the lacquer? Surely not, Mother?'

'Why, yes,' she said, making her face very innocent. 'Times were much freer when I was a girl, you see, for we still had our wicked Prince Regent, who was very much in favour of painted toenails. Unfortunately, once again, your grandmother did not approve of mine, and by the time she died I had rather passed the season for such things – so you may reap the benefit of it. Your husband may not approve, of course, for you will be rather more naked than he is accustomed to see you in public, but the surprise may be no bad thing. Few husbands actually look at their wives, I find, unless they have a reason to do so, and it does no harm, now and then, to provide a reason.'

And her tone was so airy, so totally without guile, that I knew she had something very specific in mind.

Yet the dress, when it came out of its wrappings, was an enchantment, high-waisted, narrow, the merest sketch of a sleeve leaving arms and shoulders quite bare, the muslin so light that the feeling of nakedness was at first shocking and then, as I moved so weightlessly, so pleasantly without my petticoats, altogether exhilarating. And although I doubted if, by wearing it, I would inflame Joel's lasting passion, which, in turn, would banish Crispin from my mind – as my mother clearly hoped – the thought of fluttering Emma-Jane's feathers – and Hannah's – was too much to resist.

I took the dress home with me, with the shoes and the gold paint, and I added my pearls. I arranged my hair in a casual Regency tumble as my mother had shown me – a boyish head almost, with a woman's body all too visible beneath the shimmering fabric, bare painted feet so outrageous that even Mrs Stevens, who, in her day, had paraded her nakedness every bit as daringly as this, became quite nervous.

'What will Mr Barforth say?'

And, indeed, as he came into my bedroom, busy with his shirt studs, I believe that, at first glance, he thought I was still in my petticoat and, thinking more of his own appearance than mine, was about to tell me to hurry. But the unusually heavy perfume – also borrowed from my mother – catching his nostrils, bade him look again, and Mrs Stevens had her answer, for what he actually said was 'By Christ, you don't mean to go out dressed like that, do you?'

'The Empress Josephine did.'

'Aye, I daresay. But not in Cullingford.'

'Don't you like it?'

'Yes,' he said as I turned away from the mirror to face him, letting the diaphanous, shimmering material float against my body. 'I like it. In fact, I like it so much I'm forced to the conclusion that it's not decent.'

'Well, before you judge it indecent, I'd best tell you my

mother wore it as part of her trousseau – and the young ladies of her day wore them damp so they'd cling even more. Come, Joel, you're old enough to remember narrow gowns like these.'

'So I am,' he said slowly, the tolerant good-humour draining out of his face, leaving him irritable and strangely displeased. 'So, I believe you have a shawl, at least, and you'll surely have need of one. The biggest, I reckon, you can find.'

The frowning strangeness of him – reminding me not of Joel Barforth at all, but of the pinched, tight-lipped prejudices of a Morgan Aycliffe – sent an unaccountable, altogether wicked delight coursing through me, causing me to twirl and sway once again, close to the lamplight.

'Of course I have a shawl, and I shall wear it like this, just slipping off my shoulders, like the Empress Josephine. Whatever can be wrong with that?'

'Not a great deal,' he said, most amazingly angry. 'Except that every man who sees you like that is going to be well aware that the rest is worth seeing. I'm surprised that it doesn't trouble you.'

'And I'm surprised that it should trouble you.'

And possessed again by that demon of wicked delight, I draped myself under the lamplight, threw out one hip slightly so that the fabric clung to the outline of leg and thigh, revealing one scandalously painted foot, and asked him, 'Would you like me to take it off?'

My reward was a bitten-off exclamation of anger, the nervous clenching of a fist, and a certain tightening and darkening of his whole face.

'Get your shawl,' he said in the voice he used to issue notices of dismissal at Lawcroft and Low Cross. 'And before we set out may I remind you that because you have dressed yourself up like an adventuress there is no need to assume the manners of one. Your shawl and your fan, then, if you don't mind – we're late already.'

And throughout the drive to town, as I sat beside him

wrapped in dark blue velvet, my hands clasped inside a
swansdown muff, he did not speak a single word.

The Assembly Rooms were most festively ablaze, spilling
long shafts of light out onto the road, where a good number
of the poor for whose benefit we were assembled had
gathered to jeer and stare as we disported ourselves on
their behalf; then crowed with delight when the Hobhouse
horses, just in front of ours, slipped on the frosted cobbles
and Emma-Jane, massive now both in pregnancy and out
of it, required three men to help her down.

'You'll have to get rid of them,' she told Bradley
furiously, not making it clear whether she meant the
populace or his none too sprightly, none too well-matched
greys, and taking my arm and Joel's, she allowed us to
lead her up the shallow steps into the black-and-white-
tiled hall, leaving her husband behind to see how much
harm had been done and how best it could be patched up.

She had dressed herself as a ungainly Elizabethan, in a
huge, red velvet skirt with a white ruff squashing the soft
flesh under her chin and puffing out her cheeks: a hot,
heavy costume that would exhaust her before the night
was done. And filled suddenly by a sheer, wicked delight,
determined to enjoy myself whether Joel approved of me
or not, I let my cloak slip from my shoulders, handed it to
the retiring-room woman, and, lifting a deliberately languid arm – as the Empress of the French would surely
have done – adjusted one of my boyish, kittenish curls.

'Verity,' she said, a most alarming flush mottling her
heavy cheeks, 'just look at you, Verity Barforth. If I didn't
know better I'd think you were nineteen.'

And there was anger in her, and accusation, for how
could I flaunt myself like that, how dare I be thin and rich
when she was fat and they were beginning to lose their
money?

'My word,' Bradley Hobhouse muttered, flushing in his
turn as we went to join our husbands on the stairs, his eyes

429

flickering eagerly over me from top to toe. But Emma-Jane would have none of it.

'Take my arm, Bradley,' she ordered, her plump cheeks quivering. 'You know very well that I'm to be careful on the stairs. You know what the doctor said, and I'm only here at all because you wanted to come and didn't feel right about turning up without me.'

And although Joel smiled at her offended back, his eyes were not angry but watchful, calculating, and still he had no word to say.

There would be no possibility, I knew, of seeing Crispin that night, for he was in the Midlands, on a lecture tour of country towns, staying in pleasant wayside inns and the homes of the local gentry and flirting, no doubt, with some squire's daughter, exposing me to the raw misery of knowing that nothing held us together but our combined desire, that nothing compelled him to return to me – the misery, indeed, of knowing that it would be logical, merciful even – better for him, better for me – if he did not return at all. And perhaps the shimmering cobweb of a dress and my scandalous painted feet were no more than steppingstones to help me walk away from the spectre of his loss.

'Verity,' Hannah said, a severe Mary Stuart in plain black silk and white widow's cap, looking more like a nun than a queen, 'that dress is really very skimpy. Put your shawl higher up around your shoulders and it will not seem such a bad fit.'

But pale Mr Ashley, quiet and clerical and anonymous as ever, blushed like a girl and looked another way.

I did not expect Mr Aycliffe's approval and was not disappointed, although Mr Daniel Adair, an indispensable member of the Aycliffe entourage nowadays, let his merry Irish eyes roam over me with an appreciation that was altogether wholesome.

'You're a fine woman, Mrs Barforth,' those eyes said,

'and there's nothing in the world pleases me better than that.'

Elinor was enthusiastic, vocal, generous in her praise. 'Go home,' she said, stamping a tiny, saucy foot. 'Go home at once. Nobody is going to look at me now – off with you.'

But, as she well knew, she was in no danger of being overlooked. She had come as Marie Antoinette, her costume modelled on one of her husband's china figurines, her favourite sky-blue satin with an enchanting lace apron, cascades of lace at sleeve and hem, the first Mrs Aycliffe's pearls wound tight around her throat, a high white wig that gave her pointed face the translucence and delicacy of porcelain. She had lace at her wrists too, knots of it on her shoes, lace ribbons floating from her high-piled coiffure, a wide lace sash set with fresh flowers; she was, in fact, so very much the dainty feminine ideal men dream of that even Joel – who had had no word of praise for me – put a brotherly hand under her chin, turned her face towards him, and said, 'Very nice – and if you could stop chattering for five minutes, I'd say very nice indeed.'

The room was hot and bright and very full, a jungle of potted plants lining the walls, the musicians earning their fee strenuously, a ball like the dozens I had attended here since the opening night, with hostesses fussily trying to outdo each other and the hostesses before them, and mothers bringing their daughters to market, offering them proudly, sadly, desperately, to men who knew exactly how much each one was worth; women like Emma-Jane, whose desires had shrunk to a cup of tea and a soft armchair to drink it in; like Hannah, who despised herself for needing a man at her side; and like Elinor, who, having made up her mind to live again, unashamedly wanted them all.

'Well now,' Joel said, turning to me at last, 'will the Empress Josephine condescend to dance?'

And as we moved away through that mass of anxiously stitched, anxiously compared costumes, born of ideas which had seemed so bright at the time, so totally original, until one met a dozen like them on the stairs, I saw Elinor hesitate a moment between Bradley Hobhouse and Daniel Adair, and, as she made her choice, I saw Emma-Jane flop down indignantly into a chair and Mr Adair walk scowling away.

I went to sit by Emma-Jane when the dance was over, submitting myself to the details of her latest baby's feeding, how James was almost as tall now as Thomas and little Freddie was talking and walking much sooner than the others. But she was anxious and angry, feeling the heat, hating me in my airy dress yet needing me, since not even the progress of Freddie, her favourite child, could distract her from the spectacle of Freddie's father dancing a second time with Elinor.

'I'm not well,' she said in a bewildered fashion, for she was quite unaccustomed to jealousy. 'I shouldn't be here at all. I can feel my ankles swelling, which is what the doctor said would happen. Will you tell my husband, Verity, that I am indisposed?'

And getting up, knocking over one of the spindly, gilt-legged chairs in the awkwardness of her suffering and of her vast velvet skirts, she rushed off to the retiring room, where someone would have a smelling bottle and a stool for her swollen feet, and sympathy for a woman who had always unfailingly done her duty as a wife.

'Emma-Jane is unwell,' I told Bradley when the moment came, but, shrugging those bulky, lazy shoulders, he merely swept me into the dance.

'Aye, she's breeding again and shouldn't have come. She'll throw up a time or two, I reckon, and be as right as rain after. You're looking grand, Verity – you and Elinor – what a pair you are – although I can't take to that manager of Aycliffe's, that bog-trotter, whatever his name is – Adair? Well, makes no difference to me what he calls himself, because they all look alike and they all sound alike, but if he speaks sharply to me again I'll flatten him.'

Yet Mr Adair, when he danced with me some time later,

having lost Elinor once again to Bradley, had enough finesse to conceal his annoyance, understanding that the last thing a lady wishes to discuss with her partner is another lady. And so Mr Adair, with enormous charm of manner, kept his eyes on my-face, no matter how much they wished to go looking for Elinor, and even when we collided with her and Bradley during a waltz and she allowed the impact to throw her briefly into Bradley's arms, he refused to be distracted from his task of convincing me that I alone was beautiful. A clever man, Mr Adair, I thought, who would not pursue his employer's wife without encouragement – no matter how old and frail her husband appeared to be – who would need to be very sure before he made a move, and it occurred to me, if not to Emma-Jane, that Elinor's sudden interest in Bradley might be less obvious than it seemed.

Yet Bradley it was who took Elinor to her champagne supper at midnight, sitting on the floor at her feet while his wife and Elinor's husband remained quite forgotten, Emma-Jane in the hands of the retiring-room woman, Mr Aycliffe in consultation with a group of his electors.

Rosamund Boulton was not present, although her handi-work was much on display, but Estella Chase, lately returned from almost a year in London, arrived a little before midnight, in some indeterminate costume of dull green crepe which, although I could not have put a name to it, suited her very well. She looked careless, haughty, a stalking thoroughbred too sure of herself to worry that her back hair was coming down, extending a limp, not particularly well-manicured hand to the many who rushed to present themselves to this second cousin of our manorial lord, although it was clear she remembered no one by name and saw no reason to try.

But my mother, who had been dining that evening with the Coreys and could be a Dalby any time she had a mind, was unimpressed, and slipping her arm through mine, she said, 'Dearest, do you remember Mrs Chase? Yes, yes,

433

dear, I am sure you do if you try. Colonel Corey's daughter? Colonel Corey, I believe you know my daughter, Mrs Barforth?'

'Indeed I do,' he said. 'My word, indeed I do.' And because of the money he had lent to Crispin – because he might even know that Crispin and I were lovers, since his son, Mark Corey, knew it – my mind was too busy to assess the glance Estella Chase exchanged with Joel until it was over.

He danced with her once, no more, keeping his polite distance, saying little, taking her back to her father and making his bow. Yet after that he danced with no one else, taking his stand by the refreshment-room door and helping himself from time to time at the punch bowl, a spectator with eyes half closed, watching her dance with other men and watching me too in a way to which I was not accustomed, which made me uncomfortable, half afraid, with his mouth hard, his expression morose and unfriendly.

'Has your husband's dinner disagreed with him?' my mother murmured, but before I could properly reply – before I could tell her that the shimmering, cobweb of a dress had not succeeded – there was a hand on my arm and a whispering voice advising me that Mrs Hobhouse was really quite unwell and had asked for me.

She was, in fact, on her feet when I reached the retiring room, colossal with rage, purple at the injustice of a world where she, who had never done anything wrong, who had been a devoted wife and mother, could be forgotten – simply forgotten – while a silly, mincing chit like Elinor Barforth, who had married that disgusting old man for money when she had failed to get her hands on Bradley, should be floating on air, the centre of attention, with Bradley – so at least a dozen people had told her – sitting at her feet.

'Didn't you tell him I'm not well?' she shrieked at me. 'I've been here for hours – hours – and what is he doing?

Has anybody brought me my supper? I could starve and would anybody care?'

And as the retiring-room woman and I attempted to calm her, Elinor, who had certainly followed me and overheard the whole, came tripping into the room, fanning herself with a dainty, quiet cruel hand.

'My word,' she said, 'you do look seedy, Emma-Jane. Quite green.'

'Spiteful little cat,' Emma-Jane hissed, lunging forward to strike a wild blow which did little harm. 'You've always been jealous of me – always wanted whatever I had. Well, if I lose this baby you'll be to blame.'

'Oh, as to that,' Elinor said, the trill of her light laughter somehow filling the room, reminding me, if no one else, of those far-off days when she'd had to beg a ride in Emma-Jane's carriage and say 'please' and 'thank you' for an unwanted length of cotton, 'I wouldn't dwell on that, Emma-Jane. I expect you could spare a baby or two. You'd hardly miss it.'

'Wicked,' Emma-Jane said, a sob in her voice. 'Wicked girl—' And, coming between them – Emma-Jane weeping bitterly now and Elinor shaking with glee – I took my cousin by her lovely, tipsy shoulders and bundled her from the room.

'That, Elinor, is enough. The poor woman is quite hysterical, and you don't really want her husband, do you?'

'Of course I don't want fat Bradley. Fat Emma-Jane can keep him. But it's nice, isn't it, Verity, to know I could take him if I wanted him? So nice. Take him and ruin him, because he knows I'd be no good for him, that he can't afford me, and yet he still couldn't resist . . . Verity, don't be cross with me. You've had the men at your feet tonight too, so you must understand. They own us, after all, don't they, and this is the only way we can strike back – make them desire us until it hurts them, and then run away. That's the game, dearest, isn't it? I'm no fool. I'll keep on running, keep on smiling and promising and then saying no. What else have I got to do – how else can I tell the difference between being awake and being asleep?'

'Oh, Elinor,' I said, despairing suddenly for both of us. 'Elinor, what a world this is.' And there, in the narrow landing by the retiring-room door, we flung our arms around each other, careless of wigs and laces and fine muslins, careless of prying eyes, and hugged each other tight.

'My word, how very moving,' a hard, sarcastic voice told us, startling us both since we had heard no one approach, startling me even more when I saw the taut, ill-tempered lines of Joel's face, with something written between them which I could not in any way decipher.

'You were a long time gone,' he said, tight-lipped. 'And it crossed my mind to wonder what the devil . . . However, now that I've found you, I have to say that this whole affair is quite tedious, and we can be on our way.'

'Oh, but it's only half over.'

'No, no, Mrs Barforth. I've ordered your carriage and so I'd say it's quite over.'

'Well, I'm sure I don't care either way. Good night then, Elinor. I'll call tomorrow.''

'Good night,' she said, looking nervous, tearful, her hand sketching an almost childish gesture of farewell as I went off to retrieve my belongings and then hurried to meet Joel, awaiting me in the hall.

Jealousy, could it be that? But jealousy of my affection, suspicion, or a more primitive reaction, the basic instinct of a predatory male who, while making free with other men's wives, does not wish anyone to gaze too closely at his own? Jealousy. And if jealousy meant fear of loss, as I understood it, then would losing me mean more to him than an assault on his pride? And if he cared more, or differently, than I had believed, if my light-headed flaunting of myself in my mother's old gown had indeed aroused something in him, stripped me finally, in his eyes, of my

436

aura of girlhood, of our too close kinship, if it had done that, then surely I must go as far as I could to meet him.

'I am base enough to know I would not sacrifice it,' Crispin's voice said to me from far away, an echo of our first lovemaking, but it was clear to me now that the sacrifice would soon have to be made, and would have to be made by me, not only for my children's sake but for Crispin's too. He could not exist forever waiting, wasting his talents and himself, at the Red Gin.

And, if my husband held out his hand to me I would have no right to refuse. Nor would it be wise to question his motives. Perhaps he had seen me tonight as a desirable woman who could at last challenge and excite him. Perhaps it was simply that, having had enough of philandering, mellowing now that his middle years were within view, his mind was turning to a deeper relationship, finding less satisfaction in chance encounters. But, whatever it was, I must accept it, must work with him to nurture it, must no longer be afraid of the potent male in him which I had always felt unable to satisfy. I must admit to myself, finally and forever, that I too had held back from him, unwilling to risk my emotions with a man who had aroused such storms in other women, who had so casually broken hearts and reputations. I must now take that risk, must give in order to receive.

'Joel,' I called out, holding my cloak snugly around me, covering my offensive nudity, 'I'm here.'

But as we walked out into the crisp night, there were two carriages at the door, our own and Colonel Corey's, with Estella Chase waiting peevishly to be handed inside.

'I will bid you good night, Mrs Barforth, Mr Barforth,' she said, each word a sharp-edged stone flung in Joel's face, her own face pinched with cold fury.

'Good night,' he answered brusquely, almost pushing me into the carriage, his intention to ignore her so plain, so rude, that even the coachmen must have known that there had been harsh words between them, even the coachmen must have pitied the poor little wife who seemed so unaware of the tension crackling and snarling from one to the other.

Jealousy? Of what? I had wondered. Jealousy of whom? Had it really been my lovely, gleaming gown, my painted feet, my posturings in the lamplight, or – as so often before in Joel's life – had it not concerned me at all? Had he wished to leave early on my account, thereby annoying this haughty woman who had counted on having him to herself? Or was he taking me home merely because he had had a tiff with Mrs Chase, who was leaving too? And although I had no answer I was no longer so ready to make a sacrifice.

28

I do not think it had been part of Daniel Adair's original plan to make love to Elinor. At their first acquaintance she had been a frail, capricious woman with no will of her own and very little spirit, and although it may well have occurred to him that her frequent bouts of ill health were rooted in emotional and sexual dissatisfaction, I believe he had no intention – while her husband lived – of attempting a cure. Daniel Adair, crafty and ambitious, lighthearted and warmhearted, a man for laughter rather than tears, would have been content to bide his time, for Morgan Aycliffe, by the look of him, could not last forever, and Elinor, as a wealthy widow with no sons to demand their share of the Aycliffe fortune, would be a glittering prize. Naturally, Mr Adair would have made some attempt to possess himself of her affections well in advance of her husband's demise, since there would be other bees in plenty circling the honeypot, but a woman may give her affections without risk, provided she does not give her body along with them, and Mr Adair, who could afford to buy his pleasures, was in no hurry.

But Elinor's fresh awakening to herself as a woman, her remembrance of the power her beauty gave her over the men who desired it, her delighted, determined skill in making them desire it the more, put a different face on things. Elinor the ailing little mouse, Elinor the feather-headed spendthrift, could be easily dealt with by a resourceful man, easily frightened or flattered into good behaviour, but Elinor the enchantress of other women's husbands – Elinor who, if left to herself, would certainly get into trouble and might, like Crispin before her, lose the Aycliffe inheritance altogether – such an Elinor was a threat to Mr Adair's schemes and, I have never doubted, a temptation to his own vigorous sensuality.

Perhaps Elinor had not intended him to make love to her, either. Her body, accustomed to serving an old man's hurried, awkward demands, was completely ignorant of physical fulfilment. To her the sexual act had first seemed a joke, then a nuisance, then an ordeal to be got through as quickly as possible whenever it could not be avoided altogether; and it was a man's admiration she required – a man at her feet, not in her bed.

But when Morgan Aycliffe returned to London for the start of the parliamentary session in February, she allowed Daniel Adair to kiss her one afternoon – feeling herself perfectly safe simply because it was afternoon and forni-cation, she believed, could only take place at night – and, finding the experience decidedly unusual, quite unable to understand why a man's mouth on her mouth could have such a strange effect on the pit of her stomach, she was unable to stop thinking about it, unable to rest until he had kissed her again. And even then it was a game. They dined together that night, making Elinor's account books their excuse, the Aycliffe housekeeper hovering between them, and afterwards, in the library, supposedly going through those conveniently muddled accounts, she bolted the door and offered him her mouth again, then her bare arms and shoulders, and found, to her amazement, that even by pressing herself into his arms she could not get close enough, that her thin silk gown was a barrier, as solid as a brick wall, which she could not tolerate. And so she tore the barrier down, fell on him, starved and parched by her ten dry years, and then, when her limbs had flooded with a pleasure she had not believed in, she lay purring blissfully against his shoulder, submissive and bemused, convinced beyond all question that no one but Daniel Adair could make this marvellous thing happen to her. And, in those early days, all that mattered was that he should make it happen again and again, with no thought of what could come after.

It was a wonderful spring that year, fragile, pale blue mornings, lemon-yellow afternoons, cool, hyacinth-scented evenings, opening the moorland pathways, freeing me from winter restraints, so that once again I could walk out to Old Sarah's Rock and the hut beyond it. I knew we had survived the winter mainly because Crispin had gone away at the start of it, to the Midlands and then to London, putting real distance between us, which had been far easier to bear than the few impossible miles from Lawcroft to the Red Gin.

It had offered us the opportunity to drift apart, an opportunity we should have taken and had, perhaps, meant to take, but as I pushed open the creaking door on that first blustery March morning and saw him there, still in his old blue coat, the winter months evaporated and we had never been separate.

'What I dream of,' he said, 'is waking one morning and finding you there, knowing you've spent a whole night beside me. Now, is that too much to ask – one poor little dream?'

Yet he had other dreams in his head just then, having spent the winter with men of his own kind in an immense exchange of ideas and ideals, culminating in his meeting with the radical politician Francis Place, who, although he was not to publish it for some time to come, had already worked out the themes of his People's Charter.

'Being with him was a revelation,' Crispin told me, his face thinner than ever from his December diet of good conversation. 'I can't tell you how exciting it was, listening to him expressing the views I've always shared and never quite put into words. I kept thinking: Yes, of course, I know that. I've always thought that, except that I'd kept it in the background of my mind until he released it, with just a few simple words. It was almost like falling in love – recognizing yourself in another person, as I did with you – or suddenly realizing one has a religious vocation. He drew all the loose threads together for me – after all, he's been a professional politician for a long time and he can speak convincingly and persuasively as they all do – but the feeling of actually finding a man one can believe in was quite overwhelming. And quite astonishing too, since I thought I was the cat who walks alone and had no great capacity for belief in anything except my own personal bits and pieces. It makes one feel far less lonely.'

'Good. I'm very glad for you.'

'Darling – are you jealous of an old Westminster warhorse like Francis Place? Then I shall believe in him all the more.'

'Yes, yes – but what does he believe in? What shocking things are you going to be advocating in next week's *Star*? You had better tell me, so I may keep it away from Hannah, for she upsets herself very much and goes on and on at breakfast time. Is it very revolutionary?'

'My word,' he said. 'I am more powerful than I supposed, if I can disturb Miss Hannah Barforth's tea and toast. Yes, I fear it is quite extreme and will appeal to no one in Cullingford but the residents of Simon Street. He believes, as I do, that government should be concerned with the individual, not with property, and so he advocates one man one vote, as I have always done, whether or not that man possesses a penny to call his own.'

'Definitely a measure for Simon Street.'

'Quite so. And to avoid the spectre of the millmaster standing over the new voter with a whip in one hand and an eviction notice in the other – my word, what a picture, I must get someone to sketch it for me, and include it with my article – well, the way to avoid that, of course, is to have a secret ballot. My father – and your husband – would merely say we were giving the common man the freedom to sell his vote three or four times over, and naturally, some would do that. But the majority would vote as they saw fit. Wouldn't they?'

'Yes, yes, I suppose so – they would vote for Mark Corey instead of your father.'

'They could even vote for me.'

'For you? How can you stand for Parliament yourself? You have no money.'

'Exactly. I could not support myself in office, and, in Francis Place's opinion, I shouldn't need to. He wishes to abolish the property qualification for Members of Parliament and to pay them salaries like any other professional men.'

'Oh well – I see now why you believe in him.'

'Because it is to my own advantage? Yes, and why not, if I feel I have some contribution to make? But aren't you shocked at the idea of men like me filling the House of Commons – men without property put there by the mass of the people who have no property, either? Doesn't it excite you?'

Irritated perhaps by his enthusiasm, I gave him a typically Barforth answer. 'Why should it? What advantage could there possibly be to me?'

'None,' he said dryly. 'None at all.' And then, understanding that this fine flaring of his opportunities, this opening up of new vistas, could hardly be pleasing to me, shackled as I was to Cullingford, he put his arms around me so gently that for a moment my heart stopped and I feared he was about to bid me goodbye.

I went home determined to be glad for him, for if Francis Place should ever find the means of throwing open the parliamentary career to men like Crispin, then his future could be bright indeed. And what did it matter that I would remain here, with no real future of my own, a part of Joel's destiny, since that was my fate in any case? But that afternoon, taking my usual drive with Elinor, I found myself struggling against a murky, altogether uncomfortable envy, for her love was still a newborn miracle and mine, perhaps, was coming to an end.

Next morning, having reached the same conclusion, Crispin was pale with anxiety as I walked towards Old Sarah's Rock. He began immediately to talk about nothing, a great rush of words weaving themselves skilfully, whimsically around my good intentions, telling me that our parting, like all painful events, would come in its own good time and that there was nothing I need do about it today.

He was, of course, more deeply in debt than ever, for no one seemed to pay for either his lectures or the journeys they involved, while the *Cullingford Star* and certain residents of Simon Street could be relied on to devour his meagre allowance well before the month-end. And although he would not take a penny from me, declaring no gentleman ever borrowed from a lady, his ban did not extend to all members of my sex.

He had borrowed, quite substantially, I knew, from a spinster aunt somewhere in Wensleydale, and there was always his bold-faced landlady, Mrs Dinah McCluskey, widow of the terrible, seventeen-stone landlord of the Red Gin, who had died, some two years ago, in a brawl involving her honour.

'She's a good soul,' Crispin said cheerfully. 'And pretty well fixed since her husband died. She doesn't mind if I'm behind with the rent. It pleases her to have what she calls a gentleman living in her attic, and I amuse her too.'

'I daresay. She couldn't be in love with you, could she?'

'Well, I honestly don't see why she couldn't, except that I'm a trifle lightweight for her taste. Her husband was a mighty man, and there are one or two just like him at her beck and call. And I cannot even dazzle her with my learning since she sees very well that I fail to make a decent living by it. If she were a man, you know, and loved you as I do, she would run off with you whether you liked it or not. And when your husband came to repossess you she would make short work of him too.'

And I saw no point in protesting that I was no mere object, to be repossessed like a bale of dress goods, since that was my condition exactly.

Yet my awareness of defeat corresponded with a great flowering of Elinor's spirit, a lovely reaching out that put peach bloom and rose bloom in her skin, gave depth to her voice and the colour of her eyes, thrusting her from her prolonged, neurotic girlhood to a wonderful, gold-tinted maturity. And I watched, with sympathy and envy, as she passed from her trance of sexual desire to that far more perilous state of love.

'What do you mean to do?' I asked her, as my mother, only last summer, had asked me. 'What future is there, Elinor?'

As I spoke the words, my mother's voice came to me from that same long-past season warning me – or warning Elinor through me – that melancholy men like her husband, to whom life appears a burden, are usually very slow to lay it down.

'I shall be patient,' she said. 'What else is there? I shall be sensible for the first time in my life – and patient.'

'You mean you will wait for your husband to die?'

'Yes,' she said, settling herself down against the blue velvet upholstery of her carriage, her eyes quiet, her face totally serene, as if the death of Morgan Aycliffe was as natural to her as the blending of one season into another.

'That is exactly what I shall do. Does he deserve more of me than that?'

'And will Mr Adair wait too?'

'Oh yes – can you doubt it?' she said, her eyes sparkling with mischief, her mouth gentle with the knowledge and acceptance of the man she loved. 'Of course Daniel will wait, Verity. I am not such a goose – I know how much the money – Morgan Aycliffe's money – means to Daniel. I know that is why he flirted with me in the first place and worked so hard to make me rely on him. I know, darling. But that is not the way of things now. He loves me now, Verity.'

And I had no cause to disbelieve her, for Elinor had always been lovable, and now, glowing with these new, vibrant shades of womanhood, she would have been hard for any man to resist. And Daniel Adair, at least, was not a cold man. Ambitious and hardheaded, certainly, but with a reckless side to him and a romantic side, with a heart that could be moved to love and persuaded to faithfulness.

'He will probably cheat your daughters of their dowries,' I told her, quoting my mother again. 'And he may beat you when you misbehave. But I think you'll be happy – I hope so, at any rate, Elinor. I do hope so.'

'And you'll continue to receive me when I'm plain Mrs Adair, and Emma-Jane Hobhouse turns up her nose at me because my mother-in-law was a washerwoman?'

'I will.'

'Even if Joel condemns me for giving Daniel control of the business, instead of him? Because he won't be able to stop me, Verity – there'll be nothing anyone can do to stop me.'

And clasping my hand suddenly with a fierce, desperate grip, she closed her eyes and said, 'Pray that it happens, Verity, for if I pray myself I may give offence, and then it could all go wrong. Please, Verity, it's not that I want him dead, it's just that I want to be alive myself, which doesn't

445

sound quite right, but you'll know what to say. I don't shock you, do I? It's not my fault, dearest; surely it's the law to blame, and those who made it – the ones who allow no escape from an unhappy marriage but death. No divorce, no separation without the husband's consent, just death – his or mine. I could have died, last year, many a time, without even weeping for myself, and he wouldn't have wept for me, either. But not now. I have never felt so strong, Verity. I wake up in the mornings – and you know how frail I used to be in the mornings – and now I could fly. Really I could; straight through the walls and away above the smoke. And I can't lose that feeling, can I? I can't let anything stand in its way.'

No escape from an unhappy marriage but death, yet I had never thought of Joel as anything but overpoweringly alive, a vital force dominating the lesser lives around him as my grandfather had done. And when I tried to place myself in widow's weeds, with Joel's money – my money – in my hands, and the freedom to dispose of it, and myself, as I thought fit, my mind faltered. I could not, in fact, even contemplate Joel's death, much less welcome it, and when I attempted to force myself, I was shaken, totally appalled.

Yet a great distance had opened up between us lately, a coldness that made him difficult of access and difficult to please. He was an irritable presence at table that summer, behind a newspaper, a drift of cigar smoke on the stairs, a closed study door.

Apart from his infidelities, of which I was supposed to know nothing, he had never treated me unkindly. He had been unfailingly generous, had made me lavish gifts, never questioned my spending, had praised me and protected me. But now, since the night of the dance, his easy, tolerant affection had gone.

'Is it veal again? Do we eat nothing else at this house?'

'But, Joel—'

'Damnation – I'm sick of it.'

'Then what would you like to eat? You have only to tell me.'

'The housekeeping is your affair, madam, and I'd hope, after all these years, that you could get it right.'

And when, the following evening, there would be beef or lamb, salmon or pheasant from Dalby Hall, all of it succulent, well seasoned, well garnished, he would eat in a silence I found more unnerving than his complaints.

Nor did his displeasure confine itself to the dining room. It came to bed with us too, invading an area of our lives upon which I preferred not to brood. I had feared, after Crispin's first lovemaking, that my body would be unresponsive to Joel and had been amazed, had wondered about myself, when this had not always proved to be the case. Yet now there were nights when Joel would take me roughly, without skill, deliberately denying me the pleasure he had once been so determined to arouse; there were other nights when pleasure eluded us both, when his mood would fluctuate alarmingly from annoyance to something I dared not call tenderness, from an urge to blame me for my inadequacies to an even more alarming urge to apologize, almost, for his own. And at such times, as tense and awkward as I had been on my wedding night, I was confused, intrigued, often very afraid.

'Does he suspect you?' Crispin asked, looking out over the dry, summer moor as if it made no difference.

'No. I am sure he does not. He wouldn't brood about that, not Joel. . . . Crispin, it's time, isn't it? Isn't it?'

'No,' he said, hands painfully on my shoulders. 'Not yet. I don't know why, but not yet. Just a little longer, Verity. I have a strange feeling something may happen to help us.'

But as I walked back alone that morning towards Lawcroft it seemed far more likely that something would happen to destroy us, or to destroy me, at any rate, since, if the storm broke, I would warn Crispin, somehow or other, to make his escape. And so heavy-laden was I by this certainty of my doom that I was not surprised, just terribly afraid, when Joel's phaeton, which should have been at Tarn Edge or Low Cross, swept in through the gates and hurtled sickeningly towards me.

It could, of course, be nothing more than a spot of engine grease on a shirt cuff which brought him home, to change it for a fresh one, but my whole guilty body flooded with a blind panic that, ironically, tragically, became my own punishment, the cause of my heartbreak.

'Dear God,' I heard myself whisper, and my dog, my companion of these ten years past, pressing close to my side, caught the spark of my fear and, before I could stop her, went streaking off down the drive towards the man and the carriage, the hooves and the wheels that menaced me.

He made, I think, an effort to avoid her, for his horse had cost him several thousand guineas and he had no mind to break its legs, nor his own, by taking a tumble. But my bitch, who had been a coward all her life, having found her courage, persisted, snarling at those long, lethal legs, snapping through the flying dust and stones and curses, the screaming, rearing horse, as the phaeton swayed, righted itself, and went clattering on, leaving behind a twitching sprawl of yellow limbs.

She was dead when I reached her, blessedly, for I could not have borne the helpless, bewildered ending of a good beast who has never heard of heaven, much less learned to hope for it. But even without that, it was too much and I was myself amazed at the grief that forced me to my knees on the gravel beside her, and unlocked a flood of tears I thought would never end. She was dead and, putting my face against hers, paying her the only tribute I could, I saw, on the insides of my eyelids, my brother Edwin, who had given her to me on my sixteenth birthday, a hundred years ago. And remembering him, my tears flowed faster than ever, my sobs became clamorous, painful, hurting not only my chest but my ears.

I neither knew nor cared what had happened to Joel,

whether he had overturned or bolted, or simply driven on regardless, but suddenly his boots were there, and his hand clenched around his driving whip, Joel standing over me as he had done once before, when my brother lay dying in my arms. But he had been excited then, exhilarated by the violence of the night and by another man's murder he knew he could use to suit himself, whereas he was angry now and disgusted and more than ready to be unkind.

'Get up,' he said. 'Get up – get up. It's a dog, no more. It's not one of your children lying there. It's a damned dog.'

And when I couldn't get up, could in no way explain to him that I was weeping again for my brother and my father, for Elinor and for myself – for him too, perhaps, in some recess of my mind – he hauled me to my feet and snarled, 'Stupid girl – you have no one but yourself to blame. If you can't control your damnable animals then you shouldn't keep them.'

'I could control her.'

'The devil you could. Well, that's an end to it, and I'm not sorry. You can stay at home in the mornings now, like other women, for there'll be no more dogs – hear me? – no more. Do you hear me?'

'I hear you.'

'And if you bring one into the house behind my back I'll shoot it – understand?'

'I understand.'

'Now get inside,' he said, at a point of fury where he would have struck me, I think, had not the grooms and the gardener and Mrs Stevens all come running. 'Get inside, before they all see what a disgrace you are. Get your work basket and sew, like your mother, or sort out your linen cupboard – do something women are supposed to do. Get inside.'

And recognizing my peril, I ran.

But I was bereaved, brokenhearted, inconsolable, not even wishing to be consoled, since I could tell no one what

449

that nervous, obliging animal had meant to me. And although I grieved for her own sake, her death had also been the symbolic ending of my love for Crispin, a brutal amputation performed, just as symbolically, by Joel. I had no dog now, no reason to walk to Old Sarah's Rock, and I would never have another, for even if Joel would permit it, no other dog could ever take the place of that foolish, faithful yellow bitch, given to me so casually by Edwin on the last day but one of his young life.

I dreamed of my brother that night, my sleeping brain, in the moment he fell mortally wounded across my knees, giving him Crispin's face, so that it was Crispin I mourned, cradling his body in my arms, hard gravel underneath my knees, until he became in turn my dog, my brother again, and I awoke suffocating in the heavy dark, my ears straining for a new anxiety. And there it was, the noise outside my door, a clumsiness that could not be Joel, who always entered silently in the night, whether he had been drinking or not, or who, if he wished to wake me, did it decisively, with a branch of candles in his hand. And because I had been dreaming of violence, of that kitchen knife in my brother's chest – in Crispin's chest – I sat up and waited, trembling, with no thought of escape. A sacrifice.

But then as the door was shouldered open and I saw the familiar silhouette, the height and breadth I recognized, I called out 'Joel?' enquiringly, wondering what ailed him.

'Who else?' he snapped. 'Damnation – take the filthy things from me, for I must be out of my mind.'

And suddenly, in the darkness, something landed on my chest, an amazing, squirming tangle of limbs and sharp claws and cold noses that gradually, a tail here, a bright saucy eye, an eager little tongue there, became not one but two puppies, one gold and the other a dark brown chocolate. I don't want another dog, I thought. No, I don't want either of you. But the feel and the smell of them enchanted me, and within seconds I was laughing – and crying – fighting them off and hugging them, squealing myself now as their sharp excited puppy teeth made free use of my bones.

'You said I couldn't have another dog.'

'Yes, and I meant it too. And then I got to thinking how it was your brother who gave you that crossbred bitch, so now you have two from your husband. Purebred, the very best gun dogs money can buy; wasted on you, I reckon. And I'd be obliged if you'd keep them out of my way, and make damn sure they're reliable before we move to Tarn Edge. Now, get them out of my bed, Verity. Fifteen miles I had to go for the little brutes, to Keighley and back, with half a bottle of brandy inside me or I might not have gone at all. I'm tired.'

'Thank you, Joel,' I said. 'Thank you very much.'

And by the time I had settled them down in my old dog's basket by the kitchen fire, laughed at them, cried over them, and hurried back upstairs, he was almost asleep.

'They're beautiful, Joel,' I said, my hand on his shoulder.

In that state of half sleep, half unknowing, he turned his head against my shoulder and murmured, 'Of course you're beautiful – I've always thought so.'

And I have always believed that, had it not been for Elinor, the coldness between us would have been over.

29

In July of that year the Prime Minister, Lord Grey, resigned, an event leading, some weeks later, to the return of Morgan Aycliffe, who, like others, had come home to test the mood of his electorate should the Whig government topple altogether. And the day of his homecoming brought me a hastily scribbled note from Elinor, begging me to dine with them.

'Bring Joel if you can, but if he is engaged come yourself, with Hannah or alone – please, please, don't fail.'

But when I arrived in Blenheim Lane, with Joel and Hannah and even the Reverend Mr Ashley in tow, whatever panic she may have felt at facing her husband again had subsided, and she greeted us calmly, warmly, displaying, in fact, so much self-possession that even Mr Aycliffe himself seemed impressed.

'How very nice,' she said, 'that we are all together again,' and as she shepherded us gracefully into the dining room I saw her husband's eyes slowly assessing her, wondering, perhaps, if this new, mature Elinor was a fit mate for him after all.

'The beef is excellent, Mrs Aycliffe,' he told her, obviously if pleasantly surprised, and, leaning back in her chair, eating little herself, she acknowledged his compliments with immense composure, surveying us all quite lovingly, as if, in the overflow of her heart, she had more than enough tenderness to spare.

'Really – quite delicious, my dear,' he said, and she nodded, smiled very slowly, a woman at last, serene and perfectly balanced and beautiful: a worthy partner of any man's labours.

She showed, that evening, a most enchanting courtesy to all of us, listening with a rapt attention she certainly could not feel as her husband and mine talked of business and politics, drawing from Mr Ashley the tale of the badly repaired parsonage at Redesdale, which had occasioned yet another delay in Hannah's marriage, showing more affection to Hannah herself than I had seen in years.

'My little girls will be your bridesmaids,' she declared. 'Prudence and Faith in pink and Cecilia in white, I think, since she is so much smaller – and it will all be quite perfect. We shall have such pleasant summer days together, Hannah, for I will often bring the children to visit, and Jonas Agbrigg may come with us any time he likes. I know you will wish to keep yourself informed of his progress and if I keep an eye on him you may worry less. Everything is going to work out so well, darling – everything – I feel it.'

'Are you all right?' I whispered as the confusion of leave-taking enabled us to have a private word, and, smiling once again, as if her great inner joy would be more than enough to sustain her, she pressed her cheek briefly, lovingly, against mine.

'Oh yes. He is here, but he will go away again.'

'And you can endure it?'

'I must. After all, I have endured him for ten years, and I think I may endure a little longer. If he comes to my room tonight – and it is not at all certain that he will – I shall not think of him at all. I shall think of Daniel, and by closing my mind to everything else I shall survive.'

'I do believe my little sister is growing up at last,' Joel remarked as we drove home. 'Tonight she really looked like Mrs Morgan Aycliffe, and damn me if Aycliffe didn't think so too. He'll be taking her back to London with him, I shouldn't wonder, which may not please all of us – eh, Hannah? – but you can't deny it's where she ought to be.'

And if Hannah understood his hint that her influence with our first Member of Parliament might be coming to an end, she ignored it.

But perhaps it plagued her just the same, thinning out her sleep as other anxieties thinned mine, so that we both slipped abruptly into wakefulness when the hammering started, the terrible night-wailing of some desperate creature, gone mad or pursued by violence, or by justice, to our door.

'Stay here,' Joel commanded, reaching hastily for a dressing gown. 'There's no telling who it may be.' But I think I knew, and I was there, in the hall, with the servants and the hastily lit candles, the excited, delighted yelping of my puppies, as he opened the door and Elinor, with only a thin cloak over her nightgown, ran inside, a hunted creature brought to bay, cowering from everything that

453

moved until she saw me and fell, panting and wet through, into my arms.

'God Almighty,' Joel said blankly, and Hannah, her lips chalk-white – for only tragedy of the first magnitude could cause a woman, even Elinor, to run half naked through the night – demanded, 'The children? Mr Aycliffe? Are they dead?'

And standing there with her collapsed body slumped against me, not even listening to the words she was pouring into my ear, I said, 'No. Send the servants away, Hannah – Joel – immediately.'

And when they had done it and come to stand one on either side of me, hard-eyed now and suspicious, I told them, 'She can't talk to you now. I shall take her upstairs and put her to bed.'

'What lunacy is this?' Joel said.

'What disgrace?' Hannah echoed, and drawing Elinor closer to me, I said, 'She has left her husband, or he has turned her out – and, either way, I shall take her upstairs, for she is not even half conscious and you will get nothing from her. Wait for me in the study. I will be down presently.'

And I suppose it was because they were so unaccustomed to receiving commands from me that they obeyed.

Mrs Stevens had lingered on the first landing, knowing her own usefulness in times of crisis, and together we dried Elinor's feet and the tangle of her hair, found her a fresh nightgown, a clean, lavender-scented bed, hugged her and kissed her and told her the pain would go away, the fear would go away, although we all knew otherwise. And gradually we pieced together the tale I, at least, already knew, that she had held firm, sure of herself and her ability to safeguard her future, until the moment he had put his hands upon her. And then, sickened by the conjugal rights her new maturity had encouraged him to reclaim, she had at first refused and finally, when he persisted, had lost her head and told him all.

'I couldn't,' she said simply. 'I thought I could. Until the instant he got into my bed I was sure of it, for I'd been doing it all these years, but after Daniel, it wasn't the same. For a moment or two I was mad with terror, quite mad, as if Daniel was my husband and Morgan Aycliffe was an intruder, a criminal. And so I said things, and he knew. He's an old man – he smells old, feels old. I couldn't.'

And, throwing pitying arms around her, Mrs Stevens murmured, 'Yes, darling, I know, I know.'

They were waiting for me in the study, Joel leaning against the fireplace smoking. Hannah sitting straight-backed, rigid with shock and shame and some honest anger that this would damage her own relations with Mr Aycliffe. And both of them, brother and sister more alike now than ever before, turned hard, accusing eyes on me as I came into the room, having clearly weighed me in their personal balance and, as Hannah had always expected, found me wanting.

'So,' Joel said grimly, 'are you in a position now to make explanations?'

'If you like.'

'Like? No, I don't like this at all – none of it, for I never heard of a woman who left her husband, and Aycliffe would not turn her out without good reason. There is another man, then?'

'Of course there is,' Hannah cut in, her fists clenching and unclenching with suppressed fury. 'What else, what else? Yes, indeed, and I think, Joel, that you would do well to require your wife to be frank with us, to inform us of the man's identity, since we cannot doubt she knows.'

And, meeting her eyes, nodding slightly, he said, 'Verity?' – the quiet menace of his tone making me well aware of the thin ice on which I stood.

'It is Daniel Adair,' I told him, wondering why I was so calm, why I remained unafraid even when, abruptly turning his back, he gave the short, unpleasant laugh that warned of danger, while Hannah, white then red then white again, became so tight with anger that I felt the strain of it in my own bones.

'Yes,' she said, 'a bricklayer. How apt, how typical. One would expect better judgement from a kitchen maid. And while we are speaking of judgement, Verity.'

'Indeed – are we speaking of that?'

'I fear so. And I find it an unpleasant task to be obliged to question your own. May one ask when you first became aware of this – this criminal association? For everything in your manner tells me that you knew of it long before tonight.'

'Yes, I knew. I knew from the beginning.'

'Of course you did. And failed, for reasons I am sure my brother will find hard to understand, to take any responsible action. Failed to inform either him or myself, as you should have done.'

But Joel, swinging round to face us, instead of taking me to task as I had expected, dreaded, said harshly, 'Leave that. For now, at any rate. We have Elinor to deal with first, and Aycliffe. And I'm damned if I know what's to be done.'

Hannah, the sister who had never yet failed him, met his eyes again, her answer ready.

'There is only one thing to be done, Joel, and, with your permission, there is no need for Verity to be involved in it. We must take her back, now if possible or early tomorrow morning, before it becomes the common gossip of the town. If anyone saw her running through the streets in that lunatic fashion, they will hardly have believed the evidence of their eyes. I think we can shut our own servants' mouths and feel reasonably confident that Mr Aycliffe will know how to do the same. But the longer the delay, the greater the risk. Come, Joel.'

'And if he won't have her?'

'It is very much in his best interests to do so. There may well be a general election before the year is out, and he cannot be allowed to ruin his career. He cannot afford a scandal, for although he is the victim in this case the *Cullingford Star* would not take that view. He will be well aware of that, once it is pointed out to him, once Elinor has been prevailed upon to plead for pardon.'

'He will not pardon her,' I said very softly.

Again she spun round to me, her eyes ablaze. 'No, and I do not expect it of him. No one could expect it. It is merely necessary for him to behave as if he had.'

'And she will not plead with him, either. Not tonight, at any rate.'

'What do you mean by that?'

'I mean that she will not be going home tonight. She will be staying here, as my guest.'

'You have no authority,' Hannah said, spitting out each word like an angry cat. 'No authority to offer her shelter under my brother's roof.'

'Rather more authority than you, Hannah, I think.'

And as she snapped her mouth tight shut to hold back her outraged words, Joel said coldly, dangerously, 'You will apologize for that, Verity, to my sister.'

And still I was not afraid.

'Presently, Joel. But Elinor is your sister too, is she not? And I wonder why you are so ready to send her back to that spiteful old man who does not really want her, who has not wanted her for a long time, without even hearing what she has to say.'

'She will have no choice,' he said. 'If I deny her shelter, and the decision is certainly mine, where else can she go?'

But having found my courage, like my old yellow bitch who had not hesitated to charge a horse and carriage for my sake, I knew I could go on.

'I think there must always be a refuge, Joel, if one looks hard enough. She could go to my mother, at Patterswick, I believe.'

'And if I forbid you to take her there?'

'Then she may go alone, if she is determined and sure of her welcome, for my mother is entirely free to offer

457

hospitality as she pleases. And no one but Elinor's husband may legally compel her to return, should he so desire.'

Amazingly, instead of giving vent to his temper, he stared at me for a moment and then turned his back again, the fingers of one nervous hand drumming against the mantelpiece, one irritable foot tapping against the fender.

'Joel,' Hannah said, 'we are not obliged, surely, to listen to this foolishness?'

And then, realizing that Joel was listening only to his own thoughts, refusing to communicate with either one of us, she turned again to me.

'Does it surprise you that my brother is at a loss for words? Setting aside all moral issues, you may be certain that if Elinor persists in this madness her husband will know how to defend himself. He will admit no financial claims, and she will never see her children again.'

'Ah, no. But then, how much does she see of them anyway, with the nurses and governesses you have found for them, and the house so full of precious china they are hardly made welcome in it. Do you really believe she would miss them?'

'It is her duty to miss them,' she thundered. 'And finally, one way or another, she must learn to do her duty. Joel, we are wasting time here. We should go to Blenheim Lane at once.'

But, inexplicably, Joel's back was still turned, his eyes apparently held by the fan of pleated paper that filled the summer hearth. Finding it easier to address his lounging shoulders than his scowling, brooding face, and hoping, I think, in some recess of my mind that he would finally turn to me in sympathy and understanding to take my part instead of Hannah's, I began to speak quickly, knowing that her claims on him were very strong and that she would not allow me much time.

'She is your sister, Joel, and entitled to your support. She may be foolish and capricious, and difficult, I admit it, but she was seventeen and young for her years when that

458

man married her. She thought marriage was a new silk dress and sleeping late in the mornings, and now, when she knows what it could have been, she's in despair. All I ask is that you talk to her when she's calmer, treat her like a woman for the first time in your life and give her the opportunity to defend herself. She has been badly treated too, you know. Yes, Joel, you know she has.'

When he still would not answer me, when even the slight movement of his hand and his foot ceased, shrouding him in a choking silence, Hannah shot him a puzzled, reproachful look and then spoke the words she had expected him to say.

'Yes, indeed. Very badly. A beautiful home full of well-trained servants. Three healthy children. A decent, intelligent husband with a successful commercial career behind him and what may well be a brilliant career in politics at his feet. Nothing in the world to do but issue her commands and spend that man's money. And she betrayed him!'

'It does not surprise me, Hannah.'

'I daresay.'

'And if he is honest with himself it should not surprise Mr Aycliffe, either. He will not be so heartbroken, you know, for he has never loved her.'

'I dispute that. I know him better than you do, and had he not entertained the deepest feelings for her he would not have married her.'

'What nonsense, and you know it. He married her on a sensual impulse, probably quite foreign to his nature, which he has regretted ever since, for once it was satisfied he had very little use for her. And that was his own fault, Hannah, not Elinor's, for he was old enough to have known better. And so was Joel, for that matter, when he consented to it. But she was not. Well, I suppose he is not the first man to lose his head in middle life over a girl young enough to be his daughter, and one can sympathize with that. But there was no need for him to turn peevish, to neglect her when he no longer found her exciting in his

459

bed. Hannah, he has virtually ignored her these past two or three years, and however well-intentioned your motives, you have encouraged it.'

'How dare you say that to me.'

'It seems I dare. What did he expect when he went off to London and left her alone? He deserted her – yes, yes, that is the right word, deserted her – because she bores him and ages him, reminds him of what a fool he once was, and because he feels uncomfortable with the children and is afraid of having more. Yet no one blames him for that. He is coldhearted and selfish. Whether you are prepared to admit it or not, if you are strictly honest, you must know that her loss would not grieve him. And I also think, Hannah, that you should question your own motives. Why are you so determined to send her back? Is it Elinor's relationship with Mr Aycliffe that you are so anxious to save, or your own?'

She raised her hand then, fist clenched, to strike me, I think, but the habit of dignity was too strong, and lowering it, twisting her hands together, she hissed, 'Be careful, my girl, very careful, unless you would have us question your own morals, as I have always questioned your mother's.'

And her scathing 'my girl' was, finally, too much.

'If you are making comparisons, Hannah,' I said very clearly, making sure she heard and understood, 'then you have not far to look, for your father was an alley cat where women were concerned, and your brother is the same, with no more consideration for me than your father had for your mother. And Edwin was like them. He would have led you a merry dance, my girl, and you would have had no time then for passing moral judgements on matters you barely understand. You seem to think Elinor lewd, but she has in fact bolted from her husband because she simply cannot bear him to touch her. One can hardly call her sexually depraved for that.'

'Joel,' she said, just the one word, an appeal not only for help but an expression of how deeply she had been

460

wounded, a cry which brought him instantly round to face her, the sister who had so valiantly shared his hard times, whose own life was still far from easy. And I could not tell from the tense, tautly etched mask of his face what it had meant to him to be called an alley cat, whether he had heard or cared, whether he would punish or laugh, whether he would astonish me by asking if he had hurt me, and by being ashamed. Yet I did know, with a sudden flow of feeling that softened me, weakened me, that I had been hurt and that, should he ask for pardon, I would not refuse it.

'I will go to Blenheim Lane now,' he said, his eyes holding Hannah's bending her to his will as perhaps only he could do, ignoring me entirely. 'I may do better, man to man, alone. And until we know his intentions Elinor keeps to her bed, here, under my roof, with no one but yourselves and Mrs Stevens near her. And as for what is between the two of you, you must settle it as best you can.'

He let the door slam shut behind him, and we stood there for a moment, Hannah and I, facing each other, imprisoned in her anger and my newborn freedom from restraint, which had made me cruel.

'I do not like you, Verity,' she said.

'That is your privilege.'

'Yes, and do not think that my brother will ever take your part against me, for he will not. Not in the long term. I stood by him when our father died, and he knows, had Edwin lived, that the Barforth inheritance would have been mine. My loss has been Joel's gain, and he remembers that.'

'Indeed. But the Barforth inheritance belonged to neither of you, Hannah. Samson Barforth was my grandfather, not yours. The inheritance was mine.'

'Which is why my brother married you.'

'So it was. And you, Hannah, would do well to forget my marriage, and Elinor's, and give some thought to your own.'

461

'Do not presume to advise me, Verity. I am older than you and have a great deal more sense—'

'But you are a spinster, Hannah, which ignores sense and seniority – and it does not suit you.'

And as her hand shot out at last to hurt me, I caught her wrist and, amazing myself that I could hold it so tight, could so obviously give her pain, I told her, 'I do not dislike you, Hannah; in fact, sometimes I like you very well, and what you think of me makes no difference. But, for your own good – and stop pulling away from me, for I shall hold on until I have done – for your own good, concentrate on your own life and let other people get on as they think fit. Marry Mr Ashley, if you must, although I think Mr Brand would suit you better. But marry someone, for you are no more able to exist alone than Elinor.'

There was, after that, a great deal more, a vast rooting out of grievances, of all the times I had slighted her or mocked her, my odd, unrealiable nature that made me so difficult to live with, my inability to appreciate the awkwardness of her situation, such a torrent of resentment that, in the end, Mrs Stevens flowed smoothly through the door, coaxed Hannah away with the little murmurs and gestures of sympathy she had used with my grandfather, and then came back to tell me Elinor was at last asleep.

'Poor child, she imagines Mr Adair will come tomorrow to take her away.'

'And you do not think he will?'

'Oh, dearest – hardly. What do you think?'

'I think he will not come, either.'

'Oh dear,' she said, 'dear, dear – and he will not prove us wrong, you know.'

And patting my cheek, she went sadly away.

I sat then, for a long time, alone in the study, watching the daybreak, the door slightly ajar, so that when Joel returned I could see him before Hannah, yet when he finally came, I had fallen deep asleep and woke with a mighty jolt, his hand on my shoulder.

'It's five o'clock,' he said, dropping heavily into a chair. 'I should be on my way to the mill.'

'You surely won't go this morning?'

'I surely will. I'll lose a day's business on the day I die, I reckon, but not before. So – since I can hardly flatter myself that you waited up to see me safe home – you'll be wanting to know about our brother-in-law Aycliffe.'

And it amazed me that after all I had said he could speak to me so naturally, that he could speak to me at all.

'Yes – will he take her back?'

'Oh, I think something may be arranged. He was very much mortified and felt obliged to speak at length about the wrong done him, and about the sins of the flesh in general. And one can only allow his position to be devilish awkward, for he has lost both his wife and his business manager, and I think, in the long term, he will feel Dan Adair's loss the keenest.'

'Oh,' I said, aware of his shrewd eyes on my face, knowing that although he had spoken lightly his keen brain was probing mine, assessing me, making its calculations. 'Well, poor Mr Aycliffe, for his notions of propriety will never allow him to reinstate Mr Adair, whatever he plans for Elinor.'

'Quite so. However, he means to solve the issue for the moment by returning immediately to London, although if a general election comes, he will have to make up his mind to face her.'

'And Elinor?'

'May stay with us until his further instructions, although he will not contribute one penny to her upkeep while she remains from under his roof, nor may she take anything from his house but the barest personal essentials his housekeeper will put together for her. And she is on no account to see her children.'

'And how are we to explain her presence here?'

'Illness, and the need to be cared for in his absence.'

'What illness?'

463

'Good God, how am I to tell? Women are always ailing, and you and Hannah between you can think of something.'

But he did know, had agreed to it, even though he did not like it, and, recognizing the flaring of his temper as a cover for his unease, I said quite coldly, 'There is only one illness which would suffice. A malady of the nerves, like the first Mrs Aycliffe, so that if she persists in refusing to live with him he can give out that she is mad. Joel, how could you agree to that?'

'I agreed to nothing,' he said irritably, flicking open his heavy, silver cigar box and then, changing his mind, going to the door and calling into the silent hall for tea, knowing someone would hear.

'Listen, Verity – and there's no reason why I should even explain this to you, no reason at all why I should put up with your damned insolence. I got her the best deal I could. He would have been well within his rights to demand her immediate return, and if he had and she'd bolted again, and gone on bolting – well – nobody is going to blame a man for locking up a wife like that. But I'm giving her time to compose herself, which is what you asked of me, so that when she does go back she can do it right. Get your feet on the ground, girl, for there's a lot of money at stake. He must be sixty now, or more, and feeble, and when he's gone I want Elinor to have the enjoyment of his money, not see it tied up in those girls' dowries to be handed over to strangers. She's had ten years of him. She's earned her fair share, and she wouldn't thank you, in the long run, if you talked her out of it. She's my sister, after all, as you've pointed out to me more than once tonight.'

The door opened to admit the tea tray, borne by a girl who, not having yet been chastised by Hannah, still showed her curiosity. And when she had gone and he had drunk one cup straight down and poured another, he told me with elaborate nonchalance, 'By the way, he asks that Hannah shall supervise his household while he is away.'

'Should that surprise me?'

464

'Verity, if you think I forced Elinor's marriage on her, then you have a short memory. She was more than glad to take him.'

'Yes, I remember. She talked a great deal about strawberries and champagne. I remember that very well indeed.'

'Well then – I know as well as you do that he should have married Hannah. I imagine he must know it himself. But how could I have told him so at the time?'

'You couldn't. And if you had not consented he would still not have married Hannah. I know. And if what I said to Hannah tonight offended you, then I am sorry, but she was very rough with me and I saw no reason to take it meekly. I am not sure what I have done to earn her dislike – in fact, I don't think I knew, before, how very heartily she does dislike me.'

'You are mistress of Lawcroft, that is all,' he said, going to stand by the fireplace again, fatigue showing now in the droop of his shoulders. 'It is a position she expected to fill herself – would have filled – and she has always thought herself far better suited to it than you. Just as she has always considered herself a far more suitable Mrs Aycliffe than Elinor.'

'She may be right – on both counts.'

'Perhaps. Verity—?'

'Yes.'

'Yes, indeed. By God, I don't know why I should talk to you at all. You said a hard thing of me tonight, Verity. No, no, I don't dispute it. I am not a sound man with women. I never have been – nor was my father. My mother did not take it well, and I had forgotten that she sometimes brought her troubles to your mother, and that you may have overheard.'

'Yes, that is how little girls learn about life, by poking and prying, since no one will actually tell us anything. Elinor knew all about it too, but Hannah denied it – decreed that her father was incapable of such bad behaviour and that her mother was worried simply about the war and the state of trade.'

He smiled, very briefly, his face for just a moment almost kind.

'Yes, Hannah would say that. But, at least, one knew what my mother's feelings were. They were distressing and something of a nuisance at times, but one recognized them, whereas with you, I have never been certain – was not certain until tonight, when you admitted it, that you even knew at all. And I have still no idea – not the faintest idea – what it means to you – if indeed it means anything. And I want to know, Verity – I'm damned if I know why, since I shall continue to suit myself in any case – but I insist that you tell me.'

'My word,' I said, getting up too, feeling very light, as if by a simple effort of will – this wonderful will I had discovered hiding inside me – I could transform myself into air and elude him, elude anyone who sought to hold me down.

'What is this, Joel? You have got everything in the world you have ever wanted. Are you running short of things to want?'

'And what the devil do you mean by that?' he said, his face scowling again, his fist clenching nervously against the mantelpiece.

'I mean, having stirred the emotions of so many other women, do you want mine too? Do you want my jealousy? Think carefully, Joel, for it would be a great inconvenience to you. As you say, you would go on just as you are, no matter how many scenes I made. And I cannot think my hysterics would amuse you for long.'

Once again he turned his back, as he had done several times during the long night, unwilling, it seemed, to expose more of his own feelings than he had to; and when he spoke, after a silence I bore with astonishing calm, it was to the empty hearth, the fire screen, the cold, uncomplicated marble.

'You were a child when we married, Verity. I was a man with my appetites already formed. And you grew up slowly. For a long time I was . . .'

'Bored with me?'

'Careful, I should have said – careful with you.'

'And I was most grateful. Will you not at least change your coat before you go down to the mill, for you have had a long drive?'

'Damnation,' he said, a mere whisper addressed once again to the mantelpiece. 'They should have named you Isabella, for your mother. You are not going to tell me, are you, whether I have wounded you or disgusted you or simply made you laugh – whether you hate me or you couldn't give a damn.'

'Oh, Joel, what an idea – hate and disgust. My word, such strong language—'

'Be careful,' he hissed. 'I warn you – take care – for I am not squeamish with women either, and I could find it in me to hurt you.'

But the door had opened again and Hannah looked in, dressed and with her hair done, but seeing me, she disappeared at once, taking his violence and whatever lay beneath it with her.

'It's late, Joel. The servants are all up.'

'Yes. I'll take a rasher or two of bacon, I think, before I go out again. Is there likely to be any new bread?'

'I'll find out.'

'Good,' he said, turning round, showing me his everyday face, the shadows under his eyes no deeper than when he had spent the night in town. 'And by the way, I thought I'd have a word with Dan Adair while I was about it.'

'Oh yes?'

'Oh no, because I couldn't find the fellow anywhere. Went to his lodgings, and one or two other places, and there wasn't a trace. His landlady wouldn't talk because she'd been paid not to, and being Irish, she'd rather take his money than mine, but it looks to me as if somebody at

467

Aycliffe's got word to him and he's blown – halfway across the Irish Sea by now, I reckon.'

And while I wondered how I would find the words to tell Elinor, he calmly selected a cigar, lit it, and, narrowing his tired eyes against the smoke, said, 'And if you haven't realized what a damn nuisance that is, I'll tell you, for without Adair there's no guarantee we'll have Tarn Edge ready in time. And I don't like it – not one little bit – when people let me down.'

30

Hannah set off that morning with Joel, bidding him leave her in Blenheim Lane so that she could see for herself the direction of Morgan Aycliffe's mind; and, returning some four hours later in the Aycliffe carriage, she was by no means pleased to find Elinor's door bolted against her.

'You will hardly deny me the right of access to my own sister,' she told me, her eyes hard, her tone as cold as December river water, and when I answered that it was not I but Elinor who denied her, she did not choose to believe me.

'You may think me meddlesome,' she said, holding herself as if her very spirit was stiffly corseted, 'but your view is not shared by my brother-in-law, Mr Aycliffe, who has seen fit not only to confide in me but to request my services as a go-between. There are certain matters which must be communicated to my sister, and, if she really cannot face me, than I trust there will be no objection if I slip a note under her door?'

But neither Hannah nor Morgan Aycliffe himself had any real meaning for Elinor that morning as she sat at the window of my best spare bedroom, docile and drowsy as an invalid, her hands patiently folded, her nature folded too, half asleep, until Daniel Adair should come to claim her. She was waiting, in fact, for a faithless man to prove his fidelity; for a self-indulgent man to put her interests above his own – waiting, I thought, for a miracle.

But, since miracles could certainly occur and no one had expressly forbidden her to write to him, I provided pen and paper and, quite openly, ordered her short, possibly heartrending letter to be taken round to his address. And while we waited for a reply, which I, for one – and possibly Elinor too – did not expect, I marvelled at her calm.

'He will be very angry with me on the surface,' she said, 'and very frightened underneath. He was so poor, you see, as a child – poor in a way we can't begin to understand – and so a house in Blenheim Lane, and all that goes with it, seems like paradise to him, instead of a prison. And now I have taken his paradise away. Yes, he will be very cross, and very worried about how to make a living, and about what my husband could do to him – for he has always taken Morgan for a vindictive man, but as soon as I speak to him, explain to him, then I shall make everything right. I have not always been rich myself, which he fails to take into account. I managed for years to do up my own buttons and laces, and my own hair. And you surely remember the skill I had with my needle?'

And when she had repeated it all to me for the third time I understood she did not believe a word of it.

'Emma-Jane Hobhouse called that morning, having heard a whisper from her parlourmaid, who had a sister in Morgan Aycliffe's service, but Hannah reached the drawing room before me and by the time I arrived Emma-Jane was in full possession of the facts as Hannah had chosen to display them – not lies, since Hannah never lied, but a simple distortion of the truth, for everybody's good.

'Naturally I would not say this to everyone,' she was telling an eagle-eyed Emma-Jane as I entered the room, 'but we have known you all our lives and I imagine you have always thought her highly strung – one minute up in

469

the air, the next wallowing in the mire – our mother was much the same, excitable and delicate; it was always either laughter or tears with nothing in between, and such natures, while delightful, are often fragile. And, as you know, she recovered very slowly, if at all, from the birth of her last child. Not all women are blessed with your amazing resilience, Emma-Jane – those beautiful healthy boys, one after the other, my word. But you will remember how my sister became – well – rather odd, very nearly a total invalid, after Cecilia was born? Yes, yes, of course you do, for you often remarked it, and I have even heard you wonder if it was her failure to give her husband a son which made her so morose. And you may well have been right, Emma-Jane – you may well have been remarkably astute – for these things prey on the mind and depress the spirits, giving rise to swings of mood and temper which must, eventually, result in a certain fraying of the nerves. Well, my sister's nerves are very frayed. I am at liberty to say no more than that. You may think it sudden, Emma-Jane, but we have long seen it coming, and if you think carefully you will realize the many occasions lately on which she had not been herself. Yes? I felt sure of it. No, no, we did not think our local doctors competent to prescribe in such a case. Mr Aycliffe has returned to London for the express purpose of consulting a specialist. Yes, indeed, it is a tragedy; the poor man has lost one wife, has been obliged to disown his only son, and now finds himself with three daughters to provide for, and a wife who is just a shadow – a mere shadow of herself. And on top of that there has been some trouble with the business. Yes, I don't properly understand it, but on his return from London I believe Mr Aycliffe found his affairs in a terrible state – oh my goodness, I couldn't begin to comprehend the details, and no one has mentioned the word 'embezzlement' in my hearing. I only know he has discharged his manager, or, at least, it may even be the man has run off in the night, which sounds unlikely – and would certainly be an admission of something or other. But that is what I have heard.'

When Emma-Jane had gone away, happy to spread the word and even happier to contemplate Elinor in a state of mental decay, Hannah turned to me and said very coldly, 'Do not imagine that I accuse Mr Adair falsely of theft, since he has stolen another man's peace of mind, nor my sister of insanity, since that is the only charitable view I can take of her present behaviour.'

Joel came home at noon and, calling me into his study, put Elinor's letter to Daniel Adair into my hands.

'You knew she had written this?'

'Yes.'

'Splendid. Absolutely first-rate, Verity. Tell me, are you part of a conspiracy to ruin my sister, or is it merely that you too have lost your wits?'

'I saw no harm to it since I knew he would be gone. You said yourself he would have bolted . . .'

'Yes, and so you allowed her to send this pathetic nonsense to his lodgings, to that landlady of his who was plainly sired by a vulture, and who has just extracted a hundred pounds from me for its return.'

'Oh,' I said. 'Oh no.'

And then, looking at him keenly, I said, 'No, Joel. I don't believe you.'

'And why not?'

'Because you would not have paid. You would have found something to threaten her with in return – and how much could it take to frighten a lodging-house keeper? I believe I could do it myself.'

'Aye, I don't doubt it. But Aycliffe would have paid and Elinor would have paid – a year from now when she is safely back where she belongs – and gone on paying to safeguard her good name. Because a year from now she'll value her place in the world, and she'll be terrified of anything that could remind her husband of the past. She'll have to earn her keep in Blenheim Lane after this – haven't you the sense to see it? – and love letters, my girl, are an indulgence quite beyond her means. Are there any more, do you think? Adair said not. But then, what else would you expect Adair to say.'

'Mr Adair? You saw him, then? He has not gone away after all?'

'Ah no,' he said, his mouth curving with a grim, altogether malicious humour. Opening his cigar box with a leisurely hand, he lit a cigar and inhaled deeply, enjoying his body's response to the tobacco and to the pleasure of making me wait.

'Oh, he bolted all right,' he said at last through the fragrant smoke. 'About as far as Leeds, I reckon, before he got to thinking what a pleasant little thing she is, my sister, and that if she'd had the good sense to bring her jewellery away with her, he might as well come back and dry her tears.'

'He does care for her, then?'

'So it would seem – moderately, at any rate, although five hundred pounds in his pocket and certain promises soon cured him of it.'

I sat down, oppressed not by fatigue but by an immense grey vapour of sadness, wreathing itself around me like the tobacco smoke encircling Joel's self-confident head, his complete certainty that every man could be bought, every woman sold, if the price was right.

'That was handsome of you,' I told him. 'But what if he takes your money and your sister as well?'

And because that was exactly what he would have done himself, he smiled.

'No, no. I thought of that and allowed for it. Five hundred pounds will tide him over, and certainly it was more than he expected, for he knows and I know that I could have had him for less, but it can hardly guarantee his future. He can't go back to Ireland and live like a lord on five hundred pounds – not for long, at any rate – and, if I read him aright, his ambitions are just a little larger than his capabilities. He needs someone to show him the way – like Ira Agbrigg did – and I like hungry men, Verity. I can use hungry men. If he lies low until Elinor is safely home, I may just decide to take him under my wing.'

'And he trusts you?'

'Of course not. But he wants what I can give him, and he knows that if he goes off with my sister he has no chance with me at all. And apart from making that grand gesture and giving him five hundred pounds more than I need have done, I let him know just how and why he could serve me. He can consider the five hundred pounds a retainer if he likes – nothing to do with love letters at all. That's what I'd do in his place. He's not wedded to the building trade, and he's just the kind of footloose charmer I need to sell my lightweight cloth in warmer climates than these. And, in a year or two when Aycliffe's gone, and Elinor has claimed her reward – who knows? If she should still have an eye for him then, which I doubt, I'll gladly look the other way.'

'And where exactly is he now?'

'At the Swan, waiting for me and the afternoon coach. He has a sister in Liverpool – or a woman, at any rate – who can give him bed and board, and since I have business there myself, I may as well use him as a travelling companion. And the more people who see us, the better, for if the dog had really seduced my sister – as somebody may be putting about – then I'd be more likely to knock him down than ride with him to Liverpool, wouldn't I? So you may talk some sense to Elinor, and then, when I come home in a day or two – and if Hannah has done her work well with brother Aycliffe – we may all be at peace again.'

But Elinor, it seemed, was at peace already, not with the wholesome serenity of true content but with an apparent refusal to face up to her situation that was as difficult to grapple with as a handful of thin air.

'Poor Daniel,' she said, when I gave her back her letter and told her how it had been obtained. 'I suppose he could do no other, for Joel is very overbearing, and if he insisted on offering money I know my Daniel is not the man to refuse. So, we are to go to Liverpool. Well, I confess I had not thought of Liverpool, but one place is as good as another, and I expect you will be relieved to see the back of me. Dear Mrs Stevens, do run downstairs for me, for I am certain I heard the door, and if there is a letter and it is left too long on the hall table, my sister is sure to waylay it. Naturally she will burn it unopened, for although Hannah may feel free to destroy my letters she would never dream of reading them. Do hurry, Mrs Stevens – and hurry back. Verity, I fear Hannah will be a great problem, for she got in here just now while you were with Joel, and she has the strangest notion that I must return to Blenheim Lane – to my husband. Well, I laughed a little at that. I couldn't help myself, for the very idea of our being together again is quite comic. After all, he didn't want me to begin with – hasn't wanted me for ages – and he couldn't possibly forgive me now. Even Hannah agreed that he couldn't forgive me. My going away can make no difference to him, except that it will save him money, for I have always been so spendthrift and careless. He can still be a Member of Parliament and have his apartment in London, and he can even put the good china back in the drawing room when I am not there to break it. It is not as if he cared for me, Verity, for he does not. You know that, don't you? So I shall sit here, if I may, as quietly as a little cat, until Daniel comes to fetch me away. Was that the doorbell again? Mrs Stevens has been an age – do you suppose there is a letter and she and Hannah are having a tussle over it? Verity, do run downstairs and see, for Mrs Stevens is afraid of Hannah and lacks the authority. You are the mistress of the house, after all, and if she has taken my letter and you ordered her to give it back, I hardly see how she could refuse. Oh, Verity, darling, do hurry, for if she tears it I may never get all the pieces together again, and if she should burn it – for I suppose there must be a fire in the kitchen, even in this heat – Oh dear, oh dear, run, darling. Was that the door again?'

But there was no letter, no word, and when at last she had succumbed to a soothing potion of Mrs Stevens's and fallen fast asleep, I went thankfully outside, into the over-abundant summer garden, my mind requiring solitude and my lungs very much in need of air.

There was a hazy light across the lawn, with roses full-blown, ready to spill their petals at a touch, velvet butterflies and velvet flowers, so soon to wither, and it seemed my cousin Elinor was no better equipped for survival than they. At best the rose petals would be gathered and dried for potpourri, butterflies snared and spiked, their wings pinned for display, a small crucifixion that no one called cruel, since butterflies and flowers – and dowerless women – have no purpose but to decorate, and no voice to complain. And, seeing Elinor pinned butterfly-fashion in Morgan Aycliffe's drawing room or pressed like a dead flower between the harsh pages of his will, Joel's will, Hannah's will, anyone's will but her own, her defeat, which the surface of her own mind still refused to recognize, struck out at me, suffocating me, so that I knew I needed Crispin to help me breathe again.

And what really prevented me from going to him? Yesterday it would have seemed impossible, but last night I had spoken words to Joel and to Hannah which had seemed impossible too, and I had not been made to suffer for them. And feeling once again that sensation of lightness, as if my body could dissolve into the gold-flecked, soot-flecked air and float away, I went back to the house, ordered the carriage, and calmly changed my clothes.

And all it took, like most things in life, was determination and desire. Joel was on his way to Liverpool to spend a night or two on the town, I imagined, with Elinor's lover. Hannah had gone yet again to Blenheim Lane, where the requirements of her small nieces could be relied on to occupy her for some time. And it was simple enough to stop my carriage outside Rosamund Boulton's smart, rapidly expanding shop and get down, murmuring something about a fitting, while the carriage went on to Nethercoats to take a present of fruit and flowers to Emma-Jane and her tenth bouncing baby, with instructions to return for me in an hour. I even went inside and made some small purchases, leaving the parcels behind to be collected presently, and then, crossing the dusty, empty street, found, without difficulty, without chance encounters, the dim, narrow shop front of the ivory seller Crispin had told me of, whose back door would give me access to Cropper Alley and the Red Gin.

Coming from the glare of the street the shop was cool, empty, quite dark, the shopkeeper as wrinkled and squat as his oriental carvings, showing neither surprise nor interest in my readiness to put money in his hands for the privilege of seeing Mrs Dinah McCluskey. But he sent a boy to fetch her just the same, ignoring me while I waited, ignoring her as she came striding in, swinging her hips and her long black hair, not even looking up as she said, 'Well – would you believe it,' and led me away.

The alley was worse, in the hot daylight, than I remembered it; fouler, slimier, the creaking stairway at the back of the inn narrower, noisier, the woman beside me bolder, her black eyes inquisitive and scornful.

'Are you sure he's at home?' I asked her, feeling the need to say something, and, sensing that I had no idea how to address her, her smile deepened.

'Oh yes. He's in all right. I know what goes on in my own house – not like some folks, eh, love?'

And knocking smartly on his door, she gave me a familiar pat on the shoulder, her enjoyment huge and crude and possibly dangerous.

He was sitting at his worktable, reading, writing, as I had always imagined him, his student's face pale from lack of air and sleep, his shirt open at the neck and sleeves, his shoulders very thin beneath the cambric. And for a moment, because he was completely astonished and I was completely overjoyed, we were speechless and foolish with our emotion.

'Verity, there has to be a reason.'

'Yes. I needed you.'

'Something has happened?'

'Yes. But not to me. I just needed you.'

'Then here I am. Come in and close the door. That's all you've ever needed to do.'

His arms closed then around me, cool and light; no rock to lean on, no bulk with which to defend me, but a clear honesty that did not seek to twist me or crush me into any shape other than my own.

'What would you change in me, Crispin?'

'Nothing. And you?'

'Nothing.'

'Surely, you'd make me thrifty and sensible – and ambitious?'

'No. An impractical dreamer, just as you are. I love you. Spendthrift and too ready to borrow money from men you think can spare it. Naïve sometimes, and other times too clever by half. I love you. Proud of your own complex, spiky, uncomfortable character, because the last thing you'd want to be is simple and easy. Innocent and cynical at the same time. The only person I've ever trusted, although basically your disposition is too nervous to be reliable. I love you.'

'Darling – have you come to say goodbye?'

'I don't know. But it seems natural to be here. Is it possible that it's all happened before? That we've been going round and round in circles for an eternity, because I've kept on making the wrong decision – thinking it was all so impossible when all I ever needed to do was come in and close the door like you told me? No, no, don't be alarmed. It's not the sunstroke. I feel quite well. You said I would come here sooner or later, didn't you? How nice for you, to be always right.'

'Are you going to tell me your reason?'

'Oh – I had one, or two, that seemed very pressing when I started. But now that I am here, I think it is mainly that I want to make love to you.'

'Oh yes – yes, please do. In fact, perhaps that's exactly what I need, to be bullied, taken—'

'Yes,' I told him, pushing him gently towards his meagre, impeccably folded bed. 'Sometimes you need to be a little boy again because you didn't get it right the first time.'

And once again I had dissolved in air, once again I was impossibly light, totally powerful, for I knew of no one who could put chains on the wind, which blew in whatever direction it chose and, being invisible, had only to stand still to evade its pursuers, had only to bide its time.

But afterwards, with my head on his bare, brittle shoulder, I said, 'My cousin Elinor has left your father.' And I waited, praying he would be compassionate.

'Oh – so that's it. I believe I'm sorry.'

'For her?'

'Yes, but then, I was always sorry for her. For him too, oddly enough. Perhaps I've grown up sufficiently now to stop hating him. Presumably she has a lover?'

'Yes, Daniel Adair.'

'His foreman?' he said, unable to suppress a grimace of distaste. 'Surely she could have made a better choice than that.'

And sitting up, drawing my knees to my chin and clasping my arms around them, my back arched slightly away from him, I shook my head.

'What choice? I don't think she made a choice at all. He was there. She's reached a point in her life where she desperately needed to fall in love, and so she fell in love with him. Choice? What could Elinor know about choice? You have no sisters, Crispin, and so you can't know how they bring us up. Choices are for boys, not girls. You have the bother of wondering what to do with your lives, but we

478

know, right from the start. Find a husband, they tell us; a rich one, if you can, and if not, any husband, any man at all who's willing to put a ring on your finger. And when you've got him, cheat him. My old maid Marth-Ellen told me that many a time and I never heard my mother contradict her. And I can remember Elinor's mother, my Aunt Hattie, doing her mending at Low Cross and telling us, "There are good men and bad men, girls. If you get yourself a bad one blind him in both eyes, if he's good just blind him in one. If you spend five shillings, tell him it cost you ten and pocket the difference. That's the only way to live with a man, although even a bandy-legged tinker is better than no man at all." So don't blame Elinor for running down the aisle to your father. She was only doing what she'd been raised to do. She didn't even understand why he wanted her. It just seemed a miracle to her that he did. It's not her fault, surely, that she grew up just a shade too intelligent to settle for being a painted doll? Choice. She began life as a nuisance to her father – as I did – because she was a girl and he wanted boys to help him in the mill. She was pushed into marriage by her brother, who wanted a useful connection. She was used by your father, who would have done better to work off his passions in a brothel. And now her helplessness appalls me. They will parcel her up – Joel and your father – and put her wherever it suits them best. They will discuss her and dispose of her as if she had no more comprehension than a carriage horse. And there is nothing she can do about it. You talk of your factory children, Crispin, who are put out to labour by their parents when they are too young to be called free agents, and you complain because it is the parents who profit from that labour. But what about young ladies? They marry us off before we are old enough to make a fuss, and to keep us docile they teach us nothing – nothing, Crispin – that we could ever use to earn a living and set ourselves free. They create a fashion for useless silly females, and that is what we become – useless and silly, so that if childbirth doesn't kill us, or milk fever, we die slowly of boredom. And, like my Aunt Hattie said, even that's better than being a spinster, since everybody knows spinsters die from frustration and shame.'

He put his hand on my shoulder, very gently, let it travel down my spine and back again, and then clasped his fingers loosely around my wrist.

'I am a man, Verity. Do I oppress you?'

Taking his finely chiselled face between my hands, I kissed him and quite suddenly laughed.

'No. I suppose you are just as bad as all the rest, but I chose you, which is a different matter. And I need you.'

'You have me,' he said, lying on his back and sighing with apparent content, boyish and rather frail as he often was in moments of emotion. 'Indeed you have me.'

And as I bent over him, claiming him, it was of no importance to me whatsoever that my carriage must already be waiting, the horses fretting, the driver wondering, beginning to worry. I was here, by my own choice, and I would leave, in the same fashion, as I chose. And whatever befell me next month, or next year, I would depend on no one for my salvation. I would choose to defend myself, no object of passivity and pity like Elinor but a woman who understood that, in the final instance, there is always an alternative – that if nothing else, at least one may claim the right to refuse.

31

I had not thought my relations with Hannah could worsen, but in those last hot August days, our bitterness became a solid presence, a sharp-clawed hand slicing through our good intentions, so that the entire household became irritable and cautious, the maids clumsy, the children fractious, Joel more prone than ever to eat his dinner at the Swan.

'Ah well,' my mother said airily. 'At least she will have to get married now, dear, since she clearly cannot continue to live with you in this fashion. Yes, I feel she has made all the alterations to Redesdale parsonage one could expect the squire to tolerate, so there is nothing left for her now but to name the day – although whether it will be Julian Ashley or George Brand, I am not yet certain.'

And indeed, Mr Brand once again entered the forefront of our lives when Hannah, realizing with what ease anyone could dispose of Mr Ashley, requested him to visit Elinor and if he could not coax her then to terrify her into decent behaviour.

But even the evangelical Mr Brand, the veins in his mighty neck swelling, his voice throbbing with passion as he spoke of hell's eternal bonfire, had little effect.

'Poor man,' she said, watching him from her window as he went away with tears in his honest eyes. 'He really cares, doesn't he, that I shall spend eternity roasting away. Oh dear, do run after him, Verity, and explain in your own clever fashion that I should actually prefer it, so long as it was with Daniel, to lying in the cold ground with the worms, and my husband. Do run and tell him, for he looks so sad.'

But Hannah, who had been biding her time, appeared quite suddenly in the doorway, filling it entirely, not with her height alone but with the awesome, outraged quality of her anger.

'I don't know you,' she said, her eyes fastening themselves on her sister, ignoring everything else. 'I don't recognize you. Have you no shame?'

And Elinor – who had never openly defied Hannah before – desperately seized the remnants of her courage and rushed shrilly to the attack, a downy little canary making its pathetic assault on an eagle.

'Well, and if we are talking of shame, what of you – for I know you have taken my letters.'

'What letters?' Hannah said, briefly puzzled, and then, understanding, she smiled as Joel often did before striking a blow. 'Letters. There have been no letters, silly goose, and there will be none. He is in Liverpool, with Joel's money in his pocket, praying for you to make up your mind to go home again, so that he can repair the harm you have done him. The man cannot afford you, even if he wanted you – which is by no means certain – it is as simple as that. You have robbed him of one career and unless you come quickly to your senses you will rob him of another. I think you should know that Joel has made him a business proposition which depends entirely on your return to your husband. So, little sister, if you care for the man at all – as you keep on insisting that you do – you should go home, should you not, to your husband and children, so that the man may be prosperous again, and happy. Surely, if you love him, you should desire his happiness – and his prosperity – shouldn't you? I am very certain he desires to be prosperous himself.'

'No,' Elinor said, backing away, her face ghastly, and, running to the window she leaned out, dragging the warm air into her lungs like a woman suffocating, drowning.

'No, Hannah,' she whispered, her tiny hands clinging to the window frame as if she thought we meant to prise her loose by force. 'No – no – you don't understand. I can't go back. Hannah, you can't know what it is, what it feels like. It makes me sick, Hannah – sick, now, even thinking about it. I could endure it once, but not now. If you condemn me to that, Hannah, then you condemn me to death – I warn you.'

'Nonsense – theatrical nonsense,' Hannah snorted, although she moved forward just the same, as I did, towards that wide, high, empty window, in case Elinor should really be desperate enough to harm herself. But Elinor, feeling our approach, stiffened like a trapped animal and slid bonelessly to the ground; and there, clutching her stomach, she was so distressingly and agonizingly sick that even Hannah was alarmed and, for a day or two, much kinder.

Yet when the doctor had been called – and Emma-Jane Hobhouse had been made aware of it – and Elinor, after a series of restless nights, had recovered sufficiently to take a reasonable bowlful of Mrs Stevens's special broth, the same problems still remained and Hannah – well aware that Morgan Aycliffe might yet refuse to receive his wife, even if she could be persuaded to return – set to work again.

'How busy she is,' my mother murmured. 'How utterly untiring. I feel certain that Elinor's house has never before been so well ordered, nor her children so excellently administered. I saw them the other day, taking their carriage exercise with their dear aunt, all of them dressed so exactly alike, and so impeccably neat and tidy that had they not looked so expensive they could have been charity children – eyes downcast, hands folded in their little laps, not a word for the cat – you will know what I mean. And although I intended this in the kindest possible fashion, what a convincing schemer our Hannah has turned out to be. Really, she is so very believable, for everywhere I go lately people are commiserating with me on the collapse of Elinor's health. "Poor child," they say, "so young – but then her mother's nerves were always uncertain and these things run in families." Naturally I look solemn and nod my head in agreement – for I dare do no other – but the odd thing is that I cannot remember your Aunt Hattie ever being so delicate. And that is rather strange, since I knew her far better than Mrs Hobhouse and Mrs Oldroyd did, who have both spent hours recently reminding me of her spasms and her palpitations – all of which I have quite forgotten. Well – I do remember one occasion when she took to her bed and was too ill to see anyone – yes, I remember that well enough – but when Emma-Jane mentioned it I didn't like to confess that it was not altogether the mysterious malady your Aunt Hattie – and Hannah – said it was but merely that your uncle – Joel's father – had given her a black eye. Tell me, dear, are you going to hide Elinor away forever? She would be welcome, you know, to come to me at Patterswick. She could sit in my garden, in the sunshine, quite safely, for I always hear a carriage at least a mile away and could whisk her off to bed at the very approach of Emma-Jane.'

But Morgan Aycliffe, from his bachelor apartment in Westminster, had made it clear that he could tolerate no breath of scandal. His wife might lose her health and her sanity if she chose but not her reputation, and so, throughout the fine weather, she remained on a chaise longue by the bedroom window, becoming gradually so lethargic that she could barely make the effort to brush her hair, could see no point – just as in the days following the birth of her last child – in getting dressed since she would soon be going to bed again, and, in any case, had nothing fit to wear because her husband, having sent her the very barest of essentials, had locked her wardrobe door and hidden the key.

'I'm so tired,' she would say. 'So very tired,' and, closing her eyes, she would allow an afternoon, a day, a week, to slip away from her like water.

'Oh – how wonderful. Is it really Tuesday? Do you know, I thought it was Monday.' And, gradually, there was no more talk of letters, no mention at all of Daniel Adair.

She slept, grew pale enough to convince the sharpest, shrewdest observer she was ailing, and became vague and uncertain, so that the few who did see her – our maids, who gossiped to other people's maids – were able to add substance to Hannah's hint of a nervous collapse, creating a climate of sympathy, rather than ridicule, for Morgan Aycliffe.

'Poor man,' they said, remembering that his first wife had been odd too. And before anyone had time to wonder if the gentleman himself could be in any way to blame, Emma-Jane Hobhouse, still smarting from Elinor's brief flirtation with Bradley, spoke up in his defence.

'He was too good to her,' she declared. 'He had her waited on hand and foot, put no limit on her spending, never said a harsh word about the bills she ran up. And now look at him, living in those poky rooms in London, doing his best to safeguard all our interests, and worrying himself sick, I shouldn't wonder, about her and those poor children. She hasn't seen them, you know, not once since she fell ill – not that she ever saw much of them in any case. In fact, my Bradley always says he doubts if she can tell them apart. Well – poor Mr Aycliffe. Thank goodness there's always Hannah. I don't know what any of the Barforths would do without Hannah. We all know that Joel relies on her far more than on Verity, who always has her head in the clouds.'

And when this was gleefully repeated to me by Lucy Oldroyd, who wanted to be everybody's best friend, I could have laughed and cried, for Hannah was soon to leave me, and although I was glad of it, I knew I would miss her.

I was, just then, extremely occupied, for the house at Tarn Edge, with or without Daniel Adair, would be ready for occupation by Chistmastime, and it seemed that every coach brought me curtain samples, carpet samples, sketches of plasterwork and marquetry and hand-painted Chinese wallpaper, or mysterious packages that, spilling sawdust and straw and splitting fingernails, opened to reveal an exquisite piece of Sèvres or Meissen, some treasure of Wedgwood or Coalport, ordered by Joel without asking – without apparently caring – whether they suited me or not.

I was on my knees one morning, unpacking a potpourri vase, my fingers gloating over the cloudy design of roses and pink-draped, pink-limbed dancers, when the skirt of Hannah's serviceable brown morning dress came swishing across the floor towards me and, looking up, I saw by her iron composure that she had something of importance to communicate.

'For the new house?' she said, indicating the vase with her foot.

Nodding, I got up, brushing a clinging wisp of straw from my sleeve, bracing myself, perhaps, since the new house could hold little interest for Hannah, who surely did not mean to live in it.

'Yes. I think it is one of a pair, so no doubt we shall be having another delivery ere long.'

'Oh, more than one, I believe, for when my brother starts spending there is no end to it. But you will be wanting to know my intentions . . .'

'Joel will want to know,' I said sharply, desperately. 'You should talk first to Joel, surely – if you have come to a decision.'

But Hannah in her mood of cold dignity was far more alarming to me than in the heat of her anger, and, sensing my reticence and her own power, she smiled.

'I think that is for me to decide. You, at any rate, Verity, will hardly beg me to stay.'

'You have decided to go, then?'

'I have. And before I do, I must warn you that this change in my own affairs will in no way lessen my attempt to put my sister's house in order. I am determined to see her restored to her rightful place before my own marriage, if possible, but if not, then very soon after. And I would like to make it very clear that if you persist in encouraging her in her foolishness, then you and I cannot be reconciled. Mr Aycliffe has indicated to me in a recent letter that he has managed to overcome his scruples – his natural repugnance – largely due to my own efforts in preventing gossip. And I will not have those efforts wasted, Verity. I have prepared the way for Elinor's return to respectability, at some cost to myself, since I have not enjoyed putting about these tales of her mental instability, whatever you

486

may think to the contrary. And yet, instead of helping me, as I might have expected, you have taken an attitude that I fail to understand. And I am not the only one, Verity, for Joel does not understand you either, and is most seriously displeased – almost ill at ease, whenever I mention your name. I do not wish to part from you on these terms, Verity, but in your present state of mind you give me no choice.'

I walked slowly to the open window, as Elinor had once done, but my motive was not escape, merely a desire not to be overheard; and, ascertaining that there was no gardener snipping off dead roses on the path below, no maid gathering the petals for the myriad of purposes of Mrs Stevens, I came back again knowing I had little chance of convincing her.

'Hannah, let me say two things to you – first of all, there is no reason for you to leave us unless you really wish to do so. Tarn Edge will be very large, you know, with space enough even for two women who do not always see eye to eye. But marriage – if that is what you decide on – may give you a clearer understanding of Elinor's troubles, and I must ask you to face the fact that she may never bring herself to overcome them. Morgan Aycliffe has the legal right to compel her to return, but you know, as I know, that he will never use it. He would never inflict on himself the humiliation of a captive wife. And I will not allow you, or anyone else, to bully her into thinking she has no choice. Yes, yes, Hannah, I know how sincerely you believe you are acting for her own good. I know you have always been well-meaning, even when you have been most misguided. But in this case you fail to take into account the strength of her physical repulsion – a subject on which you cannot be well informed. You accuse me of not helping you with her, but what help could I give other than turning her out and closing my door behind her so she has nowhere else to go but Blenheim Lane? Well, I have housed stray dogs and cats many a time and so I think I may do the same for your sister. And when you are married and settled at Redesdale, I doubt that Mr Ashley would make any objections to your receiving her there, for he is a Christian gentleman, after all.'

And instead of the indignation, the moralizing, the fresh reproaches I had expected, her face flooded with a scorching crimson, the most painful colour I had ever seen, and she said harshly, 'Did I mention Redesdale – or Mr Ashley?'

'No – no—'

'No, I did not. In fact, it would be most improper in me to do so, since I put an end to my relations with Mr Ashley quite ten days ago.'

'Oh – I'm sorry – at least, I suppose – but then, I have often thought Mr Brand may be more suited—'

'Mr Brand,' she said, clasping her hands together, that dreadful colour still hot and fierce in her cheeks. 'Mr Brand has been your candidate all along, has he, Verity? And your mother's too, I gather, from something she said to me the other day. It will displease you then to know that Mr Brand has engaged himself to a Miss Mayfield from Halifax, a nice enough little woman – which, really, is hardly my concern, since I must now tell you that when his period of mourning is over, sometime in the winter, I have promised to marry Mr Agbrigg, a promise I most assuredly will not break.'

And so shocked was I that I began to laugh until, seeing her face, I froze and said weakly, 'Oh no, Hannah – no, no, Hannah – you can't do that – really, you can't do that.'

She seized my wrist with her hard, unrelenting hand and dragged me as close as she could, dominating me with her height and indignation, with the veneer of Barforth grandeur and Barforth fury that still remained.

'And why not? My sister fell in love with a bricklayer, did she not? Then why should I not do the same with a mill hand – although he is far from being a mill hand now.'

'You can't mean that, Hannah – surely – not love—'

'Can't I? Why can't I? Are you brooding on physical repulsion again, Verity? Mr Agbrigg may repel you but it doesn't necessarily follow that he repels me. Perhaps I am not so nice in my notions as you and Elinor – perhaps I can't afford to be. Unless, of course, it turns out that I have rather more in my head than this eternal business of repulsion. Yes, yes, he's far from handsome and exceedingly rough-spoken, I grant you, although the speech, at least, can be remedied – a pauper brat from nowhere, who doesn't even know his real name, but a man who has risen by his own efforts – hindered, not helped, by those around him – and who could rise much further.'

'Good God, Hannah, rise where? He's the manager of Lawcroft Mill—'

Her temper flaring, she pinched my wrist hard, meaning to hurt, and with a powerful movement of her arm and shoulder pushed me away.

'Yes, he's the manager of Lawcroft, and what will Julian Ashley ever be? What will George Brand ever be? Love. Of course I don't love him. I don't love anybody. I've gone beyond that. I'm simply at a point in my life where I must marry someone. I must have an establishment of my own – must – absolutely must – and I won't confine myself to the limitations of a parson's wife. What is it, Verity? Do you want to see me at Redesdale, walking behind the squire's lady, mending and making do and being glad of your castoffs, and Elinor's? Or with George Brand, who'd take me off to some pest hole in Africa as a missionary, once he got his hands on me? Or would you really like to see me stay here and grow old and dependent on you – the poor spinster sister who does the plain needlework and has her dinner upstairs with the children when there are guests? Oh no. I was cheated of the life I should have had, Verity – the life that was given to you in my place – and now I must do the best I can for myself. I would have married Julian Ashley, make no mistake about it, or George Brand – one or the other – as soon as I was sure there was no better alternative. Oh yes, Verity, Mr Agbrigg may be plain and common and what of it? Mr Adair was handsome and common and I never heard you object to him.'

I was appalled now, beyond any hope of concealment.

'Hannah, Hannah – how will you live – oh, Hannah, take care.'

'I will,' she said, still flushed but growing hard again. 'Very good care. I shall live in the millhouse, where I would have lived with Edwin. There will be a great deal of gossip, of course, and Emma-Jane Hobhouse may not invite me to dinner, but you will defend me, I feel sure of it, just as you have defended Elinor. I have always had certain ideas about the millhouse, as you know, and in my hands it will become very comfortable – really, most pleasing. And this town is growing, so rapidly, that ere long we shall be a fully fledged city with our own council, our own mayor – and I see no reason why the first Lord Mayor of Cullingford should not be Mr Agbrigg. Newcomers to the area will know nothing of his origins, and others will forget. They will think of him simply as a Cullingford man of business, well-to-do and well connected, and I do not think anyone could dispute my suitability for the position of Mayoress. I may never be so rich as you and Elinor, but I shall be immensely respected. I shall be important in this town, Verity. People will know my name and court my favour. People will stand back to let me pass. And I shall have one tremendous satisfaction. I shall have a very clever son, for with proper guidance, I do not think there are any limits to what Jonas could achieve. Now then – I do believe I hear Joel's carriage? Yes, I thought I had timed things aright, for he mentioned at breakfast time he would be back around midmorning. I would be obliged to you, Verity, if you would give him my news.

Naturally I do not expect him to be pleased and so I will wait upstairs until his first reaction has cooled. Perhaps you will come up presently and let me know?'

But Joel, on hearing that his favourite sister was to marry Ira Agbrigg, largely, it seemed, because she wanted to be Lady Mayoress and mother to the unpleasant Jonas, was so incensed that, not caring who heard him, he strode into the hallway and bellowed her name loudly up the stairs.

'Yes, Joel?' she said, coming as slowly as she dared, and snarling something under his breath, he took her roughly by the elbow and pushed her into the study.

'I'll turn him off,' I heard him growl at her. 'I'll have him out of Lawcroft and out of the valley by nightfall.'

Hannah must have expected him to say that and, not feeling my presence to be required, I went out into the garden, putting distance between myself and such a lava flow of true Barforth rage.

I must have walked more slowly than I had intended, for it did not seem long before Joel was out on the gravel drive in front of the house, shading his eyes from the sun and calling, 'Verity, where the devil are you?'

He was still very angry, very ready to hurt, but his temper was in control now, an invisible menace chained to his will, although the horse, standing between the shafts of his phaeton, caught the spark of it and, shivering, began to toss her showy chestnut head.

'Is Hannah – all right?'

'All right? I wouldn't say that. I'd say she's as cracked as the other one. I'd say they're a pair of prime idiots, my sisters. And I'd say Agbrigg's a deep one – one I'll have to watch. Agbrigg – my God – how can she do this to me?'

'Can you stop her?'

He pulled on his driving gloves, his hands independently angry, I thought, because it was no longer possible for a man in his position to take a whip to a disobedient woman; nor was it likely that the shrewd Ira Agbrigg would oblige, as Daniel Adair had done, and part with his bride for five hundred pounds.

'I could make it damned awkward for her. I could take his house and his job and see he didn't get another hereabouts. But the world doesn't stop at the end of the Law Valley, and they've calculated I won't do it anyway. She's not Elinor. She might just go with him – calculating again that I'd fetch them back. And he's useful to me. He knows a lot about my business. It's always been at Low Cross, remember, that I've experimented with my new cloth and my new machines, where we've adapted and adjusted, and I don't really want my trade secrets put up for auction, do I? That's been part of their calculations too.'

'So you'll give them your blessing?'

'Hardly. Listen, Verity, go and see Agbrigg this afternoon. Find out just where he stands in the matter, for it strikes me it was all Hannah's idea. He still talks about his wife as if she were waiting for him at home with the kettle on instead of being in her grave, and, for the life of me, I can't believe it ever entered his head to make love to my sister. So, if he's unwilling, or uneasy, if she's bullied him into it, then I want to know, because then I can bully him out of it and still keep him on at Lawcroft. Understand? I'll be at Tarn Edge around four o'clock. See me there.'

The millhouse at Lawcroft was cool and quiet as always when I arrived, my old home invaded by strangers, one of them, the boy Jonas, coming out to greet me, his pale, narrow face and slanting, colourless eyes informing me that he was aware of the situation and gloried in it. And as he went off to the mill to fetch his father, with shoulders hunched in the fashion of one who spends much time stooping over his books, I understood that whatever private reservations Mr Agbrigg might have about taking a Barforth wife, young Jonas had no doubts at all that a Barforth stepmother was just his style.

The surviving Agbrigg girl, Maria, hastily installed me

in the parlour, much smaller than I remembered it and overcrowded now with the old horsehair sofas and ungainly schoolroom chairs of the Agbriggs, but just the same it was the room where my brother Edwin had announced his intention of marrying Hannah, where Joel, on my own betrothal day, had congratulated me on my good sense, the room where I had last spoken to my father.

'Will you take some tea, Mrs Barforth?' Maria Agbrigg enquired, a prim, plain little mouse unlikely to inspire more than casual kindness in Hannah and declining the complication of cups and saucers, I was almost tearful with memory – with the perilous, painful game of wondering what might have been – when the door opened to admit my new prospective brother-in-law.

He had first come to this house as a hungry young man, cap in hand, to lay information against his workmates, desperate enough for anything that would release the trap of his poverty. And I saw now that, beyond the dark frock coat and well-pressed, well-cut trousers, beneath the cambric shirt and the sober but expensive necktie, he was still dissatisfied. He had lost his poor, sad Ann and nine of his children, and with them, perhaps, the last thread of gentleness in his nature, the last whispering hope of any real personal joy in life. But Ann's favourite son still remained – and one of her daughters with Ann's thin, fair hair and a touch of her frailty. I needed no more than ten minutes of Mr Agbrigg's time to realize he knew exactly how useful Hannah wanted to be to Jonas, how useful she could indirectly be to Maria, and that he had no intention of denying them their opportunities. Perhaps the idea of her as a woman had not even occurred to him until she decided that it should, but once the offer had been made, once it was all there before him, he would not let it go.

He had always felt the deepest admiration for Miss Barforth, he told me, keeping his eyes on the carpet. He believed her to be a truly marvellous woman and had no hesitation at all in placing his future, his children's future, in her capable hands. He was, of course, well aware of the vast social gulf between them. She was far above him and would always remain so, he would never dispute that, nor would he dispute the right of anyone to be surprised – annoyed – at her decision to marry so far beneath her station. But – and here he did, for a moment, glance palely at me and then away again – no one could deny that he was hard-working, which counted for a great deal in the Law Valley, and good-living, which may count for rather less but which, in a matter of this kind, was surely of value. Nor was there any question of financial gain on his part, since Miss Barforth had no fortune and no expectations and would be more likely to empty his pocket than fill it. Their decision to marry had been taken logically, he felt, and carefully, and since Miss Barforth was now a lady of some maturity and immense determination, one could safely credit her with the ability to know her own mind.

A speech, I thought, which bore Hannah's signature as clearly as those delivered from the hustings by Morgan Aycliffe, Hannah's voice speaking through her half-willing, half-eager bridegroom, saying, 'I am thirty-four years old and single, and I will do as I please.'

'She is very fond of my boy Jonas,' Ira Agbrigg said as he handed me into my carriage, speaking his own words now, as if he thought some kind of emotion appropriate to the occasion. 'Thinks she can make something of him.' And I drove away quite sadly, hardly knowing what I could say to Joel.

The afternoon was fine, the treetops already gold with approaching autumn, a thin, blue sky hazing to saffron on the horizon, the road to Tarn Edge shorter than usual since I was in no hurry, and empty of anyone who could delay me from reaching the spot where Joel's house was rising from the ground like a small cathedral.

The outer shell was completed now, the graceful Gothic spires giving height and presence to massive stone walls which sprouted, in every possible crevice, a midsummer

494

profusion of carved fruit and vines and mythological heads of tangled hair. The front entrance was wider, had more steps, more columns, more ironwork on the heavy oak door than the Assembly Rooms in Cullingford; the hall, still bare, was several square feet larger and had more doors opening from it; the sweep of the staircase was grander, climbing upwards to a landing as wide as the millhouse parlour, and a mighty window of ruby and emerald and sapphire glass. Joel's house, the shop front of his achievement and success, with Joel's phaeton already standing on the uncompleted drive, and another carriage I didn't recognize, a smart equippage with a coachman lounging moodily, thirstily perhaps, at the horses' heads.

Joel's house, smelling of new plaster and new paint; vast, empty spaces, a cool refuge from the dusty, sticky day, the silence shattered, not unpleasantly, by the unseen tapping of a workman's hammer, a saw slicing busily through wood, a house beginning to come alive. Bare boards under my feet, a happy clattering as I ran upstairs, a willingness to lose myself in these unknown rooms to furnish them, in my mind, not merely with chairs and tables, but with Blaize and Nicholas and Caroline, with my puppies' excited yelping, with Mrs Stevens stirring her broths and her medicines and her perfumes, with Hannah bringing her clever, spiteful Jonas and her embarrassed husband to call, with Elinor, drawing her chaise longue to the window, forgetting about the letters that never came, forgetting everything, perhaps, except that she was weary. And, with a sudden acute pang that took my breath away, I did not know if I would ever live here and forgot, for a terrifying moment, what I was doing here now, forgot my intentions and aspirations, my very name. And, closing my eyes, I could see nothing but an alleyway leading to the Red Gin and could hear a voice – not Crispin's, my own perhaps – telling me I had only to open the door.

But it was the window that came first to my hand, the new frame lifting jerkily to fulfil my need for air, and, leaning out a little, breathing greedily, gratefully, I saw Joel coming across the as yet unlandscaped garden, with a bare-headed, long-limbed woman I recognized as Estella Chase.

I had seen her last at the Assembly Rooms, arriving late with the Coreys and the Corey-Mannings and my mother, looking at Joel in a way I understood, letting her long, narrow hand linger on his arm, displaying her lean, thoroughbred body so that it would linger in his mind. And I saw that now, recently returned once again from London, she was doing the same, offering enough of herself, as she swayed close to him and then away again, to arouse – or re-arouse – his appetite. And although there was no reason in the world why I should not have called out to them, waved from the window, and gone tripping downstairs to greet them, I drew back a little and kept silent, even when they paused almost directly beneath me.

'We are dining with the Floods tonight,' she said, 'which is always a vast production, so I must be on my way. But now I have let you know I am home again, perhaps we shall not be strangers?'

'Surely not,' he told her, ready enough, I thought, to let her go since there were stonemasons and carpenters awaiting his instructions and the claims of his house, just then, were more important, more exciting, than any woman.

'Let me take you to your carriage,' he said, holding out a hand to steady her across the rough ground.

It was then, I think, that he looked up and saw my face at the window, my eyes somehow connecting with his, so that we were still looking at each other when he drew the surprised Estella Chase into his arms and kissed her very slowly, so that I could see the tip of his tongue against her lips, her own tongue flicker greedily to meet it, the excitement of her body nailing itself to his, which may not have been excited at all.

'Joel – darling – I thought you'd forgotten.'

496

'How could I ever do that?'

'Easily – wicked as you are. I'd quite decided to forget you.'

As she lifted her face once again for his kiss I found myself pressed hard against the bare wall, invisible now to them both, fists clenched, every nerve in my body clenched, it seemed, against the onslaught of my anger, the roaring, red-flecked Barforth fury which now, pounding inside my body, needed violence to be at peace.

I'll hurt him, I thought. I'll hurt him badly. He'll pay me for this.

Through the painful clamping of my teeth on my lower lip, the clawing of my own nails against my palms, hurting myself and willing him to feel the injury, I heard my mother's cool voice telling me how it could be done. He had kissed that woman without desiring her, simply to wound me, hoping to wound me, and so there would be no wounds, or none that he could see. I would not delight him with tantrums, nor flatter him with jealous tears. I would give him what his vanity least desired, my indifference, and, hurrying, running almost, I left that bare room behind me, reaching the landing, the stairs, flew down the hall, paused to catch my breath, and, walking through the heavy, iron-studded door, met them head on as they came around the side of the house.

'Ah, there you are,' Joel said, his face quite blank, although I could feel the calculation behind it, the cruelty, the eagerness for my reaction.

'Yes, dear,' I replied, with no idea at all how I made my voice so calm and bright when everything beneath the surface of my placid skin was trembling. 'Here I am. Here you are too, and Mrs Chance. It is Mrs Chance, isn't it? How nice to see you again.'

'Chase,' she said. 'My name is Chase. Oh yes, Mrs Barforth, I was driving by, and having heard you are building a palace, I could hardly restrain myself from taking a look.'

'Of course you could not restrain yourself, Mrs Chase. I do so perfectly understand. Well then, now that you have let us know you are home again, perhaps we shall not be strangers.'

And it could not have possibly escaped her that I had quoted the very words she had used to Joel a moment ago.

'Oh,' she said, her pale eyes staring. 'Quite so. But, heavens, the time. I really must fly, Mr Barforth, Mrs Barforth.'

We watched the carriage drive away in a taut silence.

'It won't please her,' he said, 'that you forgot her name, or appeared to.'

'If that is supposed to worry me, then I find I can hardly bring myself to care.'

'So I see. That surprises me, Verity. I don't think I've ever known you to take the trouble to dislike anyone before, and whatever can Mrs Chase have done to deserve the favour?'

And growing hard suddenly, I answered, 'I merely find her type of woman tedious. She has a great opinion of herself but, really, if it were not for her London gown and her London manner, I doubt if any man would give her a shilling.'

'Ah, so you think her a light woman?'

'Yes, when I think of her at all, which is seldom.'

'That I grant you,' he told me, coming to an abrupt halt. 'She is a light woman. And what I want to know now, Verity, is why that should bother you? My sister Elinor is a light woman, too. We both know that, and yet you were a tigress in her defence. Really, I continue to marvel at it.'

'Elinor has nothing to do with it.'

'Has she not? And has she nothing to do with this change in you?'

'What change? I am not changed.'

'Are you not?'

'No, I am exactly as I have always been, and if you

498

think otherwise, then it can only be that you have never looked.'

'So, I neglect you, do I? Have you any particular complaint to make?'

And because I could hear, beneath his words, the voice of his will urging, 'Fight me, Verity. Come, girl, bite me, scratch me,' and because I had found another, infinitely more subtle way to bite him, I said with all my mother's deliberate vagueness, 'Why no, darling, absolutely not. What an idea.'

But as we went back to the house, side by side, civilized again and cool, to talk of floor coverings and wall coverings and Ira Agbrigg, I was not sure who had won or why the battle had been fought at all. I only knew I felt sick at heart, desolate and bereaved and exceedingly weary, and that I did not wish my life to continue in this way.

32

In September, after a day in the saddle clearing his land of foxes, Squire Dalby felt a pain across his chest which, growing more and more acute, not only confined him to his bed for six weeks of glorious hunting weather but, by reminding him of his mortality, increased his determination to marry my mother.

'It is all because of his heir,' she told me when I drove over to visit them both. 'It is his grandson who inherits from him since he has lost his son, and as he has never seen eye to eye with his daughter-in-law, who has married again, he feels that she and her husband will turn me out of my cottage as soon as he is dead. Dear man – the world is full of cottages, and although I tell him repeatedly that I have money enough for all my needs, he simply cannot bring himself to believe it. He is totally convinced that the young squire will order me out of Patterswick with threats to set his dogs on me if I return, and he will not be persuaded that I would simply move to Redesdale or Floxley, or even come to you.'

'Perhaps you had better marry him, then.'

'Well, dear, I think I must consider it – in fact, that is the very least I can do after all his kindness. My dear old Dalby has convinced himself he is not long for this world and it is his gallantry, alongside his whim to annoy his daughter-in-law, which inclines him to take me for a wife. But, between ourselves, I think, with proper care, he may live a long time yet, and although I had made up my mind never to marry again, I think I might not altogether dislike the position of squire's lady.'

The wedding took place at Patterswick in the middle of November, in a church somewhat fittingly decorated with the richly tinted blooms of autumn, although my mother, coming down the aisle on Joel's arm, looked young enough to cause some consternation on the bridegroom's side of the church, where certain elderly Dalbys, having been informed that the bride was a widow and a grandmother, seemed unable to believe their eyes.

She was attended, once again quite fittingly, by a procession of children, Caroline and the three Aycliffe girls in white, flouncy dresses and pink sashes, Caroline in a temper because she had wanted a blue sash or a yellow one or, failing that, a pink dress, anything to make her stand out from her Aycliffe cousins.

'It is my grandmamma,' she had said, mutiny writ large across her scowling Barforth brow. 'She's only their mother's aunt, which makes them her second nieces, and that's nowhere near as close as me. I should come first, by myself in a pink dress, and they should just bunch along behind me – they're narrow enough to get down the aisle all three together, side by side.'

And Caroline, flying off in a rage at the denial of what she considered a perfectly reasonable request, was not to know that if Hannah had had her way, the Aycliffe girls would not have been there to trouble her at all.

'It is quite out of the question for them to be bridesmaids at such a time,' she had declared. 'Altogether ridiculous when one considers the state that family is in.'

But Hannah herself was in something of a state just then, having suffered greater humiliation than she had anticipated at Cullingford's reaction to her new engagement, led by Emma-Jane, who, conveniently forgetting that Hannah had jilted both Mr Ashley and Mr Brand, expressed great astonishment at the lengths some spinsters would go to in order to get themselves off the shelf.

'I was never so shocked in all my life,' she told me gleefully, looking better than I had seen her in years. 'I wonder Joel doesn't put a stop to it. But then he and Mr Agbrigg have always been so close – always whispering secrets together – and I suppose they're just like Lucy Oldroyd and me. We can't afford to have a fall-out because we know too much about each other. But, just the same, it's going to be awkward for you, isn't it, having him in the house, using your first name and making your children call him uncle. Naturally the rest of us can get out of inviting him, but I don't see how you can avoid it, Verity. Oh dear, you poor thing, you do have my sympathy. Thank goodness we won't have to come to the wedding, because I should cry, all the way through – I wouldn't be able to stop myself.'

Having this to contend with, Hannah was perhaps less vigilant than usual in the matter of my mother's bridesmaids, allowing herself to be taken by surprise when my mother, bypassing her authority, wrote directly to Mr Aycliffe in London, informing him of her marriage to a gentleman of considerable local importance and requesting that his daughters should attend her.

'Permission granted,' she told us, floating into my house one morning with a letter in her hand. 'Mr Aycliffe congratulates me on my forthcoming marriage and although he doesn't quite say it – and I didn't quite say it either – he appears to agree with me that a refusal to allow his daughters to be my bridesmaids would appear not only churlish but rather odd. And Mr Aycliffe does not wish to appear odd. I must invite Elinor too, you know – to avoid that slight suggestion of oddity – for if we are to play happy families we must do it right. Yes, absolutely, I must invite her, and I see no cause for alarm, Hannah. We can hardly hope to see Mr Adair on a white charger come to carry her away. And since neither the Hobhouses nor the Oldroyds will be there, I think we may manage her tolerably well. You had best get her a new gown, Verity, for unless her husband agrees to release her clothes, she will be a sorry sight.'

But Morgan Aycliffe had no intention of putting into his wife's faithless hands the costly silks and satins she had extracted from him, fearing, one supposes, that she would sell them to finance her escape or wear them to attract another lover.

'Mr Aycliffe's instructions have been most explicit,' his housekeeper, Mrs Naylor, informed me when I called, keeping me standing in the hallway with such scant courtesy that I understood she did not regard me as her master's friend. 'Undergarments and nightgowns he told me to send on to her, her hairbrushes – except the silver-backed ones – such toiletries as I deemed necessary, and a change of outer garments suitable for day wear – all of which I have done. I have made a list, Mrs Barforth, which I submitted to Mr Aycliffe for his approval, and I would be glad to go through it with you. I believe you will find she has received everything to which Mr Aycliffe considered her entitled, and without his further instructions you must see that I have no authority whatsoever . . .'

And leaving that hushed, shadowy house behind, feeling a mad urge to stand in the high-walled, box-hedged garden and shout some bawdy popular song at the top of my voice, I drove straight to Millergate, purchased a length of sky-blue satin, a deep-brimmed bonnet trimmed with white ribbon-roses and a dashing white feather, and set Mrs Stevens to ply her needle.

Mr Aycliffe, of course, was far from pleased with my mother's interference in his affairs, and although he could not withdraw his grudging consent to his daughters' attendance at her wedding, he did specify – most decidedly and most peevishly – that they must have no conversation with their mother.

'Ah well,' my own mother murmured, 'that should be easy enough, for I do believe I have never heard any one of them say more than "please" and "thank you" in their lives, which is hardly conversation.'

Yet, on the day I took them to Miss Boulton's to be fitted for their wedding clothes, my own talkative Caroline did not have things entirely her own way. And when her refusal to wear a pink sash like her cousins became shrill and persistent, Miss Boulton was so sharp with her, so unprofessionally tart, that I could only conclude she was in the throes of one of her nervous headaches, or that the presence of Joel's child made her uneasy.

'I still won't wear a pink sash,' Caroline continued mutinously, knowing that Miss Boulton, however irritable, would hardly go so far as to slap her. 'I don't want to look like them.'

It was Faith, the tallest and prettiest of Elinor's children, who stepped forward and said with an unusual measure of sweet reason, 'But you'd never look like us, Caroline. We're all fair and you're dark, and you're inches taller. You don't need any old sash to make you stand out.'

Joel Barforth's daughter, however, had not been entirely convinced even then; she had gone on scowling and muttering, pretending not to understand Miss Boulton's instructions to raise her arms, turn this way and that, stand still, so that the irate dressmaker was easily forgiven when she stuck a pin – accidentally or not – in Caroline's thigh, imagining to herself, perhaps, that it was Joel – or Estella Chase – she was attacking.

But Rosamund Boulton's skill had not faded with her hopes and her good looks, and the four children who followed my mother to the altar of Patterswick Church could not have looked prettier. They came demurely in pairs, Caroline first with Prudence, the eldest of the Aycliffes, whose fine, light brown hair and thin, pointed face reminded me achingly of Crispin, honey-blonde Cecilia and silver-blonde Faith walking behind, Caroline a head taller than any of them, stronger, infinitely more alive, her dark ringlets a rich, true black against the foamy white dress and the satin sash which, as Faith had said, she did not need to make herself noticed.

Joel's daughter. And Joel himself a step or two ahead of her, giving the bride away, playing the gallant son-in-law to perfection as he raised my mother's hand to his lips, relinquished her to her elderly but ardent squire, and then stepped into the pew beside me.

The church seemed surprisingly full, although it did not take a multitude to fill it, Dalby servants and tenants sitting self-consciously at the back, the Dalby heir, young Master Felix, and his mother, in front, Colonel Corey, who was cousin to Squire Dalby as well as to Sir Giles Flood, immediately behind them with his daughter, Estella Chase, a scattering of sporting gentlemen and their ladies shuffling their feet in the pews in between. On the bride's side of the church, Joel and I, a handsome couple, occupied the front pew with our handsome sons, Blaize in dark blue velvet, Nicholas in chocolate brown, Elinor and Mrs Stevens behind us and, behind them, Hannah, impeccably turned out in brown silk with cream lace at the throat, an acutely uncomfortable Ira Agbrigg on one side of her, a much gratified Jonas on the other, the girl, Maria, squeezed into a corner, almost out of sight.

The inclusion of the Agbriggs had given rise, quite naturally, to a great deal of discussion since Joel, while making no move to prevent the marriage, had not precisely given it his blessing.

'You may take it that if Mr Agbrigg is not asked, then I shall feel obliged to stay away,' Hannah informed me in Joel's hearing, but when he refused to commit himself either way – refused to discuss anything with me these days other than the most essential domestic issues – my mother, who had championed Elinor, felt it only right to help Hannah too and, driving down to the millhouse, had delivered to the Agbriggs their invitations herself.

'Yes, you may thank me, Hannah,' she said. 'I really am a very good-natured woman, although your brother may not think so, for he scowled quite ferociously on hearing what I had done. However, since he failed to make his wishes clear, I do not see how we are to blame. And on the day, you know, when he has bestowed his mother-in-law on a Dalby of Patterswick, he will be too well pleased to make a fuss.'

And Joel, for all his scowling, had nodded quite civilly to Ira Agbrigg on his way down the aisle, nodded to Colonel Corey too and to the other hunting, shooting gentlemen who believed, one and all, that money could only come respectably from land, highly delighted, as my mother had said, at this breach in their ranks. Certainly they had their privileges and their pedigrees, certainly they had never soiled their hands with engine grease and hard cash as he had, but perhaps a time was coming when a man's best pedigree would be his bank balance, and when that day dawned Joel Barforth would tower head and shoulders above them all.

I saw Estella Chase glance at him from the corners of her eyes and saw her mouth curl with remembered satisfaction, a woman who was not really my enemy, since she probably never thought of me at all, and, remembering the killing rage I had felt that afternoon at Tarn Edge, I turned my mind hastily away from her to my mother, who, in her swathes of ivory lace, was making her vows.

And it would not do, for I had stood in a church very like this one, eleven years ago, making those very same vows to my grown-up cousin, and I had kept none of them, he only one. We had never loved each other, or even considered the possibility. He had neither cherished nor worshipped me; I had neither honoured nor obeyed him. But he had endowed me with the worldly goods which had been mine in the first place and continued to so endow me when his own skills had caused them to multiply. And, increasingly, our marriage had become a financial arrangement, a commercial enterprise which, after the move to Tarn Edge, would no longer necessitate the sharing of a bed. I was to have my own magnificent, bay-windowed apartment, separated from his by a dressing room as big as the bedroom we now shared, so that when he came home with the dawn, or did not come at all, there would be no explanations to make. Not that I ever asked. Not that he ever offered to tell. But, at Tarn Edge, in the civilized, sophisticated manner of Captain and Mrs Chase, I would be unaware of his comings and goings unless I chose to enquire. And it was a symptom of the disease between us that I would not, could not make those enquiries.

But I could question myself and increasingly did so. What, indeed, could I ever mean to Joel? To begin with, I had been Edwin Barforth's well-mannered, well-dowered sister, not intended for fortune hunters such as he. With Edwin's death I had been a prize he would have given his right arm to win. But I remembered, now, hearing these marriage vows all over again, the awkwardness of our wedding night, and understood, as I had not understood then, how difficult it had been for him to overcome the barrier a man feels with a woman who is almost a sister. He had done no more than his duty that night. And could it be that now, when I had given him three children and seemed unlikely – unwilling – to produce more, he had decided that our sexual duty towards each other was done?

Was he, in claiming freedom for himself, allowing me mine? Was he saying to me, 'I require your skills as a hostess; I require you to preside over my social engagements and my domestic comforts, and the education of my children. I require you to wear my pearls and diamonds and my furs so that the world may know me as a rich and generous man. But I do not require you as a lover and, in that respect, you may please yourself, as I shall, provided you are discreet and I never come to hear of it.'

A provocative, tempting thought, and a dangerous one too, for Joel, beneath the London sophistication of his dove-grey coat and trousers, the pearl in his necktie, the scented oil on his hair and the scented lotion on his skin, was still a Law Valley man, raised in a world of double standards, where enjoyment was a male preserve, sin a strictly female matter. In the Law Valley, only men made love for pleasure; respectable women did it because it was their duty, harlots because it was their trade, and it seemed to me perfectly possible that however skilfully Joel played the gentry's games, no matter how real his satisfaction in winning a thoroughbred like Estella Chase, she was, in the private recesses of his mind, no better than a high-class whore. And although he could enjoy a whore – respect her, even, if she extracted enough of his money – he would expect his own wife – in true Law Valley fashion – to be beyond reproach.

Joel may not want me himself – surely he did not want me? – but he would allow no one else to have me, would give no one the opportunity to laugh at him as he was himself all too ready to laugh at Captain Chase. Yet when I had thrown his adulteries in his face, he had made no real defence, had not threatened and blustered and lied as I had expected. And why had he deliberately forced me to watch him kiss Estella Chase? Had he wished to taunt me, or test me, or had it simply been a way of saying, 'This is what I am. We both know it, so now let us be honest about it. Let us be cousins again, in our private lives, and go our separate ways.' And why, since that afternoon, had he barely addressed a word to me, and not very civilly? Why had I felt that murderous rage, that dreadful unleashing of the Barforth side of my nature when, increasingly, I had little room in heart or mind for anyone but Crispin? And, most of all, if Joel was really offering me this compromise and I accepted it, how long could I remain intact? How long before my love for Crispin deteriorated into excitement and I became – like Joel – a self-indulgent adventurer?

Yet what else could I do? I went now, whenever I could, sometimes quite recklessly, to the ivory shop, to Dinah McCluskey, who cleared my way through the alley to the Red Gin. I had opened Crispin's door now a dozen times and then closed it behind me, yet I always opened it again, my mind becoming so fragmented that, inside his room, I was a girl in love who saw nothing but him, yet the instant my foot touched the creaking stairway leading back into the alley, I became a woman with a dinner-party menu to plan, a parcel to meet from the afternoon coach, a chipped vase which must be returned and replaced, a child to be fetched home from school. And I knew my danger, for he was involved now, more than ever, with political ideals which could well take him out of the Law Valley, and unless I could discover the mad courage to go with him, I would be forced, as a final act of love, to release him.

My mother left the church, Mrs Dalby of Patterswick now, to a joyous pealing of bells, my daughter Caroline preening herself on the church porch as people came rushing to congratulate the bride, seeing herself, I thought, one day leaving some vast cathedral on the arm of a prince, her Aycliffe cousins walking behind her like a flock of quiet, sad-eyed doves following a peacock. And for a while we all stood in the churchyard in the autumn sunshine, remarking on my mother's incredible youthfulness, the incredible good fortune of the squire, at his age, to get so lovely a wife, the incredible good fortune of the bride, with her common, commercial background, to get herself so gentlemanly a husband.

'How like your mother you are, Mrs Barforth,' Estella Chase murmured to me, offering two totally disinterested fingers by way of greeting. 'My father and I were both much struck by it.'

But her father, the once upright and genial Colonel Corey, much altered now by recurrent bouts of illness, looked too frail in the cruel November daylight to have much interest in anything but the cosseting of his failing limbs, and it was largely on his account that we cut our observations short and drove back to the Hall.

Squire Dalby's house was very old, quite small now to my eyes, which had grown accustomed to the budding splendours of Tarn Edge, but so very old, so overlaid with the births and deaths, joys and sorrows of so many lives, that beside it Tarn Edge was as yet no more than a costly pile of stone. To begin with, there had been a pair of towers, built for defence against Scots and Lancastrians and Parliamentarians, as well as the private feudings of ancient Dalbys, who, in quieter times, had added rooms as it pleased them, a hall with a gallery, a cobweb of corridors and terrifying stairways, creaking boards and sagging, bulging walls which even to the insensitive could have contained a secret chamber and the bones of a captured enemy, a mad relation, a faithless woman.

But today all was light and harmony, the stone-flagged hall decorated with harvest fruits and autumn branches, the fragrant crackling of logs in the plain stone hearth that had nothing to adorn its mantelpiece but an array of pewter jugs and dishes which may have seen service in Cromwell's time. There was a massive, iron-bound oak chest, a colossal oak sideboard, much scarred and knotted, a number of narrow wooden chairs offering no comfort, a table almost as long as the room itself, bearing a wedding breakfast clearly intended for men who had spent the day in the open air, in the saddle. A harsh, tough-grained, somewhat arrogant setting, in no way softened by the light of the window occupying almost the whole of one wall, its panes set with the armorial bearings of the local nobility who had allied themselves with the Dalbys, the Ramsdens of Huddersfield, the Tempests of Bradford, the Wintertons of Floxley, the Floods of Cullingford, the de Greys of Redesdale, and, in the centre, the device of the Dalbys themselves, to which my mother could only add her wit and charm.

By no means overawed, she floated serenely among her guests with a word and a smile for everyone, and, watching her, my father's face rushed swiftly into my mind and out again, leaving tears in my eyes.

'Do go and talk to the Agbriggs,' she murmured, laying a cool, happy hand on my arm, 'for no one else will, and Hannah is beginning to look fierce. And, dearest, do tell Elinor that if she wants a half hour or so alone with her children it can easily be arranged.'

But Elinor, when the offer was conveyed to her, shook her head, her eyes dull and disinterested.

'No, no. Thank your mother kindly, but, really, why embarrass the poor things? They are timid enough in any case, and heaven knows what Mrs Naylor has been saying to them lately. No. Let them run and play in the garden while they can.'

And when, worried at her apathy, I tried to urge her, she tossed her head and bit her lip, with something of her old impatience.

'What on earth can I find to say to them? What possible good can I do? They are girls, don't you see? Girls – like you and me and Hannah were once girls – and I don't think I want anything to do with girls. They'll get married – their father will see to that – and I don't think I want to know about it. And, after all, the last thing they need is my example, for who could call my life a success? No, no. I'll just go and talk to my sister. Poor Hannah, I never thought she'd need my help, but now there is something I can do for her. I'll go and say kind things to Mr Agbrigg – who really doesn't like us very much, you know – and I'll flatter his clever son, which is easy enough even for me. Look, the children are doing very well. I do believe Faith is actually skipping, which I never saw her do before. Let them be.'

Skipping indeed, silvery ringlets flying, forgetting every-thing but her enjoyment of the fresh air and her own unaccustomed freedom of movement, Prudence and Ceci-lia and Maria Agbrigg joggling along behind, grouped around Caroline, who was explaining something, organ-izing something, studiously ignoring her brother and Felix Dalby, who, with another boy – a young Winterton of Floxley – were hatching secrets nearby.

'What an attractive child your daughter is – so unusually self-possessed,' someone murmured to me, and meeting the brilliant, altogether false smile of Lady Winterton of Floxley Park, I remembered the rumour that her estates had been sadly burdened by extravagance and misman-agement, and realized that Joel's boast of being able to offer his daughter a title one day had not been idle.

'And are those your sons, Mrs Barforth? Such sturdy little men and such a comfort – such a stake in the future – when there is property to be looked after. I am so rarely in Cullingford – I find it so sadly altered from the quaint little market town of my childhood. My cousin Giles Flood's town, we always thought of it, although it seems rather to be your husband's town now. When I next come over I wonder if I may leave my card?'

And I knew that the effort it had cost this woman – a Flood and a Winterton – to beg an invitation from me, a mongrel millmaster's daughter, would be an additional satisfaction to Joel.

'Well, dear,' I could imagine her saying to her balding, rather chinless spouse, 'if Estella Chase can sleep with the man, I think I can bring myself to take tea with his wife. They have money to burn, dear. Money they can't possibly know what to do with, and it could almost be an act of charity to show them. She is quite a presentable little thing – quite well-spoken. One has no need to be ashamed of her. And one must assume the daughter will have a fortune. Naturally, dear, I quite agree, one cannot possibly want to marry such people, but one can hardly doubt how badly they would like to marry us – and in that case, they must be made to pay for the privilege.'

'They are girls,' Elinor had said, only moments ago. 'They'll get married – their father will see to that – and I don't think I want to know about it.'

But smiling, giving this arrogant, overbearing woman the answer she wanted to hear, I reached out in my mind to Caroline – tossing her dark ringlets for the Dalby boy and the Winterton boy to see – and I wanted urgently to know about her future, to stand between her and the mistakes I had already made, to stand beside her when she made mistakes of her own.

And leaving Lady Winterton behind, I walked quickly down the garden, understanding from the arrogant nonchalance of my son Blaize and the scowling pugnacity of my son Nicholas that unless I acted quickly they would very likely turn on the heir to Floxley Park, the heir to Dalby Hall, and knock them both down.

33

We moved to Tarn Edge at the end of the month, an enormous exodus, leaving the Top House unsold, untenanted, a prize Joel would bestow where and when he chose – on Hannah, perhaps, if she could find her way back into his good graces; or, if she did not, on some ambitious stranger it might please him to promote over Ira Agbrigg's head.

Both Hannah and Elinor made the move with us, Hannah clearly as a temporary measure, since her wedding date was already set, her authority already supreme at the millhouse; Elinor perhaps as no more than a fleeting visitor, since the fall of the Whig administration that November and the likelihood of a general election meant the return of her husband to Cullingford and an alteration of some sort in her affairs.

I had expected Mr Aycliffe to be seriously displeased at Hannah's engagement, shocked even, but he had written warm letters of congratulation both to her and to Mr Agbrigg, proving to me at any rate that, valuing Hannah's friendship as he did and having suffered at the speculation it had sometimes caused, he not only considered the protection of a husband most convenient but was well suited to see her marry a man who would be unlikely to complain whenever he – Morgan Aycliffe – monopolized her time. And since the engagement had also served to bring Hannah and Elinor much closer together, it seemed that Hannah would manage to arrange things in her own way.

My own time, just then, was eaten up by the demands of Tarn Edge, consumed entirely by the interviewing and engaging of new staff, the arrangement and rearrangement of furniture and ornaments, the sheer administrative burden of such a household. Mrs Stevens – a friend now rather than an employee – had gladly relinquished her housekeeper's keys, contenting herself with the care of my social commitments and other small matters between ourselves, and every morning, in her place, there was a stately Mrs Richmond to offer me the day's menus and to guide me – since she had seen service with a baronet – in the way my husband wished me to go. We had a butler now, who had taken great pleasure in bringing me Lady Winterton's calling card on a silver tray, and a pair of good-looking footmen – a danger, most likely, to the maids, who, unlike my old Marth-Ellen, who had never hesitated to speak her mind, were trained, according to Mrs Richmond's aristocratic notions, to keep out of my way.

A lady, it appeared, did not concern herself with the names and faces of her staff. She wished simply to be served efficiently, unobtrusively, by willing but anonymous hands, and required her house to be immaculately maintained but had no desire at all to see the work being done. And so I grew accustomed to lavender cotton uniforms and white starched aprons whisking themselves out of any room I happened to enter, or disappearing into empty bedrooms to avoid passing me in a corridor; accustomed to being on speaking terms with no one but the head parlour-maid, who served my tea, immaculate in her black silk dress and white cap and ribbons, and pretty, cheerful Sally, who did my hair and looked after my clothes.

And I believe that until the house was ready, fully furnished and fully staffed, even I had not realized the extent of Joel's success.

'I'll have a decent house before I'm forty,' he had told me, and now, at something less than that, he had built Tarn Edge, a monument to the power of machines and his own courage and ability to use them.

'It must be like living in the Assembly Rooms,' Emma-Jane Hobhouse told me. 'Don't you feel strange, sometimes?'

And Lady Winterton, driving over one bracing December morning with my mother, expressed her envy by ignoring the house altogether. 'What a lovely day. And how fresh the air is. One would hardly think oneself so near to town.'

But both Nethercoats Mill and Floxley Park were in decline, and their owners' pique could do no more than flatter us.

The house was set on a slight rise of the land, the grounds falling away from it like a wide, tiered skirt of lawns and flower beds and elaborately clipped box hedges, their intense dark green broken by the sudden white gleam of a garden statue. There was a summerhouse, a covered, trellised walk festooned by hanging baskets of ferns and blossoms leading from it to a stretch of quiet, lily-studded water. There would be a carpet of daffodils in the spring, forsythia, lilac, massed hedges of rhododendron shading from the palest pink to a royal purple. There would be roses and carnations to come after, a mighty oak, a dreamy willow, evergreens to see us through the winter, glass houses for rare plants and blooms so that at all times the house could be filled with flowers.

The hall now was richly, darkly panelled, the stained-glass landing window casting an almost medieval light on the life-size bronze stag at the foot of the stairs, the long-case clock of elaborately carved mahogany, the marble nymph, set in a fluted recess, brand-new yet managing somehow to give an air of dusty antiquity, as if she had been but recently unearthed from some Grecian hillside.

The drawing room, its huge bay windows turned away from the mill – only two miles distant – was a clear forty feet by twenty, its high ceiling a marvel of gold and blue mouldings, bearing the weight of two chandeliers, offering between them the shimmering, dancing light of eighty candles. The fireplace, backed by a gilt-framed mirror that rose almost to the ceiling, was pure white marble; a French clock in ormolu and enamel stood in the centre of the mantelpiece with a pair of flowery, rococo vases by Sèvres on either side.

There were wide velvet sofas, their weighty feet sinking into the carpet, balloon-backed, cabriole-legged chairs, ormolu-mounted, inlaid cabinets of dark wood, glass-fronted to display the fine porcelain of Coalport and Meissen and Sèvres we had collected with small knowledge but growing enthusiasm. Delicate, linen-fold panelling covered the lower half of the walls, with more moulded plasterwork above it, a neutral, ivory-coloured background for the heavy-framed Italian landscapes Cullingford could barely understand and the scantily robed pagan nymphs and shepherds it could not understand at all.

The dining room was high-ceilinged too, its carved

wooden walls almost black against the oval portrait of Caroline in a white dress and pink-fringed shawl, Blaize and Nicholas in jewel-coloured velvet jackets, my own bare shoulders, framed in a cloud of gauze, my pearls painted in exquisite, lustrous detail, the likeness to my mother beyond dispute. The dining table was very long, very highly polished; the sideboards, along two walls, were carved with cupids and grapes and acanthus leaves, and set with shelves and niches for the accommodation of crouching bronze animals, crystal lamps, silver, and more porcelain, each costly object doubled by the tall mirrors behind. The windows were shrouded with heavy, dark velvet, and the double doors leading to the book-lined, leather-upholstered smoking room were of decorated oak, this smaller room, which would be Joel's private sanctum, leading in turn to a wide terrace with steps directly into the garden, so that he could take his guests and their cigars into the fresh air on summer nights.

I had a sitting room of my own leading to the same terrace, chintzy and light, with all the feminine clutter of worktables and writing tables and a pianoforte covered with an embroidered shawl, which I had never learned to play. Apart from these rooms, my own creamy, lacy bedchamber, and Caroline's smaller version of the same, the rest of the house was almost unknown to me.

The kitchens, undoubtedly, were superb, crammed with every modern device, but kitchens were for cooks, as schoolrooms were for governesses, housekeepers' rooms strictly for housekeepers, and Joel's room, with its capacious half-tester bed, its vivid oriental rugs, its much-talked-of recess that contained his private bathtub, was altogether for Joel. I would not enter without an invitation.

Needless to say, the house brought Joel no popularity. Law Valley men, if they had money, did not spend it on bronze lions and paintings of near-naked women. Nor did they indulge themselves with the suspicious, very nearly effeminate habit of taking hot baths. Law Valley men invested their spare cash in far more solid propositions than fine porcelain, or they hoarded it. They washed in cold water, in a bedroom they shared with their wives, and now that Joel had chosen not only to play the sultan in his personal habits but to consort with the gentry as well, he was regarded with growing alarm. Not only were the feelings of Law Valley men truly lacerated at this squandering of hard-earned wealth, but what on earth would happen if their own womenfolk should expect them to do the same?

The Reverend Mr Brand, catching the drift of public opinion and still smarting perhaps at Hannah's defection, was quick to preach a sermon on the subject of criminal extravagance. Emma-Jane Hobhouse, whose ten little boys were bursting Nethercoats at the seams, continued to let me know she could never bring herself to live in such a mausoleum. Little Lucy Oldroyd, who had plenty of money and could hardly blame me for her husband's aversion to spending it, lectured me gently about the simplicity and humility of a truly Christian way of life, hinting at the discomfort she felt in my opulent surroundings when there was such poverty and deprivation in the world. But none of them ever refused my invitations and, between them and my host of new acquaintances, my time was rarely my own.

It was not only the Wintertons and the Dalbys who 'took me up' that year, for Cullingford was going through yet another stage of rapid growth, manufacturers and merchants moving in from all parts of the area and beyond with the capital to buy up old factories or build new ones; men of energy and ambition who were quick to appreciate Joel's achievement and sophisticated enough to allow him his hot baths and his painted nudes, and for whose wives I was a natural social target.

I took tea now not only at Floxley Hall but in the elegant new villas multiplying at the continuation of Blenheim Lane. I dined with charming, gruff-voiced men of supposedly Germanic origin, whose wives sometimes spoke little English at all but who, far from despising our pictures, were often artists themselves, devoting hours to their canvases, to the pianoforte or the violin, to matters other than the eternal production of babies and hot dinners. And if Emma-Jane Hobhouse considered their tastes decadent, their religious practices decidedly suspicious, I, for one, was fascinated, immensely encouraged, happy almost, on the days when I could convince myself that Crispin would love me forever and that Joel would not care.

Estella Chase's father, Colonel Corey, who had looked so frail at my mother's wedding, died at the beginning of the winter, making Mrs Chase a wealthy woman, and it was at his funeral that I first saw Morgan Aycliffe again, standing grey-lipped, hollow-eyed, enormously long and thin in his tightly buttoned black coat at the back of the church. And later, in the wind-raked, bitterly cold grave-yard, when he raised his hat to me, I had no choice but to approach him, grateful that Crispin, who had known Colonel Corey well – who had been, in fact, considerably in the old gentleman's debt – was not there.

Mr Aycliffe had come back, of course, for the general election, having decided to risk himself at the hustings once again, and, for a moment, he talked gravely to me about the King's dismissal of his Whig ministers in November and his sending for the Duke of Wellington, who had refused to do more than act as caretaker until Robert Peel could be fetched home from abroad. And now, even though Peel had chosen rightly to go to the country, Mr Aycliffe doubted that there would be any clear decision.

'We are a deeply divided nation,' he told me, but although he said little else I understood that, politics apart, he had heard how Cullingford was building again, new factories and new houses, more worker's cottages, more terraces for overlookers and craftsmen, more managerial villas, more palaces for those who wished to rival Joel. And then there was the matter of his wife.

Elinor locked herself in her room the evening he called to see Joel, but he made no attempt to molest her, and when he left it was Hannah, momentarily back in favour, who was called into the smoking room to receive her brother's confidences. But, knowing them all as I did, I required no great wit to see through the net they were weaving.

Six months had passed since Elinor's attempted elopement and now we were at the end of our excuses. Now she must either recover from her illness or die of it, and, recovering, must either return home or be cast out into permanent exile. And although Mr Aycliffe no longer desired the lady's fair body – had perhaps rather passed the season for such things altogether – and had nothing but abhorrence for the foolishness and depravity of her nature, he was prepared to admit the awkwardness, at this time, of fighting an election without her. The recent increase in Cullingford's population had brought new voters, new ideas, and his success was no longer the foregone conclusion it had been two years ago. This time he needed to win the support of strangers and he was decidely nervous at the idea of the vicious Mark Corey and his own ungrateful, lying son presenting him to these newcomers, in the pages of the *Cullingford Star*, as a man who had ill used his young wife. Not, of course, that there had been any ill usage, but in a world where it was considered more amusing to believe a sensational lie than the plain truth, it seemed best on the whole to remember his Christian principles, raise up the fallen woman, and take her home. And, having done so, he felt that Joel would have no hesitation in recommending him to his new friends, both as a politician and as a master builder.

So he was ready to take her back, and Joel, who knew the value, in these days of expanding trade, of a friend at Westminster, was ready to let her go. Nor, I imagine, was he prepared to tolerate the interference of his meddlesome wife, for, a day or so after Mr Aycliffe's return, Elinor was whisked away on a long-proposed visit to my mother, leaving me anchored by my social engagements at home.

'Just a few days in the country,' Hannah told Emma-Jane brightly. 'She is much improved and we have high hopes of her being able to stand up to her social obligations during the election. But you will see for yourself at my brother's party on the twentieth. Yes, yes – of course she will be there.'

And I could only conclude that Hannah, who went regularly to Patterswick, knew far more than I.

'Are you sure?' I asked when Emma-Jane had gone.

Shrugging, Hannah answered coldly, 'Has it ever been in doubt? My sister will be here, at your grand reception, on her husband's arm – not only willingly but gladly.'

And to avoid unnecessary argument, I refrained from reminding her that since we were giving the reception partly to present Morgan Aycliffe to his new electors and partly to refresh the memories of old ones, her prediction, for Mr Aycliffe's sake, had best be correct.

I had spent the whole of one dreary day in my sitting room with Mrs Stevens, writing cards of invitation, an anxious morning or two with my new housekeeper, Mrs Richmond, but her training in a baronet's household enabled her to view the feeding and entertaining of a hundred or so Law Valley notables with no particular alarm. And when she presented me with a list of all the things I had been meaning to bring up with her, and more than a few others which had not even entered my mind, I realized that she required no more of me – that Joel required no more of me – than a warm smile and a welcoming murmur on the night and a gown that would be remembered even if my conversation was not.

I bespoke my outfit this time from Rosamund Boulton – refusing an offer from my new friend Mrs Mandelbaum to take me to Leeds, a suggestion from Lady Winterton that I might like to try her dressmaker in York – for Miss Boulton had looked unhappy lately, as well as ill-tempered, and perhaps Hannah's wedding dress, already on order, had done little to ease her mind.

My confidence was not misplaced, for she designed for me a stunning confection the colour of old ivory, its wide skirt almost entirely covered with pearl beads stitched, by the several embroideresses now in her employ, into dainty outlines of flowers. There were pearls too on the foamy, lacy sleeves, a thick, gleaming band of them at the shoulders, thinning to a mere scattering at the elbows, a tracery of pearls and lace along the low neck, and an imaginative cluster of pearl-studded, ivory roses for my hair. Admiring its shimmering elegance, aware of the bustling, thriving shop around me, I wondered what case Miss Boulton really had – when she was so clever and so prosperous – to be so morose?

I took the dress home with me and tried it on again, arousing great enthusiasm in Mrs Stevens and Sally, my recently acquired maid, but when I mentioned it to Joel he either did not hear or did not think it worth an answer.

'I thought Miss Boulton looked most unwell today,' I told him and then retreated instantly into some safe discussion of Caroline's music lessons, since Rosamund Boulton could lead to Estella Chase, to infidelity, to that dressing room separating my bed from Joel's like a thick, spiked wall, real issues, real decisions, unanswerable, unthinkable just now, when I had not yet discovered the extent of my courage or whether, indeed, I was brave at all.

'I find this all decidedly odd,' my mother told me, having driven over to discuss Elinor and discovering instead, after a quick glance at that dressing room and some shrewd questioning, that my own marriage was in a more perilous condition than she had thought. 'I have no objection to separate rooms. In fact, I find the arrangement most civilized. But no man gives up his conjugal rights without good reasons, and it is no more than prudent to ascertain exactly what they are. In matters of this sort it is essential that a woman should know just where she stands, for, all else considered, my love, if you were to become pregnant now you would find it most awkward. Yes, yes, you may have discovered the uses of sponges soaked in vinegar and certain ointments – Mrs Stevens's harlot's tricks, in fact – but none of them are totally reliable. I merely mention this in passing, since if I were to be put to the torture I would hardly know how to describe either your hopes or your intentions. But, dearest, since the subject has arisen, is it not time now to let Mr Crispin Aycliffe go? I perfectly understand the superior quality of your love, but think, dearest, think well, is it not time now for you to withdraw and give him the opportunity to fall in love with someone else? Painful, of course, even to contemplate the possibility, and he would certainly swear to you that he could never love again. But life is not really like that, Verity. Time passes, and although one can remember pain one no longer feels it – which, of course, is unfortunately just as true of joy. Every aspiring politician needs a wife, Verity, and you should not stand in his way. Can you, in all honesty – in all sanity – tell me I am wrong?'

I could not. Yet the elections, in which Crispin was deeply involved, enabled me once again to put off my decision, his conversation now being political rather than romantic, our time together considerably reduced. He had spoken out this time no longer as a Tory, no longer exclusive in his support of Richard Oastler and the local issue of factory reform, but as a radical, an out-and-out revolutionary, who advocated with passion that every man, no matter what his status, should have the vote. And when he was hissed and jeered and asked how he could justify the folly of putting power into the hands of an ignorant, gin-soaked populace who could not run their own meagre affairs, much less govern a nation, he had answered simply, 'Educate them.'

Dreams, of course, according to Morgan Aycliffe, since one half of the people didn't wish to be educated and the other half was incapable of it, yet Crispin continued to speak, whenever a crowd assembled to hear him, somewhat to the embarrassment of the official Tory candidate, a portly, excessively good-natured gentleman who, while wishing to stress the alliance between the Tories and the workers, had no desire at all to incite them to riot.

But, whenever I drove through town that December on my many errands and my vastly escalating social duties, I saw groups of workmen carrying Tory banners calling for action against the abominable alliance of the Whig grandees and the middle classes, and although these men still lacked the votes to drag the manufacturers down they had muscle in plenty to attack, once again, the windows of the Swan and, on polling day, to persuade certain voters to abstain.

'We won't win,' one of them told me, thrusting himself in my way as I came out of Miss Boulton's shop, my maid Sally behind me, her arms full of parcels. 'We won't win this time, but we'll win in the end. And then it'll be God help the likes of you. It's you who'll be carrying the parcels then, and this lass here who'll be wearing your silks and getting into your fine carriage. Go and tell your husband that, Mrs Barforth.'

Had I been close enough to Joel just then even to tell him that much, he merely would have replied, 'They may knock down what I've built up – like they did in France – but they'll need me, or a man like me, to build it up again.' And, as usual, I could see right – and wrong – on every side.

On the fifteenth of December, five days before my party, his election campaign already at its height, Morgan Aycliffe declared his intention of driving to Patterswick to see his wife and, meeting no opposition from Joel, who had spent an hour with his sister the day before, or from Hannah, who had gone to Dalby Park with him and remained there, I ordered my carriage and went off to give Elinor warning.

'Ah yes,' my mother murmured, hurrying to greet me

across the uneven stone paving of the great hall. 'It is today, then? I think she is quite ready.'

And going upstairs to one of the dark, low-ceilinged bedrooms which Squire Dalby had seen no reason either to carpet or to decorate since his great-grandfather had not, I found my cousin sitting on the hard, ancient bed, her few remaining possessions set out around her.

'Today?' she said, no longer the whispering, sobbing girl of six months ago, no longer the lethargic, blank-eyed creature of a fortnight past, lacking the energy to raise her hand, but a woman I had never really seen before, hard-eyed and resolute, almost unfriendly, the impertinent tilt of her head telling me that neither my sympathy nor my impotent good-intentions would be welcome.

'Well then, one day is the same as another, and, as you see, I can be ready in five minutes. I have only these few petticoats and everything else I may carry home on my back. Five minutes . . .'

'Elinor, is this really what you want?'

'And what else is there?'

'Joel—'

'Joel will not give a penny. He told me so yesterday. I may do as I please, he says, may take Daniel Adair or anyone else who wins my fancy, once I have made sure of my husband's money. But, until then, I am to go home and behave myself. And one has to admit the sense of it.'

'And if you refused, Joel would not see you starve – whatever he says—'

'Ah no, I am well aware of that. But we are not talking of starving, are we, Verity. We are talking of living, and my ideas on the subject are very exact, very large. I find, after all, that I would like the keys to my wardrobe back again, and my carriage to drive. And Joel has arranged all that for me, has been most specific about the way I am to be treated and the pin money I am to receive. You should not have given yourself the trouble of coming all this way to see me, Verity, when tomorrow I will be back in

Blenheim Lane. Hannah is here, and she is to come home with me and spend a day or two, until I find my feet. Really – you are not needed.'

And crossing to the window, she turned her back to peer through the dull, diamond-shaped panes.

'Will my husband be very long, do you think?'

'No. Half an hour behind me on the road. But, Elinor, tell me, is it part of the bargain between your husband and mine that you and I shall no longer be friends?'

'No,' she said, her back still resolutely turned. 'No one has asked me that. No one has spoken of you at all. It is just that – I don't want your sympathy, Verity. I find it – inconvenient.'

'How is that?'

'Because you remind me, more than anyone else, of what a fool I have been. And I do not wish to be reminded. Because I confided in you the whole of my silly, sloppy, worthless little romance, and whether or not you smiled at me behind my back, it suits me to think you did. I dislike you because I dislike the memory of myself as I was six months ago. And I dislike you most of all because now you would like to see me do something heroic and altogether extraordinary, like somehow managing to support myself instead of returning to the only man who appears willing to do it for me. You want me to live up to all the threats and promises I made, and I dislike you for wanting that – and myself for not being able to do it. I think you are probably my best friend, Verity, which is another cause for dislike, since I can't help feeling I have disappointed you.'

We sat in silence for a while, one at either end of the bed, her few meagre petticoats between us, the dark December afternoon outside the window threatening rain, the empty Patterswick road offering us suddenly the sound of hooves and wheels.

'I think he is coming.'

525

'Yes. But he will spend a little time first with my mother. Elinor – what is really in your mind?'

And as she made her answer, the rain tore itself loose from the skirts of a vast grey cloud, the room becoming too dark for me to see her face.

'Oh – what has always been there, I suppose. I shall recover, presently, and learn to stop despising myself. But I have been a great fool. I had only to wait, as Daniel Adair told me. "Just you wait," he used to say. "Bide your time and you'll have it all," which meant, of course, that he intended to have it all away from me as soon as he could. Well, now I shall do just that, and when I have it, I shall share it with no one. It strikes me that the world is full of Daniel Adairs, and when I am free I shall be able to pick and choose. My husband may not leave me his entire fortune, or he may tie it up so that I shall only have the spending of a part. But there will be enough – my brother will see to that. I shall have my horses and carriage, my clothes, and I shall be courted for what I have and for what my daughters have. In the meantime I shall be fully occupied. I shall be waiting for my husband to die. I shall devote my time, right gladly, to that.'

The sound of hooves now was immediately below us, Mr Aycliffe's spare, grey figure visible on the gravel, feeling the cold, I thought, and grateful of my mother's offer of hot, spiced wine; a man too burdened, perhaps, by the demands of politics and commerce to be unduly troublesome to his child-wife, who was no longer a child.

'Well,' she said, getting to her feet, smoothing her hair and rearranging the folds of her skirt. 'I had best go and present myself as a penitent and get it over. Tears, I suppose, will be very necessary, and I may swoon a little – yes, indeed I may, for I would like to wear the first Mrs Aycliffe's pearls to your party and it will take a great deal of humility to achieve it. Don't look so sad, Verity. Don't ask yourself how I shall endure. I shall stare at the ceiling and think of sky-blue satin dresses as I have done these ten years past – as I should have done on the accursed night I ran away. And he, no doubt, will think of the votes and the contracts Joel has brought him, and remind himself that I am cheaper than a proper whore. Don't worry. My mother detested my father, and you and Hannah are not in love – not with your husbands, at any rate.'

And reaching out her arm quite blindly before her, she pressed the hand I slipped into hers, opened the door, and, composing herself as the supplicant she was about to play, walked very quietly down the corridor, down the stairs, going meekly as a nun to judgement.

34

Tarn Edge on the night of the reception was everything one had hoped for, luminous with candlelit crystal and silver, fragrant with hothouse blooms and the spicy, tantalizing odours of fine wines and foods designed to please not only the palate but the eye. There was to be no dancing, this being a serious occasion, an opportunity to discuss vital economic and social issues with Morgan Aycliffe, Member of Parliament for Cullingford, as well as to marvel at the wealth and good taste – or criminal folly and extravagance, according to how one looked at it – of Joel Barforth, his chief supporter. But seriousness had never been a bar to Law Valley appetites and, had these not been adequately catered for, few would have scrupled to ask the reason why.

Refreshments of an insubstantial nature – claret, sherry, a magnificent ice-cold punch, tea and coffee for those whose constitution or whose religion forbade them anything stronger – were to be served from the arrival of the first carriage to the moment the last one rolled away. While somewhere around midnight we were to serve a mammoth champagne supper of salmon and game, Frenchified pâtés and intricate savoury moulds that some would find irresistible and others indecent. There would be ices too, for the ladies, high-peaked mountains of cream stuffed with nuts and cherries, an epergne overflowing with fruit and ferns like a horn of plenty, and, to enable the gentlemen to retire in peace to the smoking room for their brandy and cigars, there would be a pianist, come all the way from Manchester on my new friend Mrs Mandelbaum's recommendation, to entertain us.

I had written on the bottom right-hand corner of my cards of invitation: 'To meet Mr Morgan Aycliffe,' lacking the confidence to include his wife's name, but they were among our first arrivals, Mr Aycliffe self-conscious and stern, Elinor looking at last like a politician's wife. There had been no time to acquire a new sky-blue satin gown but she had filled in the low neck of an old one with layers of creamy lace, removed a great deal of the trimming from the skirt, transforming a once dashing outfit into something infinitely more demure. The silky cascade of her hair had been tamed, its ringlets and wildly curling tendrils smoothed into neat wings coming from a centre parting to cover her ears and form an elegant but subdued coil at the nape of her neck. And although the first Mrs Aycliffe's pearls were around her neck again she seemed to have no awareness of them, no intention at all of flaunting them at Emma-Jane. She looked as if she had been very ill indeed, would be quite likely to fall ill again, but, unlike the old days when the merest hint of a headache would have taken her to bed, she remained for the whole of that long night at her husband's side, listening intently as he explained his policies, smiling when he smiled, leaving him only when his political duty called him to the brandy bottle, and hers, it seemed, was to sit between Hannah and Emma-Jane and pay polite attention to the music.

Emma-Jane, of course, so plump now that it was hard to tell whether she was pregnant or not, did not believe a word of Elinor's illness and was completely convinced, as little, sharp-eyed Lucy Oldroyd was convinced, there had been something very much amiss. But there was nothing they could prove. And although, in normal circumstances, they would not have worried overmuch about that, Bradley Hobhouse, increasingly concerned about money, might have pointed out to Emma-Jane that if he ever needed to borrow, then Joel Barforth was probably the only man who could afford to lend. Matthew Oldroyd, who had been twice fined recently for employing underaged children in his spinning mill, might have warned Lucy that it would be as well to keep on the right side of their Member of Parliament. And perhaps neither of them really had the nerve to question a situation which my mother – Squire Dalby's lady – had so readily endorsed. Certainly, in their minds, they knew Elinor had had a lover, but Emma-Jane had never heard of Daniel Adair, Lucy's imagination extended no further than the holding of hands beneath a carriage rug, a few kisses and sighs, and, as the evening wore on, even Hannah's vigilance began to relax.

'I think everything is going very well indeed,' she told me, her eyes on Ira Agbrigg, terribly stiff in his brand-new evening clothes but having no difficulty, among all these strangers, in finding someone to talk to him. Bradley Hobhouse, who had been drinking, Hannah thought, before he arrived, had indeed pushed past Mr Agbrigg on the stairs and Matthew Oldroyd had turned conveniently deaf when Mr Agbrigg had asked him how he did. But George Mandelbaum, lately come to us via Manchester and Hamburg, was pleased enough to make the acquaintance of Hannah's fiancé, and since Mr Mandelbaum would undoubtedly be of importance in our community, I thought that Hannah's social and civic ambitions could well be realized one day.

'Mr Agbrigg looks quite presentable in his new clothes,' my mother murmured. 'Really – is it possible that he came to me once, cap in hand, clogs on his feet, and his elbows out of his jacket, to inform against his friends? And now he is almost too smart. You will have noticed, I suppose, that Sir Charles Winterton's coat is decidedly short in the sleeves – one can only suppose he had it from his grandfather, like the rest of his goods and chattels.'

And, indeed, the contrast between the neat-as-a-new-pin Mr Agbrigg and the carelessly-thrown-together Sir Charles Winterton was reflected everywhere, creating a gulf between the newly rich, the 'machine-rich,' and these landed gentlemen and their languid ladies who did not feel the need of fine clothes and expensive French furniture to prove their status. Even little Lucy Oldroyd, not noted for her extravagance, had a decent diamond on her finger; even Emma-Jane had encased herself in a length of gold-embroidered purple satin that would not have looked amiss on a queen. But Lady Winterton, whose dull green gown inspired me with thankfulness that I had refused the services of her dressmaker, wore no jewellery but an antique ring which might have been improved with cleaning, while her hands, although proclaiming her a noted horsewoman, would have profited from the attentions of a clever maid.

Estella Chase was not there, being still in mourning for her father, but Mrs Elizabeth Flood, daughter-in-law of our manorial lord Sir Giles, who had looked in for a disdainful five minutes and stayed until well after supper, had only a single strand of pearls around her throat – the remainder, one supposed, having gone to satisfy her husband's passion for cards and Arabian stallions – and wore a gown we all believed we had seen before.

But, undoubtedly, it was going well. Those who wished to meet Morgan Aycliffe met him; others, like the Tory gentry, who wanted nothing to do with a Whig, contented themselves with costing up the contents of the drawing room and wondering between themselves what kind of fortune Joel was likely to give to Miss Caroline; whether, perhaps, the demands of one's ancestral estates could justify the bestowal of a niece or possibly a younger daughter on Mr Blaize or Mr Nicholas Barforth. Others, who wished merely to eat and drink, gossip, see and be seen, found their desires more than adequately catered for.

I moved from room to room, murmuring, smiling until my cheeks cracked, accepting glasses of champagne and, moving away, setting them down again untouched. Hours of rich food in my nostrils had taken my appetite away; false conversations had planted themselves on my tongue, so that I no longer needed to think as I spoke, functioning perhaps as career hostesses must, with an automatic brilliance far removed from reality.

'You're beautiful,' Bradley Hobhouse told me, meaning it, although most women seemed beautiful to him through the brandy fumes so often in his head, and when one thought of Emma-Jane . . .

'You are looking extremely well,' Morgan Aycliffe said peevishly, having had rather too much of pretty women for his taste these last few years.

'Stunning,' Sir Charles Winterton proclaimed, while my new stepfather, Squire Dalby, grew quite sentimental and shed a few tears because he had not known my mother at my age.

But Joel, his eyes sweeping brusquely over my lovely, lustrous gown, had merely reached into his pocket and tossed at me, as casually as he had once tossed me my pearls, a thick rope of gold, elaborately twisted and set with diamonds, which now was an unaccustomed weight on my arm.

I had thanked him – quite meekly, I think, having nothing else to say – and, nodding, smiling a little, he had walked past me on business of his own, giving me no clue as to his meaning. The bracelet, I supposed, had cost a great deal of money, since Joel would not have bought it otherwise, and, as with my pearls, he would not ask me what I had done with it tomorrow morning. He would not require me to return it to him for safekeeping, would not grumble if I wore it in the garden when I exercised my dogs. The bracelet was mine, although I had not asked for it and did not greatly care for it, manacling my wrist and weighing me down, for it was heavy, as this house was heavy, as Joel's apparent indifference to me, which should have been light, was heavy. And I could see no point in further resistance. I was Verity Barforth and would never be any other, and I must go to Crispin as soon as I could and tell him so. I must admit to myself that he could be happy without me; that I, without him, could be reasonable again, sensible and safe. And when I was older, quieter, surely it would not matter so much? Surely I could immerse myself in my children's lives, as other women seemed able to do, and remember him in small, permitted doses, with pleasure? Surely it would be enough to know that, recognizing his need for freedom, I had willingly, lovingly, set him free?

At three o'clock in the morning, four o'clock in the morning, when the Aycliffes and the Wintertons and other respectable people had long since ordered their carriages and gone home, the house was still full of the hard-core drinkers, some of them in small scatterings, here and there, most of them in the smoking room in various stages of intoxication. Bradley Hobhouse, who had taken Emma-Jane safely back to Nethercoats as soon as she had eaten her supper and then come back alone, was asleep now in a deep leather armchair, his legs a peril to unsteady passersby. A young Winterton cousin had collapsed neatly on a sofa; a certain young lady, her matrimonial prospects now somewhat impaired, had been obliged to retire to a spare bedroom, to the mortification of her mamma, who, quite understandably, refused to leave her side. But my presence now among men who were turning bawdy or nasty or stupid with drink was not required and, approaching a much-mellowed Joel, I asked him, 'I could say good night now, I think?'

'Yes,' he said, a warm hand on my shoulder, his body richly at ease, the wine inside him, it seemed, inclining him to a universal goodwill. 'Go to bed now, if you wish. In fact, I'll light your way, madam, as a husband should.'

He led me from the smoking room and up the stairs, which had no need of bedtime candles, his hand still on my shoulder, leaning against me a little as if his balance was no longer altogether accurate. And, having rarely seen him so completely in his cups, I smiled up at him, finding it natural, appealing almost, that he had drunk so deeply to his own triumph.

'I think it has gone very well. Are you pleased?'

The deserted corridor was like a strip of cool water flowing above the tumult downstairs, hushed and dark. His hand lingered about me in the beginning of a caress, an indication, perhaps, that once again there could be peace between us, deceiving me so totally that even when he straightened, held himself erect and well away from me, hawk-faced and keen, no longer drunk at all, I did not begin to be afraid.

'I walked up here with you to thank you,' he said, each word coming by itself, distinct and dangerous. 'For a husband should thank his wife, should he not, Verity, when she has served him well?'

'Oh – as to that—'

And still I was not afraid, but ill at ease.

'What is it, Joel?'

'Why, what should it be?'

'You seem strange. Have I done something amiss?'

'I wonder. But we'll come to that later. I am here merely to thank you, as I said, for a job well done. It went well tonight, very well. Everyone says so. And I am glad to see you still so faithful to my interests, however unfaithful you may be to me in other ways.'

For a moment in that narrow, empty space, his words danced like sharp needles over the surface of my skin, piercing a slow passage to my brain.

'Do you hear me, Verity?'

And although my mind, recovering its courage,

answered, 'Yes, I hear you, and you have only yourself to blame,' my tongue was too heavy, too cold either for protest or for defence, my body lost in a wild snowdrift of fear. Yet I knew that from the very beginning this moment had been waiting, biding its cruel time, certain of its own strength and my utter powerlessness, and, pressing my back against the wall, adopting the stance of any other trapped and terrified animal, I could hear my breathing labouring in my chest, hurting.

He took a step or two backwards and then slowly walked towards me, halting a bare inch away. 'You dirty bitch,' he said, his face quite blank. 'So it's true, then.'

And, holding me with one hand, he hit me twice across the face, viciously and accurately, so that my neck muscles wrenched in agony and my head, reeling backwards, struck hard against the wall.

'It's true, isn't it? Say it. Damn you, Verity, say it. It's written on your face clear enough, but I'll hear it, one way or another. Are you unfaithful to me? Say it.'

Appalled by that terrible blankness in his eyes, I understood that to allow him to shake a confession out of me would be to cheapen everything I had felt, tarnish everything I had valued, and lifting up my head and my voice, I whispered, 'It's true.'

'Yes,' he said. 'I know. I've known these past six weeks, known and not known. So it's true. And the man's name?'

'You must know that too.'

'Of course I know it, and where you meet him and for how long. Of course I know. Now say it.'

'He's not to blame; he didn't force me.'

'No, by God, but I'll force you. His name.'

'Crispin. Crispin Aycliffe.'

'Yes, Crispin Aycliffe. You breathe it to me like a prayer, but it won't help you, neither of you. Now get to your room and wait until my guests have gone and I have time for you. Get to your room, damn you. Get out of my sight before I indulge myself and thrash you.'

My maid was waiting, sleepy but determined to do her duty, and it was easy to let her undress me and brush my hair, somehow possible to answer her chatter with a nod and a smile as she got out my jewel case and locked away my pearls and my new bracelet. But when she had gone I took off my nightdress and put on a dark wool gown suitable for morning, twisted my hair into a low knot, similar to Elinor's, the best I could manage unaided, afraid, I think, of appearing in any way naked before him, afraid of losing control and rushing outside in my bedgown like Elinor. And sitting, hands folded, waiting as he commanded, I was frightened most by my own veneer of outer calm, my body encased, as so often before, in glass. So had I been on the night my father died, and on the next night when they had murdered my brother. So still and quiet that no one had noticed my agony. And so was I now, drugged by my determination to bleed unseen, to retain intact those fragments of myself which neither Joel nor my grandfather, in some ways not even Crispin, had been able to dominate. Yet now, perhaps, I would be obliged to sacrifice that ultimate freedom for Crispin's sake, would be obliged to plead and implore forgiveness, like Elinor. And the taste of the sacrifice was cold ash on my tongue. Joel would require vengeance, as my grandfather would have required it, and somehow I would convince him that, as the blame had been mine, the punishment must be mine too. So I would even incite him to punish me, so that, free of the need to hurt, he might even reach some measure of understanding.

I heard the carriages leaving, one after the other, until even Bradley Hobhouse had been poured into his equipage and rolled away. I saw the sky lighten with the start of a cold morning and heard Joel, I thought, in his own room; I held my breath a moment, waiting for the dressing-room door to finally open, but he did not come and I had to wait a half hour longer before one of Mrs Richmond's faceless maids came to summon me downstairs.

He was sitting behind his desk in a high-backed chair, a coffee tray with one cup, a honeypot, and the remains of a crusty loaf before him. He had changed his clothes, shaved, breakfasted at his leisure, a man as alert and refreshed as if he had slept soundly the whole night.

He said, master to maid, 'You had best sit down, although there is not a great deal I want to say and I shall not keep you long. Have you anything in particular to say to me?'

And chilled by his complete self-possession when I had prepared myself for the scorching heat of his anger, my mouth turned dry, my stomach lurched uneasily.

'Perhaps all I can say is that I thought, sometimes I was almost certain, that you knew.'

'And condoned it? Then you understand nothing of my nature. I was very far from suspecting you, Verity. I wondered at your motives for defending Elinor. But I decided it was because I had neglected you, and Hannah had interfered. And there was a moment when I was almost pleased to think you cared enough to complain. Yes, just think of that. You've contrived to make something of a fool of me, Verity, for a man believes, generally, what he wants to believe, and I didn't want to believe you false. That's why you had to tell me yourself. I believe it now.'

'Why tonight, with the house full of people?'

'Why not? The opportunity presented itself, as opportunities always do, if one bides one's time, a lesson my sister Elinor has learned to her cost and somewhat too late.'

'I am not Elinor. It is not at all the same.'

'Ah no, naturally. Her sins are mean and slightly ridiculous; yours are splendid. That is always the case. But the fact of the matter is that you are exactly the same – you less greedy perhaps, less simple, less easy to manage, but still birds of a feather.'

And, seeing no reason to be meek now that I had nothing

536

more to lose, I said, 'Yes, birds of a feather, all of us, following our family traditions.'

He brought the flat of his hand down on the table with a mighty slap, setting the coffee tray jangling, warning me that he had it in him not only to hurt me badly but to enjoy it.

To divert him, remembering that he could also hurt Crispin, I said quickly, 'May I know who told you?'

'Does it matter?'

He got up, strode irritably to the fireplace, threw his cigar into the fire, restraining himself, I thought, from immediately lighting another, and then, as if the whole conversation had suddenly wearied him, sat down again, staring at his cigar box, drumming his fingers against it.

'I heard it from Estella Chase,' he said, still contemplating the massive gold-and-onyx box. 'And she had it from her half brother, Mark Corey – a friend of Aycliffe's.'

And, each word cutting like a drop of ice water through the thick silence, I answered, 'In fact, you heard it from your mistress.'

'So I did. She has nothing to do with you.'

'Oh – I should think about as much as Crispin Aycliffe has to do with you.'

He pushed back his chair, got up again, putting distance between me and the abrupt, unleashed snarling of his temper, taking a cigar with him this time and lighting it from the fire, inhaling deeply before he returned to lean against the desk, in command of himself again, and to look down at me.

'I have kept my distance from you for more than a month,' he said, his lips hardly moving, his eyes dark slits in the gloom, narrowly glittering. 'I waited deliberately until I had mastered my impulse to flog you – not because I care about giving you pain but because a woman with a cut lip and a black eye is a pitiful spectacle and I have no mind to see you the object of anyone's pity. You are going to suffer, I suppose, but you'll suffer in private. There'll be no one to say, "Poor soul, poor lamb," because no one will even know.'

'Very well, Joel. I'll suffer. I've always known there was a good chance of it. But tell me first, what have I done to you that you haven't done to me? What has Crispin done to you that you haven't done to Godfrey Chase and heaven knows how many others?'

'Nothing,' he said, his eyes still slitted with rage, but his mouth was hard and cold and sarcastic. 'And what has that to do with it? Are you asking me for justice? I'm not interested in justice – only in reality. I'm no blustering hypocrite, Verity. Have I said a word about sin and shame? No, no. I've talked about surprise, because I didn't think you had it in you, and I've talked about anger – but as for guilt or remorse, I don't give a damn. I don't want you on your knees begging my pardon – like Elinor with Morgan Aycliffe – because all you're likely to be sorry about is getting caught. And, I repeat, let's see things as they are and forget any high-flown notions of justice. I outwit my competitors, but that doesn't mean I admit their right to outwit me. And no matter how much of a fool I may make out of Godfrey Chase, no man – understand me – no man does the same to me. You should have known that, Verity, indeed you should.'

And my fear, at that moment, must have been so apparent that he smiled.

'What do you mean to do?'

'To you? Or to your paramour? I could take a horsewhip to him, I suppose, if I wanted to. No one would blame me and he wouldn't know how to defend himself. I reckon Dinah McCluskey could stand up to me better than him.'

'You know her, then?'

'Of course I know her. Everybody knows her. She was the biggest whore in the Law Valley before McCluskey took her on. But rest easy, for if I thrash him even Bradley Hobhouse could work out the reason, and that wouldn't suit me. I don't mean to give them the satisfaction of seeing

538

me down, and what a satisfaction it would be, eh, Verity? Barforth with his mills and his money and his fancy new house – high and mighty bloody Barforth, with a wife who takes her petticoats off for a nobody like Crispin Aycliffe. No, no, Verity. You'll not do that to me. We'll keep it between the two, or three, or five, or six of us, I reckon. I can fix Dinah McCluskey and Mark Corey, and I can fix you too, my girl.'

And I knew that if I was ever to make a plea for my freedom, for my right to decide the course of my own life, for the simple right to be heard, it would have to be now.

'Joel – let me tell you—'

'Nothing. Tell me nothing.'

'Joel, you have to listen to me – try to understand how I think and feel. And you have to know you can't order me to stop feeling as I do—'

'Have I tried to?' he said. 'You haven't been listening, Verity. Perhaps I don't care how you think and feel. In fact, you may think and feel exactly as you please. It's your behaviour that concerns me. Your behaviour I can and will control. Why discuss it any further? You will do as you have always done, Verity. You will look after my house and my children and my guests – all of which you do very well. Nothing will change, except that, until further notice, you may consider yourself safe from my physical attentions – and of course you will not see Crispin Aycliffe again, nor receive messages from him, nor even open any letters he sends you. Is there anything else?'

'Yes,' I howled, jumping up, my whole body clenched tight with outrage. 'You can't dismiss me like that. You have to listen to me, hear my reasons. You have to stop treating me like a child or like an employee. I'm a living woman with a brain as good as yours, and you can't lock me away.'

But, once again, I should have known him better than to imagine he would threaten anything he could not enforce, and perhaps I was not too surprised when he

539

opened a drawer and threw a sheaf of papers heavily onto the desk.

'But I can.'

'And who will you have as my jailer? You are not always at home to watch me yourself. Who will do it for you?'

'No one. No one could. I appreciate how clever and resourceful you are – be sure of it. And who should know better than I that if a woman wants to misbehave she'll do it, one way or another. Fear of the law never stopped a hungry man from stealing a loaf of bread, nor a hungry woman from stealing an hour or two in a strange bed. However, in your case, I have the means to remove your appetite. You remember Colonel Corey, do you?'

'Why yes. What has he—?'

'And you know that he was the father of Mark Corey, as well as of Estella Chase? Not a satisfactory young man, Mark Corey – illegitimate to begin with, and sour about it. Upset Mrs Chase a great deal when he insisted on calling himself Corey instead of Smithers, or whatever his mother's name really was – although the colonel was too fond of him to complain, which upset Estella even more. Spendthrift too, our Mark, always in and out of trouble, so the colonel not only made him an allowance but lent him fairly weighty sums from time to time – most of which lost itself in that newspaper of his, and created more bad blood than ever between him and Mrs Chase.'

'And—?'

'Yes, you are looking worried, Verity. Are you already a step or two ahead of me? These documents were Colonel Corey's property – Mark's debts, in fact, and a few paltry sums advanced to one of his cronies. A hundred or two here and there, a thousand, perhaps, in all, which is the same as a million when you're living on fifty pounds a year and can't pay it. You do follow? Yes, I thought you would. This money is now owing to Colonel Corey's estate, or was, until Mrs Chase made me aware of it, when I purchased the debts from her – Mark Corey's and Crispin

Aycliffe's – to relieve her of the unpleasant duty of calling them in. If Mark Corey cannot pay me he will go to jail, and in any case, it will be the end of the *Cullingford Star*, something that has been in my mind for a long time. And what happens to Crispin Aycliffe is up to you. He doesn't strike me as particularly robust, and life in a debtor's prison is very harsh. A year or two of that and he could well find himself prone to the same nervous ailments as his mother – unless the jail fever or the rats got him first.'

And we both know there was nothing more to say.

I sat for a while, very quietly, looking down at my hands, my breathing shallow, sections of my mind closing themselves down – sections I would not need again, sections of emotion and energy that could only be a burden to me in this shrinking world – and then, nodding slightly, I asked him, 'What must I do?'

'Nothing. Look after your housekeeping. I will convey to him your regrets that the affair is over, and what more is there to be said? You will do nothing to displease me in the way of writing or receiving letters – I feel I can rely on that, unless, of course, you wish to see the poor devil in jail, in which case you have only to say the word. No? Well then, we may continue with our rich and happy lives – or, at least, I shall. You will want to sleep now, I suppose, for you look quite done in.'

As I stood up and walked to the door he stubbed out his cigar with a vicious grinding movement and said, 'Thank you, Verity – no hysterics, no excuses – most sensible of you. Really – most reasonable. And if you are thinking, like Elinor, of waiting for me to die, I shall take my time about it, I warn you – my own good time.'

'Yes, Joel,' I said, and went away.

35

Morgan Aycliffe was re-elected a week or so later with a comfortable majority and returned, quietly triumphant, to Westminster, leaving Elinor again installed in Blenheim Lane. But this time, instead of Daniel Adair to keep an eye on her, there was a long-nosed, sharp-featured Mrs Hardisty, an Aycliffe cousin, officially Elinor's companion but, in reality, her keeper.

'Dear Maud,' Elinor called her, and she was soon accepted as Elinor's shadow, a voice counting the hours of Elinor's day, a keen eye and ear checking the content of her conversations and to whom they were addressed. Not a bad woman, certainly, but too decided in her opinions for comfort, and determined to have her way not from any love of power but because she could not believe any other way to be right. And Elinor, with her new, hard-earned wisdom, chose neither to rebel nor to submit but channelled the unsuspecting lady's energies to her own good purposes.

'Dear Maud will see to it,' Elinor would say, good and quiet as a little nun, hiding the malice in her eyes as 'dear Maud' hurried upstairs to reprimand a child or a disobedient parlourmaid, went through accounts and menus, or submitted her weekly report to her cousin.

'Dear Maud, do lower the blind – the sun is in my eyes,' and Maud, barely distinguishing Elinor from Faith or Prudence or Cecilia – finding privately, in fact, that Prudence had more sense, Faith a more open disposition – would click her tongue, put down her work, and tug irritably at the offending blind.

'Is that enough?'

'Oh – yes, Maud dear – enough for now, except that the

sun will move in a quarter of an hour, I suppose. And what shall I do then?'

But at Maud Hardisty's direction, she wrote a stilted, dull little letter every Friday morning to her husband and had begun to embroider for him a pair of braces, which, if nothing else, created the right impression when Emma-Jane and Lucy came to call.

But our immediate preoccupation that winter was Hannah, who, having won Joel's consent to her marriage, if not his approval, was determined to do the thing in style.

'Surely, it will be a private family affair?' Emma-Jane asked me, oozing with sympathy. 'Bradley and I were talking of it just the other night, and we imagined she would just slip into church quietly with you and Joel and Elinor, and no one else the wiser. Naturally I'll call on her afterwards with a bride gift, but as to witnessing the thing take place – no, no. I can't think she really wants any of us to do that.'

But such a hole-in-the-corner affair had not so much as entered Hannah's mind. She meant – had meant from the start – to make her vows in the parish church, high above the town, surrounded by flowers and bridesmaids and all the pomp and circumstance that my brother Edwin would have brought her. And, when George and Rebecca Mandelbaum accepted Hannah's invitation with pleasure, when it was realized that Squire Dalby would go wherever my mother led, and that even Lady Winterton, who, insofar as manners and appearance were concerned, could see little difference between one common man and another, was willing to attend, Emma-Jane's resolve began to weaken.

And so, once again, I sat in Rosamund Boulton's fitting room with Elinor and dear, inevitable Maud, while five little girls – Maria Agbrigg this time with Caroline and the Aycliffes – were pinned into their wedding finery.

The dresses were to be of white spotted net over white satin, and from the first there was trouble, not only with

Caroline but with Hannah herself, who, for all her thirty-four years, was a virgin bride and felt entitled to make a greater show than my mother, a widow with three grandchildren to her credit. Her own outfit was a masterpiece of restraint, lace the colour of pale, milky coffee on a foundation of cream brocade, high-necked, tight-sleeved, the skirt enormously wide, regal rather than virginal; and the prettiness she could not feel appropriate to herself she wished to see in her bridesmaids, but Rosamund Boulton, looking harassed and nervous, not at all well, somehow could not get it right.

'No, no, Miss Boulton, those frills are far too narrow – not at all what I have in mind. We are dressing bridesmaids, after all, not charity children for a Sunday outing. I want these net skirts to have the appearance of clouds – fluffy clouds on a March day, not scraggy little things all limp with rain – and I don't care how many yards it takes. And on the satin underskirts, if you could stitch a few white flowers, quite large ones so they can be seen through the gauze. And I want the bonnets absolutely covered with flowers, very small ones, white and yellow, to give the effect of crocuses. I don't want to see any fabric at all, just flowers, and lace inside the brims. You can do that, I suppose, Miss Boulton?'

'Oh, by all means, Miss Barforth,' Rosamund Boulton said sourly, no longer on her knees with pins in her mouth as she used to be but standing straight-backed and eagle-eyed while her minions pinned and tucked in her place. And, in consideration for her all too obviously aching head, I felt obliged to take my outraged daughter home when, having herself pointed out that five little girls cannot walk in pairs, she discovered that Maria Agbrigg – not Caroline Barforth – was to head the procession, carrying Hannah's prayer book on a pillow of silk and lace.

Maria, of course, her colourless, lashless eyes quite terrified, would have given way; her father, had he been consulted, might not have wished her to put herself forward either and might well, in fact, have been better pleased with the quiet ceremony Emma-Jane had suggested, but Hannah, with the unwavering support of her protégé, Jonas, was unprepared to give an inch. And although Caroline, already a Barforth to her fingertips, pointed out that since her father was paying for the wedding she ought to play a main part in it, not only were the lace pillow and prayer book allotted to Maria but also a deeper-brimmed bonnet and a few extra flounces at the bottom of her skirt, to mark her status as attendant-in-chief.

'I thought you might like to get claret colour for Blaize and Nicholas,' she told me. 'I know the velvet suits they had for your mother are as good as new, but people do remember, and my brother would not thank us if we seemed to be penny-pinching. A really deep, rich claret – I have seen exactly the right shade – would suit them very well since they are so dark – with white lace collars.'

But Blaize, entering his eleventh year, wanted a proper broadcloth coat and trousers like his father, and Nicholas wanted whatever Blaize wanted, only bigger, more of it, and the claret velvet gave rise to a great deal of muttering, the lace collars to downright mutiny.

'No,' Nicholas said, squaring up to Hannah, his black eyes narrowing as Joel's did with rage. 'I won't wear that. I'll tear it up.'

But Blaize, a little older, broke free suddenly from the first level of childhood and, assessing his aunt's mood, gave her a charming, calculating smile which also held something of Joel.

'I'll wear mine, Aunt Hannah, don't you worry. I won't spoil your day.'

But, on her wedding morning, Blaize's collar had somehow disappeared, could neither be found nor replaced, and only Nicholas – whose collar had been removed for safekeeping – appeared in lace.

The evening before the ceremony Hannah spent an hour with me in the small sitting room, rendering an account of herself like a housekeeper quitting her situation rather than a woman about to become a wife.

'I have turned out all my drawers and boxes,' she said, 'and arranged with Mrs Stevens what is to be given to the maids. You will find everything in order.'

And as the February wind gathered strength behind the windows, drawing us together in the comforting circle of firelight and candlelight, I told her, 'Hannah, I wish you well with all my heart. If this is right for you, then I can only be glad.'

'Right enough,' she said, holding out her capable, square-tipped hands to the fire, and prone these days to sudden surges of emotion I found hard to control, I lightly touched her arm, knowing my question would not be well received.

'Hannah, if you could have your life over again – arrange it as you pleased – marry anyone you pleased – tell me, which man would you choose?'

'You are thinking of your brother,' she said coolly, taking up the poker and stirring the logs to a fiercer blaze. 'And that is only natural. I have thought of him myself often these last few weeks, and shall continue to think of him, especially as I shall be occupying the house where he was born. Unfortunately I am experiencing some difficulty in remembering his face.' And, replacing the poker carefully in its stand, she clasped her hands together, her face soft and rueful yet without any weakness.

'We should be friends again, Hannah.'

'Yes, of course we should. And I will answer your question. If I could have the ordering of my life, I doubt if I would marry any man. I would be a man, like my brother Joel. I'd manage his mills and drive his phaeton and take myself off to London whenever it suited me. I'd get some real work to do, take on some real responsibilities, instead of running petty parish errands and feeling myself grow as small-minded as they are themselves. I'd grapple with real issues. I'd be a Lord Mayor, if I could. I'd take Morgan

Aycliffe's constituency away from him and go to Westminster myself. And, obviously, since no woman can do any of these things, I'll content myself with the next-best thing and marry someone who can.'

'And – affection, Hannah? What of that?'

'Love, you mean? Well, I had that with Edwin and he would have made me into an Emma-Jane. Oh yes, and that was what I wanted at the time – ten children and all my linen cupboards in good order – but I shall do better now. Don't worry about me, Verity, for I am not so shortsighted as you seem to think. I am well aware how deeply Mr Agbrigg regrets his wife, and that marriage with me is more of an honour, in his view, than a pleasure. But I have nothing to fear from him. According to the law, a wife passes under her husband's authority and discipline, but in our case my husband would do nothing to offend my brother Joel, and I rather think the authority will be mine. And make no mistake about it, he may regret his dear Ann and tell himself he is marrying again so soon for the good of his children, but he wants to progress – he wants to be a mayor and an alderman and anything else I can devise. He is not doing it all for them.'

And rubbing her hands once again over the fire, she said, 'Ah well – we have a busy day tomorrow,' and went for the last time to her solitary bed.

We got up the next morning to grey skies, a high wind playing havoc among the remnants of last year's leaves, but by breakfast time there was little more than a thin curtain of rain misting the treetops and, as the decorated bridal carriage drew up to the door, a patch of white appeared among the clouds, not sunshine but an indication that the sun, at least, was there, somewhere on high.

'But who on earth is going to sit on the bridegroom's side of the aisle?' Emma-Jane had wanted to know. 'He has no relatives – or so one supposes – and it will all be most unbalanced – most odd.'

But there were managers now, of the various sections of

Lawcroft and Low Cross and Tarn Edge, a new class sandwiched between ourselves and the workers, who were prosperous enough to make a decent show and shrewd enough to keep on the right side of Ira Agbrigg and his Barforth wife. And so the bridegroom's pews were adequately filled, young Jonas – to the disgust of certain other youthful gentlemen – looking immaculate, if not handsome, in a plain grey coat and dark trousers, and his sister, Maria, playing her part to perfection.

The wedding breakfast was at Tarn Edge, the usual cold collation of hams and tongues and turkeys, which, apart from the champagne, was also standard Law Valley procedure for funerals, and apart from one regrettable, predictable occurrence, there seemed nothing to mar the day.

'Who's this, then?' Blaize asked, his eyes on his brother's lace collar. 'One of the bridesmaids gone astray?' And underestimating Nicholas's fury, he found himself on the ground, rolling and pummelling and spitting curses neither of them should have known, until Joel's well-shod foot kicked them apart.

But Hannah remained serene, between her newly acquired son and daughter, accepting congratulations with the air of one who has allied herself with an earl, confident that Joel, with his commercial instincts, would make the best of things and decide to settle matters her way. Distinctions, of course, were still being made. Jonas and Maria would call Hannah 'Mamma' but there was no question, yet, of an Uncle Joel. Ira Agbrigg, although my permission had been granted, could not persuade his tongue around my Christian name and would continue, perhaps indefinitely, to address his employer as Mr Barforth or sir when the occasion required. Yet Morgan Aycliffe, who had made a special journey from London to bring Hannah his good wishes and a Wedgwood dinner service that had considerably upset Emma-Jane, seemed able to recognize a future Lord Mayor when he saw one.

And it was no secret that Joel, no matter how distant his manner, would continue Hannah's allowance and had not yet given the Top House away.

She would, as she had said, do well enough within the limits she had set herself, and when it was over and she had gone down to the millhouse – the demands of Barforth enterprise permitting no time for a wedding journey – I was surprised how acutely I missed her. She had been a buffer between me and Joel, another person always at the table, so that conversation of some kind was possible, and her absence, giving rise to silences I could not endure, compelled me to fill the house with guests, bright people, dull people, kind, cruel, or downright half-witted people, anyone at all so that Joel and I need never be alone.

Springtime brought me the undulating carpet of daffodils the gardeners had promised, lilac and birdsong, clean-washed blue skies, my young dogs yelping their high spirits among the new grass. There were picnics that June by the lily pond, tables set out under the willow tree, starched maids bringing baskets of party food from the house while Elinor's 'dear Maud' shredded her nerves and ours with her dread of bee stings, grass stains, wet shoes, horrific tales of children drowning in ornamental garden water. There were carriage drives to ruined abbeys, one agonizing Saturday-to-Monday at Floxley Hall when Lady Winterton, with more guests than she could easily accommodate, had offered us a double bed and we had slept back to back, or Joel had slept and I had lain uneasily awake.

But there had been no harsh word spoken, simply a strange brand of politeness that at best was cool, at worst had the touch and texture of black ice. We existed under the same roof, spoke to each other carefully, whenever necessary, a business arrangement, a form of life imprisonment that aroused no pity since no one but ourselves – and a few others – were even aware of it.

'I will convey to him your regrets that the affair is over,' he had told me, but I did not know when or how the information had been conveyed, or received, how Crispin had replied, and when a boy thrust a letter into my hand one day in the town, I took it home, as I had promised, and gave it unread to Joel, not in meekness but because I did not trust him and, with Crispin's life in my hands, could not risk another trap.

There were other letters after that, reaching me in various ways, all of them delivered promptly to Joel, who, without any discussion, slid them into a desk drawer instead of burning them, so that I was not surprised when, one morning, I saw them bound up together and was required to write a covering note, explaining their return and asking Mr Aycliffe to trouble me no more. And after that – on the very day that Mark Corey was arrested for debt – the letters ceased.

I was, perhaps, eight miles from the Red Gin but I could have been in China, and, hedged around now by servants, children, friends, no longer a girl who could walk her dogs alone to Old Sarah's Rock or anywhere else, I attempted to come to terms with my private isolation, tried hard to convince myself that, having always known the penalty, I must not shirk now that I had been required to pay it. And I managed, generally, to be calm, until the thought of the barren years ahead sickened me and turned me cold.

And what would Crispin do with those years? Sometimes I could endow him with a rich, full life, with political or literary status and a wife and children to share it with him. But at other times, the hurt child in him tugged at my mind, rekindling my need to protect him, a far more primitive, more overwhelming emotion than I had felt for my own sons. Blaize, I knew, would always have his way. Nicholas would take life by the throat and squeeze what he wanted out of it. Like Joel, they were strong, deep-rooted evergreens, their growth undiminished by summer heat or winter gale. They would prosper and multiply for their own satisfaction, whereas Crispin, without their tough fibres, was less attached to life, might not take the trouble to succeed alone. He needed, as he had often told me, an exclusive relationship; he needed, in fact, to be loved, as Joel apparently did not – as Blaize and Nicholas might not – and the thought of the harm I had done him was not easy to bear.

I would never try to see him again, I knew that, but, one flowery, sun-flecked afternoon when I had taken my children and Elinor's to Patterswick, I saw Dinah McCluskey swinging her brazen hips towards me down a quiet lane, and my need to know how Crispin was – just to know that much – became too acute for caution. I didn't ask myself how she came to be in such a place, alone and bareheaded, walking as if the lane belonged to her and everyone else should be ready to make way. I simply knew that Joel was safely away in Liverpool, that there was no one else to observe me here but 'dear Maud,' who was too hotly in pursuit of my scampering children and Elinor's, too alarmed by the dangers lurking in this placid country-side, to notice what I did.

As she came abreast of me, keeping her eyes downcast, leaving the decision to me, I called out, 'Good afternoon, Mrs McCluskey. What brings you here?'

'Oh, you've decided to know me, have you?' she said. 'And what about that woman over there? I doubt she'll want to know me. But never mind. You can tell her I'm a gipsy hawking pegs.'

'She doesn't matter.'

'Happen not. But before she comes and pokes her nose in – well – how are you, Mrs Barforth?'

'Well – and you?'

'Oh, middling.' And tossing her head, her eyes bold and black as any gipsy's, she laughed. 'But you'll be wanting to know about Crispin?'

'Oh yes – please. Did you come here to find me?'

'I did.'

And pushing the gleaming tumble of her hair back from her forehead, she paused and smiled again, enjoying her power, knowing I would go down on my knees to please her.

'Well – he took it bad, Mrs Barforth. He knew it was bound to happen, but when it did he wasn't ready. You should have told him yourself, really you should, instead of sending your husband. That wasn't nice of you.'

'He came himself, then? I didn't know.'

'Of course he came himself,' she said sharply, scornfully. 'You wouldn't expect him to send his shed foreman, would you, or his butler?'

'I'm sorry.'

'So you should be. Well, we used to see a lot of your husband in the old days before he was your husband, when he couldn't afford the prices at the Swan. But that was the old days and I wasn't going to let him get near Crispin. "He's out," I told him. "Gone to Manchester on the Flyer," and when we'd had our few words, he says to me, "Right, Dinah. Tell him my wife sends her regrets. Explain to him she's seen the error of her ways, and let him know if he can't quite understand why, then I'll be happy to call again and go through it with him myself." First off, of course, all Crispin was bothered about was if he'd hurt you. But I sent somebody to have a look at you and you seemed all right. "Leave it," I told him. "Let it go. Don't put anything down on paper." But he had to write those letters you didn't answer, and when Mark Corey was arrested we understood why. I reckon it was Mark who told his sister about you and Crispin, and she told your husband. Well, Mark should have kept his mouth shut, and I'll tell him so if I ever see him again, but there's no forgiving the spiteful bitch for what she's done to him. He's her brother, after all, wrong side of the blanket or not, and she could spare him that thousand or two, after what she's raked in from her old man. Crispin went very quiet after they took Mark – very quiet. Shut himself away upstairs, thinking things out, I reckon, and it struck me he might decide to go away. After all, there's no money now to run

552

the *Star*, and to tell the truth I'm about ready to move on myself. But no. He comes downstairs with some scheme to raise the money to buy Mark out – not that it's likely to work, because Crispin has the best will in the world but no sense where money's concerned. And then he asked me to come and see you.'

She paused again, letting her eyes roam over the smiling summer fields, the leafy branches twining their arms over our heads, very obviously disliking her task, having promised to perform it for Crispin's sake but with no confidence in the message – whatever it might be – and with no faith in me at all.

'Mrs McCluskey, please. What is it?'

And I think I knew how much she wanted to stride away from me, leaving me in ignorance of the request, telling him that she had delivered it and that I had refused.

'He wants you to go away with him,' she said harshly. 'He says it will take time but he thinks he can arrange it. First he'll have to make peace with his father, which will take some crawling, but he thinks the old man would be glad to do it, now that Dan Adair's gone, and would agree to pay his debts. Then, of course, being Crispin, he says he'd have to work for the old man awhile, put his affairs in order for him before he'd feel right about taking a job in London or wherever. But, if you'll agree to wait for him, that's what he's ready to do. He doesn't think your husband would bring you back once you'd actually gone. He says it's pride with Barforth, not heart, and that rather than make a fool of himself running after you, he'd snap his fingers and set up a stable of high-priced hussies in your place. Anyway, that's what he's ready to do for you – give up everything he cares about, which he reckons is only fair, since you'll have to give up a few things too. That's what he asked me to say.'

I walked a step or two away from her, needing badly to be alone, needing the whole world to fall silent so that I could contemplate unhindered the intense joy and the intense sorrow of what she had just told me, this act of love and sacrifice, this challenge, this whispering of hope where there had been no hope at all, growing to a wild sea-roaring in my ears. And then Dinah McCluskey came up behind me and put her shapely but rough-textured hand on my arm.

'Well then, Mrs Barforth, I've given you his message, like I promised – two days and two nights it took him, staring out of his window, to make his mind up to it, so the least I could do was deliver it. So now I'll go back and tell him you said you'd like nothing better, but it can't be done. That's what you want me to say, isn't it?'

'Is it?'

'Oh yes, I think so, Mrs Barforth. You've got too much to lose, love, just think about it – those fine children tumbling about over there in the field, for one thing. You'd never see them again. And what about him, Mrs Barforth? Oh yes, he means every word he says and he'll do everything he's promised, if he gets the go-ahead from you. But I reckon, at the bottom of him, he'd as soon go to jail as go back to his dad. Can you make up to him for that?'

'Can you?'

'Happen I can.'

'Oh, I doubt that, Mrs McCluskey – indeed I do.'

'Why?' she said. 'Because I'm a common barmaid? That doesn't upset him. He thinks there's romance in the working class – and dignity – and he's right, except that he forgets we're good and bad same as everybody else. And if you put a bonnet on me, you know, and gloves, and a high-necked frock, I'm not so bad. I'd pass, in a crowd, as a lady.'

'You don't imagine he'd marry you?' I asked her, astounded, wounded, hating her, terrified of her.

And her voice throbbing now with urgency, she put her face too close to mine, offending me with her breath, the healthy fresh-air odour of her skin, the tang of spirits and tobacco clinging to her clothes.

554

'I don't know. But if he did he wouldn't regret it. You may have a lot of feeling for him, Verity Barforth, but I doubt you can give him what he really needs. Haven't you read him aright yet? He wants a woman who can be wife and mother to him at the same time, and you can't be either. Content yourself with what you've got, and leave him to me. I'll have no man but him, and no child but him, and although I don't doubt he'd take some persuading to it, it would be the best thing for him in the end. My life's been hard, Verity Barforth. They sent me to your grandfather's mill when I was five, and I was on the streets at twelve, peddling my wares for pennies, and then for shillings when I got a bit wiser, until Jack McCluskey set me up behind his bar and then married me. Big, beerswilling ox that he was – drinking his profits – finished up a raving madman, seeing spiders in his soup and thinking I was trying to kill him. Swore he'd kill me first and damn near did more than once. Well, if I could survive Jack McCluskey, nothing else is going to put me down, and there's nobody can take advantage of Crispin if I'm there to look out for him. I've had no bairns of my own, you see. An old woman aborted me with a knitting needle when I was thirteen, twenty years ago, I reckon, and there's been no sign of anything since then. So he can have that side of my nature too. You should step aside, Mrs Barforth – really you should – and give me the chance to show him he needs a woman like me.'

There was a rustling in the hedgerow, some small field animal busy about its own concerns, a bird persistently singing, children's voices rising in the distance to a pitch of high excitement, a quarrel brewing, Maud Hardisty's wail of terror at the prospect of torn trousers, a grazed knee which could lead to certain blood poisoning and heaven knew what else; a chill little wind suddenly rose up from the grass, bending the clusters of buttercups, the fragile pink-tipped daisies, and breathing down my spine.

And I saw that the children and Maud Hardisty were coming towards me very fast.

'So,' Dinah McCluskey said, 'I'll give him your regrets, shall I?'

'No.'

'No. What do you mean, no? Have your wits about you, girl? What else can you say?'

But rounding on her, loathing her, I said, 'Tell him I need a little time – not a lot – but time. Tell him I have to think it out – as he did himself – for his sake. Tell him that, left to myself, I'd come away with him in my petticoat, but that I have to be sure it's right for him.'

'Damn you,' she said, her hand fastening around my wrist like a talon fallen from the sky. 'Selfish bitch. You know it's not right for him. But you'll play with him, won't you? Use him like your husband uses his women. You're tarred with the same brush, all you bloody Barforths.' And pushing me savagely against the hedge, she strode off.

36

I went home, exercised my dogs, spent a bedtime hour with my children, sat at my dinner table, with Joel's rope of diamonds around my arm, and tried to imagine myself otherwhere. I tried to root out the self-seeking element from my love, to hold it up and examine it in a strong light. I thought of courage and punishment, and remembered the texture of Caroline's hair, her squeals of protest when the brush caught in the tangles. I thought of solitude, a deserted landscape, an empty, pale sky, and chatted to my guests. I slept, much later, in an uneasy cocoon of dreams where Crispin's face, emaciated almost beyond recognition, peered at me from behind his father's shoulder. 'I couldn't get away,' he said, and, as Morgan Aycliffe stepped gleefully aside, I saw Crispin's body, manacled, shackled, hideous, and Elinor, frantically laughing, pointing. 'We feed him twice a day,' she shrieked. 'And he sleeps in the countinghouse. What more can he need?'

I woke to a break in the weather, rain lashing my window, a listless morning of headache and tension, unable to decide on the lighting of a drawing-room fire, much less the course of my life, and Crispin's, and Joel's; an afternoon with Joel himself unexpectedly home, dressing almost at once to go out again; an early evening, fine and still, bringing news that reduced some things to their proper size, gave stature to others.

I was crossing the landing at the head of the stairs when, looking down, I saw Mrs Stevens and Mrs Richmond with their heads together, recognized the signs, and, going downstairs, was at once detained by Mrs Stevens's hand on my arm.

'Oh, Mrs Barforth – such a terrible thing. It is Miss Boulton. I fear she is dead.'

'What? Rosamund Boulton?'

'Yes, poor soul – poor, tragic soul.'

'But how—? She has looked ill lately, but so suddenly—'

'Yes, dear, so ill – we have all remarked it,' Mrs Stevens began, meaning to break the news gently, but Mrs Richmond, who was little concerned by the death of a dressmaker and knew of no reason why it should concern me, said flatly, 'There was no illness. She cut her wrists, it seems, with a kitchen knife. Quite shocking, and I am not at all sure if they will bury her in hallowed ground, or if they ought to.'

'Oh dear – dear me,' I heard Mrs Stevens say. 'Come, dearest, come and sit down.'

And while I stood, both hands clenched on a chair back, too frozen to bend my body into the chair, she hurried away, brought me a smelling bottle, hurried away again to contact her sources of information, and returned an hour later with the whole pitiful, atrocious tale.

Miss Boulton, it appeared, had slashed her wrists early

that morning in her room above the shop and had lain there behind the door until her father, quite by chance, had called with some message from home.

'Poor man,' Mrs Stevens said, tears in her eyes. 'She was still alive. In fact, she was still breathing an hour ago, but her family have been told there is no hope. Oh dear – Verity – dear Verity – I am afraid she was pregnant, there is no doubt about it. And although she has bled massively from her severed veins, they say it is the miscarriage that will kill her.'

I didn't know where Joel was and would not have dared send for him if I had, and so I waited, my sitting-room door ajar, for the sound of his phaeton, and then hurried to meet him in the hall, seeing at once from his face that I was too late, that he already knew. And when he walked past me without a word, I waited a moment, followed him, and entered his bedroom for the first time.

He was sitting in a tall armchair by the fireplace, staring into the empty grate, an unlit cigar in his hand, his face, which this morning had held all the arrogance of a man in his prime, suddenly showing the years, the strain of commercial combat, the strain of philandering, the accumulated lack of sleep. He looked spent, emotionally bankrupt, and, never having seen him in pain before, I hesitated, not knowing how to comfort him and surprised that I felt so strong an urge to try.

But before I could speak a word his narrowed eyes shot open and he almost shouted, 'Well, you will be wanting to know if the child was mine.'

'Oh no – what does it matter?'

'It matters to me. And it mattered to her, because if I had been the father there'd have been no need for this. I'd have paid – and handsomely. Why not? I've been sending money to your brother's bastard ever since he died. I can afford one of my own. I'd have set her up somewhere, away from the gossip – made life easy for her. She knew that. But the child wasn't mine – couldn't have been – and, as you say, it makes no bloody difference because I'd have seen to her all right in any case. All she had to do was come and tell me – no more than that.'

But how could she have admitted to him, I thought, when he had twice deserted her, that she had allowed herself to be used and then abandoned by another lover? And, kneeling on the rug beside his chair, not quite touching him, I said, 'Joel, were you ever in love with her?'

And it was very far from anything he could bear me to say.

'Go to hell, Verity,' he said, so calmly that, the tone of his voice bearing no relation to his meaning, I was unprepared for the swift pressure of his hands on my shoulders, dragging me to my feet and hurling me backwards against the wall.

'You'd best leave me,' he said. 'Just go – for God's sake, leave me alone.'

And glancing at his sombre face, I fled.

I sat, then, in my little back parlour, watching the evening come on, listening as the clock counted the seconds, droplets of time hurrying away, all of them in the same direction, forwards, never backwards to that vital moment of decision when one could choose again, differently, when one could lay down the knife, reject a lover's advances, when one could hope again. And I did not know how far back the fault lay. If my brother Edwin had not died, Rosamund Boulton would not be dying now; she would be Mrs Joel Barforth of Low Cross, harassed, perhaps, and hard-pressed for cash, ironing Joel's shirts herself to save a maid, pinching and scraping to make a decent show when her sister-in-law Hannah came down from Lawcroft to tea. And I, perhaps, would have been in Blenheim Lane, keeping the peace between Crispin and his father, while Elinor might well have been the spinster in Rosamund Boulton's place. And would this different settling of the kaleidoscope have made us happier, better, or would we now, from the inherent discontent of our natures, simply be calling our grievances by other names?

Perhaps I heard the doorbell, perhaps I was merely expecting someone, some new dimension to the catastrophe, so that when my door opened and Mrs Stevens, considerably shaken, told me, 'Mrs Barforth, it is Mr Boulton,' I was shaken too but not greatly surprised.

He was standing, an ordinary, elderly man, just within the empty hallway, the look of a good tradesman about him, serviceable, with big-knuckled hands, stooping a little at the shoulders; Rosamund Boulton's father, who had warned her from the start that Joel Barforth would bring her nothing but trouble and who, ever since the opening of her shop – knowing, one supposed, whose money had been used to launch it – had made a point of never being in the Piece Hall at the same time as Joel and had avoided, quite openly, shaking his hand or meeting his eye. I remembered, too, that, at the election, he had voted most surprisingly Tory, unwilling to share even the politics of the man who had first seduced his daughter.

Yet he was here now, on the eve of what must surely be his daughter's death, and despite his hesitant expression, the air of a man somewhat overawed by his surroundings, when he asked for Joel my instinct was to deny, quite amazingly to protect.

I said, much too quickly, 'Oh, he's away, Mr Boulton. He's in Manchester and won't be back until Monday morning. Mr Boulton, please, what can I do for you?'

'Nothing, lass,' he said. 'I'll wait.'

'But, Mr Boulton, surely not until Monday . . .?'

And as I stood there, transparent perhaps with pity for this man I did not really know, and with my new, astonishing need to defend the man I knew too well – who, surely, had no need of aid from me – Joel appeared at the head of the stairs. He wore no jacket, his shirt open at the neck, his sleeves unfastened, and, pausing a moment, drawing a resolute breath, he made a slow descent, walking, I thought, as a man goes to the gallows.

'I'm here, sir,' he said. 'Just arrived. Will you come this way?'

And they went into the smoking room and closed the door.

I could not let them go alone but I dared not follow. Nor could I have explained my fears, but Joel would do him no harm, and he was an old man, tough and wiry, but no threat to Joel, in full, vigorous prime. And although Joel had done Miss Boulton much wrong, her father must know, since I knew and others knew it, that their affair had long been over. Yet how much resentment had her father nourished, how much shame had he felt seeing her name above that shop doorway, hearing the rumours? How many suitors, perhaps, had she turned away because of her passion for Joel, so that ultimately her father could see no one but Joel to blame for her disgrace, the tragedy of her ending? Joel may not have been the father of her child, but what could that matter now to Mr Boulton?

Why was he here? And why was I so afraid? Was it simply the air of death around him that had unnerved me or was it Joel's own guilt-ridden distress that drew me down the corridor, my hand reaching out for the smoking-room door, knowing I must not enter yet finding that my fingers had somehow turned the handle, that a strength I had neither summoned nor suspected propelled me inside and closed the door behind me, my body leaning against the carved wood so that no one else could follow.

And what my eyes told me was, quite simply, not to be believed. Joel was standing by his desk, his head bowed slightly, reminding me more than ever of a man mounting the scaffold. Mr Boulton stood close beside him. Then I saw the knuckles clench, the old man's body hunch forward as he drew the driving whip from his boot and raised it, hissing through the heavy air.

'Oh, Mr Boulton,' I heard my voice cry out. 'Mr Boulton. No, Joel, don't hurt him.'

But Joel, who could so easily have wrenched the whip away, after an instinctive movement of self-defence stepped backwards, his whole face losing its colour again.

'Mr Boulton . . .' he said, no more than that, and then, as the lash caught him again, knocking him back against his desk, I saw his jaw muscles clench, his eyes close, and knew that he meant to submit, to allow this desperate, crazed old man to take his revenge.

A stripe of red appeared, suddenly, across Joel's chest, the fine cambric of his shirt shrivelling away at the shoulder, showing more red beneath. And then, through the hissing and whining of the whip, the dreadful beast-panting of his pathetic assailant, a whole cobweb of crimson patterning the front of him, smudging as the blood began to flow, his chest seemed to open, as my father's had once done, and the astonishment on his face was my brother Edwin's astonishment when an adversary as weak as this one had plunged a carving knife into his gut.

Joel's hands clenched white-knuckled on the chair back as he submitted to the traditional horsewhipping of adulterers and despoilers of women, his dark face shocked and set with determination neither to cry out nor to fall down until it was over. And I was proud of him. I felt his agony with him, groaned for him, and was proud of him, until a moment came when the deadly singing of the whip jolted me into calling out foolishly, 'That's enough. Stop it at once.'

Yet it was sufficient, for, miraculously, the hissing stopped, the air ceased to vibrate, and that old, grey shape dwindled suddenly, folded into a chair, an old, big-knuckled hand hanging loosely from either knee, two eyes staring, blank and blind, from a face that had no life, no colour but that of cold ash. And as I peered closely at him, Joel's voice came to me, his breath rasping with a sound I thought splintered bone might make, his words not entirely the ones I had expected. 'Look after him,' he said. 'Don't let him go. He's not responsible. He could harm himself.'

And lowering himself into the tall leather armchair where he so often sat to administer the affairs of Lawcroft and Tarn Edge, he slumped forward, tattered and bleeding, across his desk top.

'Look after him, Verity.'

But Mr Boulton, sinking into some terrible, grey twilight, was as limp now as seaweed, sodden and spent, incapable of movement, let alone of flight, and I could think of nothing to do for him but leave him in peace.

'He's well enough. Let him rest awhile. But you, Joel, oh, Joel, stay there a moment, while I send for the doctor.'

'No,' he muttered, trying to get up but then falling back into the chair with a thud that squeezed fresh blood through his shirtfront, sending a thick slug-trail of it leaking down the back of his hand. 'No doctor.'

'What—?'

'No doctor, Verity.'

'But you must have a doctor – you're bleeding.'

'No, no! For God's sake, Verity, if you fetch a doctor somebody is going to know about it, and work out why, and they've had enough to bear, the Boultons, without this. He's got to live in this town, the poor devil, afterwards, and his wife . . . It's got to be kept quiet somehow. God knows how, for I can't think straight, not yet. Help me, Verity.'

And there it was. 'Help me,' he said, and realizing that at last he was speaking to me as a woman capable of decision and enterprise, a woman whose strength he recognized, whose comfort he undoubtedly needed, knowing myself to be fascinated by that need, uncertain of it yet confident beyond question of my own ability to fulfil it, I nodded my head very slightly.

'Yes, we'll manage it. And, Joel, I think you must resign yourself, for a little while at least, to doing as you are told.'

And through all the weariness and pain I saw his grin flash out, drawing from me an answering smile.

Concealment, of course, was essential even here, for I knew none of the servants well enough to trust, and although Mrs Richmond was perhaps too grand for gossip, her disapproval could only hinder me. But Mrs Stevens, I knew, would not fail me, and finding her waiting in the corridor, whispering to her as much as she required to know, I left her to administer brandy and any other assistance she could think of to Mr Boulton, bidding her lock the door, while I, bringing Joel's jacket, helped him into it, supported him up the stairs to his bedroom, and there, where hot and cold water and clean towels were already waiting at this hour, began slowly, delicately, to cut away his shirt.

'Mind the carpet,' he said weakly as the blood began again to flow. 'It's worth a fortune.' But the separation of torn cambric and torn skin, the prising loose of the finely matted hairs on his chest caused him such agony that only when it was done and he lay back in his chair, stripped and nauseous and still bleeding, did he glance down at the upholstery and mutter, 'Christ, look at the mess. They'll never get these stains out of the leather.'

He was badly but cleanly cut across the chest and shoulders, raw weals raised thick along his back, one hand split from wrist to palm, a long, slashing wound on the shoulder, not deep but persistently oozing with red, seeping through the towels to my hands and sleeves, soaking the front of my dress.

'You need stitching,' I told him, 'and I can't do it.'

'Then bandage me tight.'

And so I did, padding him well under the linen strips, binding him round and round to the point of suffocation almost, so that he was glad, I think, to lie down on his bed while I rolled up the stained towels and hid them away, threw the rose-tinted water out of the window, disguised, if not altogether obliterated, the damage to chair and carpet, and then, crossing the forbidden barrier of the dressing room to my own bedroom, disposed of my own soiled garments, washed, dressed in something appropriate to the hour should anyone call, should the servants or the children see me, and hurried downstairs again, damp and inwardly shaking, greatly unwilling to leave him even for a moment, to check on Mr Boulton, to assess the damage to the smoking room and Mrs Stevens's ability to repair it, and to retrieve the whip.

I carried it upstairs with me, wrapped in a towel I had fetched downstairs for the purpose, meeting Mrs Richmond on the way.

'Ah, madam,' she said, her eyes fastening on the towel draped artlessly over my arm, 'may I take that for you?'

'No, thank you.'

And although she could require me to make no explanations, she had no intention of letting the matter rest there. Not that she was particularly curious, nor even cared very much what I was up to. But as my housekeeper, she felt it essential to her dignity to be well informed, to have an answer for any impudent little parlourmaid who may have seen Joel staggering upstairs in his greatcoat, leaning heavily against my shoulder.

'Is everything all right, madam?'

'Why, yes, Mrs Richmond, perfectly – except . . . Well, to tell the truth – and I see no reason for not telling the truth, since I am exceedingly vexed about it – my husband has been drinking, Mrs Richmond, which, for a man in his position, is quite shocking, and I do not at all wish the whole world to know it. Please tell the staff he is not to be disturbed on any account. Naturally he will not be dining. I will take something on a tray later, and if he is recovered enough to join me I will let you know. I am simply thankful that we have no guests tonight.'

'And the gentleman downstairs with Mrs Stevens?'

'Oh, I do not think he will be dining. He is an old and rather dear friend of Mrs Stevens's, and it appears they have something to discuss of a private nature. Really, I should leave them alone.'

And I did not care whether or not she believed me, only that she should behave as if she did.

Joel was still lying down when I got back to him, desperately uncomfortable beneath those tight bandages but breathing more regularly, sufficiently recovered to ask for brandy and raise himself to drink. Yet, even so, his first urgent whisper took me by surprise.

'Verity, can you get me dressed, do you think?'

'I suppose so – not that I would—'

'But you must. Get me an evening shirt and a waistcoat. In fact, get me two waistcoats so I can put one on top of the other and then if the bleeding starts again it can hardly show.'

'Joel, are you raving?'

'Very likely, but I'm expected at the Swan.'

'What of it? I have only to send a message.'

'Aye, and have them saying I daren't show my face because of what's happened at the Boultons' – and worse than that if it gets about the old man was here. I told you, he has to live in this town afterwards – and his wife is in poor health already. So get me my clothes, and another brandy while you're at it.'

'I'll do no such thing.'

He closed his eyes, keeping his temper, learning very slowly to cope with weakness when he had built his life on undiluted strength; and, opening them again, it seemed he had discovered frailty's chief weapon, a smile.

'Verity, I can do it without you, one way or another,' he said quite sweetly, defying me gently and with humour as Blaize did. 'No matter how you try to stop me I'll get up and dressed, order the carriage – I'll do it and you know I'll do it. I'm asking you to make it easy for me. And if I kill myself you'll be a rich widow that much sooner.'

But I was a Barforth too, capable of calling his bluff, and it was not until he heaved himself to his feet, took a few dizzy steps towards his closet, endeavoured quite drunkenly to put on a shirt, that my awareness of his pain unnerved me and brought me to his side scolding but ready to help his desperate, guilt-ridden enterprise.

'I think you are quite mad. You will do Mr Boulton no good if you collapse on the Swan floor.'

'I'll not do that,' he muttered, struggling one-handed with his cravat, looking likely to collapse there and then. It's a calculated risk, like all the other risks I take. These slashing cuts look worse than they are, and a little blood goes a damn long way. If he'd stabbed me just two inches deep I might not have bled much at all but he could well have murdered me. But all he's really done is break the skin. I'll show my face, buy my round, and then come home again. But I'll go – choose what, choose how – I'll go.'

'Then I'll come with you.'

And, seeing the surprise in him, the beginnings of gratitude, I clicked my tongue with false impatience, not ready yet for either.

'Yes, Joel, I have been thinking it over, and if you persist in this pigheadedness, then I shall be pigheaded too. What is to happen to Mr Boulton? You have not considered that, have you? Well, we cannot leave him downstairs forever, nor can we turn him loose to find his own way home, so someone must go with him. And since you cannot, and I would not lay such a burden on Mrs Stevens's shoulders, then clearly I must do it myself. I will have them get the carriage ready – unless, of course, you have any thoughts of driving your phaeton – and we will leave all three together. I will put you down at the Swan, take Mr Boulton home, see him safe, and come back for you. And you may stop frowning, Joel, for there is no other way it can be done.'

'I cannot ask you to go to the Boultons',' he said, still frowning. 'Good God, Verity, I cannot ask you to do that.'

And I replied, quite tartly, 'You have not asked me.'

I feared, at the last moment, that Mr Boulton might make some difficulty, but he was still faraway, still docile, willing to go wherever Mrs Stevens required, and it was Joel who hesitated at the carriage step, wincing, and needed my arm to make bearable the ascent. And as the coachman, far too conscious of Joel's reputation as a whip, set off at a cracking pace, he winced again, and I with him, my body feeling each jolt twice over.

'I will come back for you in an hour,' I told him as the Swan at last drew near. 'Perhaps sooner, but I will wait an hour before sending in for you. Are you in pain?'

'Soreness mainly. I believe I am on the mend.'

'I doubt it. Don't drink too much. You have lost blood and eaten nothing. Bravery is one thing, bravado another.'

'I am not playing the hero, Verity.'

'I know.'

'And do you know how sorry I am to have exposed you to this? I think I have never been sorrier in my life, nor more conscious of what I owe you.'

He got down from the carriage somehow, using his bandaged right hand to account for his clumsiness, his awkwardness of gait.

'Damn glass broke in my hand,' I heard him say to Bradley Hobhouse as I drove off, hurriedly, before my passenger's empty eyes and vacant face were recognized, before my own impulse to get down too became too strong to master.

'Mr Boulton,' I said gently, 'where may I take you? To your own house, or to the shop?'

But one place was as good as another to him just then, and, basing my judgement on Mrs Stevens's information, I drove straight to Millergate to find a lamp burning in the window above the shop, the doctor's gig outside, a harassed woman in the doorway who, seeing us, came running out considerably dishevelled and sharp-tongued with relief.

'Father, how could you? We have been looking everywhere. How could you, with Rosamund as near death as anyone can be. No, she has not gone yet, but it can only be moments— How could you? Go in now, for mercy's sake, and ease her mind, if she can still hear you. Go quickly now – unless you are too ashamed.'

And as his younger daughter's scolding pierced the fog in his brain, he blinked, shook himself like a wet dog, and went inside.

I had no intention of staying after that, no thought of anything but escape from this familiar place, rendered alien and terrible by death, from this woman in whose destruction I had surely taken part – the woman I had taunted, years ago, by wearing a dress she had not made for me and who had suffered such biting agony that same night when Joel had first looked at Estella Chase. But her sister, Mrs Bramley now, I thought, came swiftly back into the street, stationing herself between me and the carriage.

'I am obliged to you, Mrs Barforth, for bringing my father home. He disappeared, earlier on, when we were much distracted – when we thought my sister had actually passed away – and my mother has been frantic since then. Mrs Barforth, has he—? Mrs Barforth, I hope he has caused you no trouble.'

'None at all. He was merely wandering – just wandering. I think he is much shocked and requires care.'

'Yes,' she said, a tall, thin woman, neat and nervous, not unlike her sister. 'My whole family needs care, just now, every one of them, and since it all devolves on me – since I am the only one near enough in my right mind to make decisions . . . Come in, Mrs Barforth – come in a moment – please – for I have just this instant reached a decision, and there is something I must say to you.'

37

I was back at the Swan within the hour, as I had promised, reaching down from the carriage, both hands outstretched – playing the happy lover – to help him in, conscious of the hot, grateful pressure of his fingers, the cold sweat beading his brow, the cavernous sigh coming from the very depths of him as we rolled back up the hill towards Tarn Edge.

'Did it go well, Joel?'

'Aye, well enough. You'll allow that I've always been an adequate liar. And you, Verity—?'

'The same – well enough. She's still alive, and they think now that there is reason to hope – not certainty, but hope.'

'Thank Christ,' he said and, incredibly, in the flickering, treacherous moonlight, I saw that he was crying.

Mrs Stevens was waiting in the hall, hands twisted anxiously together, her eyes compassionate, whispering to me that, in the smoking room she had made all tidy – not perfect but sufficient – and I took him upstairs, walking once again as a lover, my arm around his waist, his arm around my shoulders. And when I had undressed him, washed him and bandaged him again, put him to bed, he said, 'Stay with me.' And so I sat down beside him, noting the greyness of his face, its gauntness against the white pillows, his eyelids blue-veined, black-smudged, his cheeks scoured into hollows, looking as Blaize had looked on that night of fever.

'Will you bring me a cigar?' he asked, hesitant almost, as if I were a stranger, and as I brought it, he groaned suddenly and said, 'I have to do something for her. Whether she lives or dies, I have to do something for her. Verity, what can I do?'

'You can settle Mark Corey's debts and get him out of jail.'

'Mark Corey. Dear God—'

'Yes – Mark Corey.'

And leaning back against his pillows, very weakly, almost imperceptibly, he laughed.

Some time later, when his eyes were closed and my eyelids were aching for sleep, I was jerked abruptly to wakefulness by his whisper, coming at me like a bee sting through the dark.

'Does she want him, Verity?'

'Her sister says that she does.'

'Then she could have raised the money herself, to buy him out – surely?'

'Not without your being aware of it, since she'd have had to take it from the business, and she knew how much you wanted to close his paper down. And then he knew nothing of the child, for it seems matters had come to an end between them, or nearly so. She thought his eyes were roving in another direction, and so why should she set him free for someone else—? At least, that is what her sister says. And perhaps she didn't want to beg. Perhaps she didn't want to say, "I have paid your debts so now you must marry me," I can understand that.'

'Aye,' he said quietly. 'But he'll marry her, just the same.'

'Joel – how can you? If he's not willing?'

'I'll make him willing. I'll make him damn glad. I'll get him out of jail and I'll get him down the aisle – or my money will, his newspaper will. Settling his debts won't be enough. He'll need money if he wants to print that bloody filthy rag again, and now that his father's gone, I see no alternative for him but to take a well-dowered wife. And since I'll be supplying the dowry I reckon I can pick the bride. He'll see the sense to it. He'll take what I offer and slander me in his first edition. Why not? I'd do the same.'

'Joel – Joel – how can they be happy, if he doesn't want her—?'

And setting his jaw, he snarled, 'I don't give a damn for

571

what he wants. If she wants him, then she'll have him. The rest is up to her.'

The next morning, blessedly, was Sunday, bringing me no need to dissuade him from going down to the mill. He had passed a quiet night, his bandages were clean, his flesh ridging painfully together, long, raw scars, uneven and ugly, but no longer seeping his life away; mending, he said, as I washed and bandaged them again and laid my hand across his brow for signs of fever.

'I'll live,' he told me, and because there was a question in his voice which asked, 'Are you glad? Are you sorry?' I became immensely occupied with towels and soiled linen, and hurried fussily away.

He spent the morning and afternoon in bed, staring moodily at the ceiling, endlessly smoking, but he allowed me to cancel an engagement to dine with the Mandel-baums, using my own sick headache as an excuse, and came downstairs in the early evening, appearing suddenly in my sitting-room door, to the consternation of Mrs Stevens, who, after one swift glance at his face and then at mine, picked up her work basket and fled.

'So,' he said, sitting down carefully, 'and what has our dear Emmeline to tell us today? She'll have had her spies working overtime these last twenty-four hours, I'll be bound.'

'She says Miss Boulton seems to be mending – slowly – although it is still not certain. They had Dr Overdale first of all, from Blenheim Lane, who does not approve of suicides and said there was nothing to be done. But then they sent for the new young doctor who lives in Simon Street, where suicides are ten a penny, and I suppose experience tells. That is what Emmeline Stevens says.'

'Verity, do you pity her?'

'Mrs Stevens?'

'Verity, for God's sake, I am not talking of Mrs Stevens.'

'Miss Boulton, then? Yes, I pity her intensely. I believe

I have always done so. Shall I ask them to light a fire in here, for I think I feel a chill——?'

'Verity,' he said, so violently that the effort hurt him and he pressed a hand briefly to his chest. 'Verity, will you talk to me – not of fires and the weather – talk to me?'

And I was at a loss to understand the feeling of power – of elation – that possessed me.

'I don't know, Joel, for you have never talked to me. You have given me instructions and reprimanded me sometimes, and you have teased me – pinched my chin and ruffled my hair in that abominable manner – and called me "reasonable" and "sensible" often enough. But I don't think one can call that conversation.'

'Maybe not. If I talk to you now, will you listen?'

And when I nodded he hesitated, at a loss himself in this new situation, faced – as I was – with a person he had known all his life and never known at all.

'I have to explain——'

'There's no need, Joel.'

'There is a need, dammit. I have to explain, and don't hide yourself away – don't disappear into a cloud like your mother. Listen to me. The father of the woman who had been my mistress for years whipped me last night because he believed I had ruined her – and he was right. And we can't let that go by without comment – can't lose it in discussions about lighting fires. You must want to know something more about it. At the very least you must be curious.'

'I asked you something about it last night and you wouldn't answer.'

'No,' he said. 'I couldn't answer. You asked me if I'd ever loved her, and I don't know what that means. I wanted her once, badly enough to marry her, since that was the only way to have her, but I let her go readily enough when I got the chance to marry you. I expected her to get married herself fairly soon after, and so did she, and if she had that would have been the end of it. I never gave her a thought for a long time, and then, one day, I called in Blenheim Lane to see Morgan Aycliffe, and there she was, on her knees, dressmaking for Elinor. Well – I'd like to say my conscience troubled me – and in a way it did – but when I made her my proposition about the shop I knew what I wanted out of it for myself. And if she'd turned me down I can't say for certain, if I'm honest, that I'd have gone on backing her. But she didn't turn me down – far from it – and for a while I can't deny that it was exciting – everything, her jealousy even, was exciting – mainly her jealousy. I liked her to love me. I liked to watch it – test it – and even when sleeping with her lost its excitement and was no more than convenient, I still liked her to love me – until it became a nuisance. And then I told myself she was doing well in the shop and that I'd nothing to reproach myself for. So – there's your answer – I liked her to love me.'

'And Estella Chase?'

'Estella Chase loves Estella Chase. She's peevish and tricky and unreliable and curious. That's been the basis of my relations with her – curiosity – and I reckon it's been long satisfied.'

And as the evening deepened, the house quietened, leaving us completely alone, I asked, 'Why are you telling me this, Joel?'

And he, leaning slightly forward, his eyes hesitant again, replied, 'Because I want to talk about you. I want to clear them out of our way, and tell you—'

'No, Joel. Not now. You're grateful now, and still weak—'

'Yes, Verity. I've spent the day and most of last night thinking about it, and there are things you have to know.'

'But it's not the moment – can't you see? You're tired, I'm tired—'

'I couldn't touch you, Verity, in the beginning – do you know that? – without a damned, stupid feeling that it was wrong . . .'

'Yes, yes, I know. I understand. You've told me and now, please, don't talk so much. It's not good for you. You'll start the bleeding again.'

'I felt I was harming you, Verity, and it troubled me that I cared. I was a man who'd had other women, and you were so untouched.'

'It was so long ago – it's over.'

'I felt I'd never penetrated you, Verity – you were like smoke in my hands. I couldn't hold you, and it maddened me, many a time.'

'Oh – as to that—'

'And I never lost that uncertainty. That's why I kissed Estella Chase that afternoon. You'd talked so calmly about my infidelity – so bloody calmly – and so I wanted you to see it – I thought that might make a difference. You wouldn't tell me what you felt, or didn't feel – and so I had to know. And finding out was painful. I didn't think a woman could hurt me, until that afternoon, when you came sailing out of the front door with a smile on your face. I wanted – oh, God knows what I wanted—'

'You wanted to see me sick and shaken and trembling – as I'd been two minutes before – that's what you wanted. You wanted me to love you, like Rosamund Boulton, but what were you prepared to feel for me – your new challenge?'

'I don't know. Is it true – that you were shaken?'

'Yes. And it's true that I've grown up, Joel.'

'I know it. I couldn't have got on without you last night, and today, thinking it over, I know there is no one but you I could have asked to help me, no one else I would have cared to ask.'

'Hannah?'

'No, not Hannah, Verity.'

'And is that supposed to mean something?'

'Perhaps I'm thanking you. Perhaps I'm saying we can't go on as we are.'

But emotion in Joel, the slight trembling in his voice as

he spoke those last words, held the terror of all things that are totally unknown, and I got up, walked away from him, feeling a desperate need for escape, to say, 'I am not quite well. I must go upstairs,' managing only to reach the window before he came and stood behind me, not touching me, although the warmth of his body, the odours of his skin touched me, separately, quite distinct.

'Verity – do you still care for Crispin Aycliffe?'

'Yes.'

And his sigh entered me, fanning out inside my body, warm, alien air, invading, possessing.

'Verity, if – and I say if — I were to allow you to see him – just see him, as you did before – live with me and see him – would you agree? Would it be a solution? Don't answer all at once. Think about it, for your answer matters to me.'

And, unbelievably, I swung round to him and said irritably, 'Oh, do go and sit down. Why on earth must you walk about so? I can feel your chest hurting. Do sit down.'

He obeyed me, crossing the room slowly to the fireside chair, watching me from lowered lids as I followed him, sat down too, my hands folded one inside the other, quietly, my breathing shallow, everything in me suspended some-how – waiting, waiting – letting the minutes flow by in silence until they measured half of one hushed hour, my body still tight-curled like a bud – waiting, waiting — to open and know itself.

'Why did you make me that offer, Joel?'

'Because—'

'Tell me the truth.'

'Yes. There's no trap, Verity. It seems that after all my philandering, I'm just a poor devil who doesn't want to lose his wife. That's what it comes down to.'

'That – or you want to reward me. A husband for Miss Boulton, a lord for Caroline, a lover for me.'

'You could be kinder, Verity, than that,' he said, and raising both hands, pressing them hard against my eyes, I felt tears stinging behind my eyelids, their first dampness on my fingers.

'I'd abide by it,' he said. 'God help me, but I'd keep my word. I don't say I wouldn't try to win you away from him – I don't deny there's a part of me that believes I could – if you'd let me try. I'd do it.'

'Why?'

'God knows. I'd do it, that's all. I'm as amazed as you are and it's taken me all afternoon to bring myself to admit it, but I'd do it. I don't say I love you – maybe I just think I could love you. Maybe I want to love you – and I'd go to the devil before I'd say that to anybody else. I don't want to love anybody else. And I'm a man who takes risks, you know that. If we keep on as we are he'll be between us for the rest of our lives. And it was only a game when I told you I didn't care how you thought or felt, only how you behaved – a charade, like it's been a charade these past six months, you must know that. I've always cared – selfishly, maybe, because I've always thought I could leave you for later, that you'd be here waiting – growing up – ready for me when I'd tasted everything else. And I miscalculated the time. I left it too long. And the power of the law and the power of my money can't keep you – not the way I want you. So if you want to see him, see him – stay with me and see him. Maybe I'm giving you a licence to hurt me. I reckon I've hurt you often enough.'

'Yes, you have.'

'That's not an answer.'

And once again time flowed between us, soft waves of slow-dropping water. Silence. And then: 'Is it a licence to hurt you, Joel, or a calculated risk – the calculation being that I won't use it?'

'Whatever you like,' he said, the strain of the day very clear now in his face, staining his eyelids, engraving lines I'd never seen before from mouth to chin. 'There's no reason why you should trust me, God knows. If you think I'm making a grand, empty gesture, then I can't blame

577

you. If you think it's all just because I can't bear to lose, then I can't blame you for that either. But I've made the offer. It still stands. What do you say?'

And this time the silence was airless, tense, the lowering quality of a hot summer sky straining towards thunder, until I said, 'No. I say no,' and the storm receded.

'Why not? Tell me.'

'Because I cannot accept so false a life – you with your lovers and me with mine. I thought, six months ago, that I could. I thought you were making me this same offer when we began to sleep apart – and even then I was uneasy with it. Adultery does not suit me, as it suits you. I could never take a lover, as you take a mistress, for pleasure. It would not satisfy me, and I don't know – I don't know – how much it satisfies you.'

'What do you want then?'

And for a long moment I looked down at my folded hands.

'I believe I want to be married, or not to be married. One thing or the other. And if I am married then I will be faithful to my husband and expect him to be faithful to me. I want my husband to be my lover and my friend – my dearest, closest friend. I want him to rely on me for the support and guidance it is in my nature to give, as I will rely on him in the areas where he is best able to guide me. I want him to trust me, and I want to trust him. Whatever happens to me during my days, however small or comic or momentous, I want to feel an immense urge to run and tell him of it, to share it with him, and I want him to feel the same urge towards me. I want us both to feel that no pleasure, not one of life's experiences, can be fully realized unless the other is involved – the good alongside the bad. I want his weaknesses and his faults as well as his strengths. I want him, as he is, a whole person, and I want him to want the whole of me. If I am married then I will refuse the fiction that I have only a woman's role to play and he only a man's. We must be two of a kind, the same species, giving the best that is in us to each other. That as what I want – if I am married.'

'Yes,' he said, leaning back heavily in his chair, his eyes closing on a great tide of weariness. 'And you are not talking about me – don't think I don't know it. And if you are not married?'

'Would you allow me – not to be married?'

'Allow it? No. But I don't know, any longer, if I can altogether prevent it. I should make another grand gesture now, should I not – another calculated risk? I should tell you to leave me, give you the money and the goods to make yourself comfortable – the calculation being that my generosity would touch your heart and you'd say, "Poor Joel, he must love me to distraction. I'd better stay." Yes, that's what I should do, but I find the risk too great – it scares me, Verity.'

And he was smiling now, ruefully, wistfully, drawing a smile from me, reminding me, for no reason I could name, of the man who had sat in the window of the Old Swan and raised his glass to the howling crowd below; the man who had driven fifteen miles one night and back again to throw my puppies at me in the dark; the man who, bleeding across his desk top, soiling his good shirt and his precious carpet, had said, 'Verity, see to Mr Boulton'; the man who later, that same night, had said, 'Verity, help me.'

'Do you dislike me, Verity?' he asked now, and I shook my head.

'No. I have never done that. If you had troubled to pay attention to me when I was young – because you are handsome and clever – I would probably have fallen madly in love with you and you would have broken my heart. Because if I had loved you then, when I was young and awkward and didn't know how to handle it, you would never have thought of loving me.'

'I am thinking of it now.'

'But you don't know for certain that you can. Joel,

would you allow me to visit my mother – while you are thinking about it – so that I can think too?'

'I don't want that.'

'No. But will you allow it?'

And for the final time that night silence entered the room and stood between us, its arms outstretched, holding us apart, the busy ticking of the clock a hammer beat, speeding my pulses and the beat of my heart.

'Yes,' he said at last, each word a dead weight on his tongue. 'Go to Patterswick.'

'Thank you. And I think – with your permission – that I would like to take Caroline too. May I do that?'

Although I believe his mouth opened to say, 'No. Never,' the words came out, laboured, unwilling, 'Yes. Take her,' his lips closing on the last word, biting back whatever remained in him to say.

Yet later, through all my tears and confusion, my thoughts of love and freedom, of grand gestures and calculated risks, it did not escape me that he had at no time offered to release Crispin's debts.

38

And so my life narrowed, adapted pleasantly to the small, cosy doings of Patterswick, to my mother's daily inspection of her flower garden, her tranquil afternoons when I, drowsy with sunshine and indolence, would watch her ply her needle. There was a pony for Caroline, the squire not understanding why we were here but happy if it made my mother happy, spending his last, good-humoured years in perfect harmony. And for a week, or two, then three, I wanted no one, was no longer afraid of decision but was content to let it grow naturally inside me, strengthening as my restful body strengthened in the sun and air, the tautness of my nerves relaxed, became well oiled and smooth with resolution. And gradually the things which had appeared impossible became not simple but well within my capabilities. I found the key to myself and knew, above all, that I was my own person. I discovered Verity Barforth, hiding inside me, and learned to value her.

At the end of the third week my mother spent a day in Cullingford, so clearly wishing to go alone that I made no move to accompany her. The next morning, as we breakfasted together, she had a whole parcel of news to impart. Mark Corey was out of jail, busily retrieving his printing presses. Miss Boulton had gone to Scarborough, with her mother and sister, to convalesce. At the millhouse Hannah was brisk and purposeful, giving the impression of a woman at least ten years married, while a suggestion had been made that Elinor should spend part of the winter in London, in a rented house large enough for her to entertain. My dogs were noisy and mischievous, Mrs Stevens very tender, Nicholas had blacked his eye, Blaize had been most charming to his grandmamma, both of them were dining now, every evening, with Joel, who had upset the governess by allowing them a sip of brandy. Emma-Jane Hobhouse was pregnant again. Lucy Oldroyd, who was not pregnant, was thinking of adopting a child.

'Oh, and one other thing,' she said airily. 'I think you must expect a visit about midmorning, I imagine – from Mr Crispin Aycliffe.'

'Mother, what is this? What have you done?'

And her face as she turned it towards me was as clear-eyed and innocent as the face of my son Blaize in his blackest moments of mischief.

'Well, my dear, I have meddled a little, I must confess, which is not at all my habit, so I feel sure you will excuse me. I have merely given him the money to pay his debts, that is all, for I am quite certain Joel does not mean to release them, and it struck me the other day how much easier you would find it if you were perfectly free to make up your mind. This way, my love, there is no pressure and no excuse. You can never say to yourself afterwards, 'I was forced to it. I had no choice.' Now you can all choose, quite freely. I do not wish to influence your choice, dear. I merely wish you to know that it has been entirely up to you, and as for the money, I am well able to afford it, for my dear Dalby will not let me spend a penny of my own. In fact, he still persists in believing I am quite penniless, although he knows quite well I am very far from that. Well, dear, your Mr Aycliffe must certainly have gone to see Joel last night to redeem himself, and then he has only to look to the hiring of a horse and ride over here, so I think we may safely expect him in an hour. If you wish to run upstairs and tidy your hair, I will not detain you.'

Crispin came promptly, as soon as he was able, the same frayed blue coat, the same intense feeling of harmony swaying me as I stood by my mother's parlour window, a warm tide of feeling carrying me towards him, although my body did not move. And we stood for a while without speaking, content simply to be under one roof together.

'I am free now,' he said. 'I have paid my debts.'

And no one else existed anywhere. We were alone, body and spirit blending together as rivers blend at their joining place, a complete and final moment of love, as I told him, 'The time has come now, hasn't it? As we always knew it would. Perhaps we can both bear it now.'

We walked for a while then, in the garden, although I saw nothing of the flowers or the grasses, nothing at all that I recognized but his face, his hand loosely clasped around mine, felt nothing but the same childlike wonder of our first night together which had been leading us gently, irrevocably ever since to this moment of goodbye. And I would not speak the word, had no need any longer of my voice to reach him.

I knew his destiny now, and I would not diminish him. I would believe in him and in myself. We had come together scarred and hesitant and full of need, but now, at our parting, we were free and whole, no longer self-seeking but self-sufficient, aware of the strength and the harmony within ourselves. We had healed each other, discovered our true selves within each other.

'Will you go now, Crispin?'

'Yes.'

And then: 'Verity, I must know, before I leave, how your life will be.'

'I shall be well, Crispin, and free. That is your gift to me.'

And my eyes did not see him go. My hand did not relinquish the clasp of his hand, although for one brief moment I shivered and felt the cold.

My mother came to me afterwards, held me for the first time in our lives, although I was not weeping, stroked my hair and made little murmurings over me as I did sometimes with Caroline.

'You have not harmed him, dearest,' she said. 'Don't think it, for one learns so much from sorrow. In fact, without it, we can learn very little at all, and he will know now how to use his knowledge well. Other women will fall in love with him, of course, but now, because of you, he has no need to fall in love again himself. I believe your memory will suffice to set him free as he so ardently wishes to be free. He may do great things now, or he may not, but you, darling, what now?'

I slept through the night, waking to a sun-drenched sky and my mother calling, from the pathway below my window, to bid me a good morning.

'I am gathering roses for the parlour,' she told me, 'since Lady Winterton is invited to tea. I mention it merely in case you should wish to avoid her.'

'I don't greatly care to see her. But if I decide to avoid her where could I go?'

'My dear,' my mother said sweetly, with perfect innocence, 'the thought had already crossed my mind, I confess it, and I really couldn't say.'

We breakfasted together as usual, Caroline, rapidly

583

adapting to country hours, having risen with the lark and set off long ago to race her pony in the meadow. Sipping my tea, enjoying my mother's efficient grace as she lifted the lid of the honeypot and passed me a jar of her rose-petal jam and her home-churned butter, I asked her, as I had once asked before, 'What must I do, Mother?'

'Ah,' she said, her narrow, elegant hands pausing a moment above the toast rack. 'As to that, my love, I have a notion you will do exactly as you think best.'

'And will you help me?'

'How may I do that?'

'Well, you have set Crispin free.'

'So I have. I have paid his debts, which, of course, will allow him the freedom to incur more, if he chooses. But you must know that my purpose in so doing was to widen your alternatives – not his – so you would be free to consider – well – the alternatives I mentioned.'

'Are there really so many?'

'Oh, I imagine there are always at least two: to do something or not to do it. You will know what I mean.'

And bestowing on me her lovely, pointed smile, she got up and, in her own unique fashion, melted away.

Lady Winterton arrived at the earliest possible moment at which one could decently expect a tea kettle to be on the boil. Sitting down in her brusque manner, her hands, which had clearly done their share of stable work that morning, immediately busy with the cream jug, the sugar tongs, the chocolate cake, she fixed me with her inquisitive, arrogant eye and said, 'You are still here, then?'

'Yes, indeed.'

'Well, you know your own business best, of course, but I wonder that your husband can spare you for so long.'

And she was only prevented from asking me more, having not quite shed the habit of interviewing manufac-turers' wives as if they were housemaids, by my mother's smooth intervention with a dish of almond slices Her Ladyship was unable to resist.

But the almonds and the apricot preserve served only to delay her curiosity, not to abolish it, and it was soon apparent that, having almost decided to marry her son to my daughter's dowry, she considered my affairs, matrimonial or otherwise, very much her concern.

'You will be going home presently, I daresay.'

'I daresay.'

'Yes – and what is this I hear, Mrs Dalby, about your old cottage? Mrs Chase informs me that you are having it done up, quite extensively improved, and I was bound to notice, as I drove by just now, that she is right. What is afoot then, Mrs Barforth? We wondered, Mrs Chase and I, if you were planning a little country retreat for yourself, or if Mr Barforth intended to use it for a hunting box, which surprises us, since there is ample room here at the Hall.'

And when, in all honesty, I could give her no information about the cottage, and my mother, very intent on her tea kettle, would not, she swallowed her almond slices in a great huff and went away unsatisfied.

We walked down to the village later that day, Caroline frisking ahead of us, a pair of the squire's half-grown hound puppies at her heels, my mother leaning gently on my arm, not in frailty but because she had acquired during her second, comfortable marriage the habit of being protected.

And with the sweet-scented air of the country evening in our faces, the fast-dropping twilight draping itself all around us in an illusion of privacy, I said, 'So they are gossiping about me already.'

'I fear so.'

'And are you really improving the cottage, Mother?'

'Why, yes, dear. I have walked down here with you on purpose to view it.'

And the cottage already in sight, we strolled silently to its wooden gate and the garden, where the roses my mother had planted in her early widowhood were still blooming, the honeysuckle riotously spreading, her lilac trees and cherry trees and apple trees still offering leafy shade.

'See,' she told me. 'All is clean and fresh inside – the walls new-papered – just a few chintzy covers, I think, on these chairs, and anyone could be perfectly at ease . . .'

And as Caroline raced upstairs in a wild spurt of exploration, the hound puppies rooting and sniffing outside, I asked her, 'Why, Mother?'

'Oh, just a question of choice, dear. You chose to set Crispin free, as I hoped you would, and now you may choose your own freedom, or something altogether different. This little cottage of mine could serve any one of a dozen needy Dalbys or it could be yours, just as you wish. And whether you take it or not, you will always know that you could have taken it. And I was always extremely happy here.'

'But you married again.'

'Ah yes. That is what I chose to do.'

'And Joel?'

'What of him? Joel is not at all my concern. Are you strong enough to see him now?'

'I must see him eventually.'

'Yes, and you must have your answer ready, for he is a clever man, your husband. Shall I let him know?'

But Caroline, tumbling downstairs, excitedly repossessing this cosy corner of her childhood, 'her' cottage now, 'her' meadow, 'her' pony, 'her' squire, who would pluck the moon from the sky at her asking, spared me the necessity of a reply.

My mother made another journey to Cullingford early the next morning, clearly to see Joel, although, on her return, I asked no questions and she offered me no information. And, expecting him in a day or two, late in the evening or on a Sunday – for when had Joel Barforth ever lost half a day's business on my account? – I was surprised to see him that very afternoon, his phaeton tearing up the gravel, entering the house like an invader, an imperious hand held out to me with a blunt request to 'Come out into the garden. This crumbling old pile gets me down.'

'I don't know why I am here,' he said, striding irritably among my mother's roses. 'God knows if I'm right or wrong. I don't understand myself anymore, and I've never understood you. It's just that I felt I ought to come. I've been on tenterhooks to come ever since Aycliffe threw his money at me the other night.'

'And you took it?'

'Of course I took it. Whyever not? You're thinking of grand gestures, are you? Well, that's one I wasn't prepared to make. A paltry thousand pounds I didn't need and he's desperate for, all he has in the world, I reckon. Oh no, I may not be able to stop him from seeing my wife, but I'll be damned before I'll pay him.'

'Am I your wife, Joel?'

And stopping in his tracks, he put hard, heavy hands on me, forcing me to stop too.

'He was here, wasn't he?'

'Yes.'

'What did you say to him?'

'Take your hands off me, Joel.'

'What did you say to him?'

'Take your hands off me, Joel, if you want me to say anything more to you.'

And I saw the anger blazing in his eyes, cooling slowly at the command of his reason, which also, just as slowly, unlocked his fingers from my arms.

'All right. What did you say to him?'

'We spoke privately.'

'Dear God, what am I coming to? You'll have to tell me more than that.'

'Well, I'm here, with no immediate intention of leaving. And he won't be coming again.'

Triumph first. 'You sent him away?'

And then a growl of suspicion. 'What do you mean – no

immediate intention of leaving? You've no damn fool notions of staying here indefinitely, have you? Verity – I want you to come home.'

'Yes. But you didn't answer my question.'

'What question?'

'Am I your wife? I said I would be married or not married. And you know very well what I mean.'

We walked for a moment in silence, Joel's eyes brooding darkly on the roses, not seeing them, although their colours moved me to a new awareness of life – a certain excitement growing inside me – their perfume tantalizing my nostrils, making me giddy, a girl again walking in a garden with this powerful, handsome man who had not wanted me as a girl, who had given me no opportunity to want him.

'I could say anything,' he told me, 'to get you back. Words come cheap enough. I could say any damn thing I thought you wanted to hear, whether I meant it or not. Could you tell the difference?'

'Oh – who knows? Let's try, shall we?'

And his lowered lids snapping wide open, he said, 'Verity, are you flirting with me? You'd best take care, for I'm in deadly earnest.'

'Tell me.'

'What? I'll tell you how I've lived these last three weeks. I've tried. I've dined at home every night with my sons, which hasn't always been a pleasure, and I've missed my daughter. I've counted my successes, and, commercially, they've been enormous. I've made my million several times over, and every night, these three weeks, I've felt like a poor man. I've missed you, Verity – yet I've spent so little time with you lately that the reason couldn't be simple. And so I reckon I've been missing what I think we could have together now – what I want us to have. And so I've done certain things to please you. I've given Hannah the Top House, and I've convinced Morgan Aycliffe he'd best take Elinor to London and treat her right if he wants to keep on the right side of me. I've made my peace with the

Boultons and put Mark Corey back in business. And I've put the children at Low Cross on ten hours a day, with Lawcroft and Tarn Edge to follow if it's a success, which has made me the most hated man in the Piece Hall – again – and is going to make them hate me worse if I can do it, as I think I can, without loss. So you've made a philanthropist of me, Verity. I even had a letter from Richard Oastler congratulating me on having seen the light – leading the way – impudent devil, good as told me I hadn't turned out nearly so bad as he'd thought me, and when he writes again I reckon he'll be asking for my contribution to his campaign funds. And they'll take a dim view of that at the Piece Hall – although I've yet to see what the *Cullingford Star* will make of me now.'

'Oh yes – I can't wait for the first edition.'

'I've missed you, Verity.'

'Yes—?'

'What do you want me to say now?'

'I expect you'll think of something.'

And taking my wrist again, this time very lightly, he held me in his arms and kissed me, in a rose garden, as he should have done years ago, and then kissed me again, most urgently, no longer in any way my cousin.

'Will you marry me, Verity?'

And there, in full sunlight, face to face, we laughed wholeheartedly.

'Really marry you?'

'Yes. I understand your requirements, madam.'

'And you can fulfil them?'

'I do believe so. And if I fail it won't be for want of trying.'

'Well then – I'll let you know, Joel.'

'What! What do you mean, you'll let me know? You can't say that to me, dammit!'

'Joel – I'll let you know.'

'Devil take you,' he said, his sudden tension relaxing, his mouth beginning to smile. 'Very well – very well, I deserve that – or do I? Just don't be too long. Shall I come for you tomorrow?'

'Joel—'

'Yes – yes, I understand – you'll let me know. I'll go now, while my temper holds. Will you excuse me to your mother – tell her I'll be over to see her presently?'

I watched him leave, waved to him as he disappeared through the flying gravel, the haze of the mellow afternoon, and then I walked back through the glowing roses, smiling, languorous, wanting to stretch myself in the scented air like a cat, sleekly purring. And in the doorway my mother was waiting, smiling too.

'I see you left him no appetite for tea,' she said. 'Ah well – you will be going home, then, tomorrow?'

And walking past her, my smile growing, spreading from my lips until my whole body seemed to be smiling, I told her, 'Yes, I suppose I may go home tomorrow – unless, of course, you would care to lend me your carriage, in which case – perhaps – I think I will go tonight.'

All Futura Books are available at your bookshop or newsagent, or can be ordered from the following address:
Futura Books, Cash Sales Department,
P.O. Box 11, Falmouth, Cornwall.

Please send cheque or postal order (no currency), and allow 45p for postage and packing for the first book plus 20p for the second book and 14p for each additional book ordered up to a maximum charge of £1.63 in U.K.

Customers in Eire and B.F.P.O. please allow 45p for the first book, 20p for the second book plus 14p per copy for the next 7 books, thereafter 8p per book.

Overseas customers please allow 75p for postage and packing for the first book and 21p per copy for each additional book.